CERES

CERES

L. NEIL SMITH

an imprint of

MANOR

Rockville, Maryland

ISBN: 978-1-61242-007-3

www.PhoenixPick.com
Great Science Fiction at Great Prices

Visit the Author's Website at:
http://www.lneilsmith.org

Visit the Author's Page at Phoenix Pick:
http://www.ElNeil.com

Published by Phoenix Pick
an imprint of Arc Manor
P. O. Box 10339
Rockville, MD 20849-0339
www.ArcManor.com

Contents

CHAPTER ZERO: THE MASCON

It never fails to surprise me how innovative Pallatians can be. I think it must come from the example of Wild Bill Curringer, who, for all practical purposes, invented the very planet they live on and call home. —*The Diaries of Rosalie Frazier Ngu*

SHE DESCENDED LIKE AN ANGEL, from the blood-scarlet heavens high above, into a flurry of microscopic ice crystals, swirling in great spirals all about her.

Seen through a carefully-arranged summer blizzard from a thousand feet in the air, the little crater lake didn't look like much, but she had measured it very carefully before the first time she'd used it— this was, perhaps, the fiftieth—referring to orbital photographs. She knew that it was two thousand yards across its shortest expanse (and about the same across its longest), more than adequate for the day's exercise.

The light, glittering snow continued falling. It lay, where it had already settled, in a feathery, weightless blanket that spread across the smooth, hard, level surface of the frozen lake, which was surrounded everywhere by a low, natural wall. Beyond that wall lay dense forest and unnumbered perils, including dangerous animals. By the time she hovered over the lake, the color of the snowy surface a hundred feet beneath her titanium-shod toe-tips, and of the sky—and of the very air around her—had shifted to a bright and promising orange.

These were only two of the many colors of a Pallatian sunrise.

Climate Control had done its job perfectly. The sky was thinly overcast and she knew from orbital radar scans taken by the same folks who had made it snow for her, that the surface of the lake was solid to a depth of at least eighteen inches. She'd be baking lots of peanut butter cookies for the crew manning the giant mirrors that controlled the weather on Pallas, second largest, and first settled, of the Belt asteroids.

Her gloves were made of the same slick and shiny material, in the same brilliant metallic blue, as the rest of her close-fitting exercise suit, which covered her from head to the soles of her boots. She brushed snow from the horizontal surfaces of what those who didn't live on Pallas often called a "flying belt". It was actually a toroid, more like an old-fashioned life preserver—like the ones that hung here and there on ancient ships— with two smaller toroids fused to it, 180 degrees apart. The largest toroid went around one's waist and the smaller pair each held a powerful electrostatic grid that ionized the air and pushed it through to keep the whole device and its rider aloft.

She had flown a very long way, mostly in pitch darkness, to be here at dawn. If she had to walk back it would probably take weeks or months.

At fifty feet, the silent fury of her passage, of the tiny twin hurricanes holding her aloft, had begun to scour the ice until she saw herself reflected, surrounded by a gauzy halo of brilliant canary yellow, yet another color of the Pallatian morning. The effect had something to do with sunlight refracted through the asteroid's plastic atmospheric canopy—the same phenomenon occurred at sunset, only in reverse order—but nobody seemed to know much more than that about it.

As the serried tips of her twin gleaming blades touched the ice, she toggled the dual releases of the harness that had supported her, raised her arms gracefully above her head, and let the machine that had borne her to this place, across hundreds of miles of untamed wilderness, rise gently around her until it floated free above her head.

Hanging in its holster from the same harness that had supported her was the ten millimeter pistol her mother had insisted that she take with her. Early in its history, Pallas had been stocked with all sorts of wildlife, including some of Earth's most ferocious predators. To any extent that they had explained it at all, the little world's founders had said they wanted to remind their posterity that safety is a dangerous illusion—and besides, they happened to like ferocious predators.

At her command, the little flying machine drifted to the edge of the ice, set itself down upon the shore amidst a miniature flurry of wind-driven snow, and obligingly shut itself off to await her later need.

By then the sky above her head, the very air around her, and the ice beneath her feet had turned to an emerald so deep and pure that it was almost enough to break her heart—except that it was perfectly normal to her, perfectly natural. She had arisen with it almost every morning of her

young life—more than forty-seven hundred of them, she quickly calculated—and returned home with it almost every evening.

As usual, she began warming up with several waltz jumps. It was an
easy exercise, and she could do them in either direction—a talent fairly
rare among skaters—starting off on the right foot or the left. In either
case, the trick was getting up onto the toe before the jump.

All around her, the ice, the sky above it, and the snow-covered land
were all a rich, soul-rending blue.

Suddenly she left the ice, rising twice her height into the air— a feat
impossible on humanity's homeworld—covering at least 50 feet in a long,
graceful arc. At the end of it, she alighted without a sound, indulgently
skimming another hundred feet before she prepared for another jump.

Next came the Salchow, beginning with a three-turn on the takeoff.
She remembered not to jump off the left back inside edge, as she was
reflexively inclined to do, but to turn and jump sideways, almost, off the
toepick.

By now, everything around her was bathed in violet light.

The trouble with her next jump, the toe loop, was the axis of its rotation. She took off on her left toepick, then had to flip her body around to
change the center of her turn until it was over her right foot rather than
her left.

Now for the loop. Leg position during the jump was critical, and she
had to remember to tuck the left leg over right, instead of bringing the
left ankle to the right knee.

The flip started with a Mohawk—a change from the right forward
inside edge to the left backward inside edge. On the takeoff, she pointed
her right toe toward the back to fight the natural tendency to start the
jump by kicking down with a bent right knee.

There were similar problems with the Lutz—a tendency to "flutz" it
by taking off as with the flip, as opposed to being on the left backward
outside edge. Instead, she put her right toepick in and jumped.

At long last, she came to the Axel, the prize most sought after by new
figure skaters, and gateway to the double jumps, The Axel was a turn and
a half, and she had to fight a tendency to "pop out" after only a single
rotation.

Now, as the landscape began to be bathed in the yellow-white light
that most human beings would regard as normal, she executed a double
Salchow—the same moves as before, but with two rotations. Then came
the double toe loop, followed by the double loop and double flip, ending the sequence with a double Lutz, and then the double Axel it had

taken her a year, a thousand falls, and cost her family a hundred platinum ounces to get right.

The double Axel—two and a half turns—led to a series of triple jumps, and those led to a series of quadruples, quintuples, and sextuples. By now she was soaring forty feet into the air, carrying with her, in her wake, a trail of powdery snow that made her think of a rocket's climb from ground to sky. On her home ice, the rink where she'd been skating since she was an infant, this is where she had to stop—the netting over the ice and the ceiling above it interfered with further progress.

Here, she could jump the full seventy feet she was capable of.

She had yet to land a septuple jump, although the power was there, and Pallatian gravity permitted it. One simply became too disoriented after seven turns to land on a single foot. She had already begun working on that, however, and had vowed never to stop—it might take years; it had taken years already—until she could make a dozen turns and land cleanly.

Finally it was time to go home. The snow had stopped falling, the ice had begun to look wet, and she had a long flight ahead of her. Touching a band on her wrist, she summoned her flying belt. Impellers humming and throwing snow—obscuring the pawprints, each the size of both her hands, of an African leopard she had been too preoccupied to notice inspecting her belongings—the device lifted itself into the air, obediently flew to her, and lowered itself over her head and shoulders.

She fastened the support straps and pushed forward on the control stick. Rising rapidly, she punched a course into the autopilot, and watched the uncharted wilderness roll by a thousand feet below her blades.

PART ONE:
ONE TENTH GEE

SIXTY-FIVE MILLION YEARS AGO, THE last time Earth was struck by an asteroid, everything in North America died in seconds, every tree on the planet burned, three quarters of the species then living, plant and animal, were wiped out, and the shockwave, conducted through the liquid iron core, split the crust open on the opposite side of the world, creating a range of volcanic mountains that did as much damage to the environment as the asteroid itself.

Had that bit of rock been only a little heavier, or traveling only a little faster, it could have burst the planet open like a bullet striking an egg, and evolution would have had to start all over again.

With the recent, tragic event at Ashland, Ohio, in East America, a badly-shaken humanity has now had a forcible reminder of its own vulnerability, as well as that of the planet it was born and evolved on. The question before our species now is, what are we going to do about it?

—Dr. Evgeny Zacharenko Addressing the Ashland Event Commission
Of the Solar Geological Society Curringer, Pallas, August 9, 2095

CHAPTER ONE: GEGENSCHEIN

Pallatians' fear that their kids, grandkids, and great grandkids will become civilized, urbanized, and lose the values that made their culture uniquely wonderful. Someday it'll just seem like too much trouble to maintain the "barroom justice" system that defends Pallatian individuals against governments and corporations. Too barbaric to hunt their own food. Too "macho" to carry weapons to defend themselves, their freedom, and their future. Personally, I don't think it'll happen. The asteroids offer too many new frontiers to conquer. —*The Diaries of Rosalie Frazier Ngu*

MUD-PIE PLANET.

It helped, sometimes, to remember that the broken, gray-brown surface that seemed to stretch endlessly before him, under merciless starlight, to a ragged horizon that was too far away, would be covered in lush green vegetation before another decade passed. That, the young construction worker thought, was the whole point to terraformation, after all.

Seventeen-year-old Wilson Ngu carefully examined the indicator riptabbed to the left sleeve of his envirosuit, found the spot on the asteroid's surface before him—the exact spot—corresponding to the reading of the instrument, and reached back, over his shoulder, for one of the transponders he carried on his back like arrows in a quiver.

It was a tedious, unglamorous task, but absolutely necessary. He clamped the middle of the shaft into an object that looked a bit like a pistol, pressed the ion-hardened tip of the shaft against the dark, crumbly surface—it was often described as being the exact color and texture of a slightly overdone chocolate chip cookie—and pulled the trigger. Through his suit, and the bones of his arm, he could hear the tool whine and scrape as it screwed the shaft six inches into the ground. When he pressed a release button, the top of the tool opened like a clamshell and let go of the shaft. Wilson was now ready, for the thousandth time today, to look for the next exact spot to plant a transponder.

He was "walking the tops" between craters, or "ridge-running" as it was called on his native world. On so heavily-ravaged a surface, it was the only way that made sense, on foot or driving a ground vehicle. Travelling the narrow elevations between craters avoided the necessity of going up and down constantly, and it also afforded much greater visibility. He would descend into a crater only if the survey called for it, and the survey had been designed not to, unless it was utterly unavoidable.

Nevertheless, it was important to be precise. In a just a few more weeks, once every acre of Ceres, largest of the belt of asteroids that circled the sun between the orbits of Mars and Jupiter, had finally been dotted with a transponder like this, standing on its fiberglass shaft about three feet above the ground, giant factory ships already in orbit—he could see one of them up there right now, its running lights cheerfully blinking yellow, red, and green—would use the guidance the devices provided to cover the entire world with virtually endless sheets, half a mile wide, of tough, self-repairing "smart" plastic.

Even that much was a monumental task, dwarfing the construction of the Egyptian pyramids or China's fabled Great Wall. Ceres had the same surface area as the Indian subcontinent on Earth. But what came next would be even more impressive. Just as there were thousands of workmen doing the same that job he was doing now, thousands more would follow, drawing the edges of the titanic plastic strips together, using tools any carpet-layer would recognize as giant versions of his own. The strips couldn't be more than inches apart, which was why precision in laying them was so important. The crews would weld them together with lasers and ultrasonic "torches". In days, the fresh welds would "heal" by themselves, creating a seamless transparent covering over the whole asteroid.

Although the materials and the technology had improved with time, the basic concept had been tested and proven three generations ago on the second largest of the asteroids, Pallas, which also happened to be the world of Wilson's birth. Pallas "only" had the same area as the West American "Four Corners" states of Utah, Colorado, Arizona, and New Mexico, with about a quarter of Wyoming thrown in for good measure.

Wilson found the next transponder location—each of the devices had a distinct digital signature that could be read from orbit—and locked a shaft into the drilling tool. The light that fell on Ceres' surface was only a fraction of that which fell on, say, Earth's moon, but it was bright enough to dazzle eyes adjusted to the Asteroid Belt. Boundaries between light and shadow were sharp. Once this atmospheric canopy he was helping to construct was complete, however, and filled with gases that human beings could breathe, things would be very different.

Green grass below, blue sky above, and shadows with soft edges. Farms. And cities. He wasn't altogether certain he approved of either. He planned—or at least wished—to be gone from here by then. He had reasons for his wishes. What they amounted to was a perfectly human need to leave the nest his parents had provided, strike out on his own, and make his own mark as a man. There was another reason, too, but he decided not to think about her just now—it was far too distracting.

For just a moment, Wilson looked up at the sky, grateful for the millions of microscopic nanoscrubbers that "lived" in his helmet and kept its transparent face from fogging up. The envirosuit kept him clean, too, fed him, quenched his thirst, and protected him from solar radiation. At least half of the hard little points of light he could see, hanging against the utter blackness of space, were familiar stars. Most of the other half were asteroids, all of them smaller than Ceres and Pallas, ranging from a couple hundred miles in diameter to the size of a grain of sand. They averaged about half a mile across, and about six hundred miles apart. Not one of them twinkled. But they all would, once the plastic canopy was up over Ceres, and filled with air.

There were planets out there, too, of course, and a hundred big factory ships, their highly-skilled, highly-paid crews already working in multiple shifts, manufacturing plastic for the canopy, rolling it onto impossibly huge spindles hanging in space beside the ships in orbit. He'd recently been aboard one of the vessels with his father—briefly, he wondered if it was the same one he was looking at now—and watched tender craft hauling raw material to it, in the form of boxcar-sized chunks of carbonaceous chondrite, the same substance that constituted most of Ceres itself. The ship's machinery crushed these smaller asteroids, extracting kerogen (the stuff that made chondrites carbonaceous) and a surprising amount of water—six to 22 percent by mass—that was used in the fabrication process, as well as for life support.

He'd enjoyed his brief visit to the factory ship. For as long as he could remember, spacecraft had been his real passion, and the camaraderie, the happy sense of a shared and worthwhile purpose among the men and women of the crew, was something you could almost reach out and touch. They might even have welcomed him, but he had more ambitious plans.

From orbit, it was easy to see that the entire surface of Ceres was densely covered with overlapping "impact features"—craters made by collision with other asteroids that would soon make it a world of a hundred thousand perfectly circular lakes, once the atmospheric canopy was finished. Ceres would also have a single perfectly circular ocean, 300 miles across, unless the Curringer Corporation found some other use for the one enormous crater that was the asteroid's most prominent feature.

None of that could happen, however, until the plastic canopy was anchored, folded into colossal gaskets at the outer edges of the north and south polar craters. The presence of those craters at the poles was no mere fortunate coincidence. Ceres had been carefully "nudged"—employing nuclear explosives—until a pair of suitable craters were at the opposite ends of its axis of rotation. Its rotation rate had been altered the same way, to give Ceres a 24-hour day. His father had planted each and every one of those explosives, by hand, although a computer had been used to set them off in proper order and at the correct intervals.

The crests of the ring-walls of those craters were being drilled two miles deep, at 21,600 points—one hole for every minute of the compass. Gigantic steel and titanium piers, each twice as large as the tallest skyscraper Earth had to offer, would then be set into the holes with perfectly ordinary concrete. Attached to the piers, huge twisted steel cables—exactly like those used on Earth's suspension bridges—would stretch hundreds of miles from pole to pole. When the plastic envelope was inflated beneath them, the cables would hold it in place.

While the rest of Ceres enjoyed a "shirtsleeve" environment, four seasons, sunshine and rainfall, even occasional snow, the floors of the two polar craters would remain exposed to hard vacuum and the bitter cold of deep space. They would become the spaceports of the little planet. Long tunnels, driven through the ring-walls of each of the craters (and between the piers), out onto the terraformed surface, and fitted with multiple heavy doors, would act as the asteroid's airlocks.

Abruptly, Wilson glanced up from his task.

Something wasn't right.

He wasn't sure what it was. He thought he'd seen movement against the next crater wall ahead.

There it was again!

Not movement, a faint flicker of reflected light. The sun was in his eyes. The inside of the ring-wall of the crater immediately ahead of him should have been in blackest shadow. Instead, it had been weakly illuminated for an instant, then illuminated again. What it meant was that someone or something was in the bottom of that crater, moving around, bouncing sunlight onto the wall, from their equipment or envirosuits.

Odd, Wilson thought, and annoying. He took it personally. He knew he looked the part of an adult, tall, well-muscled, agile, with that characteristic tan that could only result from being a native of deep space. He carried himself in a manner that unselfconsciously conveyed confidence and competence unusual in someone of his age, anyplace but out here, along the frontier of humanity's expansion into the Solar System.

Proud to be considered a full-grown man by everybody brought up in this pioneer culture, Wilson detested being introduced to investors' representatives from the Earth or the Moon, who refused to believe him capable of accepting adult responsibilities, and treated him like a child only because their own seventeen-year-olds were still children. He'd been told he would be in solitary charge of planting transponders in an area the size of Rhode Island. However now he suspected that his father had sent someone—or even come here himself—to check up on him.

Suddenly, something arose from the crater on a pillar of fire and smoke, and streaked upward, straight toward the cluster of yellow, red, and green lights blinking overhead.

Someone was trying to blow up the factory ship in orbit!

CHAPTER TWO: LASERFIGHT

To be a parent is to be torn right down the middle. On one hand, it's your evolutionary and social function to turn your children into fully autonomous adults as rapidly as you can. On the other—and here is why children are so often kept infantilized in other cultures—you will worry every minute they're away from the nest until (and this is the only way it ever happens) you finally exhaust your capacity for worry. I have found that living on a frontier will keep you focused on the first hand. —*The Diaries of Rosalie Frazier Ngu*

SOMEONE WAS TRYING TO BLOW up the factory ship in orbit!

Wilson felt his stomach tense as he imagined what a missile would do to the vessel and her hundreds of crew. Sickened, he watched the rocket climb and climb until it disappeared in the distance, boring through empty space toward its defenseless target, hundreds of miles overhead.

Then his heart leapt as the weapon exploded harmlessly, what must have been thousands of yards beyond the factory ship's running lights. Somehow, through mechanical failure or human incompetence, it had overshot the mark.

Wilson knew that he didn't have an instant to waste. He moved as rapidly as the lack of gravity would let him. True, it was twice what he'd been born to on his native Pallas, but the real difficulty was getting enough traction when he only "weighed" eighteen pounds—and his clumsy envirosuit didn't help. A few feet short of the dizzying cliff that was the inner wall of the crater, he climbed the little upslope at its edge, then got down on his hands and knees and peeked over, careful to keep his head down between two clumps of impact rubble.

Down on a crater floor perhaps half a mile in diameter, a dozen figures were either facing outward, keeping watch, or tinkering with the primitive-looking rocket launcher they'd apparently brought with them. Wilson could tell from the shiny, cheerfully colored envirosuits they wore that they were merely amateurs, or tourists. What was that old song his grandfather Bill used to sing him about "a red one and a blue one and a green one and a yellow one and they're all made out of ticky-tacky"?

If the intruders had been down there for any time at all, they must be miserable by now, suffering heat and cold at the same time, depending on what part of their mostly unautomated suits bothered them worst, and from accumulated moisture from condensation. To make it worse, cheap outfits like that didn't even have elementary sanitary facilities.

No doubt that was partly why they'd grounded a small, cylindrical interasteroidal spacecraft in the shadow of the sunward crater wall. It looked to Wilson like a Fiat 914SX, a cheap rental "jumpbuggy" with a single deck, shared with the fusion-ion engine. With a dozen people aboard, uncomfortable wasn't the word for it. It couldn't be from anywhere but Pallas, of course, and probably wasn't any more reliable than their suits. Out here, as anywhere else, you got no more than you paid for.

Wilson stepped up the magnifying power of his helmet's faceplate and noticed the two-handed laser rifles being held by several of the outward-facing watchers. There was only one use for lasers under these conditions—against envirosuits of decent quality—and it wasn't as a weapon's primary energy source. The surface of a properly built envirosuit was highly reflective, and would ablate relatively slowly. Moreover, the gases boiling off would tend to attenuate the beam's destructive power. That was the theory, anyway. If he'd been in their place, looking for trouble, he'd have forgotten about lasers, which were far too expensive, in any case, and brought magnetic driver weapons.

Thinking about it, he could have used something like a magnetic driver weapon himself, just now—the thought of tiny steel bullets fired at several thousand feet per second was comforting. The other figures below laboriously loaded another rocket into the front end of their launcher. Using a small finder scope attached to the barrel of the thing, they did their clumsy best to aim it straight at the factory ship in synchronous orbit overhead. Wilson watched them helplessly.

No—not quite helplessly!

Wilson glanced down, a little surprised to find the pistol-shaped transponder drill still in his hand, but useless. Carefully attaching it to one of the suspender straps of his equipment harness—no one abandons tools of any kind in an environment where all life depends on them—he withdrew a real weapon from a zippered, insulated pocket across his chest. He hadn't thought about it before now because it was very nearly new. Nevertheless it was his pride and joy, a large-framed Herron StaggerCyl "double revolver", chambered in the classic .270 REN. He'd never fired the massive weapon he carried until now, except against paper targets and the heavy metallic game animal silhouettes that represented almost a century-old sporting tradition on his native Pallas.

A true spacer's "wheelgun", the Herron StaggerCyl boasted a pair of six-inch barrels, one set above the other, under a broad milled rib supporting old-fashioned but reliable iron sights of the Patridge square-notch-and-post variety. The gun's dual firing pins alternated automatically, geared to a 12-shot cylinder with an inner and outer row of chambers, neatly arranged in a zig-zag pattern around a center ratchet.

The small brass cartridge with its tiny projectile—its true caliber was only .277—wouldn't be much good for anything on Pallas but playing games and shooting rabbits. The Herron StaggerCyl was low powered precisely to avoid excessive recoil in microgravity. But the little bullet's velocity was high enough to do exactly what it was designed to do, which was to knock over a metallic animal silhouette, although it could also handily penetrate multiple layers of envirosuit fabric.

Wilson forced himself to calm down and breathe normally. Although he could simply have pulled the trigger through, "double action", he prudently thumbed the hammer back, instead, and aligned the big square radio-luminescent iron sights of the Herron where he calculated that the tripod base was attached to the launcher far below. Only when he had a steady basic sight picture did he depress the switch-pad of the targeting laser built into the right grip of his revolver, gratified to see that it placed a bright red dot exactly where the sights were looking.

Taking half a breath, he squeezed the trigger slowly.

The sear released. The hammer fell. A bright three-foot ball of blue-pink flame blossomed briefly at the muzzle. Recoil was negligible and the shot could only be "heard" through his arms, through the fabric of his suit, and in the wave-front of rapidly dissipating gases generated at the muzzle. The small, nickel-clad hardened lead alloy projectile struck the launcher just as the larger weapon discharged, tipping it over and sending its missile skittering wildly across the crater floor, to blow up against the opposite wall, right beneath the jumpbuggy.

The rocket's double fist-sized explosive charge would have opened a house-sized hole in the factory ship overhead, killing hundreds and possibly destroying the entire vessel. Instead, its power reduced the flimsy jumpbuggy to tinsel. That the shot was pure dumb luck, Wilson was perfectly willing to admit. Some rental agent back on Pallas was going to be extremely unhappy. He don't know himself, whether to laugh or weep.

Suddenly, both options were out of the question, as he discovered he was being showered with tiny sharp-edged fragments of rock. The shooters in the crater below were firing their laser rifles at him, missing badly, and mostly striking the boulders to either side of him, instead. Intentionally or not, they were spalling off flakes of heated olivine gravel that struck him harmlessly. However, his envirosuit, which was not a cheap piece of tourist ticky-tacky, began talking to him.

"Warning! Warning! There is a Class Five breach in the right shoulder of this device, Location SDY5955! Warning! Warning! There is a Class Five breach in the right shoulder of this device, Location SDY5955!"

Damn! One of those laser shooters must have actually hit him! A Class Five breach, Wilson knew from countless hours of screen time and from classroom training that his father and mother had both insisted on (in one of their rare moments of agreement), meant that a few stray air molecules could just be detected migrating outward through the upper layers of fabric in his envirosuit. Damage like that might cause him to run out of oxygen in a decade or two. He ducked down behind a rock, switched his big revolver to his left hand, and spoke to his suit.

"Activate right wrist pickup."

"Warning! Warning!" came the automated reply to his request. "There is a Class Five breach in the right shoulder of this device, Location SDY5955! Warning! Warning! There is a Class Five breach in the right—"

"I know! I know! Shut up and activate the pickup!"

"Warning! Warning! There is a Class Five breach…"

However in a small video screen near his right cheek, he could now see what the tiny camera at the back of his right wrist was seeing. He reached toward the small of his back and seized a bright, lime-green, thumb-sized tab, pulling out an emergency adhesive patch roughly the size of his hand. Switching the big Herron StaggerCyl back to his right hand, he stripped the cover from the patch exactly like the bandage it resembled, and slapped it on his shoulder in the correct location. "Warning! Warning! There is a Class Five—"

Abruptly, his envirosuit stopped talking to him. But by now he'd noticed that his radio antenna, located behind his right shoulder, had been reduced to a shiny-ended quarter-inch stub, and wondered why he hadn't felt it when it happened. And why his suit hadn't bothered to mention it. Too busy nagging him about the big bad Class Five leak, he supposed.

Suddenly feeling pressed for time again, Wilson crept back to the edge of the crater. Sure enough, two of the laser riflemen below had begun clambering painfully up the inside crater wall, coming toward him, miniature landslides starting beneath every uncertain footstep. It was a pretty stupid move, he thought, unless they believed he was dead. As his head became visible, one of them snapped off a shot at him and missed.

Ignoring the danger more than he probably should have, he sighted his revolver on the nearest figure and shot it in the center of its torso.

Not waiting to observe the effect, he shot the other climber.

Limp as cloth dummies, the two shooters tumbled back down the way they came, raising gray-brown dust that settled quickly without air to support it. Their expensive laser rifles followed after them. His own envirosuit might be able to seal a hole like that, possibly allowing him to survive. But they weren't wearing his suit. If they weren't dead, they soon would be. Catastrophic suit failure had that effect on people.

Down on the crater floor, two more of the cheaply-attired figures began lasering at him without bothering to take cover, doing their best to keep him busy while their comrades fought desperately to get their damaged rocket launcher upright again and reload it. They must all be very dedicated, down there, Wilson thought, or extremely stupid. He began to have a suspicion about which it was and who they were.

He shot one armed figure, then the other—and a third who had begun shooting at him from nearer the launcher. The last one took his hurried bullet through the front of the helmet and was squirming on the ground with both gloved hands clasped desperately over his ruined faceplate.

Five of their number now lay dead or dying. Through it all, the other seven went on struggling with the missile launcher until Wilson finally used his own, considerably less powerful laser to line a shot up on the barrel of the launcher and hit it with one of his little .277 bullets.

He felt a bit cheated. He didn't knock it over this time, but in a proper atmosphere, that thing down there would have rung like a bell. It had the desired effect nonetheless: suddenly all of the figures in their colorful envirosuits laid their tools and weapons on the ground, stepped back from the rocket launcher, and raised their hands over their heads.

Guess they weren't so dedicated, after all, Wilson thought, or so stupid. Nevertheless, as a warning, he splashed the red dot of his targeting laser on their chests, one by one—now that was the proper use for a laser in these circumstances—while he waited for help to arrive.

Only then did Wilson remember his damaged suit radio.

CHAPTER THREE: THE GAMERA

> I used to find it mysterious and frustrating that the news media—those whose trade it is to observe reality and bear witness to everyone else—are the least capable observers and least articulate witnesses among us. Then I realized that there's no such thing as "the news"; it's just the lowest, sleaziest rung on the show business ladder. —*The Diaries of Rosalie Frazier Ngu*

"THAT'S REALLY HIM DOWN THERE?" asked Ingrid Andersson, staring into the monitor from where she stood behind her employer's desk chair.

"What Ingrid said," said Adam Ngu. Despite her name, his assistant was as thoroughly Asian as a young woman could get: high cheekbones, dark eyes that looked almost black, and glossy hair that displayed reddish highlights in the sun. It was typical of Adam that he'd never noticed she was pretty, although a civil engineer certainly should have noticed how perfectly constructed she was. Everyone else who worked with her had.

"Yes, Miss Andersson, Mr. Ngu, you're looking at him now," said the off-camera voice of Hortense Blumenfeld, manager—not captain— of the factory ship *Percival Lowell*. Like about half of such vessels presently standing in synchronous orbit about Ceres, the *Percy*, as she was called, was independently owned and operated, rather than property of the Curringer Corporation. "It appears his envirosuit radio was damaged in the gunfight."

Gunfight. Behind Adam, Ingrid let a little gasp escape her throat. She was originally from East America, where such things as gunfights were completely unheard of—because they were censored from the news.

Hortense would be the one to know, Adam thought. Although the screen was showing the surface of Ceres, he could see her in his mind, a short, compactly built woman with a cloud of tightly-curled black hair about her head. She'd grown up on Mars, a Settled World in some ways only half terraformed even now, where envirosuits were as common as raincoats, and they still had an occasional gunfight to make life interesting.

Adam leaned back in his swivel chair, gazing up for a moment through the non-existent ceiling of his office, at the underside of the transparent dome, a thousand feet high, that served as base camp and headquarters for the Ceres Terraformation Project. A mile and a half in diameter, made of the same plastic that would someday cover the entire planetoid (except, of course, for the polar craters), the dome kept a habitable environment within, while protecting Adam and those working for him from solar radiation and a constant rain of micrometeorites.

He could see a lot of tiny lights up there. Some were asteroids— this was the most densely populated portion of the Belt—but he didn't have time or patience just now to watch long enough to tell which. He saw the Curringer Corporation's factory vessel *Giuseppi Piazzi*, flagship of the fleet, affectionately known by everyone as *Joe Pizza*. Then he peered again at the big, flat, high resolution screen at the back of his desk.

"This is in real time," he said.

"Yes, sir," Hortense answered, "Real time."

The view was through a computer-assisted telescope aboard the *Percy*, looking into an otherwise undistinguished crater from which a missile had apparently been launched at the factory ship. Down inside the crater, the remains of a jumpbuggy were the easiest thing to see—little more than metallic confetti in the middle of a spoked rosette of blackened soil. Not far away, a small cluster of figures wearing brightly-colored envirosuits sat cross-legged, fingers interlaced submissively atop their helmets.

On a nearby rock that had tumbled back into the crater sometime in the last couple of billion years, keeping his prisoners in that position, sat an individual wearing a white, professional-grade envirosuit more appropriate to long-term use on an asteroid's surface. The manager of the *Percy* had assured Adam that the figure was his son, Wilson. Whoever it was—and there was no reason to believe that it wasn't his son—he held a bulky laser rifle across his chest and looked up, every few minutes, toward the factory vessel in orbit above him.

He made a decision. "Ingrid, call the motor pool and ask them to warm up a *gamera* for me, will you?"

"Right away, Boss." Ingrid went to her own desk and began pushing buttons.

"Thank goodness we had the Morse Code in our database, Mr. Ngu," Hortense was saying. They'd known each other and worked together for 15 years, and he'd never persuaded her to call him by his first name. Martians could be terribly formal, just as Pallatians tended to be rather informal. "And thank goodness your son guessed right, that at this distance, a laser rifle is safe to use as a signaling device."

Adam laughed. "If I know my own son, there wasn't any guessing to it. That young man has the quickest mind for practical math I've seen since I met his mother. Did you attempt to signal back?"

"Yes, sir. We'd seen the missile they fired at us—damn fools couldn't shoot for sour owl-shit, pardon the expression, sir. Then we watched the gunfight and the explosion. Unfortunately, there wasn't any way we could help. All of our tenders were out on rounds—still are, in fact—and we have no real weapons aboard except for personal sidearms. I think I'll write a memo about that when this is over. When the boy sent us an SOS, using that laser, we switched off all of *Percy*'s running lights and switched them back on again, three times.

"He acknowledged with his first initial and his last name."

Adam nodded, filled with fatherly pride. She could see him, even if he couldn't see her. He was a man in his early 40s, sparely-built, tall, with thinning, sandy hair and an expression of vague sadness he didn't know he wore. "Then he'll know help is on the way—which it won't be until I'm aboard the *gamera*. Talk to you again enroute."

"Okay, Mr. Ngu," she answered, "*Percival Lowell*, signing off."

He got up, seizing his pistol belt where it hung from a shelf above the desk. It held a 10mm Magnum Ngu Departure Mark Five that the inventor—his own long-missing grandfather—had given him as a gift on his twelfth birthday. He was never more than an arm's length away from it—that was the Pallatian Way—but the belt, holster, and spare magazine pouches didn't work well with the arms of his swivel chair.

"Ingrid, I'm outa here! Take the rest of the day off. I'm going to need you bright and early tomorrow morning."

"Good hunting, Boss." She extinguished the lights and shut the door behind them.

*
**

"Doctor Ngu!"

Striding across the dome at ground level—his office was at one edge, the motor pool airlock almost at the other—Adam recalled that he hadn't known why transports used here and on other large asteroids were called *gamera*, until his daughter had told him.

"Doctor Ngu!"

In his mind's eye he could see Llyra now, tall, slender like nearly all Pallatians, blonde and fair, with a light scattering of freckles across her cute little turned-up nose—but looking back at him with her lost and legendary great-grandfather's Asian eyes. She'd been exasperated with her daddy because "everybody" knew that the vehicles were named for their shape—everybody her age and enthusiastic about the latest media revival—a giant, mythical, rocket-powered turtle in silly Japanese monster movies of a previous century.

Sometimes he wondered where a 13-year-old learned about things like that. It certainly wasn't what he and his wife imported tutors to teach her. On the other hand, it had been a long time since he'd been 13 himself, and the years between full enough to make remembering what it was like a trifle difficult.

If only Ardith—

"Phone!" Adam spoke to the air more emphatically than he'd meant to. The thought of his wife usually had that effect on him. A welding crew preparing their midday meal at the worksite looked up at him. They were using an acetylene torch to heat the underside of a cast iron skillet, its handle clamped in a vise. It smelled like they were frying rabbit. It reminded him that he hadn't had any lunch yet today.

He grinned and waved as he passed them.

"Doctor Ngu!"

"*Ready*" came the electronic answer from his shirt pocket.

The dome was full of buildings, relatively skeletal in appearance to any observer born and raised in more than a tenth of a standard gravity. Here were the administrative offices, drafting facilities, workshops, and living quarters for the Curringer Corporation's Ceres Terraformation Project which he served as Executive Director and Chief Engineer. He walked rapidly through the makeshift streets between the so-far only half-constructed buildings, unconsciously inspecting them as he talked.

"Get me Lindsay and Arleigh, right away, in conference."

"I just learned about Wilson," said a voice most people heard as identical to his own. His middle brother Lindsay was one of his two "right arms" on the Project. "I'm on my way back now. You under way, yet, Ad?"

"Not quite," Adam told him. "I'm afoot, just arriving at the tunnel airlock. I'll be aboard Number 23 in three minutes. Where are you now?"

Lindsay laughed. "Look out through the dome. That's me approaching in the crawler. Some idiot excavator thought he'd found a Drake-Tealy Object. What he found was one of the original survey landing sites. I'll reach the *gamera* first. Want some coffee? Where's Arleigh?"

"What I want is lunch." Adam couldn't see him through the dome. He'd just sealed himself into the first of three airlocks between the edge of it and the motor pool. All the chambers between were kept filled with air, so the only wait was for the doors to open and close.

"I'm in the lockspace right behind, you Ad," came a third voice, tenor, rather different from those of his brothers. "If you'll wait. There's a very insistent young woman with me who's been following you from your office, screaming your name."

Adam waited as requested, until the lock cycled, and was joined by his youngest brother. Arleigh was already wearing most of a company issue envirosuit and held his helmet under his arm, with his gloves tucked into it. Adam's envirosuit—one of them, anyway—would be waiting for him in the *gamera*.

"Doctor Ngu..." There was a woman with Arleigh, mid-30s, Adam guessed, and from Earth to judge by her clothing. She wore a fairly plain business suit with a short skirt that didn't work at one tenth of a gee—or worked splendidly, depending on one's viewpoint. It kept creeping up over her hips and she had to hike it down. What most impressed Adam about her was that she wore a pair of Sony QDH-616G SuperMedia spectacles with cameras at their outer corners no bigger than a pinhead—and far too much perfume for a closed environment.

Without thinking about it consciously, he dismissed her.

Unlike Adam and Lindsay, and most Pallatians, Arleigh was almost as broad as he was tall. Their father Bill joked that he'd been born over a mascon and was built for heavy gravity. Arleigh had powerful arms and big, thick-fingered hands. His bushy hair and massive beard were black and curly. People had the impression he was short until they stood beside him. From the first moment she'd spoken, and for seven or eight years thereafter, Llyra had called her uncle Arleigh "Hagrid".

Arleigh had named himself. He'd hated his first name, Randolph. He'd hated being called Randy even worse. Going by his middle name for a while, he'd found that people assumed that "Leigh Ngu" was Asian. Not that it mattered. The brothers' paternal grandfather was half Cambodian and half Vietnamese. That was how things were in the Belt. People came for a new beginning. They met and married others—or the daughters and sons of others—who had come for exactly the same reason.

By then, nobody cared about anything about you, except the kind of person you were inside. You had to be smart and tough to survive. You had to have a decent regard for the rights of others. That was what really counted. The boys' great grandmother's maiden name had been Singh, but her father had been born and raised in Montana, part of West America.

"Doctor Ngu," the woman insisted. "Please let me introduce myself. I'm Honey Graham, of the Interplanetary Interactive Information Service. I understand there's something of a crisis going on right now, and that it involves Null Delta Em—and your son, Wilson."

Without pausing more than an instant, Adam turned away from the woman and shook his brother's hand. Ignoring her, they both hurried down the long tunnel designed to protect the dome from an explosion or fire in the motor pool. (The mechanics always said it was to protect them from an accident in the dome.)

On the phone, Lindsay spoke. "I've downloaded nav data, Ad. Are you about here?"

Adam said, "Just beneath you, cycling the elevator lock."

"See here, Doctor Ngu, you can't just ignore me like that!" Honey Graham had caught up and was out of breath. "I represent the people's press, and the people have a right—"

Adam turned to her. "This is the asteroid Ceres, Miss... what did you say your name was? Every square inch of it is private property, and 'the people' have exactly the same rights here that they have in your bedroom. Now if you'll excuse me..."

He pushed buttons beside what looked like an ordinary elevator door. It opened into a cylindrical chamber. He and Arleigh entered, looking forward to the door closing behind them.

"Please wait, Doctor Ngu! I've been on this goddamned rock for three weeks and haven't found a single story worth transmitting home! I'm in danger of losing my job—and even worse, of dying of boredom! Can't I come along? I'll behave myself, I promise."

She twisted her torso slightly to expose a bit of cleavage and even more thigh. Adam sighed to himself. After only two minutes' acquaintance, he detested this woman and everything she represented. But as Director of the Ceres Terraformation Project, he couldn't afford trouble with the press right now, especially if Null Delta Em—and their sponsors, the Mass Movement—was involved.

"What's the matter, Miss..." he asked. "If nothing bleeds, then nothing leads?"

"I'm Honey Graham, Doctor Ngu, and I'm afraid you're right. I'm hearing that your son is a hero, though, and I'd like to cover the story."

"All right," he told her. "Step into the elevator. I don't suppose you have an envirosuit with you."

Arleigh laughed. "We'll fix her up, Ad, don't worry about it."

Adam pressed a button. The door shut and they felt a slight change in pressure in their ears. By the time they'd worked their jaws to clear them, the elevator had risen 20 feet and was now inside the belly of the *gamera*. The door opened. The two men and the woman stepped out.

The door closed and another door, part of the *gamera*, closed over it. The elevator lowered itself back into the ground and circular doors on both the *gamera* and the tunnel below sealed themselves. The chamber that remained in the *gamera* could now be used as an ordinary airlock.

"What's our ETA?" Adam strode forward to the controls, while Arleigh stayed behind with the reporter, ostensibly to inspect some part of the machinery. Lindsay sat in the lefthand seat, working his way through the checklist. Like his brother, he was tall and slender, although his hair was dark and had receded to form a distinctive widow's peak.

"Point-to-point, about 36 minutes." Lindsay flipped a last switch, closed the aluminum-covered book, and dropped it into its slot beside his left knee. He shouted at Arleigh, "Grilled cheese sandwiches and tomato soup in the kitchen unit! Better buckle up back there!"

"I'm buckled! So is Miss Graham—may I call you Honey?"

Grinning, Lindsay checked radar, then checked the old-fashioned way, through what were once called windshields, for any traffic around them. He took the yoke in his left hand, put his feet on the pedals, and pulled back on a lever. The *gamera* lifted itself from the ground on a column of ionized gases, surged forward as it continued to rise, and they were off.

CHAPTER FOUR: BRODY MEMORIAL

In retrospect, it makes perfect sense, as all unintended consequences do. The parts were all there: the low gravity, the availability of temperatures only a handful of degrees above Absolute Zero, confined spaces that won't permit wider- reaching pastimes like baseball. But who could have guessed that the asteroids' favorite sport, to watch or play, would turn out to be hockey? —*The Diaries of Rosalie Frazier Ngu*

"I SEE YOU HAVE AGAIN been pond skating," Jasmeen Khalidov said. "And over mascon."

Somehow looking like a ballerina at rest, the young woman sat cross-ankled on a long, low, slatted plastic bench running down the center for most of the length of the women's hockey locker room at the Aloysius

Brody Memorial Ice Skating Rink in Curringer, principal city on Pallas, second largest body in the Asteroid Belt. She was holding, in both of her long, slender-fingered hands, her only student's left boot, upturned just now to expose the gleaming double edges of the blade.

The boots were perfectly conventional, handmade for their owner of stiff, multilayered leather and various synthetics, nominally white on the outside, but covered with scuffs and cuts from long, hard use. It was the blades that were different, especially designed for the lower gravity of Pallas. They were half again as thick as ordinary figure skating blades, but lighter because they were made from an alloy of titanium. Their under-surfaces were grooved, like those of ordinary skates, but the radius was much smaller than normal—only three sixteenths of an inch—to provide extraordinarily sharp, deep edges, necessary for control at only one twen-tieth of the "standard" Earth gravity.

The toepicks at the fronts of the blades were different, too, longer and sharper. Ordinary toepicks, meant for use on Earth, would only skid in the light gravity of Pallas, without biting into the ice properly.

The other boot lay at Jasmeen's feet.

There wasn't a surface in the room that wasn't marked where a black rubber hockey puck had bounced off it at one time or another. There were a dozen signs in the locker rooms, in the lobby, in the bleachers, in the al-leyway around the rink itself, warning in big red letters against puck and stick play anywhere at Frazier Memorial but on the ice. Nobody had ever paid the slightest attention to them or ever would.

Similar warnings not to hang on the overhead netting, forty feet above the ice—it was an easy jump for most Pallatian skaters— were similarly ignored.

Three broken hockey sticks stood, stacked together like rifles, in a corner of the room near the showers, and odd remnants of gear, armor made of fiberglass—knee guards, shin guards, elbow guards, shoulder pads, even a helmet—were strewn about the rubberized floor like bits of molted dinosaur skin.

The heavy odor of athletic sweat, suffused with adrenaline, and allowed to stand in lockers full of dirty clothing until it fermented, permeated the room, but Jasmeen and her student were as accustomed to it as anyone could get. After twenty minutes or so of adjustment, they hardly noticed it. If it were her rink, the young coach had often said nobody would be allowed to enter the rink with unwashed pads and other equipment.

Jasmeen could see herself in the polished nickel-steel mirror at one end of the locker room. (Glass wouldn't have survived in here for a minute.)

What she saw was an extraordinarily slender, rather fragile looking young woman who was not quite yet 20, and, at five foot four inches, fully a head shorter than most of the Pallatian children Llyra's age.

Appearances can be deceiving. There was nothing fragile about Jasmeen, nothing fragile at all. She was a pretty blonde—at the moment, her shoulder-blade-length hair was bound up in a couple of big pigtails—with rather strong features: enormous gray-green eyes with very long, dark lashes, and lids that were a natural lavender color and needed no makeup. Her eyebrows didn't arch, but soared up and outward above her eyes. She had a small dimple in her chin, and her lips, especially the lower one, were full. Her nose, gracefully turned up, was proportionate with the rest of her face.

Jasmeen looked thin, but she had good, broad shoulders. She was also quite full-breasted for her size, and although her hips were slender, they were set off by an exceptionally narrow waist. Just now, having not yet put on her long, black, "official" coach's coat, she wore a delicate little white cotton top—no female needed more than that at one twentieth of a gee, although in the cold of the rink it could be embarrassing sometimes—that did nothing to disguise her obvious assets. Its frilly hem left a bit of her flat belly exposed over badly faded bluejeans with the waistband turned down.

Where she stood at her open locker, 13-year-old Llyra Ngu turned abruptly, unconsciously standing on her toes. "How can you possibly know I've been pond skating, Jasmeen?" She pronounced her coach's name correctly—"yahzz-MEEN"—as many others who knew her failed to do. The 19-year-old was more than just a figure skating coach to the younger girl. She was Llyra's tutor in several other subjects, her best friend, and only six years her senior. Sometimes she was Llyra's mother.

Jasmeen looked up at her student and laughed. It was a warm, happy laugh, not intended to inflict pain. "Is elementary, my dear What'sit. Bootsoles still damp, although I know you have had no ice booked here yesterday or this morning. They are playing hockey all day long here, yesterday and day before. So I deduce you must be skating outdoors, somewhere."

"Yes, that's right," Llyra was incredulous, but delighted. She loved games like this. "But over a mascon?"

"Why else are you ever skating outdoors?" Jasmeen shook her head, indicating her student with an upturned hand. "Where you have equal chance of falling and breaking something or being eaten alive by wild animal. Possibly both. This is not happy girl unless there is small, extra risk to turn her mother's hair white—not to mention hair of little Russian coach!"

"You know why I do it, Jasmeen. Someday I'm gonna skate on Earth." Llyra gave her coach a good-natured frown and held up a stainless steel object she'd just taken from her skate bag, a Ngu Departure Pocket Ten her parents had given her on her twelfth birthday. "Anyway, I had my little pistol with me—and you aren't Russian, you're Chechen."

"Mostly, I am Martian," Jasmeen replied, with a sigh, and it was true. She was the daughter of an intrepid (and desperate) couple who had traveled to Mars under a United Nations program funded and directed by the East American government. Fleeing the political and military perils of the Earth, Mohammed Khalidov and his wife Beliita had been among only a few to survive the Red Plant's harsh environment long enough to be rescued by Pallations.

To this day, any time someone mentioned the Earth, Father spat. Due to his influence, she favored a Coprates Industries plasma-driven Express Eleven.

*
**

Outside the locker room, in the rubber-paved space between the locker room walls and the transparent "boards" of the rink, Jasmeen paused.

The surface here was unique in all the Solar System—although she suspected it wouldn't be, once a rink was built on Ceres. At what would normally have been the outer margin of the rink, it curved up smoothly, toward the vertical, so that objects tended to slide back down onto the flat. A dark-stranded net, stretching from the top of the boards, up and completely over the ice, kept hockey pucks—and the occasional involuntary skater—from leaving the rink in the low Pallatian gravity.

It was the beginning of an "open" or "public" session. The ice this morning was presently occupied by a dozen "recreational" skaters, mostly gliding around the rink in elongated circles. But they had just finished three hours' worth of hockey practice in here. The cavernous, high-ceilinged room reeked of adrenalin, sweaty bodies, and unwashed pads and jerseys. The odor was tolerable only because it was the kids' teams that had been practicing, boys and girls of Llyra's age and younger. If it had been a couple of the men's teams, the air-scrubbing machinery would be working at full tilt, and the air would still be unbreathable.

Jasmeen stood momentarily with both of her hands against the boards, one foot beneath her and the other far behind, stretching her calves. It was more than a little awkward, encumbered by the long plastic guards

31

that protected her blades from dirt and grit on the floor, but she'd been doing it all her life and was no longer conscious of the difficulty. She liked doing it out here, where she could see what was going on.

Llyra had gone to the rinkside weight room, a few doors back up the corridor, to spend a useful 20 minutes or so warming up on one of the treadmills her engineer father had redesigned for a world that had only one twentieth of the gravity that the machine had been intended for. She also enjoyed using the free weights (cast of solid tungsten, a relatively cheap commodity among the asteroids, especially for this facility) and machines, but it was always hard to get her to stretch sufficiently.

Not for the first time, Jasmeen reflected on how was amazing it was, how the lives and fortunes of their two families, the Khalidovs and the Ngus, were so deeply intertwined. Llyra's great-grandfather Emerson had been one of the founders of the settlement here on Pallas, before his notorious disappearance aboard the exploratory vessel *Fifth Force*, and had helped convey it safely through many perils in the early years.

Llyra's grandfather William and his brother Brody (named after the same individual this facility had been constructed to honor) had flown to Mars, decades later, to rescue her—Jasmeen's—mother and father, and other colonists, after the East American government and the United Nations had simply abandoned them there. Now she—Jasmeen—was here, working for William's son Adam and Adam's wife Ardith, helping to educate their daughter, whom she'd come to love as if she were a little sister.

Llyra badly needed love, Jasmeen thought, although she would never have said so aloud, to anyone. Adam, her father, was a good man, but he was absent most of the time, lately on Ceres, which he was making over as he had made over the exercise machines here—and as others had made over Pallas itself. Jasmeen wasn't absolutely certain, but she believed that Llyra's mother Ardith regarded affection as a sign of weakness. It was possible that Jasmeen was prejudiced, but she didn't think so.

She put a heel up on the little unintentional shelf, four feet high, that separated the upper and lower boards surrounding the rink. She bent, wrapping both hands around her foot. As she stretched the muscles of her back and legs, she watched three of Llyra's friends. She couldn't remember their names, but she'd seen them here before. A little boy, perhaps 10 or 11, sat on a big plastic footlocker the hockey teams used sometimes, just outside the rink gate, with a little girl, a tomboy. Neither of them looked at the other. Both stared down self-consciously at their hockey skates. It was obvious that he was working up to taking her hand, but was happy merely to be sitting beside her. That most magical of instants was only a heartbeat away when—

All at once, they were interrupted by another little boy who had just come off the ice, pink-faced and breathless. He was begging the first boy to come out into the rink and skate. "That's the reason we came, isn't it?"

A long, silent struggle ensued, played out entirely on the first little boy's face. At long last he got up, mumbled a perfunctory apology to the little girl, and dashed out onto the ice with his buddy. The little girl stared back down at her skates again, lower lip trembling.

Life's little dramas, Jasmeen sighed to herself. Something inside her wanted her to hurry to the little girl, put a comforting hand on her arm, and tell her that she wouldn't always lose this kind of struggle—that, in fact, in the end, she'd always win, that being the nature of life.

But it simply wasn't in Jasmeen to intrude. Martians were almost insanely reticent, and it had required a supreme effort on her part not to be that way with Llyra, who required affection, required human contact, as a beautiful flower requires sunlight and raindrops in order to live.

Three of the raindrops—or rays of sunshine—in Llyra's life came down the corridor toward Jasmeen now, having emerged from the girls' locker room. All three were freshly showered and dragging big hockey equipment bags behind them that they could have used as sleeping bags.

Nikki Johnson had dark, curly hair, almost black, with threads of auburn through it. Just now she wore it in a pair of braids. Her pale Celtic skin was covered with freckles from hairline to chin, across both cheeks and her turned-up nose. It always surprised Jasmeen that her thoroughly Irish eyes weren't blue. Ordinarily, she was a little chatterbox, but she'd been playing this season with an ankle injury, and practice this morning had worn her out. Her face was grim, and all Jasmeen got from her was a reasonably cheerful "Hey-oh!" as the girl, a year or two older than Llyra, but one of her closest friends, set her hockey bag down and leaned against the transparency to watch the rink.

Right behind her, dragging her own bag, followed Katie O'Hara. Katie's hair was straight and brown, and at some point in her young life, laughter had moved into her amber eyes to stay. In Llyra's absence, Katie was the clown of the ensemble. When the two of them got the giggles, it was as contagious as the Black Plague and they couldn't be shut off.

Emmy Morimura seemed to be constructed on a smaller scale than the others, with glossy black shoulder-length hair, and eyes so dark that they looked black, as well. It was impossible, Jasmeen often thought, for a human being to be so beautiful. Third and last of Llyra's trio of closest friends, Emmy dragged behind her the extra-large bag and extra-wide stick of a goalie, an odd position, Jasmeen thought, for someone so withdrawn, quiet, and small. Ordinarily, even when an adult asked her a direct question, she would simply look down at her shoes and say nothing. Emmy apparently saw Jasmeen, however, as something in between child and adult, for she sometimes engaged the older girl in long, animated conversations.

Just then, Llyra emerged from the weight room in a brilliant metallic blue leotard, with a towel around her neck, and her skate bag dangling from two fingers. The girl's dark blonde hair was pinned up, with a few escaping strands around her face and at the back of her neck.

"Here comes the ostrich!" Nikki hollered at her. The girls had recently watched an old recording of *Fantasia* together, so they all knew what she meant.

Katie echoed her. "Where're your pink toe-shoes, ostrich?"

Emmy grinned, but said nothing. That was usually her part in this ritual. Llyra stuck her tongue out at them as she passed, and patted Emmy on the head. She set her bag down on the locker, sat, and began lacing her skates. The other three girls gathered around her in a half circle.

"Watch out!" she told them, pointing a jagged toepick at them. "My toe-shoes are white—and have teeth!"

"Say," remarked Emmy, startling them all. "Wouldn't that be assault with a sledly weapon?"

There was a moment of stunned silence.

"Mighty big talk," Katie observed at last, "for somebody who skates in her skivvies."

Llyra pointed at Katie's huge equipment bag, which contained her helmet, armor, and padding. "Mighty big talk for somebody who skates wearing a canoe."

They all laughed. "Score one," Nikki grinned, "for the underwear lady!"

Jasmeen laughed, too, despite herself. She'd been alarmed until she learned that they all prepared for these episodes days in advance. She'd once caught Katie writing down comebacks on her pocket computer. Llyra finished lacing her skates, stood, and strode toward the gate in the boards where Jasmeen was waiting for her. Llyra used the public sessions to warm up for her lessons.

"Excuse me, Miss?"

The voice behind her startled her. She turned to see a young man in full hockey regalia. Judging by the smell it hadn't been cleaned in weeks.

Jasmeen patted Llyra on the arm as she passed. "Warm up and I'll be right with you."

Then to the young man. "May I help you in some way?"

"Well I was going to ask about drop-in hockey hours…" he said, just as Llyra sped by and executed a casual waltz jump that took her six feet into the air and covered a dozen yards. She landed silently and lightly as a snowflake.

"You were saying?" Jasmeen asked.

"Yeah—what the hell is *that*?" He pointed at Llyra as she did a set of "stars"—low-bending single spins that ended in an inverted camel so fast that she became a blur. Nikki, Katie, and Emmy stood close by, noses pressed to the thick plastic transparency that wrapped around the rink.

"Watch your mouth, jackass!" Katie jumped in. "That was a waltz jump and a camel spin. Unless you meant Llyra herself. She's a figure skater— the only one on Pallas—and a real good one, too! That's her coach you're talking to."

The young man shook his head, sighed deeply, and muttered. "What a waste of perfectly good ice."

CHAPTER FIVE: OLD CURRINGER

The way a culture treats its past is the best indicator of how that culture will be treated by the future. —*The Diaries of Rosalie Frazier Ngu*

"I WOULD APPRECIATE," SAID JASMEEN, "if you would not try backflip again without consulting me. Is dangerous, even when I am there to spot for you."

The walk home wasn't long. Chattering to one another about the morning's session on the ice, Llyra and Jasmeen left the rink by the south doors, following the footpath where it paralleled the east side of Curringer's main street. Chopped by a light wind, Lake Selous was at their left. Its opposite shore could be seen from the rooftops of some of the taller buildings in town, but not from ground level. From here it looked like a small ocean.

Llyra said, "Okay, coach—but I warn you, next time I'm going for a double!"

"Is fine," Jasmeen scowled at her. "You want remains cremated or buried at sea?" She pointed at the lake.

Llyra made a scoffing noise that her coach found particularly annoying. "Jasmeen, a little thing like a double backflip isn't going to kill me."

Jasmeen's eyes widened, suddenly and menacingly. It was a technique she'd learned from her father, who called it his Rasputin expression. "No, but if you try without proper preparation, *I* kill you!"

"Then how about shooting my remains into orbit?" Llyra laughed and Jasmeen laughed with her. They picked up the pace a little because they were both very hungry and looking forward to a big lunch at home. Figure skaters are always hungry.

It was early on a warm, bright, sunny afternoon. Lake Selous was dotted with small boats, many of them with brightly-colored sails, others under power. One pulled a water skier in a bright red bikini, sending spray high into the air. People of every possible sort, native and tourist, stood along the shore, and on the railed porches of lakefront buildings, fishing. Overhead, all over town, and all over the lake, others hung from flying belts like Llyra's. Some of those had fishing poles, too. The street was full of the lightweight, spindly-looking three-wheeled vehicles that were characteristic of Pallas.

On a red brick traffic island in the middle of the cobbled street, stood an heroic-scale bronze statue of William Wilde Curringer. "Wild Bill", as he'd been known, was the billionaire genius who had caused Pallas to be terraformed, even before Llyra's own great grandfather, Emerson Ngu, had arrived here with his parents. Curringer—one of his companies had created and produced the tough, self-healing plastic that the Pallatian atmospheric envelope was made of—had brought tens of thousands of human beings to the little planetoid in his great fusion-powered space liners. And he'd died here, in an ultralight aircraft accident, helping to seed the barren, crater-pocked surface with life.

Curringer's statue stood in the exact spot where he'd "screwed his little plane into the ground," as her father always put it unsentimentally. Someone had actually proposed that a bronze replica of the crash itself might be more appropriate. City builders had chosen a more conventional design and left an a empty lot, a small park, directly across the street, between two buildings, so that he could always "see" Lake Selous.

In the wild old frontier days of her great grandfather's youth, at least half of the buildings standing around her now had been notorious and historic saloons, the other half what her Uncle Arleigh referred to as "houses of swell repute". Llyra understood perfectly what that meant—she couldn't understand why anybody would want to do that for a living— and why her mother invariably scowled at Arleigh whenever he said it.

These days, it had been whispered among the older girls at the rink, such establishments had moved away from Lake Selous with its elderly tourists and its souvenir shops, up into the fashionable hills above the old town. However in one former saloon or bordello, some member of her own family had established the Drake-Tealy Museum, named in honor of Raymond Louis Drake-Tealy, the famous and innovative anthropologist who had founded the unique Pallatian culture that Llyra had grown up in.

Drake-Tealy had reckoned that the adoption of agriculture as a way of life had, for many reasons, been humanity's greatest mistake. It had given rise, for example, to the tyranny of government. He had persuaded Wild Bill Curringer (who had wanted to avoid such tyranny for reasons of his own) to avoid that mistake and charter a high-tech hunting culture on Pallas that was still going strong after more than a century.

However the principal attraction of the museum had nothing to do with any of that. Soon after people had come to the asteroid, they had discovered fist-sized oddly-shaped lumps of metal that Drake-Tealy had declared to be ancient alien artifacts, perhaps as old as a billion years. Established scientists had made fun of him until a brilliant young woman whose specialty was "speculative xenotechnology" had pronounced his theories to be correct—and presented scientific proof to that effect.

That brilliant young woman, Rosalie Frazier, born on Pallas but raised and educated on Earth, had eventually married Llyra's great grandfather Emerson. Decades later, she disappeared with him aboard the *Fifth Force*.

The museum now housed the largest collection of what were known as Drake-Tealy Objects in the Solar System. They had so far been found on every asteroid explored, as well as Mars and a couple of the moons of Jupiter. To this day no one knew what they were or why they had been created, only that they were artificial, and clearly non-human in their manufacture.

Mysteriously, the greatest number of Drake-Tealy Objects were to be found on barren Vesta, third largest of the asteroids, but made of solid granite. Vesta was not inhabitable, not worth terraforming, and was the best proof so far that the makers of the artifacts were completely alien.

Llyra exclaimed, "Okay, here we go!"

"About time," Jasmeen answered. "I'm getting famish-ed!" She'd pronounced the last word with three syllables.

They had come at last to the part of the walk home she liked best. There was a geologic fault here, resulting in a vertical drop of about fifty feet. Continuing straight ahead, where the road became a long ramp, there was a steep flight of stairs, built of stone and stainless steel. Llyra had never used them. On the Lake Selous side of the walk, two big steel poles, two inches in diameter and also stainless, stood side by side, placed there by some whimsical individual more concerned with fun than practicality. Each was cut with a single heavy square thread. One of them—the "down" pole—constantly rotated clockwise, driven by a small motor powered by a shoebox-sized fusion reactor. The other—the "up" pole—rotated counter clockwise.

At the top of the "up" pole, where they'd run out of thread, half a dozen objects stood away from the smooth portion of the pole where they'd been waggling and clanking as it turned. They were something like open ended wrenches (and indeed, that's what people called them), with eighteen inch handles. But they were made to fit the thread of the pole.

Llyra took a wrench off the "up" pole and placed it on the smooth part of the "down" pole, above the thread. Looking less enthusiastic about the whole undertaking, Jasmeen took another of the wrench-like objects and awaited her turn. Here on Pallas, the long drop to the bottom could have been safely made simply by jumping, but Jasmeen was from Mars, a world with almost seven times the gravity of Pallas. She might also have taken the stairs, but for some reason that had never occurred to her.

Llyra let the wrench fall onto the thread and stepped off the sidewalk. She hung there by one hand for a moment, with her skate bag in the other hand. Then the rotating pole carried her smoothly and gently to the ground—although the metal-on-metal squealing of the wrench and pole set her teeth on edge. She pulled her wrench from the pole and placed it on the "up" pole so that it would be there for others to use. There were already half a dozen of the things piled up at the bottom of the "down" pole, for people headed in the opposite direction, toward town.

"I love it!" Llyra shouted.

"You may have my share to love, as well."

Amidst more metallic squealing, Jasmeen alighted behind her, skate bag dangling from her shoulder, and shifted the wrench she'd used to the "up" pole. She wrinkled her nose and was about to make the same comment about the noise that she always did, when Llyra's phone rang. The girl touched the breast pocket of her light denim jacket and said, "Hello?"

"Llyra?" It was her mother Ardith's voice, sounding not quite as cool and detached as it usually did. The girl could see her mother's face clearly in her mind—delicate features and enormous dark eyes, framed by wavy dark hair. "Llyra, I've just heard from your father on Ceres. Something has happened. Something—it's about your brother Wilson."

It was Llyra's turn to wrinkle her nose. She knew perfectly well that her father was on Ceres—he was the chief engineer there. And she knew who her brother was, as well. Why did her mother always talk to her like a—then her heart froze as she realized that this was probably bad news.

Jasmeen had heard the message and put a sympathetic hand on Llyra's shoulder.

"Is Wilson okay?" the girl haltingly asked her mother. It was her second attempt at it. The first attempt had only produced a nervous squeak.

Ardith replied, "Yes, dear, Wilson is just fine, and I'm sorry I didn't tell you that right way. He's fine, but apparently he's done something … well, extremely heroic and extremely foolish at the same time. The Curringer Foundation is planning to hold a special ceremony at your father's headquarters to give him some kind of an award. Your father would like very much for us to be there when it happens, and so would Wilson."

Amazing—and a little scary. Her mother actually sounded worried and proud of Wilson at the same time. She'd mentioned their father without any trace of bitterness in her tone. She'd even called her daughter "dear".

"Then when do we start?" Llyra asked. Unbelievable! She was *finally* going to get a real ride on a real spaceship! The furthest she'd been, so far, was in a tourist jumpbuggy to Pallas B, the asteroid's tiny moon. They hadn't even EVAed. She'd had better views of the surface of Pallas B through a telescope from her bedroom window.

Her mother was speaking. " … sending an ionopter to pick us up at the house and take us to Port Peary. I'll close the lab and meet you at home. It's an eighteen hour trip from Pallas to Ceres right now, so pack your toothbrush. Oh—and please ask Jasmeen to come along, will you? Your father was quite insistent about that, although he didn't say why."

Maybe, Llyra thought, it was to save his daughter the fate of being cooped up alone in a small spaceship with her mother for eighteen hours.

But what she said was, "Okay, Mother. We're almost home right now. See you."

"Yes, dear. Goodbye."

Amazing.

⁎

The Ngu house, just outside of Curringer—some called it the Ngu mansion—had been constructed from native stone by Llyra's great grandfather, Emerson. It was here that he'd brought his bride Rosalie Frazier, the famous archaeologist, and here that their eight children had been born. Mystery still shrouded their eventual fate. They had headed for the

Cometary Halo, made a few reports that had taken hours, at lightspeed, to get back to Pallas, and then no more had been heard of them.

Their last communication had been garbled but had mentioned alien artifacts.

Llyra's grandfather William had been born here, like the rest, and grown up on the hospitable shores of Lake Selous. He'd been the eldest of Emerson and Rosalie's children. When he was barely in his twenties, he'd left the family homestead and gone with his younger brother Brody to Mars, to help keep colonists from Earth from dying of what he'd called "a faulty space program". Several years later, he'd returned with one of those colonists, former East American Marine Lieutenant Julie Segovia, married her, and settled back into the Ngu family dwelling.

Llyra's father Adam, William's eldest son, had been born here, too, although by then there was a genuine hospital in Curringer. He'd studied engineering over the Solar Internet, apprenticed himself to one of the engineers who'd terraformed Pallas, grown up, opened his own practice, and married another native Pallatian, Llyra's mother, Ardith Zacharenko.

Thus the house, to Llyra, was like another member of her family, as ancient as her missing great grandfather, but always there to protect and comfort her. Like most of the buildings on Pallas, it was built from the asteroid's native gray-brown stone—carbonaceous chondrite with the petroleum-like kerogen carefully baked out. The kiln still stood, like a concrete igloo, on a remote corner of the property. Three generations of Ngu kids and their cousins had cleaned it out and used it as a playhouse.

Unlike most other buildings on Pallas, however, the Ngu house had not been made to resemble the architecture of any other place or time. Most of the buildings downtown, for example, looked like they'd come from a western movie set.

The Ngu house was wide, where it sat along the Lake Selous shore, made up mostly of bold horizontal strokes, raw stone interspersed with balconies and broad, deep-set windows. In most places the house was four stories tall, and not symmetrical. It fell, rather, into "split levels". The design had sprung from the inventive mind of Emerson Ngu, who referred to the style as "Frank Lloyd Wright without the useless spaces".

Leaving the sidewalk from town, Llyra and Jasmeen descended a flight of broad, gentle steps, and crossed a swinging footbridge made up of huge blond-colored wooden planks and "musket-browned" steel cable. They came to the big front door, which overlooked a broad stone terrace, so closely surrounded by trees that they practically made a canopy over it. Llyra thought this was a perfect place to sit on a hot summer day, have lunch, and study. Through the trees at either end of the terrace, she could see the lake. The balcony of her bedroom looked out over the lake, as well.

The family kept several boats in their boathouse on the shore. One was a contraption with pontoons and a canopy they could go out and have barbecues on. They hadn't used it since Adam and Wilson had gone to Ceres. Another was a little canoe with an outrigger and a big wind-driven rotor that turned a shaft that turned a gear that turned another shaft that drove a propeller. It actually sailed faster into the wind than running from it—and Llyra had built it, by herself, from the keel up.

But what was truly magical about the Ngu house was the fact that from nearly every level, water fell in broad and shining curtains, sometimes onto the level below where it fell again, sometimes all the way to the ground, where it was collected, filtered, and sent back to the rooftops once more. The noise of all this falling water was deeply relaxing. Llyra had grown up with it and missed it whenever she was away.

"There it is!" Before Llyra and Jasmeen could reach the front door of the house, they heard the breathy roar of an ionopter high overhead. Jasmeen shielded her face from the sun and from wind-driven spray from the waterfalls being thrown around by the machine. Together, she and Llyra watched it begin to settle on the rooftop landing pad.

Even to those accustomed to it, it was quite a sight. Jutting out and upward at about a forty-five degree angle, two dozen feet above a boxy metal and plastic body the size of a small city bus, three large booms, two forward and one aft, cut through with circular lightening holes, each supported a twenty foot double disk—one set above the other—of metallic mesh. The upper disk put an electric charge on the air molecules above it, and the lower disk pulled them through and expelled them, creating enough thrust to lift the ionopter and pull it through the air.

Occasionally, some foreign object—a large insect or the feather of a bird—got between the disks, and there was a flash of momentary lightning and an alarming crackle as it was reduced to its constituent ions.

Ionopters were the fastest means of transportation on Pallas. Between them, various corporations and individuals maintained a fleet of fewer than a hundred of the peculiar vehicles. This asteroid was the one place in the Solar System where such a craft could operate. Mars had too much gravity, Earth's Moon had never been terraformed and lacked the necessary atmosphere, and terraformation had only begun on Ceres, for which a bigger, more powerful ionopter was already being designed.

In some ways Curringer was the System's largest small town. Both young women knew the pilot, R.G. Edd—a frequent drop-in hockey player—who waved at them cheerfully from his tinted plastic window as the big fusion-powered aircraft's ridiculously tiny landing gear touched the roof.

Precisely at that moment, Llyra's mother Ardith wafted onto the terrace in her flying belt. As her feet lightly touched the flagstones, she said, "Aren't you two inside, yet? We've got to get packed and going!"

"But Mother," Llyra protested as she felt her stomach growl. "What about lunch?"

CHAPTER SIX: SAVE THE EARTH

There are those who insist that nobody ever thinks of himself as a villain. On the contrary, I think that villains know perfectly well who they are. Don't you? —*The Diaries of Rosalie Frazier Ngu*

"BAD ENOUGH THEY WRECKED THE natural environment of Pallas with their illegal 'designer' microbes. They actually altered its rotation, first, using nuclear weapons! Nuclear weapons! All so they could have a 24-hour day!"

Anna Wertham Savage, recently chosen as the new leader of the Mass Movement, finished her signature with an angry slash, taking her pen off the page and across her desk blotter before she could stop it. She sat in her meticulously restored Victorian office, with its mellow, hand-carved rosewood wainscoting, tastefully figured beige wallpaper, and embossed ceiling high overhead set off with more rosewood, signing copies of the latest edition of her last year's bestselling book, *Massquake!*, in preparation for an enormous rally later that week in Boston.

It was hoped—Savage hoped—that the city would ban purchase and sales of all offworld items and materials—perhaps even outlaw their ownership, triggering door-to-door police searches for imported asteroid contraband. Accomplish such a thing in Boston, and the entire state of Massachusetts would surely follow. Accomplish such a thing in Massachusetts, and that would be a significant step toward banning imports from East America altogether. It would probably be followed by United Nations embargo.

She found the idea breathtakingly wonderful.

Savage felt she needed some cheering. Together, she and the guest in her office had just watched videos from the asteroid Ceres, pieced together by some enterprising soul from several different industrial cameras aboard the *Percival Lowell*, and sold to one of the 3DTV news networks.

Savage and her guest had seen a surface-to-air missile fired from a crater down on the asteroid, rising on a dense column of smoke, and rocketing past the defenseless factory vessel to explode harmlessly thousands of yards away. Then came a lone white-suited figure, like a cliché movie knight. His lucky pistol shot, dashing the missile launcher to the crater floor, had also destroyed the launching party's only way of getting back to Pallas. At that point, the white armored figure had fought a desperate gunfight with the colorfully-suited laser-wielding defenders.

These videos would never be seen on East American channels. They had originated at a commercial broadcast 3DTV station near Topeka, Kansas. Receiving radio, 3DTV, or SolarNet signals from outside East America was supposed to have been a serious crime. But since the authorities would have had to admit that places like Topeka and Denver and Houston and Omaha were no longer a part of their country, it was a serious crime that somehow never got prosecuted, a serious crime that everyone committed, every day, even the authorities who were supposed to prevent it.

For a moment, Savage looked up at her visitor, lounging in the most comfortable chair in the room, under a big formal portrait of the eternally blessed Rachael Carson, sipping at a glass of her bourbon. Coming from a long line of Temperance Movement prohibitionists, Savage never touched alcohol, herself, but kept a bountiful supply for her guests. He was a handsome young man, she thought, wearing a dark colored lightweight turtleneck, a pale gray Armani 2000 suit, and expensive Italian loafers with socks that matched his shirt. She'd never seen the man unkempt, uncreased, or with a speck of lint or animal hair anywhere on his person.

Sometimes, she wished—but on the other hand, even when she was young, it had always been something of a struggle for Savage to remain pressed and crisp-looking. Now, in her forties, she'd given it up. She kept cats—and everybody knew it with a glance at her baggy sweaters and dresses. She was a natural, prematurely gray-streaked "dishwater" blond, with flat, stringy hair that failed to cooperate no matter what amount she spent on it. She was also cursed with pale, watery blue eyes that … well, she thought, they *bulged* whenever she got excited. She had to be careful when she was on 3DTV. Worst of all, she had thick ankles and no figure. Clearly, she had been meant for something other than—higher than—romance, marriage, motherhood.

And although her feminist forebears had taught her that she wasn't supposed to care about any of those things, to her dismay, she found she cared more deeply about them with every passing year, and couldn't help herself. Savage *wanted* romance, marriage, and motherhood—if it wasn't already too late—and felt cruelly, personally cheated by a reality in which she'd was made so hopelessly unattractive. Sometimes she even caught herself promising that she would someday make them *pay*.

Whoever "they" were.

But what she said to her guest just now was, "Oh, Paul, I can't imagine what my predecessors could have been thinking of. Believe me, if it had been me in charge, if they'd had to put ten million bodies out there, protesting in the streets, in a hundred cities, and a dozen countries, I wouldn't have hesitated. They should have shut Curringer down before he ever got started, and burned his head offices to the ground!"

There. That felt better. With a little smile, she placed the newly signed book on a big stack on the right side of her desk, used a handkerchief on her palms, which had grown a little damp, took another book from a stack on her left and opened it. *Massquake!*: the very book that had brought her to the attention of the expensively-dressed men in cigar smoke-filled rooms who made decisions about the tactics and strategy of the Mass Movement, as well as a thousand other groups like it.

Her guest murmured, "The 'natural environment' of Pallas was hard vacuum at Absolute Zero, Annie. It made Antarctica—or even Mars—seem tropical"

P.E. "Honest Paul" Luegner, Savage's opposite number in Null Delta Em—an organization whose absolutist rhetoric and violent tactics she was compelled to publicly denounce at frequent intervals—set his drink on an endtable, leaned back in the most comfortable chair in the room, and put his manicured hands behind his head. The man wasn't supposed to be here; he was never supposed to be seen in Anna Savage's company, but he had brought important news of the recent unfortunate events on Ceres, where his entire Environmental Defense Brigade had just been killed or captured, not just by a boy, but by the son of Adam Ngu.

By the grandson of William Ngu of hated memory, the Martian revolutionary.

By the great-grandson of the most malignant capitalist in history (second only to William Wilde Curringer), inventor-industrialist Emerson Ngu.

"And your predecessors did try to shut Wild Bill Curringer down," Luegner went on. "Only the crafty old devil offered the United Nations a land grant for an experimental agricultural collective—that's the way I heard it, anyway—and the UN turned right around and ordered your people to lay off! Funny thing is, that UN agricultural colony didn't last long. Most of the peasants—I mean, colonists, escaped—er, emigrated to other parts of Pallas, including *the* Emerson Ngu, himself. Anyway, by the time anybody really knew what was going on, Curringer had already liquidated or abandoned most of his assets here on Earth, and shifted operations to his huge fleet of factory ships, orbiting Pallas."

Savage looked up at Luegner from the book she was signing. "Yes, Paul, I know the relevant history, and now the disease is beginning to spread, all over again! Do you realize this business on ... where is it? Ceres—could lead to thousands of asteroids being terraformed? And there's no way to stop it! William Wilde Curringer may be dead— thank goodness for small favors—but his vile corporation just goes on and on and on, despoiling the natural purity and balance of the Solar System!"

Tears welled in her eyes. The whole idea was just too painful, too infuriating, too ... She broke off for lack of suitable vocabulary. People mustn't be allowed to leave the Mother Planet, not until they'd solved all of their problems here. Then, of course, they wouldn't want to leave; they'd have no reason. Wasn't humanity ever going to learn its proper place in the natural scheme of things, instead of always swaggering around like the lords of the universe? Not with men like Curringer and Ngu to lead them into hubris and disaster time and time again!

Gasping for her mental breath, Savage gazed out her hard-earned corner windows across the timeless, changeless vista that was her own beloved Amherst, Massachusetts. It was the home of the Mass Movement, and the home of her heart, as well. It was timeless and changeless because, sometime early in the 21st century, the voters and officials of the City of Five Colleges had decided that progress had gone too far—or was about to, anyway. From that moment on, nothing visible outdoors within the city limits could appear to be from any later than the year 2000.

The cut-off year had only been arrived at after long debate and bitter wrangling. And in the end, in the opinion of the law's original advocates, the choice of the year 2000 had defeated the whole purpose of the effort. They'd have preferred the year 1900—or better yet, 1800, with electricity and the internal combustion engine purged from human culture.

Those who had opposed the new law altogether felt that they, too, had been betrayed by politicians they thought they'd bought and paid for. Thus the decision was hailed as a monumental achievement, especially by those in media and politics to whom compromise is the very spirit of democracy, and democracy the only real measure of a civilization.

The population of Amherst began to diminish steadily. That had suited Savage's predecessors, although Zero Population Growth and others like it complained that it was merely being displaced. The day would come, Savage knew, when the cowards and deserters would have no place left to run.

Outside, high over the city, a squadron of the Air Force's brand new plasma-pulse fighters snarled their way across the sky, heading northwest.

Half a century ago, Vermont and New Hampshire—and very possibly Maine, it was difficult to tell through the haze of propaganda and counter-propaganda—had taken it upon themselves to imitate the territories west of the Webb Line, and stop being part of Lincoln's sacred Union. The leaders of that movement had to be put down by force.

Even so, every few years, it seemed a handful of the inhabitants and neighbors of the "Live Free or Die" states grew restive, and it was deemed necessary to demonstrate the futility of such an attitude, not only for the benefit of New Englanders, but anybody else who might be getting secessionist ideas. These days the government made a practice of planning regular military flights across all major cities as a reminder and a warning.

In Amherst, it hadn't quite become illegal to dress in styles anachronistic to the year 2000, but people would stare and frown at you if you did. To the satisfaction of some, the new law worked—not without an occasional bobble. Popular national restaurant chains like Ali Wanna or Zeefo's, compelled by local laws to disguise themselves as parts of the quaint but long-defunct MacDonald's or Arby's or KFC franchises, elected instead to relocate, despite punitive lawsuits threatened by the city.

The minority still privileged to drive automobiles in East America soon discovered that they had to park their clean, efficient Ngu Departure Electrics and Fusion-Brasilias well outside the Amherst city limits, and rent ancient, noisy, stinking internal combustion-powered Fords, Chevrolets, Volkswagens, and Volvos that were historically faithful to the period. Some visitors were inconsiderate enough to point out that this was hardly a desirable outcome. On the other hand, vehicles of Korean, Japanese, and Malaysian manufacture were now prohibited altogether because—in the view of the Amherst city fathers—they never should have been permitted on American soil to begin with.

"You've gotta take the long view, Annie, and not worry," Luegner laughed. "We're working on young Pallatians of the third and fourth generations right now, those who know absolutely nothing about what their parents and grandparents and great-grandparents went through to terraform and settle the asteroid, who take what they've always had for granted. I do admit it would be a damn sight easier if Pallas had compulsory public schools that we could move into and take over, but they'll be ours, eventually, and Curringer's bunch won't know what hit them."

Savage made a huffing noise. "Maybe so, Paul, but in the meantime, while you're taking the long view and not worrying, Curringer's bunch are busy terraforming another, even bigger asteroid, where millions of people, maybe, will go through exactly the same struggle, learn from it, and undo everything you say we're accomplishing on Pallas. And from there, they'll go on to the next asteroid, and then to the next. And on top of that, they'll keep right on sending their tons and tons of manufactured and raw materials to Earth, every day, threatening our precious Mother Planet with crustal shifting and slippage that could wipe out every—"

Luegner held up a hand. "Earth naturally receives a hundred tons of micrometeorites every day. Don't tell me you actually believe all that crap."

For a moment, their attention was captured by a colorful West American ad for a family hovercraft. Since their de facto secession, Westerners had let their previously tax-supported infrastructure— the part that wasn't converted into private, profit-making businesses—fall apart completely. Streets, roads, and highways were now merely vegetation-covered tracks, traveled over by huge, wasteful, dangerous 350-mile-per-hour vehicles—built largely from exotic materials manufactured in space—that didn't need streets, roads, and highways.

Savage reached out abruptly and shut the hated images off. Her watery blue eyes widened and the nostrils of her narrow, knifelike nose flared. It wasn't a pretty sight, Luegner thought. Some women are definitely *not* beautiful when they're angry. Some aren't beautiful at the best of times. Of course he was accustomed to having his choice of young, succulent college coeds on the lecture circuit, always eager—anxious, really—to help 'the movement' out in any way he might suggest.

"The people who contribute money to this organization," she told him, "and help keep you in caviar and champagne, 'believe all that crap'!"

"Never cared for either, myself, but point taken, nonetheless. Annie," he admitted amiably, still thinking about those coeds. They believed it, too, dear things, and saw him as a noble, romantic, even revolutionary hero, locked in mortal combat with the evil tentacles of capitalism.

It didn't hurt that he looked ten years younger than his 45 years, retained all of his dark, wavy hair, and had a livid scar across one shoulder that he told them was where the police had shot him during an otherwise peaceful demonstration in some always faraway city. How they loved to run their fingers along that scar! In fact, a pipe bomb he'd been building in Scranton had gone off accidentally and almost killed him. It had killed the girl he'd been sleeping with at the time, whose basement apartment it destroyed. It sometimes bothered him a little that he couldn't remember her name. "I certainly can't argue with you there."

Savage opened her mouth to accept his apology.

"Me neither!" Savage's office door slammed open, threatening to shatter its carefully lettered glass, and a youthful figure virtually leapt into the room. He wore a white "ice cream" suit currently the rage in Amherst, and a matching Panama straw. Savage and Luegner both recognized Johnnie "the Fish" Crenicichla, the only individual in the world who worked for both organizations, the Mass Movement and Null Delta Em—although his paycheck came from neither group, but from an ancient Boston bank.

"You've got to stop meeting like this!" he told them in a light, bantering tone. He threw himself into the room's second most comfortable seat, a short divan on the opposite side of the door from Luegner. "You pay me obscenely—somebody pays me, anyway—to act as a credibly deniable liaison between you. You guys should let me liaise!"

"We do, Johnnie, we do," Luegner told him. "I figured this came pretty close to an emergency, and I happened to be in North America this morning, anyway … "

Crenicichla threw his head back and laughed sarcastically. "Damned right it's an emergency! The Curringer Corporation's planning to give that trigger-happy Ngu kid some kind of award, and broadcast it on System-wide 3DTV!"

"Shit!" Luegner sat up straight.

"Oh, dear," Savage muttered. It was all she could manage.

"Oh, it gets even better, folks!" Crenicichla went on. "To top it all off, like cherries on a sundae, two of the seven of our people that the kid took alive have offered full confessions in exchange for amnesty."

There was a long silence. Then: "I wasn't aware," Luegner said, very slowly and quietly, "that the Curringer Corporation condones torture."

Crenicichla shook his head. "Amnesty. That's what the Corporation is claiming, any—oh, I get it. That's our story and we're sticking to it."

Luegner nodded, but said nothing else. Savage buried her face in her hands. "I didn't hear that. I wasn't here. I didn't hear that. I wasn't here. I didn't hear that. I wasn't here. I didn't hear that. I wasn't—."

"That's the plan, then," said Crenicichla, his usual enthusiasm apparently restored. "And a damned good thing, too. Guess who the stool pigeons named as their boss, Paul! Luckily, they can't touch you here in the Formerly United States. I checked with the Mass Movement's legal people before I came here. They're the criminals—anyone who works for the Curringer Corporation, that is—in the eyes of the East American government."

"Yes, Johnnie, but we can't just react to this situation," Luegner objected. "We've got to take the offensive again, make *them* react." Unlike Savage, he knew exactly who he meant by "them", and so did Crenicichla.

"Stool pigeons?" Savage raised her eyes. She had never heard the ancient expression before, and didn't care for any of the images it brought to mind. "They didn't—"

Crenicichla shook his head. "No, Annie, they didn't mention you. You're perfectly free to issue your regular outraged disavowal of Null Delta Em."

He turned to Luegner. "Paul, it's time you got your famous and photogenic face the hell out of this building. We'll make some time for planning tomorrow. Naturally, not before we check upstairs with You-Know-Who."

That was the way Crenicichla was in the habit of referring to the individuals who had selected each of them in the first place, and from whom all other blessings ultimately flowed. He reclaimed his Panama hat.

"Take the freight elevator and leave by way of the basement."

CHAPTER SEVEN: BETWEEN THE PIERS

While it's undeniably true that not everyone who benefits from public works (so-called) on Pallas helps to pay for them, if those of us who do stopped to worry about "free riders", nothing would ever get done and we'd all be squatting in our own dung in a cave somewhere. —*The Diaries of Rosalie Frazier Ngu*

IF PALLAS HAD BEEN THE Earth, Curringer would have been right in the middle of the north temperate zone, like Brussels, or Peoria. The trip to the asteroid's north pole by ionopter took slightly less than two hours, during which Ardith and Jasmeen gave a small part of their attention to an old movie, and Llyra, having sworn she wasn't tired, slept.

It was here, around the mile-high, mountainous circumference of an impact crater ten miles in diameter, that Pallas's vast atmospheric envelope—and the mighty spun-steel cables that held it in place—dipped down to touch the asteroid's surface. (At the equator, they stood a full two miles above it.) Here they came to an end, anchored by hundreds of colossal stainless steel columns set more than a mile deep—the most massive monolithic steel fabrications, R.G. Edd, their ionopter pilot, proudly told his passengers, ever to have been manufactured.

Outside the north polar crater, inside the atmospheric envelope, it was warm. Rain fell, and occasional snow. Wind blew, and green things grew. Little children laughed and played. Inside the crater, outside the envelope, there was hard vacuum and temperatures that varied from two hundred degrees below zero to two hundred above, depending on whether the thermometer in question stood in shadow or in sunlight.

The two vastly-differing realms were separated at the lowest level by the circular mountain range, through which dozens of tunnels— with mammoth doors to seal the air in every couple of miles—had been bored.

As the ionopter approached the little town of Curley's Gulch—white houses, picket fences, and a tall church steeple (Our Lady of Discord, as it happened, Reformed)—nestled in the lower folds of the rim range, Jasmeen nudged Llyra awake and the two of them strained to see everything at once. Through the curved plastic windows in the roof of the ionopter, they could actually see the atmospheric envelope, held down by cables as big around as Llyra was. They could actually see the individual twisted strands of which they were composed. As the cables curved toward the waiting mountain peaks re-engineered to receive them, the aircraft was forced to fly lower and lower.

At one point, the ionopter actually flew close enough to the "roof of the world" for its passengers to see repairs being made to it from the outside. The "smart" plastic that W.W. Curringer had invented for terraforming Pallas was remarkably durable and self-healing, but a continuous bombardment by micro- and not-so-micrometeorites, and the steady solar ultraviolet baking it was subjected to, eventually took their toll.

Outside, dozens of skilled workmen in rocket-powered envirosuits were struggling to position an enormous replacement patch under one of the great cables—Edd informed them he had done that sort of work himself, when he was a younger man, and that the patch they worked with was the size of two football fields, side by side—employing jacks of some kind to create sufficient space between the cable and the canopy.

The patch had been lowered from an orbiting factory ship—one of the older, smaller fleet that had been employed to terraform this world three generations ago—and would be hand-welded in place using sonic "torches".

The continuous growling of the ionopter's propulsive screens made unassisted conversation almost impossible. "Once the edges have healed seamlessly to the original canopy," Ed informed them over the cabin intercom, "the section it replaces will be carefully cut away from underneath, by workmen using flying belts inside the envelope. Getting it down to the ground gently is an art in itself. The worn out section will then be cut up, taken outside, and recycled up in one of the factory ships, where it will eventually serve as replacement material elsewhere."

"Is like gigantic cataract operation." Sitting beside Llyra on a passenger seat, Jasmeen had an approving expression on her face. "Only much more economical! This is almost Martian!"

The pilot laughed. "Well, Miss, somebody once said—it mighta been me—that Curringer wanted to be called 'Every Part of the Buffalo Bill'."

"And who pays for all this work?" Jasmeen asked. "Is no such thing as free lunch."

Ardith, seated on the other side of Llyra, leaned forward and across her daughter so that she could see Jasmeen. "Why, the Curringer Corporation does, dear. Every single individual who is born on Pallas is a stockholder—as is anyone who pays to immigrate here and signs on to the Stein Covenant. The Curringer Corporation makes money from exports and from patents, and that's what keeps a roof over all our heads."

"Isn't that socialism?" Jasmeen asked. "Is called 'Social Credit System'."

Ardith sighed. "I see why you'd say that, but it's not socialism at all. For most of us, it's an inheritance from our parents and grandparents and great grandparents who risked and toiled and lived and died to have something to pass on to us. No one is asked to contribute involuntarily, and if they receive something they didn't earn and don't deserve, they'll lose it soon enough to somebody smarter."

"Shirtsleeves to shirtsleeves," Edd offered, "in only a single generation. That's progress!"

Jasmeen nodded. Things were different on Mars. For one thing, its atmosphere, however artificial, was the product of purely biological processes that required no maintenance. She knew generally that Ardith headed up an important laboratory on Pallas, experimenting constantly with newer and better means of asteroid capture, handling, and utilization. "So you are source," she said, "of Curringer Corporation patents?"

Ardith smiled. "Absolutely. Some of them, anyway. The Curringer Corporation pays me very well, and I also receive a share of the royalties."

Jasmeen looked at Ardith carefully, calculating. "On Mars we are not tolerating royalties—on Mars we are having only glorious revolution!"

Ardith frowned, blinked, and shook her head.

"She's pulling your leg, Mother!" Llyra laughed and punched her coach gently on the shoulder. "Jasmeen, you are the silliest person I know!"

Jasmeen shrugged. "This is only because you are not knowing my father. But I graciously accept compliment anyway. Is good to be appreciated."

The pilot laughed.

The ionopter flew directly over the town at just above treetop altitude. Llyra and her companions could see the upturned faces of people peering into the sun to see the aircraft. At the very foot of the crater rim mountains, it set down amidst blowing leaves and dust on a paved circular landing pad, and the roar of the ionic screens overhead died abruptly.

Now they could see a huge hangar door cut into the mountainside. It looked dark inside, and they couldn't see very far. Two men wearing coveralls marked "Curley's Gulch Air Services" ran out, pulling light cables behind them, and affixed them to the ionopter's landing gear. The cables taughtened and began to pull the flying machine into the vast hangar.

The interior, it developed, was perfectly well-lighted. It was only by contrast with the sunlight outside that it seemed dim. More figures in coveralls swarmed around the ionopter, attending to its needs, while others wheeled a short staircase to the side of the aircraft. As Llyra, her mother, and Jasmeen descended, an open car drove up, the same "Curley's Gulch Air Services" emblazoned on its side. Its driver got out and opened a back door. A member of the maintenance crew brought their luggage on a cart, and this was placed at the front of the long floor of the back seat, directly behind the driver's seat.

Marveling a little, the three passengers climbed into the car. To Llyra, the vehicle looked quite a lot like a 21st century Earthside luxury machine with the top down, but its red rubber tires seemed foreign to the design and were enormous, five feet in diameter—they stuck up above the top edge of the car—treadless, and they looked relatively soft.

"It's a 2039 Raleigh convertible, refitted for Pallas." The driver stood by his own door and grinned at them. "It'll be a twenty mile ride from here to the Marshall spaceport offices, ladies, and I can't manage over about forty miles per hour through these tunnels, so you'll have time for a short nap. I can promise you that the ride will be smooth, and I'll point out features of interest—unless you don't want me to."

"Oh, please do," Jasmeen asked, beating Llyra by a fraction of a second. "I took very different route from spaceport when I came here from Mars."

"Here we go, then!" the driver exclaimed. The car surged forward smoothly—it appeared to Llyra to be electric—as windshields along the back edge of the driver's seat, and on either side of the rear seat automatically rose a foot or so to keep the three of them from being blown on uncomfortably by the car's passage through the tunnel.

The route turned out to be less … subpallatian, Llyra decided to call it, less troglodytic, than she'd expected. In many sections of the tunnel, which was at least forty feet high, and wide enough for at least four of these vehicles to pass each other safely, well-lit and interesting shopfronts presented themselves. Streets branched off from the tunnel, down which she briefly glimpsed even more shopfronts. The sight of several restaurants reminded her that she'd never gotten more than peanuts and a Coke for lunch.

About six miles along the tunnel, the neighborhoods became residential, with broad sidewalks, and apartment complexes carved out of native stone. People strolled and walked dogs. Businesses were tiny here, the sort of thing you'd want around the corner, where you could buy a pack of cigarettes, a box of cartridges, or a carton of milk. Small trees stood at intervals in holes cut in the sidewalk—Llyra wondered if the holes were planters or the trees were rooted in the substance of the asteroid itself—basking in the glow of bright lights set in the ceiling.

Ten miles along, halfway through the tunnel, the driver slowed to point out an enormous metallic construction, buried in the wall to their right, that resembled, more than anything else, a great fuel or water tank that seemed to begin at some level far below the street and continue upward through the tunnel's ceiling. There wasn't a seam or rivet visible. Llyra knew that she must looking at one of the great piers that anchored the thousand-mile cables that held the atmospheric envelope of Pallas in place. Judging from the portion she could see, she guessed that the diameter of the thing must be at least a hundred feet.

"That's just about right, young lady" the driver commended her. "And yes, it's as hollow as a drum, but its wall thickness is around ten feet. Massive. Like I said earlier, this thing would be the largest single piece of machined chromium steel in the history of mankind and the Solar System, if there weren't three hundred and fifty-nine others just like it, set one degree apart around the crater rim."

The cross-street here, the driver explained, Carville Avenue, was the only one where the naked piers could be seen. It was ninety-four miles long, buried ten miles from the crater under its ring mountain, but stretching around its entire circumference. It had been named for the engineer who had designed the incredible structures. Llyra played with the calculator built into her lapel phone. "So what's inside the hollow?"

The driver laughed. "Argon-foamed titanium. That's one of many new substances that can only be manufactured in the absence of gravity, and a major reason we Pallatians are so wealthy, compared to the rest of humanity. The stuff weighs practically nothing, but it's stiff as it can be, and keeps the piers from deforming—as if that was likely to happen."

The open car picked up speed again and moved on. The neighborhood past the pier was no longer residential. It didn't quite appear to be industrial, but was dominated by office businesses that served industry in various ways. Like any properly schooled Pallatian, Llyra knew that her homeworld had gradually become heavily industrialized since it had been founded as a high-tech hunter-gatherer economy, but that most of the manufacturing was done safely, well outside the atmospheric envelope in the polar craters, and on the moon of Pallas, Pallas B.

At last the driver announced that the odometer read twenty miles. They had came to a broad semicircular turnout. A sign on an island planter in its middle declared it to be the Solar System headquarters of:

FRITZ MARSHALL SPACEWAYS
ESTABLISHED 2050

The driver swung the Raleigh convertible into the turnout. Above three or four steps cut from reddish stone, and a narrow landing, the entire semicircle was lined with tall glass windows. A revolving door stood in the center, but several coveraled individuals took Llyra's bags, along with those of her mother and Jasmeen, through an ordinary glass door at one side. The driver shook hands with each of them in turn, and accepted a tip from Ardith. The platinum coins clinked as they hit his palm.

Llyra couldn't believe that he actually bowed. "Thank you very much, ma'am. I hope you'll ride with me again, perhaps on your return from Ceres. It's always a pleasure to serve one of the Founding Families."

Mildly irritated as she always was by such remarks—the Ngus hadn't really been First anyway, simply among the noisiest—Ardith muttered something polite, and the three of them climbed the steps and went through the revolving door, the first Llyra or Jasmeen had ever seen.

Inside stood a curve-fronted counter, dominated by an enormous oil portrait of the company's founder, Fritz Marshall, hanging on the wall behind it. A brass plaque at the bottom of the frame proclaimed that it was "a gift from the grateful people of Mars". From behind the counter, a pleasant-looking young woman in a company blazer greeted them warmly.

"The Ngu party? Your transport is ready for you, anytime you wish to depart. There are only about a dozen other passengers, all bound for Ceres, like you."

"Where do we go?" Llyra asked somewhat absently. Through a big floor-to-ceiling window, she could watch the floor of the polar crater, studded as far as she could see with spaceships of various sizes and shapes. The light was harsh, even through tinted glass, and the shadows were coal black, with edges as sharp as a razor. The ship nearest the window was a simple cylinder, its top end bristling with antennae, connected with the crater wall by a large translucent plastic tube.

"Through that door there, Miss," the receptionist answered, "which will lead you to that tubewalk outside, which is connected with the ship. I envy you a little: you'll be travelling aboard the *FMSL Beautiful Dreamer* one of our lines' newest and most comfortable vessels."

They thanked the young woman and walked to the door, down a short, tidy corridor, and out through a series of mechanical fittings that connected the tube with the offices in the crater wall. Llyra had half expected the tube to have a round floor, and to bounce and sway as they made their way along it, but none of that turned out to be the case.

It might as well have been made of stone. Llyra wondered how it was done.

As they approached the end of the tube that was attached to the ship, however, their forward progress was obstructed by an overweight middle-aged woman wearing a garish floral-patterned pants suit. She was speaking and gesturing impatiently to a young man in a Fritz Marshall company blazer, standing behind a portable podium marked "Boarding Attendant". A middle-aged man standing beside her with a camera on a strap around his neck said nothing, but appeared to be embarrassed.

"What do you mean you recognize us and we don't need tickets?" she exclaimed. "Young man, I insist, at the very least, that we all be searched!"

"I'm sorry, ma'am, but if I did that, I'd probably lose my job for molesting the paying customers. It's against company policy and Pallatian custom. It's the grossest possible violation of individual sovereignty."

"But—" She appealed to the man standing beside her, probably her long-suffering husband, Llyra decided. He rolled his eyes and looked away.

The young man went on. "Besides, ma'am, anybody who took a job that required it would have to be some kind of pervert, wouldn't they? I mean, groping people's little old grandmothers for a living, all day long?"

"But what," she almost screamed it, "if I were carrying a concealed weapon—or a bomb?"

He shrugged. "Well, I wouldn't be too happy about the bomb, ma'am. But you can make a bomb these days that resembles an arm or a leg, and has no giveaway chemical or electronic emanations. Hire yourself an amputee to carry it—and *boom!* You can't do much about that, can you? On the other hand, if you were a Pallatian—you're from Earth, aren't you?"

"We're from Bricktown, New Jersey, United States of America, the Earth."

"I see. East Americans. Well, if you were a Pallatian, ma'am, I'd be surprised if you *weren't* carrying a personal weapon of some kind, a firearm or a laser or a plasma pistol. It's an important tradition on this asteroid—just as it is on Mars and will be on Ceres. It's considered socially beneficial, a civic duty, and an indispensible source of the individual liberty we all enjoy."

The woman looked to her husband again, but was offered little help. "B-but what if somebody with one of those guns took over your little spaceship?"

"*Tried* to take over our little spaceship, you mean," the young man corrected her. "Ma'am, the guy could consider himself damned lucky if the other passengers filled him full of holes before they spaced him."

Her eyes grew big and round. "Spaced him?" Her husband, perhaps entertaining a long-held personal fantasy, attempted to suppress a grin.

"Sure, ma'am. Put him out the airlock—the door, I mean— without benefit of spacesuit. Not the pleasantest way to die, take my word for it."

The woman shuddered visibly. "What a violent place this is!"

He shook his head. "We practically never have any criminal violence out here in the Belt, ma'am. The cost is simply too high. What's the annual rate of murder, mugging, and rape where you come from?"

CHAPTER EIGHT: THE WILD BLACK YONDER

As I dictate these words, Pallas and Mars are the only Settled Worlds, not counting Earth, and there aren't that many other places to go yet. But a day will come when dwellers in the Asteroid Belt will travel from world to little world as easily and casually as West Americans now travel from city to city by bus or in their own cars. That sort of

freedom of movement comes very close, I think, to being the definition of freedom itself. —*The Diaries of Rosalie Frazier Ngu*

RATHER DISAPPOINTING IN HER EXTERNAL appearance (at least
as far as Llyra was concerned), the *Fritz Marshall Space Lines' Beautiful
Dreamer* turned out to be a cylinder a hundred feet in diameter and a
hundred fifty-one feet long, the same proportions as a traditional tomato
soup can.

Andy Warhol would be so proud, she thought.

However, before the boarding attendant would let them pass (and as
soon as he'd managed to quiet down the lady from New Jersey) he had
a lecture he had to deliver. Along with a handful of other passengers in
the portable anteroom at the end of the boarding tube, just outside the
spaceship's main airlock door, Llyra, Ardith, and Jasmeen gave him their
polite attention.

The floor of the little room, its ceiling, and its walls were stark white,
as longstanding tradition required. Four features broke the solid white: a
window on either side, showing the crater floor, ring mountains, and a
black, starry sky; a metal airlock door belonging to the spaceship, rather
than to the anteroom, and a large digital clock counting minutes until
liftoff. Just now, a little over an hour remained.

There was also a transparent plastic lectern to the right of the airlock door, where the boarding attendant stood. As the young man began
speaking, a three-dimensional cross section of the spaceship, colorful but
partially transparent, formed in the air at his left elbow. As he discussed
them, he pointed to various features of it with a finger.

"Although it reads like it was translated from the original Sumerian
into twenty-second century English, I'm sure you've read the brochure
that they gave you up front," he opened to polite laughter. "But the Fritz
Marshall Space Lines requires me to introduce you formally to the *FMSL
Beautiful Dreamer*, latest and greatest of the fabulous Fritz Marshall fleet,
and to explain a little bit about the journey you're about to make."

He turned to the diagram floating beside him. "'*BeeDee*', as we affectionately call her, is based on what was originally a design for asteroid
mining. However, as is often the case in such circumstances, Fritz Marshall eventually discovered that it was far more profitable to provide
transportation to asteroid miners, than to mine asteroids, himself.

"This is, in fact, exactly the same process by which the Strauss brothers'
canvas trousers entered our culture three hundred years ago, during the
California Gold Rush, and have remained with us ever since."

The attendant pointed to the lowest part of the diagram. "As you can see, *BeeDee* is a cylinder, divided into eight levels, or decks. The bottom or aftmost deck houses the last word—at least so far—

in hybrid fusion reactors: the Brown Systems 1.21 gigawatt catalytic Tokamak, along with the three massive Leland-Mazda ion-rocket engines it drives, and a few other engineering utilities peculiar to space travel."

Waving his hand up and down the middle of diagram, the young man told them, "Note the central axisway stretching the full length of the ship, with its spiral escalator wrapped around the service core. The next three decks above the reactor room are intended for cargo of every possible kind. These days, of course, we haul a lot more of that, here and there, than passengers—although the company fondly anticipates that this will change once Ceres is terraformed and ready to be settled."

He grinned. "Now you're really going to like this, folks. On the next deck, that's the fifth level, the Fritz Marshall company proudly offers a recreational-sized swimming pool—the only swimming pool aboard a spacecraft in the entire Solar System—and also a fully equipped weight room, convenient centrifuge, and spa with both sauna and hot tub."

Seeing a certain look on Jasmeen's face, Llyra arched her eyebrows innocently and refrained from asking if the pool could be frozen over. "What do you mean by 'recreational-sized'?" asked another prospective passenger.

The boarding attendant grinned again, sheepishly, and adjusted the lapels of his blazer. "And here I was hoping that phrase would slide right past you. It means 'not very big', I'm afraid, as might be expected of the only swimming pool aboard a spacecraft in the entire Solar System."

"I was going to ask you about that," Llyra couldn't help herself. Her mother scowled. "Wasn't there a swimming pool aboard the explorer ship *Fifth Force*?" She should know; her great grandfather Emerson, her great grandmother Rosalie, and a great many of their friends had taken that ship decades ago, out to the fabled Cometary Halo, halfway to the stars.

"*Fifth Force* theoretically crossed Pluto's orbit long ago," the attendant replied a bit stiffly. "She isn't technically in the Solar System any more. Our pool is about forty feet by twenty feet by five feet deep. That's four thousand cubic feet of water, or about sixteen thousand gallons. That comes to sixty-four thousand quarts, or a hundred twenty-eight thousand pints. Do you remember 'a pint's a pound the System round'? The water in our pool masses out at sixty-four tons."

"All of which have to be lifted, handled correctly at turnover, and braked," Llyra suggested.

The attendant brightened toward her. "That's absolutely right, young lady, all of which have to be lifted, handled at turnover, and braked."

"Excuse me, officer," said the lady from New Jersey. "What's with this turnover business you keep talking about? I tried to read about it in that brochure you mentioned, but I couldn't make heads or tails of it."

"Well, you see, Madam—"

She almost wailed. "It sounds extremely dangerous—do we have to do it?"

The boarding attendant cleared his throat and waited to make sure she was through. "Yes, indeed, you must, Madam, if you want to arrive at your destination, instead of shooting out of the Solar System toward the stars."

He waited for an interruption, but none was forthcoming. "You see, Madam—everybody—you'll be leaving Pallas, accelerating at the same rate as this asteroid's average surface gravity, a twentieth of a gee."

"Average surface gravity?" the New Jersey woman asked. "I thought that gravity—"

"Varies," he interrupted her this time, "from point to point on any planet's surface, even that of Earth, believe it or not. But it tends to be especially noticeable out here on small worlds like Pallas and Ceres."

"He is not just whistling 'Dixie'." Jasmeen whispered to Llyra.

"But to get back to your question," said the boarding attendant, who now had a diagram of the Solar System floating beside him. "Your ship could keep going at a twentieth of a gee, gaining speed until it gradually approaches—but never reaches—the speed of light. Please don't ask me about that, folks, because it's a whole different lecture.

"Instead, when you're halfway there, the ship will flip over, its engines still running, and begin slowing itself—it'll feel just like it did before; you won't be able to tell any difference—until you arrive at Ceres."

The lady from New Jersey was insistent. "But what about this flipping over? Will we have to wear seatbelts, or tie ourselves into our beds?"

He gave her a manly chuckle. "No, Madam, you won't feel that, either. The captain and the ship's computer know how to use the attitude thrusters to turn it over very subtly and gradually. If you're having cocktails, you won't spill a drop—unless you've had too many, of course."

Llyra raised a hand and spoke without being acknowledged. "Isn't it a little more complicated than that? What about the difference in Pallas' orbital inclination and Ceres'? What about the difference in their gravities?"

The attendant nodded. "Right again, Miss. The actual acceleration of the ship will increase gradually until you're feeling the tenth gravity of Ceres, rather than the twentieth of Pallas. The actual moment of turnover will be determined, in part, by the fact that, while Pallas travels in the same plane as almost everything else in the Solar System, Ceres' orbit cuts through that plane, rising above and below it. Its 'angle of inclination', as they say, is about twenty degrees.

"Happy now?" He winked at her.

She grinned. "Happy now,", she told him.

"Okay, then, back to *BeeDee*. The two levels above the recreation deck consist of a series of large, comfortable wedge-shaped staterooms located around the central well and escalator. Our staterooms offer every modern amenity, including real showers, automassage beds, almost limitless 3DTV and music libraries, and high speed SolarNet access. In addition, they are capable, in an emergency, of serving as independent lifesaving pods."

In the holographic simulation, Llyra and her fellow passengers watched dozens of pie-piece shapes—each with a single bite taken out of the small end to make room for the central well—floating around the abandoned and forlorn skeleton of a stricken ship. She wondered if the cargo holds could be ejected, as well.

The boarding attendant went on. "At the moment, because there aren't very many of you, we're using most of the lower passenger deck for package mail and light cargo. The topmost or eighth deck—that is, the deck furthest forward—features a spacious passenger lounge, including a full service wet bar, and an automated kitchenette. A series of floor-to-ceiling windows wraps around the deck's entire circumference, affording a scenic view unrivalled by any luxury hotel —with the possible exception of the Marriot Everest and the proposed Mons Olympus Hilton.

"At its center stands a slightly elevated control deck, capped by a transparent dome, and visible from all over the lounge area. All Fritz Marshall Spaces Lines passengers are encouraged to visit and observe the captain and his bridge crew navigate and operate the ship. There will be champagne cocktails offered to celebrate liftoff and midcourse turnover."

With these words, the boarding attendant dramatically threw open a large oval-shaped door in the wall behind him. The passenger tube from the Fritz Marshall offices in the crater wall attached to the vessel at the level of the recreation deck. A transparent-walled companionway between the weight room, with all of its machines and mirrors, and the swimming pool, led them to the central well and its spiral escalator. Llyra and the other passengers found their luggage already in their staterooms, and were free to repair directly to the lounge deck if they wished.

Jasmeen and Ardith insisted that Llyra take a nap, first.

⁎⁎

Soft chimes sounded, followed by a gentle recorded female voice saying, "Twenty minutes remain until liftoff. Twenty minutes remain until liftoff."

"I believe," said Ardith, "I will have a baggie of champagne."

She was speaking to a crisply-dressed female attendant who had just offered her a flexible plastic cylinder with a self-sealing top. The attendant wore dark slacks and a brass-buttoned blue blazer, just like the boarding attendant, with her long, dark hair neatly tucked up into a French braid, just as his had been. Pallatians were familiar with containers like this, which were useful in carrying liquids and preventing messes not only in space (the lounge attendant had assured them that they would never feel less than one twentieth of a standard gravity, even at turnover, halfway to Ceres) but on Pallas itself, where one twentieth of a gee usually wasn't quite enough to make drinks behave themselves.

"What I don't understand," Ardith went on, "is how this company plans to make any money." Llyra knew that it was more than simple curiosity with her; the Ngus were major stockholders in Fritz Marshall Space Lines. "This is a beautiful room, and our suite below isn't a bit less wonderful."

The three of them were on the lounge or common deck at the very top of the *Beautiful Dreamer*. The deck had a circular floorplan almost a hundred feet in diameter, centered around a pilots' flight deck standing in the center of the room and elevated five feet above the main deck. Through its transparent doors and windows, passengers could watch the flight crew handle the ship and be invited, a couple at a time, to come up, look around, and even try out the captain's chair. Just now, captain and crew were going through the pre-flight checklist.

"It's our 'Hidden Efficiency' plan, Ma'am," another attendant told her with a proprietary grin. He was a young man in his early thirties, with thinning, carroty-colored hair cut very short, and round, shiny cheeks. He, too, wore dark slacks, a white, long-sleeved shirt, and a black necktie. But, instead of a blue blazer, he wore a red plaid vest. His accent was southern East American. "I'm glad you-all're enjoyin' it."

The soft chimes sounded again, and the voice said, "Seventeen minutes remain until liftoff."

61

"Hidden Efficiency plan?" Ardith gestured with her baggie and her eyes, asking Jasmeen and her daughter if they might like a container of champagne. Jasmeen nodded enthusiastically and accepted a baggie from the attendant. Llyra, only now beginning to awaken fully from her nap, mouthed no thanks, and took another sip of her favorite drink, Koffie Kola.

Wrapped most of the way around the base of the control deck—

interrupted only by the forward, or upper terminus of the spiral escalator—was the kitchenette and bar the boarding attendant had spoken of. There were facilities in the staterooms for preparing simple meals, as well, although Llyra had been too sleepy to inspect them closely.

The lounge attendant slipped his tray beneath his arm and squatted beside the comfortable leather-covered sofa Ardith relaxed in. "Yes, Ma'am. Fritz Marshall company policy is that nothing is ever done that will diminish or spoil our passengers' experience with us. Think about it—is this your first trip into space? I thought as much. How about your daughters—oh, I see, her first trip, her tutor's second. My point is, this is something that each of you will remember for the rest of your lives. And we want it to be a happy memory, one that you associate with us."

"I understand," said Ardith. "But the Hidden Efficiency … "

"It's simply this: if we have to save money, it must always be done somewhere else in the operation, where the payin' customers'll never notice it."

"So you might cut corners," Llyra suggested archly, "where safety measures are concerned?"

"Or perhaps on maintenance?" Jasmeen asked, like Llyra, appearing to be innocent. Sometimes, Ardith thought, they really do seem like sisters.

"Absolutely not, Miss. Havin' one of our spaceships blow up at liftoff or crash into another ship or something would sort of be the ultimate way of diminishin' or spoilin' our passengers' experience, wouldn't it? And, of course, they'd tend to notice it—for a few seconds, at least."

Jasmeen smiled. "So how *do* you reduce overhead?"

They heard the chimes again, the voice said, "Ten minutes remain until liftoff."

The attendant sighed, "I guess we'd look for bargains in deuterium or reaction mass, or peanuts an' champagne. The way they always talk about in company briefin's, is by cuttin' salaries and benefits—but only from the top down. Nobody who serves in-ship as attendants or crew, nobody who gets his hands dirty in the wrench barn, has ever taken a cut. But it's said Fritz Marshall himself worked for nothin' through a couple years in the beginnin'."

"Well," Ardith replied, "I suppose that represents some kind of progress." She turned to her young companions. "You see, the so-called Sagebrush Rebellion, the agonizingly slow-but-steady 21st century revolution against the United States government—that ended with West America separating itself from East America—was also a revolt against a handful of giant corporations that had come to believe they owned the country and everybody in it. There are still states in West America where holding a Master of Business Administration degree is illegal—or at least considered suspicious, like being caught carrying lock-picks."

The attendant chuckled. "Makes sense. Whenever a company hires an MBA, it's a sure sign they're lookin' for ways t'give their customers the least possible goods an' services in exchange for the highest possible prices."

"Regrettably," Jasmeen sipped at her champagne, "revolution is incomplete. Problem is not solved everywhere, even today. My father worked for short time in factory making … electric tooth washing machines."

Ardith blinked. "In Russia?"

"In Newark," Jasmeen replied. "When factory is owned and operated by original inventor of tooth washing machine, quality is such that they have less than two percent return of faulty merchandise from customers. This goes on for years and years. Then inventor sells company so he can retire to Florida beach, and factory is taken over by engineer."

"A man with a mind so narrow," the attendant was grinning as he quoted the old saw, "that he can look through a keyhole with both eyes."

Jasmeen asked, "Are you not engineer, Mrs. Ngu?"

The attendant paled slightly. The chimes sounded again, and the voice said, "Six minutes remain until liftoff."

"No, Jasmeen, dear," said Ardith. "I'm a scientist. Llyra's father is an engineer." She tilted her head back, emptied her baggie, and took another.

Jasmeen went on. "Engineer at tooth machine factory is also Master of Business Administration, therefore perfectly able to put whole head through keyhole."

Everybody laughed.

"One day, out of blue," Jasmeen went on, "recombinant MBA-engineer hybrid calculates that Quality Control Department—where my father Mohammed happens to work—costs tooth machine company too much. Engineer eliminates entire department, saying this will save company millions."

"Uh-oh," Ardith and the attendant muttered at the same time.

"You are both way ahead of me," Jasmeen told them. "Merchandise returns promptly shoot up to fifty percent. Engineer claims this is still cheaper than running Quality Control Department and therefore acceptable. Trouble is that tooth machine company soon acquires reputation for selling trash to wholesalers, retailers, and public. Engineer's short-term gain is erased by long-term loss. Company fires engineer, asks my father to restart Quality Control Department, but by that time, he and Beliita my mother are in training, committed to IASA Mars program."

The attendant nodded. "Introducin' 'em to an altogether different kind of quality control problem. I know—I had an uncle and an aunt who died on Mars."

They heard the chimes again, sounding a little more urgent. The voice said, "Thirty seconds remain until liftoff. Thirty seconds. Please be seated."

"Their name?" Jasmeen asked, genuinely interested.

"Sanchez—Fourth Expedition."

She nodded. "Mine is Khalidov, Seventh Expedition, rescued by—"

"The infamous Ngu brothers," he supplied, then looked to Ardith and then to Llyra. "Your grandfather, young lady?" he asked the younger female.

Llyra stood up and stretched, then sat again as the deck beneath her feet began vibrating. "That's right, William Ngu—and my great uncle Brody."

As Llyra and her companions watched out the enormous windows of her eighth deck, *Beautiful Dreamer* began to rise above the baked and frozen soil of Port Peary, as quietly and gently as an elevator in a luxury hotel. In seconds—almost without discernable acceleration—

the ship reached, then surpassed, the level of the mountaintops about the polar crater.

In the center of the deck, a few feet above the level of the lounge, the flight crew, consisting of the captain and two assistants, chattered at one another in technicalese, as they manipulated their keyboards. Llyra's heart beat so hard in her chest that it hurt. She was going to see her father and her brother! She was going to see another world!

They were on their way to Ceres!

CHAPTER NINE: THE MONKEY IN THE WRENCH

All of the new worlds likely to be settled by humanity in the near future have a considerably lower gravity than Earth: Pallas has five percent of Earth's gravity, Ceres has ten. Earth's Moon has about seventeen percent, and Mars has about thirty. That fact—and its consequences—may turn out to be the most important in human history ... or at least human evolution. —*The Diaries of Rosalie Frazier Ngu*

NOT QUITE WIDE AWAKE YET, Jasmeen took a deep breath and released it, uncertain but fearful of what she was about to confront. The young woman pushed a lighted plastic button on the panel before her, let the stainless steel door slide shut, and felt her weight surge slightly as the compartment began to rise.

The ship's centrifuge facility, strictly speaking, constituted an unnumbered deck unto itself, squeezed in between the deck with the swimming pool and sauna, and the lower, or aftmost deck of passenger accommodations, presently uninhabited and given over to cargo. The machine could be entered only when it wasn't running, by means of this small lift from the recreation deck.

Her weight grew lighter on her feet, the door slid open again almost immediately, and, as she stepped through, shut itself again. Without being told, the lift descended to the deck below, leaving an empty space behind her. She looked across the disk-shaped centrifuge deck, interrupted only at the hub, where the escalator and service core passed through it, to a clutter of various benches, chairs, and exercise equipment, all of it bolted securely to the curved wall on her right.

From within one of the cagelike weight machines, a familiar voice spoke to her. "You'll have to reorient yourself ninety degrees as quickly as you can. The new floor will be the carpeted surface to your right. Lie down on one of those couches ahead of you, strap in, and, once the centrifuge has begun spinning, you'll find yourself standing on the new floor."

Jasmeen answered. "Llyra, what are you doing down here in middle of night? I woke up just now and you were gone. If your mother knew, she'd be—"

"My mother, Jasmeen. She'd be my mother." Jasmeen saw movement ahead of her as Llyra climbed out of the exercise machine holding a remote control device in one hand. The girl pressed a button. They both heard relays thud, and a low, powerful hum began to fill the space they occupied.

Llyra said, "No room to jump in here. I want to do some floor exercises and some of these machines. Let's try the gravity of Ceres, first, okay? One tenth Earth normal, twice the gravity of Pallas. Better get into these couches, though." The girl quickly followed her own advice.

"Very well," the older female said. "But afterward we shall have some talk." Lying down and strapping herself onto the couch, Jasmeen placed the soles of her feet in contact with the carpeted wall. This shouldn't be much of an ordeal, she reflected. Llyra had experienced this much gravity at those mascons on Pallas she liked to skate over, and it was only a third of the gravity she herself had been born to, on Mars.

The noise grew quieter as it grew more complex. Jasmeen had read the brochure by now and knew there were counterweights in the ceiling, spinning in the opposite direction as the centrifuge to keep it from altering the ship's attitude and course. She also knew that, although facilities like this had been built wherever humanity settled among the asteroids, and the moons of the major planets—not to mention several dozen space stations between here and the Sun—and had once been thought vital to the survival of the species in space, it was now known there was no need for them. They continued to be built and used nonetheless. *Beautiful Dreamer* might be the first spaceship (since *Fifth Force*) to boast of a swimming pool; it was by no means the only one to have a centrifuge.

Apparently thinking similar thoughts, Llyra told her, "You know my mother spent hours and days and weeks in one of these things, just to have my brother. The theory was that human ova can't descend through the Fallopian tubes without more gravity than we have out here in the asteroids."

"I know theory," Jasmeen answered, thinking that her young student knew altogether too much, sometimes, for a thirteen-year-old. Oh well, she had been very much the same, herself, only six years ago, and it didn't seem to have done her any harm. "Theory is interesting, but completely—"

"Wrong," Llyra finished. "Because it turns out the Fallopian tubes are lined with ciliated cells, just like the bronchial tubes, and they whisk the egg along to the uterus whether there's any gravity or not. Poor Mother."

Jasmeen had never heard Llyra talk this way. "Poor Mother? Why poor Mother?"

Llyra responded with a humorless little laugh. "Isn't that silly—no pun intended? Silly-ated. All those hours, days, and weeks spent working out

66

in a giant rock tumbler—or just sitting in it knitting booties—and there wasn't any need. By the time my folks decided to have me, they knew the scientific truth and they didn't bother with a centrifuge."

"I see," Jasmeen nodded. "Although many would-be mothers still do. It has become superstition?"

"Well, you can't blame them, I guess" Llyra said. "Not with the rate of miscarriages we have out here. We're like Quito, Ecuador or Leadville, Colorado—only worse. Mother doesn't know that I know she had four of them—spontaneous abortions—between my brother and me. My father told me. She'd die of embarrassment if she knew. I think a lot of women still believe this might be a way to prevent it, and would do anything."

Jasmeen thought she heard an odd quality in Llyra's voice, but, lying in these couches the way they were, couldn't see her face. "Sad thing," she said, "is that only time and evolution can do that. And science, perhaps."

"Perhaps," Llyra agreed. By now the noise of the centrifuge had steadied, their weight was on their feet, and what had been the wall now felt like a carpeted floor. "Tell you what, don't unstrap—let's skip Cerean gravity and head straight for the Moon—one sixth of a gee."

The stateroom's shape was difficult to get used to, its current occupant reflected. One end was very narrow, its short wall occupied only by an oval door to the circular hallway and the spiral escalator outside. He'd avoided coming here for as long as he could, sitting, instead, in the passenger lounge, listening carefully to the others talking.

The wall opposite was a good deal wider, nearly sixteen feet, the room's occupant had calculated, and slightly curved, as it was a part of the ship's circumference. A pair of twin beds were set against that wall, with a porthole between them over an item of bedside furniture offering three drawers and a reading lamp screwed to its surface. At the foot of each bed sat another small chest of drawers, along with a chair that could be moved only if a small lever at the end of each leg was thrown first.

On the counter-clockwise wall, another oval door led to a bathroom shared with the occupants of the room to the right. How many passengers tripped over that high, submarine-style threshold when they got up in the middle of the night, he wondered. A door in the left, or clockwise wall opened into a surprisingly roomy closet. The passenger was mildly curious about the arrangement in the room to the left, where the closet would be where this room's righthand bed was.

There wasn't much to see out the porthole, a twelve-inch disk of thick glass or plastic set in a heavy frame. It looked a bit odd here, lacking the traditional latch and hinges that would grace a seagoing window back on Earth. (The passenger had once stuffed a dead human body through such a porthole.) This one was on the "night" side of the ship; all that could be seen through it was an ocean of small pinpoints of light. Some of them must be asteroids and planets, the passenger realized, but there was no way he could tell one from another.

If this stateroom had been on the sunward side of the ship, he knew, even this far from the Solar System's primary, the transparency would have darkened itself until he couldn't see the stars. To anyone who was even mildly claustrophobic, as he happened to be, the idea was unthinkable.

Back inside, almost any portion of the walls on either side of the stateroom could be programmed to perform as a 3DTV screen, tapping into the ship's supply of entertainment, or even realtime broadcasts from Earth, the Moon, Mars, and Pallas. At the moment, the walls were blank. The passenger had little use—and a great deal of contempt— for most of what was broadcast. The human race badly needed a wakeup call before disaster of unprecedented proportions became unavoidable back on the Mother Planet, and they weren't getting it from the mass media.

No matter, he would provide such a wakeup call, himself. It was his duty, for which he was remarkably well paid, but it was also his pleasure.

He focused his attention on the stateroom's righthand bed, where his suitcase still lay as the attendants had placed it, unopened. It was large, brown, and shiny, a stylish reproduction of the ancient classic Samsonite. Even if it had been inspected before boarding—

which local practices stupidly forbade—there was nothing in it or about it that might have given him away as an "asset" of Null Delta Em, not even the personal sidearm most of the idiots out here couldn't seem to live without.

As important as it was for him to fit in, he could never bring himself to carry a gun. He'd used guns, of course, to accomplish certain tasks, then thrown them away as far and as soon as he could. The fools out here all thought they were Daniel Boone or somebody, he supposed. It was just like travelling west of the Mississippi, only worse. He'd hated every minute he'd been forced to live in Curringer on Pallas, working at an office job provided by his real employers back on Earth. He'd managed to acquire a lot of money during that time, however, and invest it in the system he was helping to destroy. He enjoyed the irony. When this job was over, he was headed back home for good.

Opening the suitcase, he removed most of its contents—shirts, socks, and underwear—and carefully distributed them among the three drawers in the bedside table. The inside of the suitcase smelled a little funny, he thought, but that was the only indication that it wasn't exactly what it was supposed to be, and that could be taken care of simply by sprinkling a little cologne into the lining, which he did now.

The heavily-coded message sent from East America (anyone else who saw it would think it was merely birthday greetings from an aunt, which, in a way, it was) had given him a location—the Curringer Corporation's construction dome on Ceres—a date and time that coincided with an event that was already the subject of excited talk everywhere among the Settled Worlds except for certain portions of the planet of humanity's birth, and a two-digit number, eighty-six, that told him the sort of operation he was supposed to conduct: messy, with a maximum number of casualties.

His assignment was to teach these frontier throwbacks a lesson that they wouldn't soon forget, that the price for defying Nature was too high to pay. His personal pleasure would be to make a murderous shambles of the award ceremony they were holding in young Wilson Ngu's honor, for having murdered five brave activists for environmental sanity.

His electronic credentials had arrived the same day in a separate e-mail packet. They were necessary because, in violent disregard for decent, humane, and progressive United Nations policies going back more than a century and a half, the asteroid Ceres had been seized as private property (just as Pallas had been before it) and was being administered as such. As an environmentalist and someone who knew that all property is theft, that irked him deeply, but he was here to put a stop to it.

The upcoming gala, then, represented a rare opportunity to travel to Ceres, see what they were doing there, and possibly do something about it, without many questions being asked. He was now a bonafide stringer for *Boston Magazine*, practically the only openly socialist "dead tree" publication left in North America, and one of the Mass Movement's staunchest editorial supporters—accompanied by his reservation for Ceres aboard the *F.M.S.L. Beautiful Dreamer* and a reasonably handsome letter of credit drawn on a Pallas bank. He was grateful he hadn't had to pay for the ship passage himself. A double stateroom like this one was expensive enough, even with a roommate— which he could have afforded only if he'd killed him later—to share the cost. Some of the accommodations even had bunk beds to help spread the expense.

Once the deed had been done—whatever it turned out to be; that much had been left completely up to him, and he had just the method he'd been looking forward to trying—he'd been informed that getting away, off of Ceres, back to Pallas, and wherever after that, would be his own concern. He'd already made arrangements about that, of course, although he wasn't absolutely certain how well those arrangements would hold, following the catastrophe he was planning for these damned cowboys.

He also had a backup plan.

And a plan to back that up.

Long-acquired habit made him want to take his personal computer from his jacket pocket, plug it into the inside of the suitcase, and submit the resulting combination to a battery of tests. Yet another ancient habit restrained him. He'd inspected this room thoroughly when he came aboard. There appeared to be no cameras or other spy devices trained on this little space. And if there had been, and the local passengers had discovered them, most likely they'd have spaced the crew and taken the ship back to Pallas to lynch the company's other employees.

But you could never be too careful about things like that. The Fritz Marshall space lines—or the vile Curringer Corporation— might risk a hidden camera here and there to protect its ill-gotten property. They would certainly be doing a lot more things like that once he was through with them on Ceres. But meanwhile, you were dead a long time, and in prison, he knew from painful experience, even longer.

He closed the suitcase, patted it like an old familiar pet, and put it away where it belonged, in the closet. He put the clothes he hadn't placed in the drawers on hangers and hung them up, partially concealing the suitcase.

Only then did he turn on the 3DTV, filling the lonely little cabin with color and sound. Onscreen, a gray cartoon cat chased a brown cartoon mouse in zero gravity. It was late, long past time to see about getting something to eat. An impossibly compact kitchenette adjoined the bath, but its cupboard and tiny refrigeration unit were empty.

He wondered what was available that he could bring back from the passenger lounge.

⁂

"My mother and father love each other," Llyra said abruptly, her tone argumentative.

The statement struck Jasmeen as an awkward and uncomfortable one for two reasons. To begin with, they had been talking about something else altogether as they jogged along the three-hundred fourteen foot circumference of the *Beautiful Dreamer*'s centrifuge chamber at one-sixth of a standard Earth gravity—the gravity of Earth's Moon—winding every foot of their way between the facility's exercise machines. Jasmeen, whose native planet Mars had twice the gravity of Earth's Moon, had been dismayed at how easily she'd become accustomed to far less. After only half an hour of light exercise, her calves and the backs of her thighs had begun to ache and threatened to knot up painfully.

Llyra stopped jogging and turned to face Jasmeen. Silence hung in the air between them. They could hear and feel the faint rumble of the centrifuge.

As a second generation Martian, the older girl was unused to naked declarations regarding one's feelings. Her own people back home were so tight-lipped about their inner processes that the Earthers, mostly East Americans, had contemptuously declared the Red Planet "Marsboro Country". For their part, the Martians had taken to heart what had been intended as an insult, and had gone far beyond merely glorying in it.

At the age of four, Jasmeen's father had proudly taken her to the original seventh-colony landing site to see a fifty-foot sculpture of what purported to be an authentic West American cowboy, complete with faded jeans beneath sheepskin chaps, a brightly-colored plaid shirt, a huge clashing kerchief, and an outlandish hundred-gallon hat raised high above the cowboy's head in one gloved hand. His other hand held a coil of rope supposedly made of braided horsehair. The Martians had added a low-slung cartridge-studded pistol belt, a big ivory-handled sixgun—something no Earthside advertising agency had ever had the stomach for—and a hand-rolled cigarette hanging from his lower lip, emitting real smoke.

For some reason, people said the cowboy's name was Woody.

She and her people were stoics, having perfectly adapted themselves to harsh colonial conditions. Still, Jasmeen thought, it was her duty, as Llyra's friend as well as her coach, to respond sympathetically, to try to understand her. The trouble was, in this particular context, she didn't have the faintest idea how. Luckily, this time, Llyra made it unnecessary by going on.

"I *know* they love each other, Jasmeen," she insisted. "I can see it on their faces—in their eyes—every time they're back together again. My brother is there, too. We all have a big, fancy dinner, then they disappear together for twenty-four hours and when they reappear it's like a party around our house for another day or two. But sooner or later, Mother starts yelling for some reason or another, it doesn't seem to matter why, and Daddy stops saying anything at all. It always happens the same way.

Sooner or later Mother locks herself in the bedroom, and Daddy goes back to Ceres."

The younger girl sat sideways on the plastic-upholstered seat of one of the exercise devices, ignoring the machinery. Were those tears Jasmeen saw in Llyra's eyes? That was another thing Martians simply didn't do, and it was difficult to see it as anything but a sign of fatal weakness. A part of Jasmeen wanted to go to Llyra and hold her, comfort her.

The Martian part restrained her.

It was all true, though. Jasmeen had seen—and lived through— the cycle Llyra was describing several times over the years she'd worked for them. She'd never quite understood it, herself. Her own mother and father, Mohammed and Beliita, were very similar to Adam and Ardith in more than one respect: they were both professionals, both academics, both intellectuals, she supposed. And they surely must have had their differences. But they had never yelled at one another in her memory, and they had *never* spent a single night apart, since they'd been married, even at IASA's Siberian training facility.

Someday, when she found the right someone or the right someone found her, Jasmeen was grimly determined—especially since she'd come to know the Ngus so well—that it was going to be like that with them. They would be two halves of a single life, two breaths of a single soul.

Otherwise, she thought, what was the point in falling in love and getting married?

Now, overcoming the Martian part, she sat as close as she could to Llyra, on a chromium-plated steel crossbar near the padded seat. (A sixth of a gee made that sort of thing a good deal more comfortable than it might otherwise have been, she noted incongruously.) Reaching carefully through the machinery, she put an arm across the girl's shoulders.

"You cannot live another person's life for them," she told Llyra. "Not even those you love most. Is hard, but when you hurt for them, you must say to yourself, 'Not my life, not my life, not my life, not my life, not my life'. Five times, just like that. Will make you feel better."

"Is that a Chechen thing?" Llyra asked through the tears now streaking her cheeks.

"No, is thing I read in ladies' magazine at dentist's office." They both laughed.

"But I can't do that, Jasmeen, I just can't say, 'Not my life' like that."

Jasmeen shrugged. "I said is hard. I didn't say is easy."

But Llyra was continuing, more to herself than to Jasmeen. "It's like … it's … oh, I don't know. Somehow it feels like it's my fault, them not getting along. Somehow it feels like I caused it. I don't know how."

Jasmeen sighed. "I hate to tell you, little one, but is not always about you."

Llyra cracked a smile. "Okay, maybe it's because I feel there must be something I could do, but I haven't done it because I don't know what it is."

Jasmeen said nothing. She knew something important was coming. She left the bar and knelt beside her student, putting both arms around her.

"I *am* going to fix it, you know," Llyra insisted. "I'm going to go from world to world, if I have to, and you're going with me. From Pallas to Ceres, from Ceres to Earth's Moon, from the Moon to Mars, skating on each and every world until it feels just like my own. And then I'm going to skate on Earth, in the biggest, most important ice rink there is, in the biggest, most important competition they have. And I'm going to win that competition, Jasmeen, so my mother and daddy will—"

She'd begun weeping again; her shoulders shook within Jasmeen's comforting arms.

"So they'll what, my little? Is magnificent plan, I agree. Is very dangerous plan. But what can even that do to make those two act like grownups?"

"Oh, I don't know, Jasmeen!" Llyra cried. "They'll just *have* to, don't you see? They'll just have to!" The girl's shoulders slumped. She bent her head to her chest and sobbed for half an hour in her teacher's arms.

CHAPTER TEN: TURNOVER

Whether a political or philosophical undertaking happens to be for good or for evil, it's eventually done in, not by its mortal enemies, but by the "moderates" and "gradualists" within its own ranks. Ideologically speaking, swimming upstream, against the current, for any length of time, is morally exhausting. Most individuals simply aren't up to it. Sooner or later, they begin to look for excuses to drop out of the struggle and head for quieter waters, comfortably going nowhere. The trouble is, in order to feel right about it, they need everybody else to do it, too. —*The Diaries of Rosalie Frazier Ngu*

THEY COULD TELL IMMEDIATELY THAT the old gentleman was from East America, specifically from the state of Massachusetts, and almost certainly from the legendarily silly Amherst area, which had led the state (and, to their enormous disappointment, nobody, anywhere else in the System) in what the West American media had described as the "new Amishness".

Their reasoning went like this: dismayed at what everyone else saw as progress, the Amish, along with Hutterites, Mennonites, and similar religious groups, had attempted to stop time—or the world, so they could get off—somewhere around the middle of the nineteenth century. Later groups, most of them religious as well, and suffering what would later be called "future shock", had attempted to stop time at other points. In Amherst, where the dominant religion was Gaianism—Mother Earth worship—they'd voted to stop time in the last year of the twentieth.

"Would you young ladies mind if I joined you?" the old gentleman asked them politely, hooking his cane over one forearm and doffing his hat.

This close up, thought Ardith, it was impossible to mistake the old gentleman for anything but an Amherstian—and probably a college professor—in his college-professorly oatmeal-colored, elbow-patched tweed jacket, his blue, self-consciously proletarian denim work shirt, and his faded blue denim trousers—permanently pressed with a sharp crease. He also wore a bow tie, and on his head, a round floppy object that another generation had called a "boonie hat", but which had been popular among academics and fishermen long before that.

"Not at all," Ardith replied. She was something of an academic herself, of course, although she hoped it wasn't that obvious. She was inclined toward bluejeans and sweaters when she was working in her lab, but tended to shift to skirts or dresses when out in public. "Please sit down."

Both of the girls nodded cordial agreement with her. Curringer was a small town—all of Pallas put together amounted to little more than a small town—and they didn't get a chance to see new faces very often.

Ardith sat comfortably on a deeply-cushioned leather-covered sofa with Jasmeen sitting at the other end. Llyra occupied an identical item of furniture opposite them. Between the two sofas stood a glass-topped coffee table. The lights had been lowered so that the passengers could enjoy the starry view outside. Classical music played softly throughout the room—Ardith had recognized Lennon and McCartney's "Yesterday" and something she thought might be called "I Hope You Don't Mind".

The three of them had left the comfortable privacy of their suite and come up to the passenger lounge to have drinks and a snack before the girls went down for a swim in the ship's "recreation-sized" pool, and Ardith returned to her cabin to work on her current scientific paper. They were pleasantly surprised to discover that in just a few minutes, when Turnover officially began, the drinks would be "on the house".

They'd forgotten about Turnover.

Jasmeen observed, "They say they're bringing champagne in a minute or two. And in glasses, not baggies!"

Llyra added, "To demonstrate that they can turn the ship over without spilling a drop! With their attitude controls they could do it all in a few seconds—and glue everything and everybody in here to the walls—but they say they're going to take a gentle couple of hours."

"That means the engines will be pushing us sideways," her mother observed, leading the witness a little. "Won't that put us off our course?"

"Not when they've allowed for it from the very beginning," Llyra laughed.

"Very good, young lady," the old man laughed with her. Back home on Pallas, Ardith thought, he might easily have been over a hundred years old. Coming from the Mother Planet, as she was certain he did, it was likelier he was only in his mid-seventies and possibly younger than that. Gravity is harmful to human beings and other living things, she misquoted deliberately. "I came up here to see it. Say, isn't that spiral escalator something? I've never seen anything quite like it." Somewhat stiffly, and with the aid of his cane, the old man sat down beside Llyra.

Ardith nodded. "It's certainly something. My daughter, here," she indicated Llyra, "has been riding it up and down all morning, trying to figure out where the stairsteps go at the top and bottom of the ride."

"I think they must slide over sideways and go back the other way," said the girl. "I was going to mark one with bubble gum and follow it, but—"

"But I would not let her," Jasmeen finished. "Cruel monster that I am."

Both girls laughed.

"Ah, science," the old man said. "What'll they think of next? Oh, excuse me. I failed to introduce myself." He leaned across the table and offered a hand to Ardith, then to Jasmeen, and finally to Llyra at the other end of the sofa. "I'm Robert Fulton, the stringer, on Pallas, for several Earthside publications, mostly East American. I'm being sent out here by *Boston Magazine* to cover the award ceremony on Ceres."

Ardith vaguely remembered seeing or hearing the man's name before, but the champagne arrrived, Llyra wanted some, and there were other things to think about.

The sun and stars had slowly begun to swirl around the ship.

**⁎
⁎⁎**

"Robert Fulton" was the working persona he most enjoyed adopting, in part because the original, historic Robert Fulton had been among the first to use technology to exploit and pollute the natural world. The little old man, at least twenty years older in appearance than his actual age, was the very picture of harmlessness, and tended to put individuals at their ease—just before he garroted, stabbed, shot, or poisoned them to death.

At the moment, as he watched the three females prattle without really listening to them, the younger man inside Robert Fulton was considering a radical change in the orders Null Delta Em had issued him. There might be an enormous advantage in just doing the job right here and now, to the family of the young "hero" on Ceres, and of the Terraformation Project's Director and Chief Engineer. True, he himself would die. But in a sense, dying in the proper cause was everything he had ever lived for, and he had been fully prepared to do it for a long time.

Liver-spotted hands resting on the head of his cane, he leaned back and closed his eyes momentarily. The gesture was more genuine than feigned. Sometimes he felt as old as Robert Fulton was supposed to be. In a great many ways, he had begun to grow a bit tired of life lately, and putting an end to it now might actually represent something of a relief.

"Sir?" came a voice. He opened his eyes and looked up at a young woman holding a tray full of traditional glasses of champagne. The Ngu women and their servant were already opening their own. "Would you care for a free glass of champagne to help celebrate Turnover?"

He smiled and shook his head, but inwardly, preoccupied with his thoughts, he shuddered, as the saying went, as if someone had walked over his grave. He wasn't afraid of dying for himself, he knew, not really. More than anything, what he feared was that, as all groups must, sooner or later, Null Delta Em would someday decide to try and "mainstream" itself, to try and soften its ideological edges for the sake of public relations—and above all, for purposes of fundraising —and begin to lose track of the reasons it had been created. He'd seen exactly the same thing happen again and again to dozens of other organizations.

At least if he were to destroy this spaceship and her passengers —including himself—he wouldn't have to watch that happen to Null Delta Em. He was finding a great deal of comfort, somehow, in that idea.

"Mr. Fulton ... ?"

He sat up and blinked. Apparently, he'd dozed off—a bad sign. Back in the world outside his thoughts, the cocktail waitress had moved along at last, and Ardith Ngu was introducing herself, her young daughter, and her daughter's coach. The foolish woman needn't have bothered, of course, although she had no way of knowing it. He'd done his homework thoroughly, as he always did when he had a contract like this one.

The woman herself, he was aware, spent most of her time locked in a sinister Frankenstein's laboratory in Curringer, not far from the very offices where he sat every day and pretended to work, learning to extract more and more vile profit from a sky full of lovely, celestial objects that had gone untouched for so many ages before Man, pristine, and pure.

She was a wellspring, a veritable fountainhead, of evil. She was the mother of the teenage murderer whose blood-drenched acts these frontier savages were about to advertise across the entire Solar System on 3DTV. She was the consort of the destroyer who had started to plunder and wreck the asteroid Ceres exactly as Pallas had been wrenched from the breast of Nature and exploited for mere human use a century ago.

Gaia alone knew what unnatural, greed-driven, materialistic, and in-humane purposes this creature was preparing her poor little daughter for, under the innocent-appearing guise of figure skating. The young coach, too, was irredeemably corrupt, a child of murderous Chechen rebels who be-came renegade Martian colonists. A child of violent anti-social refusniks. A child of defectors. A child of traitors. That alone should be enough to pre-dict that nothing good could come from any of these three. Best to pinch their tawdry lives off now, before they could foster any more abominations.

It had sickened him to touch the foul hand of Ardith Zacharenko Ngu. At the same time, it had sent a perverse shock of desire through his body. Like most supremely evil things, he had discovered in his life, she was very beautiful. But his ultimate objective had required the hated contact.

That was another reason, perhaps, to fulfill his commission right now and be done with it. He would no longer suffer the need to resist the distractions and temptations that a perverse universe presented him with. He'd always much preferred working in Moslem countries, where they kept their women decently under cover. All modern women were whores, displaying themselves with utter abandon. If only there were some way, before he struck, to taste what this one blatantly offered to all comers.

For that matter, the young Chechen coach, with her slender waist, her narrow hips, and those remarkable breasts of hers would do very nicely.

Or even the woman's little daughter.

Reason number three occurred to him just as he was imagining what each one of these females must look like underneath the shamefully skimpy clothing that they wore: the young "hero" and his father would be left behind by the deed, shaken by its unexpected suddenness, stunned by its ferocity, stopped by its finality, and possibly ruined for life.

The lesson would be learned by others, and it would never be forgotten.

⁎⁎

"She doesn't deserve him!"

The girl wailed angrily, then looked around, a little chagrined. She was safely in the privacy of a bedroom suite that, because she happened to be personal assistant to the project's Chief Engineer, she didn't have to share with anyone else. But these dormitory walls had been shipped here under circumstances in which every ounce and every square inch came at an enormous premium, and they were notoriously thin.

"Ingrid Andersson," said a voice, "I've heard you say that at least ten times in the last hour, and that many times a day for the past two years. And it may even be true as far as it goes—I'm certainly no judge of matters like that. But hollering isn't what makes it true, dear. Even if it was, what can you do? The man has been married for twenty years, however unhappily, and he has two beautiful children. You want to ruin their lives, just because you have an itch in your breeches?"

The voice Ingrid was hearing was her own, issuing from the audio pads of a Purse-O-Nal Systems Interactive Diary she'd been using for a decade, ever since she'd turned fifteen. Sitting open on her little desk, it was designed to destroy itself if anyone else attempted to tamper with it. Buying the device with money she had earned herself had been a major turning-point in her life. Its voice and outlook had matured with hers, as they were programmed to do, although sometimes, she admitted, it seemed like the AI itself was maturing faster than she was.

"A what in my what?" Ingrid's tone was outraged. How could it possibly be so crude, if it based itself on her personality and vocabulary?

The device chuckled. "You heard me. Finally got your attention, didn't I?"

Ingrid shook her head, otherwise ignoring the remark. "If I could only get *him* to look at me! I'm prettier than she is, at least I think I am, and I'm younger. I have a better shape, and a sweeter voice. I could even give him more children—another whole family! That's important to Pallatians, isn't it? You know I dream about that sometimes."

"You don't know for a fact that you could give the man children, Ingrid," the diary replied evenly. "I know you're aware that the rate of spontaneous abortion is high enough among native Pallatians, and Martians, and Mooners, let alone recent transplants from Earth like you."

She huffed at it. "You're not supposed to say 'Mooners'. It implies—"

"I know what it implies, Ingrid. And if I'd been programmed with a sense of humor, I'd think it was funny. For what it's worth, those who live on the Moon do. But very well, let's make it the politically correct 'Lunarians'. In either case, you know I'm right about the miscarriage—"

"I think maybe I should set your argument levels lower," she told the device abruptly. The diary looked a little like a laptop computer of a century ago, except that it was much smaller and offered the user no keyboard, at least at the moment. The full color three dimensional screen served Ingrid mostly as a non-reversing mirror. "How would you like that?"

"You could do that, and I admit, I wouldn't like it a bit," said the diary, its mouth moving with the words it spoke. "But it wouldn't change the truth, now, would it?" Its tone was a little smug. It often sounded that way when it knew she was coming around to its way of thinking.

"No, no, it wouldn't." A tear slid from the corner of one eye, down her cheek, followed closely by another. "I just wish she wasn't coming here, that's all. She belongs back on Pallas. Why does she have to come here and—"

"When you've had him all to yourself? It hasn't done you a lot of good, though, has it? And you know perfectly well why she has to come here, Ingrid. It isn't even necessarily to see him, is it? It's to see her son—and his, of course—rewarded for saving lives at the risk of his own."

A forlorn Ingrid looked at the only face her diary had been programmed to present. The eyes—which were usually extraordinarily beautiful, were red now, swollen with anguish. "Why do you always have to be so cruel?"

"Who set my parameters, Ingrid? Wasn't it you? Didn't you want me to serve as your reality check—because you deplored the way your mother always evaded the facts of reality and your father let her get away with it?"

She nodded. "Yes, yes, it's true. I know it's true." Her father Thor (his mother had called him Takeshi) was plenty capable of evading the facts of reality, himself. He was a born crackpot of both the bow tie and the propeller beanie varieties, who had changed his ancient family name to Andersson because of a theory he had about the Vikings having discovered Japan. Despite centuries of anthropological evidence to the contrary, he even believed that the Ainu were the Vikings' descendents.

She wondered why he cared. The whole family had lived in Connecticut for six generations.

"Sometimes that hurts you, I know," said the diary with a more conciliatory tone of voice. "Believe me, if I were capable of feeling anything, I'd be happy to feel sorry for you, Ingrid, honestly I would. You know you're not just important to me, you know, you're all that's important to me."

Ingrid sniffed back her tears. "What a nice thing to say ... "

But it went on: "So let me ask you: this is a construction site, where men outnumber women a hundred to one. Why don't you look around for somebody who isn't married? Somebody who isn't *way* too old for you?"

The diary had hit a nerve, a very tender nerve. "Wait a minute! He isn't too—"

"He's nineteen years older than you are, Ingrid. Admittedly, that's not as bad as it once was, when people only lived to be seventy-five or so. But you should find someone who's just starting out, like you—"

"So we could make all our life-altering mistakes together, like the blind leading the blind? *Now* who's sounding like my mother?" She shook her head. "Why don't I find somebody else? Because I love *him*, that's why, and nobody else! Human beings don't choose to love the people we love!"

The diary asked, "So who does, Ingrid? Who chooses who it is you come to love?"

Ingrid took an annoyed breath. "Okay, that's enough. Shut yourself off." She resisted a temptation she often felt, to throw it across the room.

"You're the boss," it acknowledged. "And it's your funeral, too, sweetie."

*

The elderly-looking individual who occasionally introduced himself as Robert Fulton had returned to his stateroom on the passenger deck below and aft, without waiting for Turnover to be completed, or even for the escalator to move him at its own speed. He'd hurried straight to the closet, had his empty, odd-smelling suitcase open, his personal palm-sized computer locked into place within it, the paired wire leads attached and timer counting down, before a terrible thought occurred to him.

Done this way, it will only make people Systemwide, even back on Earth who were not ordinarily sympathetic to colonials, share the sorrow of the grieving husband and son, of the bereaved father and brother. Photographs of the martyred females would bring fools to tears everywhere.

Far better to obliterate them all at the same time, and their little Martian rebel bitch with them. They would be transformed into abstracts, a few among hundreds, possibly thousands of casualties, difficult to visualize, impossible to mourn. The Mass Movement's supporters in the media would work the facts around and blame the victims, rather than Null Delta Em, making the lesson clear: this was a spoiled, ruthless, obscenely wealthy family, used to destroying whole worlds for profit. Instead of sainthood, the message would be, "This is the price for exploiting one's fellow man and going against Nature.

"Go no further.

"Better yet, retreat."

For a long, timeless while, maybe ten minutes, maybe two hours, he sat motionless and limp on the carpeted floor inside the closet, next to his empty suitcase, shaken to the core of his being by what he'd almost done, trembling like the old man he appeared to be. His chest ached with the beating of his heart, and his stomach was a mass of knots.

True, he was prepared to die, but it wasn't an easy thing to bring one-self to. To approach the brink, peer over it into the abyss, then back off again, postponing it for another day, was draining, to say the least.

What a colossal mistake he'd almost made—and almost certainly for reasons that were purely personal, purely selfish! So what if he was tired of his life? Did that mean he was relieved of the duties it demanded of him? So what if looking at Ardith Ngu or Jasmeen Khalidov made him salivate like Pavlov's dog? Did that mean that he could use this mission merely as an excuse to obliterate the temptations that beset him?

A thoughtless act like that could have set the Mass Movement back a century! Just look at what those idiotic amateurs on Ceres had accomplished—for the Movement's enemies—by trying to blow up that factory ship!

He'd already switched the timer off. When his hands were steady again, and he could breathe deeply without pain, he carefully detached the leads between the inside of the suitcase and his computer, removed the computer and put it back in his pocket, closed and relocked the odd-smelling suitcase, left the closet, and closed the door behind him.

He prepared to go upstairs again, It was time for a drink.

Maybe for several.

And then he would wait until they got to Ceres, where he would make his point in spades, and maybe live to retire comfortably and tell the tale afterward.

CHAPTER ELEVEN: NO GOOD DEED ...

The hardest lesson to learn in economics is that money is "only" a medium of communication. The information it conveys is formally known as "price", and what it tells us is how much to make or how much to do if we reasonably expect to get paid for it. The trouble with governments (public transportation is a good example of this phenomenon) is that, when the data all say "zero", they interpret it as an indication to make or do *more*. —*The Diaries of Rosalie Frazier Ngu*

FOUR MEN SAT AROUND THE dinner table, one of them tall and thin, one heavyset, two roughly medium-sized. They ate, they drank, and, thanks to a remarkably efficient air filtration system, two of them smoked.

All four were named Ngu.

The tall, thin one stubbed his cigarette out in the disposable dinner plate he'd just finished with, and said, "You know they're bound to make a big fuss over you, boy. How many lives did you save aboard the *Percival Lowell*? Twenty-four, twenty-five hundred? You're a genuine larger-than-life hero! There's no way you can get out of it, now."

The younger of the medium-sized men replied, "I don't see why not, Uncle Lindsay. You know I didn't do anything that anybody at this table, anybody in this camp, or anybody back home on Pallas wouldn't have done." He took a long draw on his chocolate milkshake. He'd been offered a share of the Jameson's Irish whiskey that the others were drinking, but he didn't like it.

The heavyset man, Wilson's Uncle Arleigh, nodded. "Absolutely right, Wilson, absolutely right. But you see back on Earth, where these corporate ninnyhammers come from, everybody's as scared as a rabbit, of every known phenomenon. Those rare few who aren't scared get jailed if they even think about defending themselves or anybody else. So you're a rare phenomenon to them and you should enjoy it while you can."

"'Uncle', he calls me." Lindsay observed, almost to himself, and as if he hadn't heard what Arleigh had said. He looked at the other two men, as if soliciting witnesses. He lit another cigarette. "After all these years, the boy finally calls me 'Uncle'. But I trust you'll note that it's only when he's trying to wheedle his way out of his chores."

"'Chores!'" Both Arleigh and Wilson had said it at the same time, but it was Arleigh who went on. "Chores! You call starring in an award ceremony to be broadcast live on 3DTV, clear across the Solar System to every Settled World 'chores'? You call being handed a substantial—if so far unspecified—monetary reward 'chores'? You call being brought to the attention of every good-looking female in the Known Galaxy 'chores'?"

Wilson muttered something.

"What was that, boy?" Lindsay demanded. "Speak up!"

"I said they won't broadcast it on Earth," he answered. "And don't call me 'boy'."

Arleigh laughed.

"Oh, puh-shaw," Lindsay said. "They will, too. And sorry about the 'boy' thing, kid." He inhaled cigarette smoke and exhaled. The smoke and the odor, driven on a stream of friendly ions, disappeared almost instantly.

Adam, who had been sitting quietly, smoking his pipe, said, "No, he's probably right, Lindsay. They'll give it 'selective coverage'. Even overlooking the Mass Movement and Null Delta Em, we're not all that popular on Earth, just now, not even in West America. The good citizens have been told that they're subsidizing us out here, and that we're draining away their wealth. The truth, of course, is that they're being drained by their own governments, and that the wealth has mostly flowed the other way, from us to Earth, for the past half century."

"*Not* overlooking the Mass Movement and Null Delta Em," Lindsay insisted, "it's even worse. Thanks to them, we Pallatians get blamed for every tremor, tidal wave, and volcano that burps or hiccups down there."

"Don't forget tsunamis," said Wilson.

"Not to mention cows not laying eggs and chickens giving sour milk." Arleigh laughed again. "And they're gonna like us even less when they find out what happens when you import so much gold that it becomes as precious as lead."

All four men laughed this time.

Adam said, "I guess that none of them were taught early in life, like we all were, about what happened when the Spanish conquerors of the—"

"Don't say it!" Wilson glared at his father, then grinned.

"Okay, I won't. Of the Americas." He leaned toward his brothers in mock confidence. "Understand that Wilson, here, was scandalized at an early age, when he found out they'd had the temerity to call it the 'New World'."

"Yeah," said Wilson. "But the universe got its revenge on them. The poor simpletons shipped home so much stolen Aztec and Inca gold that it destroyed Spain as a world power for the next six hundred years."

Lindsay nodded. "Yeah, and it's gonna happen again. No matter what they claim to the contrary, Earth governments still reckon the worth of their trash-paper currencies and phony electronic credit in terms of gold. There's a disaster coming, but they don't want to hear about it."

"Or the fact," Arleigh said, "that folks out here on the other Settled Worlds divide their investments among a number of valuable commodities—"

"Of which gold is only one," Lindsay finished.

"And not even the foremost among them," said Wilson.

"No," Adam agreed with his brothers and his son. "I'm a bit behind on the market, but I believe that, at the moment, palladium is the hot commodity."

"Maybe they'll give you a great, big pile of palladium," Lindsay ventured.

Arleigh jumped in before Wilson could say anything. "Oh, the young man doesn't care about money, Lindsay, nor—even if I contradict myself—about every good-looking female in the Known Galaxy. He only cares about one, and he's afraid that she won't get to see him on 3DTV."

Blushing furiously, Wilson kept his eyes on the table. "Keep it up, Arleigh."

"I will, Nephew—until you call *me* 'Uncle'."

*
**

"No, no, no!" Honey Graham, of the Interplanetary Interactive Information Service, consulted hand-written notes on a piece of typing paper folded twice. A potentially important news story was finally breaking for her out here—a story that had everything, badguys, goodguys, conspiracies, politics, sabotage, gun battles (well, one gun battle, anyway), dead bodies, prisoners, and a real, live, handsome young hero with a famous name—and she was the only reporter within a hundred million miles of it. "Don't put it over there, put it over here!"

There was a little muttering from her reluctant helpers. It was the third time she'd asked them to move the object in question from where she'd just had them leave it, to somewhere else, a matter of inches. But it had to be right, she told herself. Everything had to be just right.

This was where she'd been told the award ceremony would be held, on the exact spot where human beings had first touched down on Ceres, where they'd first set foot. The Pallatians had somehow lost track of the analogous location on Pallas years ago. All they had was the exact spot where William Wilde Curringer had crashed his little airplane and died. They were grimly determined not to let that kind of history be lost here.

She looked up through the transparent dome, high overhead, to the stars. They'd created this little ceremonial spot before they'd even started a single building. Even now, most of the small city she saw around her still consisted of the empty frameworks of uncompleted structures. But this miniature memorial only needed a few finishing touches.

Of course there was always a distinct possibility that the network wouldn't run her story, back on Earth. News from outer space wasn't particularly popular with East America's political leaders, especially when it made the people out here or the worlds they'd built look good. It made the taxpayers restive, reluctant to go on doing what they were told, reluctant to go on giving up whatever the State required them to give up, reluctant to go on sending their sons and daughters to serve and die in the military. Hope, she knew, was the most dangerous phenomenon in politics.

Nevertheless the Wilson Ngu versus Null Delta Em story would be very popular everyplace else in the System. And before it was spiked back home, it was bound to be seen by *somebody* in the upper IIIS hierarchy who could do her some good—assuming, of course, that she could ever get this handful of clumsy idiot workmen to do their part correctly.

"All right," she said at last. "I guess that'll have to do. Now, can we move the other one?" Three of the half dozen workmen she'd been assigned by the Chief Engineer's office—"stolen" from a rough and untidy-looking crew of welders who were sitting around, seemingly with nothing to do—struggled with another of the enormous concrete vase-shaped planters, walking it along the edge opposite from where she stood, of a large, stepped recess, also fabricated from concrete. The workmen insisted on calling it the "see-ment pond", with emphasis on the "see".

For some reason, they thought it was funny.

"Another foot closer, please." She peered through the reticles of her Sony QDH-616G SuperMedia spectacles, trying to delineate a sort of informal stage that would help her frame the shots she was planning. She had begun to wish she had a real cameraman with her; she could use a little more face-time, associated with this story, for the sake of her career. The big planters were empty now, but she'd been told there was a ship with a cargo of flowering vegetation due in sometime today. That same ship was bringing the hero's pretty mother and irresistible little sister from Pallas.

This story has *everything*, she thought again, unable to restrain her glee.

Two of the other men had begun filling the stepped recess with water, beginning carefully because there wasn't much gravity on Ceres to hold it down. When they were finished in a couple of hours, this would be a kidney-shaped decorative pool roughly sixty feet by thirty. There should have been a flag, of course, maybe on a little island in the middle of the pool. And there would have been, at home. But Pallatians were notoriously anarchistic, and their world didn't have a flag.

Nor would this one, if they had their way.

No wonder these poor men were stuck out here at the bitter end of nowhere. Just look at them! Every single one of them was carrying a handgun on his hip, just like in the wild, wild west, which meant it must be a dangerous, crime-ridden place in which to try to live and work. Their clothing and hands were filthy. And they didn't seem to care whether they were pleasing her or not—she wasn't accustomed to that.

Maybe living and working in outer space had done something to their –

"Miss Graham?" Who said "Miss" anymore? Honey turned to see the Chief Engineer's personal assistant, Ingrid Andersson. (How did such an obviously Japanese girl come to have a name like she did? Was that another story worth following up? Maybe a human interest sidebar?). She was coming from the direction of her boss's office. The boss himself, Dr.

Ngu, had been in conference when Honey had gone to see him earlier, but he'd thoughtfully left instructions to grant her "every courtesy".

"Yes, *Ms.* Andersson?" The reporter emphasized the politically correct title. The girl was beautiful, Honey admitted to herself, with a smooth, clear, golden complexion, great big almond eyes—almost black, a good, straight nose, a wonderful little chin, and ripe, full lips, the lower one very European, the upper one very Asian. Her hair was long, glossy black with reddish highlights, tied up just now in a ponytail.

She's far too sensual for network news, of course, Honey thought, where one's basic female attractions had to be balanced with a certain degree of studied, non-threatening sexlessness. We mustn't offend the female audience—who do most of the shopping—while attempting to interest the males.

Momentarily, Honey allowed herself to speculate about this lovely, exotic creature and her obviously lonely boss. There were rumors about him and his wife on Pallas—then she shook it off. She wasn't here for that kind of story, she reminded herself. Not yet, at least. She noticed, abruptly, that even this highly decorative specimen carried a small, deadly-looking pistol tucked tightly against the curve of her tiny waist.

Ingrid said, "You asked me to let you know when the *Beautiful Dreamer* came in."

Honey brightened. "Why, yes, dear, I did, thank you. Is it here?" She realized that was she almost through here at the see-ment pond, anyway. Thank God.

"*She's* in orbit," Ingrid replied, emphasizing the politically incorrect pronoun. "Since there's no atmospheric envelope on Ceres yet, and nobody to meet her at the poles, she'll land near here—just far enough away to avoid unpleasant accidents to the dome. We're sending our fleet of *gamera* out to bring the passengers and cargo here."

"Oh, yes," said Honey. "That peculiar vehicle I rode in with the Ngu brothers. And ... ?"

"Anyway, Dr. Ngu asked me to ask you if you wanted to go meet the ship."

Honey's heart leapt. This was just getting better and better! The mother and the sister! More tear-jerking exclusives! "Would I ev—I mean, that would be very satisfactory, Ms. Andersson. Thank you for asking."

The Asian girl smiled. "That's quite all right, Miss Graham. And please call me Ingrid."

*
**

Ardith is here!

To his tremendous surprise and annoyance, Adam discovered that he was nervous. His palms were damp. He tended to forget about this phenomenon between … visits.

Ardith is here!

He had showered, shaved, brushed his teeth, and used deodorant. Briefly, he'd considered using aftershave or cologne, but had rejected the idea. For at least the dozenth time, he ran a comb through his thinning, sandy-colored hair, feeling like a schoolboy on his first date.

Ardith is here!

Unconsciously, he paced the few square feet his private quarters permitted, waiting to be told that the *gamera* were back from the *Beautiful Dreamer*, wondering if he should have gone to meet the ship, himself. No, no, he had to be here, as Chief Engineer, to stay on top of things.

Once again he took a step and a half to the mirror and inspected his shirt, his pants, his shoes, his gunbelt, his socks. His jacket hung over a chair, waiting to be put on. He was a credit, he thought, sartorially speaking, to the engineering profession and to manhood in general. But inside, he was a mess.

Ardith is here!

How odd, remarked the part of him that stood outside and made remarks. He'd been married to this woman almost twenty years. In many ways, he knew her much better than he knew himself. He'd fathered two children with her—six, if you counted the four that tragically hadn't made it. After all that time, all of that joy and all of that pain, she was still everything to him, everything he'd ever wanted or needed. She was more than just the love of his life, she was love itself. And life.

The hell of it was she wasn't even here on Ceres to see him, but to stand with him beside their son in his moment of glory and supreme embarrassment.

* *
*

Wilson sat in a straightbacked chair at a little two-legged desk fastened to the wall between two sets of bunk beds, in the room he'd been assigned by his father's assistant, in one of the workmen's dormitories. The facilities were Spartan, but warm, well ventilated, cheerfully decorated, and very clean, thanks to microscopic armies of nanobots.

He'd been informed that these were only temporary accommodations, intended for transients, visitors, and Curringer Corporation employees who hadn't yet found a permanent billet here at project headquarters.

Since no permanent billets had even been built on Ceres yet, everybody lived in the dormitories, including the Chief Engineer and everyone working for him.

But Adam had assured his son that he wouldn't be bothered here. Nobody else would be assigned to this room and he was free to enjoy his privacy as long as it lasted. His young life was about to be turned upside-down, but for now, he would have all the privacy he needed or desired.

Just now, privacy was exactly what Wilson desired most. From the change pocket in his bush jeans, he pulled his personal computer, a JCN OmniBorg, a device roughly the size and shape of an old-fashioned pocket watch, complete with a lanyard that attached to one of his belt loops. To be sure, there were much smaller computers available, but his mother, who had given him the powerful device a year or so ago on his birthday, believed that anything smaller was too likely to get lost.

Unclipping the computer from his jeans and placing it flat on the desktop before him—where it would draw power by induction—he pressed a tiny recessed button in one edge, and a viewing area, two feet square, nearly thirty-four inches in diagonal, sprang into being above it. Wilson's idle screen display was a commercial hologram, set against a starry background, of a Ball 500 Asteroid Scout, one of the little fusion-ion rock hunting ships he dreamed of owning, and maybe of capturing the Diamond Rogue or some other legendary treasure with when he wasn't occupied dreaming about something—or somebody—else. As usual, the hologram caused him to sigh resignedly. Even a used Ball 300 was far beyond his means, and likeliest to stay that way.

He only hoped the somebody he dreamed of having wasn't equally unobtainable.

Between him and the tiny computer, the image of a control board flowed out across the tabletop. He usually preferred writing to dictating.

"SolarNet," he told the computer, which promptly opened his 'com program and opted, as it was instructed to do, for e-mail. To his utter astonishment, he had more than three thousand messages, the vast majority of which were from people he didn't know, congratulating him for having saved the *Percival Lowell* and being properly recognized for it. The system told him he had another twenty thousand messages waiting that couldn't be downloaded until he'd dealt with the first batch.

Twenty thousand?

On the other hand, at least half were from individuals who wanted to sell him something, or simply to beg him for money. And there were dozens of offers of marriage or some other intimate arrangement, not all of them from females. Some of them even included holograms of the senders, most—big mistake—without benefit of clothing.

A few were from sympathizers of the Mass Movement and Null Delta Em, accusing him of helping spoil whole worlds, and even of being a murderer.

One or two of those contained death threats.

He glanced at the .270 Herron StaggerCyl with which he'd earned all of this dubious attention, lying on the table beside the computer. He took considerable comfort in it, but found himself thinking that maybe he ought to get something a little bigger and a lot more powerful for indoors, where people didn't wear envirosuits that could be punctured.

It occurred to him that he didn't even have an indoor pistol belt and holster for the Herron yet. He'd been carrying it in a pocket of his enviro-suit. Maybe he should get a belt with two holsters, one for the Herron and one for whatever larger-caliber gun he found. "Two-gun Ngu," they'd call him, and he'd never be able to show his face in public again.

With a few keystrokes and verbal commands, Wilson persuaded the computer to set aside any e-mail he'd received in the past 24 hours from first-time correspondents. That seemed to take care of the bulk of it. If his father was willing, maybe he could ask Ingrid—Miss Anderson, he corrected himself—to help him answer it. In most cases, he didn't have any idea what to say to these people who'd written to him. Besides being extremely decorative (his heart may have belonged to another, Wilson told himself, but he wasn't blind—or dead), Ingrid was very efficient and struck him as having a lot of class.

But, remembering the other his heart belonged to, he searched the short remaining message queue for the only bit of correspondence he really wanted to see.

And there it was:

SUBJECT: YOU MAKE ME PROUD SENDER: AMORIE SAMSON

There were earlier messages from her. This one had been sent only an hour ago. He opened it and it unfolded to reveal a holorecording of her, and a paragraph of text, which was a written record of what she was saying now:

"Willie! I just heard of what's going on there on Ceres, and what you did! I'm having a hard time not bragging about you to everybody I know!"

He hated being called Willie, but could never seem to talk Amorie out of it, and was reluctantly willing to make an exception in her case. He gazed at her hologram with an expression he knew his uncles would have made fun of. It was just that looking at her made him feel so ... so ...

Amorie had absolutely the sweetest face he'd ever seen, framed in fine, astonishingly waist-length light brown hair dancing with honey-colored highlights. Her cheekbones were pronounced and high, her nose almost straight, with a slight upward curve that made her look even younger than the sixteen standard years he knew her to be. She had a subtle dimple in her chin, and the kind of complexion that had once been described as "peaches and cream", along with great big brown eyes, white, even teeth, and warm, moist, full lips he wished more than anything he could—

What was that she'd just said? He scrolled back to the place where he'd become distracted and lost track. " ... tried to persuade my folks to head for Ceres, but we've just come on an unexpected cluster of irons, and couldn't have made it in time. My folks said to be sure to tell you you're welcome to come stay and visit with us any time you can."

Now Amorie leaned into the 3D camera built into her computer, so he almost felt he could touch those lips. He could also see far enough into the top of her blouse that, even in a room by himself, he blushed. "And Willie," she almost whispered it. "If you want, you can stay in my quarters, with me."

Wilson groaned. He wouldn't be sleeping much tonight.

CHAPTER TWELVE: THE THINGS WE DO FOR LOVE

There are those who wish to kill us out of their hatred for us, or because we have something they want. There are others who end up killing us out of what they imagine is their regard for us. The assassin-fan who murders his beloved idol comes to mind, as well as many a mother or father.

Admittedly, there is a great deal of love in my life—my husband, my children, the surrogate parents who raised me —but in most circumstances, I would rather trust the profit motive than the vagaries of what others call love. —*The Diaries of Rosalie Frazier Ngu*

ARDITH INSPECTED THE LITTLE STATEROOM one last time.

There wasn't much to inspect. She'd had it to herself while Llyra and Jasmeen had shared the adjoining cabin, and she'd never really unpacked.

One double bed, just the way it was at home. After a long while, she'd finally gotten used to sleeping in the middle. Otherwise, these quarters were about as plain, she thought, as they could get without resembling a cell in a convent, or a medium security prison somewhere.

That was pretty much the way she liked her own bedroom.

The girls had hurried through their breakfast so they could watch the landing from the passenger lounge. Then they'd bustled excitedly down to the recreation deck to await arrival of several rocket-powered hover-craft—*gamera* they were called, for some obscure reason—that would carry them, along with the rest of *Beautiful Dreamer*'s passengers, to the Ceres Terraformation Project's construction headquarters.

That phrase "the girls" had suddenly struck Ardith a bit oddly, this morning, although she employed it quite often—at least in her own mind—to indicate her daughter Llyra and her daughter's tutor, Jasmeen.

It seemed the natural thing to do. There were times when it felt exactly as if she had two daughters. And she would have been as proud to have Jasmeen as her daughter as she was with her own daughter, Llyra. Jasmeen was a very fine young woman, honest, intelligent, and hard working. The standards that governed her personal behavior (and which served as an example to Ardith's daughter) were of the highest order.

At other times it felt as if Jasmeen were Llyra's mother. Ardith knew she had laid a great deal of the burden of raising Llyra on the older girl's shoulders. She often felt bad about it, but what could she do?

What else could she do?

Not for the first time, Ardith reflected that Jasmeen seemed to be remarkably wise and patient for all that she was merely nineteen years old—fewer than eighteen months older than her son, Wilson. Possibly that came from being born and growing up on what was surely the most harsh and least forgiving frontier that humanity had ever attempted to conquer.

Or maybe it simply came from having Mohammed and Beliita Khali-dov—two old and valued friends of Adam's father William, from his days on Mars—as her parents. Ardith recognized that she, herself, hadn't been anywhere near that mature at nineteen—that was just about the time that she'd met and married Adam—although there were moments when she missed all of the energetic passions of her youth, however painful they had felt at times. It seemed like the only thing she ever felt these days was worry—with occasional flashes of inexplicable anger.

It was that anger, she knew, that had pushed the only man she'd ever loved away from her—hundreds of millions of miles away from her, in fact—and constantly kept the son and daughter she adored with all her heart and all her soul at arm's length. She felt that she would give anything to know why she did it, why, after only a day or two of blissful reunion and renewal with her husband, she would let herself become infuriated by some casual remark that Adam thought was innocent.

Ardith had come from a very warm, close, loving family, herself, so it wasn't that. Just now, thinking of her younger, more innocent self, of half a lifetime ago, she'd felt an overwhelming wave of ... what?

Longing?

But for what?

What had she lost along the way, sometime after she was nineteen, that she still longed for now, even though she didn't know what it was?

On the other hand, maybe knowing wouldn't be enough. Sometimes the truth doesn't set us free, but only makes our captivity that much more unbearable. Exhaling sharply, she tried to shake off all this useless prying and poking, all this unproductive pseudo-psychological scab- lifting, and forced herself to concentrate on practical matters at hand.

For some reason, she'd left her osmium wristwatch, the one Adam had given her when Wilson was born, on her desk back at the lab in Curringer. It seemed like too much bother to consult her computer—although it was only half the size of Wilson's, and she wore it on a pin in her lapel, like a nurse's watch. Unlike several of her younger colleagues, who looked forward to a day, not long from now, when it would be possible, she couldn't bear the idea of getting a cerebral implant. True, it would place a computer several times more powerful than this one in direct contact with her brain. She'd never need to look at a watch or a calendar, or consult a map for directions or a dictionary, again.

She'd always be connected to the SolarNet wherever she went.

But Ardith's was one of the "first families" on Pallas, after all; from her earliest years, she'd been taught the ways of governments too well. As long as even one of the things continued to exist, anywhere, it was too dangerous to wear an implant, which could become an open door to whatever some two-bit Napoleon wanted to do to one's mind. The very thought made her shudder as if she'd found a garden slug in her salad.

So this morning she'd borrowed her daughter's Timestamp (a recent high-tech Martian import) which was the last thing left sitting on the bedside table. She would drop it in her bag after using it and give it back.

She'd never played with one of these devices before, although the technology was very interesting, and she had always been curious about it. It was perfectly cylindrical, an inch and a half in diameter, and about three inches long. The flat top bore an image of what the stamp was all about—trust her Llyra to have selected the simplest pattern she could, an old-fashioned analog sweep-second clock dial without a date or any other information.

Ardith lifted the object from the table and took the cap off the bottom. It looked to her like an ordinary rubber stamp, with purple ink—again, typical of her daughter. She placed the working end on the back of her hand and pushed, firmly, just the way she'd seen her daughter do a hundred times. When she lifted the object from her hand, the purple clock image had been transferred to her skin. Amused and amazed, she watched the second hand rotate around the face for a little while, then put the cap back on and tucked the device in her large handbag.

Fun with nanobots.

The microscopic machines would stay on her hand, racing across her skin, telling her the time—oh, dear, Curringer time, and the Pallas length of day—until they wore off molecule by molecule, or she washed them off on purpose. Technology was her business, but it surprised even her, sometimes.

Technology was her family's whole—suddenly, Ardith noticed an emotion lurking inside herself that she'd been avoiding. Her entire family—Llyra, Wilson, Adam and his brothers, and yes, her "other daughter" Jasmeen—were about to be together for the first time in a long, long while, and she couldn't feel anything. Well, not quite anything—the thought of seeing Adam again filled her with abject terror.

What was wrong with her?

Yet Adam was a good man—the very best of men, in fact—and the truth was that she had been his since the day they'd met on a museum tour, when she was only five years old and he was twelve. (He hadn't really known that she existed for another decade.) Just the thought of him right now filled her full of fire and made her want to—no, no, this was not the time for that! She realized now that she'd been dawdling in the stateroom, putting off the ride to the construction dome for some reason.

She wondered if Adam had driven out to meet her and the girls.

What would it mean if he hadn't?

Despite the ship's gradual acceleration to match the gravity of Ceres, it was tiring, standing in line in the corridor that bisected the recreation deck, waiting for the shuttles, or whatever they were, that would take them to the only inhabited spot on this asteroid so far.

With any luck, it was the only one there ever would be.

"Oh, excuse me, sir!" said the middle-aged woman ahead of him, overweight, unattractive and a Pallatian, to judge from her own poor adjustment to the doubled gravity. "I didn't mean to step on your foot."

He lifted his hat. "I didn't even feel it, my dear. Think nothing of it." The gravity helped him maintain his imposture of a tired old man—although he didn't need it. Most of the time he felt that way anyway.

For a while, he was "Robert Fulton" once again, although when the time came—if it was possible—he was prepared to change his name, his age, his height, his weight, his race, even his apparent sex, if need be, and to disappear forever, never to be heard of again by anyone, especially those accustomed to hiring him to do their dirty work.

This one assignment, and he would retire, All he wanted was to gaze at the sculpture and paintings he'd collected over the years, drink the wonderful Lunar greenhouse Merlot he favored, listen to Mozart, and tend the swordtails and black mollies he'd always wanted to raise.

"Something to drink, sir?" One of the attendants was passing along the corridor, offering the passengers small plastic baggies on a tray. "We have a little wine, a little whiskey, some apple juice, and some water."

He took a small container of apple juice and sipped at it as he waited with the rest of the passengers. They'd been told it would take the machines from the dome fifteen minutes to reach them, and another five to couple up to the ship. Luggage transfer would take another ten.

Luggage.

If he couldn't get cleanly away before the end, if his operation consumed him, too, it was something he could accept. He'd arranged for his possessions—safely stored in an ancient missile silo in Wyoming that he'd purchased and remodeled—to be passed on to someone who would appreciate them. That person didn't even know him, wasn't even aware that he existed, and would be extremely surprised when contacted by his lawyer. But the precious legacy, he knew, would be accepted and cherished, if not because it had been his, then for what it was, in itself.

The daughter he'd unwittingly helped to conceive in a moment of weakness twenty years ago, would have something of her father, after all.

What a night that had been. He'd been undercover, in white tie and tails like the fabled British spy, attending an enormous cocktail party in Denver. His assignment had been to ferret out the "secret leaders" of Sagebrush Rebellion II—that had stopped western states from sending representatives to Washington—and kill them, one by one.

The trouble was that, despite the fondly-cherished beliefs of the FBI, the CIA, the NSA, and others like them, those leaders didn't exist. Sagebrush Rebellion II was the spontaneous effort of hundreds of thousands of men and women in the American west who wanted nothing more to do with the government in the east—a government capable of committing any atrocity, including sending an assassin to kill their leaders.

If only they'd had any.

He'd met a pretty girl there, a sort of West American counterspy, who'd known all about him and had almost—but not quite—convinced him to change sides. Afterward, he had never regretted letting her live.

He opened his eyes wide and took a deep breath, shaking off his reverie and returning to the present. Now, all the usual precautions were called for, and perhaps a little more. These were circumstances—it felt to him like last day of school—in which one could grow careless. He'd hurried to leave the ship with the other passengers, then held back so he wouldn't be first. Always stay concealed in plain sight, inconspicuous in the middle, that was the key to survival in his trade. Always remain as average as possible, the average of the average.

"Excuse me, sir, would you mind?" He turned to the passengers behind him, a young couple who looked like they might be on their honeymoon—although why they would come to Ceres was beyond him. The young man held out a tiny camera and asked if he would take their picture.

"I'd be happy to," he replied, finding them in the viewfield floating above the camera and pressing the release. He took three pictures and handed the camera back. "Not vacationing on Ceres, are you?"

The young woman grinned and shook her head. "Not really. We just got married, and we both have jobs here. I'm with the canopy welding crew, and Hamish, here, is a microbiologist assigned to atmosphere generation."

He nodded amiably, but was very nearly sick to his stomach. This sweet young couple were the enemy. He felt his head swim with utter revulsion.

The deck's ceiling was so low it made him feel claustrophobic, creating room, no doubt, for the centrifuge over their heads. Through one transparent wall of the corridor they occupied, he could see the swimming pool—what a ridiculous waste of resources!—covered now with a big sheet of plastic, as was the hot tub standing beside it. He turned to look through the transparent wall on the other side of the corridor, where a dozen exercise machines stood motionless and silent, as they had been for most of the trip. Not many athletes in this lot, apparently.

Except, of course, for the ice skaters.

It had pained him deeply to let somebody else handle the single item of luggage he'd brought with him, his special shiny brown plastic suitcase that, despite his best efforts, still smelled a little funny. ("Luggage"—he thought about the word for the first time: that which one *lugs*.) Not only was it dangerous, it was undemocratic. People shouldn't have to be one another's servants—this he had believed all of his life—they should all be servants, in equality, to a benevolent State, instead.

Nor should they be permitted to go running away to the Asteroid Belt or other places like it, where their proper leaders couldn't reach them, living any way that happened to come into their heads, and fomenting rebellion on Mars, among other places, opposing duly constituted government authority. Martian colonists had murdered his father, who had been a part of a United Nations military detachment sent to bring them back into line. It had been his lifelong dream to make them pay for it. If he had to do it here on Ceres, then that's the way it would be.

He reached into his left inside jacket pocket to feel the worn, folded scrap of blue and white synthetic he always carried next to his heart. It was a lightweight, low-volume flag, shipped into low orbit by the tens of thousands and returned for sale or presentation on Earth.

His had been given to his mother the day they'd informed her that her husband was dead, and that his body couldn't be recovered—another score he needed to settle with these self-made aliens. All during the memorial service, his mother had soaked it with her tears. He valued it as much for that as any purely ceremonial connection it had to his father.

He would have it with him when whatever happened.

*
**

"Here they come! I see them!" Llyra exclaimed redundantly. Her face was pressed against the plastic porthole in the outer airlock door.

The little airlock was unlit, so she could see outside better. Captain Gunther Quigley stood behind her, almost filling the rest of the closet-sized chamber, the inner door of which was open onto the well lit corridor behind him. He was not a native Pallatian, this short, heavyset individual of about sixty years' age. He had a florid face, thinning red hair featuring more than a few silver strands, a big curly red beard and sideburns, and a cheek-appling, eye-crinkling smile, like the Santa Clauses in Coca-Cola ads. Llyra had liked him the first time she saw him.

"How far away are they now?" someone behind her shouted from the corridor.

"How many of them are there?" asked someone else.

By the powers vested in him by the Fritz Marshall Space Lines, the captain had informed the passengers lined up in the recreation deck, he was appointing the youngest person onboard the *Beautiful Dreamer* Official Lookout while they were waiting for the *gamera* to arrive. This was necessary because the only view of the outside, on this deck, was through a nine-inch disk of transparent plastic. This exit hadn't originally been intended to be used as an airlock, he said, except in emergencies.

"They're just over the horizon," Llyra said, "Can't tell how many yet."

"Can you hear them, dear?" asked the woman from New Jersey. The girl bit her tongue and refrained from making the remark she felt was deserved. It was nothing but hard vacuum outside, and completely soundless. Didn't the socialist schools teach people anything in East America?

Llyra answered politely, "No, ma'am, I can't hear them." Somebody laughed.

This ship had originally been intended to ply a Pallas-Luna route, she knew, but had been reassigned to Ceres before she'd actually been finished. Llyra had been told that there were larger, far more useful airlocks on each of the lower cargo decks. Passengers had always been meant to embark and disembark from decks higher up, through extendable tubes like the one they'd come aboard through at Port Peary. Changing circumstances had forced changes in design and use.

The whole youngest passenger production had impressed Llyra as more than a little childish. She hadn't complained, because (as the captain knew perfectly well), she happened to be the youngest, and she wanted to see the *gamera* when they got here. She didn't mind at all being the first person to do so. Of course her view of the surrounding "countryside" would actually have been a lot better from the forward passenger lounge, and better yet from the bridge, a few feet higher than the lounge. It was equipped with radar, lidar, and several different kinds of light amplification equipment.

And here they came, now, three, four, five, six sets of brilliant white headlights, exactly like cars on a highway—only this highway was twenty feet above the rugged airless surface of an asteroid, and she could see the blue-orange jets of the tiny rocket engines that kept the machines aloft—and, incidentally, were the source of the vehicle's name.

"There are six *gamera*, I think," she shouted back into the corridor. "Five are holding back while one is coming right up to the door!"

"That's our cue, young lady," the captain stage-whispered. "For safety's sake, we'll back off now and close the inner door, just in case." He touched her shoulder with just the right amount of polite pressure.

The chances were better than even, she thought, that he'd arranged for her to be at the porthole, not because she was the youngest, but because she came from the richest, most important family on Pallas, and was the daughter of the Ceres Terraformation Project's chief engineer. She hated making calculations like that, but had been taught by both parents to be careful and observant. It was often hard to tell who your real friends were.

Llyra nodded reluctantly and let herself be shown away from the port-hole. She'd wanted to see if the smaller craft would hover on its jets as it linked to the ship and was being boarded, or if there was some other arrangement. Now she'd just have to ask someone. Llyra was the kind of person who would much rather see than ask, any day of the week.

"Well, I suppose they could hover," Captain Quigley told her, once she'd asked. He nodded a little, then shook his head. It was a comical ges-ture and she decided she'd give him the benefit of the doubt. "But I think it would engender unnecessary risk, and use a lot of fuel. No my dear, they have all had landing jacks attached to the undersides of their hulls, those criss-cross scissory things, if you know what I'm talking about, that will bring them up to just the level they need to be on. But first, they'll have to turn around and back up to the door."

Llyra and Captain Quigley had moved a few feet away from the outer door at this point. The corridor, crammed with people, seemed hot and stuffy to the girl. A male attendant who had squeezed down the narrow passageway, past all of the increasingly impatient passengers, helped the captain swing the inner door shut and lock it securely. The instrument panel above the door indicated there was still air in the lock.

"And now," Captain Quigley said with some sort of satisfaction, "if we have a little fender-bender, we won't lose even a molecule of air."

"Fender-bender?" the girl asked. "Isn't a fender a fireplace thing?"

Quigley grinned. "It's a turn of phrase my maternal grandfather fa-vored. He migrated to Pallas from California, after the Big One. Maybe it's something to do with that. I'm not certain what it means, myself."

Maybe the woman from New Jersey knew. She had opened her mouth to speak, when suddenly, everyone began to hear—and worse yet, to feel—a long series of loud, dull thumping noises, coming from outside the airlock. Given what the captain had said about "fender benders", it was a little unnerving. Before anyone could tell Llyra that she couldn't do it, she pressed her face against the porthole in the inner airlock door, just in time to see the outer door pop and swing away. The instrument panel above the door still showed nothing but green lights.

Beyond it, she could just make out the inside of another airlock, presumably the *gamera's*. Standing just inside it, lifting a heavily booted foot over the coaming of both airlocks into the larger craft, was a very large man wearing an envirosuit. He inspected an electronic instrument of some kind held in his hand—checking the air, Llyra thought.

Then, clipping the object to his already crowded equipment belt, the man reached up with both gloved hands, gave his helmet a twist, lifted it off his shaggy head, and reached to open the inner airlock door.

"Hagrid!" Llyra threw herself into her Uncle Arleigh's arms.

CHAPTER THIRTEEN: SURPRISE, SURPRISE

The weaker, more fragile sex are often accused of being shallow because the first thing they're attracted to in a woman is her physical beauty (I've heard some cynics argue that it's more likely to be her willingness), while women are more interested in a man's character. But they're after the same thing. What a man is looking for, although he probably doesn't realize it, is good reproductive health, in whatever arbitrary terms his culture defines it. A woman looks for traits in a man that assure her he'll be a good provider and defender to herself and her children. —*The Diaries of Rosalie Frazier Ngu*

"NEXT MONDAY," WILSON EXCLAIMED A bit breathlessly, "the factory ships will start lowering sections of the atmospheric canopy onto the surface, wrapping them around Ceres. I'll be with the first welding crew—Arleigh and Lindsay showed me how, and I've been practicing for days."

His sister asked, "That's why you've got bandages on both thumbs?" The vehicle swayed a little as he stood beside them, hanging onto an overhead support. Llyra suspected that meant Ceres had its share of mascons, like Pallas, and wondered how high the gravity measured above them.

She and Jasmeen were sitting in the first row of seats in what had only recently been the cargo hold of the *gamera* they'd boarded, in a windowless prefabricated passenger section meant to be dropped into that part of the utility vehicle and connected with life support and power. A scattering of overhead 3DTV screens showed what the pilots were seeing. About half the seats were occupied by former passengers from the *Beautiful Dreamer*. Llyra spotted elderly Mr. Fulton sitting somewhere in the middle and waved to him. The old man smiled and waved back.

Wilson had greeted the girls and his mother as they'd stepped over the threshold, through both airlocks, and into the vehicle, which bounced alarmingly on its spindly uprights as it was boarded. For a while, the noise of passengers chattering while they found seats was intolerable, although it died down as the machine fired thrusters, retracted its legs, and began moving. Wilson made a mental note to talk to his father about acoustic spray for all of the insert's hard surfaces.

Adam would ask Ingrid—Miss Andersson—to fill out requisition and work orders, and then Wilson would probably be assigned to do the job.

If Ardith had been disappointed that her husband wasn't aboard the *gamera* to meet them, she hadn't shown it. Her daughter had been disappointed but hadn't said anything, either. She trusted her father and knew he must have a good reason for waiting to greet them until they'd gotten to the dome. Wilson was a pretty good substitute. If anything, her brother was even more handsome than when she'd last seen him.

He'd hugged his mother energetically (she was up forward at the moment, visiting with her husband's brothers, Llyra's uncles, for the first time in a long while, as they piloted the machine) and his sister, as well, as if he hadn't seen them for years. It hadn't quite amounted yet to six months. He'd awkwardly shaken hands with Llyra's coach, as well. Unlike Arleigh, Wilson wasn't wearing an envirosuit, but ordinary running shoes, faded bluejeans, and a brilliant scarlet t-shirt with the Ceres Terraformation Project's logo printed on it in yellow.

Slanting from his left hip to his right thigh, he also wore a wide leather pistol belt with his long-barreled .270 Herron StaggerCyl riding in an open-topped holster—tied down to his leg just above the knee—and a pair of twelve-shot loaders high on the other side.

"How long will all this lowering and welding take?" Jasmeen asked politely. Her coach's homeworld, her student knew, had been terraformed by an extremely different method that hadn't involved wrapping the planet in a gigantic plastic bag. On such a scale, even her father probably couldn't do it, Llyra thought.

Wilson looked at his feet and swallowed. "Uh, they say it'll take about two years. That's with full crews working in shifts around the clock."

Llyra observed that her brother was a bit flushed following this conversational effort, mostly on the sides of his neck beneath his jawline. She'd noticed earlier that he'd kept his contact with Jasmeen as brief as possible, withdrawing his fingers as if he'd just plunged them into boiling water. And he couldn't bring himself to meet her eyes.

She wondered if Jasmeen had noticed it, too. The younger of the girls knew exactly what it meant. It meant Wilson had just realized for the first time that Jasmeen was pretty. They'd known each other more than three standard years (the actual years of Mars and Pallas were much longer), but Wilson had only been fourteen and Jasmeen sixteen when they'd met, an unbridgeable gap at those ages. They'd spent most of the time that followed living on different worlds, growing up. In Wilson's mind, noticing that Jasmeen was pretty probably constituted disloyalty to (what was her name?) that insipid girl on the SolarNet he thought he was in love with and wanted to marry.

Llyra sighed inwardly. The truth was that it wasn't too early for Wilson to start entertaining feelings like that, whoever they happened to center on. Young men and women tended to marry much earlier than, say, Earthsiders, out here on what somebody had once called "the final frontier". (Llyra and her brother had been brought up to think of it as merely the beginning of an *endless* frontier.) The general custom—in a place and time where there were far more customs than laws, and they were much more stringently enforced, by Mother Nature (or "Auntie Evolution", as Llyra like to think of it) herself—was that they married for life, and they had the biggest families they could manage.

Even with today's technology, taming a wilderness was a labor- intensive undertaking.

Somehow, she couldn't see that creature ... that Amorie Samson— that was her name—as anybody's frontier wife and mother, for all that she had supposedly been born to a hardy asteroid-hunting family somewhere down Sunward. The holograms Emerson had sent home to Pallas made the girl look pampered and ... well, *useless*, in some way Llyra couldn't quite define, as if she were the asteroid-hunter family's pet Persian kitten, rather than a daughter expected to pull her own full weight.

Yes, the girl had a pretty face, a very pretty face. But it was a smooth, featureless kind of pretty that wouldn't last long, despite the anti-aging advances that medical science had made in the decades since her great-grandfather Emerson had underwritten the invention of full-body tissue regeneration. It certainly wasn't like her mother's ageless beauty. Young men still sent frankly speculative glances in Ardith's direction wherever she went. Llyra had seen it, herself, and it gave her mixed feelings. Her grandmother Julie still looked like a young girl in her twenties.

Jasmeen, she thought, possessed that same kind of beauty. It began with stronger features than Amorie's miniature ones, but most of it seemed to come from what was inside her and inexorably wrote itself on the outside, more clearly every year. Llyra loved her older brother and wished he'd wake up and take a look at what he was getting into.

Jasmeen had continued asking Wilson questions about the process of terraformation. The boy hadn't exactly stumbled through the answers, but Llyra could tell that he was extremely uncomfortable. She was about to join the conversation to take some of the pressure off him, when a man she recognized from the *BeeDee* approached the three of them.

He stopped short, as if he didn't know whom to address, then saw the revolver Wilson carried, which he eyed with visible wariness. This was the weapon, he knew, with which the boy had killed five "murderous saboteurs"—his editors back home preferred the phrase "selfless environmental activists"—and spoiled the hopes on Ceres of Null Delta Em, perhaps forever. "Mr. Ngu," he began. "I'm Tim Lipton of *New Angeles Online.* Do you think it would be all right to ask you and your sister a few questions, now?"

New Angeles was one of the makeshift cities that had risen slowly out of the smoking rubble that California's "Big One" had made of what was sometimes called "Lost Angeles". Despite being about as far west in West America as a geographic location could be, the new city's people and institutions generally reflected the opinions and values of East America.

Wilson opened his mouth, but Jasmeen asked, "What do you mean, 'now'?"

"Er, uh ... " the newsman cleared his throat nervously. "Well—Miss Khalidov, isn't it, Jasmeen Khalidov? I only meant that we were all warned not to bother your party aboard the ship, but now that we're on Ceres, a number of us ... well, I'm the one who got the short straw."

Releasing his hold on the overhead stanchion, Wilson leaned toward the correspondent. "You were warned? Who exactly was it that warned you?"

"Well, it's just ... just ... that the captain—Captain Quigley—told us that if we 'bothered' any member of the Ngu family while we were aboard his vessel, that he'd ... he'd 'space' the offending individual. That man has absolutely no conception of freedom of the press."

The two young women were as surprised as Wilson, but tried to sit still, stoically restraining an urge to burst out laughing. Llyra glanced at Jasmeen. No Martian had any reason to love the Earthside media, who, during the long, deadly battle they'd fought for Martian independence— a necessity for survival on that planet—had acted like nothing more than a pack of jackals, howling and yapping for blood.

Wilson allowed himself a grin. "Sounds like he has a pretty good idea about the individual right to privacy, though. Now look here, Mister … "

The reporter gulped, but stood his ground. "Lipton, *New Angeles Online.*"

"Mister Lipton. My dad—Adam Ngu, Chief Engineer and Director of the Ceres Terraformation Project —has a press conference scheduled for a little while after we get back to the construction dome. I won't offer to space you or anything, but I'd prefer that you news people all left my mother and sister and Miss Khalidov alone. That okay with you?"

The reporter eyed Wilson's revolver again. "Very well, Mr. Ngu. Thanks."

The man turned and went back to the other media people seated at the rear of the passenger insert. But to Llyra, he didn't sound very grateful.

*
**

Adam was waiting in the airlock tunnel when the *gamera* fitted out for passenger transport arrived. Unfortunately, the little elevator that connected the vehicle with the tunnel could only hold a few people at a time, and the machine had nearly emptied itself before its airtight door cycled for the dozenth time and he finally saw his family.

"Daddy!" Llyra shouted when she saw him and came running at him. He'd thought he was prepared for how much she had grown in six months, but he wasn't, nor for the unchildlike firmness of her arm muscles. Most people didn't expect skating to produce strong arms, but one's arms were what controlled one's bodily attitude and added power to one's jumps.

"Baby! It's so good to see you! Why did you three get off last?" She had her skate bag with her. Good. He had a little surprise for her, and it was something that he'd secretly asked Ardith to make sure of.

Llyra backed up a little and reached up to straighten a strand of her father's thinning hair. "Mother thought it would give us Ngus some privacy."

"What a good idea!" And so it had. The rest of the passengers had hustled themselves off to the dome, and the Ngus—and Jasmeen—had the tunnel to themselves. Abruptly he realized what was about to happen. His heart began to race and the muscles in his legs turned to water.

He shook it off the best he could.

Jasmeen had changed, too, Adam observed. Not in size or anything else that could be measured, but where there had been a pretty and precocious little girl, there now stood an exotically beautiful young woman. As the father of a daughter himself, he was sure it made her parents proud—

and nervous. Jasmeen approached him a bit diffidently and thrust out a hand.

How very Martian, he thought.

"Is good to see you again, Dr. Ngu."

He seized the hand, bundling her into his arms. "Since when have I been 'Doctor" to you, Jasmeen Khalidov? I've known you all your life, and your folks a long time before that. They changed my diapers and I changed yours—or I might have, anyway. Now you're changing Llyra's—don't tell her I said that. You and your folks are family, young woman."

Still held within the circle of his arms, Jasmeen tried to look down at her shoes and murmured, "Please, Adam, you make my eyes to leak."

Adam laughed, gave her a final squeeze, and let her go. "Later on, I want to hear all about your folks, Jasmeen, how they are, what they're doing, and Llyra's skating. But I have to make other eyes leak first, if I can."

She laughed. "Including your own, I see. I think I'll go to dome, now." There was a little space between her upper two front teeth that had made her look cute as a little girl. Now it made her look sexy, and he experienced a moment of pity for the hordes of boys doomed to fall for her.

"I'll go with her!" Llyra exclaimed. "Wilson promised to show us around and find us the best room in the dormitory." She looked back toward the lift at her brother and gave him some not very subtle signals that he should come, too, so their parents could have a rare private moment to themselves. To Wilson's credit, he took the hint. The three of them gathered up hand baggage and were off down the tunnel.

Suddenly they were alone, she where the lift had left, he ten feet away.

"I, er ... " Adam felt weak and flushed all over, and other things were –

"Me, too!" Ardith exclaimed, grinning at him through her tears. She rushed to him and threw herself into his arms, squeezing him as hard as she could around the waist, trying to bury her face in his shoulder. Her eyes shut tightly. As Adam always did, he discovered he'd forgotten how beautiful Ardith was, how warm and soft against his body, and the way that she smelled. He crushed her to him and could actually feel her heartbeat in his own chest, through what they were wearing.

After a few moments, he lifted her chin and kissed her deeply and passionately. As she always had, she returned his kiss with equal passion. The same thrill went through him that had been there the first time he kissed her, when she was sixteen, on her parents' back verandah overlooking Lake Selous. That first time, they hadn't gotten caught.

When they broke for oxygen, Adam started to speak.

"Shhh!" Ardith's cheeks were wet and her eyes were still full of tears. Adam's own face was wet, as well, but he couldn't tell if it was from her tears or his own. All he really knew at the moment was that he adored this magical creature in his arms with all his heart and all his soul, and had been helpless for what seemed all of his life to do anything else. "Maybe," she whispered, "if we don't say anything ... "

Adam nodded, understanding perfectly, and kissed her again. He knew how this would end, eventually, tomorrow, or the day after that, or the day after that, exactly as it had always ended, and always would.

But just now, he didn't care.

*
**

" ... in an effort that makes the construction of the Pyramids in ancient Egypt or China's Great Wall appear almost trivial, many more engineering operations like these will follow before people can come to live on Ceres and create a new future for themselves and their children ... "

The area behind the decorative pool—now full and sparkling, with a little fountain at each end—where Honey Graham had asked that two man-sized planter-urns be rearranged to form a sort of stage, also had a nine foot high back wall, made of the same smoothly finished concrete as the pool and the planters, fabricated from local materials and colored an extremely pale blue, to work well with 3DTV cameras.

Standing at that wall for the moment, Ingrid Andersson, the Chief Engineer's assistant, was delivering a little lecture on the Ceres Terraformation Project, to provide background for the media people who had come here to report on Wilson's Ngu's award ceremony, planned for tomorrow.

Earlier this morning, Ingrid had recruited some office help to bring out an old 3DTV flexscreen she'd found in a storage room, unroll it, and let it adhere itself to the wall. It was somewhat obsolete—only six feet high by eight wide, with a ten-foot diagonal, and it was a clumsy quarter of an inch thick, but it was wholly adequate for her purposes.

She pointed to a floating diagram of the asteroid. "As you can see, this half represents Ceres before the terraformation process. The surface is bleak, airless, and cold. It looks like nighttime perpetually, although the sun can be seen when you're at the right place."

She could see that several of the media people wanted to ask her questions already. She knew what most of those questions would be like. She prepared answers for at least one e-mail interview a day for her boss. He would look her answers over, make corrections if needed or okay what he'd originally taught her to say, and she'd send it away.

"This half shows what it'll be like a year or two after the new atmospheric canopy is put into place, about four years from now. The sun shines, supplemented by a pair of orbiting aluminized plastic mirrors, three miles wide. Under the canopy, the daytime sky is a brilliant blue. Sometimes there are clouds and it rains. Lakes and rivers everywhere moderate the temperature and humidity. It's warm. Green things grow—although trees are still only saplings at this point."

Off to one side, hidden from the reporters behind a big stack of construction materials, Ingrid could see Adam and his wife Ardith, standing with their son Wilson, who looked extremely nervous. And who could blame him? He was a very nice young man, very polite and as smart as his father. Very handsome, too. She was grateful that he'd never developed a crush on her. His uncles, Arleigh and Lindsay, were there, too. One of the girls with them, the younger one, must be their daughter Llyra. The older one, maybe three or four years younger than Ingrid, had to be the girl's Chechen skating coach, Jasmeen Khalidov.

Together, they made a fine-looking family group, she admitted to herself.

Damn it.

"Miss … ?"

"Andersson," she replied, blinking. The questioner was a middle- aged man, obviously Pallatian from his dress and the rake of the pistol on his belt. "Ingrid Andersson, with two esses. You have a question?"

"Yes, I do, Miss Andersson. Marvin Challopy, representing KCUF, the oldest news multimedium on Pallas, and still the most connected with."

"Yes, Mr. Challopy, now that you've finished the commercial, your question?" Everyone laughed, including the middle-aged Pallatian correspondent.

Then: "My question. Once the atmospheric canopy is in place around Ceres, will this asteroid experience the same colorful and beautiful sunrises and sunsets that make Pallas the best place to visit in the System?"

There was twice as much laughter this time. Ingrid laughed, too, and smiled. She was recorded doing it by a dozen 3DTV cameras that, for the proverbial fifteen minutes, would make her the Solar System's most desirable pinup girl.

"Mr. Challopy, we just don't know. Believe it or not, nobody knows why the canopy on Pallas does what it does, although generations of scientists have tried to find out and failed. I guess that we'll just have to build the thing and find out."

There was general laughter again, and applause. Most of these people weren't used to hearing a straight truth—like "I don't know"—from members of whatever government ruled them or from corporate spokesmen.

"And now," Ingrid told them, "I'd like to introduce my boss, who will have some remarks of his own to make. Possibly he can give you a better answer to that question than I just did, although I doubt it very much."

More laughter.

"Ladies and gentlemen of the press, Chief Engineer and Director of the Curringer Corporation's Ceres Terraformation Project, Dr. Adam Ngu."

Ardith squeezed his hand in encouragement, and Adam stepped from the shadows, onto the little makeshift stage. "I'm afraid I don't have a better answer for you about the canopy than Ingrid did. I can't wait to find out, myself."

Everybody laughed.

"However this is not the day," Adam told them, "this is not the time, to consider technicalities like that, but to turn our attention to a young man who will stand in this place tomorrow morning, after his family's had a chance to visit with him, to receive the highest tribute his employer, the Curringer Corporation, can offer him, as a token of appreciation for what he did for them and all of us last week."

He could feel tears welling up again—that made twice in one day!

"I know you're anxious to meet him." Adam grinned, "He's anxious to get it over with. I want to add that it makes me inexpressibly proud to be the father of such a young man. Please welcome Wilson Ngu."

Wilson stepped out, grateful that his father remained at his side. Now it began to sound like a genuine press conference, as each of the correspondents shouted for Wilson's attention all at the same time. To Wilson, it was like facing an onrushing tidal wave (an experience he'd never had, but could imagine—it probably felt like holding a press conference).

"Mr. Ngu! Mr. Ngu!" He wondered how you got them to shut up, and which one to call on first. He wished he was back outside, planting transponders.

Adam raised a hand. "Miss Graham."

"Honey Graham," she introduced herself. "Wilson, tell me, how does it feel, at the tender age of seventeen, to have shot five human beings to death?" She nodded toward the weapon he still wore on his thigh.

Before Wilson could speak, his father, who had seen this sort of thing coming days ago, spoke instead. "If Wilson will please excuse me, I'll ask you one, first, Miss Graham. You're from Earth, aren't you?"

"Why, you know I am, Dr. Ngu," she replied warily. "Why do you ask?"

"Because anyone from any of the Settled Worlds—even in the news media—would have asked, 'How does it feel to have saved the lives of 2400 people aboard the factory ship *Percival Lowell*?' That's why."

CHAPTER FOURTEEN: MADNESS AT MIDNIGHT

There's a big difference between keeping the peace, which is something folks do pretty well themselves, and enforcing the law, which is another thing altogether. Throughout most of West America—which seems to have learned the lesson— municipal police forces have been outlawed. The sheriff's job, when he arrives, inevitably after the fact, is to make sure it was the badguy who got shot. That was the Pallatian custom to begin with, and Pallas has prospered accordingly. —*The Diaries of Rosalie Frazier Ngu*

THE INDIVIDUAL WHO SOMETIMES CALLED himself Robert Fulton peered about in a darkness that resulted as much from the fact that most of the area lights in the big construction dome had been turned off, as from the fact that the sun shone presently on the uninhabited side of Ceres.

A day would come, he was aware, when the towns here would never be this empty, when there were a hundred times as many workers on Ceres as there were now. That was their expectation, at least. His hope was to thwart their expectation, and they had been helpful enough—because they had dormitory rooms to spare at the moment—to give him one to himself on the ground floor, the closest room they had to the front entrance.

He believed that nobody had seen him leave the building with his big, brown, shiny suitcase dangling from one hand. He believed that nobody had seen him cross what would someday be a street and enter the little plaza with its decorative pool and stage area, the latter set off by a pair of concrete planter urns the height of a big man and about the same number of feet in diameter. The miniature fountains were still, now, the surface of the water was as smooth as glass.

For some reason, there were now four big black corrugated hoses of some kind snaking into the water at the closest thing the pool had to corners, from somewhere out of the light. They had nothing to do with him.

It was good to be out of his disguise, if only for a little while. No one would see him here, so it wouldn't matter. And it was much more comfortable.

During the press conference in which he'd pretended to be the Pallas stringer for *Boston Magazine*, he'd finally had his inspiration. He knew, now, how he would go about fulfilling his commission to Null Delta Em. On closer inspection, after the conference had broken up (in confusion, because that idiot network newswoman didn't know how to control an interview), he'd observed that the flowering plants growing out of the tops of the urns were actually bedded in metal pans no more than eight inches deep, designed to be set into the tops of the urns and stay there. The rest of the urns' interiors were empty, filled only with air.

A man could hide in there.

Or hide a suitcase.

Reaching the top of the urn wasn't as difficult as he'd originally anticipated. This morning's inspection had taught him that people here were careless, leaving items like tools and ladders around wherever they'd last used them or planned to use them again. That was probably a function of everybody knowing everybody else. Likewise, they didn't think twice about a stranger examining how something worked or had been built. The lighter gravity (lighter than Earth's, anyway) helped, too, although working for almost a year on Pallas had weakened him horribly.

He'd want a wheelchair or crutches for a while, and a lot of serious physical therapy, once he got back to Earth.

Although it was a long reach from the stepladder to the top of the almost spherical urn, thanks also to the gravity, it was easy to pull the planter out of the top. He climbed back down and set it to one side. Opening the suitcase—his small computer was already in place and had started counting down the hours—he removed a small tool kit. Closing the case, he took a spool of synthetic cord from the tool kit and tied each end of a length of it to a couple of spots on the suitcase.

Back up the ladder again, he had a bad moment when he thought the suitcase was too large to fit into the urn. Then, to his relief, it let itself be pushed through the short neck of the urn, into the space below. He lowered it with the cord, careful that the bottom of the suitcase was oriented away from the little stage, toward where he understood the 3DTV reporters would be all standing, especially Honey Graham.

There was a titanium plate lining the bottom of the suitcase that would shape the explosion when it occurred tomorrow. It wouldn't save the reporters, only delay the explosion's wavefront reaching and killing them until their cameras had recorded the violent deaths of young Wilson Ngu and his family. Everyone on Earth—including most of East America, watching the ceremony illegally—would see their bodies shredded to bloody pulp, and then watch it again and again, probably in slow motion, as the media beat the story to death.

The giant concrete pot would tamp the explosion—he planned to seal the planter pan in place with a tube of adhesive from his tool kit—and provide several hundred pounds of shrapnel to be thrown around at several thousand feet per second, killing everyone and obliterating everything within its reach. It was more than possible that the explosion would breach the dome itself. Meanwhile, if all went well, he would be well away from the cataclysm when it happened—by what he'd afterward call "sheer good luck"—strolling casually down an airlock tunnel, exploring the facilities that served the *gamera*.

Satisfied that the suitcase was where he wanted it, he climbed back down the ladder and carefully applied adhesive from the tube around the rim of the metal planter pan. This wouldn't keep the explosion from hurling it upward at several times the speed of sound, possibly out through the top of the dome. It would delay it happening for just a microsecond or two, while the concrete shrapnel did its job.

Carefully holding the planter pan by an unglued portion of its bottom edge, he awkwardly climbed back up the stepladder and dropped it into place, gratified to see a fine "bead" of adhesive press out from underneath, evenly all around the rim. The glue would set in seconds.

He was about to climb back down the ladder, when he heard a voice.

"Hello, Mr. Fulton," said Llyra. She was dressed in her pajamas with a lightweight bathrobe worn over them. "So you can't sleep, either?"

*
**

"Oh, pardon me," Llyra said, squinting in the twilight. Although there was a superficial resemblance, this man was twenty years younger than the old man on the ship. "You're not Mr. Fulton—or are you? Were you wearing an old man disguise, back aboard the *Beautiful Dreamer?*"

"How do you know I'm not wearing a young man disguise now, my dear?" he asked her, winking broadly. She'd caught him at the top of the ladder. He used her momentary confusion now to climb carefully to the ground. Once clear of the stepladder, he began to approach her slowly, thinking the same kinds of thoughts that a cobra might think as it stalked a bird it held helplessly fascinated with its slitted gaze.

He spoke slowly, too, very softly, so she had to strain to listen. "I enjoy wearing disguises, don't you ... Llyra, isn't it? Miss Llyra Ngu, daughter of Adam and Ardith Ngu, granddaughter of William Wilde and Julie Segovia Ngu, and great granddaughter of Emerson Ngu? A long, distinguished line, isn't it, my dear? Who says these things aren't genetic?"

She said nothing, but watched with ever-widening eyes as he took another slow-motion step toward her. As he passed by the spot where he'd left his little tool kit lying on the ground, he stooped and caught the reel of cord in his left hand. He'd discovered many uses for the stuff, and this wouldn't be the first time it had helped him eliminate a potential problem like this one. He didn't know how much the little girl had seen, but at this point in the operation, he couldn't afford to take a chance. Environmental justice must have its day.

She would have died tomorrow, in any case.

Too bad she wasn't her mother. Or her coach. Too bad there wasn't time ...

Now he held the reel in his left hand and let it spin in his grasp as he pulled out a three-foot length of the cord with his other hand. Continuing to maneuver slowly toward the girl, he surprised her by extending the free end of the cord to her. "Maybe you could help me, though ... "

Not taken in, she took a step backward and slid a hand into her dressing gown pocket. "Whoever you really are, I think you'd better stop."

"Stop what, Llyra? Just what is it that you think I'm doing?" He took another step forward and wound some of the cord around his right hand.

"I said stop, Mr. Fulton, and I meant it!" Llyra took another step backwards and pulled a small black and silver automatic pistol from her pocket.

He lunged at her hoping to catch her off guard—

For an eternal instant, Llyra was strangely conscious of minutiae. She pulled the trigger and felt it creep backward. She felt the sear break. She felt the weapon's internal striker fall and strike the primer of the cartridge in the chamber. As the gun went off, she felt its polymer frame flex in her hand, absorbing recoil. She also felt the recoil insert at the back of the grip compress its springs. She saw four bright jets of blue-pink flame blossom from the recoil ports in the muzzle brake.

Oddly, she never heard the blast or felt the recoil itself.

He'd rushed her, and she never had time to properly acquire the sights. Instead, with perfect clarity, in frozen time, she saw the brilliant flash of her gunshot reflected on the flat, almost polished rear surface of her cu-pronickel bullet as it entered his leg, and watched his left knee come apart in a gory explosion as the bullet destroyed it.

As he collapsed, time—or at least Llyra's perception of it—somehow returned to normal. There seemed to be vast gouts and loops of thick scarlet blood everywhere. The very air smelled of it, as much as it smelled of expended firearms propellant. Her would-be assailant lay twisted on the concrete-covered ground at her feet, writhing and screaming.

"Well," she heard herself ask, "what did you expect when you tried to attack a defenseless little girl? You're in the Settled Worlds, now!"

***

The noise of Llyra's shot and the man's screaming began to attract attention. The first people she saw, coming from the administrative building where he kept an apartment, were her father and her mother, both wearing robes over nightclothes and looking a bit sleepy and confused.

Each had a weapon in hand. Adam carried the ten millimeter magnum his grandfather—her great grandfather—had given him. Ardith's was a compact, powerful laser pistol, imported from Mars. They were a comforting sight. She looked down at her own gun and put it in her pocket.

"What's going on here?" Adam demanded when he was close enough. He didn't ask why his daughter happened to be up at this hour. He knew her habits well and often had the same difficulty sleeping that she did.

"It's bad enough to be shot by a snip of girl!" the man who called himself Robert Fulton complained. He lay on his side, now, with both hands wrapped around his ruined knee, blood seeping from between his fingers. "Why do I have to listen to the murderous little brat gloat on it?"

Neither Llyra nor Ardith saw the warning look that Adam gave the man, but he shut up abruptly. Ardith had given him an identical look of her own.

Llyra appealed to her father. "I didn't mean to gloat, Daddy, honest. I don't even know why I said that to him." She repeated what she'd said, as best as she could recall it. Ardith came to her side an put a warm arm around her shoulders. Just then, she and Llyra saw a very concerned-looking Jasmeen emerge from the dormitory and approach them. She, too, was armed, but shoved her pistol in a hip pocket of her jeans when she decided that the situation had already been taken care of.

112

As she came closer, she asked Llyra, "Are you all right, my little?" Llyra nodded as bravely as she could and snuggled closer to Ardith.

Jasmeen turned and knelt on the other side of Fulton, offering to help Adam. Suddenly Ingrid was there, too. Except for Jasmeen, who'd pulled her clothes on, everybody was wearing a bathrobe or something like it. Ingrid's was a silky floral print and looked just like a kimono.

"That's all right, Sweetheart," Adam told his daughter. He'd taken off his robe, folded it, and put part of it under Fulton's knee, using the other half of it to apply pressure to the bleeding wound, a job he gladly turned over to Jasmeen and Ingrid. He stood up. "People tend to do and say funny things in emergencies. You can never predict what it'll be. In case you're concerned, this guy's going to be all right—more or less. He'll wear an artificial kneecap for the rest of his life."

Fulton groaned and began to whimper, his hands and face covered with a mixture of blood and tears. By now it became apparent to all those standing close by that the man had also wet himself—and worse.

"I'm not concerned, Daddy" Llyra said it over the noise the man was making. "I meant to kill him, the way you and Mother taught me. I just didn't have time. Now he's going to be a bother and an expense to everybody."

A medical team had arrived in a tiny open truck and began tending the man's injury, preparatory to putting him on a stretcher. Jasmeen and Ingrid had gotten to their feet. Adam instructed his people to treat Fulton like the apprehended criminal he was, as much as an injured patient. He had also made a couple of calls on his personal phone.

A small crowd had begun to gather, composed of Ceres Project personnel and people who'd come here with Llyra, Jasmeen, and Ardith from Pallas. Some of them were slowly beginning to act like media reporters.

He turned to his daughter where she stood beside her mother and put a hand on each of their shoulders. "Don't worry about that for even a minute, Sweetie. I think this may be one of those occasions where somebody like him will prove to be more useful to us alive than dead."

Llyra looked around them, and then whispered. "If it turns out that I've done a good thing, I don't want anything made of it, Daddy. Tomorrow is Wilson's day, and I don't want to interfere with it in any way. If I'm in trouble, I'll take my medicine—just not tomorrow, okay?"

Adam looked down at his daughter, speechlessly proud of her behavior. He looked at Ardith, too, and shared one of those better moments parents sometimes have between them. Then he took a breath. "Okay, Baby, you've got it. You're not in any trouble, and you're not going to be. We'll

113

find out everything about why this thing happened, eventually, but in the meantime, I'll say I shot him if you want me to."

"Yes," she said with relief, "I want you to. But Daddy, one more thing—"

He put a finger to his lips. "Not now, Kiddo, here comes Honey Graham."

"But Daddy," she pointed in the direction of the big planter, where the stepladder still stood, mutely accusing Fulton, although of what, she wasn't quite sure. His toolkit still lay nearby. "What about—"

"Let's get this over with and then we'll all have something hot and soothing to drink. As you say, we have a big day tomorrow," he winked at Ardith. "And I need whatever sleep your mother will let me get."

Llyra was scandalized. "Oh, Daddy!"

***

Morning came all too soon for Llyra.

She looked around the little plaza with its decorative pool and fountains—and the pair of ominous-looking concrete planters—trying to decide what was different about it today. She looked over at Jasmeen who had somehow guessed the truth about the shooting and had sat beside Llyra's bed, holding her hand, until the younger girl had fallen asleep.

She would have told Jasmeen anyway, later today. You can't keep something like that from someone you trust as much as you must trust your coach. As much as she trusted Jasmeen. Now the older girl wouldn't leave her student's side—her folks were busy helping poor Wilson prepare for the ordeal to come, a task that she was more than content to leave to them—and Llyra took a great deal of comfort from it. For some reason, though, Jasmeen had brought their skate bags with her.

Everything seemed to be in exactly the same position as it had been the night before. That couldn't be what was troubling her—although "troubling" was perhaps too strong a word. Somebody had taken the stepladder away, picked up Fulton's kit of tools, and cleaned up the blood.

In one respect, she didn't know what was happening and didn't know what to do. She'd tried and tried last night to tell her father about the planter she'd caught Fulton fooling around with, but he wouldn't listen. It was exactly like one of those nightmares she had sometimes, where nobody paid attention and nothing worked. Only this was really happening.

He'd told her not to worry, Baby, but to drink her cocoa. Now that she was thirteen, she hated being called Baby, but she didn't press the point. She'd once promised him, when she was about four, that she'd always be his baby. She'd tried later and he'd patted her on the head—actually patted her on the head!—and told her to go to bed and sleep tight.

She supposed she had to trust him. Feeling as she did about her father, it wasn't terribly difficult, but she couldn't help being anxious anyway. It had made her feel very good to see him and her mother together that way last night. She'd seen it before, of course, and it had never lasted. But they loved each other and she wanted there to be hope for them. It was something else she couldn't help feeling.

Now, as a crowd began to gather, she noticed four big black hoses, pleated like an accordion, entering the decorative pool at different points around its edge, and wondered if they'd been here last night. She'd been sort busy then, she told herself, and couldn't remember now.

The two little fountains were running again. That was nice. She'd always enjoyed fountains, although these made the air feel a little chilly. She wondered what time it was and started to look, when she suddenly saw what was different: there was a big institutional clock hanging on the wall behind the planters and the stage area. It might be the one that normally hung in the project cafeteria. There were also microphones at the front of the stage and amplifiers off to each side.

The time was twenty-five minutes before noon.

Finally, things began happening. Her father's personal assistant, the pretty Asian lady with the Scandinavian name—Ingrid; she'd helped Jasmeen last night—came and got them where they stood on the far side of the pool, away from the stage area. It had started to fill up with media people anyway. She took them around the pool to one side of the stage, asked them to stay there, and bustled off on some other errand.

Llyra turned to Jasmeen. "Don't you think she looks at my father funny?"

"Ingrid Andersson?" Jasmeen answered, adding, "-san?"

"Yeah," Llyra nodded. "I'm not sure I like the way she looks at my father."

Jasmeen laughed. "Your father is hero, my little. Your father builds whole world here. Also, he is very handsome man. I myself would look at him 'funny', if I didn't know how very much he loves your mother. Only thing that love like that leaves room for is you and Wilson."

Llyra sighed. "You're very wise, Jasmeen."

Jasmeen shrugged, "Just observant. And as I told you, I read ladies' magazine in dentist office."

Just then her mother and father, dressed as if they were going to church, entered from the other side of the stage, with Wilson. He looked odd,

Llyra thought, scrubbed and dressed like a grownup. (Come to think of it, he *was* grown up, she supposed.) So, to her complete amazement, did her uncles, Arleigh and Lindsay, who were supporting a limping, bandaged—and very unhappy-looking—Robert Fulton between them. The injured man was pale and sweaty, but he didn't appear to be in too much pain. Somebody had found a set of clean clothes for him. What he did look was desperate, though. She thought about the planter again.

The clock on the wall said it was five minutes to noon.

"Ladies and gentlemen," Adam said into the microphone. He had to say it again, however. Centuries of electronic progress had failed to eliminate the high-pitched squealing of feedback in public address systems. He had a strong voice, and could have done without the microphone.

"Ladies and gentlemen," he persisted. "We're here today to honor an exemplary and heroic employee of the Curringer Corporation—an individual, I'm happy to say, who just happens to be my son." There was a little polite laughter and a murmur in the gathered crowd. Wilson looked down at his feet, but his sister could see the color in his face.

"But first—" Adam went on. Oh, no, she thought. Is Daddy going to break the promise he'd made her last night? Her heart began to beat rapidly. Jasmeen noticed that something was wrong, shifted the skate bag to her other shoulder, took her hand, and gave it an encouraging squeeze.

"—a word about what happened last night." Now the murmur became a low rumble. Adam put his hand up to silence them. "Please! Let's get this done and go on to happier things, all right?" The rumble died down.

"I know that there are a lot of rumors going around this morning, but I'm about to tell you what really happened. This ... this man—" He indicated Fulton, who was beginning to look increasingly nervous. "This man was caught last night, attempting to commit an act so evil that it almost defies description. He was shot, which put a stop to his activities, and he stands here now so that you—and everybody in the Solar System—can see for themselves the sort of creature he is."

At least half of the cameras present swung around to focus on Fulton. The clock said one minute to noon, and the sweep hand was moving fast.

"Stop it right now!" Fulton screamed. "We've got to get away from here!" He was jerking around frantically between Arleigh and Lindsay, and his wound had reopened. A trickle of blood began to run down his left leg onto his shoe. Llyra wondered if he was going to wet himself again.

Adam turned and looked at him. "Why do we have to get away from here?"

"Because—"

Suddenly, but from outside somewhere, there came the rumble—all of it conveyed through the asteroid's substance—of a far distant explosion.

Fulton collapsed, unconscious.

"Because," Adam finished for him, "Last night this man—whom we believe to be an assassin and saboteur for the Null Delta Em wing of the so-called Mass Movement—concealed a powerful bomb in that planter right there. It would have killed everyone in this place a few seconds ago.

"It was designed to spare you media people for much less than a heartbeat, so your cameras could send pictures of the atrocity back to Earth."

CHAPTER FIFTEEN: GRANDPA MARRIED A MARTIAN

It's possible that the expression I hate most in the English language is "passed away", which is what people say when someone's life ends. It is bland and supine—and therefore an insult to anybody whose life was none of those things.

My eldest son breathed his last trying to stop three hundred megatons of iron-rich magnesium silicate—olivine, a common stony asteroid—set in motion by an idiot amateur, from colliding with and crushing another asteroid where a family had built their home and a farm. He succeeded only because he let it crush his little spaceship, instead. His heroic act was so ordinary among Pallatians nobody thought it unusual, although, as I say, it annoys me to hear that he "passed away". Billy Ngu did not pass away, he was crushed to a paste and he died.

Nobody ever "passes away" heroically. Far better to say honestly (if still euphemistically) he "bought the farm", "croaked", or even "kicked the bucket" (I often wonder about the origin of that one), or simply that, like my son Bill, he died well. —*The Diaries of Rosalie Frazier Ngu*

HORTENSE BLUMENFELD WAS MANAGER—NOT CAPTAIN—OF the factory ship *Percival Lowell*. In this day and age, the inviolable custom aboard commercial space vessels (sea vessels, too, for that matter) was to avoid imitating military hierarchies in any manner. It was a custom Hortense approved of highly and was reflected in her attire, a plain, Navy blue (oh, well, she thought, nothing's perfect) pants suit.

And sensible shoes.

Following some generous introductory remarks by her employer of fifteen years, Adam Ngu, she stepped the center of the little stage, a medium-sized Manila-colored plastic envelope in her short-fingered hands. The crowd quieted down, and she began to speak. She was a blunt-headed, solidly-constructed individual, her voice surprisingly high and breathy, almost as if a man were speaking in falsetto. In fact, she was a widow, and the grandmother, so far, of fourteen children.

"In the control center (not the bridge, she thought to herself) of my factory ship, *Percival Lowell*, fastened to the bulkhead with the intention that it never be removed, is an inch-thick golden rectangle, about a foot on a side, commonly known as a commissioning plaque. It names the vessel herself, her original owners, as well as the company that constructed her, the architect who designed her, the location where she was built, and her first home port, Earth's Lagrange Point Five. She was meant to build space elevators to equatorial points on Earth, but as you know, thanks to ecoterrorist threats, that has yet to happen."

She closed her eyes, an almost raptured expression on her face. "I can see that plaque from my chair in the control center, and it never fails to thrill me, through and through, to be manager of such a fine vessel and have some part in creating a newer, better world here on Ceres."

Now she opened her eyes again and looked squarely at her audience. "The fact though, is that a week ago last Wednesday—shortly after the event we've gathered here to acknowledge—and, if I may say so, celebrate—that plaque was taken down, and another datum added to it: 'This vessel was saved, with 2417 crew and managers, on July 14, 2131, by the fearless, brilliant, and heroic action of Wilson Ngu of Pallas'."

She was forced to stop as most of those she spoke to applauded. It was just as well. She was surprised to discover that her eyes were moist. "In addition, an eighth of an inch of gold was removed from the obverse of the plaque before it was restored to the bulkhead, and used to cast a perfect miniature, right down to and including, the final inscription."

Hortense opened the flap of her plastic envelope and reached into it, pulling out a large, square gold medallion on a broad blue satin ribbon. She beckoned to Wilson to join her at the center of attention. "Over the days to come, those who are hostile to our efforts out here will doubtless claim that Wilson is being rewarded, not for what he has accomplished, but for who he is. This medal, I assure everybody here, is the merest token of the deep and genuine respect, affection, and gratitude that all of us aboard the *Percival Lowell*—not to mention our families—feel toward our brave young friend here, Wilson Ngu."

Dropping the envelope to the concrete, she reached over Wilson's head, draped the ribbon around his neck, and gave him a peck on the cheek. This gesture, from a Martian, was nothing short of astonishing. The applause grew riotous, and Hortense couldn't speak for several minutes.

"For the most part..." she began, then had to wait and start again. "For the most part, ladies and gentlemen—overlooking members of the media from Earth and Earth's Moon—the folks gathered here today come from three Settled Worlds that didn't even exist, as such, a hundred and fifty years ago. Those three worlds are Pallas, from which Wilson and his family hail, Mars, which is the place of my own birth and that of several others here—by the way, your parents asked me to tell you hello, Jasmeen—and a brand new shiny Settled World, Ceres, being created even as I speak. So it was not merely my crew and vessel that Wilson saved, but the hopes and dreams of everybody on those Settled Worlds, as well as their futures and their children's futures."

She took his hand to shake it. "As inadequate as it may sound, Wilson, thank you."

⁂

"As the senior member of the Ngu family living and present today, I have come here from Mars to speak to my grandson on behalf of his family."

The voice was that of a slender, willowy female with enormous blue eyes, long, straight, dark auburn hair, perfect teeth, fair skin, a turned up nose, and freckles. One couldn't look closely enough at Julie Segovia Ngu to see that she wasn't the pretty, vivacious young girl in her twenties she appeared to be, but, thanks to twenty-second century science and force of will, a phenomenally well-preserved woman in her seventies.

Julie also happened to be Adam's mother, Llyra's grandmother, and Ardith's mother-in-law. A wholesomely elfin creature whom the media had dubbed "the First Immortal", rumor had it she wore a large diamond in her navel, which nobody but her late husband had ever seen or ever would. "I take great personal pleasure in this," Julie explained. "You see, I was originally born on Earth, in darkest East America, and was among hundreds abandoned on Mars by that government when our mission there failed. "What made me different from most of the folks who call themselves Martians, was that I was an officer with a military expedition sent to put down a rebellion among civilian colonists who had come

119

to the realization that they were never going to be rescued, but would be allowed to die, instead, unless they went their own way with regard to certain matters that included receiving assistance from Pallatians to achieve a massive, lifesaving, *illegal* alteration to the Martian environment."

It did not strike Julie as odd that everybody laughed, well aware of the consternation caused on Earth by the "macaroni plant" developed by two of Emerson Ngu's daughters and spread on Mars by two of his sons. Almost by itself it had transformed Mars into a decent place to live.

"As you know," she grinned, warming hearts all over the Solar System, "I eventually married the dashing young leader of our bold Pallatian rescuers, William Wilde Ngu, and returned ecstatically with him to Pallas, where I raised a family with him and wrote something like two dozen children's books—so far—which, I've been informed, have been appreciated by three generations everywhere but East America, where, having been written by a vile defector, and being of a decidedly seditious character…" Here again, everybody laughed. "…they are strictly forbidden."

The books concerned the adventures of a little girl, Conchita, her friend, Desmondo, and her pet arachnicat, Ploogle, in a strange land of "Wimpersnits" and "Oogies". They were thinly-disguised tales of neopuritans and safetyists (the Wimpersnits) and their gleefully brutal enforcers, the Oogies. They were credited with (or blamed for) the collapse of countless parliamentary governments, and for starting at least three revolutions. The books had been translated into a hundred languages, and read aloud for transmission into East America so many times that the government had learned to weather it like a bad winter.

When her husband William had died heroically a decade ago, Julie had returned to Mars, to construct a fabulous fantasy home and write even more seditious books about Conchita and Desmondo, having agreed to license a "Wimpersnits and Oogies" theme park in a big dome on Earth's Moon, over the hysterical objections of the East American government.

Julie beckoned, and Ardith handed her a scuffed briefcase-sized box of African buffalo leather she'd brought with her from the Red Planet. If anybody noticed that Ardith looked ten years older than her mother-in-law, nobody said anything—although it puzzled Ingrid Andersson. She was never going to let herself look older than she was today.

"From our family to you, Wilson, an object that once belonged to a member of the Pallas terraforming crew, a strong man who died young and never knew that he was Rosalie Frazier's grandfather, Horatio Singh. It passed from his widow, Henrietta Singh, to your great grandfather, who gave it to his son—my husband William—for his courageous acts on Mars. I hope your father won't mind if it skips a generation. I'd love to call it the Conchita and Desmondo Award for Moral Courage, but if it has a name attached to it, it can be no other than that of Emerson Ngu."

She handed the leather box to a mystified-looking Wilson, who opened it up and nearly staggered with surprise. Inside was a mighty weapon as fabulous as the family sword of any famous European knight or Japanese samurai. It was the very .45 Magnum caliber, ivory-handled Grizzly "Win Mag" that Emerson Ngu had relied on all his adult life on Pallas. Wilson had been told many tales about it. Some of them may even have been true.

"Carry it and use it, Wilson," his pretty young grandmother told him. "It was never meant to be locked in a museum to gather dust and be gawked at."

⁂

"If you'll look overhead in about a minute, you'll see a small, powerful, constant-boost vessel formally registered on Earth's Moon as the *C.C.S. William Wilde Curringer* and, following ancient usage, known affectionately by her crew and others familiar with her as *Billie*."

The individual making these remarks was a plump, middle-aged man, dressed in an expensive Earthside business suit of the current style (although he'd told his hosts earlier that he hadn't set foot on the Mother Planet for more than thirty years): soft gray trousers, a mid-thigh-length jacket without lapels or visible pockets, and a ball cap fashioned of the same material, that he'd taken off before starting to speak. He had lots of white hair, a big white moustache, a piercing, blue-eyed, majesterial gaze, and the kind of nose often referred to as "aquiline". He reminded Wilson of somebody, but he couldn't remember who.

The visitor had been introduced to the family and well-wishers gathered in the little plaza as Sheridan Sinclair, Chairman of the Board of the Curringer Foundation, an organization distinct from, but closely connected with the Curringer Corporation. The latter had terraformed Pallas generations ago, was now in the process of having Ceres terraformed, and was undertaking several other massive civil engineering works, including an O'Neill-type habitat miles long that would orbit Jupiter, and a dozen interlinked "space elevators" to serve Mars and a Solar System grown dependent on its technological marvels. They were even talking now about putting a dome over Hellas Planitia. There was a low buzz of appreciation. Most Curringer Corporation employees here had benefitted, at one time or another, from their founder's agreement with a Biblical philosophy that it never pays to bind the mouths of the cattle that tread the grain—a philosophy that most large corporations seemed to have to learn the hard way, over and over again.

"As I observed earlier," he said, "while the Curringer Corporation directs all the work (and makes all the profit), it's the Foundation's job to make sure that the people doing the work don't get overlooked or forgotten. This often requires spending some of that profit, just as Wild Bill Curringer intended, his attitude being, 'What the hell else is it for?'"

"Here she comes now!" Sinclair pointed up through the transparent canopy overhead, as excited and enthusiastic as a little child. He didn't know it, but that was the reason he had this job. "See? I asked the captain to blink her running lights at us as she passes above the dome."

As the spaceship orbited out of sight, he grew more serious. "Over the same period of time that many of you were travelling here from Pallas at between a tenth and a twentieth of a standard Earth gravity, we headed here from the Moon. We began at a sixth of a gee and worked our way up to a full gravity—an acceleration at which we continued through turnover, until we arrived here at Ceres. As a consequence, I believe that we have set a new Solar record for Earth-to-Ceres transit time."

He placed a hand behind one hip. "Not to mention for bruises and contusions."

Amidst polite laughter, Sinclair turned from his audience, which consisted mostly of Ceres Project employees, media people, and an unseen audience of hundreds of millions all over the Solar System, to those he shared the stage area with: young Wilson Ngu and his family (including Jasmeen Khalidov), and Hortense Blumenfeld, manager—not captain—of the factory ship *Percival Lowell*, who had arrived here with Julie Segovia Ngu in the latter's private hopper.

"I'm sure you'll all agree with me that it's a very good thing to set new records, and an even better thing to undertake vast scientific and engineering enterprises that astonish our entire species, delight us personally, and promise, ultimately, to alter the course of human history. However it's equally important to assure ourselves that those who do these things for us come to no harm at the hands of others who, for numberless and unhealthy reasons of their own, envy and resent them."

Sinclair went on to describe in some detail what Wilson had done—making it sound like a 3DTV action-adventure episode in the process—at dire risk of his own life, and surviving a damaged envirosuit, bravely and single-handedly killing five armed, desperate criminal saboteurs and capturing seven more, while saving the lives of more than two thousand people. By now, everyone had heard the story—it was a good one—but if there was a time to tell it again, this was it.

Wilson looked up and across the decorative pool at the crowd of media people recording what was being said and done here. He wondered how much of it would be seen and heard back on Earth, especially in East America, where the Mass Movement and Null Delta Em were often looked on—especially by the popular media– as rascally antiheroes locked in mortal combat with nasty, exploitive capitalists, unconcerned with the future health and habitability of the planet of mankind's birth.

Wilson wanted very much to be a capitalist himself (he had his reasons, nasty or otherwise), and "exploit" the Solar System. The more crimes Null Delta Em committed out here—everybody everywhere knew that they were working for the Mass Movement, but for some reason, most people pretended not to know—the less he gave a stony pebble about what happened to the Earth. He'd learned the hard way and at an early age that all the logic and scientific evidence in the universe are impotent to persuade people to give up their irrationally held opinions.

Take the media people, here. They'd been shown several x-rays of Robert Fulton's deadly suitcase bomb, and even apparently understood the callous use that he'd intended to make of them. For the moment, at least, they seemed to be taking a different view of things than their colleagues Earthside usually did. But Wilson doubted that the lesson would last very long. It appeared to him that media people had the memory and attention span of the little green spitty aphids in his mother's rose garden.

But Sinclair was continuing. "As most of you on this world are aware, metallic asteroids, which comprise some thirty percent of the Asteroid Belt, contain not only nickel and iron, but great amounts of gold, silver, platinum, chromium, palladium, iridium, and several other precious substances. Carbonaceous chondrites, which for reasons that are still mysterious comprise about seventy percent, offer us water, for our survival, and a material much like petroleum, called kerogen."

He produced a large plastic envelope sporting the company's logo. "Having conferred at length with all of the directors of the Curringer Foundation—a somewhat formidable task, believe me, distributed all throughout the Solar System as they are inclined to be—we have come to the unanimous conclusion that it is altogether fitting and proper to reward this valiant young man with a small measure of the treasure that he and so many others like him have helped our species amass—I employ that word 'amass' advisedly, and sincerely hope that you are listening, Anna Wertham Savage—over the generations they have been out here."

He gestured to Wilson to approach. "I am given to understand, in fact, that Mr. Ngu aspires to become a hunter of asteroids, himself, a worthy ambition that requires a considerable investment of capital. Therefore in recognition of his heroic acts in defense of the Ceres Terraformation Project, as well as of the independent factory vessel *Percival Lowell* and the members of her crew, we are honored to offer him the sum of four hundred platinum ounces, to help him achieve his dream."

Sinclair opened the plastic envelope and slid a hand inside it. Wilson's already dazzled mind reeled. A brand new asteroid hunting vessel, fully equipped, would cost him almost twice that amount. He knew because he had stacks of magazines and catalogs on the subject, and thousands of files and site locations in his personal computer. But a perfectly sound and lavishly-appointed—even luxurious—used spacecraft would leave him enough money to run on for at least six months. Four hundred platinum ounces! He was rich!

Wilson suddenly remembered who Sinclair reminded him of—the actor Frank Morgan in the twentieth century classic, *The Wizard of Oz*. A brain, a heart, courage, Kansas, and maybe a 2125 Mitsubishi Rockhound 9000L.

He turned to his parents, but he had no idea what to say to them. His father was obviously fighting back tears, but his mother—even more shockingly—was beaming at him (although he thought he saw a bit of the same concern in her face that she'd shown when he was six years old and had gotten his first flying belt as a birthday present). His sister was jumping up and down, clapping her hands joyfully, while their grandmother Julie apparently had to fight the impulse to join her. Jasmeen seemed to have an unusual, evaluative expression on her lovely face.

It made him nervous.

It was only then that he noticed the way everyone in the little plaza seemed to be applauding him, even some of the media people. Quite naturally, his own hometown multimedia station KCUF loved him. They'd thrown a party for him—as they did for every other adolescent in town on such a day—when he'd killed his first big game animal, in his case a huge muley buck that had fed the family for weeks. Its antlers still graced his mother's formal dining room, at least according to Llyra, and venison spaghetti was still his special favorite.

Second only to venison sausage for breakfast.

But now he wouldn't be able to walk down the streets of Curringer any more without all kinds of people wanting to greet and talk to him. Mr. Sinclair put a big arm around his shoulder and presented him with a giant green plastic card, an official deposit receipt, he said, from the Miner's Bank of Pallas, for four hundred ounces of platinum, 999 fine.

Four hundred ounces!

In a few days—weeks at most—he'd be master of his own ship! And who knew what could happen—maybe he'd find the Diamond Rogue!

✼

Sheridan Sinclair stepped backward, taking Wilson along with him, deferring to the Chief Engineer of the Ceres Terraformation Project, who raised both his hands, asking for silence and attention from the gathering. "Before we all go our separate ways this morning—this is not a holiday, and I'd remind you that we're now behind schedule, placing survey transponders—I have one more happy item to attend to. Our guests may have noticed these four big hoses attached to those pieces of equipment over there, trailing across the plaza to what would be the corners of our little kidney-shaped decorative pool—if kidneys had corners."

There was general polite laughter. The machines that Adam referred to were the size of fifty-five gallon oil drums on wheels. They had been running quietly all this time, half hidden behind the concrete wall. Some of the media people had complained about having to step over the hoses. Honey Graham had twisted her decorative ankle on one of them last evening—Arleigh had taken care of her and gotten her to the medics– but was here this morning looking like a professional newsie.

"Our construction personnel here know what these devices are," Adam continued. "Although they may wonder why they're being used like this today. I confess that it might be seen as a minor misappropriation of company resources, but we'll enter it in the books under 'Advance Publicity'."

And if the directors of the Curringer Corporation didn't like that, he thought, they could go find themselves another boy. This was by far the most challenging, difficult, annoying—and satisfying—project he'd ever undertaken. But the notion of returning to Pallas with Ardith was becoming more attractive to him with every hour that passed. It was too early to tell, but maybe they were finally growing up.

"Ordinarily, when we're faced with drifts of dust or aggregations of loose rubble here on Ceres—or silt and mud on some other planet—and the blueprints call for putting a hole through the stuff, a hole that isn't going to collapse on us while we're working in it, we'll saturate the area first with some kind of liquid, usually water, if it isn't already wet, pull a cover over it so the liquid won't evaporate or sublimate, and freeze it solid with machines like these, so the whole mess can be dug, cut, or drilled, just like ordinary rock or soil." He turned to his wife, an expert in the field he was about to make reference to. "More or less the same process is commonly used before a loosely-aggregated asteroid or meteoroid can be deflected in one piece from a potentially lethal course and safely collected if it has value. We've been considering giving Ceres its own moon that way, like Pallas has."

Llyra had always believed that her daddy could have hung the Moon. She suddenly realized why it had felt so cold beside the little pool last evening. It hadn't anything to do with the fountains—which had just been turned off, in any case. She also knew suddenly why Jasmeen had brought her skate bag with her. It had been a family conspiracy.

"The sides of this decorative pool were designed with an outward slant," Adam observed, "so that freezing—and expanding—the water within it couldn't damage them. With four powerful heat pumps steadily removing energy from the pool, I calculate that it should freeze to a depth of about eighteen inches in just another five minutes, which is long enough for anybody who happens to have brought a pair of ice skates with them to lace them up and do a little preliminary stretching."

There was a burst of applause and delighted laughter. The media began swapping lenses on their equipment and making what adjustments they could for the harsh backlight that always made ice photography difficult.

Jasmeen obeyed without further prompting, sitting down at the edge of the pool and disposing of her shoes. She opened her bag and pulled out a well-worn pair of lavender suede S.P. Teris, with MK "Outland" blades designed for low gravity. Jasmeen had always preferred skating barefoot inside her boots. Llyra chose to wear stockings. The younger girl's heart began beating rapidly. She was about to skate on another world!

And she loved skating with Jasmeen.

A little layer of fog began forming six inches above the surface of what had now become ice. "Do I have any takers?" her father asked, unnecessarily.

CHAPTER SIXTEEN: DOWNSYSTEM

Sigmund Freud said it (or so the story goes): "Sometimes a cigar is just a cigar". So who was it who rushed to the unsupported conclusion that the so-called Venus of Willendorf—and many other objects like it that have been found—are "fertility symbols" or objects of worship? Feminists even like to cite them as evidence of some ancient, benevolent Goddess-religion, long since replaced by vile male-oriented beliefs.

Doesn't it make more sense—and strain credulity less—to suggest they were a caveman's version of *Playboy*, passed from hand to hand around the campfire after the women and children had gone to bed, to be fondled and chuckled over licentiously? —*The Diaries of Rosalie Frazier Ngu*

"IS IT PRACTICAL, JASMEEN?" ASKED Julie. "Can it be done?"

With Llyra, they occupied a comfortable corner booth in the Ceres Terraformation Project cafeteria, which had been hastily refurbished for the benefit of the visiting media. The fresh colors were bright, the fixtures were shiny, the food was all right, and the media were gone—which suited everybody absolutely perfectly. There was even a big old Rock-o-la jukebox, anachronistically playing 21st century tunes.

Llyra had just skated on the frozen pool for the third time in as many days—for the first time today without Honey Graham and the others there to fuss over her. The pool was tiny, compared to the rink back home, but she had it to herself, except for Jasmeen, and it was fun. And of course it was something that her father had done just for her.

She wished his secretary didn't look at him that way. It made her nervous. She'd meant to talk with Wilson about that, but he'd been busy.

Now, over a vanilla milkshake almost as big as she was, and a big plate of French fries smothered in homemade ketchup, Llyra had just confessed to her grandmother Julie her ambition to skate, someday, on Earth.

"Ngu family doctors say not," Jasmeen answered. "Will injure or kill self, they say. Me, I don't know, but nothing worthwhile is without serious risk."

"I agree with you completely." Julie wrinkled her pretty nose. "In the end, doctors are just like lawyers," she said. "They're always ready to tell you what can't be done—what you can't do. They don't remember that this isn't what you hired them for. What would you girls say if I were to consult the people I pay to keep me young, inside and out?"

Llyra looked at her beautiful grandmother, who didn't yet look thirty, and her eyes grew large. "I'd say thanks, Grandma Julie! How soon—"

"Well, there's just a small hitch, Sweetheart. They're down in the Moon. Your great grandfather, my father-in-law, is often credited with having invented the cellular regeneration process, just as he invented so many other things, firearms, vehicles, personal fliers. But this one improvement he paid to have done, and the DeGrey Foundation, the outfit that finally succeeded—"

"It's in the Moon?" Llyra was growing excited. "But that's where I need to go next, anyway, Grandma Julie! My native asteroid Pallas at one twentieth of a gee, Ceres at one tenth—although I had a little bit of that on Pallas, you know! And then the Moon, at one sixth of a gee!"

"Mars after that," added Jasmeen, looking almost as happy as her student.

Julie considered it. "Your brother Wilson needs to go downsystem, because that's the best place to buy a ship, at one of the Lagrange points. Your father asked me to go along and help him with that. I'm a pretty good bargainer. I don't know if your father's doing the right thing, not holding Wilson to his labor contract here on Ceres. I don't know if I would—the poor boy certainly has the fever."

"Yeah," Llyra said grimly, "and not just for a hunter ship, or even the Diamond Rogue! 'Ooh, Willie!'" she cooed in falsetto. "'I can hardly wait to see my little Willie!'"

For some reason, Jasmeen colored, but said nothing. She wondered if Llyra knew what willie was a euphemism for. They didn't discuss it much.

"I need to go downsystem to sign papers and break ground on the new Wimpersnits and Oogies theme park," Julie said, trying hard not to laugh at her granddaughter's imitation of her brother's girlfriend. "Of course I could do all that electronically, but I'd rather not. I really want to hear all the squawking from East America close up and personal."

Jasmeen laughed and clapped her hands, exactly like Llyra did sometimes.

Llyra needed to go to the Moon as her next step upward in gravity. That was all she could focus on. She knew it could mean months, maybe years, of suffering and pain, even injury and death. Nevertheless, she waited breathlessly for the next thing her grandmother was about to say.

"I'll take you and your brother and you, too, Jasmeen, with me in the Curringer Foundation ship. Sherrie Sinclair owes me a favor or two, so we'll draw on the available credit. What do you say, figure skater?"

"I ... I ... " She began to fight back tears.

"Look, just between you and me and your little Russian coach, here—" She winked at Jasmeen, whose parents were old friends of hers.

"Chechen," Llyra corrected her reflexively.

"Whatever—I started out half Puerto Rican, myself, and half Irish. Now I don't know what I am, and I don't care, because I've always known *who* I am. Anyway, you should be aware, my dear, that your kindly little old grandmother knows exactly how that Null Delta Em filth Fulton got himself shot—your father never could lie worth a damn to me—and how the shooter didn't want to claim credit for it because she didn't want to spoil her big brother Wilson's award ceremony."

"Well, I ... uh ... " Now it was Llyra's turn to blush. Jasmeen hadn't heard the whole story—she'd taken time to get dressed and hadn't caught up yet—but had deduced all of the most important facts. It never occurred to her that much of Llyra's character was her doing.

"Don't worry, your secret is safe with me," Julie said, "But for that reason, and not just because you're my cute little granddaughter and I love you to pieces—with your father's approval—I'm going to pay the bills while you train, and compete, on the Moon. If you like, sweetheart, you may think of it as *your* four hundred ounces of platinum."

*
**

"Absolutely not!" Ardith shouted, the most furious expression on her face that Julie had ever seen—and she'd seen some of her best, she thought.

For lack of any better place to gather privately, the Ngu family occupied a comfortable room in Adam's office complex that he used for staff meetings, for dealing with the representatives of the Curringer Corporation and Foundation, and for confronting (his choice of words) the media. It was very clean—for being situated in the middle of a construction site—and surprisingly spacious, given the amount of room available under the dome, offering them a long conference table made of polished Cerean olivine, and twelve almost luxurious chairs. Between virtual windows on all four walls showing how Ceres would look once it was terraformed, there was a coffee maker and a generous wet bar.

On his feet, pacing back and forth as if to make a poorer target, Adam spread both of his hands helplessly at waist level. "But I thought—"

Ardith whirled on him, the violent motion adding emphasis to her outraged words and tone. "It was you who put them up to this, wasn't it?"

Adam's eyes widened like a rodent suddenly aware a raptor was descending. Here it was at last, what he'd expected all along. What it seemed to be about didn't matter at all.

"Well," she demanded, "wasn't it?"

"No, Ardith, my dear," Julie answered before her eldest son dug his grave any deeper. It was remarkable, sometimes, what an efficient spade the human tongue made. She was sitting at the head of the table and had used both the coffee maker and the wet bar to make herself a mug of Irish coffee. Too bad there wasn't any whipped cream for the top of the mug. "It was just little old me, your nosy, interfering mother-in-law. And for what it's worth, my dear, I'd love it if you'd come downsystem with us, too. We haven't had a real chance to visit in ages."

Ardith was seated halfway down the table, which she'd had made in her lab as a gift to Adam when he'd accepted this assignment, a lovely thing fashioned from the most useless kind of asteroid material. Something from nothing; she liked to think it was her specialty. She turned very slowly, looked her mother-in-law straight in the eye, and said, "No thank you, Julie, dear. Some of us still have real work to do."

Sitting directly across from Ardith, Llyra gasped audibly. She'd never heard her mother fight with her grandmother before now, or even imagined that such a thing was possible. At the end of the long table, in the chair nearest the door, she watched her uncle Arleigh look down intently at his heavy work shoes and put a hand across his forehead, covering his eyes. His brother, her other uncle Lindsay, had apparently discovered something fascinating to examine up in the corner, near the ceiling. At Llyra's side, Jasmeen moved her chair a bit closer to her student's and, in a very unMartian way took the younger girl's hand in both of hers.

She'll definitely do, Julie thought. She approved of this young woman. And when she told them, once she got back to Mars, her parents Mohammed and Beliita would be proud of the way she'd grown in the last three years. It had cost them a great deal, emotionally, to send their only child to faraway Pallas, even to the home of longtime family friends.

As the author of two dozen popular children's books, Julie had been accused of not doing anything real for a living before, of spending her life behind a computer display instead of in the real world, even of corrupting the minds of babies with reactionary fantasies, but never by a member of her own family. She decided it was better not to say anything for the moment. She had a theory that Ardith was insane—at least temporarily—at times like this, and would later regret what she'd said, not only to her mother-in-law, but to everybody else in the room.

Poor Adam, he loves Ardith so. And Ardith loves Adam. Julie could see it clearly, if nobody else here could. But Lennon and McCartney were wrong: love is *not* all you need. Most times you need more than love. Sometimes you need a lot more. Linda could have used a cure for cancer. John could have used a bulletproof vest. Yoko could have used a .45. Ardith could use a little perspective. If she wasn't careful that overheated little assistant of Adam's was going to snatch her man right away.

That was easy to see clearly, too.

*
**

130

Alone at last, Wilson didn't waste another minute. Keeping the Grizzly, he handed his heavy gold medal and his Bank of Pallas deposit receipt over to Ingrid's—Miss Andersson's—safekeeping (in a real safe) and almost ran back to his dormitory room. Inside, with the door locked, his computer found his SolarNet account for him in record time.

Not being the most introspective of human beings himself (Wilson liked to think of himself as a man of action), he didn't like to contemplate what had just happened—what always seemed to happen—between his mother and his father. It had taken him a long, hard time to realize that their life was not his life, and that as sad (or dumb) as theirs might be in many respects, he had to put it to one side, and try to live his own. It was the only thing he had to power to do, really.

He did know that he loved them both and refused to choose between them. He was pretty sure his younger sister Llyra had made the same decision.

At last, his account began delivering the mail he wanted most to see. There she was, his Amorie, more beautiful, if such a thing was possible, than he'd ever seen her. "Hi, Willie!" her recording said, "I couldn't wait to tell you that we all saw you on 3DTV! My whole family! You're so handsome, it was just thrilling! You're a real hero, Willie!"

He'd always hated being called Willie, but Amorie's teeth were white and perfect, her lips moist and full. Her soft brown eyes were big and bright. She had the cutest upturned nose. He loved the way her little ears peeked out of her hair. And the graceful curve of her shoulders, her delicate collarbones—he shook his head to keep it from spinning and began what would be his reply, bit by bit, to her message.

She would receive it only forty-five minutes after he sent it.

"Well," he said into his computer. "I didn't think much about what I did out there, you know, I just did it. People were going to die if I didn't. I'm glad it worked, but anybody else would have done the same."

"I bet I know," Amorie's message went on, "what you're planning to do with all that platinum and gold they gave you! Cash those receipts in, melt that gold down. I wanted to tell you that they've just upped the E.L.E. bounty by almost seventy-five percent for the diversion or destruction of rocks headed toward Earth or any other Settled World—and the hunter gets to keep the rock, regardless of its composition! Hurry downsystem, Willie, hurry! And we can talk about it all in real time!"

Wilson knew from sad experience that Amorie didn't have a clue who "they" were, who paid the bounty on Earth-threatening asteroids and meteoroids. She must be a hell of a pilot—or whatever she did for her family—if she didn't follow the business details of her family trade any better than that. He'd have to do it all for himself. She never talked much about what she did, really, only about what he did, and what they'd both do provided they ever managed to get together physically.

She had a hell of an imagination that way. Good thing modern e-mail was private.

As best he could under the circumstances, he replied to that bit of her message before he ran the rest of what she'd sent him. He could see she'd been in her own quarters, a tiny one-bunk cabin aboard her family's asteroid hunter ship. She'd decorated it with filmy, floaty, sheer stuff, mostly the color of Earth's skies. They usually ran their vessel at a tenth of a gee, and the hangings rippled in the air like water.

"I have to sign off, now, my hero, but before I do, I think we know each other well enough by now to get to know each other a little better." With those words, she opened her clothes—he hadn't even noticed before this what she was wearing—more blue filmy stuff—and backed away from the video pickup so he could see all of her at once.

He nearly fell off his chair. Her breasts were fuller, firmer than he'd imagined, her belly flat, her—He wouldn't be getting any sleep tonight.

Again.

* * *

Ingrid Andersson sat at her desk with her forehead in her hands, about half a micron away, she realized, from tears or from maniacal laughter.

Why had these things started happening to her? She couldn't help how she felt about Adam, or that she'd overheard Ardith's outburst. It had been extremely noisy and the doors and walls were thin on this world. And, as Adam—Dr. Ngu—had said out in the plaza, today was not a holiday. They had fallen behind and there was work to catch up on.

Important work. Vital work. She had no choice, being here, in the next room, where she was forced to hear her boss's wife's lunatic bellowing.

As she began to calm down, Ingrid found herself mystified all over again. It was true, her boss had a beautiful young daughter and a handsome, courageous son to think about. But the children were both very nearly grown up, certainly least by Pallatian standards. So why did he put up with that screaming, hysterical bitch—there, she'd finally said it (or at least thought it)—when he didn't have to any more?

Ingrid couldn't bring herself quite far enough to imagine exactly what kind of consort—partner—mate—she might be to Adam, or even compare herself in any way to Ardith. But she'd been brought up by both of her parents to believe that a woman must try as hard as she could to be a perfect companion to a man, in any way he wanted her to be.

She could do that.

It was a very old-fashioned ideal, she knew, some might even say sexist or downright backward. But had any notion for organizing human society that had come afterward, ever produced any greater happiness for men or women? All sorts of other ideas and images suddenly cascaded into her mind. Ingrid swallowed hard, undid the top button of her blouse, and turned her desk fan up another notch. At her best, Ardith Ngu was nothing but a cold-blooded scientist. What could a woman like that possibly know about sex—er, passion?

Suddenly Adam stood beside her desk. "Please—Oh, I'm so sorry, Ingrid, I didn't mean to startle you when you were lost in thought. I get that way, too, sometimes, in case you haven't noticed. Please find Mrs. Ngu's—that is, my mother's—hopper pilot, will you? He's probably out in the *gamera* tunnels hanging around with the off-duty crews. They have a kind of a pub down there. Tell him that she won't be returning to Pallas with him and Manager Blumenfeld, but that Mrs. Ngu—my wife—will."

That shook Ingrid completely out of her unhappy (if stimulating) reverie. She tried being properly guilty about it, but the feeling simply wasn't there. Instead, a sense of even greater warmth pervaded her body, making her head spin and her hands shake. Adam's wife was going away again! So were his mother, his daughter, and even his son. For a while—a very long while, perhaps—she would have him all to herself!

Hope had bloomed again for Ingrid.

*
**

But what Adam was thinking in that moment would have disappointed her.

Perhaps, he mused resignedly, with everyone he loved heading out for Pallas or the Moon within the next few hours, he was about to have something of a break from the soap opera that his life had somehow become when he wasn't looking. It was possible that he could get back to living the safer, saner life of the mind. While the transponder planting crews were catching up, maybe he could get in some journal reading.

Ardith would eventually discover the present he'd found her and realize all over again that he loved her. Things would slowly get better.

His in-laws, Ardith's parents, had been deeply involved with the Jupiter habitat project for years. He was fairly familiar with its modified O'Neill design. Five miles long, two hundred fifty million tons of spinning metal, all alone in the night, it would combine some of the best opportunities for scientific research in history with a wonderful luxury hotel featuring the most spectacular scenery in the Solar System.

But he wanted to know all about the Martian dome Sheridan Sinclair had mentioned. Hellas Planitia was one of the lowest places on the Red Planet, with the densest air, but it was also one of the coldest. Before Mars had acquired a breathable atmosphere, frost used to gather in it—frost made of carbon dioxide. Maybe an atmospheric dome on an already terraformed planet made a little more sense than he'd first believed.

Idly, he wondered what that perfume was that Ingrid was wearing.

⁂

Well, she'd done it.

She'd finally done it.

Ardith threw what few things she'd taken out, back into her only suitcase. She wanted to be out of this room before Adam came back to it. She wished she could be gone from this asteroid sooner than was likely. She felt grateful she didn't have to wait for the regularly scheduled passenger liner. Three long weeks. That would have been unbearable.

Yes, she'd finally driven her entire family, practically everyone she'd ever loved, away from her—all at the same time! There ought to be some kind of category for it in the Guinness book of records. Adam would stay here on Ceres because it was his job, a job he loved, and because it kept him safely millions of miles away from her insane rages.

Here was a little handful of underthings that needed washing. She decided they could wait. She stuffed them in her suitcase and forgot them.

Wilson, her one and only living son, was travelling downsystem, to Earth's Moon, to buy himself a spaceship, to find himself a new life like all young men must eventually do or remain children, and no doubt to claim himself another kind of prize, as well. He was a hero, after all, very handsome and well-poised. It surprised his mother mildly that the idea of her son having a romance didn't scandalize or dismay her the way it should. Instead, she hoped sincerely that he was better rewarded with regard to that part of his life than his poor father had been.

What was this? A fist-sized gray velvet bag she didn't recognize, tucked into the inside pocket of her suitcase with her jewelry and accessories.

And Llyra, her lovely and amazingly talented baby daughter, was going downsystem, as well. The half dozen developmental physiologists she'd quietly consulted without Llyra's knowledge had warned her that, at the very best, it would take no less than two years of intensive training before

134

she could hope to be competitive against athletes who had grown up at one sixth of a gee. At worst, Llyra could destroy her beautiful little body and wind up crippled for life. And her abject failure of a mother wouldn't be there to help and comfort her if it happened.

Instead, having disgraced and embarrassed herself for no reason at all—and for the last goddamned time, she swore grimly to herself—she was tucking her tail between her legs, and heading home to Pallas, a prospect that offered her no comfort at all. Her parents were long gone—they would be among the first to live in the completed Jupiter orbital habitat.

Inside the bag, she found six rough transparent stones the size of her thumb. She knew at once what they were: asteroidal diamonds, clots of kerogen trapped in the centers of only the largest carbonaceous chondrites, crushed and heated for billions of years until they became pure, allotropic carbon. These were about eight carats each, and were accompanied by a strip a flimsy plastic certifying that their purchase by Dr. Adam Ngu from the Curringer Corporation's deep boring teams at the poles—where they were placing the cable piers—was legal and proper.

The monetary figure had been blacked out.

Adam's contract permitted him to do things like this occasionally. Without a politically powerful cartel to inflate their value by making them artificially scarce, the uncut stones were worth, at the most, a tenth of one percent of what they might have been on Earth a hundred years ago. But they were still valuable and very beautiful, a gift of love.

On the back, a handwritten note: *My darling Ardith, Adam.* She sat on the unmade bed, put her face in her hands, sobbing helplessly. How was it possible that a man like this one could waste his love on her?

She would go home, then, and do her science—it was the only damn thing she'd ever been any good at—pushing back the barriers of the unknown and all that nonsense. If the day should come that Adam asked her for a divorce, then she would acquiesce quietly, no matter how much it hurt, as a sort of penance. She couldn't kid herself that it would never happen. She hadn't missed the way that Ingrid, that little Asian secretary of his, looked at him. If not her, then it would be somebody else.

Eventually.

Aside from her professional colleagues, Ardith would remain all by herself in that big dark house on Pallas, possibly for the rest of her life.

And the Zacharenkos were notoriously long-lived.

PART TWO:
ONE SIXTH GEE

THE SO-CALLED "CRETACEOUS-TERTIARY EVENT", PUT an end to the dinosaurs sixty-five million years ago. A similar occurrence, a hundred forty million years earlier, the "Permian-Triassic Event", killed off ninety percent of the planet's species. There have been perhaps as many as a dozen of these "Extinction Level Events" in the history of the planet.

Human beings are the first species with the ability to understand these events. Since we're about fifteen million years overdue for another one, we must also become the first with the ability to prevent them.

To establish perspective, the calamity which has brought us here together, the recent, horrific cataclysm in and around Ashland, Ohio—a perfectly natural tragedy that snuffed out fifteen million lives and created a sixth Great Lake in the center of the North American continent—doesn't even come close to qualifying as one of these events.

—Dr. Evgeny Zacharenko Addressing the Ashland Event Commission Of the Solar Geological Society Curringer, Pallas, August 9, 2095

CHAPTER SEVENTEEN: GRAVITIC SHOCK

> Taking a captured asteroid apart can be rather like dismantling a whale aboard 19th and 20th century factory ships on Earth's oceans. If it's small enough to move around, it's small enough to turn beneath your tools and yield up riches, layer by layer, until it's nothing more than a handful of worthless—and harmless—pebbles. —*The Diaries of Rosalie Frazier Ngu*

"HOMEBASE, THIS IS 'CLARA BARTON' leaving ACCS Bay 13, Slip 5 as dispatched, two cases of G-shock, both young Pallatian women. Do you copy?"

All around her, it seemed, bright lights were flashing red and blue. From somewhere outside, she could hear the plaintive wail of a siren.

Despite calling itself "Clara Barton", a name Llyra thought she recognized from her history lessons, the voice coming from the front of the vehicle was definitely male, low-pitched, and a bit gruff. She couldn't see who was speaking. Strapped down, flat on her back, she was looking up through a plastic transparency at what appeared to be the ceiling of a cave ripping by overhead, surrealistically illuminated by flashing, whirling lights.

"Copy, Clara," came a woman's voice, filtered by some sort of communications system. "Treat as indicated and transport to L.E.I., stat."

"We are in transit. Say again, Homebase, L.E.I.?"

"That's correct, Clara, L.E.I."

"L.E.I. Roger that, Homebase, this is 'Clara Barton', out."

⁑

When the *William Wilde Curringer* arrived at the landing terminal of the Arthur C. Clark Spaceport, Llyra had to be carried off on a stretcher.

To her eternal chagrin, Jasmeen came off *Billie* on the stretcher right behind Llyra. After a brief, exciting ambulance ride they were both rather grateful they hadn't had to watch through a front window, they were greeted by attendants and technicians from the Life Extension Institute, the facility responsible for keeping Llyra's grandmother young.

Julie had called the facility while the ship was still in orbit.

It had been a good flight from Ceres, Llyra thought, up to a point—the point where she had to be carried off on a stretcher. On Ceres, the small corporation spaceship *Billie* had sent an automated landing pod down to the asteroid's surface, which she, Julie, Jasmeen, and Wilson had boarded via the airlock of one of the project's *gamera*, driven by Lindsay, while Arleigh had observed and offered unnecessary advice.

Goodbyes were prolonged and tearful; *Billie* had to make an extra orbit while they went on. Llyra's mother, who would herself be leaving within the hour for Pallas, came to say farewell and express all of a mother's misgivings about sending both of her children—or maybe it was all three of her children—more than a hundred million miles away. For Llyra, the worst of it was that her father didn't come to see her off. It wasn't that she didn't understand, with her mother there and all, just that it hurt so much anyway.

When the little shuttle finally reached the *Billie*, in orbit about Ceres, Sheridan Sinclair had already been aboard for some time. "It is important to make certain," he informed them grandly, "that all is made as commodious as possible for our most esteemed and honored guests."

Two of his guests, Llyra and Wilson, hadn't experienced anything gravitically more rigorous than the one tenth gee of Ceres. Two more of Sinclair's guests—Julie and Jasmeen—had spent significant portions of their lives in gravity fields twice as strenuous as the one sixth gee the ship would gradually build up to during its voyage Moonward.

"It's pretty clear," Julie observed as they came aboard through an airlock in the vessel's side near the pilots' compartment, "that none of us is going to be wandering around very much for the next few hours.

The little vessel, she told Llyra and Jasmeen, was about the size of a small corporate jet on Earth. There wasn't a lot of room, they agreed.

Sinclair conducted them to enormous, overstuffed chairs that did double service, he explained, as acceleration couches once *Billie* started moving under her own power. Instead of being designed the way *Beautiful Dreamer* had been, as a simple, utilitarian multi-leveled cylinder, *Billie*, a cylinder with a bulge at one end for the flight deck, looked to Llyra something like a wingless commercial airliner, or even an ancient bus from old movies she'd seen about life back on Earth.

"If you'll glance forward, you'll notice that there's a bulkhead with a door. It's intended as much for the privacy of this vessel's passengers as for any security purposes. On the other side of it are the traditional work stations for a flight crew of three, the ship's pilot, the ship's copilot, and a flight engineer who also serves as communications officer."

Aft of the flight compartment bulkhead were a dozen rows of three passenger seats with a broad carpeted aisle separating one of the seats from the others in each row. "Each seat features a screenfield generator on the seatback ahead of it," Sinclair told them, "so we can offer various choices of programming, either in recorded form, or transmitted in real time from the Earth or the Moon. There are also several ports for different models of personal computer or media player."

Llyra noticed that Wilson immediately got his computer out and logged onto the SolarNet, no doubt to commune with his dearly beloved (and embarrassingly boring) Amorie. Her brother would be as good as not even here, for the rest of the voyage, however long it happened to last.

"What's this?" Llyra asked, as Mr. Sinclair showed them all of the technological gadgetry available to them. It was an oddly-shaped port beside a palm-sized door in the back of the seat ahead of her. Julie and Jasmeen were already watching an old 2D movie together, a classic 21st century western starring the legendary David Boreanaz and Lexa Doig.

"Virtual Reality," he told her, opening the little panel. Inside was a fist-sized piece of tan fabric, porous and open as cheesecloth, covered with tiny, glittering metallic points connected by a mesh of fine wiring. Unfolded, it was obvious that the object was intended to cover the head and face. The wiring all came together in a slender cable ending in a plug that fit the peculiar port Llyra had asked about.

Reaching deeper into the recess, Sinclair removed a little plastic basket that stayed connected to the seatback by a lightweight bead chain.

"And here's the software!" he exclaimed. The basket offered three rows of brightly-colored plastic objects about the size of an old fashioned twenty-five cent piece. "You can be a Roman gladiator, a West American cowboy, a British seaman in the Napoleonic Wars, or any one of fifteen other things."

Llyra grinned. "How about a champion figure skater?"

"I'll talk to the manufacturer," Sinclair laughed, "as soon as we get home."

⁎

The changes came, as nearly as Llyra could remember afterward, at some point after the *Billie* had gradually accelerated to about one eighth of a standard Earth gravity, halfway between that of Ceres and the Moon. Both she and her coach had managed to endure a much greater amount of gravity than that, Jasmeen having grown up in the one third gravity of Mars, and her young student having tried out Lunar gravity for a few hours, at least, in the centrifuge aboard the *Beautiful Dreamer.*

This was different, somehow. Although, later, nobody was ever able to give her an explanation for it that satisfied her. One moment, she was wearing white denim bell-bottomed trousers, streaked with tar, and a striped sailor's T-shirt over her hairy chest. Her hands were large and callused. She was crouching in the fighting top of the *H.M.S. Victory* off the Cape of Trafalgar, on the Spanish coast, southeast of Cadiz.

It was about one o'clock, the afternoon of October 21, 1805.

With the long, heavy "Brown Bess" musket—a smoothbore military flintlock she'd just taken from the dead hands of a Royal Marine—she was trying to draw a bead on a French sniper high in the rigging of the nearby *Redoubtable*, one of Napoleon's combined French and Spanish fleet that had engaged the Royal Navy. The French sniper was about to snuff out the life of England's greatest hero, Admiral Lord Horatio Nelson.

Llyra's task was nearly impossible with the great warship rolling and pitching the way it was, even on these relatively calm coastal waters. The miniscule platform she occupied described a twenty-foot figure eight in the air over the main deck of the English flagship. In his gaudy uniform, bedecked with fresh ribbons and "stars of honor", Lord Nelson had gone to considerable pains to make himself conspicuous to his men. In real history, the French sharpshooter had made the shot successfully.

This era of Earth's history wasn't exactly famous for its light, crisp precision trigger-pulls, nor for the quality of the iron sights it mounted on its firearms. Llyra would no sooner center them on the sniper, holding onto on a similar platform above his own vessel, when something would move—her ship, his ship, the sniper, her musket—and she would have to realign the sights all over again. The sea air was cold and tasted salty, and she was not too high above *Victory's* vast main deck to avoid being sea-sprayed from time to time. It was uncomfortable and made her worry about the charge in the pan of her flintlock.

At last she had a good sight picture and squeezed the trigger. The flare from the flash pan nearly blinded her as she forced herself to "follow through", keeping the sights aligned even after the gun had gone off—highly necessary with these slow black powder ignition systems.

She felt no recoil, but heard the huge lead ball strike something meaty aboard the *Redoubtable*. The ships were nearly in collision. *Redoubtable*'s yards deeply overlapped those of the *Victory* and both vessels seemed to be wrapped in sheets of flame. She hoped it was the sniper she'd hit. As the smoke cleared before her eyes, she could see that the Frenchman was no longer where he had been. Nelson still stood on the quarterdeck, pointing across the gap between ships and issuing orders.

She'd done it—she had changed the course of history!

Stripping the VR mask from her face, Llyra suddenly noticed it was hard to breathe. She had a pain in the left side of her chest as if her heart were being crushed in a vise, and her left arm ached to the elbow.

"Jasmeen! Grandma!" Her voice was clear and strong, they told her afterward, but it didn't seem that way to her at the time. "I—I can't breathe!"

Llyra watched as Julie, rising in one swift, graceful motion from the single seat across the aisle, snapped a few words at Sinclair, who leaped from his own seat a few rows forward and hurried aft. Both of them crouched down beside Llyra. Something was happening with Jasmeen, too, but by now, Llyra couldn't turn her head or eyes to see what it was.

Sinclair stretched up to the overhead and struck a plastic panel with the heel of his hand. Llyra felt very cold and could see that her fingernails were purple, surrounded by gray skin. Sinclair shoved a plastic mask over her mouth and nose, then struck the panel above Jasmeen and started giving her oxygen, as well. Before very long, she sensed that her proper color was returning, but she was too weak to move.

"Wha—?"

"It's called gravitic shock, my dear" Sinclair told her, Julie was still kneeling on the aisle floor beside Llyra's chair. "Nobody knows a damn thing about it and there's never any predicting who'll get it and who won't—although it seldom proves fatal." He turned to Julie. "Both of these unfortunate young women have it, Miss Ngu a little bit worse than Miss Khalidov. It isn't common, but it isn't exactly rare, either. Most times, it wears off as they accustom themselves to higher gravity."

Julie nodded. "I had it, the first time I returned to Mars from Pallas."

In the row ahead of the two girls, and across the aisle, Llyra's brother Wilson, wearing earphones and a hushmike, and intent on his SolarNet communications, was completely unaware that anything unusual had happened.

*
**

" ... very careful, my dear Willie dear. As I told you, my father died in a conflict with rock pirates when I was only a three-year-old baby." Soft and beautiful as always, and agonizingly desirable, she fluttered her impossibly long eyelashes at him, straight into the pickup.

Yes, yes, Wilson thought, rereading the most recent communication that his SolarNet account had received from Amorie. Yes, she told me all about that, at least a dozen times before now. It must be a very strange experience, hard to live with in some way he couldn't imagine, growing up without a father. "My dear Willie dear" was new, however, and he hated it even worse than he did plain old Willie. If he married this lovely creature, would she be calling him her "dear Willie dear" forever?

But Amorie was going on. "Of course you have to understand that the pirates didn't kill him on purpose. They seem to have some strange code of honor about that. They broke off their attack, sent us their condolences, and left a hundred platinum ounces behind. They'll even punish their own over what they consider an unnecessary killing."

"I see the way of it," Wilson muttered disgustedly, momentarily forgetting that any reply he made to Amorie wouldn't reach her for at least an hour, and that he wasn't recording one, in any case. "They'll gleefully rob you at the point of a Gatling or a particle beamer, but they'll—"

"It was an accidental collision," she insisted, with her lower lip curled in a little pout. "As much my father's fault as anybody's, I guess. And it killed three or four of their company, as well. But dead is dead, whatever people intend. So the first thing my mother's elder brother, Uncle Anton did when he took command of our family ship was add a particle cannon, very efficient for carving up asteroids—or pirates."

As Amorie laughed at her own joke, Wilson did, too. Now, that's my kind of girl, the young man thought, soft, sweet, and terrifyingly ferocious.

At this particular moment, she and her asteroid-hunting family's vessel were further away from the Earth-Moon system, where he and his own family were headed aboard the Curringer Corporation's *William Wilde Curringer*, than he and his family were. Somewhere down near the orbit of Mercury, she'd told him. True, there were fewer profitable rocks down that far—hurricane-fierce solar winds would have swept most of the debris away at least three or four billion years ago—but what remained was brightly lit by the Sun in an enormous variety of radiomagnetic spectra, and was easy to detect in passive sensor mode.

"Running in passive mode can make the difference between life and death, sometimes," Amorie's newest message continued. "Most of the time in normal space, while you're preoccupied, trying to spend as little reaction mass as possible, patrolling for some halfway decent find, the rock pirates will just hang in orbit somewhere and listen for the active radar and lidar noise that discovery and rendezvous with an asteroid require. The returns get shorter and shorter. Once the sound and fury stops, they assume you've found your target, and that's their cue to swoop down, get the drop on you, and steal your find."

Normally, Wilson enjoyed this kind of talk with Amorie very much. She didn't shy away from all manner of dirtywork—and that included self-defense—when it needed doing. And she was the only girl he knew who conversed with him about the mechanical and economic theory of asteroid hunting, even if she wasn't much for practical details. But just now he wished she'd say something more personal to him.

After all, it might take days, even weeks or months to work their way back to the Moon. But he and Amorie were going to meet each other face-to-face eventually, and he very badly wanted to contemplate that moment, those hours, with her again, they way they had when he was on Ceres.

He paused Amorie's message to begin making a reply of his own. He'd have to remember that business about rock pirates—and particle cannons.

⁑

Billie's course had been plotted from the beginning to bring her into orbit of Earth's Moon with a minimum of dodging, backing, and filling to consume precious reaction-mass. There, at the appointed time and place, high over the crater-blasted black-and-white surface of the Moon, she made rendezvous with the strangest object in space that Llyra had ever seen, a long open framework of glittering metal, about the same length as the little spacecraft herself, and just large enough to propel her into.

Abruptly, *Billie*'s engines shut down, producing a silence more frightening, Llyra thought, than any loud noise she might have heard. For a blessed moment, all of the weight that had been crushing her was lifted, only to be replaced with the feeling that came when you hit a downdraft and your flying belt dropped you twenty feet in an instant. Only this instant seemed to last forever, as did the accompanying nausea.

When *Billie* was in the correct position, they could hear the thing lock itself into place on her hull with a series of terrifying bangs. Maybe she'd been wrong, she thought, about silence being more frightening.

The little corporate spacecraft had gone through its turnover some time earlier (Llyra couldn't remember it clearly) and had finished working its way up to the one-sixth gee of Earth's Moon. In spite of that, Llyra and Jasmeen were beginning to feel better and were holding hands for mutual comfort although they were still wearing their oxygen masks.

As soon as Wilson learned of the girls' predicament, he hurried back to their row in concern. There hadn't been much he could do to help them. In the end, he'd found them a website on the SolarNet that offered live webcam views of the most famous skating rink on the Moon. Unfortunately, there were hockey games being played on all six of its Olympic-sized ice sheets.

Now, Sinclair stood up in middle of the aisle again.

"Ladies and gentleman," he told them, "we've just acquired our wheels, as it were, and are about to make a runway landing on the Moon. Since turnover, we've been travelling backwards, decelerating with the help of *Billie*'s main engines. But the device we've just docked with will provide a very different kind of propulsion. You'll begin to feel yourself pressed gently into your seatbacks, while the screenfields on your seatbacks will show you exactly what *Billie*'s aft-facing cameras are seeing—the Lunar surface coming up to meet us, and our rapid journey down a two hundred-mile runway. At the Lunar terminal —"

"If you'll pardon the expression," Wilson suggested a bit sardonically.

Sinclair laughed. "Indeed, sir, 'if you'll pardon the expression'. But I was getting ahead of myself—which is a rather easy thing to do when you're travelling backwards at several thousand miles per hour."

Llyra and her companions laughed politely.

"This special frame we're riding in," Sinclair continued, "has a number of large wheels—fifty-six to be precise—along its sides. But it's the frame itself that's important. It consists of a battery of passive electrical coils that will interact magnetically with coils underneath the runway, slowing us down while keeping us close to the ground so the brakes on the wheels can eventually work. And should we fail for some reason to decelerate within the prescribed profile, a series of arresting cables will be raised across the runway to slow us."

"But the pilots," Ardith began. "How can they be expected to—" The notion of flying and landing the ship backwards always bothered her.

"Will be watching what they're doing using screenfields of their own. To them, as to you, it will appear as if we're all still moving forward."

"Induction braking?" Wilson asked. "What do you do with the excess heat?"

Sinclair nodded. "There isn't any excess heat, son, or we'd all disappear in a flash of vaporized metal and flesh. During our landing, all of the kinetic energy we shed will be converted directly into electricity."

"And the same hardware," Wilson said, "electrically launches a vessel when it leaves the Moon, using all of that stored energy from landings."

"Just so," Sinclair beamed at him. "The process is ninety percent efficient."

"Why don't we just land on our tail?" Wilson wanted to know. His computer held copies of every movie about space travel ever made, from the silent era until now. He was especially fond of those from the 1950s, when shiny spindle-shaped spaceships landed on huge triangular tailfins.

"Because the engineering to perform that single feat—not to mention the fuel required—would double *Billie*'s penalty weight. It's much cheaper and safer to use this electric orbiting/deorbiting cage."

Wilson grinned. "Victor Appleton would be so proud."

"The young scholar knows his classics!" said Sinclair.

Ever since the engine had shut down, *Billie* had been dropping toward the asteroid-shattered surface. From time to time, they heard the brief roar of smaller motors as she made minor course and attitude corrections.

"—But for all practical purposes," Sinclair explained, "we are falling, 'dead stick', as the aviation-johnnies have it, toward the ground."

"Excuse me," Jasmeen muttered, "if I say *yeek!*"

Wilson turned in his chair to look at her. "The trick," he said, "is that we're falling forward. The pilots are fighting right now to make sure we fall as parallel to the Moon's surface as we can. Long before the tires touch the runway, the induction coils will have us and start to slow us." He gave her an evil grin. "That's the plan, anyway."

"Even so," Sinclair added, "the wheels will touch at something close to three thousand miles per hour. Marvelous tires they make nowadays."

Outside, the Moon toward which they had been heading now became the surface over which they were travelling, a surface that could be seen to grow larger and closer with every heartbeat and blink of the eye. On their screenfields, the nose of the spacecraft seemed to come up gradually, as if she were an aircraft flaring before landing, and she suddenly began to shake violently, the noise of it becoming almost unbearable.

Now the whole structure of the vessel and the frame wrapped around it began to groan and shudder like a living organism being tortured. Through it all, instead of strapping himself back in, Sinclair calmly stood beside Wilson's chair, smiling benevolently aftward at Llyra and Jasmeen, then across the aisle to Ardith, and then back to the girls again. The harsh vibration and noise didn't seem to bother the man at all.

Through the actual port beside her, Llyra thought she could see the de-orbiting cage starting to glow with heat from the energy it was attempting to dissipate. Their conversion from kinetic to electrical energy, Sinclair had said, was only about ninety-eight percent efficient. Two percent of the energy they had to get rid of was no trifle. All systems, she knew, were imperfect and prone to failure sooner or later.

On the screen before her, they already seemed to be on the ground, a range of mountains ahead, rushing at insane speed to smash them. She looked over at Jasmeen and realized suddenly that she couldn't see clearly, because her head and eyes were being rattled around too much. Even worse, she couldn't hear anything but the terrible sounds of the spaceship coming apart around her—and what she hoped wasn't her own screaming.

There came a bump, then silence.

Sinclair said, "That's wheels down, dear friends! Welcome to the Moon!"

Llyra lost consciousness.

CHAPTER EIGHTEEN: HELPING HANDS

Economists tell us that the "price" of an object and its "value" have very little or nothing to do with one another. "Value" is entirely sub-jective—economic value, anyway—while "price" reflects whatever a buyer is willing to give up to get the object in question, and what-ever the seller is willing to accept to give it up. Both are governed by the Law of Marginal Utility, which is actually a law of psychology, rather than economics. For government to attempt to dictate a "fair price" betrays complete misunderstanding of the entire process. — *The Diaries of Rosalie Frazier Ngu*

"WELL, LADIES," SAID THE MEDICAL man. "Here's the way things stand."

Dr. "Wink" Jeffries sat in a swiveling desk chair in his office, which also served as his consulting room, one hand on the tidy green blotter on the desktop before him, the other on his knee. His hair and beard were closely trimmed. His casual shirt (nobody wore a necktie on the Moon) and dark slacks looked like they'd just been pressed.

A tall, solidly-built man, originally from Earth, Llyra guessed, and from various artifacts scattered around the room, an avid hockey player.

Llyra and Jasmeen sat comfortably, even if it happened to be in a pair of matching wheelchairs, on the opposite side of Jeffries' desk. Jasmeen's grandmother Julie sat between them in a more conventional chair. Jeffries appeared to be in his early thirties, but in this day and age—and at this facility in particular—looks could be deceiving. Julie herself was more than evidence enough of that. She appeared to be somewhere in her mid-twenties, but Llyra knew she was at last half a century older than that. Dr. Jeffries might be even older than Mr. Sinclair.

The fifth individual in the room had been introduced to them as "Bass" Williams, also a doctor, specializing in therapies devised for gravity-related illnesses. Williams was a big man, not nearly as tidy as Jeffries, but more comfortable, somehow, at least six feet six inches tall, Llyra estimated, broad-shouldered, with long blond hair tied up in a warrior's braid. He looked about the same age as Jeffries, she thought.

Jeffries had explained that he, himself, was a general practitioner, but that he was also Chief Administrator of the Emerson Ngu/Aubrey de Grey Life Extension Institute, a research facility originally endowed by Julie's famous father-in-law. This was the place that kept her looking so young, but apparently it had developed some other specialties, as well.

Williams spoke. His voice was deep, but smooth and soothing. "The gravitic shock you arrived with is a mysterious phenomenon, not well understood, even by us. It seems to affect about seven percent of the folks who come to the Moon. Fortunately, it's transient and it never recurs. Once you're over it, you're over it for good, which makes us think it may be viral in origin, although we've never found any single pathogen associated with it, nor any of the appropriate antibodies, either."

"And you've looked, I presume," Julie said.

"Yes, Mrs. Ngu, we've looked."

"In any case," Jeffries addressed Llyra and Jasmeen, "you both seem to have recovered very nicely after forty-eight hours of therapy and rest. Now I'm afraid you have a much steeper climb ahead of you: getting accustomed to three times the amount of gravity you're used to."

"But Doctor, I—" Jasmeen began. She leaned forward in her wheelchair.

He put up a hand. "Yes, Miss Khalidov, you were born and grew up on Mars, which has twice the gravity of the Moon. But you've spent the last—" He consulted the handheld before him. "The last three years on Pallas, which puts you in roughly the same boat as Miss Ngu, I regret."

"Somehow," Jasmeen protested, "that doesn't seem—"

"Fair?" Williams asked with raised eyebrows. His voice was gentle, but his words were not. "There's no such thing as fair, Miss Khalidov, certainly not in this universe. And as a Martian, you should be the last person I need to remind of that. There isn't even such a thing as linearity or proportion, where biology is concerned. Miss Ngu, here, might get her G-legs before you do, and you might never get them at all."

Llyra gulped. Jasmeen nodded gravely.

"However," Williams added, "the statistics are on your side. We've treated a good many cases similar to yours, if not exactly the same. Both of you must receive a battery of drug treatments, of course, to stimulate your bone and muscle growth. Your diet will be designed to support that effort. You'll both undergo extensive physical therapy before you can walk unassisted on the Moon. At best, you can expect to be outpatients at the Ngu/DeGrey Institute for between six months and a year."

Llyra gasped. "Six months to—"

"A year?" Jasmeen finished for her.

"It'll be an interesting experiment," Jeffries agreed. "Ironically enough, the course of therapy Dr. Williams plans to follow will be nearly identical to the one we prescribe for Moon dwellers visiting Earth."

Llyra glanced at her grandmother, who had volunteered to pay for all of this sure-to-be-expensive attention. Almost as if reading her granddaughter's mind, Julie reached over, placed a warm hand atop Llyra's, and squeezed. Then she gave Jasmeen an encouraging nod and a smile.

"And ice skating?" Llyra asked. "It's what this is about, after all."

Jeffries looked to his associate, who shrugged, then back at Llyra. "Anything like that is risky, of course—like practically anything else worthwhile." He raised a hand, drawing their attention to several photographs on the wall. In them, Llyra saw the doctor, accompanied by a pair of young girls about her own age. Some were obviously hunting pictures, of everything from grouse to grizzly bear. Llyra recognized an antique Ruger Number One single-shot rifle in Jeffries' hands; her father had one just like it, chambered for the immortal .375 Holland and Holland. Others were fishing pictures: huge salmon and strings of trout.

The settings looked familiar, somehow.

"Yes, these were all taken on Pallas, your homeworld, Miss Ngu. The place is a sportsman's paradise. Those are my daughters, Fae and Rae. They're willing to accept the risks of hunting for the various pleasures it offers. You should go ahead, I think, and do whatever ice skating you can, as you can. You'll become more capable every day, and relearning everything you know that way will ultimately be good for your art. I'm sure Miss Khalidov will help you stay safe and healthy."

Jasmeen nodded. "Was my job before we are ever coming to Moon."

"Will you do me a personal favor, Miss Khalidov?" Williams asked abruptly.

Jasmeen blinked, and answered, "Almost certainly, doctor. What is favor?"

He grinned, "Please say 'moose and squirrel', just once."

"Okay, moose and squirrel—what is so funny about moose and squirrel?"

Williams and Jeffries were laughing uncontrollably. Julie rolled her eyes. "It's a joke a century and a half old, Jasmeen, dear. Don't take it personally. They do the same thing to every Russian who comes in here."

Jasmeen frowned. "But I am not—"

"I know. You're Chechen. And they take turns being Fronkensteen and Eye-gor. But they're good doctors, judging from the bills they send me."

Llyra sighed. This was going to be a very long year.

✳

Wilson had overheard somebody back at the ACC spaceport call it a "pukemobile".

It was a downsystem version of the jumpbuggy, considerably more luxurious than he was accustomed to, electrically launched from the Lunar surface to save reaction mass, capable of reaching Lunar orbit and beyond, to Lagrange Points One, Two, Four and Five. Point Three, about 186 million miles away on the other side of the Sun, was well beyond the little ship's range, mostly for reasons having to do with life-support.

This was largely an excursion vessel. It didn't even have a name, just a number, its pilot a young college girl home for "summer" vacation. On a world without seasons, summer could be whenever you needed it to be.

Several dozen passengers sat in folding seats with their backs to the cylindrical wall of the ship. They could see out through windows over the heads of the passengers opposite them. At the moment, there wasn't much to see. They were breaking orbit and the Moon was behind them, the Earth out of sight—the spaceport boasted a spectacular "Earth-viewing" room on one of its concourses, but Wilson hadn't bothered with it—and their destination was still too small to be seen.

Stars are what Wilson saw, instead. Some of them may have been planets or even asteroids.

In the seat to his right sat his grandmother, the men aboard the ship giving her the eye, as always. She ignored it and went on reading

151

something out of her pocket computer. Wilson was tempted to hold her hand and really give the other guys something to think about. But he couldn't do it. All adults are supposed to be the same age, but she was his grandma. She'd burped him and changed his diaper too many times.

As the little craft drew closer to its destination, Wilson learned why it was called a pukemobile. He'd been enjoying the relief from the Moon's one-sixth gravity. But as the craft's pilot made adjustments to its course and speed, interspersed with longer or shorter periods of coasting at zero gee, some of the passengers became uncomfortable, and one of them pitched his breakfast at the deckplates in front of him. The odor of half-digested bacon and maple syrup was unmistakable and revolting.

Another passenger became violently sick, probably from the smell, and then another. A damned good thing, Wilson thought, that the deck was perforated like a colander and made of stainless steel. There seemed to be a light, constant air suction through the deckplates, as well.

Through it all, Wilson easily retained control of himself. It wasn't motion or the lack of gravity that threatened to get to him, anyway, but the noxious smell, and that went away as the self-cleaning deckplates—the floor was darkened for a few seconds by millions of not-quite-microscopic nanobots—and the ventilation system went to work.

Obviously, they were prepared for this sort of thing.

Outside, an enormous object of indistinct shape loomed toward them overhead, casting its shadow across them. It looked like someone had started with a core—maybe a used booster or a fuel tank—and then built onto it, bit by bit, adding whatever they felt was necessary at the time. Come back next year, the whole thing would look altogether different.

The little ship gave a last, dizzying tumble and there was a loud clank as its airlock fastened itself to someone else's airlock. Wilson noticed they were in freefall. After a few more thumps and clanks, a heavy trapdoor in the floor swung upward and a young man popped his head through the opening, looked around, sniffed, and wrinkled his nose.

"Geez, Clarice." he shouted forward to the pilot. "That's gotta be at least three, maybe four spews this time. You gotta go easier with the lead foot."

Wilson wished somebody would throw up on him.

※

It was a field of rubble, only a few hundred feet thick from top to bottom, but floating in that plane of space as far as the eye could see in any direction, each and every particle of it artificial, man-made, and man-abandoned, replaced by what would someday be better rubble.

At an average distance from each other of a hundred yards, Wilson saw a couple of old NASA shuttles and several ancient Soyuz craft from a time before Earth governments finally gave up on interplanetary enterprise and abandoned it to the private sector. Julie pointed out half a dozen Rutan spaceships of various vintages, and, in a forlorn corner by itself, for some inexplicable reason, a 1936 Ford pickup truck.

The premises, fenced off by radar and laser beams, belonged to the Guzman Brothers' Used Spacecraft Emporium, the longest-established private business here at Lagrange Point Four. Their pilot had docked and let them off at what was known as L4 Little America, a combination fuel station, rest stop, and hotel that offered showers and long range communications to what they called "travelers and truckers", as well as outfitters, shops, restaurants, several theaters, and a gambling casino.

The Guzman Brothers' headquarters turned out to be an enormous inflated doughnut-shape, perhaps a quarter mile in diameter, at the end of a long, pressurized, cable trolley ride into the middle of an endless expanse of scrap metal and broken dreams. On their arrival, Wilson and Julie were ushered inside by its proprietor, Lafcadio Guzman.

"Welcome, friends! Welcome to Guzman Brothers! What may I show— Julie? Julie Segovia? Julie Segovia Ngu? My day is made! My whole week! What brings you to this dusty and forgotten corner of the Solar System?"

Julie smiled and let Wilson describe his needs while Lafcadio pretended to make notes. What the guy really wanted, thought Wilson, was simply to stare at his grandmother. He was a big man from the waist up, with a gigantic belly and a prodigious beak of a nose. A ring of curly gray hair above his ears encircled a shiny dome of a head.

On the way here, Julie had explained to Wilson that she'd known Lafcadio for most of their lives. He didn't have a brother, but came originally from a long line of antique furniture dealers in her own native Newark, New Jersey—which was a wonderful place to be *from*, she'd always told her children and grandchildren—and that, since coming here to Lagrange Point Four, he'd never entered a gravity field again.

The way his tiny legs hung beneath his body, Wilson could easily believe the stories. He never seemed to stand or sit, just hover in mid-air, thinking up deals and making keystrokes with his handheld computer.

The salesbot wafted a hand grandly. "Here y'go young feller," it said in Lafcadio Guzman's voice "A mere three hundred forty platinum. Just for you and your lovely grandmother, I'll throw in a square klick chainlink."

The ship floated above them, a short, fat cylinder that came to a rounded point at the bow, which was made, almost entirely, of windows. It was pretty, freshly painted to all appearances, and sported three manipulation arms longer than itself on the portside, starboard, and along the top of the ship. They were folded aftward just now, and stuck out a little beyond the quadruple fusion burners. Beneath the ship was fastened the "toolbox", containing everything necessary to seize and manipulate small asteroids, and prepare them for shipment to a factory vessel or processing site.

One of these tools, common chainlink fencing, was used to maintain control over loose aggregates of rock. It wasn't all that expensive, Wilson knew, and a square kilometer of the stuff wasn't enough to cover any profitable find. He looked to his grandmother, who shook her head.

"Cotton candy," she told him and the salesbot, "meant for wealthy tourists who want to play at asteroid hunting—play and nothing more, looking for the Lost Cambodian or the Diamond Rogue. This tin can wouldn't last a dozen real hunting trips. Let's look at something else."

The robot couldn't look dejected. Its smile was painted on, along with its red pants, white belt and shoes, buttoned-down pinstriped shirt, and an antique tie that matched its pants. It wore painted suspenders, and a pencil was tucked behind its artificial ear. Why people picked the mid-twentieth century to represent the epitome of salesmanship, Wilson didn't know. It was like some restaurants he'd encountered on the Moon, whose employees affected eighteenth century attire. There were several, and all of them claimed to offer French cuisine.

"Look out!" he shouted reflexively, as another machine, identical to the one the three of them occupied, equipped with its own salesbot, flashed past them, heading straight for the pretty red airlock of the pretty red and white vessel. Wilson bet that it was pretty inside, too.

At the moment, they were riding in a "sky-raft", a saucer-shaped platform covered with something like a very large Bell jar. They both stood, their feet slid into in stirrups, holding onto a chest-high circular rail, and looking out and up, as the tiny craft was guided by the real salesman, Lafcadio Guzman, who had safely remained back in his office, looking out through the salesbot's big blue eyes, and giving them his pitch through its speakers. He'd explained that this was his busy season, and he could assist several groups of customers this way, which reduced his overhead, and therefore the price of his goods.

Yeah, right, thought Wilson.

Another silly-looking sky-raft buzzed by them, full of young kids in dark pants, white shirts, and blue, star-spangled neckerchiefs that identified them as Space Scouts. A mechanical salesman identical to this one was with them. They were probably looking for a rental for a camping trip. It reminded Wilson that the craft were self-guided to a high degree. No matter what they were remotely commanded to do, they wouldn't hit each other or approach other objects here at a velocity that could damage them or their passengers.

"And what, may I ask, is that?" Julie pointed to a floating object approximately the size of a small house, roughly spherical, very dark in color, with large projections all over its surface in the shape of rectangular solids: hexagons, cylinders, pyramids, even a piece that appeared threaded like a giant screw. The whole thing looked like a big steel weldment—perhaps a work of abstract art—covered with rust and hardened mud.

"Oh, *that*. It's a damned Drake-Tealy Object. The biggest in the system, in fact." Even through the medium of the salesbot, Lafcadio seemed almost embarrassed by what should be considered a spectacular possession.

"Biggest by a substantial margin, if it's true," she replied. "I don't think anybody's ever seen a Drake-Tealy object larger than your fist."

"It's all the same material," the proprietor sounded almost as if he were in tears. "The same spectral signature, the same ratio of isotopes, the same age, every damn thing the same as the little ones. Only nobody believes it, no university, no museum, even after they've conducted their own inspection. I think they just don't wanna believe it."

"Like they didn't want to believe in Drake-Tealy objects at all in the first place," Wilson suggested. "Until my great grandmother Rosalie—"

"I know the story, son," Lafcadio interrupted. "Knew your great grandmother—Julie's mother-in-law—too. She was a very great lady. What hurts is what I paid for it, to a miner who dragged it back from the orbit of Pluto. I thought it was worth at least a thousand platinum."

"How about that little ship right over there, Lafcadio?" Julie asked the salesbot, apparently changing the subject. "The little rock hunter you've got tucked in between those two nasty old kerogen processors?"

"Er ... " the salesbot replied, after considerable thought, adding, "Uhhh ... "

"Didn't want us to see her, did you? She does need a lot of work, which you were planning to do yourself so you could triple the price afterward?"

"Quadruple," the robot replied sulkily. "Damn it, Julie Ngu, I don't know why I always let you do this to me, every single damn time. Yeah, you're right. I'd planned to fix her up, myself, but what the hell. You want to look her over? She's older'n the hills and twice as dusty."

Julie laughed. "Save the countrified observations, Lafcadio. We're both from the same block of Darkest Newark, learned the way of the bombed-out parking lot forest, bathed in the River of the Hydrant and Lake Stormgutter. And do show us the little ship over there, if you please."

Nobody would have accused her of looking like much, Julie thought. Whatever colors she'd originally been painted, she was now a patchwork of matte metallic grays, browns, and reds the color of dried blood. Relentless decades of exposure to micrometeorite bombardment had given her an eggshell finish, the patina of neglect. Even her windows were frosted.

Julie calculated that the little ship was about the same age she was.

In shape, she had about the same proportions as an old-fashioned pistol cartridge—say, .45 Automatic Colt Pistol. About two thirds of that, the cylindrical cartridge case behind the bullet, consisted of engines. There were three of these, ancient and enormous catalytic fusion burners that, even at rest, appeared to be bulging with power. Each of the engines was tucked neatly into its own deep recess along the hull, although, as their sky-raft swung around the little vessel, they inspected heavy machinery built into the stern that could extend each engine outward several meters, providing extra leverage in the turns.

Engines very much like these had brought people to Pallas three generations ago.

As they approached the bullet-shaped bow, mostly constructed of once-transparent materials, they saw two manipulation arms, of which there were two, folded back in long grooves between engines. Along the underside, or "chin" of the command section, lay the "toolbox" containing various lasers, masers, and chainlink dispensers. This was where Wilson would put his particle cannon—if he could ever afford one.

"It's an old General Systems Procyon, isn't it?" Julie asked the salesbot in sudden recognition. "About a Mark IV, I'd guess. She's been modified so much she's almost unrecognizable." Julie noted with approval that all of the vessel's antennae, reception and transmission dishes, passive and active sensors, even handholds, had been mounted flush with the surface, an absolute necessity in denser areas of the Belt.

"An oldie but a goodie," the salesbot replied. "The DC-3 of space, in her time!"

Lafcadio's alter ego indicated the little ship's finer points. She had what long-haul hunters called a "coffee grinder", for example, to convert otherwise worthless bits of rock (as well as valuable ones in an emergency) to reaction mass. The ship's manipulation arms could be rigged and charged to sweep spaceborne particles (one or two per cubic meter) into the engines, supplementing whatever reaction mass she carried.

The main airlock, appropriately enough, was on the portside of the ship. The sky-raft gave a nauseating little flip to match the docking machinery on its underside with the asteroid hunter's. The handrail became a footrail as Wilson and Julie climbed up into the larger craft. The salesbot's head separated from its torso and followed its customers on puffs of air.

The pilot's seat was a flimsy, skeletal affair sitting on the end of a gracefully curved beam in the nose of the ship, surrounded on all sides but the back by glass. Wilson saw right away that the comm system needed updating. It consisted of nothing but audio and typo—no real video—and the sensor readouts were all flatscreens, limited to 2D. How they'd found and captured rocks with this stuff he couldn't guess.

On the other hand, there were two big bunks aft of the control area, a dining table, and excellent sanitary facilities, including a shower that drew water from carbonaceous chondrites processed in the coffee grinder. Although the mechanical life support systems were more than adequate, the high circular wall of the living area was an airponics garden, at present brown and brittle, that modified and moisturized the air, and offered the hunter welcome items like big, red, beefsteak tomatoes.

There was also a closet-sized gymnasium with good, if very old equipment.

"I'm going to call her *Mighty Mouse's Girlfriend*," Wilson declared.

"What?" Julie blinked. It was as if the boy just come to life, she thought. She knew that look, all too well. It was a good thing. A very good thing. This little vessel wasn't the Ball 500 Asteroid Scout she knew her grandson had dreamed of owning, or the Mitsubishi Rockhound 9000L he often talked about. But somewhere in the last five minutes, he'd stopped seeing this ancient, beat-up workhorse as she was, and had begun seeing her as he would make her. Her late husband Billy used to have that look a lot, maybe even once or twice—given her rough start on the mean New Jersey streets—about her. "Why not just call her Minnie?"

"Not Mickey Mouse's girlfriend, Grandma, *Mighty* Mouse's girlfriend. I don't know what her name was. I don't know if she even had a name. But he rescued her from being sacrificed to a volcano god one time. When I was little, I thought she was the cutest, sexiest thing I ever saw. I especially liked the way her little ears stuck out through her hair. I've tended to rate girls on a 'Mighty Mouse's Girlfriend Scale" ever since."

Now that explains a lot, Julie thought, remembering the holograms he'd shown her of Amorie Samson. That one probably rated a Ten—maybe even an Eleven or a Twelve—on the Mighty Mouse's Girlfriend Scale.

CHAPTER NINETEEN: STARTING OVER

I WAS SIXTEEN WHEN MY great aunt, Mary-Lou Altman Frazier—the woman who had raised me as her daughter—had a stroke and ended up in a nursing home. Her husband was long dead and all she had was me. All around her in that place, people were giving up and dying, but she wouldn't. Whenever she couldn't get them to put her in a wheelchair, she got out of bed and crawled, rather than be left helplessly dependent on others. In the end, she recovered nearly completely, It taught me a lesson I've never forgotten: *anything* is better than helplessness. —*The Diaries of Rosalie Frazier Ngu*

"Was that seven rotations, or eight?" Llyra asked in admiration—although back home she could have eventually worked up to twice that number.

Here on Earth's Moon, it was a very different matter altogether. Bad enough that her legs ached and trembled from hip to ankle at the end of every day, she thought. It was even worse to begin the day that way, as she had done each and every morning since first coming to this place. Her legs had ached and trembled when she woke up, they'd ached and trembled all through this morning's therapy session, they'd ached and trembled all the way over here, and they ached and trembled right now.

Probably thinking many of the same thoughts, Jasmeen answered somewhat abstractedly, "Was not counting, my little. Whoever she is, she is good skater. Will count next time."

Eyes on the half dozen figures out on the ice, Llyra nodded. She'd been paying most attention to the landings, and to what was happening with her own body. Her back hurt, too, and her shoulders and arms. It seemed like months, but they'd been on the Moon less than a week. She thought Jasmeen was starting to recover, maybe because she'd been born and brought up in twice this much gravity. At least she was spending more time standing up, and once or twice had even crossed the living room of the little apartment they shared without one of the magnesium alloy walkers they were using these days to get around and see the sights.

"Me, too," Llyra said. She wondered how these skaters, with their Lunar muscles, would fare on Ceres or Pallas. Probably land on their heads.

The sight they both wanted to see most was the sight they were seeing now and had longed to see every day until they'd been cleared to travel by themselves. They were visiting the Robert A. and Virginia Heinlein Memorial Ice Arena in a suburb of Armstrong, the principal city on the Moon—or "in the Moon", as the natives insisted putting it, and with justice, since its main streets lay several hundred feet beneath that world's surface, far from its heat, cold, radiation, and micrometeorites.

Heinlein had foreseen that. He was regarded here as one the great writers of the twentieth century, an early advocate of space travel and settling other worlds, a prophet. Julie had told them that there might never have been cities in the Moon—or much of anywhere else except for Earth—if he hadn't lived. Most of what he'd written—especially about the Moon—had come true, and what he'd written about settling the moons of the gas giants had come true in the Asteroid Belt. He'd even predicted that someday people—like Julie, for instance—would be virtually immortal, although he'd thought the answer lay in selectively breeding people like hothouse plants, instead of in techniques like the various DeGrey therapies. When he'd first written on the subject, DNA hadn't yet been discovered.

Heinlein and his wife had also been ice dancers where they lived in West America, another reason this cavernous facility bore their name. The space it occupied was artificial, according to a brochure Llyra still clutched, forgotten, in her hand, created by setting off some sort of thermal explosive in a hole drilled deep under the Moon's surface. The walls of the cavern were fused into glass two feet thick, and the remainder of the vaporized rock had been allowed to vent into space.

"Look at that!" Llyra exclaimed. "An octuple Axel!" An Axel was a turn and half, which meant they had just seen a jump of twelve whole turns.

At the moment, she and Jasmeen leaned on their walkers, observing (not without envy) a "contract" session through the thick, heavy plastic transparencies around the rink, one of six at this facility. This was time that individual skaters had paid for in advance, so they could practice what they'd learned in their formal lessons—with a guarantee that there would never be more than a certain number of them on the ice at any given time. The skaters (mostly girls, just as it was everywhere else) were doing fabulous things: waltz jumps that covered half the rink, and ten-turn Salchows that carried them seventy feet into the air.

The rinks were laid out in two rows of three, separated by ranks of bleachers. Bleachers also ran around the perimeter of the facility. There were plans, the brochure said, to add another row of three rinks.

Exactly the same signs were hanging here that hung in the Brody Memorial rink at home: no stick-and-puck games off ice, no hanging from the overhead netting. And, just the way it was back home, the walls everywhere in the facility were covered with black neoprene marks.

Abruptly, Llyra overheard a sort of stage whisper behind her back, in the narrow aisle between the boards—the walls of the rink—and the foot of the bleachers. "Why are those *cripples* hanging around here?" The rubber carpeting had kept her from hearing their approach, but Llyra didn't need to turn to see who was behind her, ostensibly headed for one of the girls' locker rooms under the bleachers. Their images were reflected in the transparent plastic in front of her face, almost as well as if it were a mirror. In any case, she'd seen these four young women huddled together in the lobby when she and Jasmeen had arrived. What she didn't know was that they were a type that could be found at almost any rink. They were burdened with their coats, purses, skate bags, school books, and an attitude she thought could have used some adjustment.

"Shhh!" another of the girls insisted. "I heard at the desk that one of them is an Intermediate—or was it a Novice?—and the other is her coach." That was the black girl speaking, Llyra was certain, with an English accent. One of the girls was Asian, and the other two were white, a tall blond and a redhead. Llyra was fairly certain the one who had spoken first was the redhead, skinny, covered in freckles, and with a small pointy nose and chin like a Japanese cartoon girl. They all wore the ponytail, tightly pulled back, that came close to being the uniform of figure skaters everywhere.

"I heard that, too," said another of the girls, the Asian, Llyra thought. "I heard they're from the Outer Worlds, somewhere. Maybe the Asteroid Belt or even the moons of Jupiter. Somebody said something about the Martian Figure Skating Association. I was never any good at geography." They kept walking to their locker room, but Llyra could still hear them. This place served a second purpose, as an emergency air storage facility—another Heinlein prediction come true. The air pressure was about twice what was normal in the rest of Armstrong, and sound carried.

"Not geography, dummy," The blond observed. She was tall and gangly, with angled features people sometimes refer to as "hatchet- faced". "Planetography. The coach's certification is Martian, all right, but she's also registered with the SFSU. Say that ten times fast!"

"Yeah, and you can tell which one she is by the way she stands—even in a walker." That was the redhead again. "I can recognize a born trouble-maker when I see one! Who does she think she is, the colonial trash!"

The blond snorted. "Just because your father's the East American ambassador—"

"Ambassador of the United States of America—all sixty-five of them!"

"Whatever. Look, Janna Kolditz, you're new out here. Maybe back where you come from, everything and everyone belongs to the government and people slink along the street with their heads down, like whipped dogs."

"Why, I—!"

"Out here, in Free Space, in the Moon, way out in the Asteroids, everybody holds himself up proudly and walks like a free individual—especially the Martians, who had to win their independence the hard way, if you'll recall your history. They belong to themselves, Janna, they believe in themselves. That's what you're seeing that you don't like."

The Asian girl added, "Danita is right. My parents were refugees from East America, you know. My guess is that these two are trying to get used to our Lunar gravity, like we'd have to do on Earth. I don't envy them a bit, either. It must hurt all the time, even in their sleep."

"Well I don't care who or what they are, Kelly Tran. Or what their problems happen to be," the redhead sniffed. "My father would know what to do with them back home, and they'd just better stay out of my way!"

The redheaded girl reached the end of the bleachers, pushed her way through the locker room door, and disappeared. The other girls followed her. Llyra gave Jasmeen a look of exasperated disbelief. The Martian atmosphere is thin, and Martians have excellent hearing as a result. Jasmeen had heard the whole thing, too, and shook her head in agreement. "I thought all that political stuff was settled long ago," Llyra said.

Jasmeen said, "Politics is *never* settled."

**⁕

"Okay, folks, tellya what I'm gonna do ... " Lafcadio Guzman leaned back behind his desk and clasped his large hands, fingers interlaced, over his ample abdomen. It would have been a more effective posture, Wilson thought to himself, if the used spaceship salesman had been sitting on a reclining swivel chair, instead of the same thin air that he and his grandmother were sitting on. "Three hundred platinum for the ship," Guzman suddenly looked serious. He was more impressive when his shriveled legs were hidden by his desk. "I'll pay for half the repairs and refitting, up to another fifty."

He'd nodded politely at Wilson before stating his proposition, but it was Wilson's grandmother he was actually bargaining with, and all three of them knew it. Now, giving her some time to think his offer over, Lafcadio took a heroic gulp from a baggie of steaming, heavily creamed coffee that floated within easy reach, tethered near his right elbow. In the sudden quiet, Wilson took a sip from his own baggie. He had always been partial to mocha. He was glad that he had Julie with him. He felt a little disoriented by the conditions here. For a moment he'd considered asking the man to turn on the gravity. When they'd first come in, he'd noticed huge metal pivots on which this part of the building was hung. The room was basically cylindrical, and seemed to be designed to use the circumferential wall as a floor. But aside from this desk, with its steel top and magnetic paperweights, and assorted business machinery scattered here and there, there didn't seem to be any furniture. The man's disability might be why he preferred freefall. Also, the room had been turned (no coincidence there, Wilson knew) so he could look at the little asteroid hunter as they bargained over her. It would have been an effective tactic if his grandmother weren't here.

"Two hundred," Julie answered her old friend matter-of-factly. "And you'll pay for all necessary repairs, no limit, until the ship passes a reputable insurer's inspection. If you do the work yourself, which I'm pretty certain you planned to all along, Wilson can help you out."

"What's this?" Guzman's eyes widened dramatically, and he swore briefly in what Wilson assumed was Puerto Rican Spanish. He waved his arms around, which set him drifting off at an angle. "A measly two hundred, and you would have me tutor this untried boy for nothing? Why do you always do this to me, Julie Segovia? How am I supposed to make any money out of the deal? What are my poor children supposed to live on?"

Lafcadio had precessed until the back of his head was toward them and he had to flail around and pull on the coffee tether anchored to his desk to face them once again. It was very funny, Wilson thought, but all of this harsh talk between old friends disturbed him—until he observed that both the salesman and his grandmother seemed to be enjoying the process immensely. It had to be a New Jersey thing, he concluded.

Julie laughed, "You don't have any children, Lafcadio. I know your wife from the last Ganymede venture, remember? You keep Jack Russell terriers."

"They seem to flourish," the man admitted sheepishly, "in zero gravity." "And this 'boy', here is hardly untried. Think back to when you were seventeen, Lafcadio, back on the street in Newark. Were you a boy then or a man? He had a man's job on the Ceres Terraformation Project, where he did for seven ecoterrorists singlehandedly, and captured the other five. That's why he's here; the Curringer Corporation gave him a reward."

Lafcadio raised both of his hands, palms turned up and outward, in apparent anguish. "I know, Julie Ngu. I saw the whole thing on 3DTV. Still—"

"Still," she told him, "you'll end up making quite a tidy profit, my old friend, because when I get back to my apartment in Armstrong tonight, I'll persuade the museum in Curringer—I'm on the board of directors— to take that mysterious white elephant of yours off your hands at a fair price, and cart it away to orbit Pallas. They'll end up running two excursions a day and three on Saturdays and Sundays. I'll even see that you're mentioned as a contributor, with a big bronze plaque and everything."

A look of astonishment and delight wrote itself briefly across the ship-trader's features until he caught himself and erased it with the best poker face he had. "How much do you think they'll pay?" he asked, trying to look shrewd. Will they spell my name right? One Z, and one N?"

Julie laughed. "They'll spell your name right, Lafcadio, I'll see to it myself. And we'll repeat everything in Chinese ideograms. As to their price, well, I shouldn't say it, but I happen to agree with you that it's a genuine Drake-Tealy Object, absolutely the largest ever found. It could be important, and it begs for proper examination. I wish my mother-in-law could have seen it. Anyway, it's priceless and unique, certainly worth at least five to ten times what you paid for it."

"Five to ten times ... " Lafcadio leaned forward and had to stop himself on the desk to keep from tumbling. "Then you got yourself a deal." He turned at last to Wilson. "Good luck, kid—pardon, not-a-kid. You got yourself a ride. Your grandma is a bargainer. And I, Lafcadio Guzman himself, hope that you catch a rhodium nugget the size of your head, or maybe the Diamond Rogue."

It was theoretically possible, but unlikely. Still, it was a very nice wish—for everybody but DeBeers, Ltd. Wilson accepted it with thanks.

Julie raised her baggie. "To *Mighty Mouse's Girlfriend*!"

"To *Mighty Mouse's Girlfriend*." Wilson answered.

"Mighty Mouse's Girlfriend?" Lafcadio said. "Why not just call her Minnie?"

Llyra shook her head—and nearly lost her balance. It was difficult to decide which was more humiliating, what she was doing at this minute, shuffling along across the ice like an old lady behind a trainer—a sort of icegoing walker made of lightweight metal tubing—or what she'd gone through earlier in the rink office suite.

"Welcome to the Heinlein," the woman with the frizzy red hair had told them. She was probably about her mother's age, Llyra thought, but like most people born and raised away from Earth's gravity—like her own mother, in fact—she looked younger. Virtual letters neatly painted on the virtual glass set in her virtual office door had read, "Armstrong/ Heinlein Representative, Lunar Figure Skating Association". The door had vanished when they'd started to knock. Jasmeen, who knew about such things, had explained that if they were going to buy contract ice time for the foreseeable future, it would be best to be affiliated with the local figure skating club.

One entire wall of the woman's office was transparent, and looked down on the rink area, two hundred feet or more below. The view was breathtaking—and dizzying. The woman led them from the door—back in place again, Llyra noticed—to a pair of chairs in front of her desk. Politely turning her back while they made an awkward transfer from their walkers, she went around the desk to seat herself behind it. "I'm Shirlene Hofstaedter, local representative of the Lunar Figure Skating Association. And what can I do for you ladies this afternoon?"

Llyra's coach leaned forward in her chair. "I am Jasmeen Khalidov, instructor certified with Martian Figure Skating Association and Solar Figure Skating Union. Home club is small, only fifty members so far, but growing."

The woman nodded and smiled. "Then everybody knows everybody else in your home club. That must be nice. I'm afraid we have over thirty thousand LFSA members. Figure skating is a very popular sport in the Moon."

"Hockey, too," Jasmeen observed, gazing through the windows for a moment down onto the ice. She and Llyra had stayed down in the rink area gawking for an hour before coming up here. "You do have very beautiful facility here. Six rinks under one roof. Is flabbergasting spectacle." The woman smiled again, but didn't laugh at Jasmeen's choice of words. "Why, thank you, my dear. We're building three more ice sheets on the far side of those you see. But wait until we've finished with our surface facility. Unlike our other sheets, it'll be up there in the sunshine and starlight, under a dome." She punched a few buttons on the virtual keyboard showing on her desktop. "Here you are, all right, Khalidov, Jasmeen Mohammedova, Adult Gold, Certified SFSU Instructor. Let's get your student signed up, shall we? Your name, dear?"

For some reason, she felt nervous. "Llyra Ayn Ngu—two Ls, one Y."

"You don't say. What a pretty name, Llyra. It is Welsh? No? Ayn must be A Y N, like the novelist. How do you spell your last name, dear?"

Llyra told her. It was extremely strange not to hear her last name recognized. It was the first time in Llrya's life that it had ever happened. "And you are from—not Mars?"

"Not Mars. Curringer, on Pallas." "Curringer, on Pallas. That's an asteroid, I know that much." The woman had been making quick-fingered notes on the virtual keyboard in her desktop. "Very well, dear. And what would you say is your best jump?"

"My best jump … " She glanced over at Jasmeen, who gave her an encouraging smile, but otherwise said nothing. "Well, my Salchow, I guess."

"Salchow," the woman tapped it all down. "And how many turns—documented?"

Llyra blinked. "Well, Jasmeen has movies. Best I've ever done is nineteen."

It was the woman's turn to blink. "Nineteen turns. And you landed it?"

Llyra grinned at the memory and saw Jasmeen do the same. It had been a good day, Llyra's twelfth birthday. "Yes, I landed it—that time."

The woman stopped typing and looked up her. "And how many here?"

"Here? None, now. I haven't even skated here, yet." She pointed a thumb to the walker standing beside her chair. "Here, I can hardly stand."

The woman made more notes on her desktop. "Do you think you can you manage a waltz jump? No? Then how about a bunny hop? Not even swizzles?"

Llyra shook her head slowly, feeling ashamed, although she knew she had no reason to be. In one of those unMartian gestures she was given to, Jasmeen reached across the space between their chairs and took her hand.

"I'm sorry," said the woman. "I'm going to have to put you down as a Beginner One." She sighed. "I guess you'd better have this, too—rink rules."

She reached back toward a stack of bright fabric piled on a shelf behind her desk, and handed Llyra a small vest made of interplanetary safety-orange mesh. Stenciled across the back, in fluorescent lime green, were two words:

BEGINNER ONE

The woman said, "Wear this at all times when you're out on the ice. I'll get one of our rink guards to find you an adult trainer frame."

"Please," Jasmeen asked, "to give me Beginner One vest and trainer also."

✳

Wilson was buried in antiquated wiring when he heard the airlock cycle. Twisting his torso and craning his neck, he saw his grandmother skim through the inner door, fly to the opposite wall of the ship, and seize a handhold with one hand. In her other, she held a large mesh bag.

"Good morning, Captain my Captain!" Julie had taken to calling him that ever since they'd signed the papers transferring ownership of *Mighty Mouse's Girlfriend* from the Guzman Brothers (Lafcadio Guzman, Prop.) to the partnership of Wilson and Julie Ngu. He didn't know if he liked it or not. Maybe he'd feel better about being called captain once he'd finished the classes on shiphandling he'd signed up for as a condition—one of several conditions—she'd insisted on before becoming his partner.

In the course of acquiring a spaceship, Wilson had discovered, to his dismay, that, even with the bargaining Julie had done for him, he didn't have enough money for operating expenses, port fees, initial reaction mass, provisions, and so on. Julie had offered to become his partner and "grubstake" him. But first, he had to take shiphandling lessons.

Wilson had agreed.

"Look," she exclaimed now, laughing and holding up the mesh bag. "I've brought you a shrubbery! And you didn't even have to say, 'Niii!'"

Shaking his head, he squirmed out of the utility access niche, gave a little tap of his foot, and floated toward her. He'd meant to start replacing the vegetation that had once carpeted the cylindrical walls of the ship. It was just one of those things he hadn't gotten to yet.

It was weird, sometimes, having Julie for a grandmother. Filled to the brim with energy and enthusiasm, she looked about a quarter of her genuine age. He was glad they weren't on Pallas, where he'd have to explain her to his friends before they embarrassed themselves. Then again, maybe she wouldn't want him to explain. Now there was a sobering thought.

Still, Julie was a pioneer. These were circumstances the human race in general was going to have to get used to. He certainly didn't intend to get old and die, himself. Which meant, with any luck, that he'd look nineteen when he was ninety. (He'd heard that there were sects on Earth that forbade life extension therapy to their members as evil and unnatural.) Nor did he want old age to happen to anyone he loved. If they lived long enough—say a thousand years—maybe his parents could finally work things out.

Wilson had always liked freefall. Alighting gracefully beside her on the wall just aft of the pilot's canopy, he asked, "Why would I say 'knee'?"

"No, it's 'Niii!' It's from an old movie. I brought you this, too."

She held out a bright blue metallic object the size of an aspirin tablet, meant for use in his personal computer. He squeezed it between thumb and forefinger and in the air, above his thumb, colorful letters formed:

MONTY PYTHON AND THE HOLY GRAIL
Python (Monty) Pictures 1974

Before he could say anything, a buzzer sounded. The comm system had been startling him with false alarms all day. He gave another kick and floated to the pilot's chair. It would be a long trip by ladder when the ship was underway. The screen was activated and showed a familiar face.

"Willie darling!" It was Amorie, speaking in what was almost real time. "We're headed for the Earth-Moon system! We'll be there in 24 hours!"

CHAPTER TWENTY: AMORIE SAMSON

> A surprising number of people want to know why, in my "old age", I have decided to go off exploring aboard the *Fifth Force* with my husband and our friends. Well, first, because my husband is going and there's no face I'd rather see on the pillow next to mine when I wake up in the morning than his. And second, because I'm not dead yet, and there's the sheer adventure of the thing. And third, because I don't relish ending up a dotty old woman, sitting home alone, nursing my resentments and regrets. —*The Diaries of Rosalie Frazier Ngu*

ONE OF THE MEN WAS her father's brother, Ali Khalidov.

The other was her mother's brother, Saladin Uzhakhov.

Together, the two Chechens took up so much space in the tiny living room of the modest apartment Jasmeen shared with Llyra, that it made her feel claustrophobic, like being in a coin-operated SolarNet booth.

"What is an uncle to do, Jasmeen? You never call!" Ali wailed. He appeared to be on the verge of tears, an alarming condition for an individual of his distinguished middle years and rather substantial proportions, especially one who wore a patch over one eye. "You never write!"

With a sudden feeling that she was about to sink beneath the weight of unexpected and unwanted family obligations, Jasmeen began, "But I … "

The distress must have shown on her face, because Ali suddenly pointed at her and grinned, while Saladin burst out in uproarious laughter. "You got her, Ali! You got her good!" Saladin was taller than Ali, and would have weighed at least three hundred pounds on Earth.

"You owe me," Ali said, wiping tears from his eye. "one ounce silver."

"You two are just plain no good!" Llyra scolded them, although she was laughing, too. Jasmeen had warned her, in a general way, that her uncles were a pair of incorrigible jokers, a trait that they shared in common with Jasmeen's father, Mohammed. They both remained unmarried, an ongoing source of scandal to her mother, Beliita. Jasmeen said she didn't think they were gay. Llyra had warmed to them instantly. She loved her parents and her brother, but in her family everyone was so serious.

These men, who, according to Jasmeen's mother, had worked together for years at some important scientific facility in another city in the Moon, had called their niece the day after she and Llyra had arrived in Armstrong. They had then given the two girls some time to settle in.

"Now here we are back, my little sunflower seed, to take you on Lunar excursion!" Although he was the smaller of the pair, Ali was a big, noisy man, much given to sudden, sweeping gestures that told the girls (if they had thought of it) that his living room was much larger than theirs.

"What sort of excursion?" Jasmeen asked to know. Secretly proud to do it without a walker, she'd gone to the kitchenette as the teapot on the cooktop began shrilling. She poured hot water through a strainer containing the darkest leaves she could find—tea wasn't grown here and was remarkably expensive—into tall thin-walled glasses in platinum holders made to appear woven, like baskets, a precious gift from her mother, one of the few frivolous things she'd brought with her from Pallas.

Seeing her struggle with the task, Saladin came to her rescue, offering the girl his arm, and taking the laden tray to the coffee table.

"I hear from your mother on Mars that both poor, brave girls are having plenty of trouble adapting themselves to Moon's gravity," he told her. "Call up environmental services before bedtime tonight. Order ten percent increase in partial pressure of oxygen for next ten days."

Jasmeen was surprised. "I didn't know you could do that."

"It will help," her uncle said. "Also,—although I don't like to admit it—*borscht*, very hot, lots of strong beef broth and sour cream."

"Yugh!" Ali exclaimed. "Is no good eating that Russian swill!"

"High protein Russian swill," countered Saladin. "Besides, I happen to like beets."

Ali ignored him, "Now where was I—ah, excursion!" He waited until Jasmeen was seated once again and tea had been poured, heavily sugared, and thick cream added. (Cows were grown on the Moon, and milk products were relatively cheap.) "Excursion to posterior of Moon—or ass-end of universe, depending on who says it! Graduate students are unappreciative lot. But—to marvelous System-famous Larsen Farside Observatory, where distinguished uncles poke and squeeze cold and ungenerous universe for valuable astronomical information, which they then sell to asteroid hunters and others like them at extortionate price!"

He winked his one good eye.

Llyra nodded in sudden recognition. "My brother told me about that!" she said. "I'd just forgotten about it. He's training right now to be an asteroid hunter—he's going to find the Diamond Rogue—and rebuilding a little ship he bought. So you're the people who detect and report on incoming asteroids. Wilson never said anything about the information coming from Jasmeen's relatives."

"Jasmeen's relatives plus staff numbering just under two hundred," Saladin admitted modestly. "Figure includes unappreciative graduate students. Most are to be found at Larsen Farside, some administrative personnel work here in Armstrong, a few—one or two from time to time—"

Ali seemed to give him a warning look and shook his had almost microscopically.

"—at mostly automated observatory in Lagrange position on opposite side of Earth. Humorists call it 'L-Sex', but is actually L-Three. Larsen Farside boasts largest and most powerful radio telescope array in Solar System. Also it has largest, most powerful optical telescope. Other location has radio and optical telescope, one half million miles away, for parallax—we see in three-dee!"

"Speak for yourself," the one-eyed Ali grumbled. "Sounds too much like 3DTV commercial. Never and nonetheless, you will come see what we see?"

"Oh, yes!" Llyra exclaimed. "Oh, can we please do it, Jasmeen, please? Our contract doesn't begin until next week, so our time is free."

Jasmeen nodded, excited herself, at the prospect of a trip around the Moon. "I think so—but we should consult DeGrey clinic and tell your grandmother."

Ali gave a massive shrug. "She is invited. Also asteroid hunter brother."

Jasmeen raised her eyebrows at Llyra, making her laugh out loud, and conveying her suspicion that her bachelor uncles had been looking forward to an excuse to meet the beautiful and famous Julie Segovia Ngu.

And what red-blooded human male wouldn't?

*
**

The colorful 3D moving posters outside the entrance proclaimed that it was Kirk Thatcher night at "The Edge of Etiquette", the most popular and up-to-date nightclub in Armstrong, and therefore, in the Moon.

Inside, the place was huge and dark, although there were points and pools of light everywhere, at the tables, on the ceiling (hung with artificial stalactites, since, without ground water, the real thing didn't grow here), at the bandstand, and among the dancers, themselves.

The young hostess escorting them to their table was half a head taller than Wilson, pale as a corpse—which she was made up to resemble—and so emaciated that she appeared to be a victim of some infamous twentieth century government atrocity. Her glossy black hair was cropped so short that it looked painted on her scalp. A pair of contact lenses made her eyes look like they were fashioned from dull aluminum; they brought the cruel artworks of Simon Benson and Robert Bishop to mind. Her narrow little face was pierced for metal bars and hoops more times than he was able to count in the two or three minutes she was with them.

"Tonight," she told them, having to shout at them over the raucous music, "we're happying ourselves over the hundredth annivert of the Thatcher glomphing the Nobel Peace Prize, whatever the herbert that was—"

And whoever "the" Thatcher was, Wilson thought. There were lots of old-fashioned 2D "flatties" of the man up on giant screens all over the otherwise dark and cavernous room. For some reason, most of them showed him with his hair cut and shaped into an impressive orange crest, and many of the pictures seemed to have been taken within five minutes of one another, aboard some variety of antiquated public conveyance.

"Yeah," the girl yelled when Wilson asked about it. "The Punk on the Bus. Boom. Box. Until that pointy-eared bathrobe came a-vulckin' around, anyway. He's the patron saint of punk—part of the Trinity: Johnny, Sid, and Kirk. You know this whole-in-the-wall's labed for his clatch."

Holding his arm firmly, Wilson's companion asked, "What for his what?"

"His clatch, courtney. His orch, orfah. His band, beverly. This deepdive is named for it. Where are you in from, anyway, the Ultima Asteroids?"

"Next best," Wilson told her, giving his date a glance. "Asteroid hunter."

"Oh." On this world, unprotected by an atmosphere, hunters were respected.

The girl's lower lip was pierced twice for small rings, halfway between the center and the corners of her mouth, and there was a shiny metal stud protruding from her flesh below the center of the lip. When she spoke, Wilson saw at least two shiny bits where her tongue was pierced.

A similar bauble adorned one side of her nose. The nasal septum was pierced, as well, for a larger ring hanging beneath her nostrils and touching her upper lip. One of her eyebrows had been pierced, and her ears were laden with so much jewelry, set in so many holes, that Wilson wondered why they didn't simply fold forward and collapse on themselves.

It wasn't until later that he remembered her tattoos.

"So what's this band that's playing right now?" Wilson's companion had to shout. He still couldn't believe that Amorie was actually here, beside him. She was vastly more beautiful in person—and so much tinier—than speaking with her and seeing her over the SolarNet for the past year had ever prepared him for. And her fragrance was ... intoxicating.

"Only the wazziest neopunk orch in the whole wide warren," their hostess beamed proprietarily. "It's our house clatch, don't you know, Spotty Wankers. And they're playing Thatcher's superwazziest noise ever!"

The lyrics seemed to consist mostly of "I hate you, and I berate you"! The bizarre thing, Wilson thought, was that, despite her slang and the hardware in her mouth, he'd understood every word she'd said, more or less. He'd seen earlier signs that the Moon's popular culture was currently in the throes of a revival of some of the ugliest music ever produced in the twentieth century. Listening to it made his head throb and his teeth ache. He expected his ears to start bleeding any second.

They arrived and sat at a table in the second tier along one wall, overlooking the dance floor. Just now, it looked like a great place to get killed. People, young men, mostly, were smashing their chests into one another, or diving headlong off the stage, expecting the crowd to catch them. Sometimes the crowd actually did. Other times—well it looked to him like there was a good chance of being trampled to death. The hostess told them that someone would be along to take their drink orders.

Wilson had arrived in some pain already. Both of his hands ached from the overhaul he was giving the "coffee grinder" aboard *Mighty Mouse's Girlfriend*. It was an item of heavy machinery that pulverized useless stony meteorites and other rubble, reducing them to fine dry powder that could be heated to plasma temperatures by the vessel's fusion engines and flung out as reaction mass. Wilson's knuckles stung where he'd barked them on the sharp corners and hard edges of the device. But the overhaul needed doing if his ship were ever to fly again.

As it was, he'd have to expend some of his precious and dwindling cash for his first hopper full of reaction mass, before he could gather and store more in open space, since whatever reserves *Mighty Mouse's Girl-friend* might once have contained had been bled off long since to feed some other lucky vessel in Guzman's fabulous floating junkyard.

"I hope you don't mind coming here, Willie darling." Amorie leaned forward, over the table, toward him, trying to keep her voice low. The dress she wore was a filmy, insubstantial thing. The back was open to well below her waist, although the skirt brushed the floor behind her. But then rose ... well, almost too high in front, and when she leaned forward like she did now, he could see all the way down to her navel. He could also see plainly that she wasn't wearing anything like a brassiere.

That garment had fallen out of fashion in the lower-gravity worlds.

"Wha—what?" Wilson felt himself blush deeply. Amorie had caught his eye and she knew exactly where he'd been looking. His mother and sister were both extraordinarily modest at home, and this was the first time he'd ever seen anything remotely like a naked breast in person. He couldn't quite see Amorie's nipples, but it was a close thing.

She grinned and refrained from sitting up again. Instead, she glanced down at herself and told him, "I sincerely hope you like what you see, my darling Willie. It's for you. It's all for you. I made and wore this dress especially so that you could see some of what you're getting."

"I—errm, ah!" Wilson had to clear his throat and start again. Every muscle in his body tingled painfully. There was fire in his veins. He refused to think about what was going on between his legs. And as if by some lovely magic, the obnoxious cacophony of the band had somehow been transformed into a tender ballad. "I thought your people—"

She nodded. "'The first meeting in the flesh must be in a public place,' she quoted with exaggerated solemnity. "Believe me, darling Willie, I'd much rather have put on a t-shirt and a pair of jeans and visited that little ship you're so proud of. They come off as easily and quickly as any evening dress does. I chose this place because the tourist guides all warned that it was extremely noisy. That way, I figured, we could have at least a little privacy in the middle of the crowd."

"I—errm, ah!" Hopelessly lost in the mist of her eyes and the scent of her body, this time Wilson couldn't even think of what to say.

"Later on," she told him huskily, "we can dance."

**

The gigantic billboard, five hundred feet tall, at least three times as wide as that, and bright enough to be seen for fifty miles, proclaimed:

BURNS BROTHERS COFFEE * FUEL * FOOD * AIR RESTAURANT * MOTEL * SHOWERS LAST CHANCE FOR 1000 MILES

"That is only about hour and quarter," Ali observed from behind the big wheel of his brand new pride and joy, a 2031 Rasputin Electric Moon-Master. He added, "Now that they've put new surface on highway." The process of long haul driving on the Moon, he'd explained earlier to his passengers, was about ninety-five percent automated, but from time to time, the road below or the vehicle itself signaled for his attention.

At this velocity, Llyra thought, somewhere between six and seven hundred miles an hour, the condition of the highway was very largely academic. They'd trundled along at much lower speeds through several of the underground traffic tunnels of Armstrong, when Ali and Saladin had picked them up at their apartment. And they would need a modicum of off-road capability on the dirt roads of the frontier town where they were headed.

Anywhere above a hundred miles an hour on this highway, however, and magnetic levitation kicked in. The monster vehicle's dozen tires hadn't touched the ground since shortly after they'd left Armstrong behind, and they wouldn't support the vehicle again until they'd arrived at their destination, the System-famous Larsen Far Side Observatory.

Saladin was in the kitchenette at the opposite end of the machine, just now, trying to get the ancient family samovar to work. Llyra didn't know what was wrong with the thing. Generating a cloud of colloquial Chechen epithets that no mullah would ever have approved of, he gave up and put a Pyrex container of water in the microwave, instead.

Sitting at the dining table in the MoonMaster's well-upholstered, comfortable lounge between Jasmeen and her grandmother, Llyra wished that her brother were here with them, today. But he was a big boy, now. And he was a busy boy, as well, going to the zoo or something with that Amorie creature. It seemed that he only had eyes for her, these days, and she only had eyes for him, apparently. It was both boring and disgusting. They couldn't keep their hands—or much of anything else—off of each another. Llyra shuddered to imagine what it might be like to have Amorie Samson around all the time, as her sister-in-law.

As if she knew exactly what Llyra was thinking, Jasmeen turned and grinned at her in sympathy. Julie seemed telepathic this morning, as well.

"You know what we used to say in the Marines, honey," she asked, "when one of our guys had gone missing and we were afraid he'd been captured?"

Llyra found she was almost in tears, "No, Grandma, what did you say?"

"They can kill him but they can't eat him, it's against the Geneva Convention."

Jasmeen laughed, "I would not be too sure of that!" and then shut up suddenly and blushed. It had sounded more genteel in her head. Most of Julie's military career, she knew, had been wasted on Mars, in a doomed attempt to suppress a colonial rebellion by Jasmeen's parents, among others. "But you are correct, is also what we Martians used to say."

She and Julie laughed while Llyra looked confused. She'd been vaguely aware that Julie had once been an officially sworn enemy to the Ngus and Khalidovs. She knew very few of the details because they made her uncomfortable. Her grandmother had always been a special, magical spirit to her, her occasional visits to Pallas reason enough to declare a holiday. She knew her grandfather William had won Julie's heart. That part seemed romantic and somehow made her feel sort of breathless.

Just imagine, Llyra thought, what it must be like, getting swept off your feet by your mortal enemy, an individual who'd been trying to kill you—and whom you'd been trying to kill—only a little while before. Just imagine. Billy Ngu must have been a pretty persuasive guy.

For the first time in a long while, the highway began to curve, and the MoonMaster, only a yard above its surface, curved with it, its passengers and everything else inside it banking, so that it looked and felt to them as if it were the surface of the Moon that had tilted. For a while, they could actually sense the speed of the thing—about the same as the speed of sound on Earth. Here, of course, the speed of sound was zero.

As the road straightened, they crossed an abyss—a deep crater, Llyra thought, rather than some mere crack or chasm—and for a long moment, the highway resembled nothing more than a flimsy, unsupported ribbon casually flung from peak to peak across the crater floor miles below.

She looked at a display, set in the headliner behind the driver's seat. Like most of the timepieces on public view in the Moon, it was a "terminator clock", the round face behind the analog hands (which kept Greenwich Mean Time everywhere on the Earth's satellite) representing the surface of the Moon, with the observer always at its center. A Lunar Positioning System kept track of the observer's location, a few major features of the Moon's surface, and the terminator—the hard line between a day that lasted two weeks, and a night that did the same. There was a clock exactly like this one—only much bigger—opposite the "Zamboni end", in each of the rinks at the Heinlein Center.

It was dark, just now, where they were headed, which was a good thing for astronomers, she guessed. Jasmeen's uncles had spent the observatory's daylight hours as they were accustomed to doing, in Armstrong, minding some business and catching up on any recreational opportunities they might have missed out on over the past couple of weeks.

Looking at the men, Llyra didn't want to think about what that implied.

*
**

As he pushed his way out through the swinging slatted doors, he wondered once again how he always seemed to get into messes like this one.

He'd been told, when he came downstairs from his rented room this morning, into the saloon that served the place for a lobby, that he'd had too much whiskey the previous evening, and gotten into a noisy argument of some kind with the notorious Sanddune Sandy Malloy, known far and wide throughout the southwest as the Alamosa Kid. Of course he had no memory of it, but apparently wiser, cooler (and far more sober) heads had prevailed, and the consummation politely deferred until noon today.

High noon, somebody had said, laughing.

At present, his own head ached, his guts were cramped, his hands shook, and his vision was blurry—it was the worst hangover he'd ever had. That was why, in addition to the .45 caliber 1858 Remington revolver he wore on his right hip—taken from a Union officer he'd killed during the War for Southern Independence, he'd later paid the factory two dollars to convert it to cartridge use—he carried a Winchester's lever action saddle carbine chambered for the same pistol caliber.

He also wore hand-lasted Lucchese boots from El Paso, Texas, a pair of huge-roweled Mexican spurs, what the catalog called a "pearl- gray" Stetson hat with rolled brim and Montana peak, a bib-fronted shirt, horse leather vest, a huge red paisley bandana, and over his tan canvas trousers, a pair of heavy leather chaps. He probably didn't need those today, but he felt more comfortable with them than without them.

Outside, it was so bright that it hurt his teeth. He glanced back into the dim interior of the saloon. The Regulator clock over the bar said it was exactly five minutes of noon. And there was that craven dog Sandy now, across the furrowed street, at the end of the block on the boardwalk in front of the general store, just one step away from the corner of the building where he could take cover once the shooting commenced.

The air was hot and still. It smelled of dust and horses. High overhead a pair of buzzards circled as if they knew what was about to happen.

He pulled a rolling paper and a pouch of tobacco from his shirt pocket, rolled himself a cigarette one-handed, put it in his mouth, struck a match on his belt buckle and lit it, savoring that first good taste.

Another figure stood at the other end of the street in front of the livery stable, another on the roof of the drygoods store, and yet another sat in an open window of a room in the hotel over Delmonico's. They hadn't told him he would have to face not only Sanddune Sandy, but his brothers, Durango Dave, Gunnison Gus, and Montrose Monty. Each of them was known, in his respective social circles, as the Alamosa Kid.

Sandy drew and snapped a quick shot off at him. Too quick: it hit the narrow lathe-turned column holding up the balcony over the saloon and threw off splinters and whitewash. Horses tethered at the hitching post tossed their heads in protest. He even thought he heard a woman scream.

Having anticipated Sandy's next move, he lifted his levergun, leaned its receiver against the battle-scarred column, and put a bullet precisely between where the man had stood and the sheltering corner of the general store. In effect, Sandy walked right into a 255-grain flat-nosed slug going 1000 feet per second, and went down hard with it, skidding off the end of the wooden sidewalk and over three or four steps into the street until only his mule-ears could be seen.

Times like these, the smell of blackpowder smoke was like a tonic to him. Without waiting, he shot the figure standing on the roof—he didn't know if it was Dave or Gus; the boys were twins and nobody could tell them apart, not even their mother—and the one lurking in the window. The latter ducked or collapsed back into the room, but the former pitched frontwards over the edge of the roof, hit the porch covering over the boardwalk, and rolled off into the street onto his face.

Even as he wheeled around the column to confront the man in front of the livery stable, he knew he would be too late. It was Monty, who fired both barrels of a shotgun he hadn't seen—thinking Monty only had a sixgun, he'd taken care of the other brothers first. It was a long reach, even for a 10-guage, about seventy-five yards, and when half a dozen of the pellets struck him in the leg, they only felt like bee-stings and failed to penetrate the tough, seasoned leather of his chaps.

Theodora Gibson, the handsome proprietress of the hotel over Delmonico's, with whom he'd spent many a pleasanter moment than this, leaned out the window to tell him that Gus was dead. Nodding, he raised his rifle and fired twice. So much for Montrose Monty Malloy, most alliterative of the four notorious Malloy brothers of Alamosa, Colorado.

He hadn't even drawn his revolver. He took another draw on his cigarette.

Holding the Winchester in his left hand again, he reached to his belt buckle with his right and turned it over. The scene faded, along with his artificial hangover symptoms, and he was in his comfortable hotel room in Leinster City. He pulled the flimsy VR helmet from his face, disconnected it from the computer on his bedside table, rolled it up, and put it in a drawer. He swung his legs over, stepped into his loafers, took his sportscoat from the chair, and pocketed the computer.

He lifted his pistol, a Syrtis Systems coherent plasma gun—or CPG—from the bedside table, holstered it, and stepped into the corridor.

The fastest gun on the Moon was ready for work.

CHAPTER TWENTY-ONE: THE ESMERALDA

Someday we will have the means to reach the stars in a reasonable amount of time. We will eventually meet people who will think surprisingly like us, but who probably won't resemble us at all. When they refer to the language of our planet, they will mean English. When they refer to its cuisine, they will mean Chinese.

Make mine *kung pao*—extra spicy! —*The Diaries of Rosalie Frazier Ngu*

ALI KHALIDOV'S 2131 RASPUTIN ELECTRIC Moonmaster carried Llyra and her companions into the 14-day Lunar night before she fully realized it.

Abruptly, Saladin leaned toward Llyra, "We are soon to be arriving at what has aptly been called 'back of beyond'. We are coming here in first place because of something that happened down on Earth in winter of 2089. Is something everybody on Earth knows about. You are not of Earth, little one, not for three generations. Do you know what is happening?"

Julie had started to say something to the physicist, but held her tongue, instead, and waited. Saladin's question had been addressed to Llyra, anyway. Although Ali's big vehicle had just taken them across the terminator, the sky didn't look particularly different—they weren't all that much accustomed to looking directly at the sun in any case—but the territory around them now, except for a ridge or mount with a crest or peak still standing in sunlight for a while, was lit only by the pale blue glow of Earth. And even that was just about to set.

"Everybody in the Solar System knows about that, Dr. Uzhakhov," Llyra replied. "On December 5th, 2089, an asteroid hit the Earth near the city of Ashland, in Ohio, which was a province of the Old United States. It killed about fifteen million people, and made a new Great Lake."

Saladin nodded. "Very good, young Miss Llyra Ngu. Is obvious you are having excellent tutor. Hunter Lake is large, but only great by courtesy. And most people are killed when impact triggered New Madrid earthquake fault." He sighed. "Was not even real asteroid, technically speaking."

Jasmeen grinned, hoping no one else could see it. She looked down at her feet and shook her head. She'd always thought her uncles were funny, even (maybe even especially) when they didn't mean to be. When they'd picked her and Llyra up this "morning" Ali hadn't been wearing his eyepatch, and seemed to have a perfectly good eye where it had been.

"Is artificial," he told them before she or Llyra had a chance to ask. "Also very versatile. Works in low light, works in darkness, acts as microscope, telescope—quite handy for astronomer—but gives me headache. When I do not need, I do not use. Use today for driving MoonMaster."

Now, still at the wheel, Ali told them over his right shoulder, "Was comet nucleus. Great big ball of slushy ice just like you buy in plastic cup at neighborhood convenience store—if you like ammonia flavor."

Llyra and Jasmeen both said, "Eww!" simultaneously, while Julie laughed.

"Yes, is very funny thing," Saladin went on. "Killed fish off for years."

"Not funny, 'Ha-ha'," Ali interrupted. "funny 'sheesh'."

"Funny sheesh," Saladin agreed. "Before Ashland Event, everybody knows celestial object—metallic asteroid—wiped out dinosaurs and most of their contemporaries sixty-five million years ago. Some even knew about earlier rock that came one hundred forty million years before, wiping out many more species, making empty place on Earth for dinosaurs."

"Presence of iridium in Cretaceous-Tertiary soil boundary layer gave game away," Jasmeen said. "Scientists named Alvarez discovered it."

Llyra volunteered, "Luis and Walter Alvarez. They were father and son scientists. And there's evidence of several more impact events just like those two, changing the Earth's geological and biological history."

Saladin beamed at them both. "Yes, lovely scholars, gold forehead stars all around. Some even knew that Earth was millions of years overdue, statistically speaking, for new Extinction Level Event. But Ashland Event was not one such. Was minuscule compared to K-T and P-T events."

Llyra sputtered, "Minuscule? But it killed millions and millions of—"

"Ah, but Ashland Object is actually saving many, many more lives, in final analysis, than it is taking—and please do not look at me that way, Jasmeena Khalidova. Is most unbecoming in niece who is properly respectful toward elders. Ashland frightened human species into doing something that simply knowing about great risk could never accomplish."

"And what was that?" Saladin's improperly respectful niece asked him. She knew perfectly well what, but wanted to hear him tell the story.

"Curringer Corporation and others," he replied, "organized private system of detection and defense we operate here today. Nobody wanted government—any government—involved in system, because power to deflect asteroid *away* from Earth is power to deflect it *toward* Earth."

Ali nodded. "Nobody trusted random nutball chimpanzee-brained president not to do exactly that if he began to feel his power threatened."

"In 2103," Saladin continued, "private system paid off bigtime when metallic asteroid ten miles in diameter was detected two years travel time in advance and was deflected by asteroid hunters from collision course with Earth, probably saving every living thing on planet."

Llyra nodded. "I knew about that, too."

"Ali and me ... " Saladin began.

She said, "I know, Dr. Uzhakhov, you and Dr. Khalidov were the detectives."

"And," his niece told him, "is 'Ali and I'."

*
**

Sometimes Wilson wished he didn't have a nose—or a sense of smell.

This place Amorie had brought him to was filled with cloying odors that reminded him of a visit he'd reluctantly paid about three years ago, a visit he'd almost completely forgotten until it was triggered somehow by his olfactory memory, to meet Jasmeen's great grandmother Anna.

The odors in the old lady's room at the nursing home hadn't been particularly unpleasant, he recalled, just ... strange, somehow, and, well, sort of smothery. Anna Khalidov had once been a very large woman, apparently. Now she had great draperies of pale, wrinkled, liver-spotty flesh hanging off her knobby skeleton, and breasts the size of watermelons, located, more or less, at the same level as her navel.

At the time, Wilson thought that Jasmeen's great grandmother was the most eloquent argument he'd ever witnessed for dying young—and possibly for never marrying. A part of the horror lay in visualizing his sister's lovely coach—being in love with somebody else had never blinded Wilson to Jasmeen's beauty—turning out just like that herself someday.

The Khalidov family had brought the old lady up from Argentina, where a great many of their relatives had fled Russian persecution, to Pallas, believing the lower gravity might be good for her. Upon arrival, she'd taken to her bed, and had refused to get up again.

As far as he knew, she was still there.

It was obvious that people had been living aboard this ship that Amorie called home for several generations, old people like Jasmeen's great grandmother, little babies in diapers, and everybody in between. Amorie probably didn't even notice the smell, but Wilson couldn't get it out of his mind, and it threatened to spoil everything for both of them.

The Asteroid Hunter *Esmeralda*, Amorie had explained on the way here in the hired shuttle, had been old before a systematic program to prevent Extinction Level Events had ever been adopted by a frightened humanity. She'd made her living then as she still did, plying the ways of the Solar System, collecting rocks—meteoroids and asteroids of various sizes and compositions—wherever she could find them and chase them down, stripping out whatever valuable materials they might contain, and consuming the remainder as reaction mass. She had once discovered a great green diamond, and the Samsons had changed her name accordingly.

This part of the ship was built more or less like his own, only on a grander scale. Overhead, under an enormous transparent dome, a huge control arc or panel was attended by half a dozen seats, all empty at present, even though the ship was maintaining an almost imperceptible acceleration to hold people and things down. He and Amorie had come aboard through a portside airlock aft of the base of the dome, and half-climbed, half-slid down something that was a mix of staircase and ladder.

The wall of the cylinder aft of the dome, exactly like that of his own ship, had been given over to lush airponic plantings that provided fruit, oxygen, and humidity. Its brilliant flowers were intended more simply to make the ship as pleasant a place as possible. The floor of the cylinder, forty feet aft of the dome, was a big common room where family members could prepare and eat meals, visit, watch 3DTV, and relax.

But the *Esmeralda* still smelled funny to him, as the homes of strangers often do. Maybe it was what they ate. Maybe it was the plants. Maybe there were some of those tropical flowers hidden in the foliage that attracted pollinating insects by smelling like rotting bodies.

A woman stood waiting for them at the bottom of the ladder. She looked about forty, had fairly short, curly, carrot-colored hair, and wore a mid-sleeved shipsuit, and an old-fashioned kitchen apron over that.

Amorie stepped off the ladder onto the floor, gave the woman a hug and a peck on the cheek and said, "This is my mother, Willie, Valerie Samson."

He stepped onto the floor, reached, and took her hand. "Hello, Mrs. Samson."

Amorie gave him an odd look. "Mama, this is my Willie I told you about."

Looking a little bit tired, like everybody's mother, and a maybe little too warm from cooking, Amorie's mother reached up and brushed a stray amber lock out of her eyes. Wilson could see that Valerie had been every bit as good to look at as Amorie, when she was younger. She was still quite pretty now, although not nearly as pretty as his own mother.

Valerie wiped her hands on her apron, seized him by the upper arm and squeezed hard. "He's a fine, sturdy boy, baby girl. And handsome, too!" Her accent seemed familiar. To Wilson: "I hope y'likes boiled cabbage."

She'd pronounced it "biled".

"Er, ah ... " Wilson replied, not really knowing what he should say. Was that what he'd been smelling? He'd eat anything set before him, but the fact was, he heartily disliked cabbage in nearly all of its forms except cole slaw, and he didn't care for anything boiled, except eggs.

Valerie laughed at his honest, downcast face. "Gotcha! That sorry, love, I couldn't resist. I hates boiled cabbage, meself, though I was after bein' raised on the stuff. We'll not be havin' any of it today. We'll start with a nice lobster bisque. We farm the fat rascals ourselves, y'know!"

"I'll show you the breeding pond, if you like, Willie darling," Amorie chirped. It's forward of the main reactor, to use its waste heat."

"Show him after supper, love," her mother said. "If you're still inclined. Pipe all hands to knife and fork stations. We're ready t'eat."

*
**

To the uninformed eye, Llyra thought, the system-famous Larsen Farside Observatory appeared considerably less impressive than she'd expected, a real disappointment, although she'd never have said so to her hosts. Undoubtedly, it was because most of it had either been constructed underground (as were most things on—or "in"—the Moon), was too far away to see, or was too big to be taken in all at once.

A good example of the last category was the radio telescope array that Larsen Farside commanded, the largest in the system, according to Ali and Saladin. Through the overhead windows of Ali's MoonMaster, as he drove it toward what he called the "front gate" of the sprawling facility,

Llyra, Jasmeen, and Julie could make out at least half a dozen gigantic parabolic dishes, looking like opened flowers of some kind on stalks towering a hundred fifty feet over everything beneath them.

At this particular point on the Lunar surface, at this particular date and time, except for what looked to Llyra and her companions like about a billion stars, there was little or no light coming to them from the sky. Streetlights everywhere made the little frontier town, such as it was, appear much as it would in daylight—something that would never have been tolerated at any optical observatory located within Earth's atmosphere, and therefore subject to light "pollution". The modest observatory back home, Llyra knew, lay in orbit about Pallas.

A dozen or more big-tired all-terrain vehicles, not one of them as grand as Ali's MoonMaster, were scattered around the facility, but all that could be seen of the buildings here was the same sort of thing to be seen ordinarily on city rooftops: vents, heat exchangers, antennas, several pairs of cameras that provided the inhabitants below with 3DTV views of what was going on outside their underground retreat. Llyra had looked through these cameras herself, via the SolarNet, from Armstrong.

"But this is only smallest fraction of first row of radiotelescope array," Saladin informed them all proprietarily, indicating the huge receptors that seemed to march toward the horizon. "Dishes are each one hundred feet across, half of mile apart, distributed approximately over two thousand square miles. Is equivalent to single parabolic dish, er ... well at least size of your own moon, young lady, Pallas B."

In fact, Llyra had no idea how large Pallas B was, although she'd seen the little satellite almost every day of her life (it was nearly as visible in the daytime as at night) and had even been there once, on an educational excursion. She did notice that the so-called "front gate" they were approaching stood more or less in the center of all of the visible manmade features in this place (except, of course, for the radio telescope array) and resembled, at least to her, an outsized submarine periscope sticking up incongruously out of the dry Lunar dust.

As the MoonMaster approached it, some part of the thing turned and began lowering until its end came level with the vehicle's portside boarding hatch, which had its own tiny airlock. The observatory's "front gate" latched onto that, allowed them entry, and after a fast elevator ride downward, of perhaps sixty or eighty feet, they found themselves standing in a much more spacious airlock, waiting for the surface-side door to close snugly before the inside door could be opened.

"Welcome, ladies, to what local inhabitants call 'The Spider'," Saladin shook his giant, shaggy head. "Is asterix-shaped network of tunnels underlying entire facility, allowing delivery of water, power, and scientists from one point to another. Also used—excessively, I might add—for storage. We are first going to LFO administrative offices, very sad to say, to discover what has been irretrievably fouled up in our absence—absences? Tell me, my young scholarly niece Jasmeen, are two people having singular or plural absence in English?"

"Singular, I think," she replied. "Absence, like water, cannot be counted."

Julie and Llyra gave the Chechen girl a nod of encouragement and approval. One subject that Jasmeen did not tutor her young pupil in was English. In fact, most of the time, it worked the other way around.

On the other side of the airlock door, they found one leg of the Spider, featuring the ends of a pair of broad, horizontal, rubberized moving "slidewalks", one of them coming toward them at a brisk walking pace, the other going away. Overhead were pipes and cables. The spaces either side were filled with cartons, boxes, and barrels. Saladin and Ali stepped onto the slidewalk and beckoned to their three female guests.

"Is absolute necessity, I am afraid," Ali explained when the three females had joined him and his partner on the walkway. "In community consisting entirely of intellectual types, wandering about with noses buried in books or other documents, or thinking deep thoughts like Dorothy's Scarecrow, they are otherwise walking straight into one another."

What Saladin had referred to as the administrative offices at the Larsen Farside Observatory didn't look very much like offices, at all, Llyra thought. They looked much more like the historic mission control center at NASA in Houston, or the equivalent at Curringer Corporation headquarters in Johannesburg—both facilities were now museums. They consisted of a series of very large 3DTV screens running around three walls of a room the size of a big theater, and curved rows of computer monitors, manned by several dozen individuals wearing headsets. A few also wore VR helmets like she had tried aboard the *William Wilde Curringer*.

Above it all hung a ten-foot recreation of an old black-and-white newspaper cartoon. Several big fat scientists in white lab coats were delightedly abandoning their equation-filled blackboards so they could run out to meet the ice cream truck. The artist's signature read "Gary Larsen".

Saladin and Ali stood with their guests at the rear, on a sort of low mezzanine separated from everything else by an air curtain, so they could talk without disturbing the people working. "Is here we correlate information from radio array, optical telescope—which we are to be showing you directly—and orbiting station on other side of Earth, which is giving us our half million miles of parallax," Ali told them.

Saladin added, "First two rows keep track of different sectors of Solar System, in plane of ecliptic, where planets, moons, and Belt asteroids are found. Next two rows observe above and below ecliptic, where most dangerous planet-killers live. Last two rows track mostly man-made objects: probes, private vessels, space liners, and rock pirates."

"Rock pirates?" Llyra and Jasmeen both asked at once.

"Yes, pirates," Julie repeated. "They spend most of their time hanging, as quietly as they can, at some likely location in space, waiting for a legitimate asteroid hunter to find the rock he's looking for—they can tell by the various signals he generates or gets back from the target. Then they close in and take it away from him at gunpoint."

"Or missile-point," offered Saladin.

"Or laser-point. Pirates are spending some of their time looking for unclaimed asteroids, themselves. Disguise also helps to reduce overhead."

"Pirates," Jasmeen mused. "At home we are for some time having *hooligani* and *brigandi* stopping travelers and robbing them in desert shortly after terraformation made such villainy possible. It appeared most were leftovers from military expedition sent by East American government to put down unruly colonists. No offense, Grandma Julie."

"None taken, dear. We had to shoot a few of our own bad dogs after it was clear that Earth had abandoned us and discipline broke down in our unit. They never could get used to the idea that a heavily armed civilian population tended to make, er, hooliganism and brigandage unprofitable."

She turned to the two scientists. "So tell me what keeps space pirates operating out here? Wilson and I just ordered a big particle cannon for his little ship, specifically to help deal with pirates. I should think that the same principle, of an armed populace, would apply."

Saladin nodded. "Applies fine when hunter is unbusy and can see pirates coming. You see, Mrs. Ngu, we are offering three varieties of information here at Larsen Farside—rather, three levels of billing. Least expensive data is from general survey of objects we are finding. Is offered in coded broadcasts to all subscribers, at low standard fee. Most expensive is specific information in unique codes, requested by only one purchaser.

Information on rock pirates we give away free. We try to make earliest warnings possible. Pirates do not like LFO terribly."

Everybody laughed.

"One tried to kill us once," said Ali. Somewhere along their path, he had removed his artificial eye and replaced it with the patch, in a manner analogous, Jasmeen thought, to changing into bedroom slippers when one came home from work. "Rock pirate tried to drop big one on observatory. It was carbonaceous chondrite, holding much water. We destroyed with terajoule ranging laser we use for pinpointing objects in Asteroid Belt, one hundred fifty million miles away. Instantly converted water to steam, generating explosion that left no fragment larger than last joint of little finger. Was very spectacular light show."

Saladin said, "We are then turning ranging laser on rock pirate: *Kaboom!*"

"And who is telling story?" Ali demanded. He shook his head and frowned. "Anyway, is coming no sound at all in vacuum."

"Be that way," Saladin shrugged. "Was certainly kaboom at their end!"

Ali laughed and slapped his partner on the back. "Very well, then, *Kaboom!*"

*
**

In the end, dinner had been wonderful.

Wilson had never had lobster before now. There was very little saltwater anywhere on Pallas, and not a single fish farm that he knew of. After disposing of three broiled tails and a considerable quantity of drawn butter, with a baked potato on the side and a salad that must have come from the garden wall behind him, he knew that he must have it again as soon as possible. He wasn't prepared to say whether it was better than sex, but if sex was better than this, he might not survive it.

"I think we'll wait a little for the dessert," declared Amorie's mother Valerie. "That'll give the gentlemen a chance for a nice smoke, while the daughter and I tidy up the table a bit. Grandma, you stay put."

It appeared that Grandma—the old lady was actually Valerie's great grandmother—was ready for a nice smoke, as well. She stuffed dark tobacco into a short clay pipe, almost black with age and use, while continuing to give Wilson the same evaluative look she d given him all through the meal. One of the "gentlemen" struck and held a match.

"An' where was it ye said ye was born, then, darlin'?" she asked Wilson as she drew the flame into her pipe and got it burning to her liking. It smelled all right, he decided, maybe a little bit like dark chocolate. Her accent was the same as Valerie's, only much harder to follow. She had a face all sucked into itself, Wilson thought, like a dried up apple. He guessed that she must be well over a hundred years old.

"Ngu House," he told her for what he was certain must be the fourth time since he'd met her only an hour ago. "In Curringer, on Pallas."

"I met Wild Bill Curringer once," the old lady said, but then fell silent.

The "gentlemen" in question, sitting around the table with the women, were two of Amorie's brothers, both older than she was, three of Amorie's uncles—two were her father's brothers and one was her mother's—and Amorie's maternal grandfather. With the uncles came their wives, three of Amorie's aunts. Half a dozen small children—Wilson never did find out whose kids they were—had been given their own table. The men smoked pipes, cigars, and cigarettes. Wilson had declined.

Now the grandfather reached into a cabinet under the big table and pulled out a gigantic accordion, covered with mother-of-pearl and chromium.

"Ah," said an uncle, grinning. "So that's the way of it, is it?" He reached up to an overhead cupboard and extracted a violin—although it was likelier to be used as a fiddle, thought Wilson, who knew the difference. Another uncle fetched an Irish bouzouki and another a five-string banjo. "Survive this," Amorie's fiddle-playing uncle told him, "ye're fit t'survive anything. The Star in E-flat, if ye please, gentlemen!"

There was a brief musical introduction—it was enough to raise the hair on the back of Wilson's neck; he had never heard live acoustic music performed this close before—a charming, haunting waltz, then Amorie's grandfather began singing in a surprisingly clear, sweet tenor:

> "Ye ladies and ye gentlemen, I pray y'lend an ear,
> While I locate the residence of a lovely charmer fair.
> The curling of her yellow locks first stole me heart away,
> And her place of habitation is down in Logy Bay.
>
> "'Twas on a summer's evening, this little place I found.
> I met her aged father, who did me sore confound.
> Saying, "If you address my daughter, I'll send her far away.
> And she never will return again, while you're in Logy Bay."

The bouzouki and banjo had joined in by now, with Amorie's uncles singing harmony. Wilson wondered what kind of music this was. He'd never hard anything like it. Maybe it was Amorie's revenge for the nightclub. She seemed to know all the words, and as she helped her mother clear the dishes, sang along with them. Her voice was clearly untrained, but as pure and sweet as her grandfather's, and an octave higher.

The men nodded to one another and stopped singing as Amorie continued.

> "How could you be so cruel as to part me from my love?
> Her tender heart beats in her breast as constant as a dove.
> Oh Venus was no fairer, nor the lovely month of May.
> May heaven above shower down its love, on the Star of Logy Bay"

Then they all joined in again.

> "'Twas on the very next morning he went to St. John's town,
> And engaged for her a passage in a vessel outward bound.
> He robbed me of my heart's delight, and sent her far away,
> And he left me here downhearted for the Star of Logy Bay
>
> "Oh now I'll go a-roaming, I can no longer stay.
> I'll search the wide world over in every country.
> I'll search in vain through France and Spain, likewise Americay
> 'Till at last I sight my heart's delight, the Star of Logy Bay."

Finally, Amorie's grandfather finished the tale:

> "Now to conclude and finish, the truth to you I'll tell.
> Between Torbay and Outer Cove, 'tis there my love did dwell.
> The finest girl e'er graced our isle, so every one did say.
> May heaven above shower down its love, on the Star of Logy Bay."

Everyone laughed and clapped, even those who'd performed. Amorie's mother wiped her hands on her apron. She looked at her daughter and at Wilson and said, with a neutral expression, "Now I think it's time for bed."

CHAPTER TWENTY-TWO: NEW HORIZONS

About a century and a quarter ago, there was a remarkable effort by a group of aggressively political females and their male submissives to force boys and young men to behave as if they were girls and young women.

Despite the futility of this experiment (not to mention its utter, self-evident stupidity), it continues to this day in East America, the precipitously declining birth rate of which seems to indicate that not all is well in the Kingdom of the Feminized.—*The Diaries of Rosalie Frazier Ngu*

THE CHECHEN SCIENTISTS AND THEIR guests from Mars and Pallas were on their way down one of the underground legs of the network of tunnels they called the "Spider" to see the System-famous Roger B. Culver Optical Telescope, when they first began to hear the screaming. It seemed to be several voices all at once, coming from the tunnel just ahead.

Llyra quickly found the compact ten millimeter pistol she'd used to good effect on Ceres. Unlike her grandmother Julie, she hadn't noticed that their hosts, Saladin and Ali, didn't seem particularly alarmed by the noise, although the larger of the pair of scientists appeared to wrinkle his enormous nose with something akin to disgust or embarrassment. She put her weapon away, hoping it hadn't been noticed.

Like Llyra, Jasmeen had reached for her own personal weapon when she first heard the screaming, but had managed to stop short, just before the pistol cleared the discreet concealment of her clothing.

Suddenly, for a just a moment, it was completely quiet in the Spider. For the first time Llyra consciously noticed that large, colorful 3DTV displays lined all of the passageways they had been traveling through, offering real-time views of various places on Earth, on Mars, even on Pallas. Llyra thought she caught a glimpse of Lake Selous, from the east shore opposite Ngu House. Some simply showed what the surface cameras were seeing here at Larsen Farside. Life down here, she realized, would probably be intolerable without them.

It certainly would be for her, she thought.

Meanwhile, at something like a steady four or five miles an hour, the slidewalk had soon brought them to the source of the disturbance. A large, noisy group of young people—Llyra guessed that they were all in their early twenties; most of them were boys, of course; and they were graduate students, almost certainly—seemed to be engaged in an unusually silly sport, even for a group of young male graduate students.

In each of the parallel slidewalks, their rubber-covered lefthand rails no more than six inches apart, starting about a hundred feet away from one another, the boys had placed what looked like ordinary plastic sawhorses with pillows fastened around the centers of their horizontal spans. As Llyra and the others watched, a boy leaped onto each of these contrivances. Somebody standing on the nonmoving floor beside the slidewalk handed him a long pole, apparently made from the same plastic tubing that contained the wire bundles on the ceiling overhead.

Each of the boys had a bright yellow construction-worker's hardhat with its transparent plastic face shield pulled down. Each wore what amounted to the uniform of graduate students in the physical sciences: bluejeans, synthetic running shoes, and a plaid, short-sleeved shirt. Each wore as well, fastened around his left upper arm, a colorful silky scarf that would have looked more at home draped around woman's neck.

The two dozen onlookers began to holler and whoop, cheering their respective champions onward. As the pillow-saddled sawhorses and their valiant young passengers approached each other at an aggregate speed of eight or ten miles per hour, the boys lowered their plastic tubes (they were using them as lances, Llyra suddenly realized, the ends of which were amply padded) aiming at the unprotected torsos of their opponents.

Well before the two sawhorses could draw even with one another, there came a thump, a *crash!* and one of the boys was knocked off his sawhorse, onto the handrail, then onto the segmented surface of the slidewalk, to the utter and noisy delight of onlookers on both sides—some of whom were girls. The vanquished knight leaped quickly to his feet, grabbed his trusty "steed" before it was driven off the end of the slidewalk, and shouted, "Okay, then, the best five out of seven!"

Several of the audience booed him, although most of them laughed and clapped him on the back. The victorious sawhorseman dismounted from his charger when he was only a few feet from the visitors and their guides. He gave the two scientists a sheepish look—"Doctor Khalidov, Doctor Uzhakhov, welcome back!"—then, just before he collided with them, hopped over the rail, onto non-moving concrete, taking his well-padded sawhorse and his lance with him. He then jogged back to the terminus to join his excited friends, perhaps for another match.

"Is Society for Creative Anachronism," Jasmeen's uncle Saladin pronounced disgustedly, seeming to believe it was an explanation. "We try our best not to bring it here with us from Purdue, to suppress it when we find we have failed, but when subjected to scrutiny or other kinds of pressure, it breaks itself into independent cells and goes underground."

"Is very much like slime-mold," Ali suggested, "only a lot noisier."

Around the circumference of *Esmeralda*'s common deck, where dinner had just been prepared and eaten, at least half a dozen open oval hatches stood in the floor, tight against the outer wall, with guard rails made of titanium pipe wrapped around them. They led down and aftward.

Aboard Wilson's little vessel, *Mighty Mouse's Girlfriend*, if she'd had hatches like these, they'd have opened directly into the engineering spaces. Here, he gathered, they led first to family and crew quarters, then probably to the cargo bays, and only then to the engines.

It was almost dark by now on the common deck, and the children had all been taken below. One by one the adults had begun drifting away, as well, either to bed, to their duty shifts, or to some appointment Moonside. Keeping a big ship like this in good working order, even when she was lying in port, was a full time job for many hands. Only the three family musicians—Amorie's grandfather and her uncles—remained. To Wilson's delight, they played a faster waltz now, that went:

> Oh, this is the place where the rock hunters gather,
> With magnetized boots and their suits battened down.
> All sizes and figgers, their hands on the triggers,
> They congregates here on the rock huntin' ground.

He'd especially liked the lyric, "Some are mindin' their consoles while others are yarnin'. There's some standin' up an' some more lyin' down ... " The verse reminded him of some of the people he'd met among the Ceres terraformation crew, who believed that only a truly lazy man could get the job done right, with the proper amount of labor-saving efficiency.

Amorie's relatives had also played and sung, "I's the Bye that Cons the Ship" and another with many verses about a legendary fistfight at a famous party called, remarkably enough, "Lafcadio's Soiree". It was all tremendous fun. Just now they were rendering a low, sweet ballad about a dying young asteroid hunter, apparently, called "Port Saint Mary's".

Wilson had never heard any of this music before, and wondered where it came from—although it did remind him of some of the stuff he'd heard issuing from inside the slatted swinging doors of Brody's Saloon back home in Curringer. As a boy, he'd never been permitted inside, although he'd argued with his mother that it ought to be considered educational, since so much history had been made in the place.

The accent this music was being sung in had to be some kind of Gaelic, Wilson knew, but it wasn't Scottish, he was fairly certain, and it wasn't exactly Irish, either. He didn't know what Welsh or Cornish sounded like, or even Breton, but made a mental note to feed some of the lyrics he'd heard into a search engine when he had a chance.

At last Amorie arose. He'd waited for her to do it for what had seemed like a century. She took Wilson by the hand, and pulled him up, out of his chair, and away from the table. Suddenly, remembering why he was here—or at least why he hoped he was here—his heart began pounding so hard he was surprised that she couldn't hear it, surprised that it didn't simply smash its way through his ribcage and out of his chest.

He couldn't think straight like this, not when he was so nervous. His blood felt like molten lava in his veins. He wondered if it was like this every time, and if so, how the human race had managed to survive.

Giving him a big, reassuring smile—and just the merest hint of a flash of cleavage—Amorie led Wilson across the deck to one of the hatches he'd noticed. The hatch lid, he could see now, was tilted back against the wall on hinges the size of both his fists. Amorie placed a softly-shod toe on either side of the ladder, just below the level of the floor, put her little hands on either side of the ladder where it thrust up through the deck, and gracefully slid downward, to the deck below.

Wilson, who'd been practicing exactly the same maneuver daily, for many weeks, aboard *Mighty Mouse's Girlfriend*, nevertheless surprised himself, in the circumstances, by following the girl's example without mishap.

"This is B-deck, private quarters," Amorie told him when his feet were safely on the floor again. Once more she took him by the hand. She indicated the many doors that lined the outside circumference of the circular hallway. He gathered that these were the less desirable billets, more subject to interplanetary radiation and micrometeorite penetration. He wondered what kind of crew people they put in these cabins.

"The young girls," Amorie told him matter-of-factly when he asked about it. "These walls are pretty much self-sealing, so we don't worry overly about micrometeorites. We keep hoping for some viable mutations, though, to add to our gene pool. We're pretty isolated genetically here, you know, and have been for four or five generations. This is the first time the *Esmeralda*'s put in to port for more than three years."

The opposite wall had fewer doors, of course, but was covered in colorful children's drawings. "We had dinner on A-deck," she went on, "and there are C-deck, D-deck, and E-deck below this one. Almost no one ever goes down to E-deck, it's just too creepy down there. Four more decks for cargo storage, and then the engines. We have six of those."

Amorie dimpled and curtsied sweetly. Wilson wanted her so much it hurt.

She folded herself into his arms. Her scent was intoxicating. His heart raced. She looked up at him and her eyes became his universe. "Do you want to see them now, or can you think of something better to do?"

*
**

"Is hard vacuum, other side of glass," Ali told them.

Having left the makeshift jousters and their tournament behind in the Spider, the two scientists and their offworld guests had taken a brief elevator ride upward several floors and passed through a series of heavy bulkheads to enter a large circular chamber built directly on the Lunar surface. At their backs, through a curving wall of glass so thick it appeared to be tinted green, lay the lamp-lighted hills and rilles and craters they'd seen surrounding the observatory when they'd arrived.

What immediately seized their attention, however, lay outside as well, in the center of the circular walkway they all stood on at the moment, partitioned off by even more of the thick glass (the ceiling over their heads was also glass), so that they occupied, in effect, the inside of a very large, transparent, air-filled glass doughnut. In the center of the doughnut hole stood the very heart of the Culver Telescope, an enormous, unreal-looking bowl of scintillating glass or metal, sitting on stout gimbals above a massive titanium and concrete foundation.

High above it, on three deceptively spindly-looking legs, at the focal point of the parabola below, they saw a cluster of instruments, including several cameras of various kinds, thermocouples, and other devices.

Ali continued. "We are having many 'System's only' or 'System's largest' here at Larsen Farside Observatory. Roger B. Culver Telescope is both. Is system's largest optical reflector, five thousand inches in diameter—which is also being twenty-seven meters—amounting to almost twenty million square inches. Also is System's first and only 'smart' mirror, consisting entirely of hair-fine hexagonal chromium wires, more than two trillion of them, each only three thousandths of inch across, all bundled together, their ends cut and polished by laser."

"Two trillion?" Llyra exclaimed. "But wouldn't it take centuries to—"

"Was assembled here by large team of Japanese robots controlled by artificial intelligence resident in Kenneth M. von Flurchick memorial superduper computer in Luna City, industrial suburb west of Armstrong. Comedian graduate students there let computer call itself 'Mycroft Holmes'."

Familiar with both literary references, Llyra and Jasmeen laughed simultaneously.

Saladin nodded. "Yes, yes, Sir Robert Arthur Anson Conan Heinlein. On weekends they hold sawhorsey tournaments with graduate idiots in Spider."

"But you are right, Miss Ngu," Ali told her. "Even with hundred robots and twenty-four hour supervision by Mycroft, assembling mirror took one year. Seemed longer. Chrome wires controlled by nanomachinery in base, each individually adjustable for height, allowing us to change optical characteristics of telescope and adjust for day-to-day fluctuations of temperature, instabilities of Lunar geology, and so on."

"It sounds expensive," said Julie, who was used to big, expensive undertakings.

"Was painfully expensive," Saladin told her, grimacing. "Woefully expensive. But worth every grain Avoirdupois. This is very profitable operation we are running. And from here, with image-enhancing help from our own, less-gifted computer—without foolish name—we can resolve Pluto as disk, or even see Ngu house on Pallas where niece lives."

Jasmeen's eyes got big. She was accustomed to sunbathing naked on the roof of the house when nobody else was home, or flying about the place.

"Do not worry," Ali told her in a stage whisper. "Secret is safe with us. We could find missing *Fifth Force* if we only knew where to look."

"Is not on roof of Ngu House," Jasmeen offered with an annoyed frown, "If you knew where to look, Uncle, *Fifth Force* would not be missing."

Ali looked puzzled. "Didn't I just say that?"

Wilson swept Amorie into his arms. He was astonished at how light she was, and how warm. She lay her head against his chest and murmured something.

"I'm sorry," he told her, having missed whatever she said while he was catching his breath and trying to regain control of himself. "I didn't—"

She laughed. To him it was like droplets from a sunlit fountain. "I said that's my door, right there, dear Willie. Go ahead, it isn't locked."

Lacking a hand to spare, Wilson pulled the latch handle down with one knee. The oval door swung open easily. Stepping carefully over the pressure threshold, he swung the door shut with a heel. Amorie kept her quarters warm, almost at blood temperature. A soft light came from somewhere.

There was also faint, formless music in the background, vague and insubstantial. The room was so small three quarters of it were taken up with Amorie's bed. It had decorative posts set at each corner that nearly reached the ceiling, with wispy curtains hung between them on rods.

Wilson took the single step that was required to get to the bed. He laid her down gently on the coverlet. She had draped the posts and rods with the same filmy, almost-transparent scarves, in pastel pinks and oranges, that he'd seen in the background while communicating with her over the SolarNet. Her dress tonight seemed to be made of them, as well. He could also smell an elusive, pleasant scent—somehow, it reminded him vaguely of cinnamon—but it was very subtle and not overdone.

Wilson stood for a moment, looking down at Amorie—his Amorie—the blood sizzling through his veins like carbonated water at all the beauty and the promise that he saw before him. Amorie turned on her side, her eyes downcast, one long, smooth leg exposed from the heel—he'd already noticed that she had tiny, shapely feet—to the waist, one small, well-formed breast visible to the rim of its pale brown center.

She allowed him simply to enjoy the sight of her for a long, long moment, then arose to her knees on the bed, facing him. Her dress had now fallen open completely and what he saw was almost painful to behold.

Reaching up, she put her arms around his neck and pulled his mouth down to hers. They kissed for what seemed to him an hour—an hour spent in paradise—and Wilson learned more about the power of a kiss in whatever time it really lasted, than he had ever realized was possible. By the time she finished kissing him, he was shaking all over.

Pulling free a moment, Amorie looked deeply into Wilson's eyes, took his big right hand in both of her tiny ones, spread it flat, and laid it on her left breast—she radiated heat—pressing it firmly against her. Wilson felt her heart, thudding almost as hard as his, and faster. He felt her nipple, swollen hard against the center of his palm.

Leaving his hand where it was, Wilson pulled Amorie to him for another kiss, an eon long, perhaps two eons. He shifted his hand and took her nipple between his thumb and forefinger pinching it and rolling it gently. Amorie moaned into his open mouth as if she'd been mortally wounded, and where her legs came together, pressed herself hard against him. Then her filmy dress was off the rest of the way, and she began frantically attacking the fastenings of his shirt and pants.

When Wilson's chest was bare, Amorie surprised him. She put her lovely mouth to one of his nipples, and began biting it lightly and sucking it. It felt as if a fine steel wire running the length of his body had been heated red hot. He hadn't known that girls did that to boys.

That women did that to men.

He badly wanted to do it to her. He'd dreamed of it a thousand nights, both sleeping and waking. He pressed her backward, onto the bed, to do it. Her legs were still in the kneeling position. Pushing her back onto them made her gasp—possibly with pain—and spread them wide. Possibly she even liked the pain. As he took both of her breasts in his hands and did what he had planned to do, he could feel her grow hot and damp where her legs almost wrapped around him at the waist.

"God, Willie," she gasped, "don't make me wait any longer!"

Wilson obliged, turning within the grasp of her thighs and sliding up through them. He fumbled for just a moment—he knew the mechanics well enough, but had no practical experience with them—then found her.

In an instant, they were one being, and it was his turn to gasp as Amorie proceeded to do more things to him that he hadn't known were possible.

At last came blinding release, a white light like he'd been told indicated enlightenment—or death. He had no doubt it represented an epiphany of some kind. He lay within her for a while—how was it possible that Amorie, who couldn't have weighed more than a hundred standard pounds, could be comfortable beneath him? He weighed twice what—

Then shock so sudden and complete that it felt as though he'd been dashed with a bucketful of ice cold water. "I ... oh my god, Amorie, I ... I wasn't prepared! I didn't even think—I'm so sorry! I was just so—"

She put a tiny, gentle hand over his mouth. Reflexively, he kissed it. "I don't think that's going to matter, dear, sweet Willie. Not at all."

*
**

The fastest gun on the Moon was of two minds.

An exceptionally tall man—which was very unusual in his field of endeavor—he leaned on the steel pipe rail in front of ten rows of fiberglass-topped concrete bleachers, overlooking the working floor of the Armstrong Space Traffic Control Center, a private corporation that kept track of, and advised vessels that traveled in space near and around the Moon. The cost of the service was covered by port fees. Visitors were encouraged to watch the great square dance being called here, twenty-four Earth hours every day, twenty-eight days every Lunar month.

On one hand, the man thought, there was the boy who deserved his attention, presently getting his teenage ashes hauled, likely for the first time, up there in that space-traveling collection of junk full of scavenger rats. But the scavengers would be jealously protecting him, at least for a while, which would make his job impossible. The boy had something they wanted—they'd space an obviously deformed newborn, but he was morally certain that they still had monsters chained in their "basement"—and it would take them a while to get it.

On the other hand, there was the boy's kid sister, that little ice skating devil girl who, he was certain, would someday make a great assassin. At the moment, she was visiting the other side of this freeze-dried owl pellet of a world, which was exactly the same as this side, only there were no decent hotels. If the information he'd just paid for was correct, whether she knew it or not, she'd be taking an even more exotic and spectacular excursion within the next couple of hours.

Because the boy had been spending most of his time aboard his own ship, where he was hard to keep an eye on, mostly in the company of someone he regarded as the most dangerous woman in the System—and the member of the Ngu family the little skater took after most—he'd been watching the girl and her pretty Martian coach, skating every day at the Heinlein, for weeks. He'd even gotten to the point where he enjoyed it. She had powerful protection, too, although she probably didn't know it. He wished the boy and his sister would stick together. The whole thing was putting quite a strain on his capacity for making decisions.

Amorie excused herself for a moment, but she was back before the sheets beside Wilson had cooled. During that brief interlude, he began to worry a little. This first time, it hadn't mattered to him that everyone onboard the *Esmeralda*—every member of Amorie's family—knew exactly where they were now and exactly what they were doing. It had never occurred to him, and he'd been too excited to care in any case.

Now, however, all he could see in his mind's eye were their faces. He was afraid that thoughts like that were going to keep him from … from being ready for her a second time, or a third, or a fourth … Between the perverted bragging that went on in sex magazines online, and the dry clinicality of the pamphlets his mother had given him to read when he'd turned thirteen, he had no idea what was natural or normal.

"You look unhappy, sweet darling Willie," Amorie said, startling him. She'd returned quietly through the hatch she'd left by, which no doubt led to a bathroom, one almost certainly shared with the next cabin.

"Not unhappy," he said, then explained what he was worried about. She was much more than just a girl he'd taken to bed with him tonight, after all. She was the friend—his best friend—with whom he'd shared his every secret on a daily basis for more than a year. He wanted to marry her, to keep her with him forever, have children with her, and grow old with her. There was nothing he felt he couldn't tell her.

Amorie grinned at him. "I understand what you're talking about in theory, darling Willie. There's no such thing as privacy on a vessel like *Esmeralda*, although we all try hard to respect each other's space."

"But I—"

"But nothing. Watch this." She kissed him long and languorously before she pushed him back into the pillows. She kissed his throat, his chest—when she reached his nipples again, he knew he wasn't going to have any trouble, after all. But he wasn't going to tell her, and she probably knew anyway—working her slow, tormenting way down and down and—

Damn! He *did* know that women did this to men, sometimes. He'd often wondered about it.

"Here," she said, freeing him for the briefest possible moment so she could talk. "Hold my wrists behind my back." She put them behind her.

"But Amorie—"

"Just do it! It'll help!"

He obeyed, clamping her wrists behind her as she went on giving him pleasure while pretending to struggle against him. She was right. It did help. Everything else was forgotten. All too soon, he felt an almost irresistible need to finish right there, right where he was. But he resisted a temptation to put a hand on the back of her head and take her.

Panting, Amorie slid up beside him and rolled him over on top of her again. He took her easily then, that time, and again, and again, until they were both covered with sweat, until the insides of their thighs chafed and their bellies ached from the pounding he was giving her.

He took her from behind, and that helped the pain a little. Each time Wilson reached a climax—one Amorie often reached with him—she excused herself briefly and came back to him clean and sweet- smelling.

He took a shower twice himself, but she followed him into the tiny stainless steel cubicle like a starving thing that would die without his not-so-tender ministrations, and his efforts at cleanliness soon degenerated into more violent and desperate lovemaking. The fourth or fifth time they did it, getting started was the very least of his problems. It took him a full forty-five minutes of fevered, relentless pounding just to feel that finishing was possible, and another twenty minutes to reach a climax that felt as if it would tear him in two. He didn't understand how her tiny body could take it. She was made of titanium.

The seventh, and last time took an hour and a half, all of the special attention she could give him—this final time she let him finish in her mouth while she was helping him—and left him covered in sweat again, spent in every way possible for a human being to be spent.

Tomorrow, he knew, each cell in his body would scream, each muscle and every joint, as if he'd worked out all night, or cleaned his three engines. He stroked Amorie's silky hair. What an art, to give someone this much painful pleasure. He never wanted to know how she'd learned it.

"Seven times, Willie! Seven times! I knew I was right about you! You're absolutely magnificent!" Her voice sounded odd, as if her jaw hurt. He hoped he hadn't injured her. She left the bed for the bath again. He'd wanted to say the same to her, but he was speechless and exhausted.

And *drained*.

CHAPTER TWENTY-THREE: THE EGRESS

It has long been observed that, in some sense, a true individualist should be a "citizen" of every country, a free spirit without borders, at home wherever he happens to find himself.

It's even more important to be a "citizen" of every age, the inheritor and beneficiary of every human experience, past present.

The first step in that direction is never to believe anything anyone in authority—politician, bureaucrat, most especially school teacher on the public payroll—has to tell you about history. Compared to any of them, a used car salesman is paragon of integrity and verisimilitude. —*The Diaries of Rosalie Frazier Ngu*

"ALI, THIS IS ANOTHER FINE mess you have gotten us into!"

Despite the circumstances, Llyra, Jasmeen, and Julie burst into laughter, as Ali and Saladin stared at them in perplexed annoyance. Apparently neither of the men had ever seen or heard of Laurel and Hardy. They'd been among Julie's favorites, however, growing up in an otherwise unpleasant and dangerous environment. She'd passed them on to her granddaughter, who had shared them with her mentor and best friend.

What they were all staring at, through the small, circular windows of a simple vehicle—little more than an inexpensive asteroid-hopper clumsily retrofitted to withstand the strains one sixth of a gee put on her, rather than the one tenth she had originally been built for—was Larsen Farside's remote orbital telescope facility, mostly automated as the two scientists had told their guests, in roughly the same orbit as the Moon, but on the opposite side of the Earth, in a position affectionately called "L-Sex".

There was no such Lagrange point, of course. This was actually L-Three, where gravitic forces almost balanced out, as they did at the other Lagrange points, and objects tended to stay put more or less by themselves. A small amount of fuel—"delta-V" Saladin called it, although strictly, that was an archaic Space Agency expression that simply meant a change in motion—had to be expended from time to time to keep the robot observatory in its proper place. People—graduate students for the most part—came here from time to time for various kinds of maintenance.

At the controls of the little spacecraft, apparently as usual, Ali let his fingers skitter over the pilot's keyboard, bringing the little ship to a dead stop, relative to the space station. "Here we are, friends, at L-Sex, so-called, other eyeball of Larsen Farside Observatory."

"Other eyeball?" Jasmeen asked her uncle, winking at Llyra. "How important is other eyeball when you are all the time squinting at sky like this?' She made an eyepiece out of her fist and peered through it.

"How many one-eyed outfielders are in Solar Baseball League? Same number as one-eyed goalies?" Ali held his thumb and forefinger up, about three inches apart. "Average distance between adult human eyes. Very small in scheme of things, very large in human survival. Two eyes tell brain how far off next limb to swing to is. Helps locate prey, avoid leap of predator."

Llyra spoke up. "I get it. Having telescopes both on the Moon and here widens that distance from three inches to half a million miles, helping you to accurately locate objects that are very far away."

"And that are both predator and prey," offered Jasmeen.

Julie gave her an interested look.

"In old days, Earthbound astronomers used Mother Earth for both eyeballs," Ali told them. "Take picture in December, another in July. One hundred eighty-six million miles distance. Accurate, but takes six months."

"Yes," Saladin agreed. "In asteroid-hunting business, six days may be too long, or even six hours. Not so much because of danger—we detect dangerous asteroid average of nine years, two months before collision—but because valued customers are not wanting stale information."

Ali turned to his partner and their passengers. "But we are having acute case of burglars precisely at present moment, do you not agree, Saladin?"

"I have never seen cute burglars before, Ali."

The observatory was roughly T-shaped, where the upright of the T was a squat canister the size of a small apartment building—Llyra and her friends could see light in several rows of windows—housing research facilities, operating systems and machinery, and temporary quarters.

Across one end of the cylinder lay an open construction at least five hundred yards long, looking rather like a radio transmitter tower, except that it didn't taper. At one end was a radio dish like those that filled the area around the Moon-based facility itself. At the other, was a less familiar, and much more complicated-looking object.

Llyra thought she knew what it was.

"What is there to burgle?" asked Saladin. "We are having nothing, I tell you, nothing. Some spare parts for both telescopes, nothing else."

"Air," said Ali. "Water. Rations. Toilet paper."

"Oogh!" Saladin complained, for the most part, to himself. "Have you ever actually tried to go to bathroom here? Not enough gravity, even, to hold you down. Is quite an ord—oops, pardon me ladies!"

Two of the "ladies" burst into laughter. Julie grinned. She had endured vastly worse hardships than trying to make a zero-gee toilet work.

Out the window, at the end of the canister farthest from the telescopes, a small spaceship not unlike their own had attached itself.

"Thousands of ounces platinum we spend to build this facility and has only one airlock? This tin can we are flying here has two airlocks!"

"We did not build facility, remember? We purchased from East American Space Agency. And why are we ever needing second airlock, Saladin? People are coming here only every few weeks for repair and refueling."

Saladin stole a sideways glance at his female guests. "And one other thing."

"Oh, well, then, yes. For one other thing. Must never forget one other thing. But in any event, my friend, we are never needing second airlock."

"Until today," murmured Saladin.

"Until today," Ali conceded.

"What's the 'one other thing'?" asked Llyra.

This time, it was Julie who burst out laughing. The men looked at her in dismay. "Go right gentlemen, ahead, tell her. I want to see you try."

Saladin sighed, wrinkled up his face, unwrinkled it, and sighed again. "Is L-Sex Club," he said, obviously hoping that it would be enough.

"L-Sex Club?" Jasmeen asked her uncle, pretending innocently not to understand what he'd meant. "What sort of club is L-Sex Club, anyway?"

"L-Sex Club," the scientist had begun turning red, either from consternation or from embarrassment, "Is kind of club your parents hope you do not join for at least twenty more years, young lady."

She let her eyes grow big. "You mean when I'm thirty-nine?"

"Possibly never," suggested her other uncle, trying to come to Saladin's rescue. "Have you thoroughly considered career in Catholic church?"

Jasmeen laughed. "But uncle, we are Moslems!"

"At least," he said, "by ancestry."

⁎⁎

Wilson lay on his back in the pilot's chair of his little ship, staring at the center of the instrument cluster before him. He'd been about to leave, after a hard day's work refitting the life support system, and had given the 'com number yet another try, almost on a whim.

Valerie Samson frowned at him, although he didn't know why. Again he wondered what he'd done wrong. Finally, her daughter came to the screen.

"Amorie," he demanded. It was probably natural that he didn't give her a chance to speak first. It was a bad way to start and he realized it about two seconds too late. "Why wouldn't you answer my messages or calls?"

She seemed confused, and more than a little bit annoyed, exactly like her mother. He'd thought that he'd behaved properly aboard the *Esmeralda*, at least in accordance with their customs. So why did both females look at him as if he were something they'd found by turning over a rock? "I'm answering your call now, Willie. What do you want?"

"What do I—" He blinked, speechless. What was going on? The gunfight on Ceres, even that strange business with the Null Delta Em bomber, had been easier to get through, and less disorienting. Aware that something life-alteringly terrible had happened, or was about to happen, or was happening now, he had an odd metallic taste in his mouth. "Amorie, tell me what's wrong! I thought that we—especially after—"

Amorie nodded as if she'd come to a sudden enlightenment. "Why, there's nothing wrong, Willie, nothing at all. We each did what was in us to do. We each did what we had to do. And now it's finished. Now we're done."

"Done? What do you—?" Wilson's scalp tingled, along with the back of his neck. For the first time in his life his palms were sweaty.

Amorie looked just as beautiful and desirable as she ever did. But she also seemed exasperated. "Didn't you have a good time with me, Willie? Didn't I give you a night that you'll remember the rest your life?"

There wasn't any other way that he could answer that one honestly. "Yes, Amorie, you did. For the rest of my life. But I thought … I wanted …"

She nodded. God, she had long eyelashes. "But you wanted more, Willie, didn't you? I think I understand—and I'm more flattered by it than you'll ever know. You wanted more nights like the one we had, certainly—although I don't know how we'd survive it. You wanted to be with me forever. You wanted to get married and maybe even have a family …

"Yes, Amorie, that's just what I thought. That's just what I wanted."

She took in a, long, deep breath and let it out. Behind her, he could see her mother and some of the others preparing dinner again. "And I believe you, my darling Willie. But you see, the trouble is that I can't have a family. I'm not physically capable. I can't do much of anything, really, except what I do. Do you want to know what I do?"

"Amorie, please don't—" He was afraid of what she would say.

"Oh, Willie, that wasn't very nice!" She laughed a bit ruefully. "It isn't what you think, dear. You see, my people have done very well for themselves over the past century. We're very successful, we're very rich. We own a fleet of hunters. But there was a cost. Radiation, the genetic isolation I told you about. We were about ten years away from extinction until a great grandmother of mine thought this system out."

"This system?" Now he was even more afraid.

She tipped her head to one side a little, a gesture he'd always found extremely appealing. "I have no mathematical aptitude, Willie dear, no mechanical or engineering potential. My reflexes are too slow to pilot a ship. There's absolutely nothing I can do to justify the food I eat, or the oxygen I breathe, or the bed I occupy, or the room I take up. If my family had known about me ahead of time—before I was born, or even shortly afterward—I'd have been exposed to the Void."

He'd heard this kind of thing about some hunters. "I—"

"You didn't see most of my family, Willie. Most of them stayed in their quarters the night you were here, like they always do on nights like that. You only saw the ones who can hide their infirmities under their clothing—or who can pass for normal like I do because their problems are all on the inside, and they can go out in public in the daylight."

"I—"

"Let me finish, Willie darling, please. Because it turned out that I did have something going for me, after all. I was—I am—the prettiest girl ever born into the Samson family. And that's worth something, as it happens. It's worth quite a lot. Strong, intelligent, brave young men like me, you see. They like me very much. They like me well enough—just as you did, Willie—to give me a wonderful gift."

"A gift?" By now, Wilson thought he knew what was coming, and he was beginning to get a terrible, twisted feeling in the pit of his stomach.

"It's a miraculous gift, believe me, Willie. They give me all of their strength, all of their intelligence, and all of their bravery. And because I can't make any practical use of it myself, I share it out among my sisters and my cousins and my aunts. Willie, you gave me enough of your strength, your intelligence, and your bravery for a dozen healthy girls! I don't know of any adequate way to thank you, really, except to say that I enjoyed it, too. Most times, you know, I don't."

Why couldn't he just die, and disappear, right now? He said, "Most times ... "

"Yes, Willie, most times. Most times they're big, ugly, sweaty young men—more of them hunters, than anything else—who may have excellent genetic profiles, but they have no awareness at all that the person in bed with them is a real live human being. Sometimes it can even be dangerous. But it's always worth it. Always. Every child you saw aboard the *Esmeralda* at dinner that night was *mine*, Willie. That is, in order to create them, I brought good, new, fresh DNA to my family."

There were tears in Amorie's eyes, now. He'd never seen that before. And they were tears of happiness. This was the strangest, saddest thing he'd ever heard of, and he didn't know what to say to her.

She smiled. "My mom is the statistician. She says, even though I can't have children myself, in my own way I'll be the mother—and in only one generation, Willie—of whole new healthy, happy family of Samsons!"

"So you have it all planned out, in advance?"

She nodded. "And when I'm too old to do it any more, I won't feel like I have to jump out of an airlock. I'll have earned my retirement. I'll be surrounded by people who won't have to hide whenever company comes. People who possess all of the strengths and talents that I lack, myself. People I made, who wouldn't be there if it weren't for me."

Wilson said nothing. There wasn't anything to say.

Amorie said, "I'm telling you this, Willie, so you'll understand, and maybe so you won't feel quite so ... well, hurt. And because you're the only one who ever tried to call me back the next day, or wanted to know why. You can't know how much I appreciate it that you care."

"Amorie, I—"

"Go live your life, my dear, sweet, darling Willie. Fix your ship up and have good luck with her. I'm getting married myself, next month—it's an arranged family thing. Find the Diamond Rogue. Find a girl you can love and make a family of your own with her. And maybe … maybe think of me now and again."

*
*

Llyra stepped through the airlock built into the nose of Ali and Saladin's little hopper, into the airlock built into the stern of the strange shuttle that had docked with the observatory station called "L-Sex". The interior of the latter was clean, featureless, and impersonal, almost sterile, as if it were not somebody's private property.

She was following Ali and her grandmother, Julie. Jasmeen was right behind her, and Saladin took up the rear. The two men had their guns out this time. Once inside the station, they had argued, they would know in what directions—and at what objects—it was safe to shoot.

Jasmeen, Llyra and Julie (Julie somewhat uncharacteristically, her granddaughter thought, probably serving as an example to the girls) had grudgingly agreed not to draw theirs unless they were in imminent danger.

Having secured the gasketed doors they'd come in by, it was now safe for them to open the airlock door that would lead into the station.

"Will be unfortunately noisy operation," Ali observed. "Anyone in station will know that there is company coming and have time to be ready.'

He put his hand on the heavy metal wheel, believing that it would be quieter than using the machinery that ordinarily turned it. Before he could apply any pressure, however, there was the sound of a big electric motor, and then, slowly at first, the wheel began moving by itself.

As the door swung aside, two young individuals were there to greet them.

"So is you two, Saladin told them. "I was wondering why I did not see you two poking sticks and cheerleadering down in Culversac end of Spider."

The boy's hair was tousled, and so was the girl's, although it might have been the lack of gravity. They were of opposite sexes, but they were dressed almost identically, in jeans and running shoes. He wore a plaid, cotton shortsleeved shirt with a single pocket. She wore a little white top of some kind with a bit of lace around the collar. Over that, she wore an oversized flannel shirt—probably his—as a jacket.

Llyra noticed immediately that it had been buttoned crookedly, one button out of synch, as her father put it. It had been fastened in haste.

"What are you doing here?" Saladin demanded. "Why did you not sign selves in for coming here on roster board in administrative office? Where did you get ship out there, fastened like lampfish to single airlock?"

Ali interjected himself, "Lamprey, Saladin. Is lamprey. But yes, where? We had to crawl through it like … like … through-crawling things."

The boy spoke up while the girl tried surreptitiously to rebutton her shirt. "We didn't sign the roster board because we weren't at Larsen Farside. We were in Armstrong City, Dr. Khalidov. It's our day off."

"Yes," said the girl, having succeeded with her jacket. "We just happened to check the website for this place—you know how it goes—and discovered that there was something was wrong here—very wrong."

Nodding enthusiastically, the boy agreed, "That's right. The navigation values for the optical telescope and the radio telescope didn't match, and both of them disagreed with the values at Larsen Farside."

"So we rented a commercial hopper from Avis," said the girl, "flew here, and found that the station was three hundred feet off its proper location."

Her companion said, "We fired up the thrusters and fixed that."

"We were … um … that is, we had just begun recalibrating the navs on both of the telescopes," she told them, "when you folks got here."

Saladin nodded, "All because you happened to check website on day off."

"And not because," added Ali, "you wanted to see if shore is transparent—"

Both miscreants, along with Llyra, Jasmeen, and Julie said, "What?"

"I think he means if coast was clear." Saladin suggested.

"Yes," Ali replied, "See if coast is clear for to join L-Sex Club."

The girl blushed deeply. The boy stood by her with an arm around her.

"Good for you!" Julie whispered to them. "You think that rental out there has enough reaction mass to reach L-Four?"

They nodded.

*
**

"Hi, there, kiddo! I didn't know what time it is for you, so I stopped off at Brother Mel's Zero Gee Pit Barbecue when I got back to L-Four just now and got you some breakfast, lunch, dinner, or whatever."

Wilson looked up from his work. His eyes, Julie noticed, were red-rimmed with what looked to her like unshed tears. She'd always had an uneasy feeling about that Samson girl, although it hadn't been her place to say so, and probably wouldn't have done any good if it had. Unshed tears, in her opinion, caused even worse heart trouble and probably cancer. Sometimes—not often—it was easier being a woman.

He said, "Thanks, Julie. I'm not sure I'm very hungry right now. I've got the reefer working finally, though, You could put it in there.

"Not on your life, Captain my Captain. I got you two giant pulled pork sandwiches on onion buns with extra sauce—Sweet Carolina—skinny French fries, cole slaw, and a couple of those jalapeno dill pickles they have. Refrigeration constitutes sandwich abuse, a serious crime in these parts. They need to be eaten pronto, as we say in Newark."

"Western Newark." Wilson straightened up slowly. He'd been squatting beside this access port for hours, wrestling with the stubborn devices inside, and despite the lack of gravity, his knees and back were stiff and painful.

"Okay," he told his grandmother. "I give. What have we got to drink?""

"The only thing fit to drink with hot food—ginger beer!"

"Ginger beer?"

The kicked themselves up into the piloting dome of *Mighty Mouse's Girlfriend* to watch the stars and the traffic around L-Four as they ate. Julie never tired of watching different types and models of ship going by. She'd have had one of her own if she could have thought of any good reason to. She knew she didn't have the temperament to hunt asteroids.

As they ate, she watched her grandson, too. She wanted him to talk about what had happened—she had a couple of good guesses—and start getting it out of his system. She believed he wanted to talk, too, but she wouldn't press it. She'd lived with Billy Ngu a long time, and thought that Wilson was more like him than anyone else in the family.

At last, Wilson took a big swallow from his second baggie of ginger beer, and said, "Wow! That stuff is hotter than the barbecue sauce!"

"Good, isn't it?"

"Sure is! Do we have another baggie?"

"In the 'fridge, Honey, I bought plenty. Bring me one, too, will you?"

When he had kicked his way back to the pilot's seat and velcroed himself in, he said, "It didn't go well, Grandma." Unlike his little sister, he seldom called her that when he wasn't hurt in some way.

"No?" she answered neutrally, pretending to pay attention to her pickle. 'You mean your visit with your friend aboard the asteroid hunter?"

"Her name is Amorie Samson, aboard her family's the *Esmeralda*. Actually, the visit itself went … very well. I can't tell you how well."

"Literally, I imagine. So why are you all down and out, then?"

Slowly, keeping his eyes on his shoes, Wilson began telling his grandmother about the two terrible days he'd suffered through after his visit to the *Esmeralda*, about not being able to reach Amorie—with whom he had communicated every day, sometimes several times a day, for more than a year—and then about their final, surreal conversation.

They didn't speak for a long while. The situation was much worse than Julie had imagined. "So what are you planning to do now?" she asked.

Wilson turned and looked at Julie. It was one of those rare moments in his life when he realized all over again how strange it must be to be seeking grandmotherly comfort and advice from a beautiful young woman who appeared outwardly only a year or two older than he did.

"I'm thinking maybe I should finish overhauling and refitting *Mighty Mouse's Girlfriend*, and sell her for three times what I paid for her, as Lafcadio was planning to do, and go back to work on Ceres."

"Where you belong?" Julie asked, arching her eyebrows.

He met her gaze. "Something like that, sure. If Dad will have me."

"Why shouldn't he?" he asked. "You think your father's likely to be angry or ashamed of you because you got your heart broken?"

He sat up. "Wow! You know, somewhere down deep inside, that's exactly what I was thinking."

"I knew you were. Remind me sometime to tell you some stories about him when he was your age. He was the king of broken hearts, himself."

Wilson grinned ruefully and shook his head. "Sometimes I think he still is."

She nodded. "Me, too."

Julie put an arm around her grandson's big shoulder. "Look here, Honey, you can't throw your whole dream away because one corner of it turned sour. I'm going to tell you something that you won't believe right now. But I solemnly promise you that a day will come when you finally realize that this was the best thing that ever happened to you."

CHAPTER TWENTY-FOUR: SAVE THE SKY

There is more than one kind of courage. One is the physical willingness, despite great fear, to leap into the jaws of death. The other is to maintain a difficult—sometimes unpopular—effort for years or even decades, despite loneliness, privation, or public derision. Of the two, the latter is less easy, but more likely to produce lasting results.

It is also, by far, the rarer.

When those who have earned great wealth legitimately, by demonstrating that latter kind of courage, are criticized or attacked, it is usually by those who lack it altogether. —*The Diaries of Rosalie Frazier Ngu*

THE FASTEST GUN IN THE Moon wasn't in the Moon at this particular moment.

At this particular moment, he had concealed himself in a kitchen cupboard he had folded his entire length into, onboard "L-Sex". He had held the position, knees pressed against his ears, breathing shallowly since there was no room to breathe deeply, for slightly more than two hours.

That was nothing, of course. As a young Special Forces sergeant in East America's ill-fated war in easternmost Siberia, twenty years ago, he'd been captured by a mixed force of Chinese, Koreans, and Russian mercenaries, taken to a small camp on the Manchurian border, forced into smaller boxes than this, and kept there for days, or even weeks. They hadn't bothered to interrogate him. He didn't possess any valuable information, and they had known it. They had simply wanted to see him suffer.

When the P.O.W. camp was overrun by his own side's mercenaries, he had been made to walk back three hundred kilometers to his old unit. In the hospital, his superiors had debriefed him around the clock for weeks, employing drugs and electronic "stimulation" to make absolutely sure he was telling them the whole truth concerning what he'd been put through.

The day of his discharge, he'd robbed a company armory and deserted. Alone, laden with weapons, he'd retraced the three hundred klicks to the ruins of the camp, then another hundred to where they'd relocated. The raid that had delivered him into the hands of what he'd ceased to think of as his own side had not been successful in any other respect. On returning, he'd killed every one of his former tormentors, mostly with his bare hands.

Following that, he'd walked out, living off the country, until he reached India, three years later, where he established a new identity—he'd had no money to begin with, but he was very good at certain high-paying tasks—and let his old self remain listed as Missing In Action.

He doubted by then that anybody cared.

But that was then and this was now. Hearing both ships break with the station and depart, he pushed the cupboard open with an elbow, and began unfolding his long legs above the kitchen countertop. As soon as he could, he used a personal phone (not his own) to call the computer he'd left aboard his own rental vessel, and ordered it to come get him. As he waited for ship and circulation to return, he reached back into the cupboard for an item he'd left there, and placed another call.

"Oh. It's you," said the voice at the other end. Please wait for one minute while I take this somewhere where we can talk privately."

The man sitting on the kitchen countertop heard the other man get out of a spring-loaded desk chair, open a door, and close it again. Pretty clearly, he'd locked himself in the bathroom.

"Very well. What have you got?"

"Switch on your video," the man in the kitchen replied.

"This is necessary?'

"If you want to see it." He held it before the pickup. "East American fragmentation grenade. Depleted uranium. Would have blown the place to bits, where it was, on the fusion reactor. I came because I knew one of your subjects was coming soon, found it, defanged it, got it off the reactor just in time. A pair of horny young grad students got here just before your subject did and almost interrupted me."

"Any idea who is responsible?"

"The individual who planted it I didn't recognize. With the disposable push unit I attached to it, the body will probably burn up in the sun, given a decade or so. I only have suspicions about the client. It's typical of the work and style of Null Delta Em."

"What do you mean, it just didn't go off?"

Anna Wertham Savage, world-acclaimed author of the bestselling book *Massquake!* (now in its fifty-seventh printing), and leader of the Mass Movement, wasn't having one of her better days. In fact, it was by far the worst day she could remember since that young criminal Wilson Ngu had single-handedly wiped out Null Delta Em's valiant Environmental Defense Brigade, and been given a medal and money for it.

Come to think of it, the same people were here now who were here then. P.E. "Honest Paul" Luegner, leader of Null Delta Em, occupied the sofa this time, and Johnnie "the Fish" Crenicichla, a go-between who worked for both organizations, sat in the most comfortable chair. Aside from that, the only other difference was that the portrait on the wall above her desk was that of the eternally blessed Paul Erlich, instead of Rachael Carson, who had recently fallen out of political fashion.

Savage had not thrown Carson's framed portrait away, however, but stored it in a closet. Day to day changes in the acceptability of historic personalities were unpredictable. Sometimes it seemed that some people were far more politically active after they were dead than before.

"That's right, Annie," Luegner told her. He'd just returned from a rare visit to the Moon on the very Null Delta Em business they were discussing now. "The damn thing should have been several thousand tons of rapidly-dispersing metallic confetti by now, floating around in an unnatural and decaying orbit. Instead, it's still the very picture of technological health. We have no idea why, or of what happened to our operative."

"It's so difficult to get good help these days." Crenicichla looked unhappy. "Meanwhile we're standing out in public with our flies open, and we have no effective counter-statement to what's happening on Ceres, later on this week." This pair of idiots had it easy, he thought. They didn't have to report upstairs to "You-Know-Who", the powerful and faceless men and women who were the real controllers of everything that happened, both politically and economically, in East America.

He'd just come from the paneled boardroom of the ancient Boston Bank where they met—he still felt as if he'd been chewed on—and he was expected back there this afternoon, presumably for more of the same.

In despair, Savage gazed out the office window at her beloved City of Five Colleges. In a world that often sped by at a blurring speed, this refuge from cupidity and avarice never changed, except for the better. It couldn't change, because change was against the law. The Amherst board of governors had recently managed to push the legal limit on visible technology backward, from the originally voted-on 2000, to 1950. All over town, construction scaffolds across the faces of buildings were helping to eradicate another fifty years of false progress. Streets were being scoured for automobiles of inappropriate vintage, and this time, there was a dress code to compel compliance with.

Perhaps in that spirit, she wouldn't own a 3DTV set and almost never read a newspaper or magazine, so she was often behind the times. Now she braced herself for another set of outrages. "I'm not supposed to know about things like this observatory business. And I don't know what's going on on Ceres. I've been too busy recording lectures for distribution."

"And hiding out in this toy town of yours." Luegner rolled his eyes. "Honestly, Annie, I don't see how you can hope to change the world without keeping updated on what it is and what it's turning into."

Indignantly, Savage retorted, "I know perfectly well what the world is, Paul—I do travel, you know, on the lecture circuit—and I also know all too well what it's turning into, thanks to nothing but greed."

More and more—perhaps because of forty-odd lectures she gave every year, mostly in North America and Europe, but all around the globe, and despite the studied cynicism of these two men and others like them—the threat of worldwide gravitic catastrophe was real to her.

"The danger looms larger," she would tell them, "with every ship that lands on the planet, bearing cargo from the Moon, from Mars, and especially from the Asteroid Belt. And now, despite my warnings, despite the ill-considered but understandable threats from Null Delta Em to destroy them before they can be completed, there is talk of building so-called 'space elevators' in equatorial South America and Africa, so that even more life-threatening alien mass can be imported from outer space."

Of course they wouldn't listen to her in South America and Africa, where she had never been invited to speak, and where projects like the space elevator offered false promises of ending centuries of poverty among the masses. Increasingly, in her mind's eye—in her dreams, as well—she saw the Earth's crust slow, relative to the motion of the core. She saw it slip and crumble, worldwide, so that in a single day, a single hour, humanity and all of its works were shattered and ground to dust, ending six thousand years of history, of Sumeria, Babylon, Egypt, and Rome, of Michelangelo and Mozart, in flame and smoke and horror.

"Annie!"

"What?" She blinked. "Oh, sorry. Woolgathering, I'm afraid."

"Where did you go?" Luegner asked her, looking concerned. "For a moment, there, I thought you'd had a stroke. We were about to discuss Adam Ngu. He and his company are about to do something significant on Ceres."

She nodded. "I've been concentrating hardest on space elevators for the past few weeks, Paul, and I haven't been paying much attention to Ceres. Anyway, there's never very much in the news now about the asteroids—"

"Because," Crenicichla broke in, "we arrange it that way. There's plenty happening out there all right. What Paul is talking about, on Ceres, they've got their plastic envelope down on the surface, welded together, and tested for leaks. Before they start stringing the steel cable to hold it down, they'll hold a big ceremony, and inject the first generation of tailored microbes into the soil. It'll generate a poisonous reducing atmosphere at about the same rate that they string the cables."

Luegner nodded. "They're going to throw a party at the end of the week to celebrate this stage of completion. We'd hoped destroying Larsen Farside's orbiting observatory would throw cold water on their enthusiasm. Now we've got a missing agent, his weapon—and possibly his fingerprints—in the hands of the enemy, and a party about to start."

"I told you I'm not supposed to know about these things, Paul!"

"It isn't pretty," Crenicichla agreed. "That's the plain truth. I could probably use a large dose of credible deniability, myself. The reason I asked you to meet me here today, all three of us, that is—although ordinarily, we're never even supposed to be together, let alone seen together—is that something extraordinary has happened, something absolutely unprecedented." He reached into his stylish (for Amherst) two-toned 1950s sportcoat and extracted two folded sheets of paper.

He handed one to Savage. the other to Luegner, then held up one of his own. "Careful," he warned them. "That's flash paper, tissue soaked with a nitrate and dried. There's another chemical on one corner. All you do is stomp it, or put it on a hard surface and strike it with something. It bursts into flame and burns so quick it's like it wasn't there."

"So what's so remarkable about this?" Luegner asked. "I seems to outline a basic Null Delta Em mission—albeit a rather ambitious one."

"And why am I being told about it in advance?" Savage wanted to know.

"It's remarkable because it won't happen for about eighteen months—it's partly dependent on Adam Ngu's schedule—but instead of letting us pick our target as we usually do, and decide how to take it, this mission has been planned in detail by the folks who pay our salaries."

"And I—" Savage began.

"You're being told about it, Annie, because the Mass Movement will make a case against Ngu and his cohorts for us, from now until the big moment. This will be an exceptionally violent and bloody action; we'll want at least a fraction of the voting public to believe it was justified."

Luegner peered at his sheet of paper and whistled. "Violent and bloody hardly describes it! They're looking to change the course of history!"

"That's the idea, Paul. As you see, Ngu'll hold another ceremony the day the last cable is in place and he injects the second designer microbe to kill off the first and begin generating a nitrogen-oxygen atmosphere. A few hours before that happens—we're still considering the timing—Null Delta Em will strike, stealing Ngu's thunder, demonstrating the danger of traveling, working, living, and building in space. The primary team has already been selected and has started training."

"That's enough!" Savage exclaimed. "I don't want to know any more! I don't want to know what I already know! I'll concentrate on Ngu and the terraformation of Ceres if I'm ordered to—although the space elevators are a far worse threat and there's the danger of simply publicizing Ngu and his efforts—but I demand not to be told any more!"

"Okay ... " Crenicichla rose and put on the straw fedora that went with his jacket, pleated slacks, and two-tone shoes. "We all have our orders. Read 'em and burn 'em. Paul, why don't you come with me? We have some items to discuss, and I can show my 'brand new' Kaiser Henry J."

***

Contract ice.

This morning—it happened to be Christmas morning—they were alone, not just on this sheet, but in the entire six-sheet facility, a vast cavern that always reminded Llyra of the salt mines she'd seen in photographs taken on the Earth. The music coming over the Heinlein's public address system was from Trinward's haunting *Lost Fifth Force* suite.

Wearing her long, black, heavy coat that nearly touched the ice—a tradition with skating coaches; underneath she might easily have been wearing sweats, an evening gown, or daylight fluorescent hotpants and a matching halter top—Jasmeen stood at the rink gate nearest the main lobby doors, watching Llyra and making movies with her pocket computer.

Llyra sped diagonally across the ice, from one rounded corner the other, until, almost at the boards, as the powerful music swelled to one of its many crescendos, she suddenly leaped upward, six, eight, ten, twelve feet above the ice, turning in the air once, twice, three times, then three and a half, and landing smoothly, trailing leg at full extension, light as a feather, without any impact noise, skating backwards.

For both of them, it was a wonderful moment, and fully appropriate to a holiday they were celebrating by doing the work they loved best. After a long, dry season, it was Llyra's first successful triple Axel—in the Moon. It had once been estimated—back in the century of a fifty-state America—that a double Axel cost a skater's parents ten thousand dollars, and the skater herself perhaps as many as a thousand falls.

Llyra's first triple Axel had happened on Pallas, at the Brody, a long time before she had met Jasmeen, when she was an athletically precocious six years old. This morning she'd done it in three and one third times the gravity she'd grown up in, after at least a thousand unsuccessful attempts, and "only" six months of nearly superhuman effort.

"Ta-da!" she sang as she skated back to her Chechen coach with a great big grin. Jasmeen was grinning, too, and there were tears in her eyes, as well. She grabbed Llyra when she arrived and hugged her until she squeaked. They both took a big drink of water from plastic bottles they'd brought with them, then decided to give the triple Axel another try. It was important, because it was the doorway to the quadruple jumps.

"I have often wondered what it means, this 'ta-da'."

"It means, 'Lookie what I did!'"

It was equally important because there was a new and urgent reason for Llyra to perform well and get along quickly to higher levels. She and Jasmeen had seen "the" commercial for the first time on 3DTV last night—Llyra's commercial—the commercial that Sheridan Sinclair, Chairman of the Board of the Curringer Foundation had promised to make (or threatened, it didn't make very much difference) and her father had provided recordings for, of his daughter skating her heart out on Ceres.

That day, on that little artificial pond under the construction dome, she'd done a quintuple Axel without really thinking about it very much. She'd done a heart-stopping, breath-taking double backflip, too. Merry Christmas, Llyra, now you're really going to look like an idiot.

The recording was being used by the Curringer Foundation to pique interest in investment—as well as future tourism and homesteading—on that little world. The small Pallatian advertising agency that Sinclair and her father had hired had even sent her a check for her performance. According to SFSA rules, she had to spend the money on skating expenses, or lose her amateur status where competition was concerned.

Her father had called her all the way from Pallas to wish her a Merry Christmas and tell her about the ad campaign. Thirty minutes' worth of transmission lag made real conversation impossible of course. He was there on business, but was calling from Ngu House. Llyra could see her mother in the background, not looking particularly unhappy about it. As far as Llyra was concerned, that was Christmas present enough.

"So be sure not to miss it tonight, baby," he'd said. "We'll be running it a lot over the holidays. They've also hired an artist, and you're about to become the logo for the entire Ceres Terraformation Project." His words had given her an indefinably odd feeling in her stomach.

Today—the morning after, as it were—the whole thing still didn't seem real, although she'd recorded the commercial and watched it at least a dozen times last night. She'd been able to skate much better at Ceres' one tenth of a standard gravity, of course, than she could at Luna's one sixth, but most people wouldn't understand that, and would want to see her equal the performance that they'd seen on 3DTV.

No pressure there, no pressure at all.

The next try, Llyra took off too late, slammed into the boards in the middle of her second turn, and fell onto her side from six feet in the air. She lay there on the ice for just a moment, "appreciating" her bruises (from the inside, of course—no professional athlete ever rubbed an injury in public) and trying to catch the breath that had been blasted out of her. Jasmeen skated up to her and took her hand.

"Are you going to live, my little?" she asked Llyra, hauling her up.

"Yeah," Llyra said, on her feet again, "but I promise not to enjoy it."

They both laughed.

Llyra shook herself and headed for the other corner to try the jump again.

*
**

Wilson said, "Download successful, Larsen Farside. Thank you very much."

A pleasant female voice replied, "You're welcome, *Mighty Mouse's Girlfriend*—I just love the name of your ship!—we'll send you our bill."

Actually, she had already; it had been embedded in the downloaded data now streaming past his eyes on the control console. Exclusives were very expensive. If this hunt didn't go well, his partner would be unhappy.

On the other hand, he caught himself wondering idly what the girl at the Larsen Farside end of the conversation was like. Pretty? Funny? Nice? Maybe it was a sign that he was finally getting over Amorie. He hadn't heard from her since that last time on the 'com. Her family's ship *Esmeralda* had left Lunar space and was headed upsystem shortly afterward.

She might even be married by now.

Taking a last lovely bite of his handmade gourmet ham and cheese sandwich (one thing Julie wouldn't let him scrimp on was food), and a last gulp of his Coke before letting them both float in their plastic baggies at the ends of their tethers—too short to interfere with the controls—Wilson attacked the keys before him, converting what Larsen Farside had just sent him into something his own navigational computer could use. He supposed he could have automated the process, but then he wouldn't have known the data a fraction as well as he did by the time he'd finished their manual entry. His dad had taught him that.

Satisfied, he struck a virtual key relabeled "ANY".

Seemingly all by herself, *Mighty Mouse's Girlfriend* suddenly slewed downward and sideways some forty-three degrees, fifty-seven minutes, driven by a single engine and her attitude thrusters. There came a surge of acceleration as she came into the correct alignment and her other two engines cut in. She and her owner were off, in a blaze of fusion-heated reaction mass, after their first exclusive quarry.

The targeted object had been described as dark-colored and potato-shaped. That was an astronomer's idea of a joke, of course. The same description applied to ninety-nine percent of all the asteroids and meteoroids and other space junk ever found. It was roughly forty feet along its longest axis, almost purely metallic, and unusually rich in palladium. It was estimated to be a monolith, rather than a loose aggregate, which meant that it would be much easier to capture and control.

Extra points, as well, because it was headed straight for the middle of L-Two, a sector of otherwise empty space that was occupied by some two hundred artificial habitations and fifty times that many people. For bounty purposes, L-Two was considered one of the Settled Worlds. This asteroid was no Diamond Rogue, but by every criterion meaningful to hunters, it was a find.

With a whoop, Wilson pursued his quarry, radar and lidar alive and singing to him from different portions of the musical scale. Unlike sonar, the actual returns occurred at the speed of light. They were only being simulated with sonar-like noises, rather like the false colors that are often useful in scientific photography. The return times kept getting shorter and shorter, until they froze and became a solid, disharmonious chord. He could see the target, now, through the curved plastic wall in front of him. Throwing switches, he armed the cable gun under the ship's "chin" and prepared to throw a loop on his first rock.

"What the hell kind of a name is *Mighty Mouse's Girlfriend*, anyway?" The harsh male voice came to him abruptly over his general address radio system. Unlike the encrypted female signal from Larsen Farside, it did not sound at all pleasant, and indeed, it wasn't meant to.

"That all depends, I suppose," Wilson replied evenly, stepping up his oxygen partial pressure. He wondered whether the guy was reading his transponder or could actually see him. "Who the hell wants to know?"

"*Space Viper*, out of Port Plato—the guy whose hunting territory you're trespassing in, newbie! Let go of that rock, and make contrails!"

That was stupid. You only saw contrails in an atmosphere. And to his knowledge, there was no Port Plato—probably no *Space Viper*, either.

Wilson had been warned about this, during the hundreds of hours of classes he'd suffered through at the insistence of his grandmother and her insurance underwriter. (His certificate of completion sat in a frame, fastened to the wall near the edge of the dome.) Several portside bullies—including a couple he'd gone to shiphandling school with—had already tried to warn him not to hunt "their" territories, until somebody had told them who Emerson was and what he'd done on Ceres.

His great grandfather Emerson's .45 Magnum Grizzly automatic pistol, hanging low on his right hip, had probably been persuasive, as well.

His grandmother told him that these people would probably have been muggers, politicians, or union bosses, back on Earth, in New Jersey.

Now Wilson laughed. "You know there's no such thing as personal territory out here, *Space Viper*—and where'd you get a name like that, anyway, a bubble gum machine?—according to the Asteroid and Meteoroid Hunters' and Miners' Concurrence of 2097. I've got it right here, and could read you the relevant paragraphs, but why don't you just fribble off, instead? Unless you want to be formally accused of piracy."

A snarl: "Yeah? And just who's gonna survive this to do that, *Girlfriend*?"

"I am," said Wilson. Fingers flying on the keyboard, he rolled his ship to bring her dorsal surface to bear on the intruder, rotated a big item of equipment, and raised it until it pointed at the other vessel. "You sort of forgot the Mighty Mouse part, *Viper*. I've got a brand new Coprates Electric ninety gigawatt particle cannon here, in a spiffy universal swivel mount, trained on your front windows right now."

Wilson flipped the red switch cover up and backward, and threw the arming toggle. An entire section of the control panel that had been dark before, now lit up like Armstrong's Eagle Avenue on a Saturday night.

It was impressive, considering that the particle cannon was on backorder and wouldn't be installed until late next week at the very earliest. All he had pointed at his adversary was the expensive swivel mounting.

He laughed. "What do you say, *Viper*, assuming that's your real name?"

Without another word, the ship that called itself *Space Viper* veered off and disappeared in a bright blast of fusion-heated reaction mass.

This is *fun*, thought Emerson, reaching for his ham and cheese sandwich.

*
**

The two men emerged from the freight elevator and stepped into the grimy alley behind the office building occupied, in part, by the Mass Movement.

One of them immediately reached into a jacket pocket and extracted a package of cigarettes that would have cost him twenty East American dollars had he bought it in Amherst or anywhere in Massachusetts. He had bought in Wyoming, where it had cost about one percent of that amount.

"Careful, Paul," the second man warned the first. "It's illegal to be seen smoking in public in this town. There are cameras and mikes everywhere."

Pulling the cellophane wrapper off, Luegner put it in his pocket and tapped the bottom of the pack until a single cigarette emerged. "Except for where people pay for them not to be, like this alley, for instance?"

Johnnie Crenicichla nodded. "Yeah, for instance. You get what we needed?"

Luegner held up his politically correct 1950s vintage Zippo lighter. "Got it in spades. If this operation goes all right, it'll be bigger than September 11, 2001, or what happened to Denver. If it goes smoothly, then we'll never need the stuff I recorded up there this morning."

Crenicichla laughed. "And if it doesn't, then, morally outraged at the crime your underlings committed without your knowledge consent, you'll resign from NDE. The recording, properly edited, will deprive Annie of credible deniability, and hang the crime on her. When she's out of the picture, you'll reluctantly take over and head the Mass Movement."

"Pretty damned slick," Luegner agreed. "Except for one tiny little thing. Give me the recording you made, Johnnie, while I was making mine."

"Paul!" Crenicichla pretended to wide-eyed, open-mouthed surprise astonishment, but not particularly well, Luegner thought. It was what came of not spending enough time around coeds, testing the extreme limits of their gullibility, "What in God's name can you be talking about?"

Luegner drew a politically correct 1950s vintage .45 auto from inside his coat and thumbed the hammer back. He always carried a round in the chamber. "Come on, Johnnie, I know our bosses all too well. Do it, unless you'd like to give the city's gunfire location system a test."

CHAPTER TWENTY-FIVE: MOON OF EYES

Despite the voluminous and unmistakable evidence all around me, all my life, it has taken me the better part of sixty years to reach the conclusion that all government—no matter what kind it is or claims to be—is parasitic and evil in its primary nature, and that indeed, six thousand years of propaganda to the contrary, its exists for no other purpose than to *be* parasitic and evil.

My husband Emerson seems to have understood this since the day he was born. —*The Diaries of Rosalie Frazier Ngu*

LLYRA STOOD IN THE GATE, listening to horror stories.

"Of course we only had three sheets of ice back then," one of the other coaches was telling Jasmeen. She was a slim, pretty, tiny woman with a young and energetic voice. Someone had told Jasmeen that she was in her forties, but she didn't look it. Either living in the Moon was good for a person's health, or it was simply having the right outlook.

"Back then", of course, neither Mars nor Pallas had any rinks at all.

The coach said, "I think I was about twelve. Our annual ice show had a Blue Hawaii theme, and my mom had made me a little outfit with a grass skirt, a coconut bra, a big flower lei, you know, the whole thing. The night of the show, it was missing from my locker. My friends and I, my mom, my coach, we all looked everywhere, but no luck."

Jasmeen nodded politely, and threw Llyra an anxious glance. The younger girl knew her coach would much rather be giving her a last- minute pep talk right now. Maybe this was just as well. Maybe they'd both feel less nervous this way—by now she knew girls who'd gotten ulcers just from these last few moments before competition—and they were making new friends in a field of endeavor where that could be important.

"What did you do?" Jasmeen asked the other coach. Llyra wondered, too.

"Oh, my mom had some material left over from my first costume and whipped up another. She's great. But you haven't heard the best part. Twenty years later, when they were building the other three rinks here, they had to tear down the girls' locker rooms to relocate them. Guess what they found behind the lockers when they pulled them out."

"Hawaiian costume," Jasmeen guessed.

The coach laughed ruefully. "You bet they did, honey, still on its hanger in the bag. To this day, I don't know why whoever did it did it."

"Sometimes," Jasmeen told her, "is no why."

She turned to Llyra and reached up to put her hands on the girl's shoulders. Not long ago, she could have leaned down and rested her forearms there, clasping her hands behind the nape of Llyra's neck. "Skate as if you are only skater here today, my little. Skate as if is not competition, but exhibition. Skate your proudest, ignoring other skaters. If you

219

compete with anybody, compete with yourself." She stood on tiptoe to kiss Llyra's forehead, then stepped back and grinned. "But try to make it friendly competition."

Llyra grinned back. She was aware that people were watching her this morning, curious about the "asteroid girl" (as she had heard herself called behind her back) and how she would fare in competition after arriving here the first time in a wheelchair. Some of them, she knew, wanted her to fail—that was something else she'd overheard—although she didn't have the foggiest notion why. One or two, she knew, despised what they called "colonials". Others simply hated the rich.

In general, Llyra didn't understand how people could be cruel like that to one another, possibly because she didn't have a cruel bone in her own body. Even her mother was honest enough with others, and herself, to realize that what happened between her and Adam—the bad stuff, Llyra thought to herself; she didn't really want to know about anything else— was completely irrational, and to feel ashamed of it, afterward.

Llyra had heard another story she didn't understand. One of the girls she shared contract ice with every morning was originally from West America. The day of her big sister's most important competition—in some place called Omaha—she'd left her skate bag inside the girls' locker room, believing it was safe. Minutes before her group was to take the ice, she discovered that somebody had taken her skates out of her bag and stomped them, over and over again, until the blades shattered.

Big sister had left competition and never skated again.

Llyra was about to say something to Jasmeen, when the announcer spoke, instead: "Our next skater is a member of the Lunar Figure Skating Club." The amplified baritone voice reverberated through the cavernous facility. "But her home ice is the Aloysius Brody Arena in Curringer, on Pallas. Ladies and gentlemen, please welcome Llyra Ayn Ngu!"

Jasmeen's grin had become an annoyed scowl. The announcer had pro-nounced her student's first name "Leera" and her middle name "Ann", despite a note she'd written on the card, but by now Llyra was used to it.

Adrenaline pumping, oblivious to everything else around her, she was about to step onto the ice, had a leg raised to cross over the threshold, in fact, when she felt a tap on her shoulder. Jasmeen caught her eye, glanced down at her feet. Llyra still had the plastic guards on her blades, and would have wound up on her behind within a stroke or two. She'd done it before. Everybody did it at one time or another.

She stooped to slip the guards off—Jasmeen took them; there were at least a dozen other coaches along the boards, clutching pairs of skate guards to their heavily-coated bosoms—and then was gone, soaring across the rink in a position called a "spiral", her torso parallel to the ice, one leg extended straight backward and as high as anatomically possible, arms extended outward like the wings of an airplane. That kind of thing had once been considered too flashy, but with the change in the status of judges, it had become increasingly common.

Llyra and her coach were both lovers of classical music. Over their weeks of practice for this event, Jasmeen had vetoed her student's choices of Ravel's "Bolero" and the version of Gordon Sumner's "Roxanne" from *Moulin Rouge!* as inappropriate for a fourteen-year- old.

Jasmeen favored Deep Purple's "Smoke on the Water", but she liked anything with Richie Blackmoore's guitar playing, while Llyra thought Lindsey Buckingham was the best guitarist who had ever lived, even counting 21st century stars like Kenji Yamagari and the six-fingered Maximillian Revo. With the introduction of a new kind of judging, the rule against lyrics in most skating music had been dropped. The girls had finally agreed on the Who's "Won't Get Fooled Again", with its simple, pulsing organ introduction that was perfect for starting a routine.

Llyra quickly found the point on the blue line (all of these rinks were marked for hockey, just like at home) that she and Jasmeen had chosen and show-stopped to a halt, spraying ice crystals. There she waited for the referee to find her music in the system and reset the autojudge.

*
**

There was only a smattering of polite applause as Llyra's name was mispronounced and she struck a dramatic starting pose. As with most lower level events like this one, despite the popularity of figure skating on 3DTV, the facility was only sparsely populated, mostly by the parents of the competitors, their brothers and sisters, and a few friends. Ten times this number would show up for the Lunar Youth Hockey game tomorrow.

In the highest, farthest corner of the Robert A. and Virginia Heinlein Memorial Ice Arena bleachers, the fastest gun in the Moon watched and learned and wondered how these young athletes—the best of them were here all the time and called themselves "rinkrats"—grew up eating food like this. He'd arrived hungry, but had had a hard time choosing the lesser of two evils, between a rinkburger and a rinkdog.

Bleachers: a peculiar name, he thought, considering that they were several hundred feet underground, carved out of solid stone, hidden for-ever from the harsh sun of the Lunar day. The seating in the new domed surface facility they were planning—now *that* would be bleachers.

He took a sip of his Rinkacola and pondered.

The referee, he understood—the woman presently occupying what was ordinarily a hockey box, wearing the ubiquitous floor-length black coat—was having the Ngu girl scanned, calibrating the facility's autojudge for her particular size and bodily proportions. These were being mapped onto a model skater contained in the judging software, a direct descendent of a program written in the late 20th century around the performance standards of the legendary Michelle Quon. Motions and positions within a given set of parameters were acceptable. Anything else—a lifted leg waving around during a spiral, for example—would cause points to be deducted from a total the skater started with.

The official standards were tighter for compulsory or freeskate competitions, and somewhat looser for artistic or interpretive skating.

The present judging system, he knew—he had been doing his homework, as always—had begun to be necessary when the fans of several different sports became technically capable of rerunning the events they had just watched at home, and suddenly discovered what bad calls officials often made.

In figure skating, a judge might blink and miss a quick, difficult jump like a Wally. The merest sneeze could blind a judge to a perfect Axel. A simple reach to pick up a dropped pencil could turn well- earned victory into undeserved defeat for a young skater. Then there was favoritism or bigotry, conscious or unconscious, toward a particular skater or coach, or even toward their choice of costume or music. Occasionally, especially at the highest levels, there were horrible scandals involving outright corruption.

In the end, perhaps the worst consequence of bad or inconsistent judging was a ninety-nine percent attrition that occurred between the so-called "pre-preliminary" level of relative beginners, and official, tested seniors. Only one of a hundred stuck with it all the way, and the reason almost always given was bad or inconsistent competition judging. A little girl's heart can be broken only so many times before she gives up.

Just as technology, in the form of video cassette recording, had given rise to an officiating crisis, technology in another form made it worse. Partly owing to a widespread, general rejection of authority for its own sake during the late 20th and early 21st centuries, once the technology became inexpensive and widely available, coaches and parents started bringing handheld "judging" devices to competitions, devices that, with varying degrees of reliability, second-guessed the all-too-human judges.

The media began publishing what they called "robojudge numbers" right alongside the "official" results.

And now, under a slightly different name, there were only the robojudges.

He shook his head, annoyed that he'd become distracted by his own thoughts. Even after everything that had happened to these two girls, they remained careless. He'd wager anything that they'd left their little pistols in the locker room where they wouldn't do them any good out here, where anybody with a crowbar or a laser could get access to them.

In a way, taking advantage of the carelessness of others was his profession, but it still bothered him that people could wander through their lives in a daze, the way these two apparently did. And such pretty girls, too. It was a real shame, he thought, a real crying shame.

⁑

" ... she'll be comin' round the mountain, she'll comin' round the mountain, she'll comin' round the—damn!" Wilson looked at his left hand in disgust. His fingertips were all swollen, now, and hurt like the blazes. There were little grooves pressed into them where the pain lived.

He'd been told he'd get calluses eventually. It couldn't happen too soon to suit him. Maybe he should have bought a set at the music store.

He'd bought a little nylon-stringed acoustic guitar to keep him company, with a part of his share of the ship's first earnings. A genuine Shedd, the guy at the music store had informed him proudly, handmade in Cavor City, home of the Cavor City Mooncalves—whoever they were. Probably a soccer team. Wilson regarded soccer as the silliest game ever invented—perhaps only because he'd never seen golf.

Now he leaned back in the piloting seat in the transparent nose of his little spaceship, his bare feet up on the console, struggling to learn his first song as he conned *Mighty Mouse's Girlfriend* with his toes.

It might as well have been the other way around, he thought. He was *never* going to get B7th right, without making the strings buzz on the frets or damping them to a dull, unmusical thud that hurt his newly sensitized fingers. Why would anybody make up a chord like that, let alone put it in a song? Trying to get his fingers twisted right, he peered at the screen to his left where the words and chords were displayed.

Nothing there but E, A, and B7th. Maybe if he just played in other keys.

He was about to hit the transposition icon on the screen when, suddenly, a not-unexpected voice came over the 'com system. "This is Acme

Assay and Purchase, *Mighty Mouse's Girlfriend*. Taking up musical culture, I see. But you oughta wash your feet more often." The voice was nicely resonant, happy, and female. "What can we do you for today?"

His little asteroid hunting ship had mostly brought herself into a spherical volume of space near L-Five staked out by Acme. Different property rules and customs applied in "civilized" space than was the case with what everybody (well, nearly everybody, anyway, he thought) mutually regarded was "open range". He realized that the yard operator who'd just spoken to him so cheerfully was also peering straight into the front of his ship with a pair of field glasses. He stepped up the magnification in the central area of the pilot's dome so he could peer back.

As she looked up, he saw she was a pretty redhead about his own age.

"I've got sixteen tons of number nine coal for you, Acme—or may I just call you Ac? If you don't like coal, I've got about sixteen hundred tons of assorted irons and a lot of miscellaneous carbonaceous chondrite: kerogen, water, and fine cigars. Where you want me to put it?"

"You may call me Fallon, Mr. Ngu, since the computer says that you're getting to be a regular around here, and I just gave up cigars. You may leave your load for assay and purchase at Marker Bouy 12. Be sure its transponder works. Hot meals and free showers at the Hub, ahead of you."

"Sounds good," he said. "Would you care to join me? For a meal, I mean." He had discovered that a long, successful hunt left him wanting more than food and drink. He wasn't quite the hermit he'd thought he was.

"Aw, you're no fun at all, Mr. Ngu." Somehow Wilson had never noticed it, but all of the girls tended to like him. "Seriously, thank you very much, but I just came on-shift fifteen minutes ago. Would next time be all right? Who knows, I might even tell you my middle name."

He grinned. "That would be nice, Fallon. And please call me Wilson."

High in the bleachers on the opposite side of the rink, sat a young couple—to every appearance—making use of dark spectacles that were actually high-powered electronic binoculars with light amplifiers.

The two were observing the man sitting on the other side of the rink, the man who privately thought of himself as the fastest gun in the Moon. That neither they nor their employers could discover his real name was one of their pet peeves. The fellow seemed to employ a different name and set of bonafides, not just every day, but with each and every transaction. This afternoon he was calling himself Francis P. Wilson.

That neither they nor their employers could discover who the man worked for, or even what side he was on, despite hundreds of person- hours of expert research was another of their pet peeves against him. People, in their view, simply did not have the right to that kind of anonymity.

The man with the blond moustache was frustrated and outraged. "What the hell is he watching her for? Everybody knows that it's her brother who's the murderer!"

The woman with her hair in a kerchief agreed. "And her father who took our operative out on Ceres. It must be some kind of independent contract. But who would pay just to have that little girl watched—unless—"

He nodded, having had the same idea. "They're planning to kidnap her!"

"Right," she replied, tucking a wisp of platinum blond hair back into her kerchief. "And that might very well control the whole family quite effectively. But it's like a genie's three wishes: what would you demand? That the father quit the Ceres Terraformation Project? Or maybe even sabotage it somehow? That the mother give up her research into the usage of asteroid materials? Or that the son quit what he's doing and check himself into a reformatory for incorrigibles where he belongs?"

"I don't know. All of the above, maybe. Paul was just saying the other—"

"Shut up, you idiot!" She forced calm on herself and smiled. "Don't you remember that we never use names in this organization, Sweetie?"

"Damn! I am sorry—oops! I almost used *your* name!" He looked down at the ice. "I don't know what you'd demand. I'm perfectly happy to leave that one up to the people we don't name. But I'm thinking if you bagged that little coach, as well, you could have yourself a hell of a fun time while you were waiting for whatever else it was you wanted."

Grimacing, the woman put her hands up and averted her face. "You are absolutely disgusting! Is sex the only thing you men ever think about?"

"Pretty much," he laughed. "Every two point four three minutes. That is, until we get old and start thinking about laxatives and funerals."

She couldn't help it, she laughed and he laughed with her. And while they were laughing, the fastest gun in the Moon slipped out and disappeared.

***

The brightly lighted holosign that seemed to hang out into the busy Armstrong corridor above the establishment's double glass doors read:

THE NIMROD A Hunter's Bar

Wilson was inside already, sitting at the bar by the door, nursing a green-bottled Astrobleme Amber Cider, a mildly alcoholic beverage, comparable to beer but sweeter, brewed from apples and pears grown right here in the Moon under sunlamps and light piped down from the surface.

On big 3DTV screens at either end of the bar, a presumably human entity, of indeterminate sex, with greasy-looking floor-length hair and tangled rags for clothing, moaned lugubriously that "no one can love you if you love yourself". Although it refused to make its point clearly, the lyric—East American, Wilson assumed—seemed to be a timid attack on individualism. He wondered who they thought they were persuading.

"Oh, sorry about that, love!" the bartender told him, reaching up hastily to switch the channels. He was a big, rough-looking character—with a completely winning smile—whom rumor said had once been an asteroid hunter himself, before some injury forced him to retire and open this establishment. It was early in the "evening"; Wilson was his only customer so far. "Had a bunch of Earthie tourists at lunch. You'd think they'd want t'be gettin' away from that sort of thing, now, wouldn't you? Especially as I've got over three hundred music video channels."

"Wait," said Wilson. "What kind of music is this?" He whistled a scrap of the tune and then sang, "Some are mindin' their consoles while others are yarnin'. There's some standin' up an' some more lyin' down … "

The man smiled again. "That's Newfy music! I happen to be half Newfy myself—and half 'Strine, of course. Where'd you hear that, son?"

"Aboard the *Esmeralda* last year. Some of the crew played as we ate."

The bartender gave him an odd look. "The *Esmeralda*, was it? People spin yarns about that ship, they do. You'll have to tell me yours sometime, if you've a mind. There are one or two Newfy channels, if—"

Wilson grinned. "Sure. I'd love it—only, what's a Newfy?"

The bartender gazed at the ceiling, remembering, "Newfoundland is a great big island east of Canada where me old dad was born. It's the easternmost point in North America. The Newfies are a fine, strong people—or they were that—exceptionally hardy and hardworking. The very first Dominion of the British Empire, they were, way back in 1588."

"I had no idea," said Wilson, sipping his cider.

"Nor does much of anybody else, I'm afraid." He thumbed his remote control through the music channels. "Back in the early days—even up to the middle of the twentieth century—hardly anybody lived in the island's interior. They lived in little settlements all around the shore, 'outports' they were called. The only city of any size was St. John's. They fished, mostly for cod, they were loggers, mostly for pulp for newspapers, and they harvested young seal pups to sell their fur."

Wilson nodded. "People hunt both for fur and meat where I'm from, too."

"And where might that be, son—and are you ready for another Astrobleme?"

"Sure—I'm from Pallas." Wilson discovered in that moment that he was immensely proud of it. "Hunting with my dad and uncles, I've shot deer and elk and antelope. And moose and caribou. I started on rabbits."

The bartender nodded. "Well the Newfies were compelled at last, by economic circumstances better not discussed, to become a Canadian province. Their independence and self-sufficiency offended that lot of socialist crybabies from the start. Canadians made the same jokes about Newfies that everybody else makes about Polacks. Ottawa even let a disgusting pack of American movie stars persuade them to ban the seal harvest, destroying the livelihood of about four thousand men. Newfies run to big families—Catholics and Anglicans, the lot—so it meant that more than forty thousand decent folks suddenly found themselves on the dole."

"But how—" Wilson began.

"Let me finish, son. Eventually the feds did the same thing to the fishermen and loggers. Little by little, Ottawa forced them off the rest of the island and into St. John's where they could be controlled easier."

Wilson shook his head. "Why did the Newfies allow that?"

"They didn't have any choice. They'd long since been disarmed and the government had all the guns. Besides, a welfare check is a mighty temptation."

"Not to me, it isn't." Wilson shuddered.

"Nor to me, love. Nor to the Newfies, in the end, either. Around the middle of the twenty-first century, a group of them rose up and attempted to secede. The lovely, gentle, socialistic Canadians treated them the same way the Russians treated the Chechens—they labeled them 'terrorists' and did their brutal best to exterminate them. My old dad finally had enough and wound up out in Alice Springs. Lots of the other survivors, refugees, ended up out here, bringing their fishing and logging music— suitably modified for asteroid hunting—with them."

"That's a hell of a story, Mr.—" He stuck out a hand.

"Furlong, Wally Furlong. Just remember it when you hear Newfy music."

"And when I play it. I just got a—"

"Well if it isn't our old buddy Wilson! You been waiting long?" The voice belonged to a young man about Wilson's age, coming through the door. He was followed closely by two other young men and an older one.

The first one through the door was Asian, a short, heavily-muscled fireplug of a fellow with a shaved head—except for the warrior's lock he wore at the back—and tattoos consisting of broad decorative bands of Chinese ideograms wrapped around his upper arms. He wore a long, heavy, Lumiere Model 460 ion-augmented laser pistol low on his thigh.

"Marko!" Wilson swiveled around on his barstool and exchanged grips. Marko owned and operated the independent rock hunting vessel *Mina*.

The second was taller, heavyset, with a round face, short blond hair, and spectacles, which was unusual in this particular time and place. He carried a pair of smaller .50 caliber cartridge automatic pistols.

"Howya doing, Mikey?" Wilson asked.

"Can't complain—nobody listens." Mikey owned the *Albuquerque Gal*.

The last of the younger men was also heavy, with a short beard, and long, wavy hair flowing down his shoulder blades. Wilson always wondered how he managed to get it all crammed into a space helmet. He was wearing a worn, military style jacket, a heavy revolver, and a kilt.

"Scotty!" Wilson greeted him. "I heard you were upsystem."

"I was," the man told him. "*Nessie* burnt through two chamber linings and I had to limp home on one engine, wondering when that'd go, too."

Wilson nodded. "But it held up?"

"No, it failed, too. I died of anoxia, hunger, and thirst. "He turned to their host. "Good evenin' landlord. Let's get the hell to a table!"

The fourth man, in his late forties, Wilson guessed, a balding black man, with close-cropped salt-and-pepper hair and short grizzled whiskers, followed them into the dining area and sat with them at a table.

"Sorry, gentleman," said Marko, who had assumed the role of master of ceremonies. "I failed to introduce you two. Swede Vargas of the *Swimming Venus*, this is Wilson Ngu, of *Mighty Mouse's Girlfriend*. Wilson, the Swede. I met him in the maintenance yard where they're struggling against hope to bring Scotty's shitcan of a ship back to life."

Wilson put a hand across the table. "Pleased to meet you, Mr. Vargas."

"Just Swede, kid. Does me fine. What's the food like here?"

Somehow, the man's voice was familiar, but Wilson was hungry. He was distracted when the barkeep came to the table with a PDA stamped on his wrist. "I'm thinkin' you boys'll be after startin' with some drinks."

"You're thinking right," Mikey answered. "Caught a hell of a rock today, so the first round's on me. Deal is, you gotta listen to the story."

There was some ritual moaning and groaning until the drinks came: more cider for Wilson; beer for Mikey and the Swede; a good Merlot for Marko. Then they ordered from the simple menu, steaks and fries all around.

"So there I was," Mikey began, "chasing an iron Larsen Farside had sold me, a fair-sized clinker supposedly headed straight for Rio de Janeiro."

Marko shook his head. "Why is it always Rio in these stories? Why can't it ever be Kalamazoo, Michigan, or Nashville, or even Bozeman, Montana?"

"Because it just was, that's why," said Mikey. "The data had said it was solid, but I decided to play it safe and put some chain link around it. Trouble was, it was an aggregate after all, and the edge of my net struck it a third of the way up, separating the front end from the rest, and causing the bigger back end to start breaking up. The worst of it was that it was now headed for the northern coast of the Yucatan."

"No kidding!" several voices said at once.

"Yeah. So I figured, 'Been there, done that', and pondered how to get myself and the rest of my species out of this extinction level mess."

"You didn't," Wilson guessed, looking at Scotty, "and we all died." By now, even the bartender, standing in the doorway, was listening.

"Pretty close. What I did was break out the hose and give the back end a good dousing of reaction mass—drinking, bathing, and flushing water—freezing the whole thing back together again. Then I jetted ahead—"

"On pixie dust?" asked Marko. "You used up all your—"

"On powdered olivine and happy thoughts," Mikey said. "I finally threw chainlink around the front, braked slightly, and let the rest catch up with us. Just made it to L-Five, and here I am to tell the tale."

"Tell me something." The Swede was skeptical. "What was its impact date?"

"Er, October 23," Mikey admitted. The current month was April.

"What year?" the whole table demanded.

"Okay," Mike put his face on the table, closed his eyes. "October, 2142."

The Swede threw his head back and laughed. "Eleven years from now!" Of a sudden, Wilson realized why he had recognized the man's voice.

"Well, they did pay me the E.L.E. bounty—and it makes a good story!"

At the back of the room, a man who had come in from the bar when nobody noticed took a sip of Grand Marnier, and then a drink of his margarita. The fastest gun in the Moon thought it was a good story, too.

CHAPTER TWENTY-SIX: RECOGNITION

Social scientists have determined that, far more than religion, race, nationality, or sex, people tend to identify with one another on the basis of what they do for a living. A West American plumber tends to identify with an Azerbaijani plumber more than he does with his own countrymen who are not plumbers.

That certainly agrees with my experience, and I think it explains perfectly why politicians, who derive their income from legalized plunder, are inclined to go soft and squishy when it comes to dealing with muggers, rapists, thieves, and murderers. —*The Diaries of Rosalie Frazier Ngu*

"I know you!" the young asteroid hunter suddenly said between clenched teeth. His heart was pounding. The short hair stood straight up on the back of his neck. "I know that voice! You're the Space Viper!"

Wilson leaned across the dining table and glared at the individual who had just been introduced to him as "Swede Vargas". It was all he could do to refrain from drawing his great grandfather's .45 magnum, hanging on his hip. In the crystal clarity that sometimes comes with large amounts of adrenaline suddenly surging through the bloodstream, he noticed that his three friends appeared to be having the identical problem.

They all froze in place—they'd heard the story—as had the bartender, who heard all kinds of stories. Vargas' hands stayed on the table. To Wilson's surprise, the man threw his head back and laughed again.

"You mean it wasn't my initials that gave me away?" He indicated a big, shiny, silver trophy buckle he was wearing, an oval of engraved and polished silver with elaborate gold decorations. First associated with rodeo cowboys on the mother planet, buckles just like it were also popular with long haul truckers on Earth and Mars, and asteroid hunters.

Vargas' buckle bore the large initials S.V. "To tell the absolute truth, kid, I found it in a recycle bin here at the spaceport, ten or twelve years ago. Don't know why it got thrown away, but it seemed like a waste to let it get melted down, so I decided then and there to change my name, thinking it might just change my luck, as well. Now sometimes I'm known to my adoring meteor hunting public as 'Skylark Valentine', or 'Smedley Veritas'."

"Or Sid Vicious." Wilson laid his right hand on the big, coarsely checkered rectangular ivory grip panel of the .45 Grizzly autopistol. "Mister, I don't give a roach's rectum if you want to call yourself 'Susannah Vusannah'. You're still a rock pirate, and we've got you. Now you're going to pay up for everything you've done! Scotty, call a magistrate—"

"Not necessary, love" said the bartender, matter-of-factly. He took the toothpick out of his mouth. In the background, on the 3DTV, a band was playing "Jack Was Every Inch A Spacer", about an asteroid hunter who bored a hole halfway through an asteroid with his fist, so he could reach in and turn it inside-out. "I'm a magistrate, but I prefer plain old 'judge'. What's this fellow here supposed to have done?"

"Why, he—" Wilson began, then stopped abruptly, thinking and remembering as hard as he could. "Well, he ordered me out of what he claimed was his hunting territory and demanded I give him a rock I'd found."

"And what were you after doing then," asked the bartender.

"Only what I'd been taught to do. I reminded him that nobody is obliged to recognize anybody's claim to a hunting territory and he should shove off. I waggled an empty particle gun mount at him—" He glared at the Swede. "I have the gun installed now—and then he went away."

"He went away, is it?" The bartender raised his eyebrows. "It sounds more like hazing than piracy. Was he actually after *doing* anything?"

Wilson closed his eyes, thought about it again, sighed, and shook his head. "No, I guess he wasn't—say, do I call you 'Your Honor' now? Like I said, all he did was try to lay claim to the region of space I was hunting in, and demand that I turn loose of the rock I was intercepting."

"Call me Wally," the bartender said. "And did you?"

"Did I ... ?"

"Turn loose of the rock."

"That he did not!" Vargas turned and grinned up at the bartending judge. "The kid ran me off at the point of a particle cannon that he didn't even have yet! Balls of brass, this one, I tell you! When I heard his friends here out at the repair yard mention him by name, I knew I had to meet him and buy him a drink. He'll do. He'll definitely do!"

The judge nodded. "Then I order you to apologize, and that'll end it."

"Not likely," Vargas replied. "I didn't to anything wrong."

"He has a point, there," the judge agreed. "Any ideas from you, love?"
He looked to Wilson. "I suppose he could buy me that drink."

The judge said, "How's about you buy all of these lads a drink, then?"

"Done!" Vargas answered. "One for you as well. Your honor. In fact, bring me the tab for the meal. This adventure's been worth that much."

Marko leaned across a corner of the table until he and the black man were nose to nose. "Okay, now, Ess Vee, why not tell us your real name?"

The man closed his eyes and even shuddered a little. "Believe me, you'd change your name, as well, if you found yourself in my place, I guarantee—"

"What's your name!"

"Othniel James Simpson. The original was a remote ancestor of mine."

The four young men at the table blinked at one another.

"What," asked the bartender, "is so bad about that?"

"Attention all Marsbound passengers for the *City of Newark*. That's all Marsbound passengers for the *City of Newark*. Your shuttle craft to the Marsbound *City of Newark* will begin boarding in twenty minutes."

The Armstrong City spaceport seemed unusually crowded today, Llyra thought, although she didn't have very many other visits to compare it with. Through an endless series of heavy glass windows along the great concourse, she and her family watched shuttlecraft and interplanetary vessels in various stages of preparation for wherever they happened to be going. There were also several small herds, it seemed, of ground- bound tenders, both wheeled and tracked, that reminded her of vacuum- breathing dinosaurs, as well as individuals walking around in numbered envirosuits.

The announcement repeated itself twice before it went on to inform them, "Passengers for the *City of Newark*, as well as all other ships of East American registry, are reminded that neither smoking nor the carrying of personal weapons of any kind is permitted aboard the *City of Newark* or any other vessel of East American registry. All tobacco, marijuana, cloves, kinnikinnik, or other forms of smoking substances, lighters, box or book matches, pipes, cigarette or cigar holders—firearms, offensive lasers, tasers, swords, clubs, knives, or any other object intended for violent purposes must be left here in the spaceport, checked with the ship's purser, or secured in the baggage hold."

The recorded voice repeated itself twice again, and then began to announce the comings and goings, and the rules and regulations, with regard to other ships here today. These announcements were generally a great deal shorter. Imitating the announcer, Llyra proclaimed, "Please bend over. This will be a service of the Department of Redundancy Department."

Her brother laughed. Jasmeen and Julie grinned, although they were all sad to be here at the Armstrong spaceport today, seeing Wilson and Llyra's grandmother off for nobody knew how long. She had explained to them that in the past year, she had finished her business here in the Moon. The Conchita and Desmondo theme park would be completed in two years, on schedule—excavation had begun already in a suburb near the Heinlein—with only a few minor alterations insisted upon by the author.

Contrary to certain shrill demands and violent threats made by the East American government's representatives, not a single politician or bureaucrat would be portrayed within the park with any sympathy of any kind. On the other hand, there would be a big discount for government employees and their families, and free admission for those who could prove they had resigned.

"I can't describe how much fun it was, seeing their statist faces collapse when I told them that," said Julie. "They actually thought they could just come up here and order us around. There isn't anything more laughably pathetic than an authoritarian politico without any authority."

Jasmeen grinned and said, "This I wish I had seen."

"You would have loved it, dear," Julie told her, laughing. "This whole trip has been an absolute delight! I got to give an award and a family heirloom to my favorite grandson—glad to see you wearing it; Emerson would be pleased—and watch him get himself established in the asteroid hunting trade. Then my favorite granddaughter takes two firsts and a second in open competition at an ice rink where she couldn't even walk a little less than a year ago. Medals, medals, medals!"

"Grandma—" Llyra began. She knew that she couldn't persuade Julie not to go back to Mars, but she couldn't keep herself from trying.

Her grandmother was going on. "But now I need to go back home and complete my new novel about Conchita and Desmondo, lost once again in the land of the Wimpersnits and Oogies, before deadline." Llyra had read somewhere that millions copies of Julie's latest book, *Conchita and the Brain Eaters* had already been pre-ordered, even though it was actually a thinly-veiled exposure of public school psychological counselors—the kind who travel from school to school following some disaster or another. It had been banned already, sight unseen, in East America, a kind of advertising, Julie said, good for even more sales everywhere else.

"But why do you have to go through all this East American security garbage, Grandma Julie?" Wilson wanted to know. "Turn your gun over to the purser? Leave it in the baggage hold? It'll be just like flying home stark naked." He blushed when he realized what he'd said. Julie brought that out in him. "Why not borrow the *William Wilde Curringer* again? She's a whole bunch faster than this so-called spaceliner, anyway—"

"Beautiful *Billie*? Well, that would be very nice, dear," Julie agreed. "The trouble, though, is that Sherry's taken *Billie* way, way upsystem, ostensibly for an inspection tour of the new O'Neill habitat construction in orbit around Jupiter. I suspect his real interest is following up some fresh rumor about the disappearance of the *Fifth Force*. Somehow, they all seem to find their way to his doorstep one way or another."

"Another one of those?" Jasmeen shook her head and muttered. The unexplained disappearance of that famous exploratory vessel, bound for the Cometary Halo carrying Llyra's two most famous great grandparents, Emerson and Rosalie Frazier Ngu, and nine hundred other Pallatians, remained the meat of tabloid journalism even after all these years. It had hung over the Ngu family like a dark cloud for most of Llyra's life.

Down at the far end of the concourse, they could see and hear a vendor offering various kinds of ammunition considered acceptable by non-East American transport companies for space travel, which meant bullets, among other things, that could be lethal to an aggressor without damaging the spacecraft. The East Americans must have hated that.

"In any case," Julie continued, "although they're not advertising it, except for the *Fifth Force*, this will be the longest voyage ever undertaken by a vehicle with a human crew. Sherry and his ship won't be back for at least six months. By then, his maintenance people will be foaming at the mouth to tear her apart, looking for micropunctures and radiation damage. As much as I'd like to, my darlings, I can't stay here in the Moon any longer. I write more comfortably at home on Mars."

Wilson was concerned. "But they're gonna make you go through that metal detector over there, Grandma, wave wands at you, maybe even take you somewhere and make you undress, or worse! I've heard that there's worse!"

The spaceport management itself refused to search passengers or disarm them, so the East American spacelines had to do it here, in their own boarding area. The employees of other companies often made fun of them, goose stepping past and making rude-sounding remarks in mock German.

"And it's dangerous!" Llyra put her two cents' worth in. "The only ships or aircraft that ever get taken by criminals or terrorists are the ones where the passengers have been disarmed." They all knew that was why most spacelines encouraged their passengers to travel well armed, and even offered them a discount for doing so under certain circumstances.

Julie smiled, nodded and put a hand on each of her grandchildren's shoulders. "I'm deeply moved that you care, both of you, I really am. They've backed off a little on so-called security since they began to have more competition. I understand that the Fritz Marshall company will begin serving the Earth/Luna to Mars route sometime after the first of the year, and that will almost certainly end these barbaric practices, altogether."

"But Grandma—" Llyra began.

"In the meantime, I have a connection or two, and I'll be home soon enough." She began to gather up her hand baggage and a couple of magazines.

Jasmeen interrupted, "We stay one more year ourselves, Then go home."

Julie nodded. "You're the coach, coach. You know I trust your judgment in these matters. I mean to tell your folks how well you're doing here. You just let me know whatever you need." By now she was standing and had bent to embrace Jasmeen and give her a kiss on the cheek.

"Home? To Pallas?" Llyra was completely bewildered. She wondered what she'd done wrong—or failed to do—to deserve being sent home.

"Home—to Mars, where we can see your Grandmama again. Where my mother will cook good Chechen food for us and make us eat it until we creosote. And where you, my little, will skate in a third gee—twice what you skate in now. Is necessary next step to finally skating on Earth."

"Home," Llyra repeated, "to Mars."

Her coach nodded. "To Mars."

⁑

"Just look at that, will you!" The man with the blond moustache and thinning hair was almost quivering, but with what—excitement, rage, bloodlust—his business colleague couldn't guess, and didn't know.

And she didn't like not knowing.

From where they both stood in the security line for *The City of Newark*, he indicated the nearby passenger lounge with a subtle nod, rather than by pointing. "All four of the monsters together! Just one little—"

It was hot and Krystal Sweet felt sweaty. Fresh, clean clothing she'd put on this morning now felt damp and dirty. The official wand- wielders seemed especially slow today, she thought, a dimwitted pair of unpleasant, unattractive, overweight women from the East American Projects, wearing shabby uniforms that were too tight for them and—she could smell it even this far back down the line—should have been thoroughly cleaned several months ago. She supposed that she shouldn't complain, though.

These minimum-wage genetic rejects were doing her work for her, after all, making sure that the victims chosen for her by her employers would be absolutely helpless when the time came.

She stopped the man beside her with a look. She knew him as "Brian Downs". It was true enough, what he'd just said. She could see the murderous Wilson Ngu and his little sister, plus that weird grandmother of theirs, looking half a century younger than she ought to, and the girl's coach, traveling companion, and who knew what else, all of them sitting together on the black leather, chrome-plated steel furniture, absorbed in some kind of conversation.

But even where she came from—west central New York state—especially in public places like this spaceport concourse, the walls really did have ears—although they were electronic ones—and they were connected with powerful security computers that listened hard and patiently for certain key words that could trigger a person's instant arrest.

Words like "grenade".

"Er, little device," Brian went on, knowing exactly what she was thinking about. He was from Philadelphia, the cradle of East American tyranny. "And then we'd only have the mother and the father to contend with!"

Krystal lifted her eyebrows and tilted her head in a manner saying that she didn't disagree with him. He'd been told how much she hated Julie Segovia Ngu. Any East American with a sense of political decency did.

A few positions ahead of them in the line, a fat, nasty little boy wearing shorts and a striped shirt suddenly discovered that the door to the small steel cage he was carrying was open, and that whatever had been in the cage was gone. It could have been a hamster, a gerbil, or a guinea pig—or a rat. The child set up a wail that bordered on the ultrasonic, giving her a headache, and people started looking at their feet. If it was a rat, she hoped someone would stomp on it. She hated rats. Her early training in Central America had been more or less paved with rats, some almost big enough to throw a saddle on and ride.

"But we'd have to leave the System to avoid their revenge," she told Brian, abandoning caution for a moment—or simply avoiding key words. "Look, partner, this is hard, even for me, sometimes, but while the Ngus are our enemies, they are not the cause, nor are they the mission. In fact, annoying them unnecessarily could greatly endanger the mission." It was a very difficult thing for someone in her trade to learn and remember; it made the difference between professional and amateur.

He grinned. "Well, then, how about just doing the grandmother on this trip? We could easily make it look like an innocent, if tragic, mishap.

She may not be a little old lady, exactly, but accidents do happen, and I would guess that a spaceship must be full of potential hazards."

By this time, somebody else's disgusting offspring had started to cry, a little baby. Herded together as they were in the security line, nobody could move to get away from vile, noisy children or take the repulsive little things away. One or more of them had started to smell bad, too. She hoped that they and their parents would still be on Mars a year from now, when she would be—better not think about that now, though.

Krystal closed her eyes, running a weary hand through her short, pale blond hair. Her head hurt more than ever and her clothes had begun to feel sticky, hanging on her. "Let me tell you something. That person over there just happens to be the toughest of all the Ngus! And the best trained, a Special Ops Marine! I know your resume, Brian, your background in the martial arts. It's very impressive. But I promise, you wouldn't survive a physical encounter with her for twenty seconds!"

"Hold it down, Krys—I mean, Amelia." He, too, believed that there might be microphones to throw off. "Your voice, I mean. You're starting to spit a little when you talk. People are starting to look at us funny. Let me get this straight: you're telling me that little woman—"

She breathed in and let it out again. "I know that it's hard to believe, just looking at her. I certainly wish I had her waistline. But fifty years ago on Mars, she was assigned to a U.N. military unit sent out there to put down a colonial rebellion. Not just one of the grunts, mind you, but an officer who'd worked her way up through the ranks."

"What? You must be kidding me. I didn't know you could still do that." The woman shook her head. "You can't, Brian. This was fifty years ago." "Oh, yeah, I remember. Fifty years." She wasn't sure he believed it.

"Good," said the pale-haired blond. "Understand, she's hard—so damned hard, as someone said once, that you can rollerskate on her. But she fell for Billy Ngu, and became a traitor. There are stories about what she did after she turned her coat that would curl your hair."

He nodded. "So that would mean the tabloids are right, that she's nearly—"

"In her mid-seventies, at least," said the woman bitterly. "Taking up space and using up precious resources that Nature intended for the next three generations! And there's no reason to think that she won't keep on defying Nature for another thousand years! And using her as the pretty pinup example, before you know it, everybody'll be doing it!"

"Calm down, er, Amelia! I didn't know this was so important to you. Maybe we ought to seize the opportunity of this trip to put an end—"

She smiled and closed her eyes. The feeling deep inside her was warm and comforting. "I wish we could, partner. I dearly wish we could."

Her companion tugged at her sleeve. The Ngu party were standing up, embracing the pretty grandmother one by one. Even the girl's paid companion was included in the family hug-fest. One of the pale blond woman's first professional assignments had been to serve as personal assistant—meaning secretary and maid—to a wealthy old woman in Wichita, while the old woman's favorite niece was being kidnapped for ransom by a group of colleagues. Somehow, the operation had gone sour on their end, and she'd wound up garroting her former employer with a lamp cord. She hated the way that rich people often tried to pretend that their servants were their equals. It was as unnatural as it was disgusting.

Now Julie Ngu was being accompanied by a pair of smarter-looking, better-uniformed security stooges—men, of course—to a VIP lounge where she would neither have to stand in line or have her person searched.

"Now that," Brian told her, "I find annoying."

"Don't worry, partner," said the pale-haired woman, grinning and nodding with satisfaction. "It's a good thing. Look around you. Sure you resent the abuse of power and privilege—and so does everyone else."

The tall, skinny Pallatian pilot stood in the airlock atrium of the Guzman Brothers' Used Spacecraft offices, waiting for an answer and wishing he'd made an appointment. On the other hand, after dozens of hours of fairly high acceleration getting here—time being money, after all—it felt good to relax for even a little while in zero gee.

It was a vice, he understood. Bad for the musculature and bones, as well as for the immune system. But it felt just like heaven to him, and he could never understand why other people didn't seem to care for it.

Funny, nobody seemed to be home, although the open sign was on. Helmet under his arm, politely, he reached a space-gloved hand up to thumb the doorbell once again, but a large, dark face with villainous eyes and a huge hooked nose appeared in the viewing screen before he could.

"Aha!" said the face. "A customer! I suppose we are still open for doing business for a little while. What can I do you out of today, customer?"

"Lafcadio Guzman?" the pilot asked. The man had been described to him.

The man replied, "Who else in heaven's name would I be, if I had a choice?"

"I don't know about that, sir. I'm R.G. Edd, representing the Raymond Louis Drake-Tealy Museum in Curringer, on Pallas. You know, the asteroid? I'm also captain of the Pallatian towing vessel *Little Toot*. See her right over there? I'm also the crew. I'm here to make sure that you got paid properly, and to pick up the Drake-Tealy object for the museum." The truth was, he was dreading the long lonely haul back to Pallas and he hoped the guy would ask him in for a bag of coffee.

The big oval airlock door swung open, and Edd was greeted by a strange looking individual. The man's head, shoulders, and torso appeared to be normal-sized, if not a little oversized. His arms looked extremely powerful. But his legs were those of a child. Some kind of accident to the spine, he supposed. The man reminded Edd of pictures he'd seen of the famous French artist Henri de Toulouse- Loutrec.

"Come in, come in, Captain Edd! Yes, yes, I am Lafcadio Guzman, himself! The very self! And I seem to be saying everything twice! Twice! And yes, yes, I received the museum's ridiculously generous payment! You know I had to call the bank and make sure that a zero hadn't been added by accident! You must excuse me, Captain, I am about to go on vacation for the first time since around the year you were born! I think I'm going to buy myself some new legs—and perhaps a brother!"

Edd had known some pretty odd people in his life, so he simply filed Lafcadio Guzman away with the rest of them. Everywhere he looked, shoes, socks, shirts, pants, and underwear floated through the air. Happily, the pair of shorts that lighted on his ear seemed to be clean.

Guzman offered him a baggie of champagne, imported all the way from Paris, France. It pained the pilot to turn the fellow down, just as it pained him to come all the way, almost to Earth, only to turn around and head straight back to Pallas. Somehow, he thought, you'd expect a museum to take a longer view of things. But that was what he was being paid extremely well to do. He took more frequent vacations than this fellow, here, so it would all come out in the wash eventually.

"Well, Mr. Guzman," he told his host, "I sure hope that you enjoy your vacation. It looks to me like you're off to a pretty good start. For me, it's blasting straight back to Pallas, to the tune of something like twenty years' worth of digitally enhanced recordings of *Gunsmoke*."

Guzman's eyebrows went up. "*Gunsmoke*? In full color and false three dee?"

Edd nodded enthusiastically. It was true, you never knew where you were going to find another fan. Nobody on Pallas seemed to understood it.

"You bet, pal—you can see the smoke from Marshall Dillon's Peacemaker come right out of the 3DTV and into your face. And Miss Kitty—"

"Oh, I can imagine it perfectly! Festus and Doc! And the young Burt Reynolds! Oh, I thank you so much! I believe I will look immediately into making a purchase of my own. A very good day to you, Mr. Edd. Can you find that accursed rock by yourself? It looks just like a big, dirty old potato, but it sprouts all of the expected knobs and excrescences of any small Drake-Tealy *Objet Drat*. Do you need me to—"

"No, no, Mr. Guzman. I already found it, thanks. I've thrown two layers of brand new chainlink around it, and we're all saddled up and ready to ride. You take care of yourself, now, okay? Keep your powder dry." Edd stepped back over the threshold into the building's airlock.

"Okay!" Guzman swung the airlock door. "Thanks again! Happy trails!"

That was Roy Rogers, not *Gunsmoke*, but Edd grinned and waved all the same. He turned, entered his own airlock, closed the outer door, closed the inner door, and climbed into his control seat. Separating his ship from Guzman's building, he thrust back toward the gigantic Drake-Tealy Object and let a loop in the cable that held the chainlink bag closed slip over a bollard at the rear of his ship. The vessel had originally been designed as a space tug, servicing both of the polar spaceports on Pallas, but ships were more nimble now, and didn't need help.

Edd planned to use a couple of miles of line so that he could get out of the way in case of some kind of accident. As the slack began to tighten, given the known mass and acceleration of his ship, strain gauges on the line gave him the mass of the Object within a few ounces.

Funny ... how could that be? This damned thing weighed as much as any chunk of sky-iron ten times its size. He could get it back to Pallas, all right, but someone was going to have to meet him after turnover with extra reaction mass—and maybe a spare spaceship or two.

Damn.

So be it. He entered values in the navigation and acceleration computer and hit the ENTER button. The computer thought about it for a couple of nanoseconds, then changed the ship's heading slightly and fired all five of the vessel's huge fusion engines. But Edd felt no acceleration.

Not at first, anyway.

Instead, his powerful little towing ship slowly began to travel backwards. He knew this was the case because his pilot's seat and the control console in front of it slewed around in their gimbals, and he was plastered into the big chair by acceleration. By the time he got himself oriented, the meter in the chair-arm read three point one-four gees, and, Pallas born and bred, he could hardly breathe or lift a finger.

"Controls to voice!" he wheezed.

"Controls to voice, aye," the ship responded.

Reluctantly, he cut his engines and watched helplessly in a viewscreen as L-Four and the Moon began to dwindle visibly in the distance.

"Broadcast the following on all frequencies: 'Mayday, mayday, mayday! This is the Pallatian towing vessel *Little Toot*. I am … um, under attack by an unknown object and being towed backward at multiple gees!' Add our heading and acceleration and repeat till I say otherwise!"

"Broadcast distress call, aye," said *Little Toot*.

He was headed back upsystem, where this damned thing had come from.

In a *big* hurry.

CHAPTER TWENTY-SEVEN: PREPARATION

The United States of America began to disintegrate as a political unity almost the minute that the average citizen came to see clearly that, no matter who he voted for, no matter who got elected, he—the average citizen—was screwed.

If you'll pardon the expression.

When even the tame mass media began referring to the two major political alternatives as a single entity—the "Boot On Your Neck Party"—it was, in the language of the times, all over. What was left of the original United States became known, whether it wanted to be or not, as "East America", and something altogether new, "West America"—which refused to dignify a federal government and national legislature grown irredeemably corrupt by sending representatives to it—was born. —*The Diaries of Rosalie Frazier Ngu*

WILSON FIRED THE HIGH FREQUENCY tactical laser again.

The beam was invisible, very nearly into the X-ray wavelengths, but he could see—under telescopic magnification, of course; the rock was actually too far away to observe the effect directly—a little jet of vapor where the laser struck. Hot particles and gases burst from the surface of the meteoroid, opposing the direction in which it was presently tumbling, gently bringing its rotation to a halt.

It felt a lot like he was pushing against the rock with the laser itself.

At the same time that the hot vapors slowed the meteoroid, sensors on *Mighty Mouse's Girlfriend*'s hull analyzed them, giving Wilson a better idea what his catch was made of than he had gotten from the observatory.

The call had come from Larsen Farside earlier that "morning": "Captain Wilson Ngu," the figure on the screen had greeted him. You are next in line for non-exclusive information. Do you accept this opportunity?"

"Sure, Doc," Wilson answered. It was one of Jasmeen's scientist uncles. He could never keep them straight. This was the big fat one. Funny the way his silly Chechen accent sounded sexy when his sister's coach was using it. "How come you're doing your own calling this morning?"

Jasmeen's uncle shrugged. "Is maid's day off. Here comes data feed. It looks like carbonaceous chondrite about hundred feet on long axis."

"And shaped about like a potato. Gotcha, Larsen Farside, and thank you."

"Do not thank, *Mighty Mouse's Girlfriend*, just pay bill on time, please."

"We always do, Larsen Farside, we always do. Talk to you later!" The stars whirled around him as the little ship changed its heading at the commands he punched into her keyboard. Wilson, pressed deeply into his acceleration chair in a way he always found exhilarating, was off with a mighty whoop and a rapidly dispersing cloud of used reaction mass.

It would be ninety-three minutes before he caught up with the rock. He called up the latest episode of his favorite 3DTV program, *Hong Lee, Secret Agent* that his computer had recorded and saved for him. It concerned a private operative, working for a famous Bulgarian philanthropist, against one of the last unfree countries in the world—the United States of (East) America. This week it was about Hong Lee trying to save some precious artifacts from the Whiskey Rebellion, before they could be destroyed by authoritarians desperate to rewrite history.

The proximity alarm rang just as the program ended (it originated in the Moon where programs running an hour and a half were popular at the moment) and the ship's computer began analyzing the target's several different motions. It was headed downsystem at the leisurely pace of six miles per second, rotating roughly around its longest axis while tumbling end over end. It was also precessing slightly as it tumbled.

First he stopped the precession with a series of well-timed, well-placed laser blasts. From the incandescent vapor, the system informed him that the rock (at least this section of it) consisted almost purely of carbonaceous chondrite: magnesium silicate with touch of iron, eleven percent water, and five percent kerogen. An ordinary rock it was, but a good one. It was the very stuff that made life in space possible.

More use of the laser put an end to the tumbling, and finally, to the rock's rotation. It appeared now to hang motionless in space a hundred yards from *Mighty Mouse's Girlfriend*, although both it and the ship were speeding through space, toward the Sun, at twenty-two thousand miles per hour. Happily, the Sun was many millions of miles away.

Now came the hard part. Sidescan radar and other sensor systems told Wilson that his target was solid enough simply to attach himself to it and haul it off. He had enough reaction mass to get it turned and headed toward L-Five, where it ought to fetch a pretty price, oil and water being almost as valuable as palladium and iridium. He would begin to run low on reaction mass about two thirds of the way there, but the olivine the rock was mostly made of would help him make the stretch.

As soon as the course was laid in and the correction properly made, he stood the engines down and coasted, then climbed into one of his enviro-suits. He pocketed his Herron twelve-shot revolver, and made his way out through an aft airlock. Attaching a safety line to a ring located near the door, he pushed off aftward until he came to the tow cable attachment. Laboriously relocating his safety line to a connection near one engine, he took a pick-axe from a handy tool box, and pulled himself along the cable until he reached the rock, turned, and set foot upon it.

Sophisticated "smart" microfibers on his bootsoles kept his feet on ground that no human being had ever stood upon before or likely ever would again. Thinking about *The Little Prince*, he walked around the min-iature world he'd captured, looking for a good place to dig. He wouldn't have been at all surprised, he told himself, to see a couple of tiny volca-noes that needed dusting, or a cruel rose under a bell jar.

At last he found a place he thought would do. He sank his pick into it, set the light in the end of its handle blinking, and returned to *Mighty Mouse's Girlfriend*, where he extracted what looked like a four-inch fire hose from a locker nestled between two engines. Making his way back to the place he'd left his pick, he set its business end on the ground—it looked like the mouth of an extremely toothy monster—and flipped a switch. Immediately, coarsely ground rock began to be whisked to the ship through a moving spiral within the hose.

All around him, the stars were bright and cold and absolutely motion-less. He had one of those moments of realization—too rare in a person's life—that this was what he had always wanted to do, the only thing he had ever wanted to do, and that he was almost perfectly happy.

The fastest gun in the Moon lay on the walk just outside the Last Branch Saloon and Gambling Emporium, bleeding on the weathered boards from he didn't know how many wounds. He'd lost count around four. He couldn't recall anything in his life that had ever hurt quite this much. Maybe he should have backed off a bit on the virtual sensations menu.

He'd been gut-shot, simple as that, shot through the abdomen with a pair of heavy .45 Schofield army-style revolvers, by a pale blond young woman who now stood over him, straddling him, both of her huge top-break, seven and a half inch barreled sixguns, pointed at his face.

He could even see thin wisps of smoke trailing upward from their muzzles, crenellated by especially deep rifling intended for soft lead bullets. Why wasn't she using a .41 rimfire derringer or, say. a .32-20? He should never have let the program choose the weapons for her.

The young woman wore a pale gray bib-front shirt of unbleached cotton with fancy hand-carved buttons, one corner of the bib turned down, sleeves rolled to her elbows, a homemade vest and breeches of fringed, rust-colored deerskin, and a pair of round-toed Justin boots with steeply canted riding heels. Her flat-crowned brown Stetson with its rattlesnake-skin band, rattles included, was thrown back onto her shoulderblades, hanging there on a braided horsehair cord around her neck. He'd thought from the start that the hat and band were a nice touch.

He'd added them, himself. He'd always been a big Barbara Stanwyck fan. There was also that hotheaded little girl who shot John Wayne in *El Dorado*.

Her real name, he knew—the name of the individual this part of the program was based on—was Krystal Sweet. She was a hired gun—and a big star in the underworld of terror and political assassination—who worked for what remained of the left on Earth, mostly for Null Delta Em, performing especially messy or violent tasks for which the organization's wealthy upper-class leaders and its mostly middle-class rank and file activists considered themselves too fastidious. In turn, she often employed the same half dozen ruthless thugs to back her play.

If she'd been placed in charge of that rocket attack on Ceres, he thought, twenty-five hundred people would be dead, including Wilson Ngu.

Referring to a three-inch thick dossier on the woman supplied by his own employer, plus research, realtime and online, that he'd done on his own, he'd programmed this simulated version of Krystal Sweet to be very good at what she did—otherwise practice sessions like this wouldn't mean anything—but he hadn't realized exactly how good she was.

Somehow, she'd managed to sneak up, plaster herself to the wall, and catch him flatfooted as he came out through the swinging saloon doors. They'd never be quite the same, either. They were as full of holes and had as many broken slats as he did. Both sixguns blazing, she'd shot him to pieces without a word, the way it really ought to be done. No dramatic fleering or gloating for Krystal Sweet until the job was done. He'd never gotten a chance to draw his cartridge-converted Remington.

His lever action Winchester lay unfired beside him, as useless as he was. His left arm didn't seem to be working, and Krystal Sweet was standing on his right, grinning down on him, as if she knew that the only way he could get out of this mess was by twisting his belt buckle upside-down. It worried him, sometimes, that the characters in virtual reality might someday discover who and what and where they actually were. It appeared to him that she had three shots left in each of her big Schofield revolvers, but she wouldn't use them now. She'd want to enjoy this. If she finished him—and perhaps she knew that, too—he'd simply wake up uninjured in his hotel, a sadder but wiser virtual gunslinger.

Vultures began to circle overhead, a strange sight in the middle of even a small city like this one. He couldn't recall programming them in.

"Aaron!" The voice belonged to his old friend and part-time lover, Theodora Gibson, who kept the Swank Hotel—and a highly select line of talented and expensive professional ladies—across the street over Delmonico's. He went by many names, here and in reality. She knew him as Aaron Salt. Lying on his back as he was, he couldn't see her, but he could hear the woman running to him in her high-button suede boots, across the street of rutted, sun-baked mud, up onto the boardwalk, finally kneeling by his side in a flurry of petticoats and perfume.

Krystal Sweet, somewhat more sparingly constructed, and possibly resenting it, made a sour face, kept her foot firmly planted on his good arm, nevertheless let Theodora put her face close to his. Tears were streaming from Theodora's eyes. Her ample chest pressed softly against his, and felt good. "What has this hussy done to you, my dear Aaron?"

Happy that he'd programmed several failsafe mechanisms into the system, he whispered a single word in her ear. "Parachute." Without a word of her own, or any waste motion at all, Theodora reached back and turned his belt buckle upside-down. The world began to shimmer out of existence.

The virtual Krystal Sweet barely had an instant to squawk in angry protest.

The fastest gun in the Moon awoke in his comfortable hotel room at the LeFevre Arms in Armstrong City, still in a considerable amount of pain. The strongest virtual sensations, he was aware, had a tendency to linger for a while afterward. He was badly shaken and thoroughly soaked with sweat, conditions no real mission had ever left him in. He reached to the left side of his belly where he'd been shot. The area was smooth, unblemished, but surprisingly tender to the slightest touch.

It was just possible that he was getting too old for this shit, he thought.

*
**

The computer finished the braking sequence and shut the engines off. Wilson floated free at his control panel for the first time in a more than a week of continuous and relatively heavy acceleration. He tucked his flatpick into the strings on the peghead above the nut, pushed his guitar into an overhead net he'd rigged for it, and spoke aloud.

"Acme, this is *Mighty Mouse's Girlfriend* requesting offloading instructions."

The space here was fairly crowded, as usual. As Wilson spoke, an automated vehicle of some kind passed within a few yards of his bow, taking a fragment of metallic asteroid somewhere in its sinister- looking claws. To aftward, a flock of self-powered tools, mostly lasers and mechanical drills and saws, made their robotic way in the opposite direction. He could see other many vessels above and below him.

The response came almost immediately. "Well ahoy there, *Mighty Mouse's Girlfriend*! We were beginning to wonder if we were ever going to see the Barefoot Bard again. Still torturing that poor guitar of yours?"

The pleasant female voice was officially that of the Acme Assay and Purchase Company, located (with about a thousand other businesses) here at Lagrange Point Five. Unofficially, the voice belonged to a pretty girl named Fallon (he didn't know her last name—yet), the redhead Wilson had done business with at Acme once before. He could see her now, through a magnifying portion of his ship's navigation dome, seated behind her own console, at a big window overlooking the company "yards". She was about a mile away but he planned on getting closer.

"Just put the guitar away. I managed an F-sharp diminished seventh today. 'We were wondering', did I hear you say?" The young asteroid hunter replied playfully, "I've been back here at least dozen times since

246

we first met, Fallon. Take a look at my account, which I'm sure you have up on your screen right now. But you never seemed to be around."

She laughed. "A *dozen* times, is it? That desperate to see me, were you? Maybe I should send you a copy of my duty card." In fact, this sort of hit-or-miss thing was an all too common occurrence with individuals living and working in space, who created their own time of the day, and whose working schedules tended to overlap in awkward, different ways. The un-varnished truth, however, was that he had been disappointed.

He hoped she had been, too.

All around him, Wilson realized again, as he always did when he first arrived here, there were about twice as many stars in the heavens as na-ture intended. Most were in colors that no ancient astronomer would ever have recognized. Some were blinking on and off, pulsing or scintillating unnaturally. One looked—if you peered at it and squinted—just like a full martini glass, rendered in neon. It was the sign, nearly ten miles away, of the Happy Hour Bar and Grill.

A tiny autocourier zipped past overhead, uncomfortably close.

"Not desperate at all, Acme, just inordinately successful." Wilson pre-tended to yawn and buffed his fingernails on his shirt. He knew she could see him perfectly, which was why his feet were in Reebok deck slippers, this time, and not up on the control console. "I found a garnet the size of a beachball two weeks ago. I only have a great big, lowly carbonaceous chondrite for you today, though. Absolutely average in olivine, kerogen, and water content, I'm afraid. In short, it's a cow."

It was a rock hunter's term for an unromantic find that would be "milked" of its lifegiving liquids and then ground up and consumed as reaction mass. Such objects were also known, sometimes, as CCs or "see-sees".

The hundred-foot captive was ahead of *Mighty Mouse's Girlfriend* now, as it had been ever since turnover, halfway to L-Five. Once he'd brought it to a dead stop, here inside the yard, he'd employed a touch of the lateral thrusters to turn his little spaceship around and the ventral thrusters so that he could look over the view-obstructing rock and see Fallon. He hadn't disconnected his towing cables from it yet—although they were completely slack, and wouldn't until he was paid.

"Nothing wrong with an occasional cow," the young woman told him. "We need air and water and plastics and lubricants. You can't breathe pal-ladium or iridium no matter how much we like them or how pretty they are."

She paused as she became busy at her keyboard. "There—I've got your cargo all neatly scanned and logged, *Mighty Mouse's Girlfriend*—you'll have to explain that name to me someday—they'll do a full assay later today, check for precious inclusions and Drake-Tealy Objects, and adjust your account. I can credit you now or cut you a check. By the way, not to be too forward, but my shift ends in twenty minutes."

"Pretty good timing on my part, then, wouldn't you say?" Wilson chuckled pleasantly. The fact was that he'd wrangled a cybercopy of the girl's work schedule weeks ago from another Acme employee who owed him a favor, and then wrestled with his own computer for a day and a half to produce this "purely coincidental"—and, according to an almost annoyed-seeming *Mighty Mouse's Girlfriend*, totally less than optimally efficient—result. "I prefer bullion, by the way, platinum or gold. Give me half an hour to get a shower. What kind of food do you like?"

"Beachball sized garnets and platinum bullion, is it?" Fallon laughed. Wilson discovered that he liked the sound of her laughter. "And for a cow, at that. Let's make it seafood and steak. I know a place."

"Seafood and steak," he nodded. "Where do you want me to meet you?"

✳︎✳︎

"So what troubles you, my little? Was worst practice we have in weeks." Llyra had fallen several times on jumps she had long since mastered. Her tan hose and the back of her skirt were covered with "snow". Their blades, freshly sharp, made "ripping" noises on the ice that most, hockey players and figure skaters alike, find extremely pleasurable.

In theory, Jasmeen and Llyra were cooling down from a strenuous morning's work, just skating around the perimeter of the rink, the younger of the two closest to the boards. In practice, this often turned out to be the most vigorous portion of their daily workout. They lived for the movement of their bodies in a way few others understood.

Nobody else was on the ice at the moment, although there was a scattering of individuals sitting in the bleachers, and a handful of skaters standing at each of the gates, conversing. The computer- operated Zamboni was scheduled to make "new ice" sometime within the next few minutes. Meanwhile, the public address was playing the stirring second movement of the "Rings of Saturn" by Sir Winston Lennon.

"It's nothing, really." Llyra shook her head. They reached the rounded corner of the rink and began a gentle turn to the right. "I was just having a little trouble concentrating." As if to prove her point, she stumbled on a toepick, and came close to taking a tumble. Instead, like a beginner, she steadied herself on the boards with her left hand, quickly regaining her balance and the steady rhythm of her stroking. Her dignity, on the other hand, would be a little slower returning.

Sheepishly, she glanced at her coach. "Everybody falls." Over the years, Jasmeen had told her that at least a hundred thousand times. And it was perfectly true, of course, especially for jumpers like Llyra. Supposedly it wasn't so bad for skaters on light gravity worlds like Pallas, and Ceres, and the Moon—it only felt that way, she thought. She still had the same mass here, and the ice was just as hard.

Jasmeen, however, said, "Define 'nothing, really'." They kept skating, making a second turn into the other straight side of the rink. The announcer's compartment and other hockey facilities were here.

Llyra took a deep breath. "Well, at least I hope it's nothing. I can't reach Daddy, Jasmeen. Every time I send him a message—even on his personal phone—it's answered perfectly on the lagtime by that Ingrid secretary thing of his, and she says he's unavailable and will get back to me as soon as possible. One time she even had her pajamas on!"

Jasmeen nodded sympathetically, perhaps a little disappointed, but hardly surprised. She loved Adam and Ardith but had long since given up trying to figure them out. "And you are thinking that maybe he and Ingrid—"

"No!" Llyra shouted; it echoed around the rink. "I *won't* think that!"

"Thank you, Scarlett O'Hara." Jasmeen made a hockey stop, touching Llyra on the arm so they would stop together. They were standing just outside the empty home team penalty box. "Tell me, then, Scarlett, when Ingrid secretary thing was in her pajamas, what was her hair like?"

A voice over the PA said it was time for everybody to clear the ice.

"What?" Llyra scowled for a moment, trying as hard as she could to recall something that she'd really much rather have forgotten. "Blue satin pajamas, I remember those, the shirt part completely unbuttoned. I think that her hair was up in great big light green plastic curlers. You know, Jasmeen, that's something else I can't figure out. Ingrid wears her hair perfectly straight. What does she want curlers for, anyway?"

Jasmeen laughed. "I do not know, my little, but I guarantee she wasn't sleeping with your father. At least she wasn't that particular evening." She pushed off and began skating again, but Llyra stopped her.

Llyra blinked. "How do you know that?"

For the second time, the PA system warned everybody to get off the ice immediately. The voice was obviously recorded, and they ignored it.

"Remember women's magazines in dentist's office? 'Men's Ten Worst Turn-Offs'. Number three is hair in curlers in bed. Other nine best forgotten. I sometimes think wives do this so they do not have to have sex."

Llyra blinked. She'd never heard of such a thing before now. Sex was not the problem between her mother and father. Everything else was.

"Is probably not the case with Ingrid secretary thing," Jasmeen grinned.

Llyra laughed, although there were still tears in her eyes. "You are right, of course, as usual." She turned and gave her coach a hug. Martian to the core, Jasmeen reflexively glanced around to see if there was anyone watching them. She caught herself at it, and forced herself to relax a bit. "What ever would I do without you, Jasmeen Khalidov?"

Jasmeen blinked back a decidedly unMartian tear or two of her own. "Whatever it is I would do without you, my little. My life would be much less happy, also much sadder—but it would oddly have fewer tears."

This time when she took off, Llyra had some difficulty catching up with her. They skated hard until the Zamboni stood in its own gate, its AI angrily honking the horn at them, and they had to get off the ice.

*
**

It was always a beautiful day in the "Parque".

That was what the builders, inhabitants, and visitors to Acme's recreational facility at L-Five chose to call it. It was a disk, or flat cylinder about two hundred yards across and two dozen feet deep, covered with a dome made of a plastic designed to scatter sunlight exactly the way the atmospheres of Earth and Mars did, producing a brilliant blue sky. There wasn't quite enough volume to form clouds, the way they formed on Pallas or even sometimes inside the largest buildings on Earth, but the plastic could be programmed to imitate them.

Now and again, fine nozzles set in the handrail of a decorative elevated walkway above the Parque would create a brief, gentle shower of rain. Visitors who didn't care to get wet heeded a warning peal of thunder that was always provided under darkening skies, and climbed one of several staircases, roughly wrought of meteoric iron, to watch for a while. There were tables distributed along the mezzanine, and various entrepreneurs to offer tea, coffee, soft drinks, cocktails, and other refreshments.

Other times, people enjoyed numerous fountains scattered across the Parque, followed a small, meandering stream, or sat beside the tiny lake it fed. There were fiery-golden Chinese carp in the water, and a handful of mallard ducks, the males with their shiny green heads.

The illusion of Earth was marred a trifle by the way the stars passed overhead. Wilson could just make out the cables, painted flat black, each as big around as his waist, that stretched from the rim of the Parque structure to a common point overhead, about a mile from where he stood. Its apex was connected with another, leading to another clutch of cables, fanning out to support a more conventional building housing Acme's administrative offices and a hotel. Whirling around, opposite one another at just the speed to produce a Lunar one-sixth gee, the two facilities served a non-spinning complex at the juncture of the cables, where Fallon's office was located. There were also hotel rooms in the center for those who preferred sleeping without gravity.

"I love this place," said Fallon. She and Wilson were on the walkway— the total circuit was a little over a third of a mile—not to avoid the rain, which wasn't scheduled for another half hour, but to give Wilson a better view of the Parque. They had just finished one of the best meals either of them had ever had, at a place called Canyon Avenue, located on the other side of the hub. "It reminds me of home."

Up close, she was a lot of fun to look at, he thought. She had enormous blue eyes, almost like a cartoon character, and a wonderfully shaped face. Where Amorie had been all softly rounded curves, Wilson could see Fallon's bone structure through her skin. Her cheeks dominated the shape of her face. Her nose turned up rather like his sister's.

"You're from the Earth, then?" he asked. Somehow he was a little disappointed. He guessed that what he was feeling might be called bigotry.

She said, "Oh, no. I'm from Pallas, Wilson, just like you are."

"No kidding!" He stopped walking and turned to face her. She was very pretty, he found himself deciding all over again, and best of all (at the moment) her eyebrows were copper-colored. It would have taken a year, he thought, to count all of her freckles—just the ones on her face, he meant. She kept her hair, which matched her eyebrows, pulled back in a ponytail that reached down to below her shoulder blades.

She had worn a dress, sort of an odd choice for a low-gravity environment, he thought, but he liked it. It was blue and matched her eyes.

He added, "I just realized that I don't even know your last name." She smelled nice, and he was suddenly glad that he'd taken the time to shower.

"O'Driscoll," she told him. "Fallon O'Driscoll of the Corner Brook O'Driscolls. My family runs a logging, lumbermill, and lumber company there. If you're a gentlemen, I may even tell you my middle name, sometime."

Fallon thrust out a hand. He shook it, but didn't let it go afterward.

"Corner Brook ... " he mused. "That's deep in the weyers, halfway around Pallas, down on the equator. The whole area is a huge evergreen forest, but I suppose you know that. I shot my first mule deer there, near Corner Brook, on a hunting trip with my two uncles, Lindsay and Arleigh."

"With that?" She indicated the big Grizzly in the holster low on his hip. "That'd spin even a big muley buck rack over teakettle, wouldn't it?" He should have known she was Pallatian by the way she wore her own autopistol, in a canted high-ride, just behind her right hip.

He shook his head. "This belonged to my great grandfather. I've only had it for a year," he told her. "Corner Brook. I remember that I was ten years old, more or less, and I used my dad's ten millimeter magnum."

She grinned. "That's just around the time that I killed my first muley, myself," she told him delightedly. "You know, Wilson, sometimes I miss home so much that it aches—I mean physically. You know the feeling?"

"Not so much, to be honest. I never really wanted to be anything but a rock hunter, and it doesn't matter much where I happen to do that. Also, I have family here, my sister, and, until recently, my grandmother."

Her brow furrowed. "Oh, I'm sorry. When did she pass away?"

He laughed. "She'll outlive all of us. She went back to Mars to write children's books. I don't like to brag, but she's Julie Segovia Ngu."

"You don't like to brag must be the understatement of the century, Wilson. You may not know my family or anyone else in Corner Brook, but they know the Ngu family, from your great grandfather Emerson and your great grandmother Rosalie, through William and Brody who saved the seventh Martian expedition, right down to the young gunman of Ceres, who singlehandedly—"

He put a gentle finger to her lips. "I don't want to do this, Fallon."

She nodded and looked him in the eye. "I won't mention it again, I promise. I just wanted you to know that I knew—except about your grandmother. I never made that connection. I think it's really neat. I grew up on the Conchita and Desmondo books, and learned to read from them."

He laughed, "So did I." The resumed their walk, still holding hands.

CHAPTER TWENTY-EIGHT: MEET THE PRESS, PART ONE

I don't know what it is about the mass media. Throughout history—certainly throughout my lifetime—in every possible social, political, and economic condition, they are enthusiastically hated, loathed, and despised by absolutely everyone. And for good reason. Almost without exception, they are corrupt, lazy, incompetent, vulgar, and dullwittedly arrogant swine—who happen to think they're not doing their job unless everybody hates, loathes, and despises them.
—*The Diaries of Rosalie Frazier Ngu*

"FIVE, FOUR, THREE..." THE FLOOR director counted the last beats silently.

On the monitors, there had just been a cheerful commercial for a dog-food containing microscopic nanobots similar to those that kept spacesuit faceplates clean. They would lay dormant within the pet's system all its life. When it died, they immediately went to work converting the animal from the inside, into a permanent taxidermic display.

Aside from the fact that it sounded sad and disgusting (although he'd never been much for pets and wasn't absolutely certain), Wilson was sure that he'd done business with individuals who had done that to themselves.

"Good afternoon, ladies and gentlemen, and welcome to another edition of *Where Are They Now?*", originating from the studios of the Okohverik Beamcasting Company, here in beautiful downtown Armstrong City."

The speaker was a slender young man in a three-piece gray double-breasted suit at least a century and a half out of date. He had chosen a wide, tastefully patterned necktie in subdued colors. His hair was cut short, oiled slightly, and parted neatly in the middle. He wore small, round, rimless spectacles and spoke with an English accent he hoped would disguise the fact he'd been born and raised in Purdue, Indiana.

In front of him, invisible to his 3DTV audience, stood an oddly life-like three-legged robot about five feet tall, that shifted from side to side, backed away, or approached closely at the behest of the show's director sitting in his glass booth overhead, at the back. It could also swivel and tilt its mantis-like head—consisting mostly of two enormous 3DTV camera "eyes"—and sometimes looked as if it might be peering hungrily at the guest, or even the host of the program.

Two more just like it wandered the studio floor, peering at other things.

253

"Our guest tonight…" The young host stood at stage right, a bulky and antiquated microphone in one hand, and in the other, a thick sheaf of papers that he referred to as conspicuously as possible from time to time. Now he swept the hand full of the papers back and to his left, where, in a typical 3DTV studio talk show setting backdropped by a glorious Jovian sunrise (photographed early in the 21st century by an unmanned probe and projected on the studio wall), another young man sat nervously, his hands folded in his lap, in another glass booth, in an odd chair that looked a little like a giant black plastic martini glass.

"…can't hear us yet, in his soundproofed booth," the host told his audience. In addition to whoever might be seeing the program at home, there was also a studio audience every afternoon, consisting of three or four dozen individuals who had not been selected for their manners, their grooming, their intelligence, or their beauty. One of the other cameras occasionally panned across the crowd, with merciful brevity.

The host reflected that it was remarkably difficult finding people like these in the Moon—where one had to be reasonably bright to get here in the first place, or at least arrange to have been born to reasonably bright parents—and a desperate 3DTV search for their unsavory kind went on continually. Luckily, finding them was not his department—but God help us if they ever form a union!

He pretended to consult his papers. "This young fellow enjoyed notoriety about a year ago, when he gunned down five environmentalist demonstrators on the faraway asteroid Ceres, where his father, as the director of terraformation and construction there, not only exonerated him for what he did, but also arranged for him to receive a solid gold medal and an immense cash reward from the Curringer Corporation, which the five bullet-riddled demonstrators had apparently been protesting against."

"A little while after that, still on Ceres…" He whisked the top paper to the back of the stack in his hand and appeared to read from the next sheet. In reality, nothing at all was written on it; the program's directors and producers had found that many people tend to believe anything if it's written down, and this was one way of taking advantage of that tendency. "…he was involved in yet another ugly incident, so far not explained satisfactorily, in which there was an explosion near the one settlement, and a tourist, come to witness the controversial terraformation for himself, was shot in the knee and crippled."

The audience had begun to grumble ominously among themselves. They were about ready. He looked back and raised a hand. "Daphne, if you will…"

An exceptionally well-shaped young woman, blindingly blond and attired in what might have been a bathing suit—if there had been more of it—materialized from somewhere backstage and stationed herself decoratively to on side of the door of the glass isolation booth.

The 3DTV host took a deep breath and loudly announced, "Ladies and gentlemen—and Daphne, *Where Are They Now?* is delighted to present you with that infamous space frontier gunfighter, Wilson 'Willie the Kid' Ngu!"

Daphne opened the door. Wilson stumbled out of the booth, past the voluptuous and almost naked young woman (who seemed to be wearing too much perfume, possibly in compensation for the fact that she wasn't wearing much of anything else) toward the program's host and the 3DTV program that he'd been watching but so far had been unable to hear. All Wilson could hear now were the barnyard noises of the studio audience, laughing, applauding, cheering, whistling, and, oddly enough booing.

Somebody shouted, "Murderer!" Suddenly, Wilson knew what this was all about. He'd had some misgivings about accepting this invitation, arranged for by the Curringer Foundation, to be on 3DTV in the first place. It certainly wouldn't have any effect on his business, one way or another, and he was really sorry that he'd brought Fallon with him. The host led him to another martini glass chair and sat in one himself.

"Wilson Ngu," the host intoned as the audience was threatened to temporary silence by a couple of thick-necked individuals, unseen by the 3DTV cameras, who could have been bouncers in one of the tougher spaceport bars. "Grandson of Billy Ngu, instigator of the Martian Rebellion, and great grandson of Emerson Ngu, armsmaker and industrial giant."

"That's right," Wilson replied, undaunted. He leaned forward, into the face of the startled host. "Also great grandson of Rosalie Frazier Ngu, the notorious xenoarchaeologist, and grandson of Julie Segovia Ngu, the infamous writer of children's books. Also, my dad is an engineer, terraforming Ceres, my mom is a mad scientist, and my baby sister is…" He lowered his voice to an ominous whisper, "…an ice skater!. We're a dangerous breed, all right, the nefarious Ngus of Pallas!"

Wilson had had to raise his voice a couple of times to keep from being interrupted. By the time he finished, the host looked exactly like he'd just sat on a potted cactus, Wilson thought. The "hanging audience" that had been carefully arranged for him seemed strangely quiet, as if they were waiting for something to happen that they could understand.

"Erm, um…" said the host. Nobody had warned him about this guy, or he might have prepared himself with a bulletproof vest, or at least some tranquilizers. "We'll be right back after this important message—or messages—from one of our sponsors. Any of our sponsors!."

Wilson looked toward the side of the studio where non-audience guests were seated. Fallon was beaming at him, and he grinned right back.

Maybe now she'd tell him her middle name.

*
**

"Good evening ladies and gentlemen of the Solar System and of the human race. I'm Lotus Morimura, of *Japanese I: A Magazine of Asian Individualism.*"

There followed a burst of 3DTV shapes and colors that morphed into words, exploded in the viewer's face, and then morphed into different words.

"Tonight it's my pleasure and honor to introduce you to one of the most amazing people," Lotus declared, "and one of the most amazing stories, I've ever heard. I'm sitting rinkside at the Robert A. and Virginia Heinlein Memorial Ice Arena in Armstrong, the biggest city in the Moon, with Llyra Ayn Ngu, a young athlete whom local sportswriters have begun calling 'the fourth or fifth best figure skater in the Moon."

Llyra hoped she wasn't blushing; that would be too humiliating. Sitting with the beautiful and stylish correspondent on the lowest level of the Heinlein bleachers, close enough to touch the glass, she also tried not to squirm uncomfortably. At the same time that her feet were beginning to freeze, the 3DTV lights were extremely hot and blinding. Lotus, apparently accustomed to the lights, was wearing a well-tailored black coat with a real fur collar and seemed quite at home.

Nobody was on the ice. High above them in the bleachers, sat half of the girls she knew at the rink, and all of the boys (both of them), plus their coaches and a smattering of parents. Among them were Kelly Tran, Danita Lopez, and the East American ambassador's daughter Janna Kolditz, the girl she'd overheard on her first day here, whispering behind her back about "colonial trash". There was an old song Llyra vaguely recalled…how did it go? Oh, yeah: "How do you like me now?"

"Good evening, Llyra," Lotus said with a big 3DTV smile. Llyra and Jasmeen had once watched an old 2D movie together in which one of the characters cynically described a Hollywood starlet's process of being able to smile without involving—and therefore wrinkling—the flesh around the eyes. That was exactly what Lotus was doing now. "Thank you for being with us and for agreeing to answer a few questions for our 'readers'."

That was the conceit, here, that this program was an old-fashioned "dead tree" magazine, being read by the individuals who were watching it.

Llyra could go along with a gag. She smiled back, more genuinely, because she didn't know how to do it any other way. "Thank you for asking, Lotus." She felt pretty good, all things considered. She knew she looked all right. Jasmeen had brushed her hair until it shone like fine gold wire, and then had helped her pick out the white satiny competition dress—with its tiny decorative beads of real gold—that she had worn for the last event she'd skated in. She might not be quite as glamorous as Lotus Morimura, but she'd taken a first in the event.

"Llyra, we've all seen the Curringer Corporation advertisements on 3DTV that show you skating so spectacularly on Ceres. They're really quite breathtaking, with jumps and spins. It almost looks like you can fly—"

Llyra laughed. "On Ceres, where the gravity is one tenth of that of the Moon, you almost *can* fly. You could do it, too, with a little practice."

"You don't say—" Lotus blinked, momentarily taken aback, her eyes glazed, seeing a realm of possibilities she'd never considered before. With what amounted to a moral effort, she regained control of the interview and with it, her own composure. At twenty-nine, she thought, she was much too old to start something like ice skating, anyway.

She pressed on: "Most people know by now that you came here from your native Pallas, second largest of the Belt asteroids, which has only one *twentieth* of a gee, to the Moon, with its one sixth of a gee. That's over three times the pull of gravity you were born and raised in, Llyra. Isn't it dangerous? How can you force yourself to do it?"

Lotus paused and looked encouragingly at Llyra who nodded and said, "If you have to force yourself, you shouldn't be doing it. You should be doing something else, instead, something you burn to be doing. It's three and a third times, as a matter of fact, although I did skate that little bit you mentioned on Ceres at one tenth. And I admit I had some practice home on Pallas over a mascon near the South Pole."

"I see," Lotus nodded. Maybe she was doing what she was meant to do, after all. Aside from doing interviews like this, with badguys, goodguys, and rare, sweet kids like Llyra, there was very little in life she cared about. She turned back toward the double-lensed camera strapped to her assistant's head, and to her viewers. "Mascons are places where the local gravity is greater, owing to deposits of denser minerals."

Then she turned to Llyra. "But for all practical purposes, here in the Moon, only a little more than a year ago, you were a cripple—to use a very old-fashioned ugly word—or you could say, 'gravitically challenged'. In any case, you and your coach Jasmeen Khalidov had only just graduated from wheelchairs to walkers when the two of you hobbled down here to the Heinlein and signed up as members of the ice skating club."

Jasmeen was sitting several levels above them in the bleachers, having grimly vowed not to interfere with the interview or jog Llyra's elbow.

Meanwhile, Lotus had already interviewed Shirlene Hofstaedter, the local Figure Skating Association representative, a very nice lady who was long-accustomed to dealing with the media—and therefore sort of a boring subject. Next, Lotus planned to interview that pretty young Martian coach of Llyra's, who would be less polished and considerably more interesting. Let her say three words in that sexy accent, and Lotus's male audience, the fifteen to eighty-five segment, would adore her.

"That's right, Lotus." Llyra said. For an instant, Lotus couldn't remember the question. Llyra had begun to relax a little. "Wheelchairs to walkers. I sort of had to start all over, at the Beginner level, although at home I was a Ladies' Intermediate and about to test for Novice."

Lotus nodded, understanding. When this interview was aired, there would be a sidebar chart showing the different levels of achievement in figure skating. "And yet, since you began competing, you've never failed to take third, second, or even sometimes first place in all the events you've entered, is that right?" She smiled, more genuinely this time.

Llyra cast her eyes down modestly, an unconscious gesture Lotus was absolutely certain she'd learned from her coach. "I've had a couple of fourths, to be perfectly truthful, but basically you're right."

Having established the important underlying facts, Lotus now asked one of the meatier questions that she'd been working up to all along. "So then, Llyra Ayn Ngu, how would *you* account for this marvelous phenomenon?"

Llyra blinked. "What phenomenon—oh, I guess I see what you mean. I...I just decide what I want to do, and I try it, over and over and over again, until I can do it. My family taught me that, and my coach, of course. They're the kind of people who *never* give up, either."

"Would you say," Lotus asked her, getting to the heart of this session, "that such a trait is generally characteristic of people in Pallas?"

"*On* Pallas. We live on Pallas," Llyra corrected. "Pretty much, yeah." Images formed in her mind, of her great grandfather Emerson and her grandfather William. She thought of her father and brother, too, and her uncles, who could be very silly, or formidable when they were angered.

Lotus nodded again. She'd done her homework and was also thinking about the legendary figures of Pallatian history. Maybe she should interview the brother. "So what's next, Llyra, where do you go from here?"

"Nowhere, not for a while, anyway. I'll finish the competition season and then resume testing. I also plan to try out for a part in the Lunar Figure Skating Association's annual ice show, *Winter Wonders*. In about a year, I guess, it's on to Mars, and one third gee."

⁂

"Good morning, sleepyheads! This here is Ebo Ebbs of KCUF 3DTV and radio. I'm here at the Raymond Louis Drake-Tealy museum to have a talk with Dr. Ardith Zacharenko Ngu, the System's foremost authority on asteroid physics and chemistry. Good morning, Dr. Ngu, and how are you today?"

Ebbs was a tall, thin individual, supposedly descended from some African warrior race, but like many people on Pallas whose ancestry was thoroughly mixed, appeared to be as white as the person he addressed.

"I'm just fine, thank you, Ebo, considering the hour."

Ardith ran a hand through her dark, wavy hair. It was pretty early in the morning for her, too—like all her family, she was basically a night person—and disorienting to be doing business on somebody else's territory, the museum rather than her lab or office across the street. Instead, they stood at the rail in front of a glassed-in display of some of the largest Drake-Tealy Objects—none larger than a cantaloupe—to be discovered, until the Object found at Lafcadio Guzman's.

"This morning's program," Ebbs told his audience. "was originally scheduled to concern itself something quite remarkable, wasn't it, Dr. Ngu?"

Ardith found the lights mounted at the corners of Ebbs's camera glasses a bit distracting. She was of a mind to ask him to turn them off. There was plenty of available light in here for modern 3DTV equipment.

"Yes it was, Ebo." She indicated an odd spherical object on an old-fashioned brass and oak stand beside her. "As you know, my son Wilson is an asteroid hunter, downsystem. Following up on information he purchased from the Larsen Farside Observatory, he found the thing you see here, which he was kind enough to send to his mother as a present."

"And it isn't even Mother's Day. He must be a good boy." Ebbs mugged for the benefit of a second pair of lenses standing atop a counter full of meteors in the middle of the hall. "What, exactly, is it?"

"Wilson is far more than a good boy, he's a fine young man. I'm loaning what he sent me to the Drake-Tealy Museum. As you can see, it's just a little bit bigger than a basketball, as transparent as glass, and a very pretty shade of red. It's the largest garnet ever discovered."

"A garnet! That's certainly impressive, Dr. Ngu—although it's a little large for a pendant and there's only one, so earrings are out of the question. And ordinarily, I'd have a whole bunch of interesting and intelligent questions to ask you about it, too. But today, it's going to have to take a back seat to something even more remarkable, right?"

Even so, Ebbs removed his camera glasses and passed them behind the garnet so that his other camera could see the light coming through it.

"As hard as that is to imagine." Ardith replied, "Yes."

Ebbs took a deep breath. This was very bad video, he thought, with little or no visual action, but a hell of a news story, and he was the first to report it. On the other hand, Ardith Ngu was easy on the eyes and sure to hold his male viewers' attention. He hoped she was a good story teller. "Could you describe for our audience exactly what has happened?"

She smiled—it was like the explosion of a nova, he thought. "Probably not exactly, Ebo. We're going to be a long while sorting it out. But the bare facts are these. Last year, Julie Segovia Ngu, the famous children's author, and my mother-in-law, persuaded the Drake-Tealy Museum to purchase a genuine Drake-Tealy Object—also the largest ever discovered, about the size of an average suburban house—from a dealer at L-Four. Also, she put up a good deal of the asking price, herself."

Ardith wasn't certain that Julie wanted that told, but it would be a public embarrassment to the cheapskates who comprised the rest of the museum's board of directors, and that couldn't be all bad, could it?

If Ebbs wasn't fascinated, he was faking it well. "And then what happened?"

Ardith cleared her throat. "Mostly for administrative reasons, it took until this year before anything could be done about physically claiming the object and bringing it upsystem to Pallas. Our intention was to leave it in orbit for scientific study and tourist excursions. Part of the delay was obtaining clear title to a suitable orbital slot."

"I see." The interviewer nodded. "And then what?"

Ardith said, "You know R.G. Edd, I'm sure. Everybody does, here on Pallas. Mostly he's our local commercial ionopter pilot. But he used to fly one of the extremely powerful tugs that helped space liners and freighters touch down safely at Port Peary and Port Admundsen. When engine and guidance technology advanced and rendered the space tugs obsolete, the company retired the tugs, and R.G. became an ionopter pilot."

"But what does that have to do with—?"

"When he heard of our prize Drake-Tealy Object," Ardith replied, "R.G. volunteered to reactivate one of the tugs—that took a little while, too—and fly it downsystem, collect the rock, and bring it home. He left early last week and wasn't due to return until late next week."

"Wasn't? Past tense? What happened to him?"

If it bleeds it leads, she thought.

But what she said was, "I wish R.G. were here to describe what happened to us, himself. He got down to L-Four all right, got the paperwork all sorted out, attached his towing cables to the object, and..."

"And...?"

"And as soon as he started his engines, the Drake-Tealy Object began towing him, backwards, accelerating to a velocity we're still not certain we've calculated correctly. He should have been killed by the acceleration, but he wasn't. Instead, he arrived in the correct parking orbit around Pallas approximately two hours after he left L-Four."

Ebbs swallowed. "But that would be—"

She nodded. "That would be about fifty million miles an hour," she said. "Or roughly fourteen thousand miles per second—or almost twelve hundred times the velocity of any natural body in the Solar System."

Ebbs whistled—to the annoyance of the sound man in the KCUF studio across town. "But then Drake-Tealy Objects aren't natural, are they?"

Ardith smiled. Demonstrating that extremely controversial fact, of course, had been the greatest scientific accomplishment of her famous grandmother-in-law, Rosalie Frazier Ngu. She said as much to the interviewer.

"You're right, of course. But what happened to R.G. Edd? Why can't he be with us today? Was he injured in some way, or perhaps mentally traumatized?

Ardith shook her head. "R.G. promptly detached himself from the Drake-Tealy Object, landed his tug at Port Peary, drove himself home to Curley's Gulch, and took his own ionopter to a cabin he has out in the weyers somewhere. He called to report what had happened and ended by saying that he plans to hide under his bed for the next couple of months."

"I can't say I blame him," said the correspondent.

Ardith said, "Neither can I."

There wasn't any point in trying to be sneaky.

This location had been selected after an exhaustive statistical analysis had shown that it was the least-visited location on Ceres. Or so the woman code-named "Harriet Beecher" had been told, anyway. There was no air, naturally, so she couldn't be heard. There was nobody else around from here to the horizon, so she couldn't be seen. There were no surveillance cameras to be seen anywhere, because this wasn't East America.

Harriet could look in any direction for miles and see nothing but herself and a bizarre, nightmarish landscape, somewhat Moonlike, but completely draped, from horizon to horizon, in what amounted to a colossal slipcover of tough, transparent plastic, waiting to be inflated by an injection of microbes genetically engineered for the purpose. The first would fill the envelope with nitrogen, methane, and ammonia.

If she couldn't stop it.

Just now, it was as if her grandmother had been turned loose with a whole world for her living room. Every last stick of furniture the old lady had owned had been covered with plastic. It had been a huge pleasure, watching her grandmother's face as she was suffocated with it. The old lady had had the gall to claim that she didn't have any money to give her only granddaughter when she was strung out and hurting.

Harriet had no illusions about what might happen to her after she did this job for Null Delta Em. She'd been plucked from a solitary prison cell in Darkest Connecticut—having brutally murdered three fellow inmates her first month inside—and cleansed of every trace of the stultifying behavior modification drugs that had kept her physically helpless, devoid of any will to escape, for the last seven years.

What a rush it had been to have all those good old deliciously wicked feelings come pouring back into her skull! It was exactly like the feeling of relief that comes with a long-anticipated sneeze, only it went on and on sort of like a perpetual orgasm. And now she had an opportunity to slaughter hundreds with one push of a button, and possibly end an historic social movement—humanity's long climb to the stars—that her employers believed was misguided and harmful to mankind.

She had no idea where they'd gotten their little spaceship. It was fast and powerful, yet luxuriously appointed, like a yacht. On the way here from Earth orbit she'd had one elegant meal after another. Then they'd lowered her from synchronous orbit on several hundred miles of synthetic line, in a spaceship's emergency escape pod—sort of a spherical airtight sleeping bag with its own oxygen supply and small, crinkly plastic windows to peek through. The flashing lights had been removed.

Already wearing her envirosuit with the helmet off, she'd slept easily through the ride to the surface and had to be awakened by her employers using wires in the cable to preserve radio silence. Apparently they were anxious about being spotted and wanted to move to a less-conspicuous orbit as soon as possible.

She'd put her helmet on and run through the suit's checklist, then flipped a safety cover and pulled a toggle that released the line. She didn't know if they'd reel it in or let it drift. It didn't matter. In theory, the individuals she was working for would pick her up as soon as her task here was done. In practice, of course, she had her doubts. But the amount of money they'd already paid her, let alone what she'd been promised she'd receive afterward, made it well worth taking the risk.

Meanwhile, she could afford to be fatalistic. She couldn't go back to Earth, that was certain, and she didn't think that she could stand it out here. Pallas sounded sort of nice, but given her predilections, and the fact that everybody she saw was armed, she wouldn't last a week.

Opening a double set of airtight zippers wasn't fun. Once she was free of the pod, she assembled the fifty-foot poles that would be her ticket off this rock. They had fifteen feet of line strung between them, part of a loop connecting to a reel of line on the back of her suit. When she gave the signal—again in theory—the ship that had brought her would swoop down, hook the loop, and drag her up into the sky, to be reeled in, desuited, paid off, and set down wherever she wished.

The Moon might do. Miles of dark tunnels, millions of potential victims.

This plastic the Ceres Terraformation Project used for making the atmospheric canopy was creepy stuff, Harriet thought. Not quite half an inch thick, most bullets wouldn't go through it. Even if one managed to, any hole it made would heal shut in less than thirty seconds.

Which was why her employers had been compelled to resort to the peculiar means she was about to put to work for them. From a zippered pocket on the right thigh of her envirosuit, she extracted a hollow metal cylinder about seven inches long and a little over two inches in diameter.

In the pocket across her chest, she found a base plate, square, eight inches on a side and a quarter of an inch thick, into which she screwed one end of the cylinder. From the pocket on her other thigh, she took another cylinder, three inches in diameter and about the same height.

The second cylinder contained a very special catalyst it had taken Null Delta Em or the Mass Movement or somebody fifty years to develop. It had originally been intended for use on the Pallatian environmental canopy, and might well be put to that noble purpose if it worked here. The second cylinder then screwed sideways into the top of the first cylinder.

From a pocket on the left arm of her suit, she obtained a tube of very special glue, which she spread carefully on the underside of the square baseplate, and over an area of the canopy plastic of about the same size. Counting to thirty, she placed the baseplate and cylinders on the plastic, gave them a moment, then tugged hard to make sure they stuck. An old song about wild horses went through her mind and she laughed.

At the top of the first cylinder, she flipped a safety cover over to expose a large red pushbutton. When it was pushed, two things would begin to happen. First, the catalyst from the second cylinder would travel down the length of the first cylinder at extremely high pressure.

Second, the glue would be ignited. It was more than merely glue. As it burned, it would carry the catalyst with it into the substance of the canopy plastic itself. There would be a cataclysmic local explosion, and before long, a ring of fire would sweep outward from the center, to consume the plastic canopy material.

Within a day, there would be no canopy at all left on Ceres, only a thin scattering of fine, gray ash, and everybody on this little world would be dead or waiting to die in stuffy confines of their envirosuits.

Harriet would be somewhere else entirely, of course, with a much more attractive name, relaxing on some hot, sunny, sandy beach or by a blue pool somewhere, sunbathing—even if it had to be the piped-in light of a Lunar resort—and drinking margaritas, pina coladas, or zombies. She had three minutes to escape after she pushed the button. She wouldn't press it until she could actually see her rescuers on the way.

"Mommy," she told her suit radio, "this is baby. Come and get me, please."

Seeing running lights low on the horizon before she expected it, she prepared herself for the jerk of the rescue cable, and pushed the button—

—and didn't live long enough to know there was no three minute delay. She and the ship now directly overhead were consumed, vaporized by the explosion, as an ominous fiery ring spread outward from its center.

CHAPTER TWENTY-NINE: MEET THE PRESS, PART TWO

A great woman, a philosopher and novelist insufficiently appreciated in her own time, once observed that you can find out just about anything you wish about a person by taking a good, hard look at who they sleep with. I've generally found this to be true, myself. Maybe the question we ask when we meet someone for the first time shouldn't be "How do you do?" but "Who do you do?" —The Diaries of Rosalie Frazier Ngu

A FLATTENED SPHEROID ABOUT FOUR inches in diameter flew past her face, its coin-sized camera eyes swiveling around to keep her in view.

There were at least three more of the things hovering in the room, peering at Julie's possessions, the photographs that she kept of her deceased husband and other members of her family, and of the friends and associates she'd had over the length of her long and productive life.

For some reason, the phrase "batteries not included" came to mind. She hoped they'd stay away from the knick-knack shelves, mostly occupied by mementos her children and grandchildren had created for her.

The cameras were very distracting, she thought, although they're sort of cute, in an overly technologized way. She knew they were the very latest thing—the very latest thing, technologically, very nearly always came from Mars—and wouldn't be in use downsystem for months. The broadcast media in East America might not see them for years.

Still and all, she thought, here she was again, being interviewed about her latest book in the convenience and comfort of her own front parlor. And an extremely comfortable place it was, indeed, in which to be interviewed. Most Martian homes had formal parlors like this one to keep strangers—even relatively important ones like this young 3DTV correspondent—out of the rest of a home intended to be a family refuge.

" ... Conchita and Desmondo," the interviewer was saying, "once again wandering through the land of Wimpersnits and Oogies, is that it?"

"What else could it possibly be ... " Julie smiled as sweetly as she could. Her interviewer was an attractive young black woman in her twenties, named Madison Moiré. She was dressed in the latest high summer fashion on Mars, what amounted to a silver bikini with what could only be described as miniature bead curtains hanging from both the upper and lower parts of the outfit, in front and back. "... when my young readers, their older brothers and sisters, and their parents and grandparents and aunts and uncles keep asking me so politely for more?"

Madison turned toward the nearest flying camera and declared, "The title of the new Julie Segovia Ngu book is *Conchita and the Brain Eaters.*" She turned back to Julie. "The word in the book publishing trade is that it's been banned already, without being read, in East America."

"You can't buy that kind of advertising," Julie laughed and shook her head. "But it's not quite true that it hasn't been read in East America—by East American leaders, that is. They got the book before anybody else did—believing that their operatives had stolen it from us—in the form of bound, uncorrected galley proofs. We wanted to make sure that the politicians and bureaucrats would be aghast and noisily outlaw it, so that East American kids would know it was on the way."

The interviewer was startled. "But Aunt Julie, if they can't buy it—pardon me, I mean Miss Ngu." Her parents had been neighbors for decades. Madison had played on Julie's front porch since she was three, and like every other Martian child worthy of the name, had grown up reading her books.

Julie grinned. "That's all right, Maddy. It's a small planet, and I think your viewers are already aware that we know each other. But you're right. On the official, legal open market they can't buy my book, it's true. Or any of my books. However there's an exceptionally healthy black market in East America. In fact it's the only thing keeping them alive, economically. We have advance orders for over a million copies in East America, alone. And, of course, being banned there is very good for sales everywhere else. We'll also be offering audio recordings, to be broadcast across the border from West America. In fact I've finished recording the book already, in both English and Spanish."

"And your latest idea," Madison said, half to her audience, half to Julie, "a Conchita and Desmondo theme park, is due to be completed … when?"

"Two years from now," Julie replied, "near Armstrong City, in the Moon.

Madison took a deep breath and let it out. "In their most recent denunciation of you and your works, the *New York Journal of Domestic Tranquility* described *Brain Eaters* as … now where did I put that? … okay, here it is: "a savage and ruthless character assassination of brave psychological counselors within the public school system who tirelessly and unselfishly give of themselves, in order to assist helpless children to survive the numberless and endless catastrophes that are inflicted on them and society by unrestrained individuals and individualism."

Julie threw back her head and laughed. "Yes, I read that article last week. We plan to use it as a blurb. When I was a little girl, trying to survive the New Jersey public school system, we called them 'psychovultures'."

"Psychovultures?"

"Psychovultures, traveling from school to school in the wake of some horrible tragedy, making damn sure that we kids took the 'right' lessons from whatever had happened: you must never, ever try to defend yourself, or do anything else on your own; guns and other weapons are both evil and useless; individuals who resent being stolen from or pushed around by the state are either villains or crazy; your parents are ignorant Neanderthals; your teachers and the police are your friends."

"Well then, I guess it's good that we don't have any of them on Mars," said the interviewer, unaccustomed to straightforward talk like this.

"It's even better that we don't have any public schools, and damned few private ones. I helped see to that in the early days. Most Martians are home-schooled, and therefore well-educated, properly civilized, and prepared to look after themselves, psychologically and physically."

The voice was light and bantering, calculated to a perfect tenor.

"Well, it seems that we've had a lot of Ngus in the news lately, Miss Khalidov."

"I did not know that, er ... people of your, um ... kind made jokes," replied Jasmeen, wondering why she'd agreed to this. She was certain that at some level, she ought to be feeling humiliated. "'Ngus in the news'—very clever."

"I thought so, too, actually. And I also understand that you're practically one of the Ngus, yourself: traveling with them wherever they happen to go, living with them, working with them on an everyday basis."

"Yes, that's true. They—"

"You're a sister to young Llyra, the celebrated ice skater, a daughter to Ardith, the famous Pallatian scientist. And to her husband Adam," the interviewer's tenor was speculative, "terraformer of Ceres, or to the dashing asteroid hunter and notorious gunfighter Wilson Ngu, who knows—"

The sentence came to a halt because Jasmeen had laid a hand on the ten millimeter autopistol she was carrying under her angora sweater in the so-called "appendix" position. It was a very familiar gesture to the interviewer, having come from Jasmeen's native planet Mars, and one of several reasons it was electronic and mechanical, rather than human.

In the embarrassed silence that followed, Jasmeen looked it over. It had once been enameled white, and was not quite as tall as she was, conical, with a rounded base like a child's boxing toy two and a half feet in diameter, scorched black by repeated reentries in the Martian atmosphere. It tapered to a point six inches across, the top of which was hinged back at present to reveal a pair of 3DTV eyes and several other kinds of sensors in the underside of the "lid". It stood on three spindly legs that folded into the machine, each ending in a powered wheel about a foot in diameter, with an electric motor in each hub.

In several places it was labeled "Syrtis Systems Telebot PCG 505F".

It had wanted to interview her in the apartment she shared with Llyra, who was off at a jumps clinic just now at a small rink in the little town of Leinster, a few hundred miles west of Armstrong. An underground high speed passenger train made the run in minutes, and coaches were not invited, which gave Jasmeen a rare afternoon all to herself.

The request for an interview had come by SolarNet before Llyra had left the apartment. Otherwise, Jasmeen, who was irregular in her comm habits, might not have seen it. She'd replied that she was amenable, but not here, in her home. How about a nice, wide-open restaurant, instead?

She'd been startled when the reply came back to her in only a few minutes. Obviously her would-be interviewer was not on Mars, even though the interview was being done for one of the large Martian news services.

"I'm in orbit around the Moon at the moment," she was told. "I can be ready in half an hour if that suits you, but not in a restaurant. People would stare and ask questions and we wouldn't get anything accomplished."

Jasmeen asked, "Why is that?"

"Because I'm a semiautonomous robot, the first of my kind. My name is Lucy. I get sent on these trips because I can conduct an interview without any time lag, and then transmit it back to Mars ahead of my return."

"Very interesting," Jasmeen observed. "Makes sense."

Which was why they were here now, in a small corner of a cavernous but almost-deserted maintenance bay, at the Arthur C. Clark Memorial spaceport where Lucy had just landed. The robot stood on the oil- stained floor. Jasmeen sat with her knees crossed on a big wheeled tool cabinet painted red and white with a Snap-On banner. Jasmeen had brought her breakfast in a brown plastic bag and stopped for coffee on the way. She adored the garage smells of grease and solvents and welding. It seemed a fitting environment for a conversation with a robot.

"Now we are starting all over again," she informed the machine, gently shaking her jelly doughnut at it. "This time you are being as polite as can be or you are going home full of holes. You understand this?"

"Yes, I understand, Miss Khalidov," it said. "Please do not shoot me."

"Very well. And you may call me Jasmeen. Yes, I am working for Ngu family. My parents and Llyra's grandparents—Billy and Julie Ngu—are friends from Martian Revolution. I coach their granddaughter Llyra who is, as you say, celebrated performer. She is also beautiful figure skater who never stops learning and never gives up. Coaching her is pleasure."

"You're a native Martian, Jasmeen. Llyra, your student, was born and raised on the terraformed asteroid Pallas—at one twentieth of a standard gee. Can you tell my viewers what you two are doing in the Moon?"

Jasmeen nodded. "Student Llyra wishes there to be no place in System where she cannot skate. Coach Jasmeen wishes to assist her in this."

"Quite an ambition," said the robot. "And I take it her ambition includes skating on Earth itself—at the risk of shattered bones, damaged growth plates, ruined ligaments and tendons, and perhaps even serious heart problems. Do you ever worry about Llyra surviving it, Jasmeen?"

Jasmeen took a contemplative nibble on her jelly doughnut and thought. "Is not my place to worry, Lucy. Is my place to help make happen."

They sat together "outdoors", on the decorative brick rim of the construction dome's "see-ment pond", their backs to the blank white concrete wall where 3D pictures of Ceres taken from orbit were being projected.

"So what you're saying, Dr. Ngu, is that the entire planet—er, planetoid—is now covered, pole to pole, in a single, solid sheet of plastic."

They could look up now and see the stuff draped over the dome, which had been made of the same material. The sun, never terribly bright this far away—about twice as far as it was from Earth—appeared even dimmer than usual, and it felt cold and a little sad inside.

"That's right, Miss Graham, a single, solid piece of very special 'smart' plastic, draped from pole to pole—except for the craters at the opposite poles, of course. The plastic there is firmly anchored and tightly gasketed, in very special steel and concrete clamps just below the crests of their ring-mountain rims. The crater floors will remain in total vacuum once the rest of our little world has its own atmosphere."

"And the two polar craters will become your spaceports. You see, I was paying attention, after all." She leaned toward him, displaying a deep and ample cleavage. "And Dr. Ngu—Adam—*do* please call me Honey."

Honey had finally been assigned a camera and audio man, a young fellow with tightly-curled blond hair, pale blue eyes, and a perpetually cynical expression on his face. He looked down at his feet and suppressed a knowing chuckle. The word, he was aware, around the water cooler at the Interplanetary Interactive Information Service that employed them both, was "Whatever Honey wants, Honey gets". Personally, he found that he was immune to Honey's putative charms. That may have had something to do with a certain golden-skinned, almond-eyed girl waiting for him back home in Vancouver.

They were expecting their first child in three months.

Adam surprised him—and Honey—by replying, "I guess I'll stick with 'Miss Graham' for now, if you don't mind. But you're right about the polar craters. Right now we're trying to decide what to call them. We Pallatians named our polar craters—rather, the spaceports located there—after the discoverers of Earth's poles, Peary and Admundsen."

"Peary and Admundsen," Honey repeated, as if it were the first time she'd ever heard those names. Very likely, it was. Unlike most news media people, she was relatively intelligent, but like the vast majority of her professional colleagues, she was very poorly educated and didn't really care enough to do anything about it. Knowing things, she'd found, just got in the way. "Then why don't you have a naming contest?"

He grinned. "That's a good idea, Miss Graham, we just might do that."

"In the meantime, though ... " She tried to regain control of the interview.

"In the meantime, though, with completion of the last hypersonic weldment or seam—and with it, the entire plastic atmospheric canopy—the Ceres Terraformation Project is taking a well-deserved day off, to sit back, relax, and lift a glass or two." He lifted his own. "It's official."

She blinked. She hadn't seen the glass mug. "Of ... ?"

"Of Old Pallatian Amber Ale. Look here on the label: portraits of Wild Bill Curringer, Raymond Louis Drake-Tealy, and Mirelle Stein—which is appropriate, somehow. Would you care for one, Miss Graham? It happens to be Ceres' most popular import. Did you know we have a New Belgium brewery right there in beautiful downtown Curringer? We need some rest before we commit ourselves to the next big task in of terraforming Ceres."

"And that would be ... ?" She'd like to have had a beer about now, but she couldn't even show Dr. Ngu actually drinking one on 3DTV, under East American broadcast agreements, let alone be seen drinking, herself.

"Come on, now, Miss Graham, you're smarter than that. You tell me."

She blinked again. "Well, er, placing the thousand-mile cables that hold the plastic atmospheric canopy down once there's air inside it. They'll be anchored at the poles, too. In fact you've already sunk the ... "

"The piers." He gave her an encouraging grin. "Yes, we have, along the polar ring-mountain crests, again, just outside of the canopy gasketing."

She struggled to regain focus again. What was it about this tall, gangly, slightly-balding guy? She'd have to ask that little Asian secretary of his, who was obviously completely gone on him. "Dr. Ngu, I've been here on Ceres enough times, for long enough, and seen enough by now, to understand that you're a builder to the very core of your being. You're proud of your work on this asteroid, and with reason. You've been entrusted with the most ambitious engineering job in human history."

"So far," he told her. "So far. I often have to remind myself of that."

She smiled. "So far, then. Any special problems you anticipate now?"

He shrugged. "No, it's basically the same engineering that was accomplished on Pallas over three generations ago, only on a larger scale, of course. Being the first to do it, though. I'll bet that was hard."

"No problems, then?" She sounded disappointed.

"I didn't say that. Ceres is a carbonaceous chondrite, almost one hundred percent—even purer than Pallas was; there are reasons for that I'll leave to the astrophysicists to explain—so we don't have all of the raw metal onsite to work with that we'd like to have. But the factory ships, over a hundred of them in orbit above Ceres, put out the specifications, and asteroid hunters bring them whatever we need."

Sometimes, Adam mused, he envied the asteroid hunters like his son, and regretted that he hadn't become one of them, himself. He might have found the Diamond Rogue by now, or that other legendary giant jewel, the Big Rock Candy Mountain. In any case, it might possibly have saved him a great deal of trouble later on in life.

"And we'll see you here to lift a glass to the successful cable laying ... ?"

He laughed. "About this time next year."

"Very well then, thank you, Dr. Ngu."

"Thank you, Miss Graham."

She glanced at her camera carrier—she'd given up wearing the Sony QDH-616G SuperMedia spectacles herself; they didn't give her enough face time which was death in this business—and signaled a stop.

"You see, now, Miss Graham," Adam told her before she could speak. "That wasn't so hard, was it? You're really much more intelligent than you give yourself credit for, and I think you know a deal more, as well."

Nobody had ever told her that before. She was really quite moved. Was she starting to fall for this guy? She hoped to hell not—a wife *and* a girl-friend, two hundred million miles from home. "Is that so?" she replied, as casually as she could manage. "So then, what will it take to get you to call me by my first name? Everybody else does, you know."

"It wouldn't surprise me. How about if you were to sign on as a colonist?"

"I—" Beyond that, she was speechless. "Ah ... er ... "

Her cameraman laughed. "I'll sign on, Doc. My first name is Burt."

"Well," Adam told Honey, "it's a start."

*
**

"No, sir. I didn't suppose there would be much call for a 3DTV cameraman on Ceres just yet, Dr. Ngu." Honey's assistant had left his equipment—there wasn't much; the camera itself, with its built-in lights, he had stuck in a thigh pocket of his baggy work trousers—at the decorative pool to walk back with Adam to the Project head office. "But I learn quickly and there are plenty of other things to do."

Apparently this young fellow is dead serious, thought Adam. His enthusiasm could make up for any lack of skills he might have. Maybe the Project could use a camera and audio man. I'll have to think about it.

"And your family ... ?" Of course he could always be trying to get away from his obligations, like many a settler on Pallas, a century ago.

"My wife's first name," Burt grinned from ear to ear, "means 'songbird' in Mandarin, Dr. Ngu. I don't know our kid's first name yet, because we haven't been formally introduced. I'll bring them back with me—or stay here and send for them—if you'll just give the word."

Adam nodded. "Then I think—"

Suddenly, a dozen harsh klaxons began going off, filling the air with obnoxious and frightening noises. This was the alarm ordinarily reserved—it had never been set off until this moment—for a catastrophic breach of the dome. Adam forgot about Burt, his family, and everything else but the present emergency as he hurried into his office.

Inside, Ingrid's beautiful eyes were wide with apprehension, but she had already gotten emergency self-contained breathing apparatus out of a closet for them both and was standing at his desk, playing his keyboard like a concert pianist. She moved aside when she saw him arrive.

She said, "Your brother's onscreen for you, Dr. Ngu."

"Thanks, Ingrid, will you find a chair for—" He looked back. Burt was long gone, to check on Honey or his 3DTV gear, perhaps both. "Never mind. Let's see what's happening. Is there still coffee in that thing?"

Lindsay's worried visage almost filled the screen. Behind his brother, Adam could make out the interior of one of the Project's *gamera*. At the controls, he could see the back of Arleigh's shaggy head.

"What's up, Lindsay?" Adam asked. "Was it you who tripped that alarm?"

Lindsay nodded. "Yeah, I asked one of the second shift hands to do that for me. I figured you might want a little time to gather up your possessions and precious souvenirs before you evacuate—if you're lucky. We're about a thousand miles from the dome right now, headed away."

"Evacuated? Why?" demanded Adam.

"Well, we just got word—and pictures—from the factory vessel *Herschel* that the atmospheric canopy is on fire and burning outward in a circle about three hundred miles in diameter as of ten minutes ago."

"But—" Adam found himself at a loss for words. "That plastic's supposed to be completely fireproof. I conducted the goddamned tests myself."

"Language, brother dear," Lindsay grinned. "Watch your goddamned language."

Arleigh turned toward the pickup as Lindsay moved aside. "I hate to say it, Ad, but it looks like sabotage to me. The images that we downloaded from the *Herschel* show a great big explosion right in the middle of absolute nowhere—one asks why—then a circle of fire going away from Ground Zero, initially at about six thousand feet per second.

Lindsay added, "It seems to have slowed down considerably since then."

Adam nodded. "So it's using up something it needs to keep on burning?"

"More likely spreading it thinner and thinner, I think," Arleigh answered.

Adam nodded again. "A catalyst, then. Think it'll get to the dome?"

Lindsay was looking at another screen. "The computer says it will, yes, about this time tomorrow." He looked at Adam. "What'll we do, Boss?"

His brother had never called him that before. Without hesitation, Adam said, "Each of you take a *gamera* to opposite positions on the burn perimeter. Station two more of the machines between you. We'll have to calculate the proper radius as we go, depending on the burn rate."

"Gotcha," Lindsay answered. "Then what?"

Adam explained what he wanted them to do. "I'll leave one *gamera* here for emergencies, and I'll take the sixth to the center of the burn."

"How come?" Lindsay and Arleigh had spoken simultaneously.

"I mean," he told them, "to find out exactly what sons-of-bitches did this to us. While I'm headed in that general direction, send me every pixel that the *Herschel* took. Then ask them to do another scan, of the very center of the explosion, at as high a resolution as possible. I'm heading for my transport right now. Ingrid, would you please—"

"Right away, Dr. Ngu!"

He turned to find Honey and Burt right behind him. "May we go, too?"

He started to tell them no, reflexively. Then he shook his head in resignation. "It looks like it's turning into a party. Why the hell not?"

⁎⁎

The airlock light turned green. Not knowing who was up front, he shouted toward the bow of the craft, "I got the back door sealed and locked!"

Lindsay reentered the new *gamera* they'd sent out to him, his heavy duty industrial hand laser beginning to smoke a little once it was out of the vacuum and the utter cold of the Cerean surface. His brother Arleigh had gone ahead with the original machine taking a crewman who had arrived at the arranged spot with this one, and would be running through a similar routine to this, several hundred miles away.

Conferring with Adam by radio, they'd figured the whole thing out on the fly. What they had to handle here, basically, he'd told them, was a forest fire, and they'd agreed. Lindsay had spent his teenage years smoke-jumping in the deep, endless forests of Pallas. Arleigh had once been a volunteer fireman in Curringer. All three of the brothers understood that they were trying to save the future of an entire world.

"I've made the initial cuts, and set the hooks," he informed the individual in the lefthand seat, as he set his laser aside and belted himself into the other seat. This was the individual who'd brought him the *gamera* from the dome, but the hadn't had time for introductions, and he wasn't even consciously aware of whoever was beside him, now, except in the present context. It didn't really matter. His brother didn't hire unreliable individuals. Lindsay's eyes remained glued to a screen to his right, showing the fire's inexorable progress around the asteroid.

His mind was having more than a little difficulty trying to absorb the bizarre fact that he and his brothers were fighting a fire in a vacuum.

He ran his fingers over a keyboard, then peered at the results on the screen for a moment. Outside, the sky seemed crowded with fliers of various designs and types, sweeping their lights over the surface, to all appearances at random. It didn't require much reaction mass to keep machines like these aloft at one-tenth of a gee, but occasionally he could feel the *gamera* shudder in their backwash as they passed overhead.

274

"Let's start warming up those forward lasers," he told the pilot. "Give us about twenty feet of altitude to get the right spread between them."

He peered out through a side port, wondering if they'd see the fire coming. From the tone of the reports he was receiving, it wasn't a spectacular thing to behold, simply a smoldering line of stubborn, slow destruction, gradually eating up everything that everybody on Ceres had accomplished out here over the past several years. Suddenly he knew how farmers must feel about hail—or the Mormons about grasshoppers.

Anonymous in a virtual reality navigation helmet and a pair of VR gloves, the pilot of the machine nodded, pushed forward on two big invisible levers, and the *gamera* rose smoothly to the altitude he'd specified. Lindsay liked the feel of real controls in his hands much better.

A pair of heavy lasers in the craft's chin, much larger and more powerful than Lindsay's, began cutting through the tough plastic just ahead of the *gamera*, continuing two of the cuts Lindsay had started by hand. A third cut was perpendicular to the first two, and a fourth, actually the first he'd made, and also perpendicular, lay ten miles ahead.

As the machine moved forward, now, a pair of big titanium hooks trailing behind it lifted a strip of canopy behind them, leaving a fifty-foot swath of bare rock that they hoped the burn couldn't get across.

Meanwhile, the 'comm system was full of curses and exclamations, rude suggestions, and discussions of various people's ancestry. He could see Arleigh on a screen and wondered briefly who was bossing the other two rigs. That didn't matter, either. The other vehicles were out here, now, doing exactly the same thing as his own *gamera* was, creating a wide firebreak that was intended to isolate the strange burn, saving the remainder of the atmospheric canopy—the computer said possibly two thirds of it— if they could only work quickly enough.

Twenty miles along the line, ten miles ahead of the original cut, the *gamera* began to labor under a load it had never been constructed to bear, even at a tenth of a gee. The limit had been calculated in advance. The *gamera* now had a ten-mile strip of canopy plastic in tow.

The pilot brought the craft down to within a few feet of the ground again, and Lindsay, who had never even bothered to remove his envirosuit, rehelmeted, hopped outside, and cut across the plastic again with his laser. He watched as the *gamera* pulled the stuff—he was not the first to observe it was like working with flexible glass—to the non-fire side of the break for possible salvage later on.

Once the entire ten mile strip was well clear of the firebreak, the pilot picked him up and they rode back ten miles to where Lindsay restarted the long cuts with his laser and reset the big hooks in the plastic.

Hot and thirsty, he climbed back aboard again.

He removed his helmet—his hair was soaked as if he'd just come out of the rain, although the suit's nanites had kept the inside of the helmet dry—and shouted at the pilot. "Hey, you got any beer aboard?"

The pilot pulled her flimsy VR helmet off and turned to face him briefly. "You look more like you need a towel than a beer, Lindsay Ngu. I have just heard from your brother Arleigh—between the four *gamera* crews, we're already more than ten percent done. There's some Gatorade, and a whole bunch of meal packs. No beer for us until we finish!"

Lindsay blinked. "Ingrid? What the living hell are you doing out here?"

The girl grinned. "Saving my home, sir, just like you're saving yours. Now if you're ready, we'll cut and pull up the next section of plastic."

CHAPTER THIRTY: THE ADVENTURES OF SAM O'VAR

Visitors from Earth often ask me why Pallatians have no flag. We have no flag for the same reason West America, the Moon, and Mars have no flag, for the same reason Ceres never will. Flags are the calling-card of plunderers, rapists, and murderers in funny hats and clown-suits, pretending to be benefactors, protectors, and healers. If history demonstrates anything more clearly than that, I don't know what it is.

We would no more have a flag than we would have a king, a President, a Prime Minister, or any of the stuff that comes with them. If you ever hear that Pallas has adopted a flag, you will understand that Pallatians are no longer a free people. —*The Diaries of Rosalie Frazier Ngu*

THE WHISTLE BLEW.

Outside the wet-streaked window, the empty miles lashed by, gray, bleak, rainy, and above all, cold. Springtime had come to the English countryside.

The two men sat opposite one another in a semiprivate compartment of the night train to Liverpool, one dressed in an enormous gray woolen greatcoat and matching deerstalker cap. He was both tall and broad, with the bearing and gait of a bear, and affected sideburns in the current "muttonchop" fashion. His hands appeared small and graceful, however, their long, slender fingers best suited to delicate tasks.

The other man was taller and thinner, with the manner of a natural aristocrat. He wore a stylish London tweed suit, brand new—over which he had thrown a vaguely military cape—and a felt hat with a broad brim. He had bushy red hair and eyes that were almost Asian. When he spoke, it was with the very voice and breath of the Russian Steppes.

Across his long lap, the man in gray carried an elegant stick with an elaborate silver handle and ferrule, and a subtly tapered ebony shaft that almost certainly concealed a sword. In the deep pocket of his coat, he carried the latest .45 caliber revolver from Webley & Scott.

At the same time, the distinctive "dog-bone"-shaped handle of a *kindjal*—that great curve-bladed knife or short sword of the Cossacks—thrust from under the cloak of the redheaded man, but the hand under his jacket lay upon the plowshare grip of a different sort of revolver, the Colt's Peacemaker Model of 1873, its chambers cut for .44 Winchester Centerfire.

They had established that the man in gray was a physician, on his way to Liverpool at the moment, at the invitation of the constabulary there, to examine a dead body and look into a possible case of murder. The redheaded man had told the doctor that he would take ship in that port city for Ireland, in pursuit, he said, of something resembling justice.

"Heretofore," said the man in gray, whose broad face was known far and wide, not only in the Kingdom of Great Britain, but in the world, "and despite my surname, I have endeavoured not to involve myself in the Irish Question, and I should strongly advise you to do likewise, Mr.—"

"O'Var, Dr. Doyle," replied the redheaded man. "Colonel Sam O'Var, late of the Imperial Army of his Majesty the Czar. It is, I confess—and as I suspect that you suspect—merely a *nom de guerre*. I left his Majesty's service, my dear sir, because I could no longer bear to sweep down on horseback upon unarmed peasants in their fields, to deprive good women of their husbands and innocent children of their fathers."

The man in gray sat up. "But what has that to do—"

"Nor, I find," the redheaded man continued, "can I bear any longer to witness—even at a distance, through the newspapers—what is being done to your poor serfs in Ireland, in the name of the Czar's cousin—"

"Serfs?" The gray man's eyebrows rose, and his nostrils flared. His voice was enormous. "Have a care, sir, for you are speaking of my Queen!"

"No, no, Dr. Doyle, I am speaking of her victims, of the Irish people, who have been wrongfully deprived of their land and of their sovereignty, both national and personal, as the Scots and the Welsh and countless others before them. They have not yet been stripped of their great-hearted spirit. I go now to assist them in any way I can to achieve not only their lost independence, but their individual self-ownership."

By now, the man in gray was purple in the face. "Why, nonsense! Balderdash!"

The redheaded man was placid. "We shall see, Dr. Doyle, we shall see."

"Indeed we shall, Colonel O'Var." Doyle refilled his short-stemmed Dutch clay pipe and lit it. O'Var lit a cigarette. Both men relaxed. "Self-ownership, you say? I confess I am somewhat intrigued at the concept."

The redheaded man grinned. "Let me tell you, then, what I know of it."

"Hey, that was pretty neat!" Wilson exclaimed.

The girl stepped from the shower, toweling her copper-colored hair.

Fallon (her name was so lovely he had never thought of trying to shorten it, even affectionately, as her coworkers did) was a slender and willowy creature, with a tiny waist, narrow hips, and breasts—delightfully enough—technically a couple of sizes too large for her little frame and shoulders. Over the past several weeks Wilson had more than satisfied himself that they were perfectly natural. They hung beautifully, though, and the gravity of the Moon is kind to females.

In the sallow bathroom light, Fallon's skin looked as pale as ivory. She was also covered from head to toe with freckles, which he sometimes made a game of counting—although she preferred to call it tickling. She had hips like a boy, he thought, but Fallon's bottom, although rather small, exactly like the rest of her, was utterly and charmingly female, a perfect valentine-shaped heart, arranged upside- down.

At the moment, Wilson was still lounging in her bed, half covered by a brightly-colored sheet, his attention divided between the wall- sized 3DTV screen across the room—which was presently occupied with a commercial message about surgically implanted telephones—and the far more lavish display in the bathroom as a beautiful female dried herself.

It was a spectacle that he'd enjoyed dozens of times before, of course, both here and aboard *Mighty Mouse's Girlfriend* (Fallon was at least a twelve on that scale, he calculated, maybe even a fifteen) but at this point, the bathroom was defeating the 3DTV handily. (She had the cutest little feet, he thought.) Wilson still felt slightly body-shy around her (although he didn't like it and would rather have died than tell her so) but she seemed to have no modesty at all around him.

Which, Wilson thought, was extremely generous of her.

"What was pretty neat?" she asked, grinning at him from under the towel she'd wrapped around her head. There must be at least fifty ways to dry your hair these days, he mused, including gadgets with lasers and microwaves. But women—Wilson's study of the topic included five laboratory subjects: his mother, his sister, her coach, Fallon, and Amorie.

Amorie.

For about the hundredth time this week he realized all over again that it no longer hurt to think about Amorie. He felt as if Fallon had somehow cured him of a deadly affliction. Maybe he even loved her. His sincerest wish was that she wouldn't turn out to be his "rebound girl".

In any case, they all seemed to prefer the ancient terrycloth turban, especially if it also happened to clash horribly with their bathrobes.

"What was pretty neat? You, of course," he winked at her. "But I was also channel-surfing while you were in the shower just now, and I happened to catch the last part of the first episode of something called *The Adventures of Sam O'Var*. I wish you'd been able to see it with me. It's all about this renegade Cossack, see, who runs away from the Czar and ends up fighting with the Irish Republican Army against the—"

Fallon's grin became a great big smile. "How wonderful! I know that series, very well! That was a rerun. The handsome hero is played by Maurice Gallatin, who used to be in *Tales of the Lost Fifth Force*, and not-Sir-yet Arthur Conan Doyle—who eventually becomes Sam O'var's reluctant companion and ally—is played by Phineas May. I have the first two seasons in my computer, if you'd like to have a copy."

Wilson nodded enthusiastically. "I would, very much," he said. "Thanks." It wasn't the first time they'd discovered they had similar tastes. They both liked all of the ancient action-adventure classics, Errol Flynn, Clint Eastwood, Tom Selleck, Bruce Willis, Haley Joel Osment.

"That's settled, then," she told him. "I'll finish up right away here and then get dressed. Then we'll go to lunch with your sister and her coach as we planned—I've really been looking forward to that—and then we'll go see the Armstrong Municipal Zoo. They have a real elephant!"

"Oh, yeah," Wilson said, "I forgot we were going to the zoo."

"That's a lot of 'thens', isn't it? I hope you don't mind that we have such a full schedule of 'relaxing' ahead today. We can only do this," she nodded toward the rumpled bed, "so much until it starts hurting."

He laughed, and she laughed with him. "No, I don't mind at all, if afterward ... "

"Afterward is fine with me, whether it hurts or not. But after lunch, can we visit my dad at the spaceport? I haven't seen him in, oh, weeks—I wonder why. He was a rock hunter once himself, you know, before he went and injured himself. If he likes you, well, I know he knows some special hunting tricks and maybe a secret lode or two."

"Is that so?" He got up, losing the sheet as it trailed away, locked her in his arms, and kissed her, as long and deeply as he could. The feel of her flesh against his, her fresh, clean scent was heaven.

"Oh, my!" she gasped when they finally had to have some air. "It's certainly wonderful to have an extra-long weekend now and again, isn't it?"

Wilson laughed again. "If it can be had with someone like you," he told her. He was more than a little nervous about meeting Fallon's father, but that was something else he was determined not to let her know.

"Oh, good. That was just the compliment I was fishing for. Keep it up, sir, and I may eventually tell you my middle name, after all. My computer's—"

"*We interrupt this program for an announcement from the asteroid Ceres.*" The screen went blank, then the image of a woman he knew appeared.

"I'm Honey Graham, of the Interplanetary Interactive Information Service, reporting to you from Ceres, largest of the Belt asteroids, where, just in the past couple of hours, there's been a terrible disaster."

Wilson felt a chill and the hairs stand up on the back of his neck.

Words crawled across the bottom of the screen: 42 MINUTE LIGHTLAG DELAY ...

* * *

Adam stood almost alone, breathing bottled air in the middle of an impossibly barren landscape, grateful for his lightweight envirosuit, made of modern, "smart" materials. He'd worn a few of the older kind, and it had been like trying to move around an old-time phone booth or refrigerator.

He had landed his *gamera* about a hundred yards from where he stood now, almost in the middle of an old, shallow crater perhaps fifty miles across. The rim-mountains that surrounded it were well over the horizon and couldn't be seen from here, but the jagged peak of the crater's central promontory was visible just over his left shoulder.

The sky, as always, was pitch black, the surrounding territory a mottled grayish-brown. Just as asteroids were always "potato-shaped"—and any unfamiliar meat always "tastes like chicken", carbonaceous chondrites were traditionally described as being about the color and texture of a slightly overdone chocolate chip cookie. Ceres was no different.

By Earth standards, ambient light was somewhat scarce—rather like a heavily overcast day on Earth—although the human eye and brain adapt marvelously to such conditions. Photographic contrast, however, washed out all but the most luminous stars overhead. Shining directly at Adam's faceplate, a single brilliant yellow star could be seen.

It was the Sun.

"Allow me to introduce myself: I'm Dr. Adam Ngu," he told the pair of 3DTV lenses being pointed his way by Burt, Honey Graham's camera operator and, apparently, Ceres' newest colonist. Adam couldn't say "good evening" or "good morning" or even "good day", because this announcement was meant for beamcast to the entire Solar System, where it was all of those times, and more, at once. "I'm the Director and Chief Engineer for the Curringer Corporation's Ceres Terraformation Project."

He paused for a moment, organizing his thoughts. His message was simple.

"As you may be aware by now, at roughly 15:45 GMT, our newly- completed atmospheric canopy—a product of two years of prodigious thought and labor on the part of more than a quarter of a million individuals—was deliberately set afire by saboteurs, and about a third of it is likely to be turned to fine gray ash before we can stop it."

Adam began walking, slowly, and as Burt, suffering in a borrowed envirosuit that wasn't quite as nice as Adam's, swung his hand-held camera around to follow him, it began picking up extraneous images: little piles of charred debris on the ground, clusters of twisted, scattered junk for which nature could not be responsible, and scorch marks.

Adam stopped when he came to a piece of wreckage as tall as he was.

"We're at the exact point where the fire first started. This is all that's left of a Mercedes-Cessna 736-ED, a rather small but very powerful spacecraft, easily capable of traveling all the way from Earth, say, here to Ceres. It had registration markings, but they were scraped off before it got here. Apparently it was destroyed when it flew over this area at the exact moment of a cataclysmic explosion. There are, as far as we can determine, the remains of four bodies inside."

Adam walked several yards away from the ruined ship and pointed to another, smaller object, lying on the ground. Burt tilted his camera downward.

"This is a glove," Adam said, "from an envirosuit. There's a hand still inside. The bulk of the body is missing. A cursory examination of the site indicates that someone was set down on the surface with whatever incendiary device was used to start this fire, and was about to be picked up again, when the device went off prematurely. The resulting blast killed the person on the surface and destroyed the spacecraft."

Adam walked directly toward the camera. "Between this gloved hand and the ship's wreckage, I believe that we can discover who committed this insanely destructive crime. The fact is, I think I already know who they are—and so do all of you, ladies and gentlemen—and if we're right, then the customary scenario will be changing as of this moment."

Acting as his own director, Burt brought his camera in another yard.

"Unlike a government somewhere, we will not attempt to capitalize on what might be perceived as an opportunity by declaring war on some other government, or making vague, impossible promises as an excuse to control our citizens more closely. This was an individual criminal act, no matter if it was committed at the behest of some government. We all have individual choices to make, each of us, individually. Each of those individuals responsible—and they know who they are—will be hunted down and made to pay for what they've been a part of. From now on it is *they* who will worry about odd noises coming in the night. It is *they* who will be glancing fearfully back over their shoulders."

At a prearranged signal, Burt lifted his camera toward the sky, singling out one bright dot, and increasing magnification until it resolved itself as one of the hundred gigantic spacecraft orbiting Ceres.

"I speak directly now to those individuals. You began with petty crimes of destruction on Earth. Then you tried to blow up a factory spaceship crewed by twenty-five hundred people. Then you tried to blow up my construction dome, which would have killed hundreds more. You have spies everywhere, but now your spies are being spied on by my spies."

Using special electronics, Burt's camera continued sending an image of the factory ship *Herschell*, while he swung it back to eye level. He pushed a button and Adam's helmeted face filled the visual field again. Adam walked back a few paces, stooped, and the camera followed.

"I can't speak for the company that employs me—at least not until I confer with them—but speaking for the Ngu family, I tell you now: it is time for you to run and hide. Even if you do, I will find each and every one of you. It will be as if the organizations you work for never existed, because each and every member, each and every officer, each and every agent will be rendered as extinct as the Dodo bird."

Suddenly the camera backed up to show Adam holding a sinister object.

"I'd cast down this gauntlet," he said. "But as I said, there's a hand still inside. We need the fingerprints and DNA. I will find out whose hand this was. I will find out who he or she worked for. Then I'll come after you. So forget picketing developers and sabotaging construction sites. Use all your brains and energy to try to stay alive."

He lowered his voice. "I promise you'll need them."

***

The traditionally-shaped Zamboni—beneath its skin nobody from a previous century would have recognized any part of the complex tangle of infrared lasers, high-pressure microplumbing, and field-generation electronics they found here—had just waddled clumsily off the ice toward its "barn", leaving behind it a clean new surface on which to skate.

They were playing "rock music" on the public address system this morning. Not twentieth and twenty-first century rock'n'roll, but something else completely. Faint, complex, rhythmic signals had been heard—and recorded—among the asteroids for years. Nobody knew where they came from, although attempts had been made to find their source.

Lately someone had taken the signals, added some other instruments and a vocalist, to make "rock music". It was strange, but somehow enjoyable.

As usual, Llyra was the first one through the gate. She was a bit stiff from this morning's work already—taking a break was sometimes a bit less than useful in that regard—and skating slowly toward the corner opposite the lobby gate, luxuriating in the fresh ice, deeply intent on adding another turn to her Salchow, concentrating on it and nothing else. Eight measly turns was all she'd accomplished so far. She was grimly determined to make it nine today—ten tomorrow—reach up and touch the overhead net, and make a clean landing, all in the same jump. She was startled by the hiss of blades only a few inches behind her.

"Hey, Asteroid Bitch, you just cut me off!" Llyra's concentration was suddenly shattered, and it was Janna Kolditz, the daughter of the Ambassador of all sixty-five United States of America (minus about thirty-six or thirty-seven, if Llyra recalled correctly), who had shattered it. "Or are you gonna tell me that's the way that everybody skates out there on Bunghole Sixty-nine or whatever it is you call it?"

Llyra knew that what Janna claimed wasn't true. She had long since developed that "sixth sense" that serious skaters must acquire sooner or later—like eyes in the back of one's head—that kept them from colliding most of the time, even when they were skating backwards and their minds were occupied with details of the jump about to come. "I did not cut you off, Janna, and you know it perfectly well."

In fact, from the scratches the girl had made on the otherwise flawless ice, it appeared to Llyra that she had been deliberately followed.

Llyra and Jasmeen had both been sitting on a bench in the Heinlein lobby, putting their skates back on after breakfast, when her father's speech had been broadcast from Ceres. Adam had accidentally chosen a slow news day (or maybe the saboteurs had chosen a slow news day to suit their own purposes), and several other news channels had picked up Honey Graham's feed to ISSS. There would be a great deal of trouble about it later on, and even a lawsuit or two. Meanwhile, nearly every individual in the Solar System had heard and seen what Adam had to say.

"You know that I don't know anything of the kind, Liar Ayn Ngu!" the East American girl retorted. She seemed to be without her bosom pals this morning, Kelly Tran and Danita Lopez—Jasmeen referred privately to the three of them as "the Harpies"—maybe they'd finally grown sick and tired of Janna's company. "I've got half a mind to report you to the management and get you kicked out of here for good!"

Llyra turned to face her antagonist squarely and look her in the eye. "You're certainly welcome to try. The trouble is, those cameras—" she pointed to the ceiling, "—won't back your story up. They installed them to make short work of liability lawsuits against the rink, but they'll serve nicely to show you up for the prevaricator you are."

Janna blinked dumbly, like a cow. Another product, Llyra thought, of a compulsory, tax-supported socialist education system, apparently the girl didn't know what a prevaricator was. The uncomfortable truth, however, was that Llyra wasn't entirely sure how she felt about all the surveillance cameras at the rink—or anywhere else for that matter. On Pallas and Mars—probably on Ceres, too, once things got better established—it was necessary to obtain an individual's explicit, written permission before his or her photo could be taken, even as a part of a crowd. Things were rather different here in the Moon, although not as bad as in East America.

Janna said nothing, but skated away angrily, her ample backside making disgruntled little jerks from side to side with each stroke of her skates. Llyra often wondered why she wasted her time—not to mention her parent's money—coming here. She suspected that it was her father's—Adam's—3DTV address that had set the girl off this morning.

To gullible East Americans of Janna Kolditz and her father's kind, interplanetary colonists were all evil ingrates, while the so-called environmentalist activists Null Delta Em employed were dashing and heroic outlaws, in the style of Robin Hood, Ned Kelly, Jesse James, or Ernie Hancock. Anyone threatening to expose radical environmentalists for what they were—cold-blooded saboteurs and murderers—would get no thanks from Janna.

Ah, well, Llyra thought. There wasn't anything she could do about the Jannas that skated through her life except ignore them when she could. She still had a couple of hours left to skate this "morning" and a competitive routine to work on for the upcoming Virginia Cup in two months. She began to head for the corner again. Because she needed all the room she could get, most of her jumps were done on the rink's diagonal—

—when Jasmeen skated up, surprising her again.

"Are you planning to report me for cutting you off, too?" she asked.

"What?"

Llyra told Jasmeen of her encounter with Janna Kolditz.

"Is unimportant, my little," Jasmeen told Llyra. "Very stupid, but unimportant. We have invitation to lunch. Your brother calls, to your phone. I answer in locker room. I am thinking he wants us to meet new girlfriend."

"It must be serious, then." Llyra laughed. The universe was never going to let her make this jump this morning, was it? She found she was looking forward to lunch, though. She was famished. But then, she was always famished. "And I am thinking that this one—Fallon was her name, wasn't it?—can't help being better than the last one, right?"

Jasmeen had a peculiar expression on her face, Llyra thought. "I do not offer opinion, my little. Is not my place. I am only conveying information."

*
**

For some reason he felt mildly ashamed of now, Wilson had half expected Fallon's father (a man, she'd told him, who had started out in life as an asteroid hunter, only to be seriously injured and forced to give it up) to be a janitor or some kind of maintenance man at the spaceport.

She'd driven them there in a little two-seater intended only for indoor use, and parked in front of the main entrance. From there, they'd taken a slidewalk through the crowded, noisy main concourse to the administrative section of the spaceport, and an elevator to the top floor, almost at the surface. The quiet, carpeted corridors had thick windows and skylights that looked out directly onto the Moon and sky.

Fallon stopped at a door with a plastic plaque that said, "Director".

"Now he's likely to be a little gruff with you at the beginning," she told Wilson. "Since you're dating his only daughter and all, I mean."

"I hope he doesn't know about the 'and all' part," Wilson said.

She grinned. "He'll suspect, after he sees us together, but I'm a big girl, and my life is my life." She reached up, put her arms around Wilson's neck, and kissed him lightly. "He'll like it that you're a hunter."

Suddenly, the door swung open, and a severely-dressed woman in her early thirties, with a small computer and a thick sheaf of papers in her hand managed to avoid crashing into them. To her credit, Fallon took her time letting go of Wilson and standing back from him a little.

"I'm sorry, Michelle," she said. "We were just coming to see Daddy. This is my friend Wilson Ngu. Wilson, my father's assistant, Michelle."

Wilson stuck a hand out. Michelle took it. "Pleased to meet you, Wilson," she said in a French accent. "I have seen you on 3DTV, have I not?"

Wilson sighed and shook his head. "I'm afraid so."

"You," said Michelle, "are the—"

"He's the one who nailed those would-be killers on Ceres last year," said a male voice from within the office. "You're Adam Ngu's boy!"

"I must go, now," Michelle told them. "It was good to see you again, Fallon, and a pleasure to meet you, Wilson. Just go right in, if you will." With that, she hurried off down the corridor on some errand.

They entered the enormous office, closing the door behind them. One entire wall was windows, draped, but looking out onto a sunny, mountainous Moonscape. Standing behind a desk only slightly smaller than Wilson's spaceship was a short, plump man with a cigar in his hand. His hair was short, and mostly white, but Wilson could see clearly, from his freckled and florid complexion, that it had been red.

"Falleen m'darlin'!"

The man seized his daughter around the shoulders and squeezed her until Wilson thought her eyes would bulge. She squeezed him just as hard and he was the first to squeak. Then he kissed her forehead, nose, and lips. Letting her go at last, but keeping her close, he stuck a plump, callused hand out. "I'm Terence Flaherty O'Driscoll, my boy, this lovely girl's father! And who might you be when you're at home?"

Wilson took it. "Er ... I'm Wilson Ngu, no middle name, although you've got a good one. Fallon tells me that you're all from Pallas, originally."

"And will be again someday, no doubt. I just didn't take to all that lumbering and milling and—tell me, did you ever smell a paper factory?"

Wilson shook his head. "I grew up on Pallas, too, in Curringer. I was a surveyor for my dad on Ceres. Now I'm an independent asteroid hunter."

"Is that so? A hunter! Well, sit down, the both of you, sit down. Oh, my, the stories I could tell you about your father, my boy—and I will, if the skinflint refuses to pay up! In the meantime, would you care for a wee drop of the Bushmill's—or should we make that a Coke? Coke it is, then. Tell me what you've been up to, young lady—but no more than an old man's tender sensibilities can stand, mind you."

She blushed. "Old man's tender sensibilities my—"

"Now, now, let's keep it clean, my dear, in memory of your sainted mother."

She turned to Wilson. "Mom, Katie Evelyn O'Driscoll, is in perfect health, and almost certainly at home at this minute, fixing him his dinner."

Terence shook his head. "No, dear, we're going out tonight, to a new Vietnamese place—I swear you could put lemongrass and *nuoc mam* on a cinder block and I'd gulp it down with chopsticks. Most likely she's picking out a nice, racy dress to distract me from those cute little Asian waitresses."

"Oh, Daddy!"

"Aha, gotcha! I knew there was at least one more 'Oh, Daddy!' in there!"

"Oh, Da—" She stopped herself and they both laughed. Terence went to a bar in the corner, fixed Cokes and something in a glass for himself.

"Now," he said, "would you rather have a First Class tour of the spaceport or listen to an old man ramble on about his asteroid hunting days?"

"I'd much rather hear about your asteroid hunting if you don't mind."

"Is that so, now?" Terence peered suspiciously at Wilson, then turned to Fallon. "You know, daughter, I actually believe the boy's sincere. I think you'd better contemplate tellin' him your middle name."

Wilson gulped. Then Terence and Fallon burst out laughing. "He's hardly a boy, Daddy. He fought that gunfight on Ceres, he's been hunting for better than a year, and he even found a garnet the size of a—"

"A Buick. I know. I saw his mother on 3DTV. Quite a find, and a fine thing to do with it, give it to his mother. Next thing we'll hear he'll be finding the Diamond Rogue itself. Not a boy, then, Mr. Wilson Ngu?"

"Thank you, sir."

"I'm not a sir—that's for all the aristocrats and _nomenklatura_ whom we wisely guillotined in the 18th and 21st centuries. Call me Terence, or Terry. I'll call you Willy."

"Wilson."

"Wilson it is, then. Let's go down to the Green Cheese Room. It's a restaurant. I have a table reserved at the back. On the way there's something I have to check in the main concourse, if you don't mind a detour."

Wilson shook his head. Fallon popped out of her chair and took his hand, pulling him from his. Wilson didn't think he'd ever seen her happier.

CHAPTER THIRTY-ONE: DEATH IN THE AFTERNOON

People never seem to understand that there's no such thing as "safety". There never was, and there never will be. It's no safer now than it was a thousand years ago, or ten thousand. It won't be any safer a thousand, or ten thousand years from now. Each period of history simply offers different dangers. The world—the universe—is an inherently perilous place.

Ironically, the worst danger we face today comes from those who would sacrifice anything, including their freedom—not to mention yours and mine—for the mere appearance of safety. And yet nobody can make it safe, not government, not religion, not the Wizard of Oz, not even your insurance company. All we can do is make the best preparations we can and then ride out whatever disasters may befall us from time to time. —*The Diaries of Rosalie Frazier Ngu*

"I'LL JUST BE A MINUTE," said Fallon's father. "I have to drop these datachips off at the routing desk, then we'll go back up to lunch."

"*Now arriving*," said the PA system, "*City of Newark*, from Mars."

Fallon and her escort agreed to stay put, more or less, until Terence returned. It was a good place to wait, Wilson decided. The concourse was beautiful, colorful, noisy, and absolutely bustling with cheerful travelers. The ceiling a hundred feet overhead was obscured by a multitude of overlapping sinuous balconies and hanging plants. Pools of water stood everywhere, and waterfalls, and giant, continuous windows wrapped around the area, stretching from the floor up into the rafters.

Beyond the great windows, the sun, unabated by an atmosphere, beat down mercilessly on the southwest quarter of the Sea of Tranquility, where the city of Armstrong and its spaceport were located. The site of mankind's first landing on the Moon had been preserved here, and was a frequent destination for school children and tourists. Visitors could purchase anything from miniature 50-star American flags with wire stiffeners, to plastic holographic replicas of Neil Armstrong's footprints, each of which had been carefully recorded and given a numbered label.

Blue Earth, aswirl in white clouds, hung in a sky as black as velvet.

Inside, across a vast expanse of highly polished native granite, the place was filled almost shoulder-to-shoulder with individuals headed to any of a hundred spaceports on Earth, or just arrived from there to stay in the Moon, or to continue to one of the five Lagrange points. Some were outward bound to Mars or Pallas or even the huge O'Neill habitat being built near Jupiter. Wilson tried to imagine what things would be like in here once Ceres had been terraformed and settled.

Or when they finally built the space elevators.

"First call for Nikola Tesla, *bound for Venus Observatory Station, now boarding next to the Orange Julius stand."*

Just now, they waited in traditionally uncomfortable seats, dozing fitfully where they sat, talking on their phones, answering e-mail, reading, doing other things with their computers, visiting with their temporary neighbors, reloading personal weapons with ammunition guaranteed to be ship-safe, buying their kids sticky things to eat and drink, cleaning up after them.

The great chamber was bursting with all the excitement of travel to new places and old, let out into the sunshine for everyone to see, although the place was actually seven hundred feet below ground level, and the sunlight and the view from outside were "piped in" from the surface.

Fallon asked, "When you got here, did anyone ever explain to you why this area is buried so deeply? I know the ports on Pallas are very different."

"From this? They certainly are. But I've never seen this place before, Fallon," Wilson told her. "When we got here, in a Curringer Corporation ship, my sister Llyra and her coach both had severe cases of gravity sickness, and we rushed them from the ship to see some doctors."

"Now arriving from Lagrange Point Two, Curringer Corporation survey vessel *Rosalie Frazier."* Wilson always enjoyed hearing or reading about the scientific exploration vessel named after his famous great grandmother, although East America and the United Nations had noisily condemned the undertaking as a waste of precious resources. Constructed at L-Two, once the *Rosalie Frazier* left the Moon, where she would be taking on more crew and supplies, she'd be gone for five long years, on an ambitious mission to catalog every asteroid in the Belt.

"Gosh, I'd forgotten about your sister's illness," Fallon told him. "Not forgetting Jasmeen. But with so much of the local traffic filled to the brim with various violent and poisonous chemical fuels, and incoming traffic running on fumes ten times as destructive, plus ships from further out, Earth, Mars, Pallas, using several different kinds of nuclear powerplant, and every one of them running at several thousands of miles per second, with our little spaceport as their bull's-eye … "

"Digging in starts to make a lot of sense," Wilson agreed. "It's so bright, in here, you'd never know you were actually underground, though. I think even my dad would regard this place as a marvel of engineering."

"And showmanship," she nodded. "They spent a lot of money on those windows, believe me. A *very* lot. And on a bank of a dozen high-speed superconducting magnetic elevators to zip you from the airlock of your ship, directly to this room, or back the other way, in only a couple of seconds. With computer-controlled acceleration, some people never even notice that they're underground, instead of still outside on the surface."

Wilson shook his head slowly. "Some people never even notice their own—"

"Gee," Fallon interrupted him, making Wilson laugh. "I wonder how much longer Daddy's going to be in there. I'm really starting to get hungry."

★

Adam caught up with Lindsay when the firebreak around the burning circle was nearly three quarters complete. Both men stood in their enviro-suits just outside the rear airlock of the *gamera* Lindsay was using.

They had a problem.

"What the hell do you suppose that is?" Lindsay asked his brother rhetorically. He didn't have to point or even nod in the direction he wanted Adam to look. Standing before them was a bizarre pinnacle, two hundred feet tall, placed directly in the path of the firefighting effort.

Adam said, "I don't have any idea. The geologists will have a field day with this—provided we survive the fire. Look at that slope!"

On the fire side, the peak sloped downward at an angle that would prevent the *gamera* from cutting the firebreak around the base of the peak. The machines were basically hovercraft, with a maximum altitude of fifty feet unless fitted with special booster packs. To get around the long slope, it would be necessary to cross the existing line of fire.

"We've got all the boosters we could ever wish for," Lindsay observed, knowing what his brother was thinking. "But they're back at the dome, neatly stored in stacks." He indicated a glow visible at the horizon. "There isn't time to go get them. The fire will be here by then."

Adam thought about it. "The *gamera* I left there could bring them out."

Lindsay moved his shoulders in a customary envirosuit gesture intended to convey that he was shaking his head. "I ran the numbers already, Ad. No good. We can't go around the back, either, because of *that*."

Inside his suit mask, Adam's expression was grim. Behind the peak lay a chasm several hundred feet deep. Something had struck Ceres a billion years ago, plowed the chasm and piled material up into this strange little mountain. Some of it had spilled forward to create the barrier slope. Whatever they did, by the time they finished doing it, the fire would be upon them, and then past them, uncontained and uncontrolled.

"I know what to do." Lindsay said at last. "I'll finish the slice, right up to the roots of this thing, then get out and start a new one by hand, burning as I climb. It doesn't look that steep for a man afoot."

Adam was skeptical, but nodded. "I'll go around on the fireside as fast as I can, ask whatever factory ship is nearest locate you, and then climb and cut my way toward you. I don't think there's any other way."

"Let's do it! When we meet at the top of the promontory, we'll drive in a golden spike." Lindsay finished the sentence with his back to Adam, running to his *gamera*'s airlock. Adam ran to his own and climbed aboard. Lindsay informed Ingrid of the plan. Under her hands, the machine rose to a working altitude and resumed cutting with its lasers.

Adam saw nothing of any of that. Obtaining the maximum altitude and forward speed his machine was capable of, he drove toward the fire and across it until he found a place on the mountain slope low enough for his vehicle to handle. He crossed over the almost bladelike feature, and headed back toward the theoretical line of the firebreak, controlling the *gamera* with one hand, while the other was occupied with punching up communications with the nearest factory ship in orbit.

"*Eugene Shoemaker* here. What can we do for —oh, it's you, Dr. Ngu."

"I was aware of that," Adam replied. It had taken him a moment to realize that the man he was speaking to was not a Eugene Shoemaker, but was speaking for his factory vessel, named after the twentieth century astronomer who had proved that craters on the Earth, Mars, and the Moon were not volcanic in origin, but had been made by meteorites. It seemed so simple and obvious now, but it hadn't been in Shoemaker's day.

"I'm going to need you to locate a man in an envirosuit, climbing up the west side of that odd little mountain directly to my north. You should be able to see him and my *gamera* fairly easily from where you are."

Adam knew that the factory ship crews all kept telescopes aboard, usually equipped with 3DTV cameras. In their leisure hours, they would minutely examine the surface below, submitting names for previously unnoticed features. Most of the time, Adam's staff accepted these recommendations.

Most of the time .. except for that guy who'd wanted to give all the features in this area Latin names for erogenous zones on the human body.

"We can do that," said the man on the ship. "Anything else, Dr. Ngu?"

"Yes, there is. I'm going to get out and start climbing toward him, cutting plastic with a hand laser. You can make sure my cuts are aligned with his." By this time, Adam was around on the other side of the peak. "I guess you could start by telling me where to park this thing."

"Sure thing, sir. You need to go another ... let me switch to the calibrated monitor ... another eight hundred eighty yards to the north."

*
**

At the opposite quarter of the gigantic spaceport concourse, one of the high-speed elevators Fallon had just mentioned arrived from the Lunar surface, where, according to rows of monitor screens mounted everywhere one looked, shuttlecraft from the East American commercial spaceliner *City of Newark*, so-called "Queen of the Mars route", had just landed on the vast Tranquility runway. The stainless doors hissed aside.

Among the first to step out were Krystal Sweet and Brian Downs.

" ... except that we were never really *on* that miserable yellow dustball!" Brian was continuing the tirade he had begun in this very place, even before they had left for what had once been called the Red Planet, a tirade that he had kept up, at frequent intervals, ever since.

After winning its independence, and before it had managed to become the technological center of the Known Universe, cash-poor Mars had first made itself famous, Systemwide, and prosperous, by offering certain fleshly and other delights, every one of which was illegal in East America, guaranteeing themselves a constant stream of wealthy tourists. "Instead of taking the shuttle down from Phobos to Mariner Canyon, say, we just stayed where we were for two days, totally rockbound while they serviced their damn cattle ship, and then came right back here!"

Krystal was tired of it. She'd been tired of it the day it had started.

"Now, honey," she began in a saccharine tone worthy of her name—one that struck terror in the hearts of everyone who really knew her. "I've told you at least a thousand times that neither our employers nor their sponsors are rich enough to pay for vacations on Mars for their employees. I'd like to have a vacation, myself, but I'll bet you'd just have gotten yourself in trouble anyway, between the whores and the drugs and the gambling.

We were there to case the space liner, anyway, don't you see? Nothing less and nothing more. Understand?"

"I understand," Brian muttered, "that all of the four-flushers and fat cats in the Solar System—including the suits and ties who run our own chickenshit movement—get to do anything the hell they want, any time the hell they want, and do it on a goddamn company expense account!"

"Brian, I—" She looked around to see if they were being overheard. Invisibility was a major asset in this business, and Brian was—

"I also understand that it's the working stiffs like you and me, Krystal, the people who do all of the grunt work and take all of the risks, who always end up paying for their good times, one way or another!"

"Keep it down, will you?" Krystal replied in a stage whisper. She nodded toward the carousel baggage conveyor that had suddenly started moving. "There's my bag, and there's yours. Grab 'em quick, please, Brian. I don't want to wait for this thing to go around again. I want to report in, take a long, hot shower, and sleep the clock around in a bed that isn't being vibrated by a dozen constant-boost fusion engines being operated out of synch by an incompetent Chief Engineer. Geez, I never thought I'd live to see Affirmative Action applied to refugee Californians."

Still grumbling, Krystal's associate retrieved their bags, taking them to one of several small, waist-height tables scattered around the concourse. He and Krystal each opened their luggage the minimum amount possible, and quickly extracted their personal weapons. His, a large, old-fashioned automatic pistol chambered for nine millimeter Mauser, disappeared under his short jacket. He was originally from Ontario, and still believed, at some level, that firearms were the work of the Devil and should be kept out of sight of children and the general public.

Krystal strapped a gunbelt and holster diagonally across her hips and, checking the power supply, dropped a big Westinghouse laser into it.

"When in Luna," she quipped, "do like the Loon—"

Brian screamed, "There he is, that sonofabitch! This is all his fault!"

"What—?" Krystal looked in the direction Brian was pointing. Sure enough, diametrically across the concourse from them, over the heads of about five thousand unsuspecting travelers, she saw young Wilson Ngu with a pretty, slender, redheaded girl. Before she realized it was happening, Brian had drawn his weapon from under his jacket and was pulling the trigger, over and over again. She knew she should have been deafened, but, suddenly full of adrenaline, she didn't hear the shots.

All around them, people made noises and dived for the floor.

She grabbed his arm. "What the hell do you think you're doing?" But it was too late. Ignoring the hailstorm of bullets singing all around him, Wilson Ngu, pistol drawn, was headed their way at a dead run.

※
※※

By the time Adam had labored his way to the tip of the pinnacle, a little platform about the size of a card table (even at one tenth of a gee it had been hard work, climbing and carrying the big, falsely- named "hand laser") his brother Lindsay was already there, waiting for him.

"Absolutely exhilarating, my dear old Sherpa!" Lindsay told his brother in a bad upper class English accent, his labored breathing belying every word he spoke. "I only wish I had a little flag to plahnt."

"Sure you do, Hillary old bean." Adam sat down, resting the laser across his envirosuited thighs. Briefly, he considered adjusting his oxygen upward, but thought better of it. It was a bad habit to get into, and he might need that oxygen later. "We could plahnt it in the pointy top of your head—or someplace better. So what do we do now?"

Lindsay indicated his *gamera*. It was a long way down. From here they could also see the fire advancing at them slowly but inexorably. "So I cut across this swath," he pointed to the plastic under his booted feet. They'd each made a pair of parallel cuttings in it with their lasers, which had more or less met here at the summit. "And Ingrid pulls it down and out of the way. Then we take the same route that you did, around the Matterhorn, here, and resume cutting and hauling. I understand that we're pretty close to finished with the firebreak."

"Ingrid?" Adam looked up at his brother, surprised.

"Sure," said Lindsay, perplexed. "I thought you knew."

"Knew what? What is there to know?" The idea of Lindsay and Ingrid together—

"That she's been ship-handing for me all day while I was outside doing the handcutting and hooking up. She's really good at it, Ad, an absolute natural. The construction crews have all been letting her practice with the *gamera*—on her own time, of course—for six months."

Adam said, "A secretary who also drives a truck. Well I'll be damned."

"You probably will be. All of the good stuff always happens to you, Ad. You're the boss here. You've got Ardith and the kids. The Andersson girl's hopelessly in love with you, and you've never even noticed."

Adam shrugged. "It's not the kind of thing it's good to notice, Lindsay."

"Hmmph," said his brother. "I'd notice."

Using his laser, Lindsay cut across the canopy plastic at the peak. Without warning, both ends began sliding down the opposite sides of the pinnacle. Adam dived toward the bare ground now exposed at the top. Lindsay tried to do the same, but, burdened by his laser, fell off to his right and began tumbling down the long fire-side of the slope.

Adam watched in helpless horror.

Once or twice, it appeared that Lindsay might actually be able to stop himself, but the plastic-covered slope was far too steep and slippery. As he rolled, over and over, his grunts and curses filled the electronic "air" around him and were probably heard all the way back at the construction dome, if not on Pallas or Earth. Somehow his laser got activated, and Adam had to duck the slashing lethal beam a couple of times before it realized that it was falling and shut itself off.

Still carrying his own laser, Adam hurried downhill, trying to move quickly, following the path of the sloughed-off plastic, which was now piled in a disorderly heap at the bottom. Signaling the pilot inside, he seized a handhold beside the rear airlock door and stayed on the outside of the *gamera*'s hull as it slewed around, headed for Lindsay.

By the time they arrived—Ingrid got there at about the same time Adam did and had immediately begun putting on her envirosuit—Lindsay lay on his back near the creeping fireline, one booted foot intersecting it. An anklet of slow, catalytic fire now crept up the man's lower right leg, consuming both suit and flesh exactly as it had consumed the plastic of the atmospheric canopy. The bones persisted for a moment and then they, too, dissolved into a gray powder and disappeared.

Lindsay writhed on the ground, panting into his suit mike. "You've got to stop it, Ad! It hurts like the blazes and I think I'm losing pressure!"

Ingrid threw a big emergency blanket she'd brought over it, but the blanket, too, made of synthetic organic materials, began to burn. Adam grabbed a corner and flipped the blanket over the fireline where it was gradually consumed. He then scooped up a heaping double handful of loose soil and piled it atop Lindsay's smoldering leg, but as the fire manufactured its own oxygen, that had no more effect than the blanket.

The line of fire was now above Lindsay's knee. Adam reached a decision. Unfastening the carrying sling of his laser, he fastened it around Lindsay's thigh, pulled it through the ladder buckle as hard as he could, and then fastened it firmly. He stood and motioned Ingrid away.

"Hold still, Lindsay. I'm sorry, but I've got to do this." And without another word, he triggered the laser and cut his brother's leg off. That, too, went over the firebreak and into the area already burnt.

The break was complete in another hour; two thirds of the canopy survived.

Lindsay had died of shock and decompression on the way to the dome.

✱

Ardith regarded the new sample in the tightly-sealed glass bottle she held up to the light before her eyes. Her laboratory magnifiers had slipped down off her forehead again, as they always seemed to do. She pushed them back in place without being completely conscious of it.

This was only one of several samples she had taken herself this morning from the gigantic Drake-Tealy Object now standing in orbit above Pallas, apparently of its own accord. The individual who usually did that kind of work for her, the pilot R.G. Edd, had flatly refused to go, or to have anything at all to do with the damnable Object ever again.

The man's feelings in that regard were more than understandable—the thing had whisked him a hundred million miles in a couple of hours—although since then, it had demonstrated nothing but exactly the same physical properties as any other Drake-Tealy Object she was aware of.

Except, of course, for its size and terrifying mobility. Every other Drake-Tealy object known was inert and little larger than a human fist.

The air here, in her personal facility, at the Asteroid Materials Laboratory, was highly filtered and kept as clean as humanly possible. Its pressure was a little higher so contaminants would blow out, not in.

At the moment, consistent with standing "clean room" protocols, Ardith wore a ridiculous plastic shower cap over her hair, a pair of disposable plastic booties over her shoes, a light filter mask, and rubber gloves. She also wore a tie-dyed laboratory jacket her daughter had given her for her birthday. It was very silly, but it helped her feel closer to Llyra, whom she hadn't seen in person for more than a year.

Now she must be especially careful. It had been more than a little arduous collecting these samples, beginning at the break of dawn with a hurried ionopter ride to Port Peary, another ride, this time aboard a high-speed individualized capsule that took her through the polar ring mountains, then a leaky, rattletrap maintenance jumpbuggy out to the orbiting Drake Tealy Object, and finally a couple of uncomfortably claustrophobic hours trapped within an old-fashioned suit of space armor, the previous owner of which had been overly fond of garlic and cigars.

Six hours going, two hours there, six hours back.

No, she didn't want these samples spoiled.

The simple taking of them, cutting into the substance of the thing with her little palm-sized laser, had been something of an emotional workout, since she couldn't know, from moment to moment, if the Object would stay in the place it had chosen, blow up, take off for the Oort Cloud—prudently, she had not attached herself to it in any way—or simply start singing "Hello My Baby! Hello My Honey! Hello My Ragtime Gal!"

At the end of the day, however—such a particularly long, hard day, during which, with Llyra no longer around to remind her, Ardith was unable to remember whether she had eaten anything or not—she wasn't entirely certain how much good all this sample-taking was going to do. She suspected that the active source of the Object's alarming behavior would ultimately prove to be buried somewhere deep inside it, beyond her present reach, or possibly even somewhere else, on the outside.

Now she unscrewed the bottle top, but left it in place until the bottle was over the collecting nozzle of the pulverizer on the bench before her. Quickly flipping it over, she let the sample fall into the machine, screwing the now-empty bottle into place at the mouth of the intake.

Next, she punched instructions into the pulverizer for granule size desired and sample divisions. She called for six small plastic packets of the stuff, finer than powdered sugar, but probably not as sweet. Her assistants often threatened to use the pulverizer to make espresso.

The machine did make lots of unpleasant noise, and would take at least an hour to reduce her thumb-sized sample to rock flour. She decided to go to the trouble of desuiting and have a nice cup of hot tea. She had recently taken up smoking again and looked forward to a cigarette.

As she turned toward the airlock door, Marla, the latest company receptionist, practically flew into the corridor outside the lab and started banging on the glass. She was colorfully dressed and Ardith thought briefly that she looked like some kind of frightened tropical bird.

"Dr. Ngu! Dr. Ngu!" The girl's voice was muffled by the air space between two layers of glass. "You'd better have a look at what's on 3DTV!"

Ardith shrugged. Her theine and nicotine could easily wait another minute. There was a set here in the lab, tucked up into a corner near the ceiling. She used the remote that was dangling from it by a bit of string.

" … is KCUF, the eyes, ears, nose, and throat of Pallas. We're repeating a story that we've just received. There has been some kind of sabotage of the Terraformation Project on Ceres, and a fire. We now have an unconfirmed report that one of the three Ngu brothers has been killed."

"Dr. Ngu! Dr. Ngu!" The receptionist was frantic by now, and still banging on the laboratory window. Ardith had apparently heard the news and collapsed to the floor. Now she lay on it in a small, crumpled heap.

**

Krystal's associate stood like an automated thing, firing shot after shot across the crowded concourse. The screaming all around them was deafening. Everywhere Brian's pistol pointed, he blew huge gouges out of the polished stone pillars. The big floor-to-ceiling windows he hit shattered—showering bystanders with fragments—and ceased to work, their residual ugly grayish white reminding Krystal of a blinded eye.

Without a second thought or a moment's hesitation, she seized both of their bags and made her way as swiftly as she could without drawing attention to herself, to the nearest exit, the same high-speed elevator they'd arrived in. A time eventually comes, she thought, to cut one's losses, and if this isn't one of them, then what the hell is?

Meanwhile, Brian's pistol had run out of ammunition and its slide had locked back. A thin twist of smoke arose from the open ejection port and muzzle. Very bad tactical form, he realized from his training days. Then again, this wasn't some Null Delta Em camp in the Georgian Caucuses, this was the real world, where he couldn't always count his shots.

Reflexively, he thumbed the magazine release, allowing the emptied magazine to fall free from the pistol to a seat in front of him and bounce, unheeded, to the floor. He inserted a fresh magazine, holding eighteen rounds of the long, powerful nine millimeter variant, and slapped it home with the heel of his hand. In those scant two silent seconds, people around him had begun to get ahold of themselves. One daring individual, just a few feet in front of the shooter, noticed his weapon had gone dry and …

As the man rose and crouched to leap at him, Brian released the slide, chambering a round, and fired, almost in single motion. The jumper's face exploded in crimson ruin and he fell lifeless at Brian's feet. He could smell the iron tang of blood in the air. It was like perfume.

Somebody nearby vomited, and that was like music.

Several seat-rows further away, another individual, a tourist from West America, drew the pistol she traveled with and began to align her sights on him. Even full of adrenalin and the exultation of the open kill, Brian barely managed to fire first, killing the woman with another shot to the head. Her little gun flew into the air and she vanished behind the seats. He felt pain in his side; when he looked down, there was blood, rather a

298

lot, soaking through his clothing. Why, that complete and total bitch, he thought. She's probably killed me.

And where the hell had Ngu disappeared to?

"I'm right here, you asshole!"

Wilson stood a little behind him, not six feet away, his enormous automatic pistol pointed straight at Brian's face. Brian had heard all about that gun. It had belonged to the devil himself, Emerson Ngu. Brian began to turn and raise his own weapon again, but the wound in his side hampered his movement, and everything was happening much too slowly.

He was too late. In the capable hands of his great-grandson Wilson, Emerson's mighty Grizzly roared and a 260-grain .45 caliber magnum hollowpoint took the Null Delta Em field agent through both lungs.

The last thing Brian saw was Wilson stepping forward, standing over him where he'd fallen, aiming the huge Grizzly so Brian could actually see the hollowpoint bullet up in the chamber, and pulling the trigger.

Brian never heard or saw the shot.

Blackness became nothingness.

Without a second glance, Wilson turned on his heel and made his way back to where he'd left Fallon. Oddly, he couldn't see her now. Instead, he saw Fallon's father, kneeling on the floor, cursing and crying.

When Wilson finally arrived at his side, Fallon lay on the granite floor, her head and shoulders resting in her father's lap, motionless and silent, with a nine millimeter bullet hole neatly through her heart.

Before he was consciously aware of it, there were also individuals in uniforms, bearing medical equipment. Holding some kind of scanner in his hand, the paramedic kneeling at Fallon's side looked across at Wilson and Terence. "I'm afraid there isn't any hope. She was gone before we got here. She was also pregnant—about three weeks—probably didn't even know it herself. Do you want us to try and save it?"

His chest filling with anger, grief, and ... he didn't know what else, Wilson looked across Fallon's lifeless body and caught her father's eye. In that instant, there was suddenly an understanding and commitment between the two of them. "Yes, do it," both men told the paramedic.

"Tieve," Terence said abruptly, tears streaking his face.

So much was happening. Wilson didn't understand. "What did you say?"

"Tieve," Terence repeated the word, making two syllables of it, "tee-EV". "I know she'd have wanted me to tell you. Fallon's middle name was Tieve."

CHAPTER THIRTY-TWO: CONSULTATIONS

Religious people often maintain that a proof of their god's existence is the marvelous way the world and all of its wonders are perfectly suited to us. What a miracle! Of course they refuse to understand that it is we—through four thousand million years of evolution—who are suited to the world, not the other way around.

If we had evolved—because environmental circumstances compelled it—to belly-squat on fourteen fat legs, in a ten gee field, breathing sulfur dioxide and excreting sulfuric acid, eyeless and blind in the Stygian darkness, but sensing the area around us through long, sensitive bristles on our paddle-shaped tails, they would still be burbling about how miraculous it all is, when it would only be another example of evolution-by-natural selection at work. —*The Diaries of Rosalie Frazier Ngu*

HER EYES OPENED. THE FIRST thing she saw was her mother-in-law's face.

"Morning, sleepy-head," Julie smiled down at her. "How do you feel?"

The place, Julie observed with a certain proprietary approval—she and her late husband had paid for a good deal of it—was bright and cheery, much more like a bedroom at home than what it really was. For the most part, medical equipment, supplies and appliances, had been kept out of sight. A high, wide window looked out across Lake Selous.

It was one of those bright, cloudless, mercilessly sunny days, with a little white chop. As usual there were lavishly colored sails far out on the water. People on flying belts hovered overhead. Girls in bikinis were water-skiing. It reminded Julie of how much she missed fishing.

Ardith said, "It isn't morning, and I've been awake several times already. You know how the bastards don't like to let you sleep in the hospital." Her voice was little more than a croak, and her eyes were dark and sunken. Julie had never seen her looking so ill and old and tired.

But she laughed. "They're worried about you, dear, that's all. You're the Great Lady of Pallas, and they don't want to lose you. But they tell me you're not eating, and you're refusing the drugs they've prescribed."

"'Great Lady of Pallas' my fat freckled—they want me to take happy drugs, Julie, or at least anti-unhappy drugs. And they summoned you all the way from Mars ... " Ardith interrupted herself with a kind of sigh. Inside, she felt ancient, and all used up. "To help them nag me?"

Julie shook her head. "I came all the way from Mars for the most selfish of purposes, to be with as much of my family as I can. Just now, you're it, kiddo, until Ad and Arleigh get here for the—you know. I'm usually satisfied to be something of a solitary individual, as you know, but I didn't think that I could bear being alone with this ... "

"You've lost your son, your child." Ardith paused for a breath. "I've often wondered—morbidly, I guess—what that might be like. It isn't right. Our kids are supposed to bury us, not the other way around."

Julie nodded, her breath going in and coming out heavily. In a sense, Ardith had been through this four times already. Goddamn it all, she thought, I am a *Martian!* I've defeated whole planets, both Earth and Mars. No matter how hard this gets, it is not going to break me. "And you've lost a brother-in-law—an individual you liked and respected."

"That's—"

"But what you can't live with," Julie told her, "what I came to talk to you about, is the sheer joy—the unspeakable ecstasy—you feel that it wasn't your husband. A kind of survivor's remorse at one remove."

"Julie!" Ardith struggled to sit up—and failed.

The older woman—who appeared at least ten years younger than her daughter-in-law, but in fact was twice as old—reached out to pat Ardith's hand where it lay weak and helpless on the hospital coverlet.

The fact was, she'd never had a daughter, and she couldn't have loved this young woman any more—Ardith was thirty-eight years old—if she had happened to be her own. Adam had chosen well despite the couple's many later difficulties. And it was never, ever too late for love.

"It's true, sweetheart, and I've got to make you see it. I'm certain he didn't want to die, but do you think Lindsay would want you to destroy yourself this way because you're glad that Adam is still alive?"

Ardith sniffed back tears. "N-n-no." Now she felt about four years old—a dizzying descent from the hundred and four she'd felt only a few minutes earlier. Despite her own energy and apparent youth, Julie Ngu had that effect on other people. She'd been born to be somebody's grandmother.

Ardith was grateful that Julie was here for Llyra and Wilson. Both of her own grandmothers had died when, under a new "scorched earth" policy, the East American Drug Enforcement Authority had bombed and razed an entire town in Connecticut because one resident, it had been alleged, was observed by an informer manufacturing the illegal drug nicotine. It was the main reason her parents had decided to come to Pallas.

Julie said, "They tell me that when they found you unconscious on your laboratory floor, you were in pretty bad condition, suffering from mild malnutrition, severe dehydration, physical exhaustion, and shock, that last probably from the incomplete news you'd seen on 3DTV."

Ardith shrugged and shook her head. There was little she could say. She couldn't remember any part of it after she'd switched on the pulverizer. She hoped somebody had remembered to switch it off. She wondered briefly why the hospital administration had seen fit to give Julie all that information about her—and then realized exactly why. Here and now, her mother-in-law was her nearest—if not next—of kin.

Julie nodded at the devices either side at the head of the bed—twin intravenous saline drips, one going into to each of Ardith's arms—that were practically the only medical equipment visible in the room.

"Not to mention a light dose of radiation poisoning. They're saying that your Drake-Tealy Object is doing some very peculiar things."

"Peculiar things?" Ardith was shocked at how uninterested she was.

"Yes, it's begun to pulse. Your people say it's emitting energy on all known wavelengths: heat, infrared, visible light, ultraviolet, radio, X-rays, alpha, beta, gamma, and anything else I forgot. The energies involved are very low and don't endanger Pallas. Most likely it was that old spacesuit that nearly got you killed. Two hours' backbreaking labor without water? I tracked it down, dear, and had it burned."

Ardith grinned. "Unlike my son and husband, I've never owned or even worn a proper envirosuit. But with a Drake-Tealy Object the size of a house doing odd things, I guess I'd better invest in one, hadn't I?"

"Then let the Drake-Tealy Museum pick up the tab, dear," Julie told her. "In fact I'd like to have you appointed Associate Curator, if I may, and put that damned thing out there totally in your hands. There's something important about it, I appreciate that much, at least. I take it that the jaw you just dropped onto the bed indicates 'yes'?"

"It certainly does, Julie!" There it came, the old energy. Not only did she feel like a kid again, Ardith suddenly felt exactly as if it were Christmas. And in a way, it was. She'd just been given—in an academic sense—what might well turn out to be the most important archaeological artifact ever found in human history. "When can I start?"

"Well, you'd better get healthy, first. Look, I understand your not wanting to take the mood elevators and anxiety suppressors they want you to. I wouldn't take them, myself. All they do is postpone what you eventually have to work through, anyway, and make it harder later."

Ardith said, "It's amazing how much alike we think."

"Yes, well, there's a reason for that most wives don't want to hear."

She shrugged. "They remind their husbands of their mothers?"

"Ardith, I'd like you to take the vitamins they have for you, and the medicines specifically for the physical illness you're suffering. I'll instruct them myself, if you like, to leave out the doubleplus goodthink pills. If they mess with us, the way they will sometimes, I'll take the wing of this place that Billy and I paid for back to Mars!"

Ardith actually laughed, and there was a bit of color now in her cheeks. Now for the hard part, the principle reason she'd come all the way from Mars, and why the hospital staff were all grateful to her for coming.

"I hate like hell to bring it up, but did you hear about Wilson's girl?" Julie worried that this could be the last straw for Ardith, the evil icing on her birthday cake, the rotting cherry atop the sundae, the …

"He messaged me yesterday on my personal phone. He doesn't know where I am, and I don't want him to. I can't believe what's happened, but when I get out of here, Null Delta Em and the Mass Movement will be—"

Julie burst into laughter, herself. "Don't misunderstand me. I'm very sorry for my only grandson. It's a horrible way to grow up. Like any red-blooded 19-year old, up to this point, all he really wanted—or even thought about much—was to get laid. But at least he has the suicidal decency to believe he has to be love with the girl who does it for him. He may outgrow that in time, but something in me hopes he doesn't."

Ardith said, "But—"

"But I'm as proud as I can be," Julie went on, "to be a member of this family—your family, dear Ardith. An indestructible, resilient family that we both married into to begin with, but in which neither of us was ever particularly content to be mere ornaments on a family tree."

Ardith did manage to sit up this time. "I feel brokenhearted for Wilson, too, and I wish I knew how to help him. He was all over us, all the time, about that Amorie creature, 'Amorie this' and 'Amorie that'. I realized Fallon O'Driscoll might really be the one, when he hardly ever said a word about her. But Julie, we're about to have something else in common. Poor Fallon was pregnant. I'm going to be a grandmother!"

"Boy or girl?" Julie asked automatically.

Ardith replied, "It's going to be a little girl. They—he and Fallon's father, Terence O'Driscoll—have decided they'll call her Tieve."

It also made Julie a great grandmother, of course, but she'd been mentally and emotionally prepared for that for a long time. As long as she managed to stay young, everything could be fun. Someday she would try to talk her Ardith into DeGrey regenerative therapy. To let such beauty, both on the inside and the outside, fade away, would border on the criminal.

"Tieve Ngu. No stranger than Julie Ngu. Shall we break out the champagne?"

Ardith sighed. "Guess we'd better make it Jell-O. I actually feel hungry! Pulsing on all wavelengths, you say? Why would it want to do that?"

✳✳

"Strange," Adam told his brother Arleigh. "Here we are, headed back to Pallas to bury our brother, and all I can think about are my kids."

The gravelly hiss, like frying bacon, of the ship's constant boost fusion drive permeated its structure, but by now, they were used to it. Adam pulled his pipe out of his jacket pocket, opened the little screen that prevented it from spilling coals in zero gee, and filled it.

"Not so strange," Arleigh replied. He opened a red plastic box of dark brown cigarettes, oval in cross section, and slipped one into a holder.

The brothers sat on jumpseats locked into the deck either side of a long metal canister that had been manufactured yesterday by one of the construction shops under the Ceres dome. It was painted a smooth, lustrous metallic charcoal gray, with a red double racing stripe along its upper surface. Ingrid, whose idea the racing stripe had been, was forward, giving the brothers some privacy, occupying the righthand seat, learning what she could about conning a jumpbuggy from the pilot. She'd told them ten minutes ago they were twenty minutes from turnover.

"What do you mean, 'not so strange'?" Adam asked his brother. He closed the screen, found his lighter, and put flame to the pipe tobacco.

Arleigh lit his cigarette and said, "Plenty of folks, when they stare death in the face, feel an urgent need to have sex, afterward. It's supposed to be a confirmation—more like a reassertion, I guess—that they're still alive. I think this is the same thing, really. Kids are what sex is all about, after all, theoretically. Lindsay dies, you want a confirmation that life is going on somewhere, that's all."

"That's all?" He wondered if Arleigh could be right. First, last, and always, he was an engineer. Psychology—except for whatever it took to run a major engineering project—had never been his long suit.

The younger brother exhaled smoke, which was immediately drawn into the purification system. "That's all. I've never had any kids, myself—at least none that I know of. Guess I was afraid to, when you come down to it. I had a professor in college who talked about having kids as 'giving hostages to history', and it kind of stuck with me."

"What a cheerful notion." Adam drew on his pipe and thought about it, then said, "You know, Arleigh, when the kids were younger—I seem to recall that Wilson was about fifteen and Llyra about eleven—I used to be pretty concerned about the two of them, having to grow up out on Pallas in a little one stop-sign frontier municipality like Curringer."

"Some folks go out of their way to bring their kids up in a small town, rather than some big city," Arleigh said. "We grew up that way, Ad, when Curringer was even smaller. Fishing, hunting, swimming and boating and diving in Lake Selous. Doesn't seem to have done us much harm."

Arleigh immediately began twitching and making distorted, hideous faces, his tongue hanging out. It was an old joke between them, and he'd done it out of sheer reflex. Adam didn't laugh this time—it was a joke they'd shared with Lindsay—or even grin, so his brother stopped.

Lights began blinking on a panel set in the bulkhead between the flight deck and where they sat. Having assured themselves that the coffin was properly secured, both brothers fastened their four point seatbelts.

Adam nodded. "It was about that time that Llyra came to me, very diffidently, mind you—I don't know if she had the same talk with her mother; we were starting to have real problems then—to reveal certain spectacular ambitions of her own which, given her character, I decided to take very seriously. Remember, she was only eleven years old."

"The ice skating thing," Arleigh said, inhaling smoke. "Most grownups I know have considerably less resolve than your daughter does."

Adam shook his head. He'd forgotten his pipe and it had gone out. Now he relit it. "Not just the ice skating thing. She'd been doing that on her own at the Brody ever since she was about four. Her mother used to take her there a couple times a week. No, I mean the ice skating on Earth thing. She meant not only to skate on Earth, but do something important there, win a big competition or something like that."

Arleigh shook his head. "In twenty times the gravity she was used to. That's a pretty tall order, even for her, and a damned dangerous one."

"That's it, exactly: bones, growth-plates, internal organs. I immediately started looking around for somebody to help her—or maybe talk some sense into her. That's when I heard that my dad's old friends from the

Mars rebellion, Mohammed and Beliita Khalidov, had a daughter only a few years older than Llyra, who was also a figure skater."

The lights on the panel changed. Turnover would be coming quickly now.

"So that's how that happened," Arleigh said. "I always sort of wondered. Uncle Brody used to talk about the Khalidovs. She's a nice kid."

"She's a very nice kid," Adam nodded enthusiastically. "Jasmeen's been absolutely perfect, as a teacher and as a companion, and I knew better than to interfere any further than I had, even when it turned out that Jasmeen thought Llyra could actually do it. But I've been worried ever since, that Llyra might destroy herself, physically or mentally, pursuing something that isn't really any part of her fondest dreams."

Arleigh raised his eyebrows. "This is news to me. What do you mean?"

He sighed. "I mean that for some perverse reason, kids often feel responsible when things go wrong in a marriage. They think maybe they can repair the damage. It hurts me deeply to think that my little girl might be doing herself harm in an effort to fix something she didn't break."

A buzzer sounded. They braced themselves for a turnover they never really felt. They didn't learn until later that Ingrid had been at the controls.

Adam unfastened his seatbelt and stood up. He had to relight his pipe again. "I think it's time for an adult beverage. You want beer or tequila?"

"Most definitely," Arleigh said, standing up and stretching, "tequila."

*
**

"But Mom, Wilson promises he can get us there on time in his own ship." She wasn't used to hearing Llyra whining at her through her nose.

Ardith shook her head. This was insane. Two burials in the family—well, almost in the family—within a day of one another. Lindsay and … what was her name? Oh, no! Why couldn't she—Fallon! That was it, Fallon! Her baby son's lost love had been named Fallon. Fallon Tieve.

Something made her want to throw her computer at the wall and then hide under the bed. She didn't know how much more of this she could take.

Then she noticed Julie, sitting in the shadows in a corner of the room, in a straight-backed chair pushed against the wall, crocheting something ugly and grotesque out of coarse blue yarn the color of a robin's egg. She seemed to be scrutinizing every move Ardith made, every word she said. She also seemed to be pulsing on all known wavelengths.

Her Martian mother-in-law still insisted on coming here to the hospital to visit her, as she had every single day since her poor, poor daughter-in-law had collapsed in the laboratory. Ardith wasn't certain, from moment to moment, whether that was such a good thing or not.

Probably not.

True, she felt much better physically, now, but she also still felt like screaming, throwing things, and tearing her hair in double handfuls. What a splendid picture that would make for Adam to compare with that gorgeous, picture-perfect, predatory Japanese assistant of his!

What the hell was her name again?

What was her name?

Through the window, she could just make out the planet Earth, where all three of her children lived in the Moon now, so far, far away.

"Sweetheart," she told her daughter, trying to control a pathetic, teary quaver in her voice. "You tell your brother for me to take care of his responsibilities down there on the Moon. I know that he's got to be feeling terrible about what happened to … to … But if he's going to keep the baby, there are preparations to make. I've read that the reclamation process leaves them with all kinds of deficits. I want you and Jasmeen to stay down there with him and help him, will you, please?"

It was so strange to think of Wilson being pregnant.

Llyra apparently thought it over, and then said, "Where are you, Mom? You're not at home, are you? That doesn't look like anywhere in the house to me. Are you somewhere else? Where are you? Where are you, Mom?"

"Where are you, Mom?" demanded Wilson.

"Where are you, Mom?" demanded Jasmeen.

Julie woke with a heart-wrenching snap, breathing hard, sweating. She looked around the room. The blinds were drawn, so she had no idea what time it was. Nobody else was there in the room with her at the moment.

Her personal computer, about the size and shape of a man's pocket watch or a compact makeup case, lay quiet and unused on the bedside table.

She knew she'd been dreaming. Transmission lag to the Earth-Moon system was almost an hour now. She couldn't have been talking to Llyra. She realized that, at some level, she felt that Julie was … what? Spying on her? Violating her privacy or her need for personal space?

She didn't know, exactly, but the whole thing made her feel horribly guilty. To be truthful, she'd always felt closer to her mother-in-law than to her own mother—who in any case was with her father at the moment, in a half-built O'Neill habitat, orbiting the planet Jupiter. That seemed more like a dream than reality, but it was real enough. What was the transmission lag to Jupiter, a couple of centuries?

Come to think of it, if she squinted just right, she could just make Jupiter out, as well as its four Galilean moons, and a big red Budweiser sign on the habitat. She could also hear her mother saying the fateful words she'd sworn she'd never say to her own kids: "You never write!"

No, that was the dream again. She must have dozed off for a moment.

Fundamentally, Ardith was beginning to realize, *everything* made her feel guilty. She would remain in this damned hospital bed—at least mentally—fighting off the implacable purveyors of happy medicines, until she could find some way to deal with that and other things.

Something was very wrong with her, of that much she was aware, something that had caused her to ruin what would otherwise have been her idyllic marriage to Adam. Nobody knew that she'd tried psychiatric therapy a couple of times after Adam had had enough and gone to Ceres, but it hadn't helped. She'd found that she couldn't take advice about her life from individuals she perceived as less intelligent than she was.

She felt guilty about that, too.

Julie, whom she saw as at least an equal, might be of some help, but Ardith didn't know how to ask her—didn't even know how to begin.

Oh my god, she thought. I dreamed that Wilson was pregnant!

Krystal had been sitting on the cold metal bench for at least an hour. It was hard to tell, exactly. She'd been blindfolded before they brought her here, and in any case, she was pretty sure the room was dark. It was quiet and cold. The only reason she couldn't hear her own heart beating was that it was drowned out by the chattering of her teeth.

Maybe she'd made a mistake this morning, calling an emergency number that had been tattooed upside-down and backwards on the inside of her eyelid, so she could flip the eyelid inside-out (you acquired a knack for it after a while) and read it in the bathroom mirror—provided you had magnifying spectacles and a source of ultraviolet light.

"Haircut," she'd told the public payphone in a Tibetan restaurant they'd chosen because very few people, aside from Tibetans, liked Tibetan food, and none of the regulars spoke English. "This is Two Bits. Please let Shave know I'm red hot and want to come in from the cold."

"Understood," answered an electronically distorted voice. "Stay there." The connection had clicked in Krystal's ear. She bought a cup of some horrible tasting tea, sat down at a table in a corner, and waited.

They'd taken all of four minutes to come to her, three men in a late model ElectroLux with deeply smoked back windows. One of the men got out of the car, stepped halfway into the restaurant, looked around, and signaled for her to follow him. She abandoned the tea gratefully.

The instant she got into the car, they were on her, the one who'd fetched her from the restaurant and another, binding her hands behind her back with a plastic cable tie, shoving a black cloth bag over her head.

"What the hell do you people think you're—"

She felt a sharp explosion of pain in her temple and saw little purple sparks before her eyes. "Keep that noise up and I'll smash your head into a bag of chunky red paste. Nobody will complain and you won't be missed."

She nodded, afraid to say anything. While the man in front drove, the two in back with her went over her methodically and without regard to her dignity. They were wordless, swift, and thorough. They didn't really hurt her and they didn't bother her sexually. They found and took her phone, her PDA, her main weapon, her backup, and her backup's backup. They found and took all four of the knives she kept handy on her person.

They found all of the normal things, as well, credit cards, keys, cosmetics, tissues. They took her shoes, hurting her a little as they did.

They didn't find—better not to think about that right now. At some point the car stopped. Her captors pulled her out of it and into some building, to a fast elevator that went down and down, seemingly endlessly, until it came to a stop, a hundred floors, she guessed, below street level in Armstrong. She didn't know anything in the Moon had ever been dug this deep. It made her wonder who she really worked for.

Now, after two hours of sitting on a hard metal bench in the cold, she heard a door unlatch, a metal door, she thought, and swing open. At least two men came toward her and stopped immediately in front of her.

One of then said, "You didn't tie her ankles." It was not a question.

"No reason to," said the other man. "Where's she gonna go?"

"Tie her ankles now, and get out of here."

"Okay, okay!" The leader's instructions were duly followed and in only an instant, she was even more uncomfortable than she'd been before.

"Krystal Sweet?" the man demanded. Now it began.

"Of the Sour Lake, Texas Sweets," she replied, mustering all of her courage and trying to remain chipper. The back of a gloved hand smashing into the side of her face rocked her until her head hit the wall.

"I'd advise humility," said the voice. "You're here because your underling made several stupid mistakes for no apparent reason. We want to see if you've been irredeemably contaminated, or if you can be salvaged."

"Then shoot me now, Jackoff! I'll be damned if I'll be threatened by some pussy who has to tie me up to hit me, and hired me to do his wetwork in the first place so he wouldn't get his own precious pinkies soiled. Gimme that last cigarette, now, Dickless. I happen to like Birminghams."

There was a long pause, during which Krystal expected to be shot, or at least stricken again, every second. Nothing like that happened. The metal door opened and swung shut again. There was something to be said, she thought to herself, for being badder than the rest of the badguys.

They came back for her in only a few moments, and when they did, they cut the wire-enforced plastic strips binding her ankles and her arms. They stood her up. The door swung open, and this time they took her through it into another room with carpet on the floor and decent heating.

They sat her in a leather-upholstered chair and left her. The room was silent, except for an old, familiar noise she hadn't heard for years.

"You may remove your blindfold now, Krystal." It was an old, familiar voice she hadn't heard in weeks, that of P.E. "Honest Paul" Luegner, the leader of Null Delta Em and her boss for the past several years. She loosened the drawstring, skinned the bag off, and ran a hand through her short, pale blond hair. "We have a mess to straighten out."

"And you've decided not to make me pay for it. That's very good, Paul, because it wasn't my fault—I don't have any idea why it happened—and I was going to make it really expensive for you to blame it on me."

Luegner nodded. "I'll bet you would have, at that. My men are all terrified of you, you know, not just because you're skilled and tough, but because you're intelligent. You're going to pay for what happened at the spaceport in a way though, Krystal, because it happened on your watch."

"That's acceptable," she said, noticing her purse and all her personal possessions were laid out on Luegner's antique walnut desk. Wood. The whole room was paneled with the stuff. It must have cost a king's ransom—probably a real king's ransom—to bring it all up from Earth.

There was the source of the noise, a real fire, burning in a real fireplace. Burning wood.

"For now, Krystal, I just want you to tell me what you think happened with Brian Downs. Why did he snap like that? The sonofabitch probably set the movement back fifty years, gunning down a pregnant girl, the way he did. The spaceport manager's daughter, of all things! And, of course, we'll have the goddamned Ngu family to contend with—again."

Krystal shook her head ruefully. "I warned Brian about that very thing, Paul. I didn't know him well, aside from his personnel jacket. I met him about a week before we went to Mars aboard the *City of Newark*."

"And ... ?"

"And, well, he complained about the assignment every inch of the way."

"What did he complain about, specifically?"

"The fact that we had to stay with the ship for an immediate turnaround, and wouldn't be taking a shuttle down to enjoy Mars like tourists."

"I see, Still, it doesn't sound like much to go on a killing spree over."

"No, it doesn't, does it? Do you have anything warming to drink? I'm still freezing to death. In the end, Brian was making Marxist noises, sort of, about the movement's 'fat cats'—that's you, Paul—being able to go anywhere they want, do anything they want on the company expense account."

"I've never been to Mars," Luegner went to a sideboard and poured them each a generous drink. As he handed Krystal's glass to her, he said, "Jameson's. Twenty-five years old. Say, those plastic binders really cut into your wrists, didn't they? I'm almost sorry about that, but I had to determine that I was dealing with the Krystal Sweet I remembered."

"Meaning ... what?"

He reached into an antique wardrobe cabinet behind his desk and pulled out a light rug or small blanket, which he put over her lap. "Meaning if you hadn't given my man such a hard time out there, daring him to go ahead and shoot you and all, I probably would have had you executed."

"It's nice to know I'm appreciated. But we were talking about Brian."

"So we were. Do you know specifically what set him off?

"Well, he always had a sort of a special jones for Wilson Ngu and his family. Seeing him at the spaceport after two weeks confinement aboard ship—which he somehow twisted around to blame on the Ngu boy—that's what seemed to make him ... have a psychotic break, flip out, whatever."

"So he was trying to shoot Wilson, rather than the O'Driscoll girl?"

"Yes, he was. Although if he'd realized that she was his girl and was carrying his child, he might well have chosen her as a primary target."

"Well, it's an incredible mess, that's what it is, and there's no time at present to clean it up. We won't claim credit directly, but we'll have Anna Savage denounce us as angrily as she can. In the meantime, it would have been nice to have two of you familiar with that ship, but you'll just have to make do with the crew you've picked."

"They're all good people, Paul. They'll do."

"That's what we thought about Brian Downs, isn't it? Still, we have no choice. You have to be back on that ship, your crew in place, by—"

He named a date that made her gasp. "That soon?"

Luegner nodded. "Or it'll be completely pointless. You have to teach them a lesson, Krystal. You have to make them all see the truth."

"Count on me, Paul. Trust me. I'm a *good* teacher."

PART THREE:
ONE-THIRD GEE

ALTHOUGH WE ARE UNIQUE IN our species' ability to foresee and even to forestall cataclysmic occurrences like the Permian-Triassic and Cretaceous-Tertiary Events, we face unique, unprecedented hazards, as well. The power to divert an asteroid or comet from its collision course with Earth is the power to divert an asteroid or comet *onto* a collision course with Earth.

There are plenty of individuals and groups, disappointed that the end of the world didn't arrive on schedule, who would be perfectly satisfied to make up for nature's shortcomings. And there are plenty of governments who have noticed that falling rocks smaller and slower than the P-T and K-T objects are capable of erasing limited portions of the Earth—an enemy country, for example—with none of the unpleasant side-effects of nuclear weapons.

Before we can approach the problem of preventing natural celestial disasters, we must first solve the perhaps greater problem that such a capability represents.

—*Dr. Evgeny Zacharenko Addressing the Ashland Event Commission
Of the Solar Geological Society Curringer, Pallas, August 9, 2095*

CHAPTER THIRTY-THREE:
CONFRONTATIONS

Some human beings seem to love competition, especially when it's somebody else—their children, for example—who has to do the competing. I love a good hockey game, myself, and Martian baseball is a thing of beauty. On the other hand, I don't know what it is about some of the members of our species who feel compelled to take every pleasant, impromptu activity, like sliding along a freshly-frozen body of water, and turn it into a life-and-death, bloody, cutthroat battle in order to "justify" it.

I'm not talking about hockey, here, of course, but figure skating. —
The Diaries of Rosalie Frazier Ngu

"HERE IT IS!" SHOUTED LLYRA.

Every sheet of glass in the lobby of the Robert A. and Virginia Heinlein Memorial Ice Arena—they were many and large—seemed to be covered with pieces of self-adhering typing paper. But they only adhered at the top—each time someone opened a door to the street or the cavernous rink below, they all flapped and fluttered in the breeze like so many flags.

Jasmeen answered, "Where is? I do not see!"

The place positively thundered with the presence of hundreds of young girls, from the age of four to the age of about nineteen, attired in flesh-colored tights, brightly-hued, highly stylized, traditional dresses with short skirts and plenty of sequins and glitter, standing in skates that made them look taller and even longer-legged than they were. The air was charged with the odors of hairspray, makeup, and perspired adrenaline.

Llyra was no different in many of these respects. Her hair was done up in a classic ponytail, slicked down with aerosol plastic, well garnished with fine gold glitter (buns and short haircuts were also acceptable). She wore an expensively tailored dress her grandmother had sent her, of fuchsia crushed velvet with spaghetti straps over her shoulders and a short, sheer skirt of paisley that complimented the bodice.

Like every girl there, she had put on enough makeup that morning, as her father had once observed, for the entire road company of *The Mikado*

Here and there, outnumbered at least a hundred to one and looking very self-conscious, were little boys in tight pants and baggy-sleeved shirts. They were tougher than they looked, willing to put up with constant teasing and bullying from non-skating boys, in order to skate.

Jasmeen wore her customary "official" coach's coat, long, black, almost ice-length. The only difference between hers and those of other coaches here today was that the other coaches wore quilted synthetics, fake furs, or heavy cloth, the only fur-bearing animals in the Moon being sheep and long-haired dogs. Jasmeen wore genuine Pallatian sable she'd paid for herself out of her first several paydays from the Ngus.

Some of these young athletes were about to skate, and were focused tightly on whatever it is inside a person that allows them to compete with others. Everywhere, signs had been posted: "NO FLOOR JUMPS", and everywhere, just as many heads bumped by the ceiling because their owners had ignored the signs. Still, they had to warm up and get in some last-minute practice somehow. There was talk of building a high- ceilinged jump room.

Others here had already skated and were waiting for results, waiting to be photographed with their competitors, waiting to go home or back to their hotel. Many of them were red-faced and sobbing, having done less well than they—or their parents and coaches—had expected. In some, it was a reflexive, preemptive reaction, in order to avoid being scolded or yelled at.

The all-important results were what was printed in neat columns on the pieces of paper sticking to the glass. Each consisted of the place, date, and name of the event, the group if there were more than a dozen or so skaters in the same competitive category, the skater's name, her placement within her group, and her "ordinals"—the place given her by each of the six automated judges that had watched her skate. Sometimes these numbers varied, owing to the different angle each judge saw her from, but disagreements like this were fairly unusual.

"Junior Ladies' Final Round!" Llyra was so excited that she could hardly control herself, but didn't want to shout her results to a roomful of girls who hadn't done as well as she had. Jasmeen caught up in a heartbeat. "First Place!" Llyra seized Jasmeen's arm and squeezed it.

"Oh, my little," said Jasmeen. "Just look at the ordinals!"

All six robotic judges had given Llyra first place, just they had for her Long Program and her Short Program that had preceded it. Being the only figure skater on Pallas, Llyra had often wondered why, when the judges were completely cybernetic, the results were posted in such an old-fashioned manner. Shirlene Hofstaedter, of the Lunar Figure Skating Association, had explained that this 200-year-old touch was one of the things that had first made automated judging acceptable to skaters.

She remembered—partly because it hadn't been that long ago—the day she'd passed her Junior Ladies' test, which had qualified her to compete at that level in this competition. It had been a general testing day, every testing skater and her coach horribly tense. The whole rink had been steeped in a mood to make this competition seem festive.

Jasmeen had been with her every step of the way, of course, watching her as she warmed up, offering final advice on the fine points of technique, reminding her, as every coach must remind her students, "Smile!" The judges were actually programmed to watch for that.

It was a strange, strange world, she thought, and growing stranger daily.

She'd been well coached and had practiced hard, getting through the test with an ease that had made her feel unsettled and suspicious of herself. Some skaters were called back to reskate a portion of their test. Llyra was not, which could either mean she'd skated well or very badly.

They'd found a little niche just off the lobby by the snack bar in which to sit and wait. Jasmeen had gotten out her PDA and begun working this week's *Syrtis Major Times* crossword puzzle, the only reason she subscribed. As with the old-fashioned posted scores, a real human being would come out in a little while to tell them how Llyra had fared.

The real human being, Mrs. Hofstaedter, as it turned out, had informed them that Llyra had passed brilliantly. "Although I must confess, I never held out much hope for either of you, that first week you were here."

Llyra had laughed and let Mrs. Hofstaedter buy her a celebratory Coke.

Jasmeen had immediately pressed ENTER on her PDA, electronically sending Llyra's entry form for the competition upstairs to Mrs. Hofstaedter's office, a full three minutes before the deadline, six whole weeks before the event today, which Llyra had won with flying colors.

Now, standing at the windows, Jasmeen caught Llyra's eye. "My little, you have just won tenth competition in Moon. You know what means?"

Still stunned at her results and filled with joy, Llyra shook her head, a smart-alecky remark about Disneyland dying unuttered on her lips.

"Means our work here is done," Jasmeen grinned. "Is time to move on."

"To Mars?" Llyra's heart raced. One-third gee! Twice that of the Moon.

"To Mars!"

*
**

"Step over here for security inspection!" The woman's voice was sharp.

Not sure exactly what she'd heard, Llyra asked, "What did you say, ma'am?"

"Be quick about it, and save your sexist remarks!" the woman ordered. "We have a schedule to keep!"

Llyra made a point of looking behind her. They were early, and there was nobody in line with her but her coach. Llyra had never seen a balding woman before. This specimen had greasy, thinning, gray hair through which the girl could see more shiny scalp than she cared to. The woman was repulsively fat in a way few Pallatians ever were. She also had a better moustache than her brother Wilson would likely ever grow.

The brim of the military-style cap the woman wore unmilitarily on the back of her head was covered with smudgy fingerprints and gold decorations her grandmother had once told her real soldiers called "scrambled eggs". The woman's medium blue uniform shirt had epaulets, with braided gold and navy blue cords hanging from them almost to her waist. And although the shift had just begun—Llyra and Jasmeen had watched the "changing of the guard" as the earlier crew clocked out and the new one clocked in—the armpits of her shirt were already salt- and sweat-stained from the previous day's work, and she smelled sour.

As the girls complied, they passed between a pair of chromed metal contrivances of about Llyra's height, a head taller than Jasmeen. An alarm sounded. The security woman and the slight, anemic-looking man who shared her shift, rushed around the rostrum they had been waiting behind.

"Drop your baggage," the woman screamed at them, spraying droplets of saliva at them. "Hold your arms out at shoulder height—do it now!"

She ran an electronic object down Llyra's body until it beeped loudly. "What's this?" she demanded, reaching for the edge of the light coat the girl had decided to travel in. Llyra backed up half a step.

She dropped her arms and turned to face to woman squarely. "Not that you have any right to ask me, but that's my personal defense weapon."

318

"Come here, Missy, you're going to be adding to our collection!" The woman reached for her again. Llyra noticed she had garlic and alcohol on her breath. The girl backed up another step. Before the woman could advance, Jasmeen, smaller than either one, stood between them.

"Let her alone, cow!" Jasmeen told her.

The woman turned on her heel, faster than Llyra would have expected. "I guess that qualifies you for some special attention, too, dearie!"

She laid a fat hand on Jasmeen's shoulder. Llyra just had time to notice that her fingernails were dirty. Then there was an explosion of motion, and when it was over, in less than a second, the woman lay on the floor, her huge breasts squashed out sideways by her weight. One arm was on the floor, the other stretched straight upward behind her, being twisted about half a turn farther than Llyra would have thought possible.

Jasmeen's foot was on her neck and the side of her head.

Llyra bent nearly double to look the woman in the face. "Jasmeen, I think you're right. She does look just like a cow." The woman's eyes were bulging with surprise and terror, as if she were about to be branded.

"You shouldn't have touched her, you know," Llyra said to the woman. "She's Martian. They like being touched even less than they like being yelled at and ordered around. They probably like being disarmed less."

Llyra looked up. It appeared they were surrounded by the entire East American garrison in the Moon, guns drawn, shock rods held high. Most of them wore spacelines livery in as shabby condition as the woman's.

One of them was brandishing a clipboard.

"Go ahead, stupids, do what you have to do," said Jasmeen grimly, shifting the foot on the woman's neck a little and pulling harder on her arm. Something popped. Something else crackled faintly. The woman groaned and whimpered. "Your colleague will be dead before I hit floor."

"And maybe three or four of you," Llyra added, drawing the ten millimeter pistol she hadn't wanted to show them, "will be joining her."

"Hold on! Hold on! One side! One side! Make way! Make way!" The strong tenor voice came from the rear of the crowd, which opened up to allow a short, plump man with curly white hair and copper eyebrows to pass through them. "Everybody stand down now, before somebody gets hurt!"

At his back were half a dozen spaceport security guards, in neat, simple gray uniforms—they wore no helmets or body armor—without a sweat-stain or a thread of lint among them. Each was armed with a .50 caliber semiautomatic pistol and carried a short, fully automatic Remington shotgun with tandem magazine tubes.

319

"Er, somebody else gets hurt, that is." As he drew even with the dramatic tableaux that Llyra, Jasmeen, and the unwilling security woman seemed to have struck, he clearly suppressed a delighted grin, demanding in the sternest voice he could, "Just what's going on here, Ermintrude?"

The woman mumbled something into the carpet.

Llyra reholstered her pistol. Jasmeen didn't let go of her captive. "They wanted to search us. Take our weapons. This one laid hand on me."

"And you are … " He had a suspicion, already.

"Jasmeen Mohammedova Khalidov."

He nodded. "And you, young lady—no, no, let me guess. You would be Llyra Ayn Ngu, Wilson's sister and Adam's little girl. I might have known it—in fact I did know it! I'm Terry O'Driscoll. I run this place, despite what this scurvy lot thinks. Let's go someplace we can talk."

Jasmeen released the woman who remained where she was, a liquid stain soaking into the carpet under her hips. O'Driscoll turned to one of his security staff, issued instructions, and then led the girls away.

"We have time," he told them. "Do you like cappuccinos?"

*
**

"Attention! United States' Vessel *City of Newark*, now boarding on Concourse A-5. United States' Vessel *City of Newark*, now boarding on Concourse A-5. Passengers must display their tickets and some valid form of photographic identification, or they will not be permitted aboard."

The pre-recorded message repeated itself in a pleasant, if brisk voice, using Spanish, Japanese, Mandarin, and … he guessed it must be Urdu. If some traveler who spoke Inuit, Serbo-Croatian, or Finnish had been included on the passenger manifest, the spaceline's computer would have duly noted it, and that language would have been used, as well. It might be fun persuading them to do it in old, dead Cornish sometime.

The individual who thought of himself as "The Fastest Gun in the Moon" hadn't joined the security inspection line just yet. He never had any trouble, but he preferred spacelines that didn't require it. The *City of Newark* was a large vessel, an enormous cylinder of some eighty decks. It was usually a 24-hour task to get everybody ticketed, searched, boarded, and nicely settled in for their four-week ride to Mars.

He'd approved of the plan he'd overheard Llyra and Jasmeen making, to board the spaceship as early as possible, get comfortable in their stateroom—his own was right next door—catch up on their e-mail, watch a movie, order a light supper, and go to bed. It made his job a great deal easier, and in such an enormous ship as this one was, even if it was East American, there would be plenty to see and do tomorrow.

It had always been his habit to hang back in lines like this for as long as he possibly could, in part, until the minimum-wage slugs whose livelihood consisted solely of violating the rights and lives and persons of other individuals were physically worn out—most of them were grossly overweight—mentally exhausted (which never took terribly long), and inclined to make the most entertaining kinds of mistakes.

Today, however, the slugs had made their entertaining mistake a little early, messing with Jasmeen and Llyra. He'd had to duck into the nearest men's room, locking a stall door behind him, in order to avoid rolling all over the concourse floor, convulsing helplessly, unable to breathe right, and with tears of laughter pouring from his eyes.

His ribs still ached and would probably bother him all the way to Mars.

Sometimes life could be truly worth living, if only for the sake of the comedy that happened along the way. For the rest of his, he would treasure the golden memory of that slovenly pig's face squashed sideways into the indoor-outdoor carpeting under Jasmeen's delicate foot. Or of young Llyra, holding off an entire horde of armed, uniformed bullies with her little pistol. What a pair they'd turned out to be!

He was extremely grateful that the spaceport manager—the father of Wilson's lost love (how tangled life can get, sometimes)—had arrived just in time, before he, himself, was left with no choice but to interfere. He had a little item with him this morning that electrically fired beryllium copper needles—short bits of hair-fine wire a quarter of an inch long—coated in curare. The magazine held three hundred rounds.

The effect was transitory, but it would probably have ended his usefulness to his current employer, which would have been too bad. He'd found that he was enjoying this job more than any other in recent memory. It was pleasant to know that those you had been hired to defend—even little girls—were more than capable of defending themselves.

He used the bathroom for its intended purpose, tidied himself up, and peeked out on the concourse. The line of boarding passengers to be violated was back in place, each of its occupants quiet, passive, and sheeplike, just the way the official spacelines of the East American government preferred them. He could even make out the overhead music system playing an upbeat, bouncy version of Barry McGuire's "Eve of Destruction".

It was too bad nobody within the borders of East America knew the words any more. They, and others like them, had been big a part of his home schooling in English Literature where he'd grown up, in Tucson,

West America. His mother had almost worshipped the mid-twentieth century poets.

Emerging from the men's room, he glanced around cautiously, just in case someone was watching him. There were advantages, he supposed, to being as tall as he was, six foot six, but he was far too old for basketball, now, and it could be a real liability, sometimes, in what he always privately thought of as the SVS—"spy versus spy"—business.

He caught sight of the two girls—Llyra and Jasmeen—sitting in the coffee bar across the concourse with the spaceport manager. It had always struck him as odd, having coffee to calm down, although people in the nineteenth century had similarly regarded alcohol as a stimulant.

None of them were laughing it up, but it was clear the girls were in no trouble. Their lives and O'Driscoll's had been touched, and somehow braided together by the same senseless tragedy, the brutal—and apparently accidental—murder of O'Driscoll's only daughter and, if his sources were to be trusted, the mother of Wilson's unborn child.

The Fastest Gun in the Moon deeply regretted what had happened to Fallon, for personal reasons of his own. The responsibility had been his, after all, to protect Wilson's life, and, by extension, Fallon's life, as well. All the more so if she were carrying Wilson's baby, although apparently even Fallon hadn't known it. And to think she'd been taking Wilson to meet her father for the first time. But even the Fastest Gun in the Moon couldn't be in two places at once.

He'd spoken with his employer within an hour of the shooting— someone needed to get busy inventing a faster-than-light communication system; he knew that it was at least theoretically possible—and his employer had agreed. Perhaps there should have been a second bodyguard. But it was doubtful much could have been done, even if he'd been there, himself. The only thing now was to watch over the two girls.

And there was good reason to do so. Looking the other way, he saw Krystal Sweet and some new companion or henchman or whatever at the back end of the security line, exactly as he'd thought he might. They probably had some other people around here, too. He'd have made this trip with the girls anyway—Wilson was big enough to take care of himself safe in his little ship—but now he was certain that he'd be needed.

He'd quietly looked into this smelly business of Krystal and Downs going to Mars but staying with the *City of Newark* and coming right back. Maybe nobody else knew what they had been doing, but the Fastest Gun in the Moon did. Fact was, he'd called in an anonymous bomb threat the next day to make sure that they hadn't left any little surprises behind.

***

The waitress put their drinks down, accepted their thanks, and left.

"Ah, there's no help for it, I'm greatly afraid," Terry told Llyra and Jasmeen with a deep, Celtic sigh. He folded up his phone, having just made several calls with it, and put it in his pocket. "You'll be having to surrender your personal weapons for the duration of your passage to Mars. I don't envy you ladies at all, I don't. Two long weeks of having to depend upon idiots and drunkards for your physical wellbeing."

"That doesn't seem right," Llyra objected. "How can they get away with—"

"They're a private corporation—at least they are in theory. In plain, despicable truth, they're a wholly-owned subsidiary of the East American government—and as such, they have the power, if not the right, to make their own rules."

The three of them were sitting on high stools at a tall table in one of the many bars, restaurants, and coffee shops set conveniently around the perimeter of the main concourse. Llyra and Jasmeen were having mochas (it was Llyra's favorite), Terry's was an Irish coffee. He seldom drank on duty but felt the East Americans had driven him to it.

"You mean if corporation made rule, 'fly naked', would have to fly naked?" It was Jasmeen protesting, while Llyra watched and listened. "I have heard from parents about horrible East American crime rate. One person in, well, one gets robbed or worse at least once in life. What if East American criminal aboard ship attempts to rob us—or worse?"

O'Driscoll laughed. "It appears to me that he'll be having his arm wrenched out of its socket for him, and his face stepped on. It'd be that humiliating for a would-be rapist. The spaceline management folks will argue, of course, that you've no need for self-defense, since they maintain a large and well-trained security staff aboard to defend you."

"Like large and well-trained security pigs over there?" Jasmeen tossed her head back toward the boarding area they'd just left. "They can't fight. Weapons handling is to laugh. Smell like hockey players at end of losing season. Would it hurt them sometime to do some drycleaning?"

Terry laughed. "The hockey players or the security people? More importantly, where the blazes did you learn to fight like that, young lady?"

"On Mars from parents and friends of parents. Old revolutionaries who didn't want kids ever to be threatened by government 'security' bullies."

"The trouble is," he nodded, "they don't think of themselves as security people, or even law enforcement officers. They think of themselves—"

"As military," Jasmeen supplied. "They think of themselves as military."

"You're quite correct, my dear, and even worse, they're garrison troops, suffering all of the same deficiencies as garrison troops everywhere."

"They'd actually like much better to think of themselves as occupying forces," Llyra observed suddenly. "Wouldn't they, Mr. O'Driscoll?"

Terry was surprised. Llyra and Fallon would have gotten along well. "Well. whatever they may be or want to be, and however they may smell—"

"Or want to smell!" the girls giggled together.

"I'm afraid that we're stuck with them as long as East America maintains the only passenger service to Mars. I still don't understand exactly how that happened. I'm not sure anybody does. But just between the three of us, I don't believe that their monopoly is going to last them too much longer, not if your grandmother, young lady ... " He nodded at Llyra. " ... and the Curringer Corporation's Sheridan Sinclair have their way."

Llyra immediately sat up. "Mr. Sinclair is back? Then maybe we could—"

Jasmeen nodded her head. She'd had the same idea, herself.

"I'm afraid not, Miss Ngu. The silly fellow's still out there among the flying mountains, somewhere, counting asteroids, taking their pictures, and giving them all cute little alphanumerical names. The grand plan, at least as I understand it, is to keep on doing exactly that until they're finally relieved by the lovely vessel *Rosalie Frazier*, which only now just left the Earth-Moon complex, headed upsystem."

Jasmeen nodded. "Yes, we heard of that. So we are having no choice in this matter? Must use Soviet spaceline from hell or stay here in Moon?"

O'Driscoll chuckled sympathetically. "Yes, Miss Khalidov, but I may be able to make it a little less burdensome." He pulled his phone out of his pocket. "Flight Control, this is Terry O'Driscoll. Oh, hello, Gertie. Thank you, m'dear, we all miss her already. I can't tell you how much I appreciate the thought. Would you please raise Captain Alan West for me, aboard the *City of Newark*? Thank you, Gertie."

He waited for a moment, then: "Al you old space pirate! It's me, Terry O'Driscoll. Have you started your checklist yet, or are you still making improper suggestions to the stewardesses? ... What do you mean that they're all male on this route? What kind of a politically correct way is that to run a spaceline, anyway? You have my extremest sympathies."

Llyra looked a question at Jasmeen. Jasmeen shrugged.

"Look, Al I need a big favor from you. Could you come down to Boarding Lounge C in a minute? I know it's a royal pain in the sitter, but it could turn out to be important. And be sure to bring your navigation case with you."

He hung up, and instantly punched in another number. "Michelle? Crank up your press release program and get ready to send e-mail to every 3DTV outlet in the Moon. Headline it 'Born and Raised at 1/20 Gravity, Pallatian Skater Defeats Luna's Best, Now Sets Sights on Mars'."

He went on to dictate four or five paragraphs, in proper inverted pyramid style, then hung up and turned back to the girls. "That should guarantee a crowded, noisy boarding area for the dashing Captain Alan West to escort you through. He's not an East American, you understand, he's from Chugwater, Wyoming, or something like that. I went down there one time to go antelope hunting with him and had to do all my shooting from a damn wheelchair!"

"So why does antelope hunting friend work for East Uglies?" asked Jasmeen.

"East America has a critical shortage of competent pilots, so he flies for the pay. He's one of the goodguys, I promise, Miss Khalidov. He'll take care of your unmentionables himself, until you get to Mars."

⁕

"Next!"

The line today seemed extremely long and slow-moving.

When they were roughly halfway to the East American security inspection point, the phone on Krystal's hip began vibrating. That disturbed her. In the first place, she didn't care for the sensation, not at all. And more importantly, very few individuals had her number—in fact it didn't officially exist—and all of them had been very severely cautioned never to use it unless there was some kind of emergency.

They pushed their carry-on luggage a few steps further along the line.

She gave her new associate the briefest of glances. Unlike this fellow's late, unlamented predecessor, Brian Downs, "Brazos" Jeffries was nothing if not totally level-headed. Even better, he was perfectly willing to follow her lead in the field, without any argument. He was an excellent shot, well-trained in knife fighting, as well as unarmed combat.

He was also a handsome devil—she thought he was cute, anyway—tall and dark in a whitebread sort of way. He looked a little younger than his personnel jacket said he was, well-scrubbed, short-haired, clean-shaven, and tidy without being obsessive about it. Krystal thought he might have passed as a graduate student in accounting or theology.

She, herself, was in a kind of disguise this morning. You could never tell what security cameras might have picked up that day Brian had flown off the handle. She had abandoned the one-piece pants suit or faded Levis she preferred, for a long, colorful "broomstick" skirt, an off-white, home-spun top with lace trim, thick-soled sandals, and large-framed glasses she felt made her look like a bug.

She carried a purse that had been woven or braided by hand out of Yeti hair or something. Her long brown wig had been put up into dozens of tiny braids when wet, allowed to dry, then combed out to produce a striking wavy appearance. She even wore a scent that mimicked that of marijuana smoke.

Reluctantly, although there was no indication who was calling—in her line of work, there wouldn't be—she answered her telephone, assuming the ultra-pleasant tone and demeanor that went so well with her name, and never failed to strike absolute, mind-numbing terror in the hearts, both of her enemies and of those with whom she chose to work.

"Hello … This is she … Oh, it's you! How very pleasant to be speaking with you in this way—so unexpectedly, I mean … " She listened intently. "Oh, you don't say! Well I must confess, that's certainly very interesting. I was annoyed, at first, that you'd rung me now, but it was mercy, believe me. Thank you very much for calling, dear."

She pushed buttons, put her phone in her purse, and turned to Brazos. They were only a few paces from the spaceline's security inspection station. "Well gosh. You'll never guess who that was," she said.

He blinked. He didn't get the saccharine act. It made him nervous. He'd been told it usually preceded an act of bloody violence. "Who was it?"

"It was our Jocelyn." she said, pretending to be excited by the news.

Brazos nodded. He was the new guy here, and was only beginning to know these people. Jocelyn was the short, brown Asian woman (Krystal had said she was Vietnamese) who would be boarding *City of Newark*, too, in due course. Presently she was only a few paces away, keeping a watchful eye on their backs, as well as on the Ngu girl and her Martian companion.

"Jocelyn tells me," Krystal said, "that an old friend of ours is here at this very spaceport, this very morning, watching us—no, no, don't look back!—and that he might even possibly be planning to board this very ship with us. Let me tell you, that could turn out to be a pretty darn interesting development." She suddenly felt a strong craving for a cigarette. "I swear, I just don't understand how a guy can do all the lurking around that he manages, when he's so gosh darn tall."

Brazos grinned. In a twinkling, he became a totally different individual, a natural, instinctive predator, utterly without qualm or compunction. His eyes were like those of a shark, uncaring, cold, and voracious. Krystal adored that in a man. He said, "Would you like me to—"

"No, no, no. Wait'll we're underway, sweetie. We'll have all of our toys then, and a much freer hand than we have now—that's for sure. For the time being, let's just do our darnedest to look and act like ordinary tourists, honeymooners, even. We'll get on board the pretty spaceship as if we didn't have a care in the Known Galaxy, and let our friends Jocelyn, Donna, Denise and Minde all do what they do best."

Although she liked having someone like Brazos around, Krystal much preferred working with other women. They were always so thorough and attentive to detail. Donna and Denise and Minde were already aboard, filling posts that would stun the media and the government, once the facts were allowed to come out. Just as no one can stop an assassin if he's prepared to die with his victim, Krystal thought, no one can stop hijackers if they're willing to spend enough money. It made her proud that this was already the most expensive op she'd ever been involved with.

She winked. "Thanks for the thought, though."

Brazos raised his eyebrows, obviously fighting the urge to peer around. Krystal noticed that he looked like a young graduate student again.

He asked her, "So who is this tall guy, anyway?"

"That's right," she observed. "I tend to forget that you're new around here. Well, sweetie, we don't even know his real name. He has nine or ten aliases. He's sort of an odd kind of a stealth bodyguard. I can't begin to guess how expensive he must be. More than I could afford."

"A *stealth* bodyguard?"

She nodded. "In more ways than one. The kind of soft, pampered rich folk he protects often don't even know that he exists, since he's usually been hired by some interested third party. In this case, the smart money is saying that it's either Adam Ngu, the little girl's father, or Julie Segovia Ngu, her grandmother. Nobody's quite sure which, but I can promise you, the man is going to be a great deal of trouble."

You'd damn well better believe I will, Miss Sweet, mused the remarkably tall individual who thought of himself as the Fastest Gun in the Moon.

He'd been listening to everything via a tiny microphone and transmitter he'd planted on Krystal's purse. *You may count on it!*

CHAPTER THIRTY-FOUR: BEER AND SYMPATHY

One good reason to get rid of politics is the traps that politicians are always setting for one another. Ordinary people get ensnared in them and it ruins their lives. In the 17th century your career could be ended if you backed the wrong semicolon in some verse in the Book of Common Prayer. Nobody really cared, it was just another way to discredit your opponent.

Lately, gene-sorting scandals have been the ruin of many an East American politician. It's what stem cells and cloning were back in the 21st century, or abortion or philandering in the 20th. It's not illegal, it's just expensive and elitist. If they can afford the price-tag, they'll suffer a brief bout of "self-improvement flu", after which they'll be handsomer or taller, and their kids will never go bald, catch a cold, or get cancer.

But there's another price. If they're unlucky enough to get caught by the predatory media (who happen to be hooked on the stuff themselves), they lose the proles—the beer and Prozac vote—and have to use their acquired charms to sell used cars. —*The Diaries of Rosalie Frazier Ngu*

"EVERYTHING TASTING ALL RIGHT, HONEY?"

The waitress was a tall, good-looking strawberry blonde, with long hair and freckles across the bridge of her turned-up nose. The skirt of her peach-colored outfit was only about a quarter of an inch longer than it absolutely had to be, and the rest of it did nothing to conceal her other ample assets. She also wore a handkerchief-sized apron.

Naturally, when she asked the question, Wilson's mouth was full. Waitresses and dentists. He'd chosen the open-faced hot Martian-raised turkey sandwich with homemade bread, sage dressing, mashed potatoes, and a dark brown gravy that seemed to be the signature of this eatery, which for some peculiar reason, referred to itself as "Deep Space Little America". Later, he'd promised himself, there would be lemon meringue pie.

The dining room was all right, nothing special, a maze of booths with little windows, or partitions above the backs, made of wood-framed pebbled glass. The ceiling was high, with a dozen slow- moving fans. The light was just right. The floor was a polished synthetic.

Wilson grinned back at the waitress and nodded satisfaction. Someday, he reflected, a horde of microscopic robots would be mining the insides of his cardio-pulmonary vessels for their accumulated hydrogenated lipids. But here and now, he had his lunch before him, and was already looking forward to dinner: a whole twelve ounces of t-bone beefsteak, medium rare, a crispy-jacketed steaming baked potato with everything on it but sour cream (which he detested), stir-fried asparagus, and a tall, cold margarita on the rocks with salt on the rim.

Just now he'd settled for a Coke, also on the rocks. At "tea" he'd treat himself to red beer—Negra Modelo and Clamato—tortilla chips and guacamole.

None of it made him exactly happy—for a moment he'd considered asking if the waitress had anything else for sale (she was quite acceptably pretty and had those long, long legs), but only for moment—it dulled the pain, especially the tequila, which was all he felt he had a right to expect. He was determined to go on living his life just as he had before he'd met Fallon, having learned—from Fallon herself—that you never know when or where you'll find your heart's desire.

Again.

He wasn't sure he'd ever get over Fallon's death, not the way he'd gotten over Amorie's ... odd behavior. He wasn't sure he wanted to. There had been some satisfaction seeing her killer's face come apart around a bullet which had expanded to the diameter of a two-ounce gold coin, but less than he'd anticipated, and it was fading away.

The worst of it, the hardest part to live with, was that he wasn't sure whether he'd loved her. It was pretty clear that she'd loved him. Apparently she'd stopped taking contraceptives pretty early in their relationship—one reason Terry O'Driscoll had more or less adopted him as a son—but he knew her well enough to understand she wasn't trying to trap him. She'd simply loved him and wanted to have his child.

Which still struck him as utterly amazing.

He'd chosen this particular place to eat in because, relative to all the others, it was quiet, the only one he knew of in the station that didn't have a row of slot machines—or a full-blown casino—at the back of the room. He didn't disapprove of gambling—someone had once referred to it as "the thrill of bad mathematics"—although he never gambled himself, considering it a waste of time and money. He did dislike the noise it generated, with its interminable bells and sirens.

Holbrook Station was famous all over the System because it circled the Sun in Earth's orbit, 180 degrees ahead of (or behind) the mother planet. Hidden by the Sun's mass and glare, it was the most isolated spot imaginable that didn't lay outside the orbit of Pluto. Depending on the constantly-changing positions of the other Settled Worlds, it was very popular with asteroid hunters who'd worked their way around this far or simply seemed to need a different set of walls, every now and again, than the ones they'd been stuck between for weeks or months.

The station consisted of two thick disks, joined at their hubs like a set of dumbbells, rotating at the right speed to produce one sixth gee at the outermost level. Each of the ten or twelve floors above that level had less apparent gravity until, nearest the hub, one could feel no gravity at all.

The hub itself—a core that went through both disks—didn't rotate. A docking ring of steel, titanium, and carbon fiber, held in place by a dozen spokes of the same material, was attached to the hub where it passed from one disk to the other. One was free to enter the station the expensive way, by docking for a metered time at one end, or more cheaply, by mooring at the docking ring, which was stationary, relative to the station—the apparent gravity there was zero gee—and riding one of its many elevator pods up the nearest spoke to the hub.

Here on the outermost level, Wilson could look down through a large window in the restaurant's floor, and see *Mighty Mouse's Girlfriend* every time the station completed a rotation and started another. She was moored by the rings and bollards she used to tow asteroids, and what he saw was her stern and the huge orifices of her engines.

What Wilson thought of as the upper half of Holbrook Station had been given over to restaurants, bars, dance halls, all kinds of shops—exactly the same kinds of enterprises that could be found at the LaGrange points or any self-respecting tourist trap in Arizona or New Mexico—and to other necessities of life, as well, like showers, luxurious baths, barbershops, and massage parlors that actually performed massages. It also offered several long rows of 3DTV phones that depended on a pair of relay satellites, also in Earth's orbit, but a quarter of the way around the sun, to communicate with the Earth/Moon system and whatever else happened to be out of reach at the moment.

He'd already inspected the swimming pool, a cluster of hot tubs, saunas, and the inevitable centrifuge full of brides and young matrons from the outer worlds, hoping to conceive and to avoid miscarriage. He'd also found a handball court, a tennis court, and a shooting range with its own gunsmith. He badly needed practice, he felt, with both his Herron Stag-gerCyl .270 and his great grandfather's .45 Magnum Grizzly. Llyra—she and Jasmeen should be starting for Mars right about now—would be disappointed to learn that they had no ice-skating rink here.

He'd been happy to find a well-equipped gymnasium and weight room. His muscles had long ago adapted from the one tenth gravity of Ceres to the one sixth of the Moon. He'd recently started using the engines aboard *Mighty Mouse's Girlfriend* to work his way up, a few digits at a time, from the Moon's point one, six, six, six, et cetera, to the point three, three, three of Mars. He thought it might make a nice surprise for his little sister and her coach if he showed up on Mars, at some point, able to get around on his own, without mechanical assistance.

There was a fuel desk, the main reason for the station's existence to begin with, where asteroid hunters and other travelers paid for reaction mass and other things to keep their catalytic fusion powerplants sizzling.

Most importantly, there were extensive ship repair facilities here. Wilson believed that one of his engines had a hairline crack in its rocket nozzle liner, which had already reduced that engine's power by eleven percent and would eventually cause a catastrophic failure in the field. That was the main reason he'd come here. They actually had a pressurized facility large enough to accommodate *Mighty Mouse's Girlfriend*. This was good because, as expensive as hangar time could be, paying a mechanic suit-time was ruinous.

There was a water desk, as well, half a dozen movie theaters, a multifaith chapel with facilities for weddings, funerals, and bar mitzvahs, offices representing banks from all over the Solar System, the law firm of Mercot, Flambingo, Creasing, and Plavnivs, and several establishments dedicated to the needs and comfort of lonely traveling men.

These establishments also made housecalls, to the rooms in the lower cylinder—actually an enormous hotel with a twenty-bed infirmary and a fully equipped operating theater—or to ships docked at the ring. The infirmary specialized in the diseases of insufficient gravity: deteriorating skeletons and muscles, ailing immune systems.

Holbrook Station offered at last fifty places to eat, ranging from many standup counters and familiar fast food joints like Zeefo's or Ali Wanna, to a genuine five-star restaurant that required its customers to wear a necktie, a formal pistol belt, and other suitable attire. It served fresh vegetables it grew in a greenhouse, and lobster, which it raised in a tank.

Abruptly, it wasn't as quiet in the restaurant as it had been. An indeterminate number of noisy voices erupted behind him—somehow, Wilson thought, it seemed a bit too early in the day for that sort of thing—he peered around the back of his booth to see what was going on.

"There he is!" said one of the three young men coming toward him. It was his old friend Mikey Mitzvah with his round face, short blond hair, and spectacles. With him were Marko Fang, the tattooed warrior with a scalp lock, and Sean Ian Scott, otherwise known to everyone as Scotty.

"What the hell are you three doing way out here?" Wilson asked. "Are you aware you're making enough racket for a dozen guys your size?"

"Hot turkey sandwich and a Coca-Cola!?" Marko said, flinging himself into the booth opposite Wilson. "Looks like it's lunchtime for Mr. Ngu. We're eight hours out of synch. It's way after suppertime for us."

The other two were right behind him. Mikey sat by Marko. Scotty said, "Shove it on over, Sport," adjusted his kilt for sitting, and slid in beside Wilson, who hated being trapped on the inside of a booth. Nevertheless, he moved over, taking his plate and drink with him.

The waitress materialized almost immediately. "What can I do for you gents?" she asked, expecting—and receiving—the usual round of fresh answers. She'd noticed the original customer at this table looking at her legs and her breasts (who wouldn't, considering what she had to wear) but at least he'd been a little shy and perfectly polite about it.

"They've just arrived from the depths of interplanetary space and it's past their bedtime," Wilson told her. "Perhaps warm milk all around?" The intended witticism only made matters worse, and embarrassed Wilson thoroughly.

When the waitress had departed with their orders, Scotty leaned toward the center of the table. "Did I hear you ask us what we're doing out here, Wilson? Because I'll tell you, if you can keep it to yourself."

Wilson leaned into the center of the table, nose to nose with Scotty. Mikey and Marko followed his example. "Okay." He sat back again.

Mikey complained, "The wise guy! Always the wise guy! Tell him, Marko!"

That individual looked around cautiously and lowered his voice until Wilson could barely hear. "We think we've found the Diamond Rogue."

Wilson shook his head. "That's a hunter's myth. My mother—"

"Is an expert on asteroids," Scotty finished for him. "And a very nice, very pretty lady, if you don't mind me saying so. I've met her, and I know. And yet you yourself found a giant—"

"Garnet. The size of a basketball. My grandma used to tell me the Diamond Rogue is bigger than a house—or a castle. In Transylvania. So is this object that you think you've found an aggregate, or one huge, gigantic diamond? And exactly how big is it? Bigger than a breadbox?"

"Bigger than one ship can haul. Bigger than three ships. That's why—"

More noise issued from the other end of the restaurant, and four young men, talking loudly and walking a bit uncertainly made their way toward Wilson's table. The four newcomers were dressed much like Wilson and his friends and were similarly armed. They walked with what people who didn't hunt asteroids for a living called a "spaceman's swagger".

"This is a hunter's bar!" The obvious leader spoke up. He was the shortest of the lot and the most in need of a shower and a shave. He breathed alcoholically on Wilson. "Whadda you think you're doing here, Pinky?"

"I'm having my dinner, formerly in peace." Wilson didn't appear to look up. He knew that the expression "pinky", among hunters, meant an inexperienced beginner. He also remembered this little man, who'd taken spacemanship courses at the same time he had, downsystem, in the Moon. "Look around, Shorty. This isn't a bar, it's a restaurant, Deep Space Little America, and the only asteroid hunters here are at this table."

Which could be taken as an insult or not, as the little man preferred.

Starting to anger, Shorty said, "You're no hunter, rich boy! Prove it!"

Wilson pointed to the window in the floor, where *Mighty Mouse's Girlfriend* was coming around again. "There's my ship, Shorty. And you know perfectly well that I've been doing this exactly as long as you have."

Shorty snarled, "You didn't earn that ship, Pinky, you bought it!"

"Way I heard it, you inherited yours. I bought mine with money I earned." In some locales—what was left of southern California, for instance—"inherit" was a euphemism for killing somebody and taking their property.

"Oh, that's right." He got his friends' attention with his elbows. "I saw it on 3DTV. Look out boys, we've got the Cereal Killer among us!"

Later, Wilson didn't remember how he'd managed to scramble over Scotty. All he knew was that, before he realized what he'd done, he was standing in the aisle between tables with an extremely sore right hand. The fellow who'd insulted him was lying on the floor ten feet away, where he'd fetched up against another booth, following a long skid.

Almost immediately, one of Shorty's pals, the one Wilson thought of as "Boils" rounded on him, his arm cocked back, telegraphing a punch. He never got to make it, however, as Marko seized his elbow from behind, spun him around, and punched him hard in the solar plexus. Boils sank to his knees, pitched over, and made retching noises.

While Boils was preoccupied vomiting on the floor, another of the four thugs, the one Wilson thought of as "Fatty", jumped up onto the seat of the booth, and from there, dived on Marko. Unfortunately for him, Marko moved at the last moment, and Mikey helped by grabbing Fatty's foot. He landed hard on Boils, making a worse mess than before.

The last of the four, whom Wilson thought of as "Beanpole" was tall and lanky, even for someone born in the lower gravity of the Settled Worlds, but there was nothing wrong with his muscles. He reached across the table, grabbed Mikey by his shirtfront, and hauled him out onto the floor, where he began hitting him in the stomach and face. Mikey, who seemed impervious, returned punch for punch, face and stomach.

Having nothing better to do at the moment—although by now, there was plenty of fighting all around him—Wilson stomped on one of Beanpole's feet, as hard as he could. Beanpole raised his head and bellowed. Mikey kicked him in the crotch, and he let go and grabbed himself between the legs. Mikey delivered a good solid punch and Wilson heard Beanpole's nose break with a satisfyingly cartilaginous crunch.

By now, Shorty had gotten to his feet and jumped back into the fray. He'd picked a fiberglass tray off another table and was about to brain Marko with it, but Marko ducked out of the way and tripped him. The tray-slinger struck Wilson at waist-height and both of them went down.

"Sorry 'bout that," Marko said, punching Boils, who had gotten up again.

"'Sokay," Wilson flipped the serving tray up into Shorty's face. He scrambled to his feet and kicked Shorty in the jaw before the thug could get up again. Beanpole was down and staying down, thanks to the pain between his legs and his broken, bleeding nose. Boils, decisively punched by Marko, and Fatty, who'd never recovered from his crash landing on Boils, were out of it, as well. It appeared the fight was over.

It was then that Wilson realized that Scotty had spent the entire time sitting in the corner of the booth, sipping his tea, watching the fight.

Scotty looked up at him and grinned. "Some do the work, while others are—"

They all heard a clacking they recognized and looked up. There, at the end of the aisle, was the waitress, in her hands, a heavy laser- augmented particle beam projector with a pitted .90 caliber emitter orifice.

Swinging it up at them, she asked, "Okay, who wants to get cut in half first?"

*
**

The business card read:

> John F. Crenicichla (Pronounced "krenny KICK la") Consultant
> Hotel Nelson Mandela, Johannesburg, S.A. e-mail: thefish@liaison.
> com telePHONE: 0-010-456-7392

The man who handed it to the uniformed hostess as he stepped through the shuttle's inner airlock door was crisply dressed in an expensively understated blue suit of the latest cut. Well groomed and manicured, he appeared to be in his middle thirties (he was actually a decade older than that) and most women in his experience found his boyish grin irresistible.

As usual, East American Spacelines had set up a sort of boarding office in the airlock of the shuttle that had brought him and a couple of dozen other passengers to the place where the company's City of Newark flagship stood in stationary orbit about the Moon. Boarding a big passenger vessel like this one was a lengthy process and would require many shuttle visits from several destinations. Beyond the outer airlock door, he could see into the open airlock of the larger ship.

Crenicichla believed in traveling light. Today he carried with him only a small African buffalo leather briefcase containing his East American travel papers (it was the last country on Earth that still required anything resembling a passport) and his personal computer, a flat, platinum- titanium alloy square from Sony, perhaps a quarter of an inch thick and three inches on a side, with rounded corners and edges. He had checked in with one additional bag, very small and also of African buffalo leather, containing a change of clothing and various personal items.

"I find the card saves a lot of trouble with pronunciation," he explained.

The hostess nodded, gave him the obligatory welcoming smile, and immediately shifted her attention to the next passenger coming through the airlock door from the shuttle. Crenicichla was prepared to give her excellent marks on her performance. She had seen him on several occasions, most of them at recent Null Delta Em tactical briefings, but no casual observer would ever suspect it. She was another of Krystal's Sweet's protégés, a young woman he knew by her cell-name, Donna.

Just this side of the shuttle's outer airlock door, a small folding desk had been set up for another young woman, whose nametag declared her to be "Denise". Sitting at the front edge of the desktop before her, a tastefully-engraved strip of gold, an inch wide, six or seven inches long, and at least an eighth of an inch thick, attached with small gold nails to what was in Lunar orbit, an even rarer and expensive strip of dark-grained hardwood, identified her as "Purser's Assistant".

"Welcome aboard East American Spacelines' flagship, the *City of Newark*, sir," this young woman said, scarcely looking up at him, but eyeing his meager luggage as if she expected to see a tag hanging from it declaring "No animals were injured or killed during the production of this briefcase". The majority of East Americans were no longer accustomed to seeing animal products openly displayed. "Is there anything you'd care to have locked in the purser's safe? Money? Valuables?"

"Just my vest—it's made from real gorilla chest." Her eyes grew wide and the color went out of her face. "I'm only kidding! No thank you, dear, nothing at all." He smiled down at her (she was another of Krystal's people and like all of them, remarkably good at what she did) and stepped aboard the vast cylinder that was the *City of Newark*.

Something about that solid gold name plaque lingered in his mind. In an earlier era, it would have been made of engraved brass, or even of the kind of plastic that was one color, usually black, on the surface, but another color, usually white, when writing had been cut into it with a special routing machine. Here at a LaGrange point, high above the Earth, a plaque of laser-cut wood would have constituted conspicuous consumption all by itself. That gold plaque was a symptom, he knew, of everything that was wrong with today's Solar System-wide economy.

For all of the alarmist rhetoric spouted daily by that hapless idiot Anna Wertham Savage and her so-called Mass Movement—not to mention Paul Luegner's Null Delta Em—concerning the mythological environmental dangers of importing objects and materials from other worlds, the concerns of both organizations' ultimate sponsors were far different, far more specific and practical. The more gold that was produced by collecting operations in the Asteroid Belt, for example, the less valuable the gold already mined on Earth became. Exactly the same was true of silver, platinum, iridium, palladium, rhodium, and other precious commodities. Handfuls of diamonds were being found out there, as well, and DeBeers, among others, were desperate to keep them offplanet.

Economists called it the "Law of Marginal Utility", although it was actually more of an observation about human psychology. The more there is of anything—tennis shoes, comic books, pistol ammunition—the less any individual unit of it is worth. If iron were scarce and palladium abundant, the two metals would swap positions on the scale of value. It had actually happened, on occasion, with gold and platinum.

Reflexively, unconsciously, Crenicichla reached up and touched a spot on his expensively tailored shirt that covered a series of small but curious scars midway between collar bone and nipple, where he had once been in the habit of attaching the symbol of his membership in the most secretive fraternal organization in the world—a precious metal pin featuring a death's head—to his naked chest whenever he went swimming or did anything else without his clothing on. Although it had nothing to do with the reasons he valued it, the metal in the pin was now worth half as much as it had been when he was a Junior at Yale.

Someday, if individuals continued to be permitted to live and work in space, it might very well be worth nothing at all. And so might be the accumulated fortunes of his sponsors. A nickel-iron asteroid a mile in diameter, he recalled someone saying (and there were hundreds of thousands, if not millions of them), contained more gold—merely as a trace element—than had ever been mined on Earth in ten thousand years of human history.

The idea made him shudder. In many ways, his life so far had been a lucky one. Born into abysmal poverty in a working-class slum of New Bedford, he had supplemented what little the public schools had taught him with a course of study designed by his mother—a public school teacher, until she had been fired for teaching more than just what was required by the official Massachusetts state curriculum. He had won a scholarship to Yale, and in time, attracted the attention of a certain fraternity.

Once he had endured the initiation rituals, they had taken him in and treated him as if he were one of their own, a scion of ancient and unspeakable wealth and power. They had seen to his mother, forcing the educational system to reinstate her with back pay and benefits, making her final years lavish. Now a wealthy man himself, he had sworn many oaths as a part of his initiation, but had privately vowed, as well, to protect the interests of his adopted class, with his very life, if necessary.

After all, they had given it to him.

Some of the flight crew had ventured off the flight deck to greet the latest flock of passengers as they stepped aboard the spaceship. The couple ahead of him were obvious newlyweds, giggling and snuggling, off on a Martian honeymoon. Watching them, he was grateful that they would be dead in two weeks, and not contributing to the human gene pool.

The elderly couple behind him was almost as bad. All they could talk about was returning to the Moon for another set of DeGrey regeneration therapies as soon as possible. Apparently, they were in their nineties, and she hadn't been able to walk for the last twenty years, but had now abandoned her wheelchair. In time, they would come to look and sound just like the couple ahead of him. It was unnatural and disgusting, another abomination that, once they had sufficient political and military power, he and his sponsors would put a stop to.

Except, of course for him and his sponsors.

Captain Alan West was a physically enormous individual, both wide and tall, middle-aged, but without a single gray strand on his head. West shook Crenicichla's hand and welcomed him aboard in an accent that seemed to the younger man to be half Texan and half big-city Jewish. NDE intel said he was from someplace called "Chugwater" in the West American state of Wyoming.

The Captain's second was younger, shorter, slimmer, but completely gray. The tan-line slanting across his forehead said he liked to be outdoors when he wasn't helping to drive a spaceship between the Moon and Mars, probably riding a horse with a sixgun on his hip and a rope in his hand. That hand was rough with calluses when he reached out for Crenicichla's.

The flight engineer (a position entirely as redundant as a fireman on a three hundred mile per hour electric bullet train, but required by the East American unions) was a pretty blonde, leaning more to the voluptuous than the slender or athletic. Like the others, she, too, shook Crenicichla's hand and smiled at him. This would be Minde, he understood, another of Krystal's oddly-assorted collection of female henchpersons.

Glancing at the boarding pass someone had handed him, he noted his stateroom number, 4-3, but, not enjoying Krystal's advantage of having already traveled on this ship, had to consult with a big interactive chart mounted on the bulkhead once he'd exited *City of Newark*'s airlock.

Like all large deep space passenger vessels, East America's *City of Newark* was nothing more than an enormous, flat-ended cylinder, divided into a number of decks built around a service core that housed two or three elevators, numerous cable runs, plumbing for various gases and liquids, and an emergency staircase. The basic design, he knew, had been stolen from shipbuilders working for Pallas' Fritz Marshall Spacelines.

On most of the decks, running around the outside of the service core, there was a circular corridor lined with the numbered doors of passenger compartments. The higher within the structure of the ship—which also meant the further forward—the fewer compartment doors there were, and the larger and more luxurious the compartments behind them. No one ever commented on this peculiarity aboard a passenger liner belonging to what was supposed to be a classless society. In history's last "classless" society, the highly pampered passengers, those possessed of the most power and greatest wealth, had been called _nomenklatura_.

Crenicichla was unapologetically grateful that he qualified for such a title. The airlock he'd come aboard by let out on the lowest of the passenger decks. While he waited for an elevator, he noticed that the facilities were nominally clean and sanitary—eight bunks to a "stateroom", two rooms to a bathroom—but that they were dismal and depressing. An earlier culture had called it "steerage".

Other decks served other purposes. Toward the bottom of the entire stack—aft, as the crew called it, but forward of the engineering spaces—there were a great many cargo storage decks, one of them all of three storys tall for the transportation of heavy equipment, building materials, and vehicles. There was a kennel deck, dedicated to housing pets and livestock, and a gymnasium—although it had no swimming pool.

All the way forward, almost at the top of the stack, there was a big hotel-style restaurant and bar, and forward of that, accessible by a fancy spiral staircase of wrought iron, a comfortable observation lounge.

The flight deck, or control room, or bridge (the brochures and the crew used the expressions interchangeably) was walled off with a thick, circular, bulletproof transparency. It stood in the center of the observation lounge, but the only access to it was by a secured elevator from the service core.

Crenicichla's ticket was for Deck Four, the second most comfortable and expensive passenger accommodation aboard the ship. If he hadn't acquired it so late in the game—having been abruptly ordered by his sponsors to do so—he'd have demanded Deck Three. Years ago, he had very carefully arranged for his undercover identity to be wealthy, accustomed only to the very best. This not only gave him open entry to any social level he desired, but served to gather all the most decorative and compliant women. His undercover identity also required that he attract a lot of women.

In the two weeks he had before the real action began and he had to abandon the *City of Newark* along with the Null Delta Em people he was supposedly watching over, he had plans to enjoy this excursion thoroughly.

Passenger Deck Four, the boarding pass specified, Stateroom Number Three. Crenicichla opened the gasketed door—right, he recalled, these wedge-shaped cabins could detach from the service core, becoming lifeboats if it was required of them—and went inside, closing it behind him and double-locking it. He looked around the small room very carefully, making certain no one was waiting to ambush him. Although it looked a great deal like any hotel room, there were no big windows on the curved outer wall, only a porthole, covered by a small, silly curtain.

Crenicichla set his briefcase on the small writing table and extracted his computer. He called up the virtual keyboard and display screen, and activated a security program. It would detect hidden cameras and listening devices, rendering useless those he chose to leave in place.

In the bathroom, he looked inside the medicine cabinet and found a screw holding it to the wall. The paint in the screw's slot had been slightly chipped and he could see bare metal. That was a mistake somebody should probably be gigged for. Extracting a ten dollar coin from his pocket, he turned the screw. The entire cabinet swung away from the bulkhead on hidden hinges. Inside the compartment he found behind it, was a large manila envelope, sealed with a common bronze office clasp.

This was a principal reason he'd acted to defeat any surveillance devices that might be in the compartment. Inside the envelope, which he laid on the vanity counter, was a special pistol, the most recent weapon to be issued to the East American and United Nations military. It held cartridges in a magazine and shot copper-jacketed lead bullets like most handguns still did, even in this century, but each of them had been treated with an extremely fast-acting neurotoxin, released only by the energy of the bullet's impact, and would also be charged, on its trip through the barrel, with three hundred thousand volts of electricity.

Deal with that, Wilson Ngu, Crenicichla muttered to himself, surprised at the vehemence of his feelings concerning the bloodthirsty boy from Ceres. On the other hand, the Environmental Defense Brigade had been his own pet idea—he mourned its several fatalities; many of them had been friends, and only hoped the survivors wouldn't identify him as their mentor—a fine and noble idea that the wealthy young gunslinger had erased from the board before it had even gotten started.

He put the pistol back in its envelope, closed it with its bronze fastener, and stowed the package away again behind the cabinet. He wouldn't be needing it yet, not for two weeks. But it certainly was a convenience, he thought, having so many people in so many sensitive positions.

About now, Krystal's operatives should be finding their weapons, too—those who had just come aboard. The others—copilot, purser's assistant, and hostess—were the folks who'd stashed these deadly toys here to begin with, proving once again that you can't prevent crime, you can only move it, in this case from the passengers to the crew.

Someone knocked on the door. The small screen on its inside showed the face of Denise, the Purser's Assistant. She shouldn't be here like this.

He swung the door aside and opened his mouth to reprimand her.

"Good day, Mr. … Krennykickla." She studied a clipboard in her hand intently. "I hope I pronounced that right. We're letting all of the higher deck passengers know that it's only a few minutes before departure."

She *was* good. "Thank you, Miss. Do I have to do anything special?"

"No sir. For a moment, you'll just feel a little like you're in an elevator. We'll start at a sixth of a gee and accelerate gradually to a third of a gee at Turnover—that's the same as Mars' gravity—and remain at that rate of acceleration until we arrive at Mars' orbit."

He nodded. "Well, thanks again, Miss—Denise. Do you require a tip?"

"Oh, no, sir. East American Spacelines' tariffs strictly forbid it." She turned a little, as if to take her leave, and fluttered her eyelashes.

"I see." He slipped her a hundred dollar bill exactly as he would have been expected to by anybody watching. "Very well, then, thank you again."

"Thank you, sir."

He closed the door, got a flask from the one small piece of check-through luggage he'd discovered waiting for him in the stateroom, and poured himself a healthy drink. The ship's 3DTV system followed East American "broadcast standards", which meant that there was virtually nothing on worth watching, but he found a soccer game, reclined on the bed, drank his drink, and eventually took a nap, missing the thrill of takeoff.

CHAPTER THIRTY-FIVE: THE DIAMOND ROGUE

We've all heard it said that people who've been married for a long time tend to look like one another. I can't really testify to that, but I do believe that people who are *going* to be married for a long time tend to think like one another from the beginning. That's why they fall in love in the first place, and that's what makes it work. —*The Diaries of Rosalie Frazier Ngu*

"WOULD YOU CARE FOR A little more of this cocoa?" Adam asked.

A breeze off Lake Selous stirred, bringing more leaves down from the trees. Pallas was having an Autumn, courtesy of Weather Control, and it would be enjoyable. The breeze was warm. An efficiently quiet machine the size of a small suitcase traveled between the lake and the house, cutting the grass and converting the orange and yellow leaves it found to a fine powder.

Ardith replied, "No, thank you, dear, I'm about cocoaed out." As he put the Thermos down, she snuggled into the red plaid blanket he'd covered her with when she'd sat down on the recliner, so that only her dark eyes showed. She felt better now, but she was still weak from moment to moment, and got chilled easily. "But I don't want to go back indoors just yet." She glared back toward the house. "My phone's in there, and more reports from my lab people that nothing has changed up there."

She used her eyes to indicate the giant Drake-Tealy object orbiting Pallas.

A few yards away, a fat red squirrel scampered over the backs of a pair of ship-lapped rowboats that had been pulled out of the lake and turned over. Birds sang in the kind of sunshine peculiar to Fall, and an occasional whitecap on the lake showed it was breezy out there, too.

Their lives were here, Adam thought. Not far off, screened by a row of trees, lay the final resting places of most of the Ngu family, excepting Emerson and Rosalie, who had disappeared, and their son Bill, his own father, of whom there had been nothing left to bury. Rosalie had had her mother, Gretchen Singh Altman, reburied here, as well. Adam had played among the markers as a child, and so had Ardith. Now his brother Lindsay was here, too. It was hard to believe it, sometimes, let alone endure it.

Sitting in an upright chair beside his wife, Adam nodded. "Mine, too. I'm grateful Arleigh was willing to oversee repairs to the atmospheric envelope for a while. I need time to think. And breathe. And keep you company. Whatever else has happened between us, I owe you that, and I want it, too. You're still by far the most interesting person I ever met."

On the lake, a small squadron of mallard ducks made an impressive amphibious landing and immediately began bobbing for food until, in their very midst, a huge fish jumped into the air, scattering the flock. Beneath the edge of her blanket, Ardith smiled. "That's about the nicest compliment I've ever received." She sighed and tilted her head over to rest it on his arm where it lay on the arm of his chair. "Why the hell can't we get along for more than about three days, my love?"

He shook his head. "My darling Ardith, if I knew that … "

"You could die a happy man?" she asked, mischief in her eyes.

He looked at her. She was also the most beautiful woman he'd ever known, but for some reason she never seemed to like to hear it. "Yes, I believe I could. Whenever we are getting along, well, I carry the happiness of that around with me for months afterward. Sometimes for years."

"Me, too." Against a feeling that her heart was about to stop beating, she took a determined breath. "Adam, we have to do something about this. And no, I don't know what. We've been married for twenty years and we've spent, I guess, about ten percent of that whole time actually living together. I don't want to do it that way anymore, do you?"

He didn't want to, and said so, hoping all of this wasn't leading up to a divorce. If it did, he wasn't sure he would want to go on living.

"For what it's worth," she added, "I think the whole thing's my fault."

He blinked, his train of thought derailed. "What makes you think that?"

Ardith took another deep breath. "I believe it was that visit that your mother paid me in the hospital that got me started thinking about it. You know, I've had a lot of time lately, in the hospital at first, and then resting here at home, to examine every aspect of it in fine detail."

"That doesn't sound particularly healthy. I've never much cared for—"

"Sooner or later, Adam, sooner or later, as I begin to feel closer to you, some little nastiness inside me starts to exercise its evil influence. It makes me willfully misinterpret the most innocent thing you say. It makes me feel angry at you and everything else in sight. I'm ashamed to say I feel the same thing when I'm close to our kids. Whenever I find myself getting close, then this core of rage takes over."

"My mother the marriage counselor." He sat silently for a moment. Then: "Rage?"

"Yes, rage. That's what I said, and ... and who the hell are you to— damn it! It started up again, all by itself. You see what I mean, don't you? This must seem perfectly insane to you. In all honesty, Adam, I can't understand why you've stayed married to me so long."

"Because, my very dear, of that first time I kissed you on your parents' second floor deck." He nodded in the general direction of the Zacharenko house, the next residence north along the Lake Selous shore. It was dark, empty, and locked up at present; its owners were upsystem at the Jupiter habitat. "Since then, I never really looked at another—"

"Really?" she grinned. "Not even your sexy little Asian office assistant?"

"Ingrid?" Adam shrugged and looked perplexed. "You think of Ingrid Andersson as sexy? Hmmm ... Well, I suppose you could look at her that way if you really worked at it. She's kind of young, though, don't you think?"

She laughed. "The other woman usually is, Adam."

"But that's exactly what I'm trying to tell you. Since you were seventeen, there hasn't ever been another woman for me. Sometimes I've wished—"

"I'll bet you have."

His hands were up: "Not fair, my dear, not fair. You set that one up, yourself."

"Most first wives do," she replied. "Okay, how about before I was seventeen?"

"What? Well, you've got me there. Sarah, this blond in my Spanish class—"

"Adam Ngu, you were home-schooled, just like me, you complete, utter, and total fraud! In fact, we learned Spanish together, you and I, from our neighbor old Mrs. Gonzales." She punched his shoulder, hard.

"Well you know what they say, 'Spanish is a loving tongue'."

"You keep your tongue out of it—at least until we're back in the house." Then she reddened at what she'd said to him, and fell silent.

Adam slipped out of his chair and knelt beside hers, so he could hold her in his arms. She put her hand on his cheek and he kissed her fingertips. Her recent illness was one of the most frightening things he'd ever experienced; the thought of losing her was unbearable. "I guess I shouldn't admit it, but your first time was my first time, as well."

"Our first Spanish lesson?"

"No, you know what I mean—in the boat house over there."

She blushed again, into his shoulder. "Hey, I knew that."

"Did you also know," he asked her, "that in all those years—twenty-two of them—we've never had a vacation together? Not even a honeymoon?"

She crinkled her forehead. "That's right. They'd just brought in a whole load of Drake-Tealy Objects loaded with beryllium, and you were working on the refit of Marshall's *Lady of Spain* for the Jupiter route."

"What would you think about taking a vacation together? The canopy fix will take months, and even if you have a giant Drake-Tealy Object alive and pulsing in orbit, nobody's demanding that you go back right away."

"Thanks a lot! It's nice to feel indispensable … Where would we go?"

"How about Mars? Llyra will be there pretty soon, and—although I can't believe it when I'm saying it—we haven't seen her in two years. Our beautiful little girl, and we haven't seen her in two years."

Ardith considered it. "Or Jasmeen, for that matter. But we'd be helpless there, Adam, in a third of a standard gee, almost seven times what we were born to and grew up in. We'd be wheelchair bound at the very least. And if both of us were invalids, who would take care of us?"

Adam answered, tentatively, "My mother?"

This time when she hit him, he said, "Ow!"

*
**

"I never would have stumbled across it," Marko told them as they left the security office, following the fight in the restaurant, "if it hadn't been for that frigging short circuit in *Mina*'s command console."

He looked at each of his three friends expectantly. Wilson refrained from repeating what Marko had just told them, but neither Mikey nor Scotty could resist: "A short circuit in your command console?"

"Is there an echo in here?" Marko laughed. "Yeah, that's exactly what happened, all right. For some reason all my communications were going out at radar frequencies, while my radar was trying to operate on comm frequencies. People must have thought that First Contact had finally happened."

"That's what you get for drinking soda pop while you're at the con. Sooner or later, you're gonna squirt a baggie in your keyboard, and—"

"Thanks, Mikey, shut up. Anyway, this Big Black Rock happened to be passing—close enough to singe my frigging hair—but it doesn't seem to absorb comm frequencies quite as well as it does radar. Thanks to the radio-absorptive quality of its surface, it was impossible to peer into the interior, determine whether it was an aggregate of some kind, a solid, or just a gigantic overcooked marshmallow. I watched it with my lidar, too, and let my computer plot its line of flight. Then I unsnarled my wiring and skedaddled back here to Holbrook to enlist some help."

"Guess it's a good thing Mikey and Scotty were handy," Wilson observed. Holbrook was a very popular place in this half of the Solar System. In fact, it was the only place, until you got to the orbit of Mars.

"No such a thing," said Marko, shaking his head. They reached an elevator, got in, and Wilson pushed some buttons. They were headed for their rented quarters and a decent night's rest in the other half of the station. Wilson hadn't been up that long, himself, but he could always catch up on his reading, his correspondence, or watch a movie. Once again, he was tempted to purchase some female companionship, but he didn't know how, and it had always struck him as a little shabby and demeaning, although whether to him or to the lady or both, he wasn't prepared to contemplate.

In any case, at present, they were taking an elevator "upstairs" to the hub. There, they would take another car—traveling at right angles to the first, and in zero gravity—to the residential half of Holbrook Station.

And finally, another elevator would carry them down to whatever floor they'd been assigned. Wilson had chosen one third gee.

The brief voyage gave them all a chance to talk.

"Matter of fact, I was downsystem, mooching around the junkyards at L-Three, looking for spare parts," Mikey told him with a straight face. "Poor *Albuquerque Gal* had a catastrophically failed flux capacitor that was gradually fractionating her dilithium crystals, and seriously decalibrating the matter-antimatter ratio in my portside interociter."

"At one point twenty-one jigawatts?" Marko inquired, deliberately mispronouncing it.

"Ah, the classics endure forever," Scotty observed. "As for me, *Nessie* and I were in the middle of the Belt, checking out rumors of gold on Vesta. Guess what: there's no gold on, in, or around that dumb chunk of granite. If this expedition doesn't turn out to be something wonderfully decent, I'm seriously out of pocket for reaction mass and consumables."

The real surprise," Marko told Wilson, generating a hurt sort of tone, "was finding you sitting in that eatery, complacently munching a hot turkey sandwich instead of coming out treasure hunting with your old friends who have absolutely nothing but your best interests at heart."

The elevator reach the top of its shaft. A recorded voice reminded them that they were in a microgravity section of the station. The door opened.

Wilson slapped his backside. "Just checking that my wallet's still there."

Marko gave him an evil laugh. They floated out.

As he grabbed a nylon handstrap—there were several of them, color coded, and running in different directions along the corridor—Mikey shook his head. "No, the surprise was we didn't get fined or jailed for that fight. Happily, Shorty and his pals are well known troublemakers and Security just assumed that they'd started it."

Wilson protested, "But they *did* start it!"

"No, Wilson, " Marko replied. "All that guy Shorty did was insult you verbally. 'Sticks and stones' and all that. You threw the first punch."

Wilson thought about it. "You're right. I guess I did."

They reached the door to the hub-length elevator. As the panel slid open, Scotty raised his eyebrows. "Think we should have told them?"

As they swung up and into the car, Marko, Mikey, and Wilson laughed.

⁎⁎

At my advanced age, Julie lectured herself, you'd think that I wouldn't get so excited. That was the problem with modern science keeping the juices flowing, she had found. Although she reasoned and acted, in most respects, like the seventy-eight year-old grandmother she happened to be, she often experienced the emotional roller coaster ups and downs of the twenty-three year-old child-woman she physically resembled.

Ah, well, she thought, my only granddaughter is finally coming to see me, here in my home, on the adopted native planet that I love. If that didn't constitute something for a little old lady—or a twenty-three year-old child-woman—to get all excited about, she didn't know what did.

At the moment, Julie stood in her favorite room, the uppermost cupola of her famous Victorian fantasy house—like most of the older homes on Mars, it was capable, in an emergency, of being sealed off and pressurized in only a few seconds—looking out through curved glass windows, over a vast prairie covered in yellow plant-life, the alien fungus that had made it possible for people to live and breathe on Mars.

Take a deep breath, Julie, someone extremely important to her had told her once, *and inhale a dream.* That someone had been Billy Ngu, only a few days after she'd deserted the United States Marine Corps.

Inhale a dream. The dreamers had eventually become her sisters-in-law, Mirella and Teal Ngu, scientists who had developed that stuff out there, starting with a not quite microscopic lifeform that they had discovered among the airless, frozen, rocky crags of Ceres itself—long before anyone had thought of terraforming it—and later, on many other asteroids, as well. The Belt had turned out to be crawling with it.

It was amazing how persistent life had proven itself to be, Julie reflected. The organism growing out there on the Martian prairie had been flourishing, thanks to a photosynthetic process (highly unusual in a fungus) leaching minerals and absorbing infinitesimal amounts of water from the carbonaceous chondritic soil. In a hard vacuum and at nearly Absolute Zero, the stuff had grown very slowly, but it had grown.

She ran a finger along a dusty window sill. Llyra would be here in only two weeks. Better get somebody in to clean. It was clearly beyond the capabilities of her little old house robots. There were better machines now, she knew. Sometimes it was difficult to remember to keep up with the latest technology when the next-to-latest seemed to serve adequately.

Julie wondered if her granddaughter would want a room to herself, possibly this room, at the very peak of the house, or would prefer to share a room with her coach—Jasmeen, a very pretty name for a very pretty and accomplished young woman—as she had in the Moon. Julie's own teenage years had been so very different from Llyra's—basically bringing herself up in the dirty, cutthroat metropolitan jungle that was Newark (ironically, the name of the interplanetary liner that was bringing Llyra to her)—that she couldn't anticipate the girl's wishes.

Calm down, set it aside, wait.

Think about something else.

The most important feature of the yellow photosynthetic fungus was that it generated and stored great volumes of oxygen in its branching tubules as a defense against spacegoing bacteria and virus that no one had even suspected the existence of before the macaroni plant itself had been discovered. On Mars, in an environment that it may well have considered lushly tropical—had it been capable of considering anything at all—at a hundred thousand times its original size, and growing at a rate that had astonished even its creators, the peculiar organism soon became the very breath of life for a planet that had been violently stripped of its atmosphere roughly four billion years ago.

Evidence of that violence remained. It was the lowest, coldest spot on Mars.

Out across the prairie, Julie could just make out the highway that ran between Bradbury and Coprates City. She ordered the windows to magnify the view. Truck-trains of seven or eight trailers, double-wide and double-tall, blurred by at five or six hundred miles an hour, carrying goods from city to city, where an airless wasteland had existed only two generations earlier. Just as they once had on Earth, truckers dressed their own way, told their own stories, sang their own songs.

Billy and Brody Ngu had brought their sisters' improved fungus to Mars as a part of their effort to rescue the seventh U.S./U.N. expedition, where it ultimately came to be known variously as "oxymold" "happy-grass", "tubeweed", "kudzuroni", and "Shmoogunk". Most of those who called themselves Martians simply called it "macaroni plant" because, by the time the Ngu sisters had finished with it, it was the size, and shape—arranged in branching networks—of that favorite children's' food. Bright yellow chlorophyll gave it its cheesy color.

It could also be pressed for the water it contained, boiled, pan-fried, baked, or eaten raw in an emergency—or woven into a pair of boots.

The Red Planet soon became the Yellow Planet, infuriating Earth's environmentalists, and prompting the launch of a punitive military mission of which Julie—as a young officer of Marines—had been a part.

Until she'd witnessed at first hand the savage slaughter, the barbaric cruelty of which the joint U.N./U.S, punitive mission was capable, under the direct orders of the Secretary General and the President.

Until she'd fallen in love with Billy Ngu.

Sometimes, Julie had noticed last year, she could see Billy looking back at her when she gazed deeply into her granddaughter's eyes.

Two weeks.

**

This blasted rock was *fast*, thought Wilson, relative to the Sun's center, which was used out here as the theoretical stationary reference point. Its orbit, a flattened loop that lay mostly outside the System at a forty-five degree angle to the ecliptic, was just ... *strange*.

What Wilson said, though, was "But I don't *have* that much chainlink!"

"Neither do any of us, Wilson," came Mikey's harried-sounding reply over the intership communication system. Apparently Marko and Scotty were having similar shiphandling problems, both with equipment and the rock's remarkable velocity, about forty miles per second. It had come from somewhere outside the Solar System, perhaps. "You've got the most powerful engines of the three of us, my fine feathered fiend. Just see if you can't snag a little bitty corner of the goddamn thing, okay?"

Wilson protested. "It's a *round* goddamn thing, Mikey! It doesn't *have* any corners!" Nevertheless, he decided to give the idea a try. Perhaps if he dragged his steel mesh net over the target—provided he could catch up and match velocities with it—it would find some kind of a snag that he hadn't seen on instruments or with his naked eye.

Not entirely trusting his computer in these unusual circumstances, Wilson laid in a course correction that he'd calculated in his head, and punched the ENTER button. As his trio of powerful engines burst fully into life, kicking him back in his seat, and the stars reeled around *Mighty Mouse's Girlfriend*, he couldn't quite resist shouting "*Yee-haw!*"

"I'll see that 'Yee-haw!'", exclaimed Scotty, making a similar course correction, "and raise you a 'Yippie-kiyo!'" Mikey and Marko immediately followed them. Four nuclear fusion-powered raptors stooped on what Wilson enjoyed thinking of as a poor, innocent, helpless asteroid.

It seemed to grow ominously as he drew nearer.

This was the first time Wilson had followed a lead that hadn't been given to him—or more accurately, sold to him—by the Moon's Larsen Farside Observatory. At the beginning of the undertaking, he'd been full of trepidation about that. Somehow, knowing that the famous Lunar observatory was operated by Jasmeen's comical Chechen uncles had become important. The two had become a kind of surrogate family to him.

But the information that had been supplied by his three hunting pals had certainly proven accurate. He didn't know whether this was the legendary Diamond Rogue or not, but it was one weird hunk of space junk.

As he reclined in his pilot's chair pushing buttons, suspended within the big plastic bubble that constituted the nose of *Mighty Mouse's Girlfriend*, the stars slewed dizzily around him and his little ship once more, until his outboard floodlights fell across the rock.

And there it was in all of its lack of glory, less than half a mile away now, and just as he'd observed to his three friends, the asteroid was an almost perfect, almost featureless sphere. It was, of course, rather larger than most of the objects that might ordinarily interest the average asteroid hunter—unless, of course, they happened to be on an attractively bounty-paying collision course with Earth or one of the Settled Worlds. It was roughly the size of a fifteen-or twenty-story downtown office building back on Earth, not anywhere near large enough for its own gravity to have pulled it into that spherical shape.

There was some physical law about that, although at the moment he couldn't remember it. He only knew that some other force or forces must have shaped it. Was it possible that it was some kind of alien artifact?

Another giant Drake-Tealy object?

Now that the floodlights of all four ships shone across it, he could see that it was the darkest object he'd ever come across in space (except for those objects that he hadn't seen at all, he joked with himself, because they were so dark). Asteroids tended not to reflect much light in any case. Carbonaceous chondrites were a dark grayish-brown, about the color and texture, as everybody out here always enjoyed putting it, of a slightly over-done chocolate chip cookie.

By comparison, this bizarre object was an utter, pitch black, the color of freshly-poured asphalt. Many of the moons of the gas giants upsystem, beyond the Belt—Jupiter, Saturn, Uranus, and Neptune—were very nearly this dark. Maybe this thing had originally come from Out There somewhere. That might account for its extreme velocity. The hunters had to keep their floodlights on it constantly or risk losing it. Even then it was pretty difficult to see, which meant that it must be covered with, and probably contained, an awful lot of relatively pure carbon.

Carbon, of course, is uncooked diamonds.

But Wilson realized he was getting ahead of himself. Who could tell what this big black object was before they actually brought it in and cut it up? (Briefly, he imagined a crisply-faceted and highly polished diamond the size of a twenty-story office building.) Why, it might be nothing more than a gigantic lump of anthracite intended for the Christmas stocking of a naughty—and extremely large—little boy.

Another item that made it … well, the term was "anomalous" … was that radar didn't seem to work on it. It appeared to absorb the wavelengths most often employed by human beings for finding things in space.

Sometimes hunters' vessels disappeared for no discernable reason. Wilson wondered how many of these things he'd come close to hitting, himself.

*
**

The letters embossed into the card read:

> Will you please do me the honor of gracing my table
> with your presence at dinner this evening?
>
> Alan R. West,
> Captain *City of Newark* East American Spacelines

"For second time?" From the bathroom, or "head" as the crew called it, Jasmeen entered the small but cozy cabin she shared with Llyra, elbows in the air, trying to do something with her hair. Neither of them had anything resembling dinner clothing, but they were making do with what they had. The fact they were young and beautiful helped a lot.

The fact that they didn't really know it helped even more.

"Apparently," Llyra answered. She was wearing a colorful summer dress with spaghetti straps and had borrowed a big, sheer scarf from her coach for her shoulders. With her hair up, and earrings, Jasmeen thought Llyra looked at least eighteen, three years older than she was.

"I overheard that unpleasant woman," she told Jasmeen, "you know, that Mrs. Erskine down the hall, complaining to somebody in the sauna that she and her family hadn't been invited to dine at the Captain's Table yet. I think she believes that there are rules that he has to follow."

Jasmeen chuckled. "If I were Captain, would invite her to eat in spacious, comfortable airlock, with outer door open for splendid view." Six years older than Llyra, she had brought the "little black dress" she took everywhere, along with a pair of black pumps good for all occasions. She had lent her student a pair of stockings, but could do nothing for her in the shoe department, since the girl's feet were larger.

Llyra laughed, imagining the waiter and the wine steward wearing envirosuits. She picked up the impossibly tiny purse she'd bought in the gift shop the first time, four days ago, that she and Jasmeen had been invited to the Captain's Table. Jasmeen gave up on her hair, took the black, se-quined bag that went with her dress, and a black mesh wrap.

Opening the stateroom door to the circular hallway outside, she held it for Jasmeen, closed it behind them, checked to assure herself it was locked, and headed for one of the elevators in the utility core. There were several people from this deck waiting for it to arrive.

Upstairs—"forward" as the crew called it—they found the dining room on Deck Two, entered, and went directly to the Captain's Table. He wasn't there yet. He was often late and sometimes had to leave his own table early in order to deal with some problem in shiphandling. Not wanting to sit down at the moment—Jasmeen's dress hadn't really been meant for sitting, and could be uncomfortable even at one sixth of a gee—Jasmeen and Llyra went to a small bar in the corner.

"And what can I do for you ladies?" the bartender asked with a cheerful politeness. "And how old is the young lady in the flowered dress?"

Jasmeen shook her head. She'd heard of this East American nonsense from her folks. You had to be eighteen or twenty-one or thirty-five or something to purchase alcoholic beverages. These days, most of the rest of the Earth left that up to a child's parents. On Mars—and she knew it was this way on Pallas, too—young people could buy and drink anything, from the first moment they could shoot straight.

"My friend is eighteen last December. Me, I am old lady. I am twenty-one."

"And you have an honest face," replied the bartender. "So what can I—"

"We will both have strawberry daiquiri," Jasmeen said. "Keep little umbrella."

"Right. Two strawberry dacks coming up! That'll be two hundred neobucks."

*
**

"Maybe we oughta call you 'Spider'," Marko observed to Wilson as they crawled across the face of a net made of all the chainlink the four young asteroid hunters possessed. "Since this was your bright idea and all."

It was hard work—oxygen and water intensive—and the nanobot scrubbers that kept his faceplate clear were working just as hard as he was.

It had been a simple matter—at least in theory—to take four pieces of the material, squares of steel mesh a quarter of a mile on a side, and fasten them together at their edges into a square half a mile on a side, us-ing thumb-sized clamps originally intended to repair the stuff. They felt lucky to have enough of the clamps, but the truth was that they tended to accumulate the same way wire coathangers will in one's closet over a year or two, while other things—at one time in history it had been beer can openers—similarly tended to evaporate.

The steel mesh squares had come from each of their little ships as standard equipment of the trade. The four hunters had left their vessels, now falling along the same course as their unusual find and slightly ahead of it, to erect their screen in front of it. Wilson had insisted on overlapping the pieces of chainlink at least a yard deep, and using every clamp they had, to make it into a single, larger piece.

He and Marko had accomplished that much, while Mikey and Scotty had started at the center of each square and woven steel and titanium cable through the mesh, toward the outside corner, with another mile or so of cable floating free. These they would attach to each of their ships.

"That," Marko announced, "was my last clamp. What now, glorious leader?"

"That's 'Imperious Leader', and don't you forget it," Wilson told him. "You just can't see my bright red eyeball flicking from side to side inside this helmet. The next thing we do, once our colleagues are through with their half of the chores, is hook the four cables to our ships."

That, Wilson knew, would only be the beginning of the grueling, horribly gradual process of slowing the mysterious rock down. He'd already run the calculations. It would require two and a half months of steady, gentle deceleration to get it down to the right velocity and course to bring them all—eventually—back to the Earth/Moon System.

If he recalled correctly, the East American spaceliner *City of Newark* would be at Turnover pretty soon. which meant that he wouldn't be greeting his little sister when she arrived on Mars, as he'd planned.

Oh, well, he'd been taught all his life, by his parents and his uncles, and his grandmother, that doing the job came first. He hoped that this rock would turn out to be worth something. The scans looked promising, but they hadn't had a chance to set foot on it yet and find out for sure. He looked forward to doing that, once it was no longer decelerating.

"I'm all done, here," Scotty told his friends. He sounded as if he were exhausted. Suit work is hard work. "I'll take this cable back to *Nessie*."

Mikey said, "Me, too. I'll take the cable opposite his, to keep this giant window screen in one place. You guys, too: we need to get this done pretty quickly, because I'm running out of air and delta vee."

Wilson looked back to the center of the net, a quarter of a mile away, where all four pieces met. Floating on a short tether, a large bag of spaceworthy material was rigged out with flashing lights. "It's nothing to worry about, Mikey. We've got extra food, air, water, and fuel here. After everybody's safely aboard their ships, I'll take it in."

"In the immortal words of Carlin Himself," intoned Scotty, "'Spare air is fair'."

"That's 'Spare *hair*'," Mikey corrected him. "I've got my end and am heading back to *Albuquerque Gal*. Once we've started decelerating, I'm for a long shower—suits make me itch—and about twelve hours' sleep."

"Sounds like a plan, to me," Marko observed. "I'm the highest in the alphabet. I guess I'll take the first watch. Mikey, you'll be next."

"Now isn't that sweet?" said a fifth voice that Wilson didn't recognize at first. "And here we all are, just in time to tuck you in!"

It appeared they'd been caught flat-footed, outside of their respective ships, and utterly helpless. There was no way to see what direction the voice was coming from, but they found out soon enough when a bright yellow laser beam lashed past them to impact on the surface of the asteroid. The huge puff of smoke it made quickly dissipated.

CHAPTER THIRTY-SIX: STAND AND DELIVER

It's important to remember, when you're trying to figure out who to trust to protect you from things like piracy and terrorism, that despite the culprits' protestations to the contrary, the vast majority of such crimes—perhaps 999,999 incidents out of a million—are committed by governments themselves.

Between sovereign nation-states and planets, for example, it's called "customs".

Moreover, what precious few resolutions that do not bring about the utter destruction of the very people, places, and things they're intended to protect, are invariably achieved by private hands. —*The Diaries of Rosalie Frazier Ngu*

JUST LIKE EVERY OTHER PASSENGER ship in the solar system—with the single, notable exception of Fritz Marshall Spaceways' *Beautiful Dreamer*—East American Spacelines' *City of Newark* had no swimming pool.

What it did have, if not accurately describable as even better, or even just as good, was nevertheless different and enjoyable and soon came to be a favorite place for almost anyone of any age to rest and relax.

Its official title was the "Solarium Deck". Its windows ran around the hull, just below the passenger decks, for its entire circumference and broke the liner's neatly tubular silhouette by thrusting outward, their down-slanting top halves meeting their up-slating bottom halves at least a dozen feet outboard, beyond the principle outline of the hull. They could be retracted if need be—for example if the ship's radar detected a swarm of meteors ahead—and covered with armored shutters.

Part of the Solarium Deck had been partitioned off—mostly with glass—and were occupied by numerous exercise machines and weight racks, half a dozen showers, and a good sauna. The inevitable ship's centrifuge was smaller than that of *Beautiful Dreamer*, and located immediately beneath the Solarium Deck, accessible from the service core.

The walls and floor were beautifully tiled and decorated in bright colors and various plantings. The temperature was maintained at a steady ninety degrees Fahrenheit, the humidity at around eighty-five. Ambient sunlight was supplemented with an impressive optical fiber array and plenty of artificial light. There were deck chairs and recliners to be found everywhere, full of people sunbathing. Everybody seemed to wear sunglasses, and the air would have been heavy with the odor of various tanning preparations, had it not been for the excellent air exchange facilities demanded by the first class passengers.

But the most attractive feature of the Solarium Deck was its "stream", a depression five feet wide down the center of the whole deck, through which perhaps eighteen inches of clean, warm water coursed energetically. Passengers couldn't swim in it, but they could lie or sit in it, or along its tiled edges. Children could play in it and splash each other. A three-foot "waterfall" marked the place where water was taken out of the stream, purified, and put back into the circuit.

The man who thought of himself as the Fastest Gun in the Moon relaxed in a recliner under a potted palm tree, pretending to read a best-seller. Over the bathing trunks he'd just purchased—which made him self-conscious; he hadn't gone out in public this way, almost naked, for decades—he wore a towel from his room in which he'd concealed a plastic and glass fiber knife he'd smuggled aboard the *City of Newark* on his back, under a carefully contrived medical back brace.

He'd waited until the last minute, when the crowd of boarders was thickest and the security drones would be exhausted and reluctant to risk a lawsuit by harassing someone who was obviously seriously handicapped.

The knife, an outsized copy of the old mid-twentieth century Buck "Kalinga", had a curved, nine-inch blade much like a Middle Eastern sash-dagger, with a wickedly sharp point and—an innovation—a serrated edge. It had been produced in its original form for tasks like skinning elephants. He thought of it as his "Brown Recluse" because it was cast in that color, and treated with selenium salts to delay healing of the wounds it produced. He'd cut his thumb with it six weeks ago, and it still hadn't healed.

At last, through a pneumatic door from the ladies' locker room there emerged the reason he was here today, exposing his fishbelly white flesh to an unwitting public. (He'd always felt his feet looked funny, too.) Llyra Ngu and Jasmeen Khalidov looked around, commented to each other on the brightness, heat, and humidity just as everybody did, and picked out a couple of fragile chairs to drape their towels over. He might have regarded them both as outrageously beautiful, if he hadn't been thinking of them as his "daughters" for the past two years.

The two girls went to the "stream", sat on its edge, and let their feet down into the swift-moving water, until Llyra finally stood up in it, lowered herself to her belly and her elbows, and let her feet and legs float behind her. The fast-moving water formed a wave around her chest and chin, and she appeared to be supremely comfortable and at ease.

The Fastest Gun in the Moon looked around carefully, as he had when he'd first arrived. None of Krystal Sweet's henchpersons were here, of that he was reasonably certain. Within sight, he counted fourteen women, most of them middle-aged and very fat. (If the fascist East American government ever wanted to do something legislatively about overweight women in bathing suits, he might just forget to protest.)

There were also two dozen children of various ages, sexes, odors, and decibel ratings, and half a dozen men, mostly older than he was, mostly paler, hairier, balder, and spindlier than he was. He was at least a head and a half taller, on the other hand, than any of them.

Which was why he was slouching beneath this sad, captive desert cycad. His extreme height was definitely a handicap in his chosen profession.

He didn't notice anybody watching the girls, so he returned to his bestselling novel from the gift shop. It concerned a valiant federal bureaucrat who had been taken—and was being brainwashed—by vile Pallatian anarchists. The writing was poor and the story ridiculous, but it bore a seal of approval on its cover from the United States' Department of Literature. The East American PTA probably liked it, too, except for the naughty bits.

As he pretended to read, he adjusted a device that looked like an advanced hearing aid, but was designed so that he could eavesdrop on girl talk.

"Didn't you think he was dreamy in his white jacket?" Llyra asked Jasmeen.

The coach adopted a sour look and shook her head. "Dreamy? I do not get silly over East American pretty boy assistant purser. Besides, was obviously not Pallatian. Was a head and a half shorter than you, my little."

Although she faced directly away from him, he could almost hear Llyra bat her eyelashes. "Not a head and a half shorter than you, my even littler."

"Blech!" Jasmeen shook her head again. "When I get silly over male of species—if ever happens, which is extremely not probable—will be over full-grown man, not mere boy. Man who already knows way through life. If capable of septuple Axel and hitting playing card at one hundred yards with pistol, so much the better."

"So speaks Martian Woman, ever practical, ever sensible, never romantic. You'd probably like him to have broad, child-bearing hips, too."

Jasmeen almost laughed, but caught herself and retained her grim demeanor. "Women—females—must be practical, sensible. Life on Mars, even now, is too harsh for anything less. Women are conservators of gene pool in which too many dirty feet and ingrown toenails are dangling."

The Fastest Gun in the Moon had trouble not laughing out loud.

Llyra shot her a raspberry and splashed her in the face with water. "Well, who do you like, Miss practical sensible gene pool conservator?"

"I like Captain West," she replied solemnly. "Too bad he is already married."

*
**

The spacecraft out on the open crater floor was being fueled just for him. Enough magnesium iron silicate dust to take him a hundred million miles.

Inside, watching through the glass walls of the south polar office of Fritz Marshall Spaceways, Adam wondered, *How in the sacred names of Marx and Lennon did we let this happen again?* As he waited, he'd been thumbing through a travel magazine he hadn't read a single word of so far. His sparse luggage was piled beside him on the chrome and leather sofa. He wasn't taking much, but then he hadn't brought much. Despite every expectation to the contrary, he was headed back to Ceres.

Now the maintenance crew was detaching the big plastic hoses out there, and sealing up the fueling ports. Around the rim of the Port

Admundsen crater, ten miles wide, he could see at least a dozen similar operations in progress, homesteader families headed back after a few days of shopping and recreation in the "big city", prospectors ready to go out searching for hidden treasure once again, maybe even a few pirates.

Who could tell?

Maybe even some like him, headed back to wherever they'd come from with a great big black hole in the middle of their existences. He'd tried several times to reconstruct what had happened with Ardith. He'd thought that this time would be different. He always thought that. But as usual, it had taken about three days—three absolutely miraculous days—for her to find an excuse to blow up, screaming and throwing things, her beautiful face reddened, contorted, tears of fury streaming.

Exactly like every single time it looks like maybe we're finally going to make it, he thought, every single time we start getting closer.

Every.

Single.

Time.

He couldn't recall the exact sequence of events. He never could, afterward, and he was willing to bet she couldn't, either. A willfully misinterpreted word or phrase, her hysterically exaggerated reaction, and he was out the door, onto the roof, boarding an ionopter flown by his old friend R.G. Edd, who knew them both well enough to keep his mouth shut. A phone call established that there was nothing headed for Ceres from up north, Port Peary, but that he could charter a jumpbuggy at the south pole and be back on Ceres—back in exile—in a few days.

And so, here he was.

This was, Adam reasoned, probably the last performance of this particular farce. No man had ever loved a woman more than he loved Ardith. Even now, the thought of her, of her scent, of her voice, of her body, of what they'd done over the last couple of days, inflamed him. He loved her as he loved the lovely pair of children she had given him, even the four she had tried to give him. He'd promised himself solemnly, before he'd come back to Pallas this time, that if the same old cycle began to happen again, he'd remember what started it.

No such luck. Once again, his relationship with his wife had exploded in his face at the very moment that everything seemed to be going perfectly, and he had no more idea why this time, than the first time it had happened, a couple of years after Llyra had been born. This time, one moment they'd been laughing, wrestling gently, talking about a honeymoon on Mars and of seeing the daughter they both adored. They had both regretted deeply that their son couldn't be there, as well.

The very next moment, she was screaming at him, calling him vile names, and accusing him of vile acts, or at least of vile intentions. The name of his goddamned assistant had come up again, despite the fact that he had never looked on her as anything but a girl, like his own daughter or her coach. Finally, Ardith was ordering him out of his father's—and his grandfather's—house. Bewildered as usual, he'd left.

Outside, he watched a crew in envirosuits pulling a boarding tube toward the jumpbuggy's airlock. Aside from the pilot, the copilot, and an attendant they'd insisted on sending with him, only one individual would be using it today. The way his luck was running, the attendant would turn out to be gorgeous and it would somehow get back to his wife. He realized that he should have rented a jumpbuggy and flown it himself.

Somewhere, deep down inside, he knew that whatever had happened, it wasn't Ardith's fault. He'd seen her face as it began. She'd seemed absolutely bewildered at what she was doing. She hadn't wanted to say the things she'd said, any more than he'd wanted her to say them. If he'd been a religious kind of man, he might have guessed that she was possessed.

But at some point, the very best intentions, the most tender and ardent affection, didn't cut it any more. His home life had been a living hell for twenty years, despite all he'd done to try and push it in some other direction. He couldn't live this way any more. He was a decent human being, too old for this shit, and he deserved something better.

The conclusion made him feel sick and empty inside. What was there in the universe that could be better? Even with all of their troubles, for all of his adult life—and a good deal of his youth—Ardith Zacharenko the lovely, exotic, sexy, bright girl who lived next door, the one with the great big dark eyes a man could fall into and drown in, had been the very definition, at least for him, of desirability, of womanhood.

"Excuse me, Dr. Ngu." The receptionist had come out from behind her counter. A pretty thing, he realized dimly, tall and slender like most Pallatians, she was probably no more than twenty. She was black, with hazel-gray eyes, a turned-up nose and freckles, and a small gap between her upper front teeth he'd always found provocative. She wore her dark, glossy hair in a complex braid curled up on the top of her head.

Adam looked up from the magazine that he hadn't been reading. "Yes?"

"I just wondered if I could get you something, sir, coffee, tea, a Coke?"

He took a deep breath, suddenly aware that there was a whole world outside of himself, a good world that wasn't mourning in abysmal despair.

"Um, no thank you," he told her. "And Miss, I'm not a sir, I'm Adam."

She smiled. A very pretty thing, he realized. "Well, Adam, if you want anything, please let me know. I shouldn't tell you this, but the head office at Port Peary said to take the very best care of you we can."

He nodded. He didn't realize it, but a large measure of Wilson's amazing popularity with the ladies had been inherited from his father. "Well, you're doing just fine, er—" The tag on her blazer said her name was Emily. "You're doing just fine, Emily, and I thank you very much."

As the receptionist walked away, Adam suddenly noticed the girl's miniskirt and her long, shapely legs. *I guess I'm not dead yet*, he thought. The fact was, he'd never been with another woman sexually, which was looking more and more like not such a good idea, maybe. He wondered (it was too long ago for him to remember) what it would be like to make love to a beautiful female without anticipating—like a male mantis or a male black widow—having your head torn off shortly afterward.

He began to think back over the years he'd been with Ardith. Been with Ardith off and on, that was. Many of those years—at the start—had been everything that any man could wish for. More than that, even. Ardith had loved him as he had not been aware a man could be loved. There was nothing she wouldn't do to make him happy, even lots of things he hadn't known he'd wanted. She'd always said she read a lot. As inexperienced as he'd been, back then, he'd known that he was lucky.

But then ... when had it started? She'd been almost suicidally depressed after the last miscarriage. The fourth miscarriage. Those graves were out behind Ngu House, too. Their children that never were. But they'd had Wilson to keep them going, and eventually Llyra. Not for the first time, he marveled at the courage it had taken for Ardith to become pregnant a second, third, fourth, fifth, sixth time—and to endure nine long months of terror every time.

Each second must have been agony, enough to drive anybody mad.

Adam had thought that Llyra's arrival—ten fingers, ten toes, every feature in the right place, every organ functioning perfectly—would make everything better. And for a while, it had.

But only for a while.

*
**

The voice sounded familiar.

"Now," it said, "if you don't wanna get yourselves vaporized like bugs in a bug zapper, you'll do exactly what I tell you, nothin' more, nothin' less.

You're gonna slow this rock down, all four of you, just like you meant to, at which point we will kindly take it off your hands."

Okay, thought Wilson, that probably constituted real piracy. His suit gear was relatively feeble, compared to that of *Mighty Mouse's Girlfriend*, but it did show him four small ships in the immediate area. He felt almost helpless hanging on the chainlink screen he'd built.

The voice continued in an insultingly casual drawl. "Now just haul those tow cables you got there to your ships, and bend them around your towing bollards. But don't go onboard your ships after that, until one of us gets there to make sure that you don't try nothin' stupid."

Almost helpless, Wilson corrected as he pushed two of forty-two small buttons on the left forearm of his envirosuit. He watched his own ship roll over a few degrees, and the plasma gun mount rise and swivel around, at his command, seeking the origin of the radio signal. The weapon's hot beam thrust outward and lit up a small vessel no more than a mile away, burning a ragged, yard-wide hole through its stern coaming.

"Hey, you sonofabitch, those are my engines you're shooting—*yeek!*"

Mighty Mouse's Girlfriend had expressed herself again. Now the would-be pirate had one less engine to complain about. Unlike her own powerplants, half-buried in the hull, his stood out from his ship on stanchions, one set of which she had burned through. While it slowly floated away from the rest of his vessel, leaving the pirate with only two engines, Wilson was finally certain that he recognized the man's voice.

"Now you're gonna do exactly what *I* tell you, Shorty," the young asteroid hunter announced. "Or I'll do what I have to do—again! Power down your remaining engines and take your weapons offline. Turn on all of your running lights while you've still got the power to do it. And tell your three little friends hanging out there to do the same thing, right now, if they don't want a similar dose of their own."

Wilson knew intuitively that individuals like Shorty lacked the temperament to work by themselves. He was willing to bet anything that the same three thugs Shorty had had with him back at Holbrook Station—whom he thought of as Boils, Fatty, and Beanpole—were with him now.

The young man was running something of a bluff, himself. *Mighty Mouse's Girlfriend* couldn't shoot anybody she couldn't see, and she was seeing passively, by radio, just now, and by memory. But maybe—Oops! He remembered just in time to disable the ship's targeting system, so Shorty could reply to his ultimatum without getting shot at again.

"Okay, okay!" Shorty surrendered grudgingly to Wilson and his particle cannon. "Hey guys, do what he says. Switch on your running—wait!

Wait! Wait! He can't see you! That's why he wants your running lights switched on. Forget about that crap, and cut the bastard to pieces!"

"But—" said another of the pirates.

Wilson tapped forearm buttons again, reactivating his ship's targeting system. Remembering what had happened on the radio while it was turned off, the particle beam cannon swiveled around to shoot at whoever had just spoken, punching a big hole through his living spaces, then fired on Shorty again, nearly cutting away another of his engines.

Her first beam had struck deeply into the second ship. The way Wilson had set it up, the particle cannon "listened" for a target by radio, but "looked" for an engine's heat signature. The targeted vessel, however, got a laser beam off that nearly cut Wilson out of the chainlink he was clinging to. Fortunately, he was a small, very quiet target, and the blow to the aggressor threw its pilot off his mark.

"Stand down, the both of you," Wilson said. "Unless you want much worse."

That there were at least two other hostile ships out there, Wilson was certain. At any moment, he realized, they'd be backing Shorty, firing on him and his friends. He wondered where his friends were now, and why they weren't fighting, but didn't want to break radio silence again.

As Wilson clambered awkwardly across the chainlink like a clumsy spider, looking for someplace where he could throw himself free of the stuff and "run" for his ship, a third enemy vessel maneuvered slowly through the group consisting of the other seven ships, the chainlink Wilson was climbing along, and the odd black asteroid this whole thing was all about. As the intruder moved, rolling and jerking this way and that to avoid becoming a target, it fired a laser at Mikey's little craft. *Mighty Mouse's Girlfriend* used the fellow's laser emitter as a target and blew that weapon out of the side of the vessel with her particle cannon. Air, vapor, and bits of debris spewed from inside the ship.

"Yeehaw!" cried Mikey. "You missed me! Nyaah nyaah nyaah nyaah nyaah!" Apparently he had made it back to *Albuquerque Gal*. Voiceless microphone clicks indicated that Marko and Scotty were still alive, as well.

Somebody—the fourth pirate—finally collected enough nerve to fire on *Mighty Mouse's Girlfriend*. A thin green laser beam took her in the nose, straight through the pilot's canopy. *There goes my herb garden*, Wilson thought, *and my tomato and strawberry plants*. The enemy ship managed to peel away before Wilson's could draw an accurate bead on her. That meant there must be some damage to her targeting system.

Drawing his .270 REN, Wilson fired at the enemy's stern, hoping to crack her fragile ceramic nozzle liners. Seeing no effect, he put the gun away, cast himself free of the chainlink, aimed himself at his ship, and fired a short burst from his suit rockets. In a few seconds, he was through the portside airlock, headed forward to inspect the damage.

As he floated forward, toward the transparent nose of the little spaceship, he reflexively drew his Herron StaggerCyl again, rolling the massive cylinder out into his left hand. With an index finger, he pressed the ejector rod, dropping the twelve-round moon clip, with its empty cases, into his right hand. That went back into an insulated pocket of his envirosuit, and from another, he took a new clip with twelve fresh rounds, dropped it into the cylinder, and closed the weapon.

The beam had missed his pilot's seat and console, and there was a surprising amount of air left in the ship. Jetting to the entry hole, he found that the plastic clipboard he usually wore Velcroed to his thigh while piloting had drifted over the hand-sized hole and closed it.

The other hole, on the opposite side of the nose, was clogged with papers—printouts of last Sunday's *Lunar Times* funny pages. Next time, he wouldn't worry so much about keeping a tidier ship than he did. He got a couple of emergency patches from a box on the rim, where the canopy attached to the rest of the ship, pulled the wad of papers from the almost perfectly-round hole the laser had left, and slapped the patch in place. Similar to the plastic "sky" of Pallas, in a day or two, he knew, it would blend with the plastic of the canopy and disappear.

Repeating the process at the portside of the canopy, he glanced at the gauges on the arms of his envirosuit and started to take it off—until he realized that there were rock pirates out there, somewhere, still engaged in a ridiculous slow-motion battle with him and his friends.

Clearly, they were *amateur* pirates.

Maybe even amateur amateurs.

Wilson swung himself up into the pilot's seat. Apparently there wasn't any damage to the targeting system. Somewhat like problems he sometimes had with his pocket computer, the ship had simply confused itself when called upon to aim at the badguy, sound a decompression alarm, and then cancel the alarm because the pressure-drop had stopped itself.

He carefully inspected the navigation and location system screens, marked Shorty's presence, those of the other two vessels his little ship had fired on with her great big cannon, and some places that the fourth ship might be. The transponders on his three friends' vessels, Marko, Mikey, and Scotty, had protected them from his ship's particle cannon. He didn't know where the boys were, however, relative to their ships.

He set *Mighty Mouse's Girlfriend*'s sensors to look for the heat signatures of three deep space envirosuits, found them almost immediately, and found a fourth hanging from a strap near one of his own engine's service ports, prying at it with something that resembled a crowbar.

⁎⁎

"What?"

Whatever had been going on in Adam's sleeping mind popped like a bubble as he awoke. He couldn't remember anything about it—but he did recall that it had been a lot more pleasant than his current reality.

"Dr Ngu—I mean, Adam?" The girl was bending over him, touching his shoulder. "I'm sorry, but your flight will be ready in just a few minutes."

This time, the young receptionist—Emily, her name was—had awakened him, rather than merely startling him out of a reverie. She'd also brought him a baggie of very hot, very dark coffee, with ampoules of half-and-half, Pallatian honey, chicory liqueur, and dark chocolate syrup.

Oh well, he thought, at least he hadn't drooled on anything. As he sat up, the magazine he hadn't been reading slid off his lap, onto the floor.

"Take this with you if you wish," she told him, picking up the magazine.

"No, thank you, Emily. I never want to see it again as long as I live."

He didn't know whether to be happy or not that his family line had a habit of nodding off during moments of high stress. On the one hand, it had always made time wasted in waiting areas like this one go by very quickly. And, he'd been told that his father—captured on Mars by a UN/US combat unit (led, ironically, by his mother)—had pulled two benches together and taken a nap before facing interrogation. It had terrified the Earther forces who had mistaken it for a fearless indifference.

On the other hand, it often seemed as if he were missing half his life.

Maybe if he led a less stressful one …

"Would you care for some assistance with your baggage?" Emily asked.

Injecting his coffee with cream and chocolate (Adam could take chicory or leave it), and unfolding the sipping tube, he stood, shook his head, and took a drink. He didn't want to ask for it but he wished he'd been offered brandy to put in his coffee. He had fallen asleep tense and was now stiff all over. Sleeping that way had also cut off circulation in his legs, and her question made him feel at least a hundred years old. "No, thanks, Emily. I'll just carry it on. Good exercise."

The girl chuckled politely, and in that crystalline instant, Adam discovered that, as often happened with him, his unconscious mind had solved a problem while he napped. On most occasions, naturally enough, it happened to be an engineering problem, and he'd learned, over the long course of many years, to trust his unconscious mind—which he'd come to believe was rather a better engineer than his conscious mind was.

This time, however, it was a completely different matter, and it made him wonder. At its best, love never makes a lot of sense, he knew, and yet, somehow, it makes all the sense there is to be found in life.

Almost hating himself for it, but certain it was the right thing to do, he thumbed a single button on the wallet-sized pocket computer that also served him as a phone. He saw Ardith's pretty face on the tiny screen, startled, her lovely eyes reddened, her eyelids still swollen.

"I got as far as Port Admundsen," he told her. "May I please come home?"

Walking to the reception counter, he scribbled a note in the margin of one of the tourist brochures: *Can this ship make it to Mars?*

Emily raised her eyebrows, then wrote back, *Maybe, but could you? Can't land except on Deimos or Phobos. No facilities for that long a haul.*

Adam nodded, then wrote, "I'm sorry. Please have them stand down." He gave her an apologetic look. She smiled back at him, trying to understand. She knew it had something to do with his wife, but nothing else. Her father and mother fought all the time, and always made up spectacularly.

Meanwhile, Ardith had made a strange little noise it was hard to interpret. She turned her handset to scan the luggage laid out on the bed.

"I was coming to get you."

Wilson opened the portside airlock cautiously. When he'd come back to *Mighty Mouse's Girlfriend*, he'd approached it as a door in a wall before him. Now it was a trapdoor in a floor he was about to climb up through.

References were always changing like that in a strange world of weightlessness. In ordinary circumstances, he found it absolutely charming.

Now, as well as he could, given the bulky helmet of his suit, the young hunter peeked through the narrow crack he'd made by opening the door as little as he could and still see aft. Sure enough, there was a human figure out there, wearing a patched and battered envirosuit, thoroughly intent on prying his portside engine access panel open. He seemed to be having a great deal of trouble at the task, because he was weightless and his feet came off the surface every time he exerted himself.

Magnetic boots, that age-old favorite of the movies, were no good, of course, most of a spaceship's surfaces being non-ferrous. Instead, a suit was held as firmly in place as its wearer wished it to be by billions of microfibers, copied from those on an insect's foot, This fellow's boots must have been as old and worn out as the rest of his suit.

In an instant, Wilson was through the airlock door, up onto the outside of the ship. with his enormous revolver in his hand, its laser designator splashing scarlet on the chest of the would-be saboteur's suit.

"You make any dents in my ship with that thing," Wilson warned the intruder, "and you'll pay to have them fixed!" It took a few moments for his communications system to cycle the message through all of the likely frequencies, during which his aim with the twelve-shooter never wavered.

Without a word, the stranger threw his prybar straight at Wilson, slapping his chest in an attempt to draw the weapon he carried there. The five-foot bar came at Wilson end-over-end. In the frozen moment, aware of every minute irrelevancy, he observed that one end of the thing was sharply pointed, while the other end had been forged out into a spatula shape. It must be some kind of geological tool, he reasoned.

Or a giant manicure instrument.

Wilson stepped aside easily and snatched the prybar with his free hand. It was titanium, the shaft between the ends octagonal in cross section.

His laser beam lit up the back of his antagonist's right hand, where it lay on what Wilson could see was an autopistol grip of some kind. The beam was followed by a 90-grain .270 bullet that struck the pistol grip, entirely by accident, rather than the offending hand. It must have stung, because the figure jerked his hand away and cried out.

"You almost hit my goddamned suit, you sonofabitch!" The voice, just as Wilson had expected it to be, was Shorty's. "You coulda got me killed!"

"I meant to hit your suit, Shorty." Wilson kept the laser on him. "I figured a little explosive decompression might be just the thing for what ails you. If you lived, you could always change your name to 'Lefty'."

The smaller man emitted an infuriated shriek and launched himself at Wilson with all of his strength. When the pair of figures collided, Wilson lost his footing, fell on his back, and let go of his revolver, although it remained fastened to his equipment belt with a four-foot lanyard.

Shorty was on top of him, straddling his chest. The microfibers on his knees seemed to be in better shape. Wilson let go of the prybar, as well, this time deliberately, snatching, instead, at the half- exposed autopistol in Shorty's chest pocket and wrenching it free. He pushed it into Shorty's belly and began putting pressure on the trigger. Shorty grabbed the prybar before it could drift away and held it high overhead to strike Wilson in the faceplate with the pointed end.

In another instant, one or both of them would die.

"*Maidez! Maidez!* This is the East American spaceliner *City of Newark* to anyone on these frequencies. I repeat, this is the East American spaceliner *City of Newark* to anyone on these frequencies! We are in midflight Earth to Mars, just following turnover and are being hijacked! I repeat, we are being hijacked! Here are our precise coordinates—"

The voice cut off suddenly and was not heard again. Shorty shifted his prybar to one side and let it go, to stand more or less where he left it. Wilson handed him his pistol—an Eveready 6000 hand laser—found his own revolver at the end of the lanyard, and stowed it in its pocket. Shorty said, "Go ahead. I'll make what repairs I can and follow."

"Let's sort our friends out and I'll help you with repairs. Better get that bar back, Shorty, you may need it. My little sister's on that ship!"

And her coach, Jasmeen, as well, Wilson thought.

CHAPTER THIRTY-SEVEN: CONVERGENCE

Principles are not meant for times or circumstances when abiding by them is easy. They're for when it's hard. They're not meant to be thrown over in an emergency, or suspended "for the duration", but to be honored no matter how dangerous or difficult it gets.

Otherwise, what the hell good are they? —*The Diaries of Rosalie Frazier Ngu*

"AND SO I HOPPED UP on the back of the wagon and said, 'It's technical!'"

The Captain's table erupted with laughter, and many of the guests applauded, including that awful Mrs. Erskine, who had finally had her invitation.

Captain West made pushing motions with his hands indicating his humility, but nobody believed him. The man was a great storyteller, and he had polished it to a fine art over many years of mastering shiploads of often-difficult passengers whom his crew privately called "beasts".

"Now," said the Captain, "since they're just about to serve us a spectacular dessert, who will enjoy a little of this hundred-year-old East Texas brandy with me?" He took Llyra's glass. "You can't learn if you don't have a chance to learn, can you? Then again I've forgotten that you're a Pallatian." He poured and then reached for Jasmeen's glass.

There were no liquor laws, nor much of any other kind, on Pallas. Llyra didn't really like the stuff (she'd tried it first at home with her mother three or four years ago) but she sipped at it to be polite to the Captain—as spectacular in his own way as any dessert—whom she and Llyra had come to adore. She was interested, speaking strictly scientifically, in the way the brandy seemed to crawl all over her tongue.

"Mrs. Erskine?" Across the table from Llyra, the woman handed the Captain her glass and even managed a smile. When he had finished with serving the ladies, he announced, the men would all have to fend for themselves.

Llyra was seated next to the Captain, on his right—again—and well aware of the honor it represented. The first night, he'd told her how he missed his family back in Wyoming, and pulled out a long plastic wallet insert, with dozens of holograms of his wife and three children.

Seated between Llyra and Jasmeen was that nice old man they'd met on the Solarium Deck a few days ago. He was almost tall enough, she'd informed him, to be a native Pallatian. He'd just smiled warmly and told her he was originally from Tucson, Arizona, out in western West America.

Although these days, for the most part, he lived and worked in the Moon.

"Then why do you go to Mars?" Jasmeen had asked him. "If is not too—"

"It's not 'too' anything, dear Miss Khalidov," he'd told Llyra's coach. "I welcome the question, especially from one as beautiful and gracious as you happen to be. Since I was just a little boy, you see, I always wanted to see Mars—especially a Martian baseball game. I had been a Diamondbacks fan back in Tucson. Nobody plays baseball in the Moon, I don't know why. But you know how it is, I'm sure: somehow I never managed to get around to making this particular excursion before now."

"Diamondbacks?" Jasmeen blinked. "I have never seen baseball game, even at home on Mars. Is diamondback not some kind of poisonous big snake?"

The Captain, who'd been listening to the conversation, laughed. "Big snake *totem*. I was a Colorado Rockies fan, myself, when I was a kid, until the team moved to Juneau and became the Malamutes. I never quite got over that one—baseball on ice. I'm told they have a dome there, built exactly like the one on Pallas and the one they're building on Ceres."

"Is not dome on Pallas, is sky. Rockies. More totemism?" asked Jasmeen, winking at him. "You are not saying mountain range moved to Alaska."

"Yes," he said, enjoying her banter, "I am not saying that." A uniformed crew member appeared at his elbow with a folded scrap of a note. "Excuse me, ladies, it appears that I have to make a happy announcement."

West stood up at the table, resplendent in his white captain's dinner jacket, and tapped his water goblet with a spoon. "Ladies and gentlemen, while you may not notice it when it happens—in fact I sincerely hope you don't notice it—I'm told we are just about to initiate Turnover, since we're now halfway to our destination. From that point on, we will be decelerating until we reach our berthing on Deimos."

There was polite applause and chatter. Captains of passenger liners apparently took pride in smooth turnovers. It was a good thing to take pride in, thought Llyra. This one should be even better than the one aboard *Beautiful Dreamer* what seemed to her like so long ago.

"Now fill your glasses," said the Captain, "and make sure we don't spill—"

As if on cue, masked, black-clad figures appeared in each of the doorways to the dining room, two at the elevators, one on the spiral stairs to the forward lounge, one at the entrance to the kitchen. The intruders were armed with a variety of bullet and directed energy weapons.

A young woman strode forward among the tables, submachine gun on her hip, pale hair streaming. She was not masked, but was also wearing black.

"Ladies and gentlemen, my name is Krystal Sweet. I represent Null Delta Em, an organization I'm sure you've all heard of. I'll be taking over from the good Captain for the rest of this voyage, but if you all behave like good little hostages, I'll be delighted to let him live. I may need him anyway, to drive this big tin can exactly where I want it."

She took another step forward. "However, just to convince you that NDE means business—" She shifted to one side, seized a middle-aged man at one of the tables by his collar, and quickly dragged him off his chair toward the center of the room. When he reached inside his jacket for something, she stepped on his arm. Everyone could hear it break.

Without another word or wasted motion, she shot him through the temple, spraying the people at the tables to her left with blood and brains.

Some of them screamed until she waved her submachine gun in their direction. "Now don't you nice folks get all upset," she told them. "That wasn't one of your fellow passenger, that was only one of the drunken bums—I mean, so-called 'Space Marshals'—that this vile corporation has spared absolutely no expense at all to hire for your protection."

Stooping slightly, while remaining alert, Krystal went through the dead man's jacket, extracting a bulky automatic pistol of some kind. "We know that there are three other individuals like this aboard. They will, of course, be turning themselves and their weapons over to us in the next three minutes, or I'll just have to pick somebody else to kill."

Two bulky men stood in different parts of the room, opening their jackets with their left hands to reveal their issued weapons. A woman also stood and held her purse up. Krystal nodded to her people, who disarmed the Space Marshals and shoved them back into their chairs contemptuously.

"Very nice," said Krystal. "Now I'm going forward to the flight deck while my friends keep you company. If the good Captain will join me … ?"

*
**

"You're from Earth," the young man said. It was a statement, not a question. His pale blond hair was cut short, in what was once called a "flat-top". He wore a beautifully tailored dark gray suit, a matching turtle-neck, expensive black leather shoes, and tight black leather gloves.

The young man stood over him. Luegner, sitting, answered, "Yes, why—?"

"How recently?" asked the young man, folding his arms in front of him.

Luegner shook his head. "How recently? Why do you … well, I guess—"

For the first time, the young man showed emotion. His face screwed up in anger. "How recently, you useless parasitic cretin? Answer the question! Answer it now!" He balled up a fist in front of Luegner's face.

"Six weeks! Six weeks! What the hell is this all about?" Luegner sat back in the straight-backed chair they had shoved him into. He wasn't used to being treated this way. Was the young man from some government?

In the beginning, he had thought he was being arrested, although by whom, he had no idea. All the policemen in the Moon were privately employed, and were required by one of the few laws that existed here to wear uniforms on duty at all times. This was something else, very bad.

They hadn't threatened, injured, or even handcuffed him. Four young men had collected him from his hotel room. All of them were dressed exactly the same way and might as well have been brothers—quadruplets. Only one of them had spoken. None of them had shown him a weapon.

So far.

He'd been brought, in a big, black, unmarked Frontenac hovercraft, to an empty storefront near an industrial park just off Grissom Drive. The "For Rent" sign in the window had been thick with dusty cobwebs. He'd been taken into the back where four more young gray-clad men, or possibly six, searched him thoroughly—although they hadn't taken anything from him except the small pocket pistol he was required by his sponsors to carry at all times, probably, he had reasoned, to commit suicide with. He loathed all guns and resented having to carry this one.

Guns were for minions to carry.

By turns, the eight or ten young men had fingerprinted him, toeprinted him, and photographed his face and both retinas. His identification—East American, of course—had been minutely examined.

The young man nodded. "Six weeks. Not too bad. Almost certainly you'll be able to survive what's in store for you. You're going for a long ride, in a private spaceship, accelerating at one full standard gravity."

Luegner bit back an impulse to echo his captor. How ironic, that he'd put Krystal Sweet through something like this recently. He hadn't liked doing it to her. He liked and respected her. He was the only one he knew who didn't fear her. In a different life, who knew what they might have been together? However, he liked having it done to him even less.

He was angry. "Do you have any idea who I am?" he asked the young man.

"Decidedly. You're the chief executive officer of Null Delta Em, a terrorist, and a murderer. For what it's worth, we happen to represent the people who pay your salary and tell you what to do. They say that you're going for a ride—" The young man hitched the sleeve of his gray jacket back to look at his wristwatch. "—in about twenty-three minutes."

Luegner sagged. "Can you at least tell me where?"

"Yes, as a matter of fact, I can," the young man nodded. "You're going to rendezvous with the East American Spacelines' vessel *City of Newark*, in midflight to Mars. By the time we get there, it will have been taken over by your people—at least in theory. Their recent record isn't good. As this is the most important and spectacular act ever taken by NDE, it was decided that you should be there to claim responsibility."

Luegner gulped. "'Me'?"

The young man nodded again. "*All* of us here will be going along to make absolutely sure that everything happens the way it's supposed to. As I said, their recent record. After their mission is complete, we'll give you and all your people a ride back home. Take your gun. Let's go."

Luegner examined his pistol to make certain it was still loaded and operational, earning him a small grunt of approval from the young man. He made a cynical bet with himself about him and his people actually being rescued.

"You'll lose," said the young man, as if he could read Luegner's mind. "You're already worth considerable to NDE and its sponsors. After this, you and yours will be celebrities, like Carlos the Jackal or Yasser Arafat or Suheiro Gwenji or Henri McNabb, too valuable to friend and foe alike to waste."

Luegner could hardly disagree with that. What his people were about to do dwarfed every terrorist act in human history—put together. This time, the identical young men in gray escorted him out with dignity. There seemed to be at least a dozen of them, maybe more. Waiting for them in the street was a pale gray Clinton town car, the notorious American president's unmistakable profile incised into the hood ornament.

Two of the young men sat in front, three in back, one of them on a right-hand jumpseat. The seats were comfortable and Luegner had plenty of room. The big gray hovercraft was followed by another just like it, as it made a U-turn and headed straight for the spaceport. Luegner started to ask the young man another question, but received an answer first.

"You've been checked out of your hotel and your belongings packed. Some are in the back and will come with us. The rest are in storage. You'll be fine for the trip, which won't last that long. You'll be required to wear some special clothes once you join your people aboard ship."

"Special?"

Another nod. "So you'll look like a space pirate or a terrorist or whatever."

"Special." Luegner considered the word, turning it over with his tongue. "No eye-patch or shoulder parrot or anything like that, I trust."

The young man kept a solemn face. "No parrot or eyepatch. Here we are."

They had arrived, by a steeply descending underground highway, at the big parking garage of the Arthur C. Clark Grand Concourse and the private end of the spaceport. Two of the gray-suited young men took his meager luggage from the back of the first Clinton. All of them—he thought there might even be more than a dozen—entered the concourse and took the first elevator on the left. At the surface, several hundred feet above the concourse, they entered an airlock—the spaceport's—stepped through it into another airlock—the spaceship's—and they were suddenly aboard the vessel that would be taking them all halfway to Mars.

It was more like a small airliner on Earth, Luegner thought, than any spaceship, with a dozen rows of seats behind a closed crew-cabin door. Through the window he could see a section of streamlined delta wing. In the rear, where they had entered, he saw mountains of gear in tough-looking black boxes, piled up and tied down. The logo stenciled on the boxes looked very familiar to anyone born and raised in East America.

"WRCH?" he demanded. "You guys are a fucking 3DTV camera crew?"

The young man shrugged. "Did we ever say or imply we were anything else?"

*
*

He was incredulous. "Don't tell me that nobody briefed you about my being here. Well, that's just typical of this damn outfit, isn't it?"

Johnnie Crenicichla shook his head ruefully as he stubbed out a ciga-rette and lit another—Gallatins he'd bought in Armstrong City, at just one tenth of the overtaxed price they went for back in East America. He'd been awakened by pounding on his cabin door and realized at once what was happening. Luckily, Krystal Sweet had decided to join the stateroom-to-stateroom search for passengers who hadn't come to dinner, so he'd avoided an unpleasant interlude with her underlings, who had no reason to know that he was in overall charge of this operation.

He'd napped through the initial phases of the hijacking. Now he went to the bathroom, closed the door, used it for the purpose it was built for, then removed the package from behind the medicine cabinet, carefully reclosing the door to the hidden compartment. He didn't know why he did that, considering the fate that had been planned for this ship. It was just a silly, unwonted tidiness that was a part of his character.

Opening the door again, he opened the manila envelope, removed the pistol there and tucked it into his waistband, and took out one more item before he threw the envelope away. It was a high capacity memory stick.

"You need to get this to the command deck as soon as you can," he told Krystal. "Did anybody bother to tell you why you've hijacked this vessel?"

Krystal shook her head. "No, sir, they didn't. I saw ... well, you prob-ably know who I saw, just two days before departure. He reviewed my plans without much comment, handed me a data packet with names and pictures of everybody I'd be dealing with, told me to be as ruthless as necessary—he didn't really need to tell me that—and take over the ship immediately before Turnover. I mean the very *minute* before Turnover."

"And so here we are," Crenicichla nodded. "Surely they told you that this was to be the most spectacular stunt that NDE has ever undertaken?"

She shook her head. "I sort of gathered that, though."

He held out the memory stick. "Let's take this to the bridge. Give it to your person there, the flight engineer, and have her enter the data on it into the navigational system. We've got a three-hour window to get it done right, and we've already used up forty-five minutes of that."

Krystal's brow wrinkled. "Sir, if I may—"

He smiled. "Ordinarily, I'd tell you that you don't need to know. Once we've got things set up here the way we like, we'll be picked up by another ship, taken off and back to the Moon where we can enjoy the fireworks."

"But ... "

"But, seeing as how you've done so much for us, and will again in the future, I think it's only right to tell you and let you enjoy the anticipation."

Krystal grinned widely. She loved it. Then, nodding toward the memory stick, said, "Sir, shouldn't we be getting that up to the bridge?"

"Right. Just a moment." He reached for his off-white silk jacket where he'd draped it over a chair, turned it inside out so that it was now a black windbreaker, and put it on. From a pocket, he extracted a scrap of fabric. It was a black mesh bag, which he pulled over his head.

"I will need to preserve my anonymity for afterward. In a way, I'm standing in for ... well, you probably know who, who should be showing up in a couple of hours. He'll be making the public statement for the cause."

Krystal raised her eyebrows.

"Let's go," he told her. Entering the hallway, they nodded to the guard Krystal had been doing her rounds with. She instructed him—it was Brazos—to carry on. The doorway to the service core was directly across from Crenicichla's stateroom door, one reason he'd accepted this cabin. They entered the elevator and she started to punch the button for the dining room, which was as high as this car went.

Supposedly.

He pushed several buttons, and the system bonged its acceptance of the code. "This," he told her, "will take us straight to the command deck." He exhaled. It was very odd, seeing and talking through the mesh bag. "Krystal, the reason this is such an important mission is that we're going to rearrange the Solar System just a little bit today."

"Sir?" Her eyes were wide, and for a moment she looked just like a small child talking to Santa Claus. He hadn't noticed before, but she wasn't at all bad looking, even cute, if you could overlook the machinegun.

"That's right, Krystal. We're going to prevent our brave Captain and his valiant crew from turning this great luxurious obscenity of a spaceship around, and keep it accelerating toward Mars, instead." He held up the memory stick. "It's all right here. Actually, it'll be accelerating toward one of the Martian moons, Phobos, and not just aiming at the moon itself, you see, but for a specific spot on that moon."

"And ... ?"

"And when this ship hits it, there will be a titanic explosion which will slow the moon in orbit, and drop it, if we've done our homework right, into Valles Marineris, the warmest, most oxygen-rich, densely-populated region on all of the formerly Red Planet.

"Barsoom go boom!"

Krystal laughed, transparently anxious to hear more. He guessed that she was becoming sexually aroused by the plan as he revealed it. That was exactly why Null Delta Em's sponsors hired people like her. Briefly, he contemplated taking advantage of the opportunity, but decided it would be too much like taking a scorpion into his bed. The elevator car stopped, but he pressed a button to keep its door from opening.

"It won't really matter where it hits, though, because wherever it hits, it will kill every living thing on Mars, including all of that goddamned yellow fungus. Together, we will put an end for all time to human efforts to colonize other worlds because, if a small handful of terrorists—assisted by the United States Government and the United Nations—can destroy a world, it's clearly much too dangerous to colonize."

She laughed and clapped her hands. "Oh, I like it! I like it!"

He grinned and nodded. "I knew you would."

*
**

"I don't think these stanchions that we repaired can take another tenth of a gee, Commodore." The voice over the radio was strained, in part because the lungs behind it were experiencing eleven tenths of a gee. "I can feel them wobbling hard where they were reattached to the hull."

Shorty had been referring to Wilson as "Commodore" ever since they'd cobbled together this little fleet of eight asteroid hunting vessels and pointed them up- and cross-system to rescue the *City of Newark*, at as high a rate of acceleration as they—and their owners—could tolerate. Marko had argued that technically it was only a task force, not a fleet, and that Wilson only rated being called "Admiral".

Scotty had argued that an admiral ranked higher than a commodore, who was only a regular captain, after all, in charge of more than one vessel.

Asked for his opinion, Mikey—who had once been in the Navy—had only deigned to transmit snoring noises to the rest of the "fleet".

Shorty's three companions hadn't had much to say, so far, although they'd helped with Shorty's repairs enthusiastically enough. They'd accepted Wilson's leadership immediately, without question, and he was trying to get to know each of them better now. This not a particularly easy task (he finally understood) by means of the electronic media. He wished he'd anticipated that when he'd first met Amorie Samson on the SolarNet.

Shorty, it turned out, was one Manuel Echeverria Gavilando, born and bred in "Lost Angeles", a portion of West America's largest city that remained in overgrown ruins today, more than a century after the devastating earthquake that everybody still called "The Big One" had killed twenty million Californians and paralyzed the American economy for more than a generation, precipitating the East-West political divide.

Shorty had scrimped and saved, he'd told Wilson (much likelier burgled and mugged, Wilson suspected) to earn passage to the Moon, and had been hired afterward by an asteroid hunting corporation that had supplied him with a ship, taking nine tenths of whatever he found with her.

In the Moon, lacking certain customary legal powers and immunities traditionally granted to it by nation states like East America. the corporation Shorty worked for had soon gone bankrupt. Manuel—who appeared to like being called Shorty—had whisked his little ship off to the faraway Asteroid Belt before anybody came looking for her, renaming her *La Diabla*, and claiming to anyone who would listen that he'd long since paid for her by using her for what she'd been built for.

Wilson wondered where Shorty had sent the checks. He had decided that he could work with him—but it would be necessary to keep an eye on him, as well. As someone famous had once put it, "Trust—but verify."

"Beanpole" had turned out to be a musician, of all things, and kept an acoustic guitar aboard his little ship, *Lady of Spain*, the same way Wilson did. He was a more experienced player, however, and had a sweet, clear tenor voice. His real name was Casey McCarthy, he'd told Wilson and his friends, from Joe Batt's Arm on Pallas. By the time they'd reattached Shorty's engine, he'd begun teaching Wilson elementary harmony—it was an eerie thing to *sing* chords, Wilson thought—and started singing traditional Pallatian Newfy songs with him.

The real surprise was "Boils", a self-confessed former seminary student from the mysterious Shadow Monastery atop Mars' Olympus Mons, and, as he called himself, an avid philosophy buff. His real name, he told them with a verifying hand over his heart, was Merton Kwembly, and he delighted in arguing about absolutely anything, interminably, taking whatever side pleased him at the moment. However he refused to say a word about what went on in the Shadow Monastery. Wilson would dearly like to have known where the brothers got their oxygen at that altitude.

"Fatty", on the other hand, or Pimble S. Pharch, as he called himself, would need close watching. Originally a native of West America, he was unkempt, slovenly, and so grotesquely obese that he'd had to have a pair of envirosuits cut and remade into a single suit that fit him. He also had the most evil eyes Wilson had ever seen. He talked slowly, deliberately, provocatively, slitting those evil eyes to watch for the other person's reactions to what he said, probing for any sign of weakness.

In the end, Wilson had called a conference with his three original friends aboard *Mighty Mouse's Girlfriend*, before they'd begun their rescue mission. Despite the urgency of what lay before them, they had to make plans and preparations. The repairs had only taken them eight hours, in all. As the work had progressed, he'd tried hard not to think about his little sister and what might be happening to her in the cold, cruel depths of interplanetary space. He tried not the think about Jasmeen, as well, for many of the same reasons and perhaps one or two more.

Most of the talk now involved what to do if any of the pirates—Fatty being the likeliest in everyone's opinion—tried to betray them.

"Even his buddies are afraid of him," Marko had advised Wilson. "Just keep that big particle beamer pointed at him. He'll be a good boy."

And that was exactly what Wilson had done, arranging his little fleet—or task force—so that the gesture didn't look quite as threatening as it was, but in a way that Fatty would still get the message. As Marko had predicted, he'd been a good boy, at least so far.

It was a good thing. Following the big black whatever-it-was, their heading and velocity had been almost perfectly wrong for the task of intercepting the hijacked spaceliner, ninety degrees away in the inappropriate direction, headed sharply south of the plane of the ecliptic.

They'd begun by cutting material from the asteroid they were chasing to use as reaction mass, grinding it up, filling their tanks to capacity, then stowing more raw material in steel baskets on the outsides of their ships. They had not run into any diamonds—which would have jammed or damaged their grinders—and had started calling their bizarre high-velocity discovery the "*unusually* carbonaceous chondrite".

Nonetheless, they marked its location and course before abandoning it and accelerating in a corrective direction, at one third of a gee, something they were all accustomed to and could tolerate. Each of them went over his ship carefully, making certain nothing was amiss, and then they added a tenth of a gee and checked their ships all over again.

They repeated this routine until they were at ten percent higher than one full gee, and the colonials among them began to have trouble breathing, let alone moving about their ships. Wilson suspected that the former Earthers were having problems, too, but wouldn't admit it. In any case, it was also very dangerous, since a fall from the pilot's chair to the deck, forty feet below, would almost certainly prove fatal.

Turnover, Wilson thought, was going to be interesting.

*
**

"Mr. Luegner?"

He stirred uncomfortably, opened his eyes, and looked up at the young man standing over him, realizing there wasn't any way to tell if it was the same young man that he'd been dealing with, or one of the others.

Maybe they were clones. Of course Null Delta Em and organizations allied with it were opposed to cloning, or any other form of genetic manipulation. It was another of science's excesses that threatened to artificially prolong human life, and was therefore a threat to the natural balance. But, he supposed, using technology like that to wage war against technology in general was probably a morally acceptable hypocrisy.

Probably.

"Why aren't we accelerating?" he asked. "Are we preparing for Turnover already?" One of the reasons he'd decided to sleep most of the way was that the seats on this spacecraft faced forward, which meant that when it was underway, it was like lying on one's back on a shelf.

In his experience, only prison transports and military troop carriers were built that way. Thank somebody there had been a urinal "relief tube" built into the left arm of his chair. The aisle between the rows of seats was built like a ladder, but he didn't want to risk killing himself climbing up and down on the thing, even to go to the bathroom.

Another reason he'd slept was that there seemed to be something wrong with the 3DTV system. The screen on the back of the seat ahead of him worked well enough, but all it would show were reruns of the immensely popular situation comedy *Happy Dog*, about a politically correct family owned by its pet, rather than the other—evil—way around.

It made Luegner bilious.

He simply adored the exciting shoot-em-ups of his youth, and kept a secret collection of them carefully hidden in his home. It was just thrilling to watch legendary heroes like Crazy Horse and Sitting Bull and Geronimo and Osceola driving European intruders from their native land. Sadly, even that kind of violence had fallen out of style on 3DTV.

In East America, anyway.

"We aren't accelerating any more, sir, because we've arrived at our destination. We never underwent Turnover, because for the entire transit, we were catching up with the *E.A.S. City of Newark*, which has continued to accelerate since the moment it was taken by your operatives."

Luegner nodded, unlatched his seatbelt, and started to get up. The young man took his arm firmly, before he could crack his head on the ceiling.

"Zero gravity, Sir," said the young man. "Now if you'll allow me to assist you, aft of this section, we have a change of clothing for you, more appropriate weaponry, and you'll have ample time to look over the script that's been provided for you while we dock with the liner."

"Script?" Luegner shook his head, feeling a little dizzy. He'd never cared for zero gravity, although most people he knew thought it was lark—until they began throwing up. There was a cover over the aisle ladder now, and handholds on the top of every seatback. He relied on them, as much as on the young man, to keep his feet in place.

"Yes, sir. It's the feeling of your sponsors that this operation has to conclude perfectly. The script was written by an associate of yours, using the latest Packard-Dell hypercomputer, with the aid of several dozen opinion polls and focus panels. The good ladies and gentlemen of the Solar System will hear only what they want to hear, nothing that will tend to upset them. It's a masterpiece, if you ask me."

They passed through the bulkhead into the boarding area where he'd seen all the media traveling gear. The containers had been rearranged now, and the equipment distributed among the gray-clad young men. Across one of the big black boxes, someone had laid out his new clothing.

Maybe they were personal valet clones. The idea was horribly attractive.

What they had chosen for him to wear was classic. It began with a pair of soft black high-top running shoes like the ones he'd worn taking firearms instruction in Mexico. He'd always liked those shoes, which looked surprisingly dressy. Maybe he could take these with him afterward. The black stockings were knee-length and woven to aid circulation.

He guessed he'd keep his underwear. None had been provided. He was always very careful to cut the tags out in case he got hit by a bus or something.

The trousers were black bush-wear, with a bewildering number and variety of pockets. For some reason, each of them had been fitted with a block of foam rubber to make it look full. Maybe some focus panel had decided that would make him appear more dangerous and sinister. The belt he recognized. It was what his firearms instructors in Mexico had worn, black nylon with a peculiar V-ring buckle. This one had a number of different pouches on it, also stuffed with blocks of foam rubber.

A black cable-knit turtleneck completed the ensemble, along with black skin-tight leather gloves, and a black Balaclava that could be worn as a watchcap, or rolled down as a traditional terrorist's ski-mask.

Luegner changed in the head, emerging to find the gray clad young man waiting for him, an exotic and intimidating weapon in his outstretched hands. It was of black plastic and metal, with a front handgrip.

"You look good, Mr. Luegner. I especially like your shoes. Take this. It's the latest, a cartridge arm, but a .14 caliber ultrahyper- velocity piece that does just a little over five thousand feet per second and generates just a little over a ton of kinetic energy at the muzzle."

"Five thousand … " Luegner accepted the weapon. "Er, thank you—I think." As he had been trained to do, he looked for the right button and ejected the long, curved magazine from underneath the gun. "But there aren't any bullets in this thing! What am I supposed to do with—"

"Say 'cartridge', Mr. Luegner, not 'bullet'. Otherwise you sound like an idiot. You're supposed to smile, sir, and look pretty for the camera. Just deliver your little speech. And don't worry, you've got plenty of well-armed personnel around you for protection. You might as well give me that little pistol of yours. We'll keep safe it for you until—"

"Absolutely not!" Instead, he handed the young man a block of foam rubber. "I'm supposed to be in charge of this operation. I've decided that I'm keeping it in one of the many pockets you have thoughtfully provided. While we're' at it, you can hand me one of those big knives over there."

"Anything you say, sir," the young man nodded, surprising Luegner with his sudden mildness. Luegner had no idea what he'd do with an edged combat weapon if he were called upon to use it, but it looked splendidly menacing, went with his outfit, and the concept of having his demand fulfilled and putting an underling back in his place was important. "I think we'd better go now, sir, if we want to stay on schedule."

Luegner put the sling over his neck, to carry the weapon across his chest. At the young man's suggestion, he rolled the Balaclava down to make the right impression when he took it off in front of the camera.

He attached the knife scabbard to his belt and took a breath. "I'm ready."

CHAPTER THIRTY-EIGHT: LIFEBOAT ETHICS

Edmund Burke once said. "All that is necessary for the triumph of evil is for good men to do nothing." I would only differ with Mr. Burke by adding that those who do nothing in the face of evil cannot be good men.

Or women, for that matter. —*The Diaries of Rosalie Frazier Ngu*

"GOOD HEAVENS!"

As Luegner passed from the airlock of the smaller ship he'd arrived in, to the airlock of the *City of Newark*, the first thing he saw, through the black balaclava bag over his head, was the body of a middle-aged man, all but decapitated by the blast of some powerful weapon.

The body had obviously been dragged here from somewhere else. It wore a suit and necktie. An empty leather shoulder holster lay between the torso and the left arm. A bloody streak on the airlock floor led from what was left of the man's head toward the inner door of the airlock.

Luegner stumbled, and felt an urge to throw up. He was not a violent man, himself, but was employed to direct others to perform violent acts in a righteous cause. Although he knew that making history is an often messy process, he had never seen a dead body before, except on 3DTV. Why hadn't anybody ever warned him about the smell?

Two of the young men took his elbows and helped him get past the horrific sight, and into the bowels of the hijacked spaceliner. There they summoned an elevator in the service core and escorted Luegner to the second level where he would unmask himself and read his statement. Leaving the service core, they passed one of Krystal's heavily-armed cohorts into the elegant dining room, not quite as elegant as it had been.

Two other young men in gray had set up in that room, swiftly and violently clearing tables away from the curved outer wall and piling them in a heap, with their dirty dishes, leftover food, and soiled linen, near the double swinging doors to the kitchen. Every chair in the room had quickly followed. The men had then made everybody sit, huddled on the floor under the huge windows with their starry view. They had directed their camera so the 3DTV audience would look past Luegner, their main focus, to three hundred terrified and cowering passengers whimpering every time one of their captors made a sudden move.

That, of course, was the substance of the message.

One of the young men in gray directed Luegner to a place in the middle of the floor marked with an X made of blue gaffer's tape. He was turned about, pulled this way and that, and generally treated like a window-dummy in a storefront until they were satisfied with the camera angle, placement, and lighting. One clipped a microphone to his jacket lapel, another made hand signals and counted backward silently from five.

Two … one … now.

"People of the Earth," Luegner began. One of his assets was a partially eidetic memory. He'd only had to read the speech they'd written for him once to know it by heart. "My name is P.E. Luegner. I am the executive commander of Null Delta Em." He used one hand to pull the black mask off his head, wondering what it had done to his hair. "I am speaking to you now from the East American Spacelines passenger vessel *City of Newark*, on course for Mars from the Earth/Moon system."

The young man acting as director signaled to him to throw the bag away, not twist it between his hands. He nodded encouragingly. Luegner was glad he'd taken plenty of public speaking courses in college and no longer feared to address an audience, either in person or by media. He'd begun as one of the many who would rather have faced death. Thank heavens his fraternity at Yale had helped him overcome his fear of speaking.

Resting his gloved hands on the weapon slung across his chest, he said, "We ask for nothing. We make no demands. We have taken control of this ship to get our point across that space is too dangerous for human beings to live and work in, and that, as long as they continue to try, we of Null Delta Em will continue to make it even more dangerous."

On cue, two of Krystal's assistants had stepped forward abruptly and begun sweeping the muzzles of their weapons across the huddled passengers, causing many of them to cry out or try to bury their tear-stained faces among their fellow captives. Luegner gave them a few moments to quiet down before he continued.

"From now on, whenever you contemplate that cruel illusion they call progress, whenever you think of that foolishness they call space exploration and settlement, consider the fate of those you see behind me now, for they are victims of that illusion, of that foolishness. They, like so many others, thought they could defile space and other worlds as their ancestors did the Earth. Here is our message to you: there will be no more progress, there will be no more exploration or settlement. We of Null Delta Em stand in the way, and we are in control."

Suddenly, from beside the pile of tables and chairs near the kitchen door, there came a brief flurry of motion. Luegner opened his mouth to continue speaking and stopped. He put a hand to his face. A common table knife stood quivering in his right eye socket. He pitched forward onto the floor, driving the knife the rest of the way into his brain.

By reflex, Krystal's associates sprayed the tables with machinegun fire, reducing them and every chair to rubble, smashing every dish and goblet in the heap, filling the room with the haze and unmistakable odor of smokeless gunpowder. Women passengers screamed and covered their ears, and so did more than one man. But it was too late. The powder smoke was clearing. The kitchen doors were swinging back into place.

And the knife-thrower was gone.

Huddled close to Jasmeen—who had not screamed—with her arms around her, Llyra looked this way and that for the nice old man from Tucson.

And couldn't find him.

*
**

On the flight deck, they heard the machinegun fire from the dining room below. The flight deck was centered in, but several steps above—or forward—of the carpeted level of the luxurious lounge, which was now empty of human occupants, but brightly lighted to prevent any surprises.

From anybody's point of view, the noise could only mean some kind of disaster had occurred.

Looking up from where she'd been standing at the pilot's console for the last half hour—adapting the preprogrammed instructions for the final flight of the *City of Newark*—Krystal turned to the Captain, who was also standing.

"How do I get down from here—not by the elevator?" Johnnie had already started back toward Engineering.

Everything about this mission was strange. Whatever was going on down in the dining room, she could afford another moment or two. It didn't really matter. Minde, the flight engineer, was seated in the pilot's chair that she and the Captain stood on opposite sides of. The girl had just made the final alterations to the ship's digitally predetermined course, then shut the navigation computer down, and disabled it by ripping out half the wiring behind it. The information stick she'd used, she broke in half and threw in a wastebin under the console.

Two dozen lesser computers, located aft within the engineering spaces, had received their orders and would follow them now, to the end.

To the death.

Nothing could be done now to alter the doom of the *City of Newark*.

Nothing.

Already, it was beginning to get cooler—or was that just one's imagination? Down in the engineering spaces, two of Krystal's people were busy shutting down unnecessary systems—life support foremost among them—so that the vessel's engines would have every scrap of energy available for acceleration. Stopping a moon in its tracks, even a relatively tiny one like Phobos, was going to take a great deal of power.

All that was left now was to get her people safely into the escape vessel.

Resignation showing on his face, the Captain showed Krystal an emergency latch. Once pulled, a curved section of the glass wall around the control area swung away. Cradling her submachine gun and laying a steadying hand on the pistol in her holster, she jumped to the carpeted floor of the lounge and ran toward the dining room staircase.

"Keep an eye on that rascal, Minde!" she shouted as she started down the wrought iron spiral. Her mind was already concentrated on whatever was happening below, and she didn't even slow to hear the answer.

"Don't worry, Krystal, I—"

Minde didn't have a chance to finish her sentence. Before she became aware of it, the Captain had taken her little chin in one powerful hand and the back of her head in the other, and twisted as hard and quickly as he could. Alan West was a very big man and an exceptionally strong one. He had only done this sort of thing once before—to a calf on his ranch born with its internal organs on the outside—but he felt the bones crack in her neck, heard her last breath rattle through her lips, and watched her eyes begin to glaze over.

The girl was dead as dead could be.

For just an instant, the Captain poked around inside himself for any signs of guilt or regret. Finding none, he shrugged and moved onward.

There was nothing else that he could do up here. The ship was done, and they had even disabled the system that let individual staterooms act as lifeboats. They required the mass, Krystal had explained, of staterooms and human bodies, to smash Phobos from its orbit.

No, no regrets at all.

He lifted Minde's weapon from her lap. It was a Heckler & Sauer nine point five millimeter automatic pistol, so new it wasn't broken in. The fearsome terrorist hadn't even been carrying spare magazines. He turned, opened the inconspicuous safe under the engineer's console, and pulled three more pistols from it. His own was well-worn, indeed, a long-barreled BNU ten millimeter magnum hunting pistol. And there was the brace of smaller pistols belonging to Llyra Ngu and Jasmeen Khalidov.

If he knew them by now, the girls' spare ammunition carriers were probably still in their luggage. There was something about these colonials he loved. He pocketed three spare twenty-round magazines for his own pistol and also took his personal phone. There was a relay right here inside the ship that might make it useful in overcoming this gang of murderous criminals. He adjusted it to tell him quietly if anyone was calling.

Thinking hard for a moment, he decided, unlike Krystal, to ride the elevator, which had just returned. But he would enter the besieged dining room through the kitchen, where he could use the big round windows in the swinging doors to get a feel for things and maybe even preserve the element of surprise.

Somebody, he swore, somebody was going to be very sorry about all this.

*
**

"I'm here."

Crenicichla answered his telephone. Not that many people had the number. He was standing at the service core in the engineering spaces where he'd just supervised two of Krystal's people as they carefully disabled the local controls. Satisfied that his work was thoroughly finished down here—there were broken wires and components underfoot all over the deck—he was waiting for a car forward to the dining room.

The E.A.S. *City of Newark*'s six mighty fusion engines would now hurl her inexorably to her destination and her destiny. Nobody could change that, short of utterly destroying her, and it was far too late for that. By the time anybody was even aware that she'd been hijacked, let alone caught up to her, she would have struck her mark on Phobos, instantly vaporizing herself and dropping the little moon from the Martian sky, incinerating or smashing everyone and everything on the planet.

If by some extremely improbable miscalculation she managed to miss Phobos, she would still hit Mars, doing damage both incalculable and irreparable. Either way, it would spell an end to human aspirations in space.

For Null Delta Em, it was a splendidly no-lose situation. They could claim—whatever way it happened in the end—that it was exactly what the organization had intended in the first place. It struck him that this was one of the last few spaceflights in human history.

Something to tell his grandchildren.

" … you there? We're having a whole buncha trouble up here, Johnnie!" He'd almost forgotten the phone. The voice on the other end was Krystal's. He'd never heard the woman in a state of panic like this before. If it frightened her a little, it frightened him a lot. "One of our passengers just wasted Paul Luegner—on System-wide 3DTV!"

"*Shit!*" He felt his legs give way and his midsection turn to water. These operations were about psychology and very little else. They'd just lost the advantage, even if the rest of the mission went perfectly.

He wasn't using video, in order to retain anonymity and prolong battery life. A good thing, he thought, that she couldn't see his expression. As it was, it was disturbing her two people here in engineering.

On the other hand, Luegner had always been a worthless lump, in Crenicichla's view. He'd never managed to figure out why their mutual sponsors had hired him in the first place. If it had been left to Crenicichla—and finally, it had—he'd have killed the man just before they departed this ship and let him become a martyr to the Cause.

He'd be a hell of a lot more useful that way than he had been alive.

Now some fool had beaten him to it, and the timing couldn't be worse. To have a spokesman killed onscreen, just as he was declaring the dominance of Null Delta Em—that had been the plan, anyway, and Crenicichla had approved the speech—was very bad. He hoped Krystal understood that it wasn't going to help the cause to murder innocent passengers simply out of revenge—at least not over System-wide 3DTV.

The guilty on the other hand …

"Did you catch whoever did it?" he asked, somehow knowing the answer in advance. She would have reported it completely differently, otherwise. The stainless doors slid open, and he stepped into the elevator, followed by Krystal's people who were coming forward with him.

"No, no, he disappeared and probably didn't even wait to see the knife hit. I guess it coulda been a she. I don't have a passenger manifest here. Talk about your ego not being involved in your work! I have to confess it was so prettily done that I almost wish I'd done it myself."

A thrown knife and an assassin on the other side who respects and admires the opposition. There speaks a real pro. Crenicichla laughed—

Krystal was certainly his kind of girl—but he let her go on. He punched the button that would take them to the dining level she spoke from.

She said, "I've got as many people out looking for him now as I can spare, including some of your pretty boys in gray. But I'm thinking that anybody who can kill a man with a thrown table knife is going to be hard to find and harder bring in. I'm tempted to leave him alone to hole up somewhere, rather than waste the time, effort, and manpower."

He would have made very much the same judgment. "Except that you don't really believe he's going let you or yours alone, any more than I do. The man's got to be found, and as quickly as possible." The elevator stopped with a subtle whish, but the doors seemed slow to open.

"I gotta agree with that, boss," Krystal replied, "I—oh, my God!"

As much through the door as over the telephone, Crenicichla heard sharp blasts of powerful handgun fire, followed by short bursts from more than one automatic weapon, and then several more pistol shots. Careful not to use her name, he shouted at Krystal over the phone. He could hear people move around and make noise, but her only reply was silence.

He punched buttons again.

*
**

The individual who thought of himself as the Fastest Gun in the Moon slipped out of the service core as inconspicuously as its doors allowed.

He didn't know exactly what Krystal and her crew were up to, but he did know Null Delta Em. Obviously, another ship had arrived, with its crew of gray-clad young men, to pick them up, which meant they planned to set some kind of destructive course and then abandon the *City of New-ark* intending her to serve as some kind of a battering ram. It certainly wasn't the first time something like this had been done.

Perhaps if he could get down to the engine room, he could stop them.

Sometimes he had to work to remember what his real name was. It didn't seem to fit him any more, somehow. Luckily, neither did old age. Most men born five years either side of his birthday were slowing down a bit. None would dream of climbing down a steel-runged ladder in the heart of a spaceship to bring terror and death to a collection of hijackers. Yet that was just what he—Aaron Manzel—planned to do now.

Aaron Manzel. I am what I am and that's all that I am. Pass the spinach.

Escaping from the dining room through the kitchen had been relatively easy, although he'd wished he'd had time enough to watch his thrown knife hit the target. He'd been looking for a chef's blade, but he was confident that even a badly-thrown table knife would have created the effect he'd wanted. In a fraction of a second, on System-wide 3DTV, the group from Null Delta Em had gone from boasting conquerors to just another gaggle of blunderers.

They might as well not even have tried.

Gaining the corridor outside the kitchen, he avoided the elevators and opened a door in the service core. Inside the core were the cylindrical shafts and mechanics for three elevators, two of which wouldn't go any higher than this level. A third, with the right key and the right code, went all the way to the flight deck. From inside the core, he could see where each of the cars was and what it was doing.

He preferred the ladder.

He took the pipe-like outsides of the ladder in his hands, locked the inside edges of his feet around them, too, and slid easily down to the third deck. He had brought no real weapons of any kind on this voyage, and he had no weapons now. This was where he would acquire what he needed.

Leaving the core on the third deck, he stepped cautiously into the corridor, using every one of the senses he possessed—senses that had been expertly trained and that he exercised and tested frequently—to the maximum. He couldn't see or hear anyone at the moment, but it was interesting (to him, anyway) how often someone would give their position away with the smell of their food, or the stink of their fear.

Just now he could smell butter and garlic and Oregano. That wasn't what was being served in the dining room. It might well be an intruder—who were those cloneboys, anyway? Where had they come from and brought Paul Luegner with them?—but it might be as simple as room service.

Sliding around the inner wall formed by the outside of the service core, he could only see about a quarter of the corridor at a time. At last he heard a door lock function. There were only four suites in this deck. He heard someone come out, into the corridor, humming to herself.

As quickly as he could, he slipped around the core to confront one of Krystal's people, a young woman, brunette. Her arms were full of plunder from the room she'd just broken into. He recognized a tortoise shell barette he'd seen Llyra wearing. Before she could get her weapon cleared, he'd stepped in beside it, pulled a combat knife from a scabbard on her belt, and thrust it into her solar plexus, working it a little, from side to side, to find the big artery running behind the stomach.

She slipped forward to the floor and was dead.

Quickly, he wiped the knife off on her clothing, put it back in its scabbard, removed her pistol belt and readjusted it to his own size. He checked the weapon—a simple laser—and its spare charges.

Time to move on.

Leaving Llyra's and Jasmeen's possessions on the floor, he took the body by its heels—nice boots, he thought—and dragged it back the way he'd come. Opening the door, he pulled the body onto the tiny steel landing provided at each deck, and dropped it straight down the shaft.

Krystal and her people were stretched Angstrom thin all over the ship. Null Delta Em was one of the cheapest groups of its kind that he'd ever had to deal with. This wouldn't do much to improve their morale.

On the fourth floor, he found absolutely nothing. Most of the half-dozen doors were swinging open, meaning that they had already been looted by the young woman he'd just killed or another of her group.

Entering the service core again, he watched what he thought of as the executive elevator—the one that served the flight deck—going upward. Neither of the other two was moving. As he slid down to the access to the fifth floor, it opened before he could reach it and one of the strange young men in gray stepped through and shut it behind him.

The man whose real name was Aaron Manzel had long observed that while hunting, or traversing dangerous pathways, no animal or human ever seems to remember to look up, even predators, who take frequent advantage of the fact, and ought to know better. This young man was no different.

Silently repeating "ten feet per second per second" to himself—the rate at which objects fall at the one-third gee at which the *City of Newark* was presently accelerating—Manzel drew the fighting knife from his confiscated gun belt, let go of the steel ladder, and fell feet-first on the young man, striking him on the head and one shoulder as he went by. Reflexively, the young man gripped the ladder tighter—the little sheet-steel landing was only about two feet on a side—which made him all the more helpless once Manzel reached his level.

He didn't waste time or effort, but stopped himself by throwing his left arm around the young man's neck, pulling his head backward, and plunging the knife into one of his kidneys with his right hand, producing massive shock and instant unconsciousness. Before his victim could fall, taking both of them down the intimidating length of the core—even one third gee can be lethal—Manzel seized the ladder and held them there for an instant, as he searched the young man's clothes.

He carried no identification, and as far as Manzel could tell, there never had been any tags in his clothing. He had a medium-framed automatic pistol and a couple of spare magazines—which Manzel took—and a set of electronic keycards, probably for this ship. Manzel pulled the knife out of the young man's back, wiped it clean on his otherwise tidy gray suit, and let him go to join the young woman below.

He wondered what else was happening on this floor. He guessed he'd better find out. Opening the panel as little as he could, he peeked out to see another gray-clad young man, apparently waiting for the first. He was unaware that the door had been opened because his back was to it, and he was talking quietly to yet a third gray-clad young man.

Manzel silently closed the panel to think about his options. Before he got very far with that, the panel opened, and a young man's head thrust into the opening. "Karl," the young man shouted. "What is keeping—"

Manzel grabbed him by the wrist, pulled him all the way into the core, and let him fall screaming, but paying most of his attention to the door, where an all-but-identical young man repeated his clone's mistake. Manzel seized him and threw him down the shaft which echoed with his screams, as well. In an instant, both were silent, and Manzel was waiting for a third figure to make itself manifest. But nobody followed.

Now Manzel crept out of the door. There were a dozen compartments on this level, and each of the doors was open. The deck was silent and unoccupied. He reentered the core and began climbing aft, to the next level.

Captain Alan West left the elevator on the third level and made his way as quickly and quietly as he could to a little-known staircase—normally used to bring room service to the most elite passengers—he used to go back up to the kitchen. He recalled that the upper entry was hidden from the rest of the kitchen by several moving racks of pans and utensils. He'd argued with the chef about it just before departure.

And lost, for which he was now annoyed to feel grateful.

The kitchen was deserted, although he was willing to bet the hijackers had sentries posted just outside, in the dining room. He made certain that Llyra and Jasmeen's pistols were secure in his pockets—for some reason it was important to him—took his own ten millimeter in his right hand and the weapon he'd taken from the dead flight engineer in the other, and approached the swinging doors with their frosted porthole windows. Sure enough, someone was standing to the left of the doors, but no one to the right where the tables were piled.

He saw two hijackers on the perimeter where they'd put the passengers—the Ngu and Khalidov girls were at this end of the crescent they formed—and somebody was in the middle of the room, striding up and down, waving a submachine gun around, and haranguing the prisoners. No matter the cause, these idiots were all alike, somehow.

West took a deep breath, grateful for all the combat ranch time he and his wife had put in, back home in Wyoming, strode forward, and pushed the right-hand door open. His left hand was already raised, and he shot the sentry through the skull with Minde's gun without even looking. He also had his right hand raised and used it to kill the haranguer.

Blessed silence.

Before the other hijackers could react, he ran to the passengers, firing both guns as he did. He saw one of the hijackers go down—he couldn't tell which gun he'd done it with. It didn't matter. On his knees, firing back at the remaining hijacker who'd taken cover behind an upturned table, he let go of the weapon in his left hand, extracted the other pistols from his pockets, and tossed them to the girls, then regained Minde's gun and made sure that the hijacker kept her head down.

Suddenly, there was a burst of noise beside him. Llyra had her pistol raised and pointed at the kitchen doors, where a body—one of the gray-clads—now lay on the floor between them, propping them open.

Jasmeen had been shooting at the individual behind the table, and was less surprised than anyone else when intermittent gunfire started coming from the opening in the ceiling where the spiral stairway stood.

Briefly, a female face appeared, upside-down, seeking targets. It disappeared and suddenly a hand was visible, filled with lethal hardware, spraying the dining-room down in hopes, apparently, of hitting somebody—anybody.

Bullets sang around Jasmeen—she heard a grunt behind her, but didn't dare look back—as she held her fire, waiting for the right moment. Finally, the shooting stopped. Krystal stuck her head down again, and Jasmeen shot her. The woman sagged, then tumbled down the stairs.

Jasmeen's impulse was to get up and run to her, to make sure she was dead, if nothing else, but Llyra took hold of Jasmeen's arm to stop her.

"The Captain's injured!" she whispered.

"Oh, I am not! I've hurt myself worse in my basement woodshop."

"Is possibility," Jasmeen answered. "Human sacrifice makes good bookends."

Captain West's white dinner jacket, already smudged and stained from his adventures getting here, now had a neat hole beneath the center of his right collarbone, and was soaked with blood. Jasmeen found a couple of clean linen dinner napkins, folded them, and pushed them under his jacket, front and back. She then turned to Mrs. Erskine.

"Make him lie flat on floor," she told the older woman. "Keep steady pressure on wound—here's another napkin—until I find help."

The woman looked terrified until Jasmeen showed her what to do. Llyra smiled, remembering all the times that Jasmeen's first aid training, a mandatory study for skating coaches, had come in handy. She'd even set a broken bone once—not Llyra's—at the rink in Curringer, using a pair of lip-balm tubes as splints.

Only then did the two girls get up. Several other people were on their feet by now, milling around the ruined dining room, most of them avoiding contact with the dead bodies. More than one of the male passengers was attempting to convince the others that he was in charge.

In a clear, commanding voice, Jasmeen announced to the crowd, some of whom were still huddled on the floor, "Is best you all stay here. Worst may be over, but we don't know. We will be back as soon as possible."

"Two little girls?" said a large individual, pretty obviously from Earth. "Not on your life! I'm a retired police chief. Give me those guns!"

A head taller than the man, Llyra leveled her pistol on his face. "You're not in New Jersey any more, Chief. We do things differently out here. Sit down and shut up."

Grinning, Jasmeen glanced over at Llyra. "We are great big girl now?"

"No," Llyra whispered back, imitating Jasmeen's accent. "We are little girl with great big gun!"

"She's still alive!" The cry came from the spiral stairwell where Krystal lay draped along the lowest half dozen steps. "She's still breathing!"

People began to get up, if they had still been sitting on the floor, and drift slowly in the direction of the stairwell. They had things in their hands, now: knives, forks, broken plates. One woman had even taken off her shoe and was trying it for weight and balance—the heel could be a deadly instrument. Looking at each other, Llyra and Jasmeen followed them, but there wasn't any way to slip ahead of them.

There was no easy way that they were going to prevent what was about to happen. Nobody would listen to them now. A noise ceased abruptly which they hadn't even noticed before now. A couple of the big dining room windows had been penetrated by gunfire. All this time, they'd been whistling shrilly as air escaped through them into space. Now they had automatically resealed themselves, and the whistling stopped.

The passengers gradually surrounded Krystal, determined to have their revenge on her. By a kind of evil magic which was still not very well understood, even in the twenty-second century, they had been transformed—or had transformed themselves—into a mindless herd, waiting only for one of their dullwitted number to make the first move. The woman with the shoe was closest now, raising it high over her head. Jasmeen and Llyra could no longer see Krystal through the crowd.

"Hold it right there!" said a voice from nowhere. "Don't come any closer!"

The voice was a man's. The face that went with it, once he'd started down the stairs, was one they'd never seen before. He was relatively young, Llyra thought, and, well, extraordinarily handsome, wearing a white summer suit—stained black here and there, and splashed with blood—and he carried with him a submachine gun in each hand, tucking the short shoulder stocks under his arms at his sides. He walked down the spiral stairway from the lounge, stopped, and now stood over Krystal, threatening the passengers.

"You two!" He waved one of his submachine guns at a couple of the people up close. "Yes, I mean you! Pull her down very gently and carry her over to that elevator! Be careful!" He indicated the elevator that couldn't be seen from the Captain's table where Llyra and Jasmeen had been sitting at dinner, what now seemed like a year ago. Llyra thought hard about shooting the man, but feared that he might just massacre the rest of the passengers to get to her, if she missed. She glanced over at Jasmeen, who shook her head, agreeing with Llyra's tactical assessment.

"Anybody else makes a move toward us, I'll kill them where they stand!" Llyra hated being ordered to do what she'd already decided to do.

The stranger followed the two passengers with Krystal into the elevator, ejected his unwilling helpers, let the doors close, and was gone.

"Life support!" the Captain said suddenly. His voice was still strong and his eyes were clear. "Miss Ngu, Miss Khalidov, can you hear me?"

"Yes?" Llyra turned to him where he lay. Mrs. Erskine was still there.

"They've shut down all the life support systems—air, heat—I saw it on the bridge consoles. I got a distress call off, early on. You must move these people to the core where they'll stay warm longest. Collect every emergency oxygen bottle from the ship—they're scattered around with the fire extinguishers—and take them to the core, as well."

Jasmeen nodded. "Trust us. You will be all right?"

"I'm less hurt than I am pissed off," said the Captain.

"Then we'll start by getting you to the core," Llyra said.

CHAPTER THIRTY-NINE: SPACE OPERA

A person had better be prepared to defend himself in this world, because, thanks mostly to the laws of Physics, nobody—not your neighbors, not your friends, not even your family, and especially not the police—can be counted on to be there when you need them.

I've repeated this observation many times in speeches I've given over the years. When the day comes that someone in the audience asks me, "What's the police?", I'll know that someone was listening. — *The Diaries of Rosalie Frazier Ngu*

"*WARNING! CATASTROPHIC ENGINE FAILURE IN thirty-two seconds! Warning! Catastrophic engine failure in thirty seconds! Warning! Catastrophic engine failure in twenty-eight seconds! Warning! Catastrophic—*"

Wilson reached to his left forearm to switch the channel his suit radio was receiving on. Shorty saw him, and signaled to Marko and Scotty.

"You here, Commodore?" Shorty asked, having switched frequencies, himself.

Wilson said, "None of us is going to be here if we don't get this done!"

The four of them were laboring, tools in hand, in the two-foot space between Shorty's vessel and its bad engine—the one Wilson had shot off, then helped reattach to the ship, *La Diabla*, or *She Devil* as Wilson now thought of her—before it exploded, taking most of the vessel with it. *La Diabla* had been warning them like this for twenty minutes, during which they'd discovered that the mechanism for jettisoning engines that were about to fail catastrophically had failed catastrophically itself during the firefight or afterward, when the engine had been rewelded onto its four stanchions, each of which now had to be cut manually.

"Okay, here we go, gentlemen!" Mikey chose that moment to jet into the center of the narrow space with a package under his arm. "One Gabney Mark Four probe motor, sans probe! Very expensive—I'm sure glad it isn't mine. I'll just install it at the center of gravity and back away. You guys sing out when your stanchions are cut and I'll fire!"

It was hard going, as the stanchions—in effect, each bore a twelfth of the ship's mass, multiplied by acceleration—were tough. There weren't enough torches available—Scotty and Marko had them—so Wilson and Shorty had resorted to hacksaws to cut the bad engine free.

"I'm clear!" Marko shouted. He shut his cutting torch off to back away.

"Me, too!" cried Scotty. He had a bad moment with a tangled hose, but got it clear of the engine and itself, and joined Scotty where he hung.

Wilson was only about halfway through the stanchion. It had just occurred to him the try the particle cannon or one of the lasers he had aboard *Mighty Mouse's Girlfriend*—but only too late to do any good. In some ways, he thought, it was the story of his whole life so far.

"I'm clear!" shouted Shorty.

"Then the three of you get out of here!," said Wilson. "Away from the—"

In that instant, the stanchion broke free, Wilson jetted backwards, away from *La Diabla* as fast as he could, and Mikey fired the probe motor which, slowly at first, but gathering speed rapidly, took the failing engine away. At about two miles, by Wilson's estimate, it exploded.

"That was close," said Scotty.

Marko managed a relieved whistle.

"Hey, you guys, we've got the board finished, in here," said Casey McCarthy, the person formerly known to Wilson as "Beanpole". He and Merton Kwembly—"Boils"—were aboard *La Diabla* now, making all the adjustments necessary for thrusting on two engines instead of three.

They'd taken Pimble Pharch—"Fatty"—with them, mostly to keep an eye on him, but he'd proven himself helpful. It had been his idea to use the probe motor—he'd had it in his "junk" compartment—when they couldn't get the explosive bolts to work.

"Okay, gentlemen, good job!" Wilson said. "But the coffee break's over for now! Everybody back to your ships! We've gotta make gees again!"

They were about three quarters of the way to catching up with *The City of Newark*, but had had to drop out of acceleration to deal with this problem, and they'd lost two hours. As Wilson plunked himself back in his pilot's chair, *Mighty Mouse's Girlfriend* was showing an image.

"I've still got a radar lock on her! Shorty, are you ready? Good. Then it's blast on five, four, three, two, one, now!" He hit ENTER on his keyboard and slammed backward into his chair at one point two gees.

"Hey, Commodore!" It was Scotty. He was going to have trouble keeping up. "We haven't discussed what we're gonna do when we get there."

"Second the motion," replied Mikey.

"It wasn't a motion," Wilson replied. "And this isn't a body that accepts them. I don't know what we'll do, because we don't have any information on which to base plans or decisions. Just keep your eyes and ears open and maybe something will come to us in the time that's left."

Over the next several hours, they batted it back and forth, but, as Wilson had predicted, they couldn't plan without more information. He had a couple of meals, he slept, and so did the others, by turn. A break came when his radar, programmed to warn him of any changes, beeped.

"Seems we've got ourselves *two* targets out there! We're close enough to resolve that many blips. Somebody has docked with *City of Newark*."

"Judging from the profile and proportion to the liner, I'd say she's a *Swan*-class private hull," said Marko, who had the highest resolution radar in the little squadron. "They're built flat, like a cockroach or a manta ray, with enough power and structural integrity to land anywhere but Earth. We're seeing her stern-on. I toured one once at L-Five. Not as much room as a liner, but what there is is choice!"

"What do you suppose she's doing with the *City of Newark?*" asked Mikey. His *Albuquerque Gal* was just to Wilson's port and a little ahead.

"Mating?" Scotty, aboard *Nessie*, suggested.

Shorty said, "No, it's the getaway yacht. And probably a stolen one."

Quickly, Wilson checked on the SolarNet, looking for stolen spaceships. Sure enough, a *Swan*-class vessel was missing from Lunar orbit.

"It's the *White Winged Dove*, gents, out of Armstrong City," he announced. The owner is some Earthside mining corporation. I wonder what 'gypsum' is. She's been gone for two days, and they found the chairman of the board and his girlfriend, plus the pilot and co-pilot, floating in stationary orbit over Armstrong, enjoying space without a spacesuit."

"Geez," said Shorty. "Wow. Just gimme plain old robbers every time. These guys with political agendas gimme the creeps." He shuddered, and the others could hear him do it over the intership radio.

Lights lit by themselves across his control panel as *Mighty Mouse's Girlfriend* made large and small adjustments to match the *City of Newark's* acceleration, velocity, and course. Suddenly, Wilson was experiencing a third of a gee—Martian gravity—and it felt relaxing.

"Everybody else make the change?" he asked.

One by one, the others reported in. They were all on course for rendezvous with the hijacked *City of Newark*, and arming their weapons.

✳

Unbelievable, thought Crenicichla. It's absolutely unbelievable. They're all dead, every single last one of them. Her gaggle of ragtag hooligans, my overpriced and overrated clones, everybody but me and poor Krystal, and I can't get this godforsaken spaceship started by myself!

At least it wasn't a matter of security systems and passwords. The stolen yacht had been deserted when he'd carried Krystal over from the *City of Newark*. Her engines were cold and she was being pulled along at one third gee by the liner. He'd meant to look at her commissioning plaque when he'd come aboard, but had forgotten to. It was peculiar, not knowing the name of the vessel you were attempting to start and run.

Some kind of bird—White Swan—or was that the class of the vessel?

He'd also intended for at least two of the clones to remain aboard and ready for a quick getaway, but apparently, given the flexible, ad hoc way Null Delta Em liked to run things, in the rapidly-growing crisis aboard the *City of Newark*, Krystal had found other uses for them, and they'd eventually met their individual fates. What a damn waste.

After taking care of Krystal as best he could and running forward to begin the start-up cycle, he'd closed all four airlock doors and securely bolted those of the yacht. At least he and Krystal were safe for a while. The wretched, world-wrecking, capitalist reactionary bastards who'd messed up the radical environmentalist statement of the century would perish, freezing, gasping for breath, or in a splendid collision.

He almost wished that he could be there to see it. He hoped that they lasted long enough, even without the life support he'd ordered powered down, to watch Phobos looming bigger and bigger outside their windows. Imagine the screaming, when they figured out what was going on, the hair-tearing, the soul-rending anguish. It was a heart-warming thought.

His hands raced over the keyboards, slowly eliciting the desired responses. Not much longer, now, and they would be away from here at last. He began to think about where they would go, to let things cool off. Someplace isolated, lonely, a little romantic, but with good restaurants.

But another thought intruded on him ...

Where the hell had they gotten all those guns? He'd thought East American Space Lines strictly forbade weapons in civilian hands, just as the East American government, with its "a metal-detector in every doorway" policy, did at home. In fact he'd counted on it. Governments always make it easy to prey on the weak because they need the weak, themselves, to prey on. The kind of people who run governments would rather see a woman raped in an alley, and strangled with her own pantyhose, than see her with a gun in her hand. He'd thought that Null Delta Em was safe to do exactly as they wished with the ship and with its passengers.

Something had gone very, very wrong.

Krystal was badly wounded, and that begged another question. When had he developed feelings for this woman? Usually he viewed women as a disposable convenience. He simply loved them and left them. In fact he hadn't had sex with the same girl twice, in the last twenty-five years.

He hadn't had sex with Krystal at all, and yet ...

The ship, whatever her name was, had good first aid facilities. He'd laid Krystal on a work table in the aft section and looked to her wounds. One of them, high in her right forearm, she'd get over. The slug was still there, just under the skin. He made a tiny incision and the bullet practically popped out. Another, across the very top of her left shoulder, was trivial. The projectile had passed almost harmlessly through an inch and a half of flesh and was long gone. He had the distinct impression they had all come from the same damned weapon.

Where the hell had they gotten all those guns? What's the world coming to, when your potential victims are all armed as well as you are?

But a bullet had grazed her left temple, leaving a long, shallow furrow, crackling the skull beneath it. It was as if its energy had poached her left eye, turning it a horrifying opaque white, and she would probably never see out of it again. But he would take care of her.

And of Llyra Ngu and Jasmeen Khalidov, in a different way, when the time came. He'd seen them from the stairway, with those *things* in their hands. What the hell did ice-skaters need with high-capacity ten millimeter semiautomatic pistols, anyway? Back home, they'd be doing a long stretch for illegal gun possession, washing prison laundry, and servicing the matrons.

And now, of course, they would just be dead. In a way, his hands were around their throats this very minute, suffocating them, freezing them, ready, in a little while, to fling their frozen bodies at an alien world.

Krystal remained unconscious, stirring now and again, murmuring, with a sweet smile on her lips. That was probably the morphine he'd given her, the only drug he'd ever been tempted by, himself. She was getting extra oxygen from a slotted mask. As best he could, he'd dressed her wounds—there were some remarkable medicines these days, and he'd applied them well before covering her up—and strapped her down to the table, which was bolted to the floor. The ship's aft section was spherical, he observed, on gimbals, and would keep her quiet, safe, and perfectly flat, whatever the rest of the vessel happened to be doing.

Now, he was back on the flight deck, going through the check-list one item at a time. He was not familiar with this particular class of ship, but he could fly a lot of different aircraft and spacecraft. He estimated it would take him no more than another hour to complete the tasks required of him by this big aluminum-covered book and get her moving.

A couple of days and they'd be back in the Moon, battered but unbowed. There was a restaurant he knew that served vegetarian haute cuisine. He wondered if Krystal would like that, or a rare, bloody steak.

She was his kind of girl.

Odd, someone had just sent a narrow-beam text-message to the little ship, addressed to NDE, while he was below with Krystal.

***

Virtually the minute that Wilson came within visual range—admittedly through a thousand-power electronic telescope—of the *City of Newark* and her companion, presumably the stolen yacht *White Winged Dove*, the latter detached herself from the former, and veered away at high acceleration on a different course than the passenger liner.

White Winged Dove had two hybrid fusion engines, according to her published specifications, one stacked atop the other, and half a dozen thrusters in her nose that would have served a lesser ship as engines. She was hard to mistake now. Marko had said that she would look like a manta ray or a cockroach. To him, she looked like a "miller" moth, the kind that come out by the millions in the Pallas summer, with graceful delta wings.

Wilson thought furiously, torn between his concern for two of the most important people in his life, and the badguys who were getting away.

"Marko! Mikey!" he shouted into the radio. "Get after that ship! Use lasers and target her engines. Remember there might be hostages. I'll see to the liner. Take Casey with you! That all right with you, Casey?"

"Well, sure! I—"

"All right—go!" Wilson could see the navigation program play out on his console, as *Mighty Mouse's Girlfriend* matched the liner's acceleration, velocity, and course precisely. Having skipped Turnover, she was going faster, by now, than anything he'd ever seen, except for that mysterious black asteroid they'd been chasing only hours ago.

One of his auxiliary radar systems informed him that Scotty's *Nessie*, Shorty's *La Diabla* Merton's *Whispers of Divinity*, and Pimble Pharch's *Lilac Waffle* were matching up, as well. He hoped the four of them would be enough, and brushed his hand across the front of his envirosuit to feel the outline of his .270 Herron twelve-shooter. He'd bring his Grizzly magnum .45 with him, too, when they boarded the *City of Newark*.

"I have a blueprint of the *City of Newark* up on my system, now," Scotty told them. Wilson saw an icon appear on his screen that was an offer to share the image, but he left it alone for the moment "There's only one passenger lock, believe it or not, near the stern, between the engines and the cargo spaces. They don't need any more than that, it says here, because the individual staterooms act as lifeboats in an emergency."

"And you can see how well that's worked out," Shorty observed. The space liner, of course, was completely intact, without a single cabin missing.

"None of our airlocks will mate with that big passenger entry," said Wilson. "It's half again the height and four times as wide as mine."

"It says here there's a smaller door built into the outer one," Scotty said. "There's also an emergency lock for the flight crew, an L-shaped tube from their deck, out through the kitchen level to the hull. It looks like it has the same standard dimensions as our own."

"There's an airlock on each of the freight levels, too," said Shorty.

"All right, Scotty, you and Pharch take the lock in the passenger door. Shorty and Merton, work the cargo locks. I'll tackle the one for the flight deck. Before you go, gentlemen, take a good hard look at your sensors. Life support in that ship is failing. It's very cold, without much oxygen."

"Pretty much," said Scotty.

"Don't you worry, Commodore, we'll wear our long, red, winter underwear."

Wilson was gratified that his voice hadn't wavered. His sister was in there, where it was so cold and the oxygen was gone, and so was Jasmeen.

Making tiny movements with his fingers on the joystick, he turned his little ship over so that his portside lock was close to the ship, and maneuvered *Mighty Mouse's Girlfriend* along the hull of the *City of Newark* until he found the emergency flight crew airlock. An inch at a time, he brought his ship closer to the other, until the locks triggered mutual responses, extended short tubes, and engaged each other. Maybe Scotty's remark about spaceships mating hadn't been so far off, after all.

Automatically, the larger vessel informed the smaller vessel of conditions inside. The temperature was a hundred ten degrees below zero, air pressure was normal, but the water vapor and carbon dioxide had long since frozen out of it, and the oxygen level was at only two percent. It almost appeared that it was being systematically removed.

Wilson slowly reduced his own ship's thrust until the *City of Newark* was accelerating for them both. He ran an electronic diagnosis of the stresses on the airlock connection and found them to be within tolerances.

He reached for his helmet, his gloves, and his other gun, which he strapped around his envirosuit. He knew what he was going to find over there, but couldn't bring himself to believe it—all the while he wondered what he was going to tell his parents. Llyra was their darling baby, which was all right with him, she was his darling baby, too.

And if lovely Jasmeen were dead, he suddenly realized, it would extinguish the light of the universe, a light he'd taken for granted—and hadn't really been aware was shining—until the horror of this moment. Jasmeen was the prettiest—and funniest—girl he'd ever known.

He was glad he wouldn't have to be the one to tell Uncle Mohammed and Aunt Beliita. Or Mohammed's brother, Ali, or Beliita's brother, Saladin.

Trying to shake off what could well become a paralytic mood, he climbed down the ladder into the living space. then back up to the airlock. Lights inside his suit told him all his seals were good and all his systems were running properly. He opened the inner door, climbed in, and shut it behind him. Pressures were already equalized, give or take a pound per square inch, but the air over there was no good.

He opened the outer door of his own ship, the outer door of the other ship, climbed through and closed both doors behind him. He then opened the inner door of the *City of Newark*'s airlock and crawled through, into a tunnel, circular in cross-section, that formed the end of the flight crew's emergency escape system. He closed the inner door, adjusted his boots to adhere as best they could to a surface intended for escapees to slide on, and began a slow crawl inward and forward to the flight deck.

On the way, he spoke to the others. Scotty and Pharch had found the small door set in the larger door of the passenger airlock, and had engaged with it and powered down, but they were having trouble getting it opened up.

Shorty and Merton had teamed up to work on the same entry, about amidships, where cargo would be stowed. Wilson had suspected that Shorty would be a good man with doors, and he was. Their trouble was that their own ships, tethered loosely to the liner, were still blasting away at a third of a gee—the highest boost, apparently, of which the *City of Newark* was capable—and they would have to be attached to the liner rigidly, somehow, before they could shut her down.

"We're into the passenger lock," Scotty said abruptly. "There's a headless—"

Merton and Shorty made noises that went with a grimace and Wilson sincerely hoped he wasn't listening to Scotty or Pharch throwing up inside their helmets. It would take the nanobots at least an hour to clean it up.

"—Oh, geez. Almost lost it there for a moment. There's a, uh, headless body in the main airlock. Looks like it could be one of the East American government's spaceship cops. We'll go on into the ship, now."

*
**

"Where do you suppose he's headed?" Casey McCarthy asked nobody in particular. Marko could see Casey's *Lady of Spain* running to port of his own asteroid hunter *Mina*. Mikey's *Albuquerque Gal* was on his starboard.

He replied, "Looks to me like he's circling back to the Earth/Moon system, or possibly one of the Lagrange points. He seems to be sending encrypted signals back that way. I don't believe he's gonna make it, though."

"Not gonna make it?" Casey asked. "Why? Is something wrong with his—"

"He's not gonna make it," said Marko, "because I'm not gonna *let* him make it!"

"Oh," said Casey. "I see—you're not gonna blow the guy up, are you? Don't do that. What about the reward?"

Mikey snorted. "What reward? Nobody said anything about a reward. Doesn't 'Action is our reward' mean anything to you guys?" It probably didn't. The reference was almost two centuries obsolete.

Marko said, "Okay, when we get caught up to the *White Winged Dove*, carefully shoot for his upper engine. Less chance of hitting his pressurized spaces that way, and don't fail to remember that he could be carrying hostages."

Mikey quickly signaled his assent. For a long moment afterward, however, there was complete silence over the intership radio.

"Casey?" Marko demanded.

"I was the guy who wanted to keep 'em in one piece, anyway."

"That you were, Casey," said Mikey. "That you were. There may yet be a reward, who knows?

"Oh yeah, who from?" asked Marko.

"That's 'whom from'," Mikey corrected him.

Casey rushed in. "From the East American spacelines whose passenger ship was hijacked. They'd probably like to get it back. It's only worth seventy or eighty quadrillion East American funnybucks."

"And so is my little baby sister's tricycle!" said Marko. They laughed.

"Or from the owners whose yacht was stolen," said Mikey. Then he remembered the chairman of the board and his secretary. They were probably having a pretty good time, up until they died. "Or their heirs."

Marko suggested, "Maybe even from the Curringer Corporation, it-self, for saving all those lives and all that infrastructure on Mars. Biggest terraformation project ever done, and the cheapest, but still ... "

"I like the way you guys think," Casey said. "Howya figure that last?"

"From the course the *City of Newark* was on," Marko told him. "Mars was pretty obviously the target, but I checked with my cyber-ephemeris, and I think they were planning to deorbit Phobos and kill Mars."

Mikey and Casey both whistled.

"Like the dinosaurs," Casey said. "Neat, if it's physically possible."

Marko began, "That's why—Hang on a minute, I've got a visual. Now to get my crosshairs on that upper engine ... fire!" They both saw his tracer splash the ship ahead. The working beam that ran parallel to it, of course, was invisible. "Damn! No apparent effect."

"You're shooting right down the bore of the engine. You can't fight a plasma torch with a laser," Mikey said. That's like a water fight where one guy has a fire hose and the other has a squirtgun."

"I believe you—hang on!" Marko accelerated until he had drawn even with the stolen pleasure vessel, then fired at the side of the upper engine, which obliged him by coming apart in a hail of rocket parts.

"Watch him! Watch him!" Casey shouted. "He's turning again! He's turning!"

* * *

Crenicichla had just transmitted his acceptance of the mysterious of-fer he'd received by text message, along with the number of a Swiss bank account containing a hundred thousand ounces of platinum, when the explosion of the upper engine lifted the tail of the stolen space yacht in a way that he didn't know how to compensate for. The ship was still going full blast—apparently the engines were completely independent—but at a lower rate of acceleration, and it was slowly beginning to describe a large vertical circle as the pitch—

Pitch. That was it, pitch. His eyes devoured the console slanting up before him, until they came to section labeled "Pitch Management". Yes, there was some kind of indicator built into the panel—an inset red light that was blinking furiously; he wondered why he hadn't seen it before now—and it agreed with him about what the spacecraft was doing.

He reached over to his left and flipped a toggle labeled "Auto Pitch Control", heard noises from the thrusters under the vessel's nose, and the ship slowly stopped falling forward the way it had been doing.

But the heading … the heading … the goddamned heading …

Radar said that his attackers, three of them, had overflown him and were coming back around now for a second pass. It took him what seemed like an eternity to find out what the heading had been, how far off course they were now, and how to get back on course. He began pushing buttons.

At least he knew now that his original mission was a guaranteed success.

"I wouldn't bother with all that stuff if I were you," said a voice from behind him. It was a man's voice, with a quality something like peanut-buttered sandpaper. Turning around in the pilot's seat as far as the four-point seatbelt system would allow, Crenicichla reached for the auto-pistol under his jacket, but it was gone. He remembered taking it out and setting it aside somewhere when he was working on Krystal.

"Looking for this?" the stranger asked, holding Crenicichla's pistol between thumb and forefinger. It was the plastic kind that required little training or practice to operate, intended for people who didn't like guns much. The man's other hand held some kind of plasma weapon with a huge, pitted orifice. "I found it down in your makeshift hospital."

Crenicichla put his hand out. "Nice of you to bring it to me."

The man grinned and put it in his pocket. "Do you have any idea how hard it is to climb that aisle ladder at the one third gee you're doing?"

"Well, gosh, if I'd known—"

"That was a good job you did with Krystal, by the way. I was a medic in the last war my country ever fought, and I should know. She's pretty badly busted up, but my guess is that she'll outlive both of us."

Crenicichla was about to respond by reflex to the compliment, but stopped himself. The interloper was in his late fifties or early sixties, incredibly tall and lanky. He stood casually behind the co-pilot's seat, his head brushing the ceiling. "Who the hell are you, and how did you get on my ship?"

"Your ship? Stolen fair and square from—oh, well, we'll let that pass." He looked down modestly. "I go by a lot of names. Call me Ishmael."

"*I will not!*" He discovered he'd pounded both fists on the chair arms.

The newcomer laughed. "Then call me Aaron. I got in because you had other errands to run and didn't secure the airlock the very first thing. It's a common error. I might have made it myself, given the circumstances."

Crenicichla was furious. "What do you want?"

"Not a lot, really. My job here is more or less finished. I was hired to protect a couple of young people from you and yours, becoming very fond of them in the process, and I figured that the best way to help them, at this point, is to come along with you and make sure you don't get into any more trouble—at least any trouble that involves them."

"Llyra Ngu and Jasmeen Khalidov—or Wilson Ngu. I should have known."

"No point denying it," he shrugged. "It's been one of my most interesting cases, and one of the most educational, what with all the figure skating and asteroid hunting. A person should never stop learning."

"It's an outrage, that's what it is! Why, they're nothing but parasites! Spoiled, wealthy children of privilege—they're just plain bad luck!"

"For you, maybe, but what does that make your backers, and their centuries and generations of ill-gotten plunder? Say, we're about to have company again. Why don't you get to work now and put us on a new heading?"

"Why should I—oh, that's right. Because you have the guns. What heading?"

Aaron looked thoughtful and smiled. "How about Mars?"

"Mars?" Crenicichla was shocked. "But if I do that—"

"We'll be destroyed when the planet is? You know, somehow I doubt it, Johnnie. My guess is that we're being fired on by a little group—probably working with Llyra's brother Wilson—who are also doing something about the *City of Newark* right now. Those are asteroid hunters out there, my young friend, and they're accustomed to dragging large celestial objects traveling at absurdly high velocities, off course."

"But the Cause! All of my plans—" Suddenly he felt grateful to his mysterious and mercenary correspondent. Maybe he hadn't spent all that money in vain.

"They'll board that space liner, get her engines shut down, and if anybody they care for has been injured, let alone killed, then they'll track you down like some kind of animal, Johnnie, pull your intestines out through a hole in your navel, tenderly roast them over a slow fire while you watch, and feed them to you an inch at a time. What do you think of that for a plan? You'd be better off on Mars even if it does explode."

Hardly able to function for the icy terror pumping through his veins—he couldn't remember ever being more frightened than this—Crenicichla let the computer tell him how to get to Mars from where he was, and—

just as Marko and his three friends passed again, spitting fire and metal—ducked under on a new heading to the formerly Red Planet.

CHAPTER FORTY: SURVIVORS

Catastrophe is a peculiar thing. It might take an individual who has been a complete failure in life and turn him into a hero who, once the emergency is over with, slides comfortably back into failure again. That's a fairly common chain of events. Or it can take a competent, successful individual and turn him into a blubbering weakling. I've seen that happen, too.

The thing is, you can never predict exactly how it'll turn out. You can only watch—and laugh or weep—as it happens. —*The Diaries of Rosalie Frazier Ngu*

IT WAS *COLD* IN HERE.

Wilson could tell that in several ways. Among them, the little microscopic scrubbers inside his helmet were having difficulty keeping up with the frost that wanted to form on the inside of his faceplate. He tried hard breathing downward, away from the faceplate, but it didn't work very well.

He, himself, was warm enough. This was an exceptionally good envirosuit his grandmother had insisted on, and these were considerably milder conditions than it had been manufactured for. He paid close attention, however, to his toes and fingers, and had his suit monitoring their temperature.

When he had crawled the full length of the escape tunnel—an easier job than he had expected it would be—he ran into a circular door at the top. Featureless, it didn't yield to pressure, nor could he fit a finger into the crack that divided the two halves, to pull it open.

He hadn't thought to bring a tool belt along—a major failure in his estimation. So much for the great rescuer. He had a caliper that would have worked perfectly. He considered using one of his guns, but suddenly realized that he didn't know what the conditions were on the other side of the door. In the tunnel, it was a hundred and ten below zero, and while there was plenty of nitrogen and traces of rare gases, the carbon dioxide had frozen out—he could look back at the trail he'd made in the dry ice frost—and the oxygen fraction was all but gone.

He opened the control panel on his left arm and pulled out one of many thermocouples that informed his suit of conditions outside of its protection. He gently teased it out, without yanking hard on the fine wires connecting it. He pulled out his field knife, a heavy nine-inch titanium alloy blade recommended specifically for use in space, formed into the shape that knifesmiths and their clients often refer to as a "sharpened prybar".

He adjusted the microphones outside his suit to the maximum, and began working the knife, slowly and deliberately, into the fine line that separated the halves of the circular door. He heard no hissing or rushing noise, which meant that the atmospheric pressure levels on each side of the door were more or less equal. When he could see a tiny glimmer of light through the space he'd made, he inserted the thermocouple into it along the unsharpened back edge of the heavy knife.

Brrrrr! The same miserable hundred and ten degrees. He reclaimed his thermocouple, tucked it away, and began prying in earnest at the door halves. At some point, the electronics in the door must have decided that somebody had caught something important in the gasketing while trying to get away, and it opened, surprising Wilson, releasing his knife, and nearly spilling him back down the tunnel, the way he'd come.

Hanging on by his elbows, he thrust himself up into the control area, put his knife away in the scabbard built into his suit, and pushed a labeled button that reclosed the door. To his left, he saw a human form still sitting in the pilot's chair. Expecting the worst, he approached the seated body, turned the chair, and looked down at a lifeless face. She had been blond, almost pretty, and wore an East American Space Lines uniform. But she hadn't died of cold or anoxia. Her head hung on her chest in a manner suggesting that her neck had been broken. It would have been easy to prove if she hadn't been frozen solid.

The navigation computer in front of her had been ripped loose of its system of sensors and servos, and was probably worthless. He wondered if she'd done it—a forensic inspection would tell, he supposed. He found a panel that gave him views of various areas throughout the ship, which seemed, except for this young woman, to be deserted.

Then he began finding bodies here and there, an inordinate number of young men wearing identical gray suits, almost like a uniform, and an ununiformed individual here and there. They were all dead and covered with frost.

Finally, he found a view of the service core. At the very bottom, nearest the engines, he saw a sight that nearly made him collapse in despair.

Dozens, maybe hundreds of bodies were huddled together in the failing warmth, probably having breathed their last breaths of decent air. Green cylinders were scatted everywhere. It looked like they'd collected and exhausted every canister of emergency oxygen in the ship.

There was more than one camera in the service core, but, try as he might, he couldn't see his sister or Jasmeen. That was probably a good thing.

He spoke. "Scotty, do you hear me?"

"Indeed, I do, Commodore. We're aft in the engineering spaces, Pharch and me. These pirates, or whatever they were, really knew how to screw up beautiful machinery. All six engines are at full throttle, producing one third of a gee, but there doesn't seem to be any easy way left to control them."

Wilson said, "Well, whatever you do, don't open the service core yet. There are hundreds of bodies in there, hundreds, just forward of where you are. They're all almost certainly dead—" It had been extremely difficult to say that. "—but I don't want to take a chance. Think about how we can access them without killing them, will you?"

"Aye, aye, Commodore. "Did you see—"

"No, I didn't. Shorty and Merton, did you copy that? Don't enter the—"

"I may have a solution for you, Wilson." It was Merton, who was turning out to be surprisingly resourceful. "It looks like there's some kind of emergency refuge on the cargo deck where they normally carry heavy machinery. It's someplace they could go if a Caterpillar tractor got loose and went out through the hull. I'm looking at it now—it's tiny—but it seems to have an inner hatch connecting to the service core."

"It wasn't in the blueprints," Scotty added. He had a memory for engineering.

Merton replied, "It has the look of a retrofit, and a fairly clumsy one."

"You want us to go in?" asked Shorty.

"No, no," said Wilson. "Wait for me. We'll all go in at the same time."

"I'll stay below," Pharch volunteered. "And keep an eye on the engines."

*
**

Conditions in the cargo hold were much the same as everywhere else aboard the *City of Newark*, with slightly higher concentrations of oxygen than on the upper decks—the organisms that consumed it were further away—but not quite enough to sustain life. It was abysmally cold.

Wilson joined his friends at the makeshift airlock, having moved *Mighty Mouse's Girlfriend* to a closer mooring. Everything inside the hold was covered with a thin layer of carbon dioxide snow. On this deck, it seemed to be mostly heavy construction equipment, bound, he guessed, for Mars, or perhaps even for transshipment to the Jupiter project, or Ceres. Some of it looked like machinery that his father had argued about with the Curringer Corporation and had planned to order.

"Gentlemen," Wilson told his friends, reaching for the airlock door, "I'll be going in first. After all, it's my kid sister in there."

And Jasmeen.

Nobody wanted to challenge Wilson on that point. He opened the outer door, squeezed into the small amount of space available inside—the airlock had been hastily constructed from common sandwich panels, relatively thin titanium alloy on the outsides, half an inch of foamed aluminum on the inside, the panels welded together into a box with ragged edges and corners that could tear an envirosuit if its wearer happened to be careless—and told the others, "Okay, who else is coming? There may be room for one more in here, as long as they're pretty small."

"As much as it pains me to admit it … " Shorty didn't finish the sentence, but managed to squeeze in beside Wilson. The door swung closed.

Wilson looked at Scotty through a porthole inset in the door. "Why don't you and Merton stay out here and watch our ships—unless we call you? It's probably not going to be a very pleasant sight in there."

Scotty nodded. "We'll just be sitting here, all alone by the telephone."

"No," Merton said. "I'll be back at my ship, collecting oxy canisters, just in case."

"Good thinking. Check mine, too. Here we go." Wilson opened the inner door and stepped onto a tiny steel platform. A ladder beside it ran the length of the core, a little over a thousand feet.

"Whoa!" Shorty had nearly missed the platform and fallen into the core. They both knew that a fall like that, even at one third gee, was fatal.

Down at the bottom, they could just make out the huddled bodies, looking a bit like they were lightly covered with snow. Wilson was tempted to use the magnifying feature of his faceplate, but he decided against it.

Instead, he swung around so that his hands were on the outer uprights of the long ladder, his feet clamped around them the same way.

"You okay, Shorty?" In a way, he was asking himself the same question.

"Sure, Commodore. I'll be right behind you." The tough-guy from Lost Angeles sounded a little scared.

Wilson loosened his grip on the ladder just a little, and began to slide down toward the two or three hundred human bodies lying at the bottom of the core. Shorty was directly above him. It didn't take long until they reached the last of the platforms, just inside its access door. This would be another cargo level, forward of the engineering spaces.

There were people lying everywhere, close together, some of them bloodied, some of them not. There were green emergency oxygen bottles everywhere, as well, a few of them still hissing. It looked to Wilson as if the passengers had all covered themselves with table linen from the restaurant. His suit gauges told him it was twenty-five degrees in here—above zero—and that there was only enough oxygen remaining for—

Suddenly, an old man lying directly at Wilson's feet shivered and pulled the tablecloth over his face, settling deeper into the huddle. His movement stirred those around him, and a wave of motion slowly made its way out across the mass of bodies lying on the floor below Wilson.

"Holy crap, Commodore, looks like they're alive! Well, most of 'em, anyway!" He didn't know what he was feeling, but Wilson would surely remember this moment for the rest of his life, and so would Shorty.

Wilson shouted into his suit mike, "Scotty! Merton! Pharch! Get that spare oxygen down here right away!" To Scotty: "Later on, we can run a line from one of our ships if we have to. Hell, it looks like they're all alive!"

"We'll do it," said Scotty. "But I'll have to climb back into my envirosuit. I have life support back up! Air and heat. Believe it or not, there are auxiliary controls on every deck of this ship! And this cargo bay is at eighty degrees *above*. It's actually starting to get hot!"

One of the forms below looked up at him. In some ways, it was like a scene out of Dante. "Wilson, is it really you? I knew you'd come, somehow!"

"Llyra!" Then he checked to see if he'd switched on the speakers mounted on the outside of his suit. He had, but how was he going to get down to his baby sister without stepping on somebody with his heavy boots? How cold was the outside of his suit? He didn't want to give her frostbite, or anybody else. Where was Jasmeen? Why weren't the damned nanobots taking care of the condensation that was suddenly blurring his vision? "Yes, yes, it's me! I'm coming. I'll be right there!"

Somehow, he managed to make his way down to her. Instead of trying to embrace him, which would have been difficult, considering his suit, she simply wrapped both of her small arms around one of his. When she sat up, she lifted the cloth. He saw Jasmeen beside her, her eyes on his own, sparkling and beautiful. With his free hand, he took one of hers.

"Oh, Wilson," Llyra told him, "I'm so happy we're not going to die!"

"Me, too, kid." He was having more of that faceplate problem. "Me, too!"

⁂

He is not little boy any more, Jasmeen thought, looking across Llyra at Wilson. *Has not been for long time. He is full grown man, for all that he is two years younger than I am. He appears to be natural-born leader, natural-born hero of variety my mother and father once told me about. He is space pilot, asteroid hunter, gunfighter, businessman, and, oh yes, he is father—or will be in another few weeks.*

He is Llyra's brother, for Allah's sake!

Wilson had ordered the survivors all taken, a few at a time in the elevators, to the forward observation lounge. There was plenty of room there for rest and treatment, and he hadn't wanted them to have to see the dining room again, with its smashed furniture and bloodsoaked carpet.

It looked like somebody had been decapitated down there. Probably the someone on the passenger lock.

Scotty had managed to shut the engines down from an auxiliary control space by cutting off their reaction mass—East American Space Lines used Lunar granite dust—then pulling the catalytic palladium rods from the fusion reactors. They weren't floating all over the ship because she was now under tow by four asteroid hunters, including Wilson's, at about one tenth of a gee.

For some reason, Pimble Pharch couldn't be found. His ship. *Lilac Waffle,* was gone, as well.

Just now, Wilson didn't give a damn about Pharch. He was sitting with Jasmeen and his sister on a huge, deep, comfortable sofa. The girls were wrapped in a warm blanket together, sipping hot chocolated coffee. He'd taken off his helmet and gloves. Merton and Shorty had gotten the kitchen restarted somehow, and had plenty of hot food and drink for anyone who needed them.

At present, they had lots of customers. Two-hundred eighty-five individuals had taken refuge in the service core, not counting a small handful of thoroughly dead bodies that the passengers all swore were part of the hijackers' gang. Some had broken necks, others had been stabbed or simply shot. Wilson believed that someone here had killed them.

And for some reason, was keeping quiet about it.

His phone rang. "Talk to me."

It was Scotty. "I believe we can do it, Commodore. I've got the course calculated and ready to send and found all the good attachment points."

"Let me talk with the Captain," Wilson told him, "I'll get back to you."

He stood up and looked down at Llyra and Jasmeen. Their color was beginning to come back. "We're about to turn this ship over and get her decelerating, but I need to confer with Captain West. It won't be too rough, but it won't be unnoticeable like it was meant to be. When the time comes, both of you find something that's bolted down and hang on."

Jasmeen cast her half of the blanket aside and stood up, fully recovered—or giving that impression, anyway. Somehow Wilson had forgotten how appealing her tight little body was, half athletic, half voluptuous. It was even possible that he'd never really noticed until now.

Llyra rose with her. "You confer with Captain," Jasmeen said. She'd pronounced it "Keptin", which he found irresistibly appealing for some reason. "We will help everybody else find bolts to hang on." Llyra seized her brother's hand, and before he knew it, her coach had taken the other. "Thank you for saving lives," the older of the two girls said. Was that a tear in her eye? "Some cultures would say that you own them now."

He swallowed. "Neither of you owes me thanks. You're my family. You have no idea what it was like to find you two alive, after what I'd ..." He turned and walked away, wondering exactly what had just happened.

If anything.

He found the Captain at the opposite side of the lounge with his crew, most of whom seemed to have survived the attempted hijacking. They had pulled several pieces of the comfortable lounge furniture together and were sharing warm blankets and hot drinks with one another.

"You know," the Captain said to Wilson. They had seen each other several times since the asteroid hunters' arrival, but had not been introduced. "I was offered a fireplace for this room, one of those round ones with a conical hood? Next time I'll consider it more seriously. I think I like the idea of a spaceship leaving a trail of smoke behind from its chimney."

Looking down at the Captain's blanket-covered form, Wilson told him, "As soon as you can give me a list of your fatalities, sir, I'll have them beamcast straight back to your company in the Earth/Moon system."

"Don't 'sir' me, son," he told Wilson. I take it you're in charge of the rescue party, and you command more vessels than I do. Call me Al."

"Okay, Al, but it's vessels I lead, not command."

"A fine distinction, but an important one. To begin to answer your question, we lost a Space Marshal and two people from the kitchen. I don't know if that's complete, but I'll find out and let you know. At the moment, nobody's at their duty stations." He waved an arm, taking in his shaken crew, sitting around him. "I wouldn't have it any other way."

Wilson nodded.

"The opposition fared a lot worse," West suggested.

"Yes, Al, nineteen dead and still counting. I'd like to talk to you about that sometime. But we're ready now to get your ship turned around. I need you to send somebody down and round up all those oxygen bottles. I wouldn't want to be turning this ship over, and have one of them come sailing out through the wall of the service core. I also wanted to discuss the possibility of restarting her engines after turnover."

The Captain nodded.

"The boys and I could probably decelerate you all the way to Mars with our ships, and we've got three more coming back to join us right now. But we were at high-boost almost on the opposite heading when we got the message, we're all getting a little short on reaction mass, and ... "

"You would appreciate our helping ourselves, to whatever extent we can. Very well ... I heard your people call you 'Commodore', is that right?"

"It's a joke." He reached a hand down to the Captain. "I'm Wilson Ngu—and yes, Al, it's *those* Ngus, including my baby sister over there."

"She handles a Ngu Departure Mark Two pretty effectively for a baby."

Wilson laughed. "My sister Llyra is probably an East American's worst nightmare. She came about as close to being born with a gun in her hand as anybody ever has. She's a much better long-range shot than I am, and I'm a three-tournament *silhueta* winner, back home."

The Captain nodded and began to get up off the overstuffed sofa. "I'll be down to inspect the engines as soon as I can move my legs again."

*
**

Four hours later, through the transparent dome of his own little vessel, Wilson could see Captain West sitting in his chair on the flight deck of the *City of Newark*, flanked by a couple members of his bridge crew. The bodies of the young woman and the other hijackers had been put away in cold storage on one of the cargo decks until they could be properly identified.

Somehow, he doubted if they ever would. Only East America still kept files of fingerprints and retinal patterns. The rest of humanity had moved on too quickly for that to follow. From what he'd learned from the passengers, a couple of hijackers were missing, including the woman who'd been at the spaceport with the assassin who'd murdered Fallon. He very badly wanted to have a private conversation with her.

There was a passenger missing, too, an old man who had befriended and defended Llyra and Jasmeen, and who could kill with a thrown table knife. A private conversation with him would probably be illuminating, as well.

Pimble Pharch seemed gone for good.

Once they'd started, it hadn't taken West's technicians—with the aid of Shorty—half an hour to repair the dense network of plugs and cables that connected the navigational computer with various systems it controlled, or that sent it information. In fact, it had taken the Captain somewhat longer to reprogram it. Other bridge functions had been restored, as well. It would be the Captain who gave the Turnover command.

Meanwhile, the ships Wilson had sent after the yacht were back, safe, if empty-handed.

"Very well, my fellow captains," West spoke to Wilson, Marko, Mikey, and Scotty, whose ships presently stood at the ends of long lines attached to the larger spaceship, every engine silent. "Captain West has given the word. If it's agreeable, let's make it thirty seconds on my mark. Are you ready? Mark!"

Wilson watched numbers, hanging in the air before his face, count down.

Mighty Mouse's Girlfriend and Marko's *Mina* (named after a Chinese movie star, Wilson had learned), were attached to towing bollards near the front end of the space liner, *Albuquerque Gal* and *Nessie*, at her stern. The pair forward—Wilson and Marko—would pull at her, taking her ninety degrees off the line she presently occupied, turning her on an imaginary point amidships. Mikey and Scotty would gently brake her, until she had completed a full one hundred eighty degree rotation, confirmed by her Captain.

"Five, four, three, two, one!" *Mighty Mouse's Girlfriend* fired one of her three engines. The other two would be unnecessary—and perhaps too much—for this job. He could see that Marko's ship had done the same. The stars reeled about them as the collection of ships pivoted on the liner's horizontal axis. In seconds, she was halfway where they wanted her to be, and the two ships at the bow stopped blasting.

The Captain said, "Cut!" abruptly to Mikey and Scotty, after they had braked her practically to a halt. He then let his fingers play across his own keyboard—Wilson could see it under magnification—firing powerful thrusters fore and aft that brought the ship to rest, her stern now pointed at where Mars would be about ten days from now. The asteroid hunters cast off—their lines would be gathered in later—and hovered, waiting for her six hybrid fusion engines to fire.

There was a fugitive flickering, and then there they were, six big frying pans at the stern of the ship, filled to their brims with a brilliant blue-white hell. The *City of Newark* worked her way up to one tenth of a gee—Wilson and his friends kept up—and stayed there for the next four hours, as her badly-abused systems were checked.

And double-checked.

Wilson took a shower in the comfort of his own ship, had a hot meal, and then called his sister. The spaceliner had some kind of communication relay that made ordinary phones work perfectly. It was a nice touch, and one he wouldn't have expected from anything East American.

"Llyra Ngu's telephone. Is Jasmeen Khalidov speaking." She sounded extremely serious, exactly the way they always portrayed Martians on 3DTV.

For some odd reason, Wilson's heart began beating a little more quickly in his chest. "Uh, hello, Jasmeen. May I speak with my sister?"

"No, Wilson," she said, still very serious. "You may not."

Was that humor in her voice or was that just wishful thinking on his part? "Okay," he told her at last, "I'll bite. Why can't I talk to Llyra?"

"Because telephone is not waterproof. Your sister is taking shower."

He laughed. "Okay, I'll call back later." He started to thumb it off.

"Is good idea," he heard her say. "Is better idea if you come over and have dinner with us here. They have dining room almost fixed now and kitchen works perfectly. I do not think that they have room service. Llyra needs to see you around, Wilson. Makes her much less afraid."

"I'll be happy to come over. I was just going to lock onto the *City of Newark* anyway and shut my engines down for a while. Save a little reaction mass that way. But I have to tell you, Jasmeen, I don't believe there's anything in the universe that my sister's afraid of."

There was a pause at the other end, then, "Do it for me, then, Wilson."

An odd thrill went through his body. "Dinner it is, then, in an hour." What the hell was wrong with him? He'd known Jasmeen for years and never felt this awkward and tongue-tied in her presence before. It must be a reaction to nearly losing her and his sister.

That was it, only a reaction.

Hands above the keyboard, he was about to head for one of the larger ship's airlocks, when there was an explosion—a big one—he actually heard it as the wavefront of expanding gases rolled over his ship.

Backing away on his thrusters, he saw that one of the *City of Newark*'s six engines was missing, an impossible tangle of fiery wreckage taking its place. Chunks of shrapnel were flying in every direction.

The Captain had his wits about him, though, and cut his other five engines almost instantaneously. "*Mighty Mouse's Girlfriend? Mina?* Anybody else? Did anybody happen to get the license number of that bus?"

Wilson answered, "Your number four engine just blew up, Captain, with what appears to be minimal damage to the rest of the ship. You don't appear to be venting atmosphere. You are off course again. How are you for air pressure?"

"We look fine, on the boards. You gentlemen want to give us a little inspection? That had the feel of deliberate sabotage to it—or am I just being paranoid? Nope, I just checked and there *are* people out to get me—or my ship. I'm not going to trust those engines again until I tear them apart and put them back together again with my bare hands.

"I don't think you're paranoid, Captain," Wilson said.

Scotty added, "And even paranoids have enemies."

"How reassuring," said the Captain.

"We'll inspect the hull for you, Captain. What will you do for power—"

"We may have to depend on you, sir, although it grieves me deeply to—"

"Don't give it a thought. We'll inspect the ship and then I'm coming aboard. Ngu out." He picked up his phone and punched a single button.

Jasmeen again. "You two all right down there?" he asked. "Slipped in the shower, did she? Only a bruise? I'm glad to hear it. But the *City of Newark* just lost an engine, and I'm going to be a little late for dinner."

*
**

Aaron Manzel, the individual who sometimes thought of himself as the Fastest Gun in the Moon, fired an opposing pair of thrusters in the little spaceship's stubby wings, rolling her so that she appeared to be orbiting *over* Mars, instead of under. He'd always hated it the other way around. Somehow it never failed to make him feel gloomy and claustrophobic.

"There, that's better, isn't it?" he asked his companion.

His companion didn't answer, but gave him a murderous look.

The *Swan*-class yacht *White-Winged Dove* groaned alarmingly as she rolled in response, her backbone severely bent, if not completely broken. She'd held together so far, but she'd probably been dealt a mortal blow, he thought, when her angry pursuers had destroyed her upper engine. They'd looked like a squadron of asteroid hunters, and he wondered if Llyra Ngu's brother Wilson had been among them. In any case, the ship would almost certainly come apart when he tried to land her.

Manzel attempted to be philosophical about it. After all, he'd lived to see, and do, quite a number of wonderful things—certainly far more than his fair share—in his long and adventure-filled life. Unfortunately, he didn't believe in that nonsense about fair shares. There was quite a number of wonderful things remaining for him to see and do—and quite a number he wanted to see and do again.

He'd lied to his new friends: Mars was not one of them.

Unlike the Earth, all swirly blue and white—and most beautiful when she was stormiest—Mars was unpleasant to gaze upon at the best of times. To begin with, under a cloud cover that was only occasional even now, the world was covered with meteoric scars large, medium, and small. A mottled orangey-pink in the few remaining desert regions, and a sickening mustard yellow where the macaroni plants had taken over altogether, the whole planet closely resembled a gigantic infected wound, centered on the three thousand mile gash that was Valles Marineris.

"Unidentified spacecraft," came a powerful radio signal from the ground. They could probably roast an ox on a spit close to their antenna.

The ship was presently over Valles Marineris, that vast and complicated system of equatorial rifts and prehistoric river canyons, now filled once again with coursing water. It was the most highly developed and densely populated region of the Formerly Red Planet, because it was very nearly the lowest, and possessed the richest atmosphere.

"This is Coprates Spaceport Control. Do not approach without permission and instructions. I say again, do not approach without permission—"

"This is *White Winged Dove*, Coprates Spaceport Control," Manzel answered. "Lately out of Port Armstrong in Luna. Your message heard and understood, but probably not doable. I've only got four or five orbits left in this poor crippled bird, and then she's for the long singe and a messy landing. I'll try very hard not to ugly up any of your runways."

"White Winged—I thought I recognized that Swan-class profile! So you're the one! You're hot, whoever you are. I'll come and arrest you, myself, for the reward! That's a stolen ship you're flying! She's implicated in the hijacking of the East American space liner and cold-blooded murder!"

"Well she's since been stolen back, Coprates Spaceport Control, Scout's Honor and sorry about your reward. By the way, if you're in communication with *City of Newark*, have them inform Miss Ngu and Miss Khalidov that their friend Aaron made it this far. I have references to back up what I'm saying, and a pair of Null Delta Em prisoners."

"Null Delta—"

"Furthermore, Coprates Spaceport Control, *White Winged Dove*'s owners are more than welcome to recover any of her that's left after I set her down. Almost certainly, I won't be in any condition to protest."

Martians loved to see themselves as fatalists and stoics. They loved that kind of talk, although, for the most part, he really meant it this time.

Manzel winked at Crenicichla, gagged and taped into the copilot's seat. Crenicichla glared back. Manzel grinned at his prisoner.

The radio said, "We only *have* one runway, *White Winged Dove.*" For shuttlecraft from both moonports. Manzel shrugged to himself. In many ways Mars was still a frontier planet and would probably always remain so. For reasons dating back to their brief war of independence from Earth, Martians didn't like things hanging over their heads in orbit and had developed ways of dealing with them.

"Okay, then, Coprates Spaceport Control," he told them. "I'll try hard to miss it if it's at all possible. Can you recommend a nice, soft desert nearby, where your emergency vehicles can reach us in a hurry?"

"Locate Coprates Chasma in the eastern half of Valles Marineris—you should have charts. Look for a horseshoe-shaped astrobleme tight against the south canyon wall—that's where we are: Coprates City and Coprates Interplanetary Spaceport. There's a large sandy basin to the west, between the horseshoe crater and an isolated set of little mountains. Land anywhere in that basin, we can be there within half an hour. Sooner, if we start now!"

Manzel displayed one chart after another on the navigation screens until he found what he wanted. He then overlapped the view from one of the ship's exterior pickups on the screen. There it was. He would land as close to the horseshoe-shaped crater—and the spaceport—as he could.

"Got you, Coprates. A nice little desert, as ordered, and a gentle turn to starboard at the bottom." He wondered if the structure of the ship would survive it. "Should be interesting. Follow us down if you can."

"Will do, *White Winged Dove,* and good luck. You're gonna need it."

"You're telling me."

CHAPTER FORTY-ONE: FESTIVAL OF WRECKAGE

It's one thing to smile at other people's customs and tell yourself how liberal and broadminded and multicultural you are for putting up with them. It's quite another thing to suffer—or to see your loved ones suffer—because of some savage, idiotic practice that's sacred simply because it's been going on for decades or centuries or millennia.

A real civilization is *not* "multicultural". It *has* no arbitrary customs or practices that put your life, limb, and luggage at risk. It got rid of them all a long time ago, and it will never welcome them back again. —*The Diaries of Rosalie Frazier Ngu*

"SO IT WAS SABOTAGE," HE said, mostly to himself.

Wilson sat in the transparent nose of *Mighty Mouse's Girlfriend*, looking down on *City of Newark*, watching sparks, vapor, and debris still coming out of the ragged place where one of her engines had just exploded.

"Can't be any question about it, Wilson!" Shorty was aboard the crippled liner, in the engine room. He'd gone there originally to survey the damage from the blast. Instead, he'd found five suspect packages—about two and a quarter pounds apiece—carefully hidden in each of the engines.

Wilson wished he was using a video pickup so he could see Shorty's face.

"I knew something weird was going on," he told Wilson. "I never saw a hybrid fusion reactor let go that way before, and neither have you. It's one of the reasons we use them. No, it was C-17, an old-time military explosive. Almost nostalgic, kinda like using dynamite. Looks like a heat-sensitive detonator. The engines start running, they reach a certain temperature, and *Ka-blamm!* Captain says Number Four always tended to run a little bit hotter than the other five. He's lucky it did!"

The man must really be rattled, Wilson thought. He's forgetting to call me Commodore. "Okay, Shorty, I agree with you on all points. Whoever did this, it has to be somebody who didn't know about Number Four running hot. And it has to have been done after we originally shut the engines down. I know what I think. What does the Captain think?"

"The Captain's momentarily indisposed. He was closer to Number Four than I was when it blew, and picked up a little shrapnel. Nothing serious. Your sister and her sexy friend are patching him up. He was the first to say the word 'sabotage', even before we found these other five bombs."

Wilson wasn't sure he liked hearing Jasmeen talked about that way. On the other hand, Shorty probably didn't know any better, growing up dangerously, as he had, in old Lost Angeles, so he decided to let it slide.

This time.

He asked, "So you don't think it was a present Null Delta Em left behind?"

"What the galoshes, Commodore," Shorty answered. "You said it yourself. When Null Delta Em hit the road—the two that made it—all six engines were running full out, hot and heavy, pushing three gees."

Wilson nodded. "Yeah, I did say something a lot like that, didn't I?"

"Besides, Commodore, they were gonna smash this ship into a flying mountain. What did they need military explosives for? I hate to say it, but this looks a lot more like some kind of inside job to me. I got me one other suspicion, but I don't really wanna say it over the radio."

Wilson heard with a sinking heart. He'd hoped there'd be no more trouble on this journey. He was pretty sure he knew what Shorty was going to tell him. "Well, do what you can, Shorty. If you think you've found all the bombs, we can start her up again. If not, I guess we can tow her to Mars of we have to—we may have trouble recovering our costs."

"Then we can always keep her! We'll take turns being captain—oh, Captain West. You weren't supposed to hear that—I was only kidding!" To Wilson: "Funny thing—he was standing right behind me all this time."

"Alan West, here, Captain Ngu," said the Captain. "Thanks to your sister and her friend, I've just missed needing a jaunty, piratical eyepatch."

Wilson grinned. "My condolences, Captain West. What can I do for you?"

"Well, I've decided to let your colleague here live, despite the fact he wants to steal my ship. I'll also see, personally, that all of your costs are covered if you tow my ship to Mars. Water and oxygen we can make, but we can't do the kind of safety inspecting we have to do to restart these engines, not and get to port before our food runs out."

Wilson sighed, but only to himself. Although he'd rather be chasing rocks, a job was a job. "I'll talk to the others. We can be underway again in a couple of hours. Reaction mass is going to be problematic."

"Perhaps not, sir. Have each of your asteroid hunters stop by the cargo lock that you came in by the last time. We'll have a sizeable load of freshly-chopped dining room furniture for you, dishes, table service, linens, and whatever else you think your coffee grinders will handle."

"How about dead hijackers," Shorty asked. Wilson hoped he was kidding.

"We need to keep them for evidence, son. Let's make this happen, Wilson."

"That we'll do, Al," Wilson laughed. "That we'll do. This is going to turn out like one of those Mississippi paddle-wheel racing stories."

"Racing story may not prove necessary!" announced a familiar voice in a heavy Chechen accent. Wilson's fingers busied themselves across one of his keyboards, trying to find out where the new signal was coming from. The lines crossed at a point where the radar showed him two big blips, half a million miles back along the track toward Earth.

"Yes, it is I," said the voice, "Saladin Uzhakhov, himself, also colleague Ali Khalidov and new associate, Lafcadio Guzman. In Moon we are seeing on 3DTV niece Jasmeen in less than salubrious circumstances. We come to rescue. Also to tell that fellow was very nice knife-throwings."

"And what ship are you, sir?" asked Captain West, probably out of habit.

"I am not ship, I assure you, sir. But I am riding in one. Lafcadio is pilot. He is not ship, either. Neither is colleague Ali. We are astronomer, physicist, used spaceship dealer. And we have present for you!"

"And what might that be?" the Captain asked suspiciously.

"New engine—General Atomic hybrid fusion PCG-FX140. Normal power output equal to all six of your engines—when you still had six."

The General Atomic PCG-FX140 was a legendary monster, a famous white elephant of spaceflight, rather like Howard Hugh's *Spruce Goose* had been to aviation. Not even the engines of the lost *Fifth Force* had been as big and powerful, although they came close. No doubt Lafcadio had had it hanging around his orbital junkyard for years.

Wilson heard three men laugh uproariously, and in the background an odd kind of barking noise. Perhaps one of Lafcadio's Jack Russell terriers?

Somehow, he didn't think so.

"Hang on, now, here comes the hard part!" said Manzel to his unwilling companion.

It seemed as if he had just turned the little ship around, fired her remaining engine to deorbit her, and then turned her back around again to handle the atmospheric entry, when several other elements of the landing started demanding attention before he was quite ready for them.

Outside, the thin Martian atmosphere was screaming past the little spaceship, beginning to tear at her very fabric and heat her leading edges. But it was nothing comparable to landing a spaceship on Earth. and it had turned out to be a great deal less trouble than he'd originally anticipated.

Manzel flipped half a dozen toggles on the console and overhead, grabbing the small black steering yoke with both hands as it rose with a reedy mechanical whine from somewhere inside the control system. Unfortunately, it came up vibrating hard. It hurt in his hands and he needed every bit of his strength just to hold onto it. The ship began to vibrate, too, swaying from side to side a little like a body in a hammock.

Crenicichla's eyes, meanwhile, grew bigger and bigger with terror. He emitted a kind of thin, gibbering squeal as the *White Winged Dove* began to bank steeply to the right and the ground below became a wall. Manzel had removed his gag, "So you won't drown in your own puke," but had ordered him to keep quiet. Somehow, Crenicichla obeyed, although he hated flying in any atmospheric craft, and hated it this way even worse.

Just before the ship releveled herself and achieved the heading Manzel wanted, east by southeast, she began to shudder violently and fell off on her left wing. He fought hard and got her back where she belonged, but by then she'd lost ten thousand feet of altitude she needed badly.

The little ship had been designed for space and was atmospheric-capable only as a contingency. She had few control surfaces and they were small. When he pulled back on the yoke, thrusters fired under her nose lifted and it. This wasn't at all like flying an airplane, he decided. Goosing her remaining engine a fraction got most of her altitude back.

He let her nose down again and flew on.

"That was fun," he lied to his captive audience, peering ahead through the windshield. They were just about to plunge into a section of Valles Marineris between Melas Chasma and Coprates Chasma. The whole place was filled with light fog—or more likely it was minute particles left over from a recent dust storm—that made it hard to see.

He watched the altimeter and the proximity radar as carefully as he could. He had plenty of room on either side. The enormous rift and river valley was at least eight hundred miles wide at this point. It was six or seven times deeper than the Grand Canyon at home, and it was that—keeping track of altitude and groundspeed—that worried him.

The ship's wings and nose began to cool as her speed dropped. The air pressure was about half of Earth's at sea level. Newcomers here often put superchargers on their homes to keep the pressure higher indoors—it also helped to keep the Martian dust out. Flare and ground effect weren't going to amount to very much. He had to land by reducing his speed and altitude to dead zero at precisely the same time.

He'd played video games like this.

He always lost.

"Whoops! There's our little mountain range, you see it?" He pointed to an odd double collection of isolated peaks standing up in the middle of the canyon. To his prisoner, it must have looked like they were about to crash into them. He put some effort into trying not to whimper audibly. "And here's where we start getting downstairs real fast!"

More toggles, more adjustment. A distinct roaring began to be heard from the nose, different from the noises the ship had made entering the atmosphere. Thrusters were firing to reduce the ship's velocity.

"Groundspeed seven-ten, six-eighty, six-twenty, five-fifty—wow! I sure didn't see that hummock! Altitude is now two hundred feet and holding. Groundspeed four hundred, three-fifty, two hundred—hold onto your hat, Johnnie! We're running out of thruster fuel about *now!*"

Johnnie didn't have a hat, so he simply screamed and wet his pants when what had become a comforting roar at the nose shut off abruptly.

White-Winged Dove took the crest of the first dune just behind her chin. There was a good, solid, spine-wrenching thump—although her structure seemed to hold—and then she took to the air again. Manzel held her there. He didn't want her diving into the base of a dune.

"That's odd, I'd have expected sand to—wait, it isn't sand, it's macaroni plant, a lubricant when crushed. It's like landing in foam!"

She took the second dune amidships, and this time there was a deep groan as her already tortured framework began to come apart. Manzel held her level, skimming another dunetop, and another, until at last she skewed off to one side and rode the contour down to a sliding halt.

"Well I'll be damned," said Manzel, we—"

Clank! He stopped because something struck him hard on the left side of his head. He slumped forward against his four-point seatbelt and was unconscious.

With approval, Krystal examined the stainless steel skillet in her hand that she'd found in the galley on her way to the flight deck. What a walk that had been! The pan had made a perfectly good cudgel, used properly, and a wonderful ringing thump, as well. She turned and looked at Crenicichla with her good eye. The other was still white, without even the pupil showing, and would probably remain that way forever.

"C'mon, honey," she told him, slashing with a nine-inch chef's knife at the gray tape that bound him. "You rescue me, I rescue you. I want you free to help me finish this corporate capitalist sonofabitch pig."

"I'd love to, Krystal," he said, thumping his own shoulders to get his circulation back. "but we're out of time and we've got to leave now. This wreck could explode at any moment, and if you'll look out the window, there, you'll see three rescue helicopters just about to land."

"Damn! I'll just get his gun and—"

"We have to go, now!" He dragged her from the flight deck to the airlock. Maybe they could hide under the ship until the rescuers were gone.

"Careful," she said, standing on tiptoes to kiss him as the lock cycled. "My mouth hurts." Even wounded and bloody she looked good to him.

"Your mouth hurts?" He grabbed as many portable survival kits from the wall as he could carry. Each contained a compressed and canned poncho tent, rations, water, a surprisingly ample first aid kit, and small containers of oxygen, each about the size of an aluminum cigar tube.

"Yeah," she told him, looking proud of herself. He closed the inner door and started the airlock cycling. "I had to chew my way through one of those damned safety straps holding me down."

The pressure began to drop. It grew colder in the lock. They found warm clothing in a locker and put it on. "Four inch synthetic straps? Crenicichla shook his head in admiration. "Baby, you *are* my kind of girl!"

***

"Well, I wonder where Fatty went," Wilson suddenly said to no one in particular.

Casey looked down on him—as he did on everyone—and asked, "Fatty?"

Everybody else was here: Wilson, Scotty, Marko, Mikey, Shorty, Casey, and Merton. The asteroid hunters. Captain West was here, as well. He had a heavy bandage across his forehead and down one cheek, thanks to the exploding engine, and his left arm was in a makeshift sling.

They were gathered in the big passenger airlock aft of most of the ship and just forward of the engineering spaces, to plan how to use the giant engine Lafcadio and the two Chechen scientists had brought with them. Their ship actually had an airlock of the right size and shape to dock with *City of Newark*, although they hadn't come aboard yet.

"Sorry, my personal name for Pharch—Pimble S. Pharch. You know, *Lilac Waffle?*" Wilson was frustrated. He'd always felt there was something wrong with the man. If only he'd acted on that feeling, instead of treating him as he had the other would-be pirates. Now he was sure that the guy had almost killed Jasmeen and Llyra all over again.

"Are you saying," Scotty began, "that our friend Pharch was the saboteur … ?"

"You would condemn the poor fellow in his absence?" Merton asked—rhetorically, Wilson thought. His hands were prayer-folded together at his solar plexus, and he looked more than ever like a statue of Buddha.

"You would *defend* him in his absence?" Marko replied. "The guy's a rotten egg, Merton, and furthermore, you know it. He'd cut his mother

424

up and eat her with a plate of hash browns and gravy if he got hungry enough."

There was a long pause while everybody struggled to live with the thought.

Kwembly shook his head sorrowfully. "To my deepest regret, I cannot help but agree with you, Marko. What's more, I know he had military explosives like that."

The men surrounded him. "How do you know?" asked Mikey.

"Because he and I partnered together on a big nickel-iron rock, recently. That's how I met him. We were in a bar at Lagrange Point Four. He knew where this asteroid was, but his ship lacked the power. We began talking, and I offered to help him with it. When we found it and started it moving in the correct direction, he cut it in half with C-17."

"And you didn't tell us until now?" asked Wilson.

"Many hunters use obsolete military explosives," Merton shuddered. "I have used them, myself, although I could never afford C-17. In any event, at the time, with a ship full of dying people, I thought it relatively unimportant."

A tone sounded, and the Captain went to an intercom box set in a nearby wall. It had a flashing blue light to tell people in the lock that it needed attention, even when the lock was open and completely airless. Wilson supposed that it also relayed signals to one's suit radio.

The Captain punched a button. Silence, and the light went out. "West."

"This is the bridge, Captain." Wilson didn't recognize the voice. West hadn't tried to replace the purposeless but union-required flight engineer, so this must be the first officer he was speaking with. "Our next door neighbors are asking for permission to come aboard. They say that they'll cycle their own airlock so you and the hunters can stay put."

"Please tell them they may come aboard," said West.

"Aye, aye, sir. Also, radar has a pair of objects coming our way from upsystem. The computer thinks it's a pair of asteroid hunting vessels."

The Captain looked around the room. The hunters, including Wilson, shrugged. Maybe some opportunists had heard the row and were out for salvage.

"Any transponder data yet?" he asked the intercom.

"Not yet, sir. They're just out of range." At that moment they heard a series of thumps, rushing noises of pressure being equalized, and another series of loud thumps. The outer lock door began to swing open.

"Very well," said West. "We'll greet our friends and decide what's next."

"Aye, sir." The voice cut off a fraction of a second before it was through.

"Wilson, my boy! Please to introduce us to friends!" Jasmeen's paternal uncle was exactly as Wilson remembered him, an energetic man with flailing arm gestures, an uproarious sense of humor, a lead foot behind the wheel, and an eyepatch. Wilson wasn't sure whether he was the astronomer or the physicist of the two, but hoped it was the latter.

"Yes, yes," said another man in exactly the same accent. Wilson suspected that they practiced it together when no one was observing them. It was Saladin Uzhakhov, Jasmeen's maternal uncle, a head taller and twice as wide as his professional colleague and friend, Ali. "Tell us, who are all of these *hooligani* you appear to have fallen in with?"

Wilson indicated West and began to say, "Well *this* hooligan is the—" when he was interrupted by a loud noise coming from behind the two scientists. It was the same barking noise he'd heard on the ship-to-ship.

A peculiar figure moved out from between the two men, none other than Lafcadio Guzman, in a lightweight wheelchair, and behind him, a sleek, furry creature Wilson had never seen before. Lafcadio was a big man—at least from the waist up—but he was dwarfed by the two Chechens.

Wilson stepped forward. "Captain Alan West," he said, as he had been taught by his mother. He also named each of the asteroid hunters present. "This is Lafcadio Guzman, an old friend of my grandmother's. He sold me *Mighty Mouse's Girlfriend* and helped me fix her up."

There were sounds of greeting all around.

"And these gentlemen are Jasmeen Khalidov's uncles, Ali Khalidov and Saladin Uzhakhov, scientists and proprietors of the Larsen Farside Observatory."

The hunters all rushed forward to shake the hands of the two men who were responsible—however expensively—for so much of their livelihood.

"And who is this?" Captain West asked Lafcadio, bravely reaching down to stroke the streamlined head of the animal he'd brought with him.

Lafcadio laughed. "Roger. He's a seal, and the ideal zero gravity companion. When the weight's off, he can swim through the air like a fish and so can I. My lovely wife has Jack Russell terriers, but Roger is my buddy."

Roger's back rippled from tail to shoulders and he gave a leap, in the one-tenth gravity being maintained by the hunters' ships moored to the liner, that took him into gentle contact with the overhead, where he twirled around twice before settling to the floor at Lafcadio's side.

Wilson laughed. "My sister should see him! I think that was a double Salchow!"

The intraship intercom went off again suddenly, amidst all the joviality, silencing them all. The Captain hurried to the flashing box.

"West."

"Bridge here, Captain. We've got a transponder number from one of the two ships headed this way. It's Pimble Pharch's *Lilac Waffle*, sir."

"Fatty." Wilson spat the name out.

"Bringing a buddy," Scotty said, "probably to try and finish us off."

⁂

Julie hated waiting.

She had been sitting just like this, she reflected, the night the news came that Billy had been killed, saving a gaggle of useless idiots from themselves. That wasn't the way at all that evolution was supposed to work, and it would eventually be the species' undoing, she suspected.

Waiting came especially hard to an individual who, due to the science commissioned by her famous father-in-law, still had the physique of a girl in her twenties at age seventy-something. She'd enlisted in the United States Marine Corps at the age of seventeen (or had it been fifteen—she'd have to think; she'd lied about her age in any case), become a young pioneer wife on an alien planet, gone on to another world, and back to this—and started a whole new career as a bestselling author.

Some people loved her, governments everywhere hated her, nobody was neutral or indifferent. That probably meant she was doing her job right, she thought.

Even her writing wasn't all that sedentary. She often went for long walks through the rolling hills of Melas Chasma, the center stretch of Valles Marineris, dictating to her pocket computer. She even had a keyboard rigged on her exercise bicycle. She fenced saber and epee, Florentine, and still practiced with the big knife she'd brought to Mars as a young Marine. She went target shooting—rifle, pistol, shotgun, more exotic, modern weapons—on a regular basis. She had even been known to hit a baseball. Sitting still, even to watch a movie, and sometimes even to read a book, simply wasn't a part of her life, except at horrible times like this one—an emergency beyond her control—when it seemed she had no other choice.

At the moment, she was waiting for more news about the *City of Newark*. She'd already arranged with some of her influential friends this morning to see that no decent port in the Solar System would accept or service any East American ship again, unless the searches and the weapons bans—which had let this mess happen—stopped immediately and were never resumed.

When would they ever learn that disarming individuals guaranteed that they would be victimized, and that putting their lives in the hands of hired gunsels only meant they would be victimized all over again?

She'd also offered a reward—two thousand ounces platinum—for those responsible for the abortive hijacking. Dead or alive, as the old-time saying went. Here on Mars it worked for everybody, but she wouldn't have been allowed to do it back in Jersey. The authorities and the media would be pissing all over themselves once they heard of it.

Now, now, remember you're a lady, Julie.

She was waiting to hear from her granddaughter, aboard the *City of Newark*. She knew—and exulted in—the naked fact that Llyra and her companion Jasmeen had survived. She also knew that there was a long line of passengers waiting for a chance to communicate with loved ones, friends, and business associates, and that the Ngu family, in the middle of the alphabet, had a long tradition of waiting their turn democratically.

Julie was also waiting to hear from her eldest son, Adam. Unable to reach him by telephone, she'd recorded a couple of voice messages—not immediately disclosing the fact of the hijacking; voicemail was no way to hear about something like that—and let it be. Adam was so stable and reliable she sometimes worried about him. He'd have a good reason for not having answered, and he'd call her back as soon as he could.

Meanwhile, she sat uneasily, watching fleeting images on the wall across from her favorite chair, alternating between the news—which she usually avoided like the life-shortening plague it happened to be—and a ballgame. Syrtis Major Carpet was playing Coprates Muffler today, at Old Survivor Stadium. The score was tied at zero in the seventh—

Her phone rang, and, surprisingly, a message on her 3DTV screen said that the incoming call was visual, as well as auditory, and that the party was within range for two-way conversation. She answered it, "Hello?"

"Mom? This is Adam." The lag was less than five seconds, annoying but endurable. "We just got your phone messages. What can we do for you?"

Behind her son she saw what looked like a small stateroom aboard a spaceship. Adam appeared to be sitting at the end of a bed, leaning toward a dresser where his personal computer must be sitting. Beside him sat Ardith, looking a good deal healthier and happier than Julie had seen her in a very long while. It seemed a terrible shame to spoil it.

Julie asked gently, "Where are you two, anyway?"

"Aboard a charter we booked on Pallas." He grinned at Ardith, then at his mother. "We're headed your way, as you've guessed by now. In spite of some pretty exciting developments with that big rock you bought her, Ardith locked up the materials lab. I left Arleigh minding the store on Ceres."

"Yes," Ardith continued, momentarily carried away. "You see, the pulse rates vary for each form of radiation, but not according to any pattern we can discover. Computer analysis indicates the rates are converging—"

Julie nodded. "The whole thing has gone public, Ardith. Similar pulses are being observed from a point source out in the Cometary Halo. Sherry Sinclair has pointed the *William Wilde Curringer* in that direction and will investigate."

"It's very exciting, Mom, but nothing we can do much about for a while, so we thought we'd surprise Llyra and Jasmeen. Sorry I was out of touch. We were—"

"Never mind what you were," Julie laughed. "You're your father's son—"

Ardith grinned and said, "Thank heavens!"

"Thank decent genes, young lady." Her expression changed as she came to her real reason for calling. "I assume you haven't seen 3DTV for—"

Adam blinked. "Absolutely not. What's up?"

"Understand first, that Llyra and Jasmeen are both perfectly fine. Other folks were hurt or killed, but they weren't. In fact, they have helped—"

"*Mom!*"

"Oh, pardon me, dear. Their ship was hijacked by around two dozen Null Delta Em people. Most of them were killed. A couple managed to escape."

Now the lag was really annoying. She watched their faces change, too, as they received the news. Ardith bore it pretty well, which was why she'd told them first that the girls were all right. She hadn't gotten the news that way, herself. It felt like she'd lost ten years from her most recent rejuvenation. She really ought to talk Ardith into—

"What can we do?" Adam asked his mother. Ardith was sitting closer to him now, biting her lip just a little and leaning hard against his shoulder.

"I've done about as much as can be done at this remove, dear." She told him about the ban on East American ships, and the reward she'd offered.

She went on. "Apparently they're having some difficulty—I don't have any coherent details, mind you—with getting the spaceliner's engines started again, or shut off, or something. I learned what little I know from a news media creature here in Bradbury who wanted to interview me, to ask what I *feel* about this, and *feel* about that."

Five seconds later, Adam nodded. "We'll be docking at Deimos in about three hours," he told her. "You know the routine. Down in a shuttle to the Coprates spaceport. Then a sandskipper ride to your place."

"Don't bother with the sandskipper to my place. In fact, don't bother with the shuttle to Coprates. I'll be meeting both of you at the transfer port on Deimos itself. I intend to be there when the *City of Newark* arrives."

*
**

He said, "They're finally gone!"

"Yeah," she replied, spitting sand. "How long does it take to rescue a guy who oughta be dead and write a crashed ship off as a total loss?"

Crenicichla and Krystal had used the folding latrine shovels they'd found in their survival gear to dig into the sand behind a car-sized rock, and hidden there for hours while rescue crews who had arrived in three giant helicopters pulled their unconscious enemy out of the pilot's seat, patched him up, got him onto a backboard, and transported him to some hospital somewhere to the east of the landing site.

"I never saw choppers with such enormous rotors!" Crenicichla had exclaimed as they'd roared overhead. The machines had had a set of eight broad blades at each end, about twice as long as anything they'd ever seen before. Between the local geology—make that "areology"—and the machines adapted to it, he was finally convinced at the gut level that he was on an alien planet.

These days, the Moon didn't seem that alien; it was like living in the Earth's attic.

Digging had been really weird, he thought. They'd gone through two inches of the plant called macaroni—nasty, slimy stuff, altogether too much like the real thing—then another nine inches or so of soil, bound by a network of eerie white tendrils the size of a human hair. Then sand, apparently bottomless. For something like four billion years, the Martian wind had carried the powder-fine stuff—at less than a single millibar, that was all it could carry—from the plateaus eight miles above, down into the chasm. It was a wonder it hadn't filled the place right up.

Maybe, now that Martian air was five hundred times as dense, it would.

"Oh, look!" Krystal wiped ineffectually at the outdoor clothing she'd put on. It wasn't quite a spacesuit. Its rubbery texture was more like what a scuba diver would wear. "I got this cheese stuff all over me!"

They'd actually been quite comfortable in their premature grave, he thought. Especially compared to some of the camps he'd trained in. The

430

soil had been relatively warm, and the air fresh and rich with oxygen. They hadn't had to touch the survival canisters they'd brought.

It wasn't that way everywhere. On the surface, out of the canyons, there were places—elevations like the four titanic volcanoes that could be seen from Earth—where it was safe to wander in the day. But when the sun went down and photosynthesis stopped, a person could end up like a goldfish that had accidentally flopped out of its bowl.

He stood up and helped Krystal to her feet. Their kits had also been provided with global locator modules. Pressing the combination for Mars linked him to a network of satellites above the formerly Red Planet.

"Let's go," he told his companion. "That old man was a better pilot than I thought."

"Yeah?"

"Yeah. It's only a four mile walk—at one third gee—into town."

CHAPTER FORTY-TWO: ON THE MEND

> The attempt to substitute policy for character—in the form of alcohol control, drug control, gun control, speed control, wealth control, all of them amounting to life control—is the root of all nanny-state evils. It's amazing—and sometimes amusing—how indignant the nannies become when they discover, over and over and over again, that it just doesn't work. —*The Diaries of Rosalie Frazier Ngu*

"THEY ESCAPED?"

The man who thought of himself as the Fastest Gun in the Moon sat up in bed and immediately regretted it. His head began to throb and a cluster of electronics on the table at his elbow began making worried noises. Immediately, the supercharger that kept pressure in the room a couple of pounds higher than what it was outside, went to work with a whir.

He felt his ears go "pop!".

"Is so," replied one of his new visitors, the one with the beard. "Was rescue mission, not criminal apprehension. They search spacecraft—part that is not squished flat—but nobody even looks for tracks. To save myself, my friend, I cannot help thinking this is most tragic and disgraceful oversight."

"Nobody" being the crews that had pulled Manzel from the wreck-age of the yacht, where he might easily have died without their speedy ministrations.

"I trust you will forgive me, if I remain grateful in my own small way."

For decades—perhaps even for centuries—popular fiction had encouraged the public in the strange belief that an individuals might be rendered temporarily unconscious, but left otherwise unharmed, by a judicious blow to the head. The ability to do this was sometimes attributed to priests or priestesses of ancient healing cults in the classical world.

Manzel's first visitor this morning had been a young doctor whose description of the injuries he'd suffered gave the lie to that popular belief.

"You have a serious concussion, Mr. Manzel," the doctor had said. "That's somewhat like a bruise," she told him, "that the brain often suffers when the head is struck by a twelve-inch stainless steel frying pan, which they found lying on the deck beside the pilot's seat that you were taking your little snooze in. Some of your hair was found sticking to its underside."

"Yech!"

She nodded. "I think that puts it reasonably well."

He liked her, even though she appeared young enough to be his daughter's daughter (if he'd had a daughter). He guessed that she was originally southern Chinese, even if her name happened to be Rachael Abernathy. (He wondered, as he always did, how that had happened.) The young woman was unabashedly straightforward and businesslike with him, but with a sparkle of humor in her eyes and a pleasant lilt in her voice.

"I don't know why you don't have a depressed skull fracture," she'd told him, examining the computer display in her hand. "I think you came about as close to it as humanly possible. You must be taking your calcium supplements, or have a pretty hard head in general. They didn't even break the skin, although you've got yourself a spiffy bruise."

"Spiffy?" He hadn't heard the expression in decades.

"An old-fashioned word I'm trying out this week. Last week it was 'singular'."

"You're not kidding."

"I'm not kidding. You don't seem to have suffered any permanent damage, although one never knows. All of that pain and swelling will gradually go away, but please pay attention to them, and rest. We'll keep an eye on you against stroke—you don't live here on Mars, do you?—but I've filled your circulatory system full of damage-control nanobots to help clean up your brain-bruise and prevent dangerous clotting."

"And ... ?"

"And I'm going to discharge you to outpatient care early tomorrow morning."

"Tomorrow?" He'd felt worse than this before and managed to work. "Why not this evening, Doctor? Why not right now? I have things I have to—"

"What you *have* to do, Mr. Manzel," she said, "Aaron, is relax. Let us watch you for the rest of today and tonight. You'll have lunch and supper with us—all our meals are catered by Maxwell's, the best restaurant in the Solar System—and the best night's sleep you ever had."

"Because ... ?" He knew what she was going to say.

"Because after I get a little more information from you for our records—"

"Sorry, Doctor, but I already declined." She looked frustrated. During the brief period when Mars had a formal government, one measure it had stringently enforced was the right to absolute privacy of its citizens. No one could keep a dossier on anyone else, or even take their photograph, without their explicit, written permission. Another was the strict separation of science—especially medicine—and state.

"I'm going to give you some morphine anyway, to help your brain heal."

He shook his head—which hurt. "And make me groggy and useless tomorrow."

"You're supposed to take it easy. Want to pop one of those damaged capillaries?" He didn't know if she was persuasive because she was so pretty, or just because she was persuasive. A good night's sleep was tempting.

"How about VR? I can't stand 3DTV," he asked.

She took a breath and let it out. "I'm inclined to say no. Those things can be pretty exciting; they tend to raise the blood pressure. 3DTV's okay. The news is full of the hijacking, and there's always baseball."

"Baseball. I can always fall asleep during baseball. You're the doctor."

"Don't you forget it." She'd taken her little computer and left.

Now, he had a couple of real visitors who had flown here all the way from the western end of Valles Marineris to see him. He felt he had some explaining to do to them, since they were the individuals who had hired him to look after Llyra Ngu and their own daughter, Jasmeen Khalidov.

"Escaped?" Mohammed Khalidov repeated the word. He was a short man, slender, but with powerful arms and hands. As he spoke, his huge walrus moustache blew out with his consonants. "They were never even caught! People who rescue you do not know they are aboard spaceship. Perhaps, by time rescuers got there, they were not. Survival gear and supplies are gone from airlock. Two pairs tracks lead west, then vanish."

"How do you know this?" Manzel asked. He liked these people very much, and it hurt him—almost as much as his head—to have disappointed them.

"We just came from there," said Mohammed's wife, Beliita. Where her husband was slight, she was tiny, perhaps no more than five feet tall. In her middle years, her looks had coarsened a little, as looks tend to do, and she was plump. But Manzel could see that she had once been a real beauty, like her daughter. "We stopped on way to Coprates City. Was in unclaimed area, so we do not trespass, and broken spacecraft is very hard to miss."

Manzel nodded. "I imagine." He had told them of his decision to board the Null Delta Em getaway vessel. It had contained the last two people who had any wish to harm the girls. He deeply regretted losing Johnnie Crenicichla and Krystal Sweet and still didn't quite understand how she'd managed to get loose from the ship's makeshift infirmary.

"Simple," Mohammed said. "She chewed her way out of uppermost strap. This I think I could not do, myself." He bared his teeth which were very large, white, and shiny. "Also climbed all the way through ship while you are making with vigorous landing maneuvers. She must be strong."

Beliita shook her head. "Strength, is nothing. She must have will of iron."

"Or teeth of iron," Manzel suggested. Nobody laughed.

"In any case, friend Aaron, we have determined is not your fault. Two dangerous criminals are loose in Coprates City. We would rather you help us find them than berate—is this the word, 'berate'?—than berate you for what you could not foresee. Four inches wide of zylicon belt! It makes my poor teeth ache just to think of it for too long!"

Manzel glanced up at the 3DTV screen—the volume was turned down all the way—where coverage of a baseball game was being interrupted by news, apparently, that the *City of Newark* was finally under way again. Photographs showed the ship under tow by a cluster of asteroid hunters. No doubt Wilson Ngu's *Mighty Mouse's Girlfriend* was among them.

The channel then went back to baseball.

"Mohammed, Beliita," he said. "I think I know how to catch our criminals."

*
**

"Here we go again," said Shorty.

Wilson hung in the control dome of *Mighty Mouse's Girlfriend*, his engines hot, but at zero acceleration relative to the space liner, all of his senses on high alert, wondering if this was ever going to end.

Scotty said, "Pipe down! Keep the frequency clear!" They were having some trouble with a strange, pulsing interference across all bands.

"What?" Mikey asked. "So we can hear them holler '*Tora! Tora! Tora!*' as they come in? We've tried talking to them and they won't play."

Shorty laughed. "What he said."

Two ships about the size of Wilson's—hunters' ships, maybe even pirates' ships—were presently braking toward the *City of Newark*. Sensors of his own and the other seven vessels in his makeshift fleet, spread wide for the best resolution, were fairly sure that one of the newcomers was actually an oldcomer, Pimble S. "Fatty" Pharch's *Lilac Waffle*.

Not for the first time, Wilson shook his head. "Why *Lilac Waffle*?"

It was impossible to be absolutely certain, of course. Six very powerful hybrid thermonuclear engines—the spacegoing equivalent of swift coastal cutters and big oceangoing tugboats combined—pointed directly at the observer and bathing his electronic instrumentation with fragments of disassembled atoms, tended to confuse them. Wilson thought he might have seen the other guy's subatomic signature before, as well, but he hadn't been keeping a record of such things—until now.

Mikey was right, of course. Even as he'd prepared his battered ship as best he could for combat—not much could be done; she wasn't even remotely any kind of fighting ship—Captain West had tried continuously to communicate with the pair of vessels about to arrive, but there had been no reply. At the urging of his comrades, Wilson had tried, too, in his capacity as "commodore" of the little hunters' fleet.

It was possible to see them now with the naked eye, two bright stars so close together that they almost looked like one. Projecting their course and changing velocity, his ship's computer told him that they'd stop here, at this arbitrary line in space along which they were all still plunging toward Mars at a horrific velocity, rather than speeding past, after having delivered bombs and bullets, rays and beams.

Wilson had his doubts. He didn't know how good a tactician *Mighty Mouse's Girlfriend* was—although she regularly beat him at every kind of combat game he could download from the SolarNet. Braking to a stop—relative to the spaceliner, of course—might be just the way to attack, if you didn't know any more about tactics than your ship's computer.

He'd prepared as well as he could, he thought, putting all seven hunters in a disk-shaped formation between the liner and the oncoming ships. He occupied the center of the disk because he had the most powerful weapon, his particle cannon. As he'd learned, an engine's plasma flare was a pretty good defense against it, but show him any other part of another ship, he'd slice it off and cut it up for French fries.

They'd even put to good use the five plastic explosive bombs Shorty had found in the *City of Newark*'s engines, five of the hunters having loaded them into their chainlink launchers, exactly like torpedoes. They had been adjusted to detonate from the heat of impact.

Wilson had requested that Scotty be the only user of lidar among them, relaying his results to the rest of the ships, because seven sets of returns would be impossibly confusing for men and machinery. For the same reason, Merton would be the only user of active radar on this day.

Wilson also had lasers potent enough to shear off slices of stony or nickel-iron asteroids. As with the cannon, he could point to a few pixels on his main screen, and that was where they would direct their energies.

"Ten miles!" Merton and Scotty sang out simultaneously. That was almost the useful limit of lidar, Wilson knew. The two vehicles were moving, now, at a slow crawl relative to the little squadron and the helpless passenger liner they were protecting. Wilson felt a tingling in his trigger fingers as they rested lightly on the firing studs of his control yoke, and decided that it might be time for a brief lecture.

"Remember, now," Wilson told his little fleet. "We need to figure out what their intentions are *before* we start shooting. After all, they might just be coming to offer help. I know that waiting for the other guy to draw first sucks, but we're the goodguys. That's what we do."

"Remind me to apply for a transfer," Casey muttered. "Pay's better, too."

"Hey, amigo," Shorty answered, deliberately thickening his native Lost Angeles accent. "Be careful—I never said I was no goodguy, man."

Wilson said, "No, you never did. But I could tell it by your grammar."

"You leave her out of this!" He broke into a fit of giggling. It was funny, Wilson thought, but not that funny. They were all tired and nervous, and trying to deal with it in their own different, individual ways.

Suddenly, the flares disappeared as the engines were shut off. The hunters blinked their eyes, watched as attitude thrusters turned the newcomers over, and presently two ships hung before them, dead in space, relative to the *City of Newark*. Lidar indicated that they rested about twenty-five feet apart, cabled together.

One of them was, indeed, Pharch's *Lilac Waffle*.

The other vessel was equally familiar—to Wilson. It was the *Space Viper*, Swede Vargas' ship. Its portside airlock door swung open and a dozen large items of what appeared to be white fabric spilled into space. Each seemed to be about six or seven feet on a side.

"Hold your fire, guys!" Wilson abruptly shouted to his friends. "It's the Swede! Swede Vargas! I think he's trying to show us a white flag!"

"Yes," Mikey said. "And he's got Fatty in an envirosuit, with his arms and legs spread wide, attached by his hands and feet to his navigation dome—just like a kid's stuffed animal in a car window!"

"Would somebody give me a hand?" Swede's voice came over a short range suit frequency. "Those are my bedsheets floating away! We had a little firefight over reaction mass out there, and knocked out both long range transceivers."

✻
✻✻

Facilities on Deimos were "rudimentary", Ardith recalled.

That was what the travel guides all said, Ardith thought, and none of them stressed it nearly enough. Earth held a grudge against Mars it hadn't forgotten in half a century and didn't seem likely to forget soon.

On the flattest surface the little moon offered—it was an unusually dark carbonaceous chondrite that circled Mars every thirty hours, its longest dimension was ten miles, its shortest seven and a half—East American Spacelines and a handful of other interests had grudgingly constructed a radial series of tubes, two dozen altogether, of various lengths and diameters, for the transfer of passengers and cargo from incoming vessels to shuttles designed to take them down to the Martian surface.

One of the few laws still remaining on the Formerly Red Planet forbade the landing of large vessels there. In another time, it had helped the fledgling Martian culture avoid military invasion by its enemies from the Mother planet. These days, it served mostly to keep shuttle operators wealthy, and there was growing pressure to rescind it.

In the meantime, there was the facility on Deimos.

At the point where all the tubes came together, like the spokes of a wheel, a simple, cylindrical, barn-like structure had been erected, two high-ceilinged stories tall. It was on the lower level that cargo of all kinds was transported by moving "slidewalk" from one vessel to another.

Similar transportation for arriving passengers took them upstairs (at several points, Ardith had noticed places where metal detectors had only recently been ripped out; most of the people she saw carried weapons) where there were bathrooms, what were supposed to be quiet waiting rooms, a few locker-like Japanese-style sleeping cubicles, and a mostly-automated restaurant serving execrable food and unimaginably bad coffee at ruinous prices. The place itself was dirty and smelled even worse than the food.

There were a few automated bank tellers and similar conveniences of modern civilization. Having made whatever transactions they didn't have any choice but to make, passengers were then routed down whatever tube would take them to a ship going wherever it was they wanted to go.

Mostly away from here, Ardith thought.

Individuals native to Pallas are known System-wide for a tidiness and cleanliness almost Dutch in character. Ardith was shocked by what she saw here at Deimos. She thought that it must be like having to eat in the restroom of a dilapidated filling station back on Earth.

"How much do you suppose it would cost us to buy this place?" She was speaking to Adam, who was with her at a circular wrought iron table with a glass top, near a mezzanine rail over which they could watch what was happening on the ground floor. The iron was almost paintless, the glass was scratched and smudged and had chewing gum on the underside.

They sat close together, holding hands like newlyweds. Each knew that something had changed in their marriage, but each was reluctant to speak of it, or even think about it too much, for fear it might go away.

"To fix it up, I assume, and make it a pleasant place to stop?" he asked. He was enjoying this time with her—he had enjoyed simply being with her since they were school children—and it didn't matter, for the moment, why they were here or what they were talking about.

She nodded. "Something like that."

"I can't say I haven't considered it, myself," He shrugged. "The real trouble is that it was built, primarily, for shipping high-tech industrial products off planet, and almost nobody else uses it. If they can, they stay aboard whatever ship brought them here until the last minute, when it's time to take a shuttle. They hardly see the place."

"Then there's the monopoly East America holds on the Earth-Mars run," said a familiar voice behind them, "which guarantees shoddy services."

They both turned where they sat, and Adam, from courteous reflex, jumped to his feet, coming close to throwing himself into the air. There was some gravity here, he reminded himself, but damned little of it.

"Mom!" said Adam.

"Julie!" said Ardith.

Looking as young as she ever did—unknown to Adam as yet, Ardith had begun considering asking her mother-in-law about this DeGrey rejuvenation process—Julie rushed forward to embrace both of them in turn, then pivoted lightly on her heel and said, "I thought this would be a good place to meet without media attention. Just look who I've brought with me!"

Behind her were Mohammed Khalidov, with his cloth workman's cap in hand, and his wife, Beliita, in her native Chechen dress. For just a moment, the thought flashed through Ardith's mind that they looked like a quaint pair of salt and pepper shakers. She shook her head to rid herself of the vision.

"Mohammed!" Adam said, holding on grimly despite the older man's vigorous handshake. "Tell me what's with the peasant dress all of a sudden?"

Adam had good reason to ask. Respectively an engineer and a scientist to begin with back on Earth, Mohammed and Beliita Khalidov had been part of growing secularist movement within what had once been a uniformly Moslem civilization. Unpopular with the Russians because they were Chechen, they had sometimes suffered as badly at the hands of their more religious neighbors, which had motivated them to help colonize Mars.

Hanging from Mohammed's waist was a very unpeasantlike plasma gun. Most of the time, Mohammed dressed as Adam did, in what had been called "engineer casual" for almost two centuries. Beliita favored bluejeans.

"Partly is joke. Our daughter is always thinking—I can tell this, although she will say nothing—her parents are hopelessly old-fashioned."

Beliita added, "Partly is to make our Jasmeen feel happier, after everything she has been through, with something warm and familiar. We often dress like this—our daughter, too—just for the fun, on holidays."

A tenet of the secularist movement was that *everybody's* holidays should be enjoyed to the fullest. It was an attractive notion, Adam thought, unless you were trying to get a construction project finished on time.

"That means I'd have to dress up like the Easter Bunny," he told them.

"Wilson and Llyra never cared much about Santa Claus," Ardith explained with a grin. "They used to call him 'God with training wheels'."

Ardith suddenly realized that someone else had come with Julie and the Khalidovs, a man who, despite his unusual height and distinctive appearance, had somehow managed to remain inconspicuous until he wished otherwise.

She looked at him and said, "And you are ... ?"

"Oh, forgive me," Julie answered for him. Ardith, Adam, this is Aaron Manzel, an old friend of the Khalidovs, who's been looking out for—"

Mohammed shook his head. "Not old friend, Julie, new friend. We hired Aaron to look out for Jasmeen and Llyra. After this we became friends."

Adam nodded. "You're the one who threw the—"

"The table knife," Aaron answered. "Yes, guilty. It was I. And it seemed like such a good idea at the time. But no matter what I do from now on, that's what people are going to remember, isn't it?"

"You're damned right, Aaron." He reached out for the man's hand. "You killed the sonofabitch who's been trying to kill my family for the last two years. Whatever Mohammed and Beliita paid you, it wasn't enough!"

"Thank you, Dr. Ngu, very much. But It isn't over, yet. Two of them escaped, and they're loose on Mars, right now. They may just want to disappear, but it's more likely they'll want to finish what they started."

Adam blinked. "Finish—oh, I see what you mean. Who are these people?"

"Johnnie 'The Fish' Crenicichla," Aaron said. "He served as the liaison and 'credible deniability' man between the late unlamented Paul Luegner of Null Delta Em, and the Mass Movement's Anna Wertham Savage. The other is Krystal Sweet, an accessory to the murder of Fallon O'Driscoll. She led the assault on *City of Newark*."

Ardith asked, "How dangerous can they be if they messed that up so badly?"

"Plenty, Dr. Ngu. It was a good enough plan, they just failed to count on me, or on a ship's captain who refused to let himself be disarmed."

"A common enough error among East Americans," Julie observed.

As everyone sat and ordered something to drink—mostly things in baggies, given the lack of local sanitation—they compared notes on what they knew of the hijacking. Some were saying that the entire bridge crew had been massacred, others that the passengers had massacred the would-be hijackers. Manzel set them as straight as he could.

"On any other ship, the latter would be likely," he told them. "The problem, of course, is the East American Spacelines tariffs that, in effect, prohibit individual self-defense. But the Captain had a gun, and he returned the weapons that belonged to Llyra and Jasmeen as quickly as he could. As for me, I can make practically anything into a weapon."

"Perhaps silliest aspect of gun control," Beliita observed. "I notice are no more weapons detectors here. Just wires hanging, in front of unpainted sections of bulkhead. What do you suppose is going on?"

Julie laughed. "I am, among others. East American has partners in this, uh, enterprise. I spoke to them about sharing liability for what happened on the *City of Newark*. I offered to buy East American out on Deimos and fix the place up, as long as they pulled the detectors out."

"See what I mean?" Adam asked his wife. "There's always some sharp operator—"

His mother leaned toward him and peered into his face, "Don't finish that sentence, Sonny, and I'll cut you in for twenty-five percent."

"Thirty," insisted Ardith.

"Done. And I'll bet you have some cute decorator ideas already, dear."

"Yes, Julie, I have. They start with several hundred gallons of disinfectant."

"Dr. Ngu! Dr. Ngu!" Suddenly there was a commotion at the door they'd entered by. A young woman already familiar to some of them thrust by Manzel and the Khalidovs, a small recording device in her hand. "Remember me, I'm Honey Graham of the Interplanetary Interactive Information Service. Is this a private party, or can anybody jump on in?"

Together, Julie, Adam, and Ardith groaned.

⁂

"Gold," observed the doctor. "How quaint." He glanced at the coins in his soft, pink palm and put them away in his pocket. He went to the sink to wash his hands and returned, pulling on a pair of syntex gloves.

Annoyed, Crenicichla frowned. "Is there something wrong with our money, doctor? Or is there something else you'd prefer—blood, possibly, or a pound of flesh? How about our firstborn?" It had taken them most of a day to find this part of town—there was always a part of town like this, except perhaps in Amherst, Massachusetts—an inexpensive hotel that didn't ask questions, and a physician of ill repute who makes housecalls.

Things hadn't turned out too badly, so far. Everything on Mars was fresh and new, compared to everything on Earth. So in spite of it all, the hotel room they'd chosen was clean and so was the doctor. He was also sober. When the window wasn't blackened all the way, as it was now, you could look right down into the Old Survivor baseball stadium several stories below, with its highly unMartian emerald green field, and its impressive stainless steel statue—four times life size—in the forecourt.

Just now there was no ball playing going on. Instead, machines and men labored over the grass, fighting to keep it alive in an unfriendly environment.

The hotel even offered room service, of a sort, delivered from a cafe next door that specialized in soups made of macaroni plant. They created dozens of variations, the proprietress had told him on the phone, based on stock grown under glass so it would have less need to make oxygen and could dedicate itself to making protein. He had ordered a soup with mushrooms, turning down an offer of macaroni plant beer. The remnants of the meal he'd shared with Krystal were on a tray in the hall.

The doctor raised an eyebrow. "You have a firstborn?" Scanning had indicated that despite being in her thirties, his latest patient was a virgin.

"We have a firstborn?" Krystal asked. She was sitting in a hard, straight-backed chair near a dresser where the doctor had laid out his instruments. She'd been drugged heavily, both for the pain and the examination.

Or the pain of the examination.

"Oh, I see what you mean. The saying out here is 'As long as it bends, it spends'. That doesn't count government paper. The rule there is, 'If it crinkles, it stinkles'. I'm just accustomed to being paid in platinum. The only individuals who ever use gold out here are you Earthers."

On Earth, at least in East America, gold was the officially favored "illegal" currency, and a legislated value had been established for it. Else-where in the System, the inflation caused by discovering so much of it among the asteroids had driven its value down considerably. Sitting on the nearby bed, Crenicichla sighed. "We're really that obvious?"

"I'm not from Earth," Krystal protested with a slur. "I'm from Wisconsin."

"Obvious in small ways," shrugged the doctor. "You still move as if you were born and raised in a full one-gee field, although you've both recently lived in less gravity than that. At a guess, I'd say the Moon?"

"That's some pretty damn good guessing." He now had to decide whether to kill the man or not. For the time being, although he hated to admit it, even to himself, he'd had more than his fill of killing. Maybe when she was feeling better, Krystal would like to do it.

"Not really. There's a reward bulletin out on you. Two thousand plati-num. It includes photos, artists' sketches, backgrounds, and a fair estimate as to the young lady's injuries. It seems you're wanted for ship theft—my word, that was you two out in the desert, west of town, wasn't it?—hi-jacking, hostage-taking, and murder."

"Now we have to kill him," Krystal observed, but they both ignored her.

Crenicichla nodded. "But, of course, Doctor, you're far too humanitarian—"

The doctor drew himself up into a semblance of dignity. "I happen to believe that everyone deserves whatever medical attention they require. Also, Mars is famous for being the place for a fresh start in life."

Crenicichla laughed. "Especially if you get paid up front, and in cash."

"Especially. Don't worry, I won't turn you in. I make more than this on the average plastic surgery, and I don't want my reputation spoiled among people who need their faces and fingerprints changed quickly."

"So you do fingerprints, too," Crenicichla shrugged. "I can see that."

The doctor nodded. "Well, I could keep this up all day, but do you want—"

"Yeah," said Crenicichla. "Give it to us, straight, doctor."

"Yeah, give it to us straight, dokker," said Krystal. Crenicichla wasn't amused to see her like this, in fact it hurt him a surprising amount.

"Very well. Your young lady friend, here, is completely blind on one side, but needn't be for all her life. The eye is thoroughly gone, of course. The vitreous humor looks as if it had been boiled, poaching the inside of the eye, including the retina. The good news is that the optic nerve is intact. It will take two weeks to clone her another eye."

"Two weeks," Krystal repeated.

"Two weeks." Cloning was against East American law, and among the major reasons people traveled to the Moon and Mars. "And until then?"

"She can wear sun-glasses. Lots of Martians do. We don't have a nice magnetic field like Earth, or a selectively permeable canopy like Pallas. We get higher doses of radiation, even down here in the gloom. She may prefer a rakish eyepatch, although it could give you both away."

"Sunglasses it is, then. How much do you want for the cloning, up front?"

The doctor snapped his glove off. "Plenty."

CHAPTER FORTY-THREE: OF FREE WILL AND CHOICES

You can discover everything you need to know, about a people or their culture, simply from their attitude toward torture. Any group or nation with a policy that encourages—or even tolerates—torture is worse than any evil it claims to be fighting.

The ends do not justify the means. The means help to insure that the ends are just. —*The Diaries of Rosalie Frazier Ngu*

"OKAY," WILSON STARTED. "WHY?"

"How about none of your fucking beeswax, you half-slant son of a chink?"

"That's one-eighth slant, Fatty, and great grandson. I think it's important for people who fly spaceships to get the numbers and names right, don't you agree?" It was the first time in Wilson's life that anyone had ever referred to his racial background that way. He knew it was supposed to be painfully insulting. Pharch had already used the nastiest words for Asians that Wilson had heard of. But it only seemed pathetic.

With the Captain and what remained of his bridge crew, they were gathered in the battered dining room of the *City of Newark*, most of Wilson's gang still wearing parts of their suits, weapons of various kinds slanted across their hips, on their thighs, or carried in chest harnesses. They looked like gladiators, and maybe that was what they were.

On the screen, and in real life, they were the cowboys of the twenty-second century.

For the most part, the place had been cleaned up—the Captain had ordered it done, even at the cost of losing evidence—and the broken furniture and table furnishings ground up for reaction mass. There were dark, ugly stains in the carpet, however, that would never come out, no matter who the spacelines bought their nanotechnology from.

With the exception of his weapons, which had been taken from him by Swede Vargas, Fatty was no different from the rest. They'd also taken his helmet, his gloves, and his boots, but none of them had been willing to go further than that. "The man smells bad enough," Mikey had observed accurately, "with most of his blubber still sealed in his suit!"

Pharch had been duct-taped securely into a straight-backed chair with arms, taken from one of the staterooms. The chair had been attached to the red brick base of the wrought-iron spiral staircase leading up to the lounge. Most of the observers stood by the walls or sat on the floor. Wilson paced a little in the open space between that they'd left for him.

"Don't call me 'Fatty'!" the prisoner screamed. It was difficult not to, Wilson thought, looking at the man wearing pieces of at least two suits, cut and retailored to contain what he had let himself become.

"You'd rather I called you 'Pimble'? I think I'd rather be called 'Fatty'. But I asked you a question, Pharch. You're going to give me a real answer. Why did you sabotage this vessel? What did you stand to gain?"

"Or what? You'll talk me to death? I know your kind, Chinaman. You want people to believe it's your ethics, or some damn high-falutin' thing, but you're just too spineless, too gutless to go for what you want."

"We don't have any more time for this," Wilson spat impatiently. That wasn't quite true. At the moment the passenger liner was being decelerated by six of the seven asteroid hunting vessels on remote control. Casey's was being used as a shuttle between all of them and the larger ship, while Pharch's and the *Space Viper* were being towed.

Wilson glanced over at the Captain, who nodded magisterially, then at Scotty and Shorty. "Leave him in the chair, boys. Take him to the airlock."

There was a collective gasp from the liner crew as the two moved to comply, Shorty drawing a huge curved knife on his way across the room.

"Bullshit!" yelled Fatty. "You're bluffing!"

Together, as he continued to abuse them verbally, questioning their manhood and ancestry, they wrenched Fatty free of the stairs, tilted his chair back and dragged him to the elevator. It wasn't hard at one-third gee. Wilson, Mikey, and Marko crammed themselves into the car. The room emptied itself as everyone else joined them, some of them taking the elevator from the kitchen.

As the elevator cycled closed, Fatty screamed, "You don't have the nads!" He was still screaming when the doors opened on the airlock deck. Wilson pressed buttons that opened the inner door. Shorty and Scotty dragged Fatty, in his chair, into the center of the garage-like chamber.

Here, too, the Captain had ordered the bloodstains cleaned up. The cleaners had enjoyed more luck with the stainless steel and titanium floor.

While everyone watched him from the semicircular atrium between the airlock and the elevators, Wilson strode to Fatty with an electronic object in his hand, which he duct-taped to the front of the man's suit. He pressed a button on it, and a small green light came on.

"This is a walkie-talkie, Pimble," he said. "As long as there's air in this room, you can communicate with me. You'll have about three minutes, which I'm sure will seem like three hours to you. Then it'll be too late. We'll pitch your dead body out, have your ship fumigated and rechristened—where'd you get that *Lilac Waffle*, anyway?—and be done with you. The Captain has okayed this and he's the law out here."

Pharch sneered up into Wilson's face. "I still say you don't have the—"

"Have it your way." Wilson turned on his heel, walked to the inner door.

"You don't have the nads!" Pharch shouted at his back. The door closed and Pharch sat alone in the middle of the room. He tried to see if they were watching him through the porthole in the inner door, but it was bright in here and light reflected from the glass in the porthole.

"You don't have the nads," he said quietly, almost to himself.

Suddenly, there were klaxons sounding, so loud it hurt his teeth, and big red and yellow lights swirling and flashing. He began to reconsider.

With a huge thump, the gaskets at the bottom of the outer airlock door unsealed, and a great rushing noise could be heard. The air was being spilled out into space. It grew colder almost instantly, and the noise of the klaxons grew less and less. There could be no question. They—or rather Wilson Ngu—was going to do it. He was going to die.

"All right! All right!" he screamed. "I'll tell you! I'll tell you!"

For a long, unendurable moment, it seemed as if he had waited too long, and nobody had heard him. As miserable as his life was, as it had always been, he didn't want it to be over with. He tried his best not to whimper. He tried harder not to let his sphincters release. He failed in both of those efforts. He knew that he had been reduced to something less than human. The worst was that he knew that he deserved it.

He was torn from his dying contemplations by another loud slamming noise. The outer door had fallen again and locked. The rushing sound was gone, as were the klaxons and the flashing lights. It began to feel warm again.

The inner door opened and Wilson strode toward him. "Okay, Pimble, talk."

*
**

Krystal gradually awakened for the half-dozenth time so far tonight.

Although it was very nice to have a mind again—drugs had never interested her much; she considered them obscene—she was having some trouble making hers up. Somehow, she and Johnnie had gotten clear of the absolute catastrophe that the *City of Newark* operation had become.

She lay beside him now in the darkness of their rented room. A place like this on Earth or the Moon would smell bad, and they'd be unable to avoid hearing their neighbors arguing, watching 3DTV, having sex. But it was quiet here, and clean. She'd awakened several times as the drug wore off, sweating hard, thirsty as a camel, scarcely daring to reach up and touch the heavy bandages covering her nearly fatal injuries.

On the table at her side of the bed, she found a self-cooling container full of sweet electrolyte replacement, she sipped through a straw. Johnnie had added ice, even though it wasn't needed. He was so sweet. She loved ice. He'd told the doctor he wanted to buy her a new eye.

She hoped it would be the same color as the original.

She'd been told that she'd rescued both of them from the wreckage of the stolen yacht. It was true, she had extremely unfocused memories of being tied down, of chewing her way free—was that why her gums were so sore?—of struggling through a long tunnel that writhed and bucked and tossed her from side to side like some angry living thing, and finally of smacking somebody on the head with a frying pan, of all things.

Oh yes, and kissing Johnnie in the airlock. He'd said she was his girl. Or something like that, anyway.

However the last thing she remembered clearly was looking into the angry eyes—and the automatic pistol muzzle—of Jasmeen Khalidov, fresh out of ammo herself, and unable to reload in the awkward position she was in. Then came the unbearably bright flash, the roar, the pain. If it was the last thing Krystal did, Jasmeen was going to die as slowly as possible.

Johnnie had been sleeping in a chair. She saw how uncomfortable he was and insisted that he sleep on the bed with her. He was a man of honor, she knew, and she wouldn't really have minded much if he weren't. Across the room, the 3DTV was playing with the sound turned down almost all the way. The captions were on and she'd awakened to an old movie about soldiers with little capes on their hats, fighting guys in dresses in the desert.

What was that all about?

By now, they'd both seen the horrible news that the passenger liner *City of Newark* had been snatched from extinction by a heroic squadron of asteroid hunters, led by that nasty little capitalist killer, Wilson Ngu. In a few days it would reach Phobos in a different way than Null Delta Em had meant, and, except for the shouting, the celebration, and the self-congratulatory media coverage, that would be that.

It was going to be very painful—but irresistible—to watch. As far as they knew, she and Johnnie—and of course that horrible old woman in Amherst, Massachusetts—were the movement's only surviving leaders. For some reason she hated that old woman as much as she did Jasmeen.

She'd never realized that before.

Of course on a personal note, it was nice for her and Johnnie that all life on Mars would not be annihilated. For some reason she had yet to fathom, he had come to love her. Of his sincerity, she was totally convinced, both by his manner and his deeds on her behalf. He was very chivalrous, and she was reasonably certain that she could come to love him, as well. Mars was a good place for new beginning. They were young. He could grow a beard, she could dye her hair, and they could start a macaroni farm and populate it with a dozen kids. She thought that might be very good.

Or it might be just like the family farm life she'd escaped from back on Earth.

On the other hand. there *was* Jasmeen, Wilson that nasty killer of a capitalist dog, his show-off sister, their smug, destructive parents, and that witch of a grandmother—where did she get off staying in her twenties for half a century?—all of them sitting around in some expensive restaurant probably this very minute, surrounded by servants and fawning reporters, gobbling lobster farmed on Mars, with imported caviar and truffles, swilling champagne, laughing at her and Johnnie and all the brave martyrs of the Mass Movement and Null Delta Em.

A small flame began to glow within her breast. Would it be right to run away and start a new life and do nothing about all that? Would they even have a right to a new life if they didn't try to even the score?

She looked over at the man sleeping so soundly, so sweetly beside her. Should they start a new life together, or finish the old one off properly?

What would Johnnie think?

*
**

"It was Null Delta Em," Fatty began.

Wilson pulled a folding metal chair up and sat down for the first time in hours. The cavernous passenger airlock was warm once again, and seemed almost festive, compared to the way it had seemed when his prisoner had been alone in here with the outer door slowly opening. It was festive compared with the dining room, the way it looked at the moment.

Someone had brought folding tables, as well, and coffee urns, and heated frozen pastries from the kitchen. Almost all of the liner's crew was here now, as they deserved to be, and some of the passengers, too. Most of the East Americans had declined the invitation with a shudder.

Wilson had cut the tape holding Pharch's hands to the chair (his torso and legs were still secured) and given him food and something to drink.

"It was Null Delta Em," Wilson repeated. The room was as silent as if no one else were in it. "Tell me exactly what you mean by that, Pharch."

"I couldn't stand it. I stumbled in here, into this lock, when I thought everybody else was gone, looking for a way to get back to my ship and away from this place."

"Desertion?" Shorty shouted at him.

"Hey, asshole, I didn't volunteer to be in anybody's goddamned army. I was coerced, if you'll remember, and you all just assumed I was going along. But I had as much right to leave here as you had to stay."

"You were making restitution for an act of attempted piracy," Wilson said. "But never mind that, you're right, you weren't in any army. None of that is important now. How did you end up working for NDE?"

Fatty took a huge bite of a Danish, an enormous gulp of heavily sugared coffee, swallowed, and sighed. "I checked the security recorder. The last two survivors—I didn't know it at the time—had come down here to board their escape vehicle. He was carrying her, and she looked to be in pretty bad shape."

"So you did what?"

"Hey, I tried to do my duty and apprehend them—I sent them a text message ordering them to come back."

That statement brought sounds of disbelief from his listeners, along with several loud, obscene comments calling his veracity into doubt.

Wilson held up a hand. "An encrypted text message. So what happened?"

"He offered me money—a whole lot of money—if I let them go."

"And even more if you would sabotage the liner behind them?"

Pharch held his chin up. "So what if he did? It was one side or another in a war. I had a chance to choose which side I'd be on, is all."

"Who's 'he'?"

"I don't know. A very neat, tidy kind of guy, from the recordings, dark, wearing a white suit—or what had been a white suit, anyway. I don't know who he was. She was a platinum blond with a bad head wound and a ruined eye."

Wilson nodded. "Krystal Sweet. What happened then?"

"He e-mailed me the code for Pallatian warehouse certificates for five hundred ounces of gold, and said there'd be another five hundred waiting for me when he heard that the charges had gone off. I had to supply my own explosives."

"So you traded the lives of three hundred innocent people, lives you had no conceivable right to trade, for five hundred measly ounces of gold and the possibly empty promise of five hundred more? What was the idea? Wasn't this spaceship headed for a big show on Phobos and Mars?"

"That *was* the idea," Fatty replied. "Knocking out the engines would ensure there was no easy way to alter the course to Phobos. They didn't count on you guys—on us—and I sure wasn't gonna tell him. I just called my ship to the small lock, planted the charges, and got away as fast as I could."

Wilson looked at Swede. He could tell the man was thinking, "But not quite fast enough," but he didn't say it, and Swede rose in his estimation.

Wilson took a deep breath, dreading what was coming next—nobody else knew what was about to happen—but also looking forward to how he would feel afterward, no matter how it ended. He needed to cleanse himself. He didn't want his parents or his sister or his grandmother—or Jasmeen—to think of him as they were probably thinking of him now.

"All right, Pharch, I believe you. And I'm also in your debt—your moral debt, I mean. My family doesn't believe in torturing people."

Shorty rushed to his side. "What're you talking about, Commodore? You didn't—"

"Sure, I did. He thought that if he didn't talk, I'd let him die as slowly and painfully as it's possible to die, short of an operating theater. It's a moral debt I can't live with—that I refuse to live with."

Suddenly Llyra and Jasmeen were in the atrium, fighting to get in. Reluctant to injure their leader's sister, the hunters let the girls in.

"Wilson Ngu! What do you think you are doing?" Jasmeen seemed more upset than Llyra, probably because Llyra understood and would do the same.

He took Jasmeen gently, by the upper arms. It was the first time he'd ever touched her, except by accident, or a chaste little peck on the cheek every New Year's Eve, and he was surprised by the firmness of her muscles—and the feeling of electricity that tingled through him.

"I'm trying to repair a damage that I've done. My sister will explain."

She looked down at Pharch with contempt on her face. "But he is just—"

"A human being with rights," Wilson finished. "Rights that I have violated. But even forgetting that, Jasmeen, there's a hole inside me for having done it, and I have to repair that, if I want to go on living."

She nodded. "I understand," she told him, looking up through long, dark lashes, tears trembling on her lower eyelids. "Is perfectly Martian." She put her hands up on his forearms. "Please to go on living."

Wilson could only nod and, reluctantly, let her go. He cut the duct tape holding Fatty to the chair. "Stand him up." There was a fine line, he knew, between doing what he believed right, and appearing to aggrandize himself at the expense of someone's life.

Never mind that maybe the life needed expending.

After what had happened, what now seemed like a lifetime ago on Ceres, and what had happened at the spaceport in the Moon—both events recorded for the entire Solar System to see—he didn't want to be remembered, no matter how it came out, for what he was about to do. Planning ahead, he'd asked the Captain to make sure no surveillance cameras were running.

West had refused, saying that neither of them owned history.

Casey and Merton now stood either side of Pharch, almost holding him up. The man knew that he was probably about to die, and he seemed to be having trouble controlling his fear. Yet who knew, the young asteroid hunter thought, in Pharch's position, what he himself would do?

It never occurred to Wilson that he was constitutionally incapable—too honest, decent, principled—to ever find himself in Pharch's position.

"I want all the duct tape taken off him," Wilson told his two new friends. "Every scrap, even when it doesn't seem like it'll make a difference. I don't want anyone saying later he was restrained in any way."

Wilson's wishes were law at the moment. He wasn't sure he liked that. He had, however, even asked the Swede to give the man back his boots. Pharch was well rested. He'd been fed and had something to drink. His suit was taking care of any other necessities he may have had.

Wilson heard himself say, "Give the man his gun."

A shudder went through the people crowded into the airlock and the atrium behind it. Nobody wanted Pharch to have his gun back except for Wilson. Pharch's former partners in piracy finally drew their own weapons as Scotty handed Pharch's long-barreled particle beamer to him.

In addition to the airlock door, there was a big window, into which Wilson's sister and her coach had forced their way. Now Llyra had her eyes shut—he knew her; she'd open them before the shooting started—and very unMartian tears were streaming down Jasmeen's face.

"Keep that down at your side until you're given the word," said Scotty.

"How do I know it's even loaded?" Pharch demanded. Clearly, he wanted to inspect the gun. "Or that you haven't sabotaged it in some way?"

Scotty drew his own weapon and held it out, butt forward. "Take mine."

"Thanks—I will!" Pharch reached out for Scotty's weapon. Scotty didn't let go of it until he had Pharch's weapon firmly in hand in exchange.

"Okay, Pharch, here's how it's going to be." Wilson reached to the chest pocket of his suit, grasped the Herron StaggerCyl .270 REN, and tossed it to Marko. His great grandfather's Grizzly swung at his right thigh. "I want this to be beyond fair. You'll have your gun in your hand. I'll have mine in its holster, with the safety-strap fastened down. The Captain agrees that if you kill me, you'll fly away a free man."

"Now why do I have trouble believing—"

"Shorty's going to do the counting. He'll count down from three, say 'Fire!' and count back up to three. You can shoot any time after the word 'fire', but after the second 'three', the duel's over, No one can fire."

"What if nobody fires?"

"Unlikely, but given the occasion, we'll just start over. You ready?"

"I—"

"Shorty?"

"One—!"

"Wait, wait!" Pharch exclaimed. "I won't play! Something's fishy here! Something's rotten! I won't let you salve your conscience for torturing—!"

"Fine." Wilson said abruptly, and turned on his heel as if to walk away. Pharch swiftly raised his weapon, leveled it on Wilson's back, and—

Wilson kept turning on his heel, thumbing off the safety strap, wiping the safety with his thumb, and got a shot off before Pharch could. The man's arms flung wide and his back arched as he was thrown against the stainless wall behind him. For just an instant, Wilson could see the wall through the hole his slug had torn through the man.

Pharch slid to the floor and it was over.

*
**

"Things are going to start changing around here," Julie explained patiently to the girl in the grease-stained food service uniform. Her nametag, cluttered with colorful but irrelevant stickers, said "Amee". "If you truly want to keep your job, you'll have to start changing, too."

The girl was close to tears. She wiped a dirty hand across her eyes, smearing them with kitchen grime and mascara. "But ma'am, I don't—"

Julie said, "I know you don't, dear. You're East American, aren't you?" The woman looked around at the daunting task that lay before her.

"Yes, ma'am, Lancaster, Pennsylvania. The judge said if I came out here—"

Julie shook her head. "This is Mars, dear, or as close as you can get without actually being there. We don't care why you came. Many of us came out here for similar reasons. I did. You might think about being a Martian."

The girl nodded dully. "Yes, ma'am, I—"

"To begin with, I'm not ma'am, I'm Mrs. Ngu. Or maybe even Julie. Now I want you to throw every bit of this so-called food away, as quickly as you can. Clean the air filters and then set that system on full. Take everything the food was in—the coffee maker, too—and run it through the dishwasher, twice, on the high medical sanitizing setting."

"Yes, ma'am—Mrs.—Julie."

"Don't worry, I'll find you some help if I have to go down to the loading floor. While the kitchen is disassembled, scrub every square inch of it with soap and disinfectant. Scrub and mop this floor, as well. I'll get somebody to work on those nasty tables and chairs and railings."

Seemingly content to have something specific to do, Amee hurried off into the kitchen area. Julie strode over to the table where Adam and Ardith were sitting. She had her computer open, going over the radiation being generated by the Drake-Tealy Object orbiting Pallas, and the signals coming from the Cometary Halo. From time to time, she received long-delayed messages from Sinclair, aboard the Billie, as well.

Adam sat close beside her, looking over her shoulder. His mother hadn't seen him happier since thirty seconds before she'd caught the pair of them in the boat house—twenty-one or twenty-two years ago—and pretended that she hadn't seen them doing anything untoward.

She always thought of it as an extra birthday present she'd given him.

Adam looked up. "Anything we can do, Mom?" He knew that she had asserted proprietorship of the place so she could receive Llyra and Jasmeen in a manner she felt proper. Honey Graham had taken Mohammed and Beliita to a meeting room. He wished her a lot of luck. He'd often watched Mohammed lead reporters in four-cornered circles, telling them nothing, learning everything they knew, and sending them home confused but happy.

To avoid the reporter's badgering and prying, Manzel had found a dirty baseball cap to put over his bandage, drifted back, away from the Khalidovs, and was scrubbing away as if he had been a janitor all his life. From time to time, he turned around, looked at Adam, and grinned.

Julie shook her head, indicating her daughter-in-law. "She's doing science," she told her son. "Take care of her while she does it and we'll clean around you. I'm going down to the cargo floor to see if anybody wants more money than East American is paying them."

She went back the way they'd come, retraced her steps, almost to the airlock where her rented shuttle was docked, and then followed a tape line on the floor until she finally reached the cargo handling area. It was extremely noisy, with large metal objects bashing into one another, and machinery of various kinds straining to move heavy containers. Not surprisingly, it was cleaner here than on the passenger level.

"Lady!" someone shouted. "This is a hardhat area, not a scenic route!"

She looked up to see a thickset individual in bluejeans, a plaid flannel shirt, and a yellow titanium hardhat. He was on a level a few feet above her, operating one of the noisy loading machines. He had five o'clock shadow that was very nearly blue, and was smoking a big cigar.

"Then give me a hardhat, if you've got a spare!" she shouted back. "I'm Julie Segovia Ngu and as of just about an hour ago, you work for me!"

The man blinked, stopped his noisy machine—she saw a union pin attached to one of his suspenders—and started to dispose of his half-smoked cigar.

"Don't waste that!" she told him. "It costs too much to ship them out here." It wouldn't forever—there would be tobacco farms on Mars next year.

"What can I do for you, Mrs. Ngu?"

"Julie. I've got a load of catered food coming up from Maxwell's, and I need some volunteers to help me overhaul the restaurant and kitchen. I'll pay half again whatever they're paying you now to help me."

"The cargo will get delayed … Julie."

"An hour to help me, another hour to share the meal. What do you say?"

He started climbing down from his machine. "Hey, boys!" he shouted into a comm button attached to his other suspender. "Come and meet the new boss-lady! We got ourselves a special assignment!"

Julie grinned and led a dozen men and women back with her to the slidewalk. When she got to the restaurant area, it already looked and smelled a great deal better. Adam and Ardith had moved to a table that had apparently been cleaned. She turned to the man with the yellow hardhat. "That's Amee, over there. Ask her what she needs for you to do."

The man nodded. Julie was happy to see that Amee had already recruited a couple of helpers on her own. Two slender blondes, one in braids, one in pigtails, wearing greasy aprons over their everyday clothes, were scrubbing and mopping industriously at the filthy tiled floor.

Then a shock went through her.

"Llyra! Jasmeen!" The two girls stood, put down their sponge and mop, peeled off their aprons, and ran to her, both of them throwing their arms around her. Adam and Ardith both got up from the table, laughing.

Wilson peeked from behind a huge refrigerator. "Can I come out, now?"

CHAPTER FORTY-FOUR: THE HOUSE THAT NGU BUILT

Most individuals simply can't abide the notion of blind evolution. They desperately want to believe that there's a Great Plan, even if—judging by the evidence with which a cruel universe presents us every day—it's a Demented and Evil Plan. They refuse to understand that, if there is no Plan, then human beings are free to subdue the universe, and to make of themselves whatever they desire. —*The Diaries of Rosalie Frazier Ngu*

ALI KHALIDOV PEERED INTO THE monitor intently, even going as far as lifting the patch over his right eye. "Why do we not go and join them?"

"Yes," Lafcadio Guzman agreed with Jasmeen's uncle. "Did you hear her say she's having food flown up from Maxwell's? I've never been to Mars and yet I've heard of Maxwell's!" His lovely wife Eladia was many things, he thought, most of them very nice, but she was not a cook. He stroked the head of his pet seal Roger contemplatively. The animal looked up at him with huge, warm, trusting eyes and made a low, growly noise.

"Will join them presently," said Jasmeen's other uncle, Saladin Uzhakhov. "But just now is for nuclear family. Kerosene family later. See how closely Llyra sits to both her parents? Wilson sits close to his father. Jasmeen sits next to Ardith who has arm around her shoulders. Splendid, lovely Julie orchestrates demolition of kitchen with assistance of Khalidov's tame assassin."

"Anti-assassin," Ali insisted. "Manzel is anti-assassin. Is very different. One is ethical, one is unethical. Is good at what he does, too. Would break his Texas heart if he knew that we know all about him."

"Arizona," Saladin shook his massive head. "Tucson, Arizona. Is *our* business to know things, Ali," he informed his colleague. "And we are very good at what we do, too. Is this not so, Lafcadio? But we will not stoop so low to break good man's southwest American heart, no."

"Looks like somebody tried to break his head," Lafcadio observed.

"Yes," Saladin replied. "My second laboratory assistant Wu Yiing Abernathy has cousin who is physician on Mars. She asked her cousin for advice concerning tall, thin male patient from Moon who will not cooperate with bureaucratic data-gathering. Yiing struggles with nosy records on SolarNet for two hours, to no avail, then tells doctor to give it up. Doctor says she thinks she will, anyway was only fish wound."

"That's *flesh* wound," Ali corrected his friend with a disgusted expression. He rolled his eyes, then went back to scrutinizing the monitor. Not many people knew—and even fewer would have believed—that the man wore an eyepatch only to guarantee his night vision for the telescope.

"Flesh wound," Saladin tried the words on for size. "Flesh wound. Flesh wound. Very good, flesh wound. Makes more sense that way."

Deimos barely had enough gravity to hold itself together, let alone anything else, and that not very well. The ship was moored to the rock beneath her, as well as the airlock. Sitting in the pilot's seat—the flight deck was separated from the rest of the interior by bead curtains kept in place by magnets in their ends—Lafcadio drank red wine from a baggie. The scientists had hot chocolate, augmented with vodka.

All three were aboard Lafcadio's ship, the *Gay Deceiver*, which had powerful engines and was heavily armed, but looked like a pile of junkyard debris on the outside. Inside, the ship was furnished like a luxury hotel. They had tapped into the Deimos facility's rudimentary security system. The fact they were watching meant that Julie didn't know about the cameras yet. If she had, she would have torn them out, herself.

There were dozens, if not hundreds, of cameras. Together, they'd watched Julie hire a dozen men and women from the loading floor. What a pity, they all thought, that there was no sound. They'd watched Llyra and Wilson's tearful reunion with their parents while Julie was still downstairs. They'd watched the tender—but silly—way she and her companion, Saladin and Ali's niece, Jasmeen, had chosen to greet her grandmother.

They were two families of jokers, the Ngus and the Khalidovs. The universe would probably implode, Lafcadio thought, if they should ever interbreed.

The scientists and the used spaceship salesman were also watching—on another cluster of 3DTV screens—the development of certain events occurring in orbit around Ceres, and from somewhere beyond the orbit of the Pluto-Charon System. That was the real reason—both Lafcadio and Ali suspected it—that Saladin wanted to stay put for a while longer.

According to Sheridan Sinclair, aboard the Curringer Corporation's far-ranging yacht, the *William Wilde Curringer*, the unexplained energies were coming from a Drake-Tealy Object 500 miles in diameter, nearly the size of the third largest asteroid, Vesta. The pulse rates were definitely converging and should be synchronized in another day. Sinclair was keeping *Billie* at least a thousand miles away from the Object.

"Sinclair," Ali observed, "looks like little man in Monopoly."

Saladin chuckled. "Yes, he does."

"Dr. Ngu's watching the same thing you guys are!" said Lafcadio.

Cameras on the opposite side of the mezzanine-like structure had caught it. Ardith's virtual screen was displaying the same images, from Ceres and the Cometary Halo, that were on the screens here in the ship: a string of colorful bar graphs, indicating frequencies all the way across the electromagnetic spectrum, displaying strange pulses of energy. Saladin had determined there were gravity pulses happening, as well.

"Should we communicate with her?" Ali asked his partner. "Should be unobtrusive enough. We know things she does not know. Perhaps she knows—"

"All right, all right, I get it!" Saladin was occupied with what was on the screen before him—pulses in energies he hadn't known existed.

"Touchy, today?" asked Ali. "Did we get up on wrong side bed?"

Saladin gave a great sigh of exasperation. "Go ahead and contact her, then—only leave lag time, as if we were still back home, in Moon."

Lafcadio asked, "But why?", then ducked the man's powerful glare.

"Who knows?" said Saladin. "In addition to touchy, I am also today sneaky."

"Hungry, too" Ali suggested. "Here comes caterer's shuttle."

⁎⁎

"I'd rather have stayed in town," Adam told Ardith as she unpacked their luggage and put their clothes away in closets and drawers. He'd have helped, but they were both in wheelchairs, and the clash of wheels would have been awkward. The house seemed to be built of closets. Julie had designed it.

It had been a good many years since Adam had visited his mother on Mars. The woman might have told him, he thought, when he'd mentioned hiring a sandskipper, that there was no further need for sandskippers, at least not here. A straight, beautiful, six-lane highway, paved with tough, black plastic, stretched past her house between Coprates City and Bradbury, entirely paid for by the trucking companies whose giant freighters blasted along its length, bringing food and other things from the spaceport in the city to the towns far out on the macaroni prairie.

The paving plastic, derived from macaroni plant, had many other uses, and was just one of many things that the big freighters were reloaded with—the System's highest-tech industrial and consumer goods were another—when they roared back to the city and its tiny spaceport.

"You don't want to stay here," Ardith observed, not looking up from the bed where she was refolding what she took from their luggage, "because you're embarrassed to make love to me in your mother's house."

"That's not it at all," he replied. Actually it was, at least in part, but he didn't want to admit it. It might not even be possible for them in this planet's gravity field. "I just don't know if the place is defensible."

Ardith chuckled. "Oh, it's defensible, all right, my darling, if Julie designed it. Are you kidding? A Marine who fought a revolution and then managed to survive all the looting and murdering that followed?"

"I concede your point. We had our troubles with Earth, too, but nothing like that. The house I was raised in, the house my grandfather built, was a lot of wonderful things, but it was not defensible. It did have lots of nice little nooks and crannies to hide and play in, though."

"I remember that," she said. "And a boathouse."

"Ah, yes. And a boathouse." Suddenly he realized, if everything went the way he hoped it would, he'd never live in the house on Pallas again.

Neither would Ardith. Some other Ngus would. Ardith had brought up the subject of moving her lab to Ceres once the terraformation process was complete. That was for the future. They had other problems now.

There was a gentle knock on the door. "Come," they both said. The door slid into the casement. Llyra stood outside—impossibly tall and grown-up looking—on the hall carpet of a balcony looking out over the great room. Mounted on the ceiling-high stonework above what Adam had always thought of as his mother's "walk-in fireplace" (it burned macaroni plant, compressed into logs) was the head of a southern greater kudu his father had killed on Pallas. Through the balcony railing, Adam could see the tips of its corkscrew horns from where he sat.

He still remembered how that animal had tasted.

"Grandma says to tell you she's ready to go," Llyra informed them. Adam could see that she wasn't comfortable in this amount of gravity, but she was handling it without any artificial support. Of course she and Jasmeen had had the voyage here, at one-third gee. She came into the room and sat on the bed so she could be at the same level they were.

Ardith took her hand. Llyra looked startled for an instant. Her mother had never been very physical with her, but Llyra understood that things were starting to change—that her mother was struggling to change them. It was the very kind of struggle Llyra had been brought up to admire.

"I still don't know," Ardith said, "about taking you and Jasmeen with us. It could be very dangerous." She looked over, appealing to Adam.

Llyra protested, "But that's the point, Mom, isn't it? We're the tastiest bait. Wilson stopped them from hurting the factory ship. I shot that man in the knee. They might not bite, if we aren't there. Especially the woman that Jasmeen shot. I'd be pretty pissed off, myself."

"Please don't say 'pissed', dear." It was a reflex. Llyra giggled.

Risking what might once have touched off an explosion, Adam agreed with his daughter. "I don't like it much, either, but I'm afraid she's right."

Ardith sighed—things *were* different, both her husband and her daughter realized—and nodded reluctant agreement. "Make sure you have—"

"My gun? It's right here, Mom. Jasmeen is armed, and I imagine you two—"

Ardith laughed. "Your father is better-armed than I've ever seen him!" He grinned and showed her the ten millimeter magnum he wore cross-draw at his waist, along with a pair of forty-five caliber weapons that had belonged to his father. Julie had insisted on his having them. He had tucked them away in the arm compartments of his wheelchair.

"Will not help much with thrown bomb." The door was still open. Jasmeen stepped into the room. "I come to help with chair if you permit." It was oddly humiliating to think of this tiny, slender young woman helping him with his wheelchair, but that was what his daughter was here for, too, he realized. When it was over, this afternoon, he'd get himself a walker.

"That's what Wilson and some of his friends will be watching for. Yes, you may help us, Jasmeen, thank you. You remember what this was like."

On Moon, yes. Was embarrassment—but not so much as Gurney!"

With Jasmeen pushing Adam, and Llyra pushing her mother—who said she hated leaving such a mess behind: clothing folded neatly on a bed—they went to an elevator that took them to the ground floor. Llyra and Jasmeen were delighted to be staying on the third or fourth floor (there was any number of half-levels, and Adam could never keep track) in what Julie called "the cupola", the highest room of the house.

Wilson was standing beside his grandmother in the entrance to the great room, near the front door. The house was an amazing construction of red-gray field stone—one could tell it was native Martian, because there was no lichen on it and never had been—and what appeared to be wood. Adam suspected it came from the same place as the fireplace logs.

The front door itself boasted an enormous, colorful window made of stained glass, depicting her two literary protagonists Conchita and Desmondo, and their pet arachnicat, Ploogle, slaying a gigantic gray dragon. Adam loved that picture. It was the cover—stained glass and all—of an infamous book in which his mother had taken on organized religion.

His son looked even more grown up than his daughter, Adam thought. It wasn't a matter of size—Wilson had been full grown three years ago, back on Ceres—so much as the set of his face and the way he carried himself. He'd been through a lot in those three years, Adam realized.

Wilson was dressed well, for a hunter, in a dark, collarless shirt, trousers tightened in the Martian way at the ankles, and a sportcoat that came halfway to his knees. It was thrown back on the right to expose the big, low-slung .45 Magnum that had belonged to his great grandfather. On the other side, high on the waist, he wore his twelve-shot revolver.

From the front hallway, Adam could see into his mother's front parlor, where the 3DTV had been left on, and where the bait was being cast.

" … Old Survivor Stadium where later today, as special guests of a local semi-professional team, the Coprates City Warlords, many of the survivors of the recent, horrifying takeover of the East American Spacelines' *City of Newark* will relax and enjoy a day of sunshine, hotdogs, local beer, and exciting baseball as only Martians can play it."

The camera zoomed past the correspondent to a section of the bleachers that had been cheerfully decked out in bunting of Martian orange—the original color of the planet before the macaroni plant arrived. Banners waved, and signs proclaimed it "Survival Day At Old Survivor."

"We'll stay with the story and have some interviews later this afternoon. Honey Graham, Interplanetary Interactive Information Service."

*
**

"It's a trap, of course," said Crenicichla.

He was looking out the window, down into Old Survivor Stadium. A moment before, he'd been watching Honey Graham on 3DTV. He could see her still, if he peered hard enough—or used the field glasses from their survival kits—standing on the pitcher's mound, facing right field.

"Of course it's a trap," Krystal answered him calmly. At the moment, she was cleaning their weapons as well as she could, given that she had no specialized supplies or tools. "She used to be on our team like all of the media, but she's becoming a tad unreliable, isn't she?"

"A tad and a half," Crenicichla answered her. "It's what comes of spending too much time with the Ngu family. You know we could still just disappear, Krystal. They're starting to stock some of the local running water with trout. I have enough money to last us a long, long time."

She nodded. "I know. I used to go fishing for bass in a lake where I lived. It sounds tempting. You go fishing. I'm going down there." She nodded at the window and the stadium. "I won't blame you, honest, honey."

Crenicichla turned, quickly strode across the little room, and took the woman—his woman, he realized—by both shoulders where she sat working at the little correspondence table. He bent so that his face was beside hers. "Don't you dare say anything like that to me, ever again! Wherever you go, Krystal Sweet, I go! No matter where it happens to be, or what happens as a consequence!"

She grinned. "I was kind of hoping you'd say that, darling." She ran a hand through his hair, then placed the slide of a disassembled autopistol back on the frame, slid it all the way to the rear, let it lock, then released it into battery. She loaded the gun. "You know the same goes for me, Johnnie, though I never thought I'd hear myself say it."

He nodded, stepped back, and took a deep breath. He was a man capable of intense loyalty, he knew, but for the first time in his life, he found himself transferring it. "The ballgame doesn't start for a couple of hours. Let's get something to eat—and then go get married."

Holstering her weapon, she giggled. "How romantic! I'll wear my formal sunglasses."

*
**

In the plaza, the statue of the Old Survivor stood four times larger than life. It was made of coarsely-brushed stainless steel. If someday it rained a hundred inches a year in Coprates, it would never tarnish. Pigeons stayed off—years of research had been dedicated to that—because they didn't like the texture of the metal under their feet.

From a cobbled sidewalk across a downtown street, Julie looked up at the faceplate where his eyes should have been visible. She had known this man as well as anyone had. He had saved her life on several occasions, as well as those of countless other people in a colony struggling to stay alive.

She could see him now, in her mind's eye, sitting with them around the electric furnace in the dimly-lit common hut, his pale blue eyes twinkling in the glow of the heating elements. His seamed face was framed in an untidy mass of gray and yellow hair and a prickly-looking beard.

Nobody knew who the Old Survivor was, not even the Old Survivor, himself. He'd come to Mars with one of six expeditions preceding the one that Julie had followed as part of a military contingent sometimes called the seventh and a half. He couldn't recall which had brought him. His envirosuit was a patchwork of suits from all six. If the seventh hadn't made it, his suit would have wound up with salvaged pieces of theirs.

She could hear him, even now, telling stories in a raspy brogue that made it seem as if he'd been with every one of the expeditions, in turn. He'd spoken of individual acts of heroism and sacrifice that had raised the hair on the back of her neck, and of cruelties and stupidities that defied reason.

Nobody knew his name. At the base of the statue. a plaque read, "THE OLD SURVIVOR" and under that, "John Carter, Jeddak of Jeddaks". Sometimes that was who he thought he was. He'd worn nothing under his suit and carried the enormous, curved-tipped sword she saw replicated here today.

She could see him now, sitting with them around the furnace in borrowed clothing the others had insisted that he wear. When he left, they found it neatly folded in the airlock, where his sword stood when he visited.

Nobody knew where he came from or where he went. It was believed he'd found a cave somewhere in Candor Chasma. He must have somehow sealed it, warmed it, filled it with oxygen. One day he'd simply shown up at the seventh's landing site bearing a few items of technology as gifts. Later he'd disappeared, to reappear whenever he thought he might be needed.

She could see him now, trying the same kindness on the military encampment, several miles away. The civilians called it "Derbyville" for the color and shape of its inflated domes. The sentries had nearly killed him before she stopped them. He had never come back to Derbyville.

Nobody had ever found the Old Survivor's cave. At first, there was no time or energy to spare shadowing him to it, even if it could have been done, during the early days of Martian settlement. Today it was the Holy Grail of Martian archaeology and history. One day he'd simply disappeared, never to return. Sooner or later, it was assumed that he was dead.

Julie remembered it all. She shut the limousine door, instructed the car to return in two and a half hours, turned, and followed the rest of her family into Maxwell's, the best restaurant in the Solar System.

Looking more like a hockey player than a System-famous chef, Maxwell himself greeted her at the door with a glass of high desert wine. He'd promised her family the best duck they'd ever eaten—and to initiate them into the mysteries of salad dressing made with truffle oil, worth more on Mars, ounce-for-ounce, than the purest palladium.

*
**

"Okay," said Honey. "Let's have one with everybody waving at the camera!" It was a sunny day in Coprates City. Orange banners and bunting flew in the soft, warm breeze of a typical Valles Marineris summer.

She didn't have to shout to be heard. Except for those she was photographing, and attendants preparing the grass, the stadium was empty. The members of the Ngu family sat together in the three middle levels of the first tier. Llyra and Wilson sat together, roughly in the center, flanked by Adam and Ardith on Llyra's side, and Jasmeen on Wilson's. Above them sat Julie, the Khalidovs, and Jasmeen's scientist uncles, Mohammed and Ali. All of them were wearing Warlord baseball caps emblazoned with the Old Survivor's sword.

Never had there been a greater assemblage of rented wheelchairs, walkers, and canes among a group of essentially healthy individuals, most of whom, coming from the Moon or the asteroids, were simply not accustomed to the one-third gravity of Mars. Whoever had said it was right: more than any other force, gravity would shape the future social history of the species *Homo sapiens*.

On two rows of seats beneath them, sat Wilson's hunting friends, Scotty, Marko, Mikey, Shorty, Casey, and Merton with their own walking aids. All had declined to give Honey their last names. Shorty didn't want to be photographed at all. One of them, she understood, was missing because Wilson had killed him in a duel aboard the passenger liner. What she wouldn't have given to see—and air!—that video. But the Captain had forbidden it. Busy boy, Wilson. He was soon to become a full-time single father.

Surrounded by asteroid hunters, Lafcadio Guzman grinned and banged the little Japanese plastic noisemaking tube he'd been given on the next seat below him.

It was great news footage, Honey thought, and an even greater story. Just too bad the whole thing was as phony as a three ruble note.

"They can't really jump to their feet, but how about one where they raise their arms and shout as if someone has just hit a home run?"

It was Aaron Manzel, standing beside her, who made the suggestion—another great story she couldn't tell. More than anyone except the vessel's captain, he'd saved the lives of three hundred passengers. But he didn't want anyone to know about it and wouldn't tolerate being photographed.

She passed Manzel's idea on, took the pictures, and sent them to the wireless address specified. She was folding her headset camera and mike when Adam arrived at her side.

"Thank you, Miss Graham," he told her, lifting a hand to shake hers.

She didn't know what to say. In terms a professional journalist understands, she had sold out to this man and his family. She could continue her career only because nobody important in her circles knew what she had done to participate in the news, rather than simply record and comment on it. The trouble was that *she* knew.

She had worse problems. "I guess you're welcome, Dr. Ngu. I hope I never have to do anything like this again, for as long as I live."

"You're saving lives," he told her. His wife Ardith was beside him now, along with his son Wilson, and the two girls, Llyra and Jasmeen, whom Honey had thought of as Adam's daughters since she'd met them on Ceres. "But you're packing up. Aren't you going to stay and watch the game?"

"Whichever game you happen to mean, Dr. Ngu," she replied. "No, I promised Arleigh I'd get back to Ceres as soon as possible. He says he misses me. And do you know what? I miss him, too. Now how the hell did that happen?"

Adam and his family laughed. "I'll see you back there in a few days. I can't really thank you enough, Honey, I owe you a very big one."

"Yes," she said. "And I plan to collect."

*
**

"We don' need no stinkin' tickets!" Krystal laughed. And she was right. When they'd gotten married in the storefront wedding parlor next door to the Chinese restaurant they'd had lunch in, they'd been given a week's worth of complimentary passes to the Old Survivor stadium.

Johnnie grinned at her. "No, all we need is these!" He flipped his jacket open to reveal, for just an instant, the autopistol he was carrying.

They stood at the entrance of a tunnel that led to the first tier of the stadium's left field seats. They'd seen that Honey woman on 3DTV, interviewing the Ngu family and others who had just arrived on Mars after their harrowing journey. They had been invited here today by the Coprates Warlords. Behind them had flapped an enormous banner, hanging from the second tier railing, proclaiming *"City of Newark Survivors' Day"*.

Krystal had a big smile on her face. Wearing sunglasses, no one would know she'd been hurt. "All you need is love—and a big enough weapon!"

Through the dark tunnel, they could see the right field seats, jammed with spectators yelling their heads off, even though the teams were only warming up. From time to time, the name of one of the local heroes would be announced, he'd strike a pose, throw a ball, or swing a bat, and they'd go crazy. Johnnie tried to remember the name of the visiting team, but couldn't. He was too nervous, and he didn't really care.

A huge 3DTV screen over on the other side filled itself with portraits and statistics that changed constantly. Crenicichla had always believed that baseball was a game invented for the benefit of accountants.

At the sides at the opposite end of the tunnel, he could see big orange banners waving in the breeze, part of the decorations he'd seen on 3DTV, honoring the survivors. Their orange color was an insult and a perversion. It was the original color of the planet Mars before it had been contaminated and despoiled by the vile fungus covering it now.

"Do you want this tunnel," Krystal asked him now, "or should I take it?"

"No, I'll take it," he told her, feeling his heart race, his knees shake.

"It's the right thing to do, you know." She stood on her tiptoes and kissed his cheek. He took her in his arms and kissed her properly, just as he had in the marriage parlor. She was right. Others before yourself.

"I know. Let's do it." He released her, turned, and started down the tunnel. He watched her walk to the next tunnel on his left and disappear into it. He looked at the crowd on the other side of the stadium, enjoying themselves so thoroughly their cheers and stomping made the stadium rattle. The giant 3DTV screen over right field, which had been showing someone at bat, was suddenly filled with colorful three-dimensional static.

He ignored it.

Unconsciously counting his steps, he came close to the end and finished his count. He took a deep breath, stepped out into the stadium and drew his gun, holding it in both hands as he swung left, taking the muzzle where he knew that it would find the key members of the abominable Ngu family.

He saw Krystal doing the same at the next tunnel mouth, but swinging right, a few dozen yards away. Only there was nobody between them. The seats were completely empty.

The giant screen behind him suddenly showed the image of a young Asian man a little older than Wilson. Beside him was a curly-haired brunette of about the same age, holding a baby in her arms. They looked strangely familiar.

"What the hell?" Crenicichla demanded of nobody in particular, until Krystal yelled to look at the right field seats and the rest of the stadium. What he saw gave him the feel of icy fingertips up his spine.

The entire stadium was empty. All the noise and shouting he'd been hearing were recorded, the spectators only a image being projected onto a huge translucent curtain hanging down from the tier of seats above. Only the flags and bunting flapping in the breeze around him, and the image on the giant screen behind were real. Everything else was—

"It's a fake!" Krystal screamed.

The young man on the screen grinned. "Hello, people of the Solar System. I apologize for breaking into whatever you were watching. I'm Emerson Ngu, captain of the interstellar exploration ship, *Fifth Force*. This is my lovely wife Rosalie Frazier Ngu beside me, and our youngest son, Harrison, in her arms. We and our friends have been on a very long trip, and have returned now to tell you all about it."

Crenicichla rushed toward his new wife to comfort her. She rushed toward him. They met in the middle of the section, beside the bottom rail.

"Oh, Johnnie, what are we going to do?"

"You're going to drop your weapons and put your hands on your heads," said a commanding voice. It was the Captain of the goddamned *City of Newark*, pointing a pistol at them. He came out of the tunnel—there must have been a janitor's room or something he'd been hiding in—and stepped into the seating section, ten or twelve rows above them.

Unaware that nobody—at least in the Old Survivor Stadium—was paying attention, Emerson went on. "There's a gigantic Drake-Tealy

Object in the Cometary Halo, about as far from Pluto as Pluto is from the Sun. When we approached it too closely, it seemed to open out into a doughnut shape, and pulled us right in. When we saw the stars again, we were in a different Solar System, with not one but two lovely, livable worlds circling a warm, cheerful yellow star a lot like our own."

"Do what he said—drop your weapons!"

Wilson Ngu had followed the Captain and now stood beside him. Others emerged from the tunnel Krystal had entered by. Together Johnnie and Krystal saw the entire Ngu family, except for the brother on Ceres, come out and stand on the same level as the Captain. Some of them were in wheelchairs. All of them were armed.

"Lose the weapons now," Wilson said, and live. Otherwise, you'll die."

"We've spent the last decade and a half exploring those worlds," said Emerson, "while our physicists struggled to get us back home. There's a giant Drake-Tealy Object there, too, and they think, somehow, its the same one that took us there."

Krystal looked at her husband. "I'll get the two girls, you get the mother and the son. Then we'll go for the grandmother and whoever else."

Emerson said, "We're back, now—having left eight hundred folks on those two worlds—to invite more people to join us, to come and settle the new worlds."

"On the count of three!"

They raised their guns and fired. The other side seemed slow to react— perhaps they were distracted by the return of the *Fifth Force*—but none of them fell. The one Krystal referred to as "the mother" pulled the trigger. Crenicichla watched a bullet take Krystal in the throat, just where her collarbones came together. As she fell backwards, over the rail, Ardith's second shot took her in the solar plexus.

Krystal flipped over the rail and fell fifty feet onto the top of a concrete dugout. There was a lot of blood. Crenicichla screamed and charged the Ngu family above him, leaping across the tops of the seats, firing as rapidly as he could at Ardith and Julie. He could see his bullets striking the seatbacks around them, chipping off bits, then the unnaturally young Ngu grandmother folded and fell, holding her belly.

Adam, Wilson, Llyra, and Jasmeen pulled their triggers at the same time. Crenicichla saw the flashes, but never heard the noise of the gunshots.

PART FOUR:
ONE FULL GEE

SINCE NO GOVERNMENT "LEVIATHAN"—AND VERY few corporations, if any—can be trusted to protect the Earth and its progeny from
"Extinction Level Events" without exacting a price for such a service too
terrible to pay, the question remains, who will do the job, and by what
means.

After long consideration, I have come here to propose that we limit
ourselves to two measures, and otherwise let the market take its course.
The first is that an observatory be established, probably on Earth's Moon,
with the idea of finding and tracking all sorts of space debris—planet-
threatening or otherwise—and making this information available for a
modest price.

The second is that a fund be established—initially by the Curringer
Foundation, but encouraging other corporations and individuals to contribute—rewarding those who capture or deflect celestial objects proven
to be on a collision course with Earth or any Settled World.

—*Dr. Evgeny Zacharenko Addressing the Ashland Event Commission*
Of the Solar Geological Society Curringer, Pallas, August 9, 2095

CHAPTER FORTY-FIVE: NGUS IN THE NEWS

> Ultimately, all individual behavior is about sex and all group behavior is about eating. All government behavior is also about eating—the individual. —*The Diaries of Rosalie Frazier Ngu*

ADAM AND ARDITH SAT ON their new front porch drinking Pallatian wine. It grew darker by the minute and they were waiting for the big show.

"Someday, you know," Adam spoke into the gathering evening air, mostly to himself, "there'll be a highway running past this property, from the Construction Village three miles over that way—we took the dome down yesterday, it was almost sad—to wherever Cereans want to go."

"Cereans," Ardith laughed. "And great big shade trees standing in our front yard, with tire swings hanging from their longest limbs, for grandchildren."

"More grandchildren?" Adam asked.

"More grandchildren," Ardith told him, as she glanced down at the visicard in her hand. About four by seven inches, it could be loaded from the SolarNet, then taken away to be viewed somewhere else at some other time. She'd already watched it several times, and would leave it on her nightstand. It was from her son Wilson, holding two-year-old Tieve in his arms. "It's so hard to believe that it's already 2136, Adam, three long, busy years after all the things that reshaped our lives there on Mars."

"Time flies when you're having fun," he told her. "They had just learned that Anna Wertham Savage, former leader of the now-defunct Mass Movement had been arrested for embezzling contributed funds. Also for smoking tobacco within the Commonwealth of Massachusetts. She'd gotten six months in prison for the former offense, and six years for the latter. "A little too fast to suit me. There's so much left I want to do. And seeing my grandfather look the same age as my son helped me make a decision."

"And that would be?"

"When we're through with the aerial plantings, and the last of the watercourse surveys, you and I are going to the Moon for regeneration. Hell, we might even go out and take a look at the planets Emerson discovered."

"So you'd abandon me for a younger ... me?"

"I'd be younger, too. Maybe we could even ... "

"More babies?" Ardith laughed. She'd finally come to understand that losing four out of six children had made her keep all that distance between herself and those she loved. It had made her crazy. It hurt too much to love someone and lose them.

"Not unless you wanted them, too."

"More babies, then. Our children are a challenge we hurl in the face of a hostile universe."

"Wow! Who said that?"

"I did, my darling Adam, I did. Hey, there goes one, now! See it?"

"No, I—wow! Who could have predicted that?"

They were looking up into the sky, their sky, the sky of Ceres. High above the rugged landscape, just beginning to be softened by teeming lifeforms—everything from earthworms to sequoia seedlings—the plastic atmospheric canopy was displaying behavior similar to that of Pallas.

Only different. It seemed to be a matter of magnitude and resonance. There would be no fantastic sunrises and sunsets on the largest of the asteroids. Instead, whenever the self-healing canopy was struck with even the smallest micrometeorite, it sent multicolored ripples outward in rainbow order, toward the entire horizon.

The discovery had been made just after the harsh "primordial" reducing atmosphere of nitrogen, methane, and ammonia, generated by custom-tailored microbes feeding on the raw carbonaceous chondrite soil, had been replaced with a mixture of oxygen, nitrogen, and carbon dioxide, also manufactured by microorganisms. The larger the bit of rock, the faster it was going relative to Ceres, and the harder it impacted, the brighter the colors and the longer they lasted before fading.

"It's a hell of a show," Adam told Ardith. He squeezed more wine from the commercial baggie through the valves of the baggies they were drinking from, then put an arm around his wife. "I wish I could claim credit."

"You can—it would never have happened without you." She kissed him passionately. They occupied themselves that way for a considerable amount of time. Finally: "I think it's time to go indoors, wouldn't you say, dear?"

"For more reasons than one. Here, hold this." He gave her his drink and the larger baggie as well, then swept her off her feet into his arms. He strode across the porch—which was the only part of the house constructed yet—across a plank, and into a large, temporary yurt made from modern materials.

Inside, they had a big roomful of inflatable furniture, and in the center, below the chimney hole, a tiny one-piece kitchen that also heated the place. They went to a beanbag sofa located in front of a twelve-foot 3DTV screen. They sat down and he fiddled with a remote control.

"Knock, knock!" said a voice at the door. "Am I interrupting anything?"

"Not yet," Ardith replied. "Please come in, Julie. The show's about to start."

"It's actually been over for forty-five minutes already, but thank you." Julie found a chair that suited her, pulled off her flying jacket, leather helmet, and goggles. "It's maddening, the lightspeed lag, but so far, it's all we've got."

It was highly possible, they all knew, that several discoveries made by the *Fifth Force* were about to give birth to instantaneous interplanetary communication. It was also possible that the velocities of spaceships were about to be raised several orders of magnitude: Earth to Ceres in under an hour. Then they'd get to see their granddaughter a bit more frequently.

Flaming red hair for the first time in the history of the Ngu family. Life was wonderfully unpredictable.

"We're back, again," said the announcer, "At the EPIC Center in Fort Collins, Colorado, West America, to bring you the final event in System-wide competition, the ladies' long program. Eight women are just about to skate, and for the first time, one of them, the up-and-coming Llyra Ayn Ngu, wasn't born on Earth. Here's a video from yesterday as she prepared with her coach, Jasmeen Mohammedova Khalidova—a native of Mars—for her short program, which, as you may recall, she won handily."

There followed brief interviews with both Llyra and Jasmeen, then a series of what seemed to Ardith unusually obnoxious commercials. She noticed that Jasmeen's pregnancy still wasn't showing yet. The sooner she got off that godforsaken planet and out of its vile gravity well, the better.

Looking into her lap, Ardith squeezed a corner of the visicard for perhaps the fiftieth time, as Adam rolled his eyes in disbelief—and then grinned. From the control space of *Mighty Mouse's Girlfriend*, Wilson spoke for a while both to her and to his father, and also to Tieve, who held both her hands charmingly folded in front of her, made word-sounding noises at the audio pickup, and waved. Ardith's heart melted all over again.

"We're completely outsystem, here, but almost finished," Wilson said. We finally caught up with the Diamond Rogue again, and this time we were ready for it—show Grandma and Grandpa, Tieve." Between the little hands was a raw diamond at least the size of a softball.

"The whole asteroid is made of at least a million chunks that size. We even swept up the carbon matrix they were in, for later analysis. This should put DeBeers right out of business, while assuring our future."

And a good thing, too, Ardith thought.

"And a good thing, too," her son said. "I'll get to Earth just in time to pick Jasmeen up. She wants our baby born on Pallas. She also wants me to take her hunting again. Of course that's what got us in a family way the first time. Shared work is an aphrodisiac. Llyra says, win or lose, she'll take time off to write about what happened aboard the *City of Newark*."

Also on Pallas, Ardith found herself hoping. She'd be packing up the lab about then and would want some company. Rosalie and Julie had promised to help her. Three generations of Ngu women in one room—five if they could get together with Jasmeen and Tieve. Absolutely amazing.

With practical immortality there was a lot more of that around the corner.

On the 3DTV screen before them, Llyra stepped onto the ice, lifted her arms in salute to the audience, and began her long, exhausting routine. What a life it had been for her, her mother thought. And what a life still lay ahead of her.

What a life still lay ahead for all of them!

EPILOGUE: THE LONE AND LEVEL SANDS

I met a traveler from an antique land
Who said: Two vast and trunkless legs of stone
Stand in the desert. Near them, on the sand,
Half sunk, a shattered visage lies, whose frown,
And wrinkled lip, and sneer of cold command,
Tell that its sculptor well those passions read
Which yet survive, stamped on these lifeless things,
The hand that mocked them and the heart that fed;

And on the pedestal these words appear:
"My name is Ozymandius, king of kings:
Look on my works, ye Mighty, and despair!"
Nothing beside remains. Round the decay
Of that colossal wreck, boundless and bare
The lone and level sands stretch far away.

—*Percy Bysshe Shelley, "Ozymandius"*

The guard said, "Pardon me, Miss Ngu, may I please have your autograph?"

Llyra stood on the slowly-moving slidewalk with her husband Morgan and their three children, taking in the amazing sight of the famous Leaning Monument of Washington. The guard—who was no more than a ticket-taker, in point of fact—had apparently run all the way from his glass booth at the entrance of the Mall to catch up with them. Now the man bent over, hands on his knees, trying to catch his breath, as well.

By special arrangement with the Seaboard Weather Control Company—a holosign over the entrance had informed them—the onetime capital city of the Old United States and East America was kept authentically hot and humid all year round. As a result, all of them—including the guard, it appeared—felt authentically sticky and uncomfortable.

"Sure," Llyra told him cheerfully over the alarming sound of his wheezing. "Are you all right? Do you have something for me to write on?"

He levered himself upright again, looking flushed. Except for a fringe of reddish hair above his ears, he was totally bald, and bright pink from his chin almost to the back of his neck. He needn't have been bald, of course—practically nobody in the rest of the Solar System was these days—old-fashioned laws forbidding genetic therapy had long since been repealed, or were simply ignored, but the East American people largely remained prejudiced against "fooling Mother Nature".

He fished around in his antique gold-buttoned blazer—a patch on the breast pocket displayed a System-famous company logo surrounded by the legend, "EjTofz Entertainment Enterprises"—producing a scrap of paper.

"I'm okay, thanks, Miss Ngu," he told her, looking to her husband, as well. "I'm originally from Flagstaff, see? Old Arizona? Eighteen years I've lived and worked in the D.C. and I'm still not used to the damn artificial climate." He glanced down at the children. "Pardon my French."

Morgan laughed. "That's okay—Fred." He'd looked at the man's nametag. "We speak a lot of French, ourselves." In his way, Morgan was just as illustrious a personality as his wife, but she was the one who got asked for her autograph and he'd long since grown accustomed to it.

Llyra spoke up. "Sorry, Fred. Where are my manners? My husband, Morgan Trask, my son Emerson, my daughter Julia, and our baby daughter Ardie in the pram." As she spoke, she signed the paper scrap, dating it July 2, 2145. A sudden wave of nausea and foreboding swept through her, as it did sometimes—she'd had another hijacking nightmare last night and awakened shaken and sweaty—but she struggled to ignore it.

"It's very nice to meet you all." said the guard, shaking hands with the couple's eight-year-old son and five-year-old daughter. "Thank you, Miss Ngu. You know, we see quite a few celebrities here, but … " He held up the autograph. "Well, my wife will be so pleased." He departed at a considerably more leisurely pace than he'd arrived.

They all looked up at the monument again, sitting about a hundred yards away. The only thing holding the tower up seemed to be a pair of structural carbon cables, stretching from the pyramidal top, against the direction it was leaning, and anchored in the ground. They were smaller, but similar, Llyra realized, to the big cable, over 22,500 miles long, that they'd ridden down on from synchronous orbit this morning.

It was hard to believe that, in times past, thousands of groups—military veterans, racial minorities, trade organizations, labor unions, animal rights advocates, and environmentalists like the Sierra Club, All Worlds Are Earth, and the Mass Movement—had rallied here, sometimes by the millions, to state their case and make their demands. Now it was just a huge empty space Llyra and her family had, almost to themselves.

"EjTofz Entertainment Enterprises must be too cheap to spring for antigravs," Morgan observed. He'd pronounced the name "Eye-Tovs". Llyra thought it must be Hungarian or Lithuanian or Serbo-Croatian or something. The company had just bought the entire city—everything inside the legendary Beltway—intending to make a theme park out of it.

"They're still relatively expensive," Llyra replied. "And power hogs."

"Yeah, but if nothing is done to prevent it, someday this monument will collapse, leaving a long, broken line of rubble—the Washington Wall."

Between them and the monument, a life-sized hologram in quaint early 19th century clothing politely introduced itself as Parson Mason Weems. It spoke of General Washington, about the monument itself, and apologized for an apparently famous untruth it had once told about a hatchet and a cherry tree in its biography of the first American president.

"Just think." Llyra said. "One little fib, not quite three and a half centuries ago and he'll be apologizing for it until the sun burns out."

Morgan laughed.

"When Washington retired after two terms," the hologram continued, "He—"

"Be quiet, now." Llyra's husband told the hologram. "And please go away."

The hologram promptly vanished.

Morgan Trask was tall by nearly anybody's standard, six feet nine inches. Although he was heavily muscled and in excellent condition, strangers usually thought of him as skinny, owing to the proportions involved. He had strong Nordic features—although most of his ancestors were Irish—and long blond hair presently pulled back in a ponytail. He wore what served as casual street clothes in the Moon's largest city, Armstrong (to natives of Earth they looked like pajamas or surgical scrubs) and a small, potent plasma pistol on his right hip.

Born and raised in what might as well have been an interplanetary colony, a village built under an atmospheric dome east of L'Anse Aux Meadows on the northernmost tip of the Great Northern Peninsula of the Unanimous Consent Confederation of Newfoundland, Morgan had been the Solar System's Olympic champion in men's figure skating a dozen years ago.

Now he turned to his wife, catching the eye of his two older offspring, as well. The third, baby Ardie, was in her stroller, more or less oblivious to anything except her toes. "Somebody told me once that when Washington was a Revolutionary general, the Continental Congress put him on an expense account, rather than paying him a salary, which he used to buy livestock for the farm he shared with Martha."

The baby began to fuss a little, interrupting her father's story. Increasing the flow of the air curtain that protected her child from the climate and flying insects, Llyra raised her eyebrows. "Is that true?"

He shook his head. "Don't know—just what somebody told me. When he got elected President, he wanted the same deal but they turned him down."

"Gosh, I wonder why."

Twenty-eight year old Llyra Ngu Trask was nearly as tall as her husband, six feet seven inches, and similarly muscled, although with all of the curves appropriate to her sex. She, too, had been an Olympic gold medalist, in women's figure skating, at the age of sixteen. Blond and fair, with just the faintest hint of her Asian forbears in her hazel eyes, her height was nothing extraordinary where she came from. She'd been born and brought up on the terraformed asteroid Pallas, at one twentieth of a standard Earth gravity. It had taken her years to work up to skating on Earth, but in the end, she'd been the first female to perform a quintuple Salchow in a one-gee field.

For the past ten years, she and her husband had been coaching young Olympic hopefuls, as well as future show skaters, at the Robert and Virginia Heinlein Memorial Ice Skating Arena—"the Heinlein"—in Armstrong City in the Moon. The waiting list for their services, famous from Mercury to Pluto, was long and those on it would now be disappointed.

They had returned to Earth with their three small children for what could possibly be the last time, to see a few sights they thought were important. After Washington, their plan was to visit a handful of other North American cities and pay a visit to Morgan's parents in Newfoundland, before heading for Egypt. Next month they would board the *C.C.V. Prometheus*, bound for an ancient alien interstellar jump device recently discovered at the edge of the Solar System. It would take them to another star system and the beautiful Earthlike planet, Paradise.

Those who wished to retain a sense of perspective had named the planet's single extraordinarily dark and smooth-surfaced moon "Parking Lot".

One sight they wanted their children to see was the former capital of the former United States of America, the last government of any consequence on Earth, and the end of eight or ten thousand years of dismal coercive history. EjTofz Entertainment Enterprises had begun its renovation of the mostly abandoned city by restarting the famous moving walkways that took visitors from one point of interest to another.

As they'd seen, holograms of important biographers acted as guides to the various monuments and memorials. Cameras, computers, and other electronics were welcome in the park (in a city that had once required a police permit for a camera tripod) but only at their owners' risk. Uncountable trillions of electronics-eating antisurveillance nanites were still active from about a century ago, when people finally grew tired of being scrutinized and eavesdropped on constantly by the government.

"Mommy, what's that?" Emerson asked suddenly.

"Don't point, dear, it's not polite. Anyway, your eyes are better than mine. I can't quite—why, I think it looks like somebody in a hoverchair."

The instant the whole family turned to look, the figure took a right angle and vanished behind a statue of Hillary Rodham Clinton that, in the style of her times, had been made from crushed aluminum cans.

"Maybe somebody from your neck of the woods, Honey," Morgan suggested. "Somebody who can't tolerate the new treatments for gravity." All five of them had suffered numerous injections, tests, physical therapy, and other indignities to be here, including the baby.

"Maybe," Llyra answered. There was something unsettling about that figure, but she couldn't put her finger on what it was. "Let's go have some lunch, shall we? I saw a little cafe over by the Schwartzenegger Pavilion."

—TWO—

"YOU THINK THERE'S BUGS IN there?" Llyra's five year old daughter Julia asked as they approached the next memorial on their itinerary, a site mostly known, these days, for its appearance on antique coins and currency.

Not all such collectibles were rare. During its final days, the East American government had cast this particular president's likeness into a thermoplastic five million dollar coin, circulating enough of them, went an old joke, to fill one of the smaller Great Lakes. In the end, the vast majority of them had been shipped to West American thermal depolymerization plants where they'd been broken down into petroleum.

Emerson gave his sister a nasty snicker.

"This is a good climate," said Morgan, "for all kinds of nasty bugs."

They'd seen some of the city proper, before coming to the Mall. So far they'd visited the apartment building where Wesley Snipes had supposedly lived in the twentieth century movie *Murder at 1600*, the basement parking garage where "Deep Throat" had met reporters Woodward and Bernstein, and a Catholic girls' school where the barricaded twenty-first century President Horton Willoughby had finally been persuaded to surrender and resign from office over the Martian scandal.

There was still a military tank—long since rusted and inert—standing at every important intersection of the city, left over from the turbulent final days of the Homeland Security era. It was difficult for Morgan and Llyra to keep their 8-year-old son and 5-year old daughter from climbing them—it looked like fun for adults, as well.

Later this afternoon they planned to visit the Hall of Fictional Presidents, with its host of robotic and holographic images from Raymond Massey to Harrison Ford, Gene Hackman, Ronny Cox, and Martin Sheen.

"And snakes!" Emerson added excitedly. "I wanna see some snakes!"

One of the few drawbacks to living in the Moon was that the Trasks and other children like them could only see wild animals by going to the zoo. The boy devoured everything he could read and watch on the subject. He was especially interested in predatory mammals. That had been one of many reasons Llyra and Morgan had decided to head for the stars, and a new planet. On Paradise, the kids could climb mountains, run through the woods, paddle through swamps, and see new life very few children—or adults, for that matter—had ever seen. There was some danger in that, of course, but pioneers like Arctic colonists and Pallatians welcomed it, for the freedom and opportunity that came with it.

The monument before them was a gigantic rectangular building entirely surrounded by columns. Inside, one of the presidents sat on what was unmistakably a throne, looking down at the visitors who came to see him. The monument, however, was overgrown with semitropical weeds and vines, beneath which two centuries of grafitti had left not a square inch of stone unmarked. One of the columns at the entrance was broken, leaving a gap like a missing tooth in the face of a street tramp.

Before they came within fifty yards of the memorial, another holofigure appeared before them, both of its arms extended, palms outward.

"I'm sorry," said the hologram. "The public may not enter this structure, as it's overrun with dangerous insects, snakes, rats, and bats."

"Bats!" exclaimed both older children at the same time, Emerson with excitement, Julia in apparent horror. In that moment, Llyra felt that same nameless dread wash through her again. It had been like this for half of her life, ever since her ill-fated journey to Mars. She shook it off, as she always did, and concentrated instead on the hologram.

"I was Thomas DiLorenzo," the figure wore an early twenty-first century jacket and tie, "one of Abraham Lincoln's last biographers. Over the past century or so, the man's image and place in history have become somewhat tarnished, as it has become clearer what he did and why. Fundamentally, he allowed six hundred twenty thousand individual human beings to die violently—and many more to be wounded, raped, and impoverished—in order to preserve an artificial political construct."

"But he freed—" Llyra began. Earth history wasn't her strong suit.

"A claim," the hologram went on, "was often made that Lincoln ended slavery, but not only did his Emancipation Proclamation free nobody, all throughout the war, Washington's capitol dome was being renovated—by slaves. Lincoln stated frankly that if he could have preserved the Union by keeping slavery in place, he would have done so. What he did, instead, was to spread it everywhere across America, by introducing military conscription and income taxation, the two most pernicious forms of slavery, ones that continued for another hundred and ... "

The hologram's voice was overpowered by a roaring noise overhead. They all looked up to see one of the new antigrav shuttles—its underbelly polished like a great curved mirror—clawing its way into the midday sky, headed for the Moon, or possibly one of the Lagrange positions.

Some people still preferred spaceships to the orbital elevator the Trask family had ridden down on. Those like the vessel overhead were faster and more direct, but a great deal more expensive. The Trasks had taken a small space hopper from Armstrong City in the Moon to the pinnacle of the nearest space elevator—there were now six of these, altogether, every one of them built by Llyra's father, who had also terraformed Ceres—and ridden it to Fernandina in the Galapagos Islands on the Earth's equator. From there, a hypersonic atmospheric cruiser had flown them to Baltimore in East America. After visiting the system-famous H.L. Mencken Shrine, they'd taken an almost empty hoverbus to what had been the capital of the world's most powerful nation.

Antigrav technology, a leftover, archaeologically, from some ancient civilization gone for a billion years, had come back from the stars with Mankind's first interstellar exploratory vessel, the *Fifth Force*. The shuttle overhead was lifted by antigrav, but driven by fusion engines that human beings had invented all by themselves. The lower portion of the vessel's hull was reflective because, for a great many years, the dying East American government had taken to using tactical lasers to shoot down aircraft it believed had violated its airspace.

Eventually one of them—a freighter full of frozen buffalo meat from Omaha, Nebraska bound for Lagrange Five—had been shot down and crashed, wiping out the town of Bricktown, New Jersey. Several heavily armed parties of West Americans had infiltrated the laser installations and destroyed them. Now the lower hulls of spaceships were polished, partly as decoration, but partly as a reminder and a warning.

The hologram continued its lecture through the ragged noise of the swiftly climbing vessel, but it was a movement in the corner of her eye that suddenly captured all of Llyra's attention. "Don't look now," she told her family quietly, "but that person in the hoverchair is back."

The apparition was closer now, less than a hundred yards away. The chair was big and bulky, technology at least a century out of date. Despite the temperature and humidity, the figure in it was swathed in a heavy blanket, with a scarf over its head and a muffler around its neck.

Once again, as Morgan and the children turned, the chair lurched abruptly to one side and vanished behind a commemorative stele dedicated to Helen McClellan Willoughby, sometimes known as the "Fist Lady".

Llyra discreetly checked the weapon she carried under her short jacket, a hypervelocity .11 caliber electric pistol. She'd been one of several hundred victims aboard a hijacked spaceliner when she was younger. Half a lifetime later, she was still having nightmares about it and had solemnly sworn that she would never let herself be disarmed again.

Although she and Morgan strove to live as normal a life as they could, especially for the sake of their children, they were both as famous as any figure skating champions had ever been, and they were accustomed—and tried to stay prepared for—odd behavior from the public. Llyra had experienced trouble before with innocent but overly enthusiastic fans, and even genuine stalkers, although learning that she could handily defend herself and her family usually discouraged them.

"Next on your itinerary," said the hologram, "is the monument to one of the last Chief Executives of the United States—although by then, most people called it East America—President-for-Life Maxwell Promise."

—THREE—

THE TRASK FAMILY HAD NOT lingered long at the Maxwell Promise "memorial". It was a grim, windowless cube, one hundred old-fashioned meters on a side, constructed of welded and riveted metal at least six inches thick. Nobody seemed to remember anymore what was on the inside. One small door apparently required a special electronic ID card to open it, but such cards had not existed for decades. In the open, there were surveillance cameras every couple of yards around the perimeter, gutted long ago by technology-devouring nanobots. There were doubtless many hidden cameras and microphones, as well, equally non-functional.

The sides of the huge, imposing building were scorched and scored by firebombs and grenades, pocked-marked by bullets. The holographic guide to Promise's life and time, an exiled historian who had lived in the Moon, had taken perverse delight in describing the way the man's lifeless body had been dragged through the streets by his bodyguards, to demonstrate to the public beyond question that he had finally been deposed.

Gratefully, the family shook the dreary hologram off and skipped ahead to the monument dedicated to the best-remembered of the American presidents, Thomas Jefferson, whose ideas and ideals had finally triumphed after nearly three bleak centuries of shrinking human freedom.

"It could never have happened," opined Jefferson's holographic biographer, one Albert Jay Nock, a man dressed in early twentieth century clothing, "without the other Settled Worlds to preserve his memory and his ideas, to practice what he preached, and, eventually, to bring it back home to Earth. Jefferson had his predecessors—his close friend Thomas Paine certainly influenced him strongly, as did Trenchard and Gordon, the authors of *Cato's Letters*—and he had his successors, but he was the very first to tell a king where to get off."

"What about William Tell?" said Emerson, irreverently.

Perhaps she was biased, Llyra thought, but it was a beautiful building, sparkling white, circular in floorplan, with a graceful domed roof supported by columns, and a classic *stoa* or covered porch. Three short flights of gentle steps led to the entrance. Inside the center of the monument, a bronze statue of the third president stood—there was no throne in this place—under his own words, inscribed high on the wall above him: "I have sworn upon the altar of god, eternal hostility against every form of tyranny over the mind of men."

a small group of individuals was busy sweeping the floor, cleaning the walls and columns, gently polishing the coppery brown statue of the author of the Declaration of Independence. "Any of the workers you see around you," explained the holographic biographer, Nock, which had followed them inside, "represent Thomas Jefferson clubs from all over North America, the planet Earth, and even the Solar System, who, since the collapse of the East American government and Park Service, have taken it upon themselves to clean the monument and maintain it in good repair."

"That's kind of nice," said Morgan.

"Unfortunately," added the hologram, "those groups, at least here in North America, seem to be dwindling in number and enthusiasm. It's feared this monument may eventually begin to decay like all the others here."

A cool, mildly swampy-smelling breeze blew in from the front of the monument, off a small body of water called the Jefferson Basin. Turning to look out over the water, Llyra saw one of the strangest sights she'd ever seen. It was that mysterious hoverchair person again, and the chair was somehow climbing on a dozen mechanical legs, awkwardly and haltingly, up the lowest tier of steps leading to the monument.

She'd known that such a thing was possible, but had never actually seen it before. Among the other Settled Worlds, individuals who were seriously injured or ill depended on medical technologies that had often been outlawed on Earth, relying, as well, on gravity that was only a fraction of the Earth's to help them recover. What was more, on Pallas, sick and healthy people alike commonly used so-called "flying belts".

"I'm going to see what this is all about," she told her husband, sweeping away the feeling of dread and panic that had arisen in her. He put out a hand and brushed her arm, but didn't try to stop her. Instead, as she descended the two flights of stairs, he watched her back.

The person in the chair had seen her coming. As soon as the chair reached the landing between the first and second flights, it pivoted and headed back toward the basin again. Before Llyra could catch up—a scattering of other tourists on the steps looked at her oddly—it had reached the slidewalk and sped away on a cushion of compressed air.

Morgan and the children joined her on the landing.

"I don't know," she told her husband, sitting on the steps. "Maybe it's just me. But this business is giving me the oddest, unsettled feeling." Something about it kept reminding her of her girlhood ordeal.

"It isn't just you, kiddo. We're definitely being followed by somebody with what my old psychology professor at Memorial called an 'approach-avoidance' problem. You know we could skip the rest of this, and go back to Baltimore. I'm having a hankering for a big seafood dinner—stuffed red snapper, maybe, or broiled lobster. What do you say?"

She shook her head. "It goes against my grain, is what I say. If we do that, I'll always wonder what it was all about. Wouldn't you, too?"

Sitting down beside her, he laughed. "Other people can have all the psychological problems their little hearts desire, my love. They're absolutely free, and the supply is endless. All I give a damn about is you and these street urchins we seem to have picked up somewhere." He tousled the hair of his son, who looked up at him with trusting eyes, then hugged his older daughter. "I'll be happy just to get them—and you, too—away from this pathologically civilized planet."

"Spoken like a true Newfoundlander," Llyra said. He laughed again and began whistling "The Star of Logy Bay", his favorite Newfoundland song.

The truth was that, coming from the tiny town of Curringer on Pallas, she shared his feelings on the subject completely. She'd grown up flying hundreds of miles by herself, over an untamed wilderness haunted by dangerous animal predators, just to skate on a frozen pond, and she longed for her children to be able to thrive in such an environment.

"So what do you say," Morgan asked, "shall we shuffle back to Baltimore?"

"I believe that's 'shuffle off to *Buffalo*', my dear—and not on your life. There's a mystery here of some kind that has to be solved before we move on, Morgan, or I'll never feel right about it." She put a hand on his arm. "And I need you to back my play, all right?"

"He's sunk," Emerson stage-whispered to his sister. Julia nodded, giggling.

Morgan straightened his back, attempting to regain some dignity. "Unaccustomed as I am to thinking of myself as anybody's sidekick—even yours, darling girl—when have I ever failed to back your play?"

"Very well, let's go on with the tour and see what happens."

—fOUR—

MORGAN WAS THE FIRST TO notice and comment on the fact that the automated slidewalks seemed to be taking them from monument to monument in a pattern that made no sense. Washington's tipsy obelisk was at the opposite end of the Mall from the weed-grown Lincoln Memorial. Promise's scorched metal cube was on the opposite side of Jefferson's gleaming memorial, which was all the way back, around the Basin.

"I'll bet I know why, too," Llyra suggested. "Millions of people used to come here. Some centralized computer somewhere is running a program designed to prevent too many tourists at a time from visiting any one of the memorial sites. Each time we stop somewhere and start again, it takes us to the least-crowded site that we haven't seen yet."

Morgan grinned and nodded. "All that, and she's good-looking, too."

"But there's hardly anybody at all here today, Mommy," Emerson protested.

"That's right, dear," she told the eight year old. "But the system isn't quite smart enough to realize that, so it keeps shifting us all over the place as if it were a hundred years ago and there were still thousands of people sightseeing on the Mall." Llyra looked to her husband. "I guess that's sort of a parable about government in general, isn't it? Or a metaphor. Govern, and if there's no real governing to do, then govern anyway. I'm glad we Pallatians gave it up."

"You gave it up before you had it," he agreed. "And we Newfies headed north to get away from it. Though not before the Canadian federal government raped the outports." It was an old story and a bitter one that began with the seal fishery being outlawed at the behest of a handful of Hollywood stars—throwing thousands out of work—and nearly ended with a formerly proud, hardworking, outdoor people being into the fetid capital city of St. John's and put on welfare.

Until the northern colony movement began in protest.

Now the family came to the Ronald Reagan Memorial, probably the most photographed object in North America, a hundred-foot titanium statue of a western-style rider on horseback, with the traditional high-heeled, pointed-toed boots and spurs, broad-brimmed hat, bib-front shirt, calfskin vest, and fringed leather chaps over his jeans.

About the former president's waist in an elaborately tooled belt, he wore a pair of giant single action Colt .44/40 revolvers. There was a colossal Model 1892 Winchester, presumably chambered for the same cartridge, in his saddle scabbard. The alloy had turned purple over the years—or had been that color to begin with—but in a triumph of art and science, both of the horse's front feet were high in the air.

Unfortunately, the monument was thickly covered with decades' worth of bird lime, and there were nests in the cowboy hat, the saddlebow, and the lariat coiled on the saddle horn. There were also the inevitable grafitti, and everything on the stature below eye level looked as if it had been pounded on and dented with a thousand sledgehammers.

Llyra wasn't certain what the monument was supposed to signify, and Morgan, who grasped it intuitively, was at a loss to explain it to her verbally. Emerson shouted "It's a *cowboy!*" which seemed enough explanation to him. He loved western movies and was looking forward to having his own horse—or some alien equivalent—when they reached Paradise.

Julia, perhaps with her grandfather Adam's instinctive eye for engineering, wanted somebody to tell her why the horsie didn't fall down.

"Cantilevers," her brother told her smugly.

"Why can't it lever?" she asked.

Emerson peered at her suspiciously. She returned an innocent look, but was not too young, not in this family, anyway, to make atrocious puns.

"What do you know about this guy Reagan?" Llyra asked. Morgan was from what had once been Canada, and might not be expected to know about this man, but all she knew about Earth history herself was that her ancestors had left the planet to avoid seeing any more of it being made.

Morgan said, "I know my granddad used to go on and on about him. He gave people an illusion of liberty, an illusion of progress, an illusion he was getting government off their backs, while all the time it grew larger and freedom shrank. He was proof, to Granddad, that politicians are all evil, no matter what they mean to be. That's why civilizations fall and this place is a ghost town. It reminds me of Palenque, somehow, a deserted Mayan capital I visited when I was a teenager."

"That's pretty harsh, don't you think?" She winked at him.

"Reagan and his administration made possible every government atrocity that happened to Americans afterward. He shifted their war on drugs into high gear and destroyed the Bill of Rights. That's what's harsh, not telling the truth about him. This monument to him is a joke."

Llyra shook her head. It took a lot to make her husband lose his sense of humor. Then again, his grandfather had been close to him and still was. He had taught Morgan to fish and hunt and survive in the Arctic.

In many of the same ways that Morgan's grandfather had mentored him, Jasmeen Khalidov, a second generation Martian colonist of Chechen extraction, had been Llyra's girlhood companion and role model, part time sister and, at need, part time mother, as well. Everything Llyra knew about figure skating she had learned from Jasmeen, or they had learned together on the long, hard road from Pallas's one twentieth of a gee to Earth. Only a few years older than Llyra, the two had more or less grown up together, especially during the dark ordeal that had been the hijacking of the spaceliner *Newark* by environmental terrorists.

No one had been particularly surprised when Llyra's older brother Wilson had proposed to Jasmeen, married her, and carried her off with Tieve, his daughter from a previous tragic relationship, to his large and growing fleet of asteroid-hunting ships which had recently begun to work the previously unexplored Kuiper Belt region of the Solar System.

Now the two were talking seriously about following Llyra and Morgan to the stars, to the system Paradise was a part of. There were asteroids there, too, to be hunted, captured, and mined, and planets in need of protection from them. Jasmeen would be so surprised—and delighted, her former protégé hoped—to learn that the fourth child Llyra had been carrying for eight weeks so far would be named after her.

Llyra shook her head. Woolgathering again, she scolded herself. This pilgrimage seemed to be engendering entirely too much of that kind of thing. They were about to leave for the next stop on the tour, when the figure in the hoverchair appeared again from around one end of the Reagan monument, where it had been concealed by an outsized hoof.

This time the apparition bore straight for them. Morgan put all three children behind him and laid a hand on the plasma weapon at his waist, while Llyra stood to one side, well prepared to set up a crossfire.

The figure raised both its hands, crossing them and waving them, as if to say, "Don't shoot!" Then it reversed itself and disappeared around the horse once more. By the time the Trasks followed it, it was gone.

Again.

—FIVE—

THE FRANKLIN DELANO ROOSEVELT MEMORIAL lay on the opposite side of the Basin inlet from the Jefferson Memorial, as well s the opposite side of the political spectrum. Instead of a single great structure, it was composed of a series of low outdoor "rooms" full of bronze sculpture and relief carvings, each of which had been intended to commemorate a distinct phase in Roosevelt's presidency, from the Great Depression through the Second World War, and formed a sort of half-maze along the shore. At one time it was said to have been the most popular of the attractions along the Mall. I was empty and neglected now.

Weeds grew up between the paving blocks.

Dry waterfalls and fountains gathered leaves that had obviously been there for years, rotting and turning into black soil. Again, grafitti defaced the monument, blotting out the former president's famous sayings that had been inscribed there late in the twentieth century.

"Look, Mommy and Daddy, a doggie!" It was Julia who was excited this time, rushing to the oversized bronze replica of Roosevelt's famous Scottie Fala, not noticing the dramatically cloaked president sitting to its left. Llyra thought it didn't look quite as cute once the scale was established. The expression on its face seemed rather menacing.

Roosevelt struck her in much the same way. Whoever had created this memorial had imagined the man as benevolent, but Llyra knew—because Morgan had told her—that, imitating several of his predecessors, his policies had actually prolonged the economic crisis for twelve years. In the end, to bail his failed administration out, the man had done all he could to precipitate an unnecessary war that killed sixty million people, worldwide, and left Europe and Japan in ruins.

That was what Morgan said, anyway.

The sculpture here was fascinating, though, she thought. Llyra's mother, a scientist specializing in finding new uses for asteroidal materials, had taken to sculpture recently, using the iron, nickel, cobalt, and other metals so abundant in the Asteroid Belt. The sculptures in this place were of traditional material, but the long line of hungry men waiting to be fed, for example, was beautifully done, and the voluminously caped president looked like a fictional arch-villain.

"*Mommy!*" Julia screamed, pointing back the way they'd come. The five of them were suddenly trapped, hemmed in by the walls of the monument. Julia hid behind the outsized bronze dog. Emerson wedged himself behind the president, and Morgan pushed Ardie's pram in with him.

The hoverchair was here again, headed directly for them.

Llyra drew her pistol, noticing that Morgan had drawn his own. The person in the chair seemed to bear an eerie resemblance to the figure of Roosevelt behind her. The chair drew up, almost to Llyra's feet and stopped, without its occupant making anything resembling a threatening gesture.

There was a long silence, then, "Please don't hurt me. I mean no harm." It was a woman's voice, a weak and quavery one at that. "All I want to do is thank you, and ask you to forgive me, if you'll be kind enough."

"Forgive you?" Llyra tucked her weapon away, counting on Morgan to protect her if she'd made a mistake. "I don't even know who you are."

The woman reached up slowly and unwrapped the muffler from around her neck. She then uncovered her head and face to reveal an aged but otherwise unremarkable countenance. "I'm sorry, I get so cold these days."

Llyra blinked. Somehow the woman looked familiar, but the younger woman couldn't place the older woman's face. "Are you all right?" she asked.

"No, dear, I'm not all right. I'm very old and I'm very ill. But that's actually the reason I wanted to thank you. You'll have to excuse my earlier shyness; this isn't an easy thing to do. But I read that you and your family are going to leave the Solar System, and I called in every favor I had left to track you down here before you go."

"But why?"

"You may not recognize me. We never met. But years ago, when you were just a girl, I was the international director of the Mass Movement."

"Anna Wertham Savage," Morgan supplied. He holstered his weapon and stood beside his wife, putting a protective arm around her. "Your people claimed that by importing raw materials, agricultural products, and manufactured goods from the Moon and the asteroids humanity would change the mass—and therefore the motion—of the Earth's crust, relative to that of the molten core, causing slippage and buckling that was sure to destroy civilization and maybe even all life on the planet."

Llyra remembered hearing about this woman. It had been a violent splinter of the Mass Movement, Null Delta Em, that had hijacked the liner. Several people had died on both sides. And now she wanted to apologize?

"I didn't approve what was done to you, Miss Ngu—Mrs. Trask—even when I believed all that about the Earth's fragility. And yet they went ahead and did it without my approval. They're all dead now, and there is no more Mass Movement. I saw to that last, personally. Later, I acquired this degenerative disease I now suffer from, a very old-fashioned one that can be cured in a few hours most places in the System."

Llyra began, "Then why—"

"But not in the former Commonwealth of Massachusetts, and most certainly not in the city of Amherst, where I have lived for most of my life. I was just supposed to remain quiet and die, slowly and painfully, because some individuals—I used to be one of them—loathe technology and loathe themselves, and all human life, even more."

"What does all this have to do with me?"

"You showed me the way, don't you see? You went from one twentieth of the Earth's gravity to become a champion here. You survived a crime that nobody was supposed to live through, and you helped to turn the tables on the criminals. Now you and your little family are going to the stars. And if you can do that, young lady, then I can go to the Moon where, even as sick as I am, I'll be able to walk again, and where they will soon cure what's wrong with me and give me a new life."

Llyra stepped forward and knelt down beside the woman's powered chair.

"And you went to all this trouble—"

"I had to. Because no matter what they accomplish for me in the Moon, I wouldn't feel right in myself until I did. They say everybody has at least on great leap in them. Let this be mine. I may never do anything adventurous or daring again, but at least I will have done this."

Llyra shook her head. "I don't know what to say."

"I do," Julia chirped. "Say, 'You're welcome.'"

L. Neil Smith at Phoenix Pick

Tom Paine Maru (Special Author's Edition)
The Venus Belt
The Crystal Palace
Pallas
Hope (*with Aaron Zelman*)

www.PhoenixPick.com